We All Hear Stories in the Dark

We All Hear Stories in the Dark

Robert Shearman

WE ALL HEAR STORIES IN THE DARK
VOLUME III

Published in May 2020 by Drugstore Indian Press an imprint of PS Publishing Ltd.

ISBN
978-1-786364-62-3

Design & Layout by Michael Smith
Printed and bound in England by T. J. Books Limited

PS Publishing Ltd
Grosvenor House, 1 New RoadHornsea, HU18 1PG, England
editor@pspublishing.co.uk
www.pspublishing.co.uk

INTRODUCTION

THE SHORT STORY, as its devoted practitioners cannot fail to notice, is often disrespected, and why? Because it is not a novel. Or "a full-length novel" as the phrase has it, with the implication that anything less than 50,000 words is somehow cheating. I've even heard people dismiss awards for short stories as lesser, even invalid, e.g. "I mean the *real* Hugo winners." This lengthist prejudice is limited to prose fiction, so far as I can see; poetry lovers do not value a book-length poem over a perfect sonnet, nor do music lovers disparage a song because it is not an opera.

Financially, for writers, the contrast is stark. No one nowadays, no matter how prolific, can expect to make a living writing short fiction. But even in the golden age of magazines, when American writers from Ernest Hemingway to Kurt Vonnegut made more money from one short story than they ever did from their first novels, the novel was the benchmark of literary respectability. F. Scott Fitzgerald lived extravagantly well off short stories in the 1920s, but fretted over the poor sales of the novels he expected to be his lasting legacy.

When I was starting out—maybe it is the same now—short stories were promoted as the way to begin, the training ground in which to learn how to write, get published and attract attention, despite the fact that the short story and the novel are different forms. And if your short stories were successful, you were expected to stop writing them and concentrate on becoming a novelist. I hadn't sold more than half a dozen short stories the first time an editor offered to take a look at my first novel.

If only I'd had one! At that point in my life, I had no idea how to attempt such a feat. Scaling up from 3,000 words to 60,000 was daunting, yes, but it was not a simple matter of producing more pages. The short story is not a stunted, under-written novel, not a broken-off piece of something that should have been longer—anyway, I liked (and still like) writing short stories. I did try.... but it was years before I was ready.

Harlan Ellison was a great inspiration to me, and my Mentor-in-Chief. That demonic genius of the short story form, one of the few contemporary writers whose fame rested almost entirely on short fiction (setting aside—if that's even possible—his personality) was a full-time professional writer who published many books, but none of them novels. Yet he frequently talked about the novel he was going to write, which gave me the impression that for all his success and fame Harlan still felt he needed to prove himself—as if, until he published a novel, there would be a faint, mocking question mark over his identity as a serious writer. It was bad enough to be categorized dismissively as a science fiction writer (something he often railed against), but possibly it was just as bad to be a non-novelist who only wrote short stories and television and film scripts. I found this dispiriting. Harlan wrote what he wanted to write—what he felt driven to write—and he won awards and made a living from it. To me, that looked like success.

A few years ago I heard a rumour that Robert Shearman was writing a novel, and I felt a little twinge of unease. Only a twinge, because, of course I wanted to read it, and it didn't have to mean that he would stop writing those astonishing short stories—but that twinge was my fear that our most amazing contemporary short story writer had given in to the pressure of public opinion that only "full-length novels" count as proper writing.

Of course, there are other reasons besides the domination of the novel why a short story writer might stop. They might run out of ideas. That was certainly the opinion of Roald Dahl, whom I interviewed back in the early 1980s. He explained that he'd spent twenty-five years dedicating himself to the short story form and: "I found probably thirty-five plots, and then I ran out of them. I don't think I could sit down and write a short story now—it's very hard." He felt this was the fate of everyone who wrote proper short stories—"the sort I wrote, you know, with a beginning, middle and end"—as opposed to all the contemporary writers who wrote what he called "mood pieces" in which nothing happened.

I wish Dahl could have lived long enough to read the stories of Rob Shearman—any one of his collections—*Tiny Deaths* or *Love Songs for the Shy and Cynica*l or *Everyone's Just So So Special*—would have been enough to make him (cranky and opinionated as he was) admit that here was the exception to his rule.

Rob Shearman is a truly exceptional writer—astonishing, inventive, with an amazingly fertile and surprising imagination.

That rumour about the novel was wrong; for the past five or six years he was working instead on the book, one of the volumes of which you hold in your hands. And what a book! *We all hear stories in the dark* just might be the longest single author short story collection—not a "collected works"—ever published, but its length is not the most amazing or unique thing about it. This is a collection of short stories —not a novel—that includes a connecting framework and Big Idea behind it that emphasizes the role the reader plays can be just as important as that of the writer in creating a book.

As for me—I'm one of those readers, but for some reason I've been chosen to "introduce" the book to you, my fellow readers.

Well, here goes:

We All Hear Stories in the Dark, I am honoured to introduce you to your readers—I hope you'll forgive me for not naming them all, but, as you would be the first to agree, it is rather dark in here.

Readers, whoever you are, it is my very great pleasure to introduce you to *We All Hear Stories in the Dark*. You are in for an experience like no other. Buckle up—it will be a bumpy ride at times, but I know you won't regret a single thrilling, scary, hilarious, upsetting, amusing, heart-warming, terrifying, peculiar, unique moment of the journey ahead. Enjoy!

Lisa Tuttle

We All Hear Stories in the Dark

Once upon a time
there was a man
who lost his wife,
and tried to find her
by reading all the books
in the world.

68

THE CIRCUS OF THE INCURIOUSLY DRAB

YOU'RE NONE TOO IMPRESSED by the posters up all over the village. 'Andrew Loving's Circus of the Incuriously Drab', they say, which you concede is certainly arresting. But there's too much colour to them, the posters are too loud, too garish. You decide not to go to the circus. But when you see it set up on the village green you're quite surprised—it looks smaller than you'd imagined. The big top is a subdued grey. And you find yourself buying a ticket at the little kiosk at the front.

The old woman who sells you the ticket does so quite vacantly. She asks you whether you want any popcorn, and doesn't seem to care when you say no. An unsmiling clown tears your ticket and leads you into the circus ring, and to get to your seat you have to cross the sawdust floor, and it feels light and spongey beneath your shoes. You feel the urge to take off your shoes and walk in it barefoot, you think that would feel nice, you can imagine sinking deep in it and the sawdust coming up between your toes, you feel the urge to dance in it. You don't. You take your seat. You can't tell whether the unsmiling clown is unsmiling because the downward curve of his mouth has been painted on, or because he is genuinely unhappy; you ask him a simple question, something like, "How's the show going?" or "Will it last long?" or "So, you're a clown, then?", not because you care, but just to get his mouth moving. But he doesn't reply.

There is no one sitting next to you. There is no one sitting in front of you, and when you bother to check, you see there is no one sitting behind you either. The tent must seat five hundred people, maybe a thousand, maybe more, it is hard to see in the dark. You wonder whether you're the only one in the audience. You wonder whether you should leave. You wonder what would be the most embarrassing thing to do, to stay and sit through the show quite alone, knowing that each and every one of the acts is directed at you exclusively and is done to win your sole approval—or to leave, and have to walk back past the unsmiling clown and the vacant woman at the kiosk and let them know you're rejecting them.

And then you see, the other side of the circus ring, with the whole stage between you, another figure in the audience. You squint at it. You try to make it out in the dim. It's a woman. What is she doing? She seems to be leaning forward, there's a strange expression on her face. You realise she's squinting at you. Is that what you look like? You'd better stop.

At some point a ringmaster walks on. Is this Andrew Loving? It might be. Andrew Loving is wearing a red jacket and tails. He has a top hat, but he doesn't bother to put it on his head, he carries it uselessly like it's a bag of shopping. You sit up straight, you feel a rush of adrenalin, something is going to happen. And you're excited, and you're glad you stayed, and you're nervous, and you wish you'd left. The ringmaster walks out on to the sawdust, shoulders slumped, looking down at the ground. Then he stops, hesitates—and walks back off again, as if he's forgotten what he was doing there. Not once does he look up at the audience.

You wish you had brought a book. There isn't the light by which you could read a book. You wish there was more light, and that you'd brought a book to take full advantage of the light with.

You try not to look at the woman again, but sooner or later you just have to—and she catches your eye, and she smiles. You smile back, then quickly look away. You don't dare look again for a minute or two, and when you do she's still looking at you (or has she been looking away too and only just given you a second glance?), and still smiling (though, again, this might be another smile altogether, she might have taken a break between the two smiles, you weren't looking at her to tell), and God, now she's waving. She's waving at you! Or she's waving at someone else, maybe someone is behind you, and you turn around to see, but you know no one has come in, the unsmiling clown hasn't been back with fresh audience.

You don't know what to do. You smile. You think maybe that'll be enough. It doesn't seem enough, a smile hardly equals a wave, and in the moment of the action it feels a bit mean and unfriendly. You wave back, then, but try not to put too much effort into it.

She gets up. She gathers her things, and begins to move. Is she leaving? Has she had enough? Or, no, is she coming for *you*? You don't want her sitting near you. You don't know her. You don't know what you'd say. And it'll take a while for her to get to you, she's got to walk a whole semi-circumference before she's with you. And you feel that if you got up right now, and begin walking in the opposite direction, then maybe you'd keep ahead, you could both keep circling the circus ring forever without needing to meet. But you think that she'd catch you up eventually, your leg is a bit sore, and you're tired, you didn't sleep so well last night. Your wife doesn't seem happy any more, and during the day that doesn't seem such a big deal and you can ignore it, but somehow in the still of the night it occurs to you it might be quite important, and you have the urge to nudge her awake and ask her if she's all right, but you're not sure how she'd like that, so instead you just lie there beside her and you close your eyes and try to sleep but thoughts keep churning around in your head. No, it's best to stay put. You just hope the woman doesn't sit right next to you. You hope she doesn't try to start a conversation.

She reaches you. She sits right next to you. "Hello," she says.

"Hello," you reply.

"Do you like circuses?"

"Not really."

"Nor me."

And at that she shrugs. She's brought popcorn. She offers you some. You thank her, but refuse.

So she eats some popcorn. She eats it perfectly silently, the popcorn is soft and marshmallow, and she doesn't even rustle the bag.

You feel bad for refusing her popcorn. You feel it might have seemed rude. You say, "Do you think it's going to start soon?" And she doesn't answer, and you think you must have offended her after all, and you look at her, really for the first time, and she looks at you, and her face breaks into the broadest smile, and she doesn't seem particularly offended.

You try to work out whether you find her attractive or not. You decide you do.

She looks nice, she's wearing lipstick, and her hair is done up in a nice cute bob, she might have just come out of the hairdresser's, and she's got on a pretty dress. You begin to wish you were wearing better clothes. You wish you'd sprayed deodorant under your armpits that morning.

The ringmaster shuffles on again, and he doesn't make it far into the ring this time. He seems to think better of the venture and is about to leave once more, and the woman whispers to you, "Do you think he even knows we're here?" and you whisper, "I don't know," and she whispers, "I think we should tell him," and you whisper, "Yes, we should," and then you wait for her to call out to him, and she doesn't, and the ringmaster has nearly disappeared now, he's nearly left the ring and you'll have lost him, so you say, quite loud, "Hey. Hey." And your heart's not really in it, you don't want to be a nuisance.

The ringmaster stops, and turns around, and looks towards you, and shields his eyes from a bright light that isn't there. "Sorry for the delay," he says. "Ladies and gentlemen, boys and girls. There's been a delay." And off he's gone again.

"Thank you," the woman says to you.

"That's all right," you reply.

She offers you some popcorn. This time you accept.

You don't say anything for a while, and nor does she, but it's not awkward, it's very friendly. You wonder how the two of you look together, all alone in the big top. You suppose the ringmaster would have thought you were a couple. You wish you'd brought a book, but not because you're bored, you just think it would be nice if you read a book beside her, and she was reading a book too, and that would be nice, and at the end of each chapter one of you would look up and smile at the other, it would just be so very nice.

You look at the sawdust. It really does look so soft and spongey and inviting.

The ringmaster returns. He still looks ashamed of the ring, and when he speaks he doesn't quite look up at you, but at least there's an announcement of some sort. "Sorry for the delay, ladies and gentlemen, boys and girls. We've had problems with the trapeze artist. The trapeze artist, ladies and gentlemen, has got a case of vertigo. The vertigo has shaken her up something chronic, boys and girls, it's a terror to see. But we're dealing with it. We know what to do. In the mean time, sorry for the delay."

He leaves. You try to make conversation. "Do you have vertigo?" you ask the woman.

"Sometimes," she says. "It depends upon how high up I am."

"Yes."

"If I'm up too high, then I do. If it's not high at all, then I'm all right."

This seems to you very wise.

"Me too," you tell her.

The bag of popcorn is finished. It's all right, she's bought another.

"I wish I'd brought a book," she says.

And then there are lights! And drums! And out comes the ringmaster again, except this time he is walking tall, and the top hat on his head makes him look like a giant, and he strides to the exact centre of the ring and flings his arms out wide. "Ladies and gentlemen!" he calls out to the empty rows facing you, to the empty rows to your right, to the empty rows on your left, to you. "Boys and girls! *Mesdames, Messieurs! Les enfants, peu importe ce que le sexe!* We take great pleasure in presenting for your especial delight, La Trapezette, the queen of the trapeze!" And he applauds, and the woman next to you applauds, and you join in.

The trapeze artist is young and pretty, and her dress is sparkly, her teeth white. She strikes a pose to the whole ring, and in doing so turns her back to you mostly, but you clap just the same. She takes out a piece of rope, unrolls it, lays it upon the ground straight. She stands at one end. A drum roll begins. She takes a deep breath. And then she walks across the rope, her arms stretched out to keep her balance, and she does it so painstakingly, so slow, you can really feel the tension, and once or twice she wobbles. But she's reached the far end, and you applaud once more, because had the tightrope been suspended fifty feet in the air she would almost certainly have survived. And is it any less impressive because the rope is on the floor? Surely the skill is the same, that she was able to walk the rope without falling off, regardless of which height the rope was hung—why should she risk her life to demonstrate it? Would you prefer that? Are you really that selfish?

And then the drum roll gets heavier, more omninous, and she produces a blindfold. And the woman next to you gasps, and clutches on to your arm. And it's the first time you've touched, and it feels good. For the remainder of La Trapezette's death-defying return across the tightrope, with nothing but her own innate skill to guide her across, the woman holds on to you—and La Trapezette certainly makes a meal of it, she keeps on having to stop and steady herself and sways side from side as she finds new courage, she drags out that return journey across a line in the dust, making it last ten full minutes—and you can't complain, you're giving some comfort to the woman beside you, she feels better for your company, you could have wished the act had lasted even longer.

At the end of the act your new friend gives the trapeze artist a standing ovation, and you don't think it quite deserves all that, but you hate being the only person left sitting in a theatre. So you get to your feet too, and you both applaud, long and hard, and the trapeze artist beams and takes four full curtain calls before you are rid of her.

The ringmaster seems to suck up your applause, he stands proud and his chest puffs out. But as soon as you stop, he starts to wilt again, even his smile sort of collapses in on itself, and he mumbles whilst looking at the ground: "And now there'll be a delay. Ladies and gentlemen, boys and girls, yes, a delay. We're sorry. We're sorry." And he shuffles out of the ring, the trapeze artist following, now shuffling too, her arms gangling and awkward and her sparkly dress refusing to sparkle.

Since there's a delay, you wonder if you should leave the ring for a while, get some air, stretch your legs. Would the woman come with you? Could you ask her, "Fancy a stroll?"—what would she make of that? You turn to her, and she turns to you too, and she's smiling, she's perfectly happy, oh, she's happy where she is.

It's at least another hour before the ringmaster comes back.

You think you should say something to your companion. You should ask her name. Ask her what she does for a living. Ask her if she likes her job, finds it challenging, or fulfilling, whether she regards the colleagues she sees each day as actual friends or just people she has to make the best of. Ask her whether it's a job she'd chosen, something she always wanted to do as a child, or whether those child ambitions are still out of reach, and what she is doing now is just something temporary to make ends meet and that somehow 'temporary' has stretched its definition already to fifteen years and counting. Ask whether she's good at her job, in spite of her lack of enthusiasm, and ask whether her proficiency at it offers any real compensation for the nagging fear that she's sold out her hopes and dreams. You should ask whether she has a cat. You like cats.

Instead, she's the one to speak, and she asks, "Are you enjoying yourself?"

You say, "Yes." And you mean it, and that's good.

Andrew Loving is back with another presentation of the incuriously drab. He looks defeated. His announcement is apologetic, but not too apologetic, it's all gone beyond a simple sorry now, if he let loose his profound regrets he'd burst into tears, it's better that he keeps his composure blank and his voice numbed. "Ladies and gentlemen, boys and girls. We present for you the menagerie de Loving. We do not present them proudly. We are not proud. They were damaged in transit. Enjoy." And then he does a flourish anyway, as grand as you like, and he rolls his top hat up his arm and on to his head, and that deserves a little applause in itself—and the lights in the ring get brighter, there's a drum roll, and the music starts. And on traipse the animals. Lions limping on sore paws and wincing with every step. Tigers with broken tails, some jutting out at sharp angles, some drilling straight down into the sawdust floor so that the tigers don't so much walk but drag. Elephants with their trunks bandaged, elephants with eyepatches, elephants with entire legs in slings. Depressed bears.

The music plays on. And the animals walk around the perimeter of the ring, in single file, again and again and again and again.

She's touching your arm. "I like that elephant!" she says. "It has a face just like my old geography teacher!"

You point out a lion. "And that's just like my postman."

"That tiger looks like the woman in the sweet shop."

"That bear looks like my wife!" You wish you hadn't mentioned the wife.

At one point a tiger just keels over to the floor. It might be asleep, or sick, or dead. The bear is right behind it, and stares down at it impassively. Then it seems to roll its eyes, ever world-weary, and sidestep the body, and continue the march. The lion behind the bear isn't so forward thinking; maybe it isn't good at contingency strategy, maybe it's just not concentrating hard; it tries to climb over the slumped tiger, staggers, falls. The elephant behind the lion has no chance, it's hard to slow an elephant in parade mode, and it slams right into the back of the lion, and then the lion into the tiger—and after that the traffic just starts to pile up, some animals crashing into each other when they brake too suddenly, others having to crawl to a snail's pace and get stuck in the ensuing jam. By the time the bear makes it all the way around the ring there's no way it can continue its journey; it looks thoroughly pissed off by this, and sits down upon the ground, and sighs.

It takes ages for all the animals to get off, and you're still not sure whether that tiger is dead or not. The ringmaster leads the applause. "Give it up for the Andrew Loving menagerie!" Delighted, the woman jumps to her feet, and her clapping is fast and loud. You stand up beside her, try to match her for speed and volume. You wish you could ever be as happy as she is now.

"Delay," then says the ringmaster. He can't even be bothered to make it part of a sentence any more. "Delay," he says again, he's off, that's good enough.

You're on your own with her again.

You think you should say something. You should ask her name. Ask her whether she likes her name. Asks her whether, when she looks into the mirror, she really believes she's called x when she sees herself as a y. Ask whether she has any siblings—whether she's an only child (like you, before you were eight), or has brothers and sisters (like you, after you were eight). Ask whether she has a favourite aunt or uncle. Ask whether any of her grandparents are still alive. Ask whether she has a lover. Ask whether her lover loves her back. Ask whether she's straight, or gay, or partnered, or single, and if she's straight and single whether she'd like to go to the circus with you again some day, and if she's straight and partnered whether she'd like to go to the circus and keep it as a secret, and if she's gay whether she's *properly* gay or whether she could be turned. Because that can happen sometimes, apparently.

Instead, she offers you some popcorn. She's got a third bag. You take a handful. Some of it is sweet, some of it is salted. "When I mentioned my wife earlier," you say—and then you don't know what to add. She's very close to you, her leg is brushing your leg, you can smell her and you're not sure whether that's perfume or just that she naturally has a faint whiff of flowers about her.

There are more acts. A fire breather with a sore throat. A mime who prefers to work with real glass boxes and struggle against real gusts of wind. Each time the woman gives them a standing ovation, and there is nothing ironic about it, she's celebrating them as they are, warts and all, and it's forgiving and kind and beautiful. For the next act you jump up to clap even before she does, and you think she smiles at you approvingly. It's not such a bad act anyway; he's a juggler who tells you he can juggle seventeen balls, but only one at a time.

And in the silences you think you should say something. You should ask her name. Just her name. Nothing else. That'd be enough.

You find out her name soon enough.

The ringmaster looks more embarrassed than ever. "Ladies and gentlemen," he says. He cannot even bring himself to appeal to the boys and girls who might wander in, he wants to protect the innocent. "The next act... I'm sorry. It's shit. It's just such shit." He opens his mouth to say more, to explain, to beg forgiveness maybe, but then he closes it again, shakes his head, what's the point? He shouts out the name of the next performer. It's a woman's name. The woman next to you rises from her seat.

In the spotlight you can now see she's old, and plump, and plain. No one bothers giving her a drum roll.

She kicks off her shoes. Her feet look big and calloused, before they sink beneath the sawdust surface.

She begins.

At first you think she's just fidgeting. Maybe she has an itch? She's swaying from side to side, once in every while she'll shuffle her feet a bit. And then it dawns on you she's dancing.

There's no music. Music might help. She doesn't seem bothered by the silence, she opens her arms to you, and she claps. She wants you to join in. She wants you to set the rhythm. So you do. You clap out a beat, she shuffles some more. And then after a while you just sort of stop, because it doesn't matter, she can't even keep time with that—and when you try to vary the pace to help her, go faster, go slower, anything, her gyrating body seems to slip away from whatever new rhythm you establish and chase after something bizarre and random of her own.

And when you stop clapping she just closes her eyes, and she's dancing to the music she hears in her head, and she's smiling so hard now, she's so proud.

It seems to go on for bloody ever. But, at last, it's over. It's really over, it's not just one of those mad pauses she takes, she's actually stopped moving, the dance is done, and she stands tall awaiting the audience response.

You clap, of course you do, and you try not to sound sarcastic. She bows. Then she *curtseys.* She's really milking it.

You wonder how long you have to go on with this for.

You feel a sudden wave of love for her, all alone down there, a bit faded, a bit ugly, but enjoying her moment, as godforsaken and benighted a moment as it is.

She waits for the standing ovation.

And you'd really like to give her one, but there has got to be a limit.

You look at the sawdust, and you think how good it'd be to put your bare feet in it, and just dance.

You stop clapping altogether. There's silence. Still, she waits. Still, she looks proud. And there's silence for ages, great yawning minutes of embarrassment. And you wonder whether you should start clapping again, but let's face it, the moment has passed. The spotlight fades. The ringmaster enters the ring, tries to usher her off. Still, for a while, she is expectant. She believes in you.

And then, quite suddenly, she just turns and marches off.

She doesn't come back to join you in the audience.

You sit there in silence for a few minutes. You wonder if the show is over. You wonder if that was the grand finale. You hesitate. You don't want to miss anything. Even now, you think, something good might be on the way.

The woman's things are under her seat. A cardigan, a handbag, five more boxes of popcorn. You wonder whether you should take them with you, but then think, no, best leave well alone.

You leave. Just as soon as you're through the exit, and the unsmiling clown has given you a blunt nod, and the woman at the kiosk has stared you down with utter disinterest—just as you leave, you hear the drum roll is starting up again. Bugger.

Your wife says to you, "Where were you this evening?"

"Andrew Loving's Circus of the Incuriously Drab."

She thinks about this. She says, "Will you take *me* to the circus?"

"No, I don't think that's a very good idea."

That night, before she turns off the lights, she actually tells you what's wrong. She doesn't say anything you weren't expecting. Really, you agree with her. Really, you'd understand completely if this is the last time you will ever share a bed, a house, a conversation.

"We'll talk about it more in the morning," she says.

You lie there, wide awake, try to think of things you want to say. The promises she wants to hear, the ones you might be able to keep, or at least, the ones she might believe you *can* keep. Clever things that will win back her love. You practise arguments, you mouth them softly in the dark. You tell her it's easy to be good at something, where's the challenge in that? What's hard is being mediocre, and getting on with it anyway. Getting on with life in spite of all.

You think you sound so smart and persuasive, but know that it doesn't matter, by the time she's awake you'll have forgotten it all.

You get up, go downstairs to the kitchen. From the fridge you take out all the eggs. You'll give juggling a try. That'll be easy. Especially if you do them one at a time. It's harder than it looks, and you create quite a mess for your wife to clean up in the morning.

And the old woman says:

- *The menagerie of animals depicted in this story are a pretty sorry lot. To read an account of creatures that are winners, turn to* **The Monogamy of Wild Beasts** *(story 26, page 437).*
- *To read a further tale of bears and tigers in reduced circumstances, turn to* **The Cocktail Party in Kensington Gets Out of Hand** *(story 69, page 1199).*
- *Delays that occur during a circus performance could arguably be used to build up atmosphere and suspense. When delays affect public transport, they only cause misery. See how a man's entire grip on reality is changed because of them in* **Blue Crayon Yellow Crayon** *(story 37, page 615).*
- *Some people get standing ovations they don't deserve. Consider the consequences of sitting down and refusing to applaud in* **The Touch of Baby Stalin's Skin** *(story 67, page 1165).*
- *For more tales of lovers that meet, dance fleetingly, then move on, turn to* **101 Heartbeats** *(story 101, page 1695).*

69

THE COCKTAIL PARTY IN KENSINGTON GETS OUT OF HAND

STILL NO DISCUSSION OF a fee, but that in itself didn't worry Alex Fitch, that usually played to his advantage. Once it was all over a client would incline towards generosity—either in gratitude of a job well done (and Alex always made sure the job was well done), or, frankly, in an embarrassed rush to get him off the premises. But the latest client didn't look the sort to embarrass easily. She had a Kensington confidence, all brusqueness and matter-of-fact superiority—there was none of the self-justifying brashness you might get in Bloomsbury, and she was worlds away from the needy guilt of Maida Vale. He'd got the usual speech prepared, the one full of the reassuring stuff, the one where he'd say she shouldn't be ashamed of what she wanted, everybody had their kinks, it wasn't his place to judge. He didn't dare to give the speech. She didn't need his speech. Even for a Kensington bitch, that threw him, just slightly.

She was an old woman, they were often old—but quite how old he couldn't begin to guess. She could have been as young as seventy. It wouldn't have surprised him if she'd been a hundred. The face was the usual mess of wrinkles and pits, but for all that, the skin was unblemished, and her eyes were so bright. He doubted she'd ever been beautiful, but attractive—yes, certainly. She cleared her throat, he realised he was staring. She said, "You might think you recognise me. I'm telling you right now. You don't." He agreed.

"Strip," she said, and he didn't have to take orders, he hadn't accepted the commission yet, but she didn't say it rudely, and he obeyed. He stood there naked before her. "I don't need to look at all that," she said, "that's not relevant. Lie down on the ground the way I'll need you, get into position." He did so, flat on his stomach, chin flush against the floor. Just the way she had shown him in the diagram. The floor was cold, he flinched at that, she told him that during the actual performance he'd be quite comfortable on soft thick carpet.

She didn't touch him, but still he thought he could feel her, as she stood over, staring down at his pasty white body, as she assessed him in detail. "It really *is* pasty white," she said, and she sounded pleased, "they got that bit right. And no tattoos? Not even any little ones, I know sometimes you hide them away between the folds of your joints...?" He confirmed that he had no tattoos. "Good," she said. "I don't want anything to distract the guests. I want the pasty white to be pristine."

A little while longer lying there, he heard her walk about him from side to side. "Good," she said, "it's very good," but she didn't seem to be speaking to him, and he didn't reply. "We'll need the mouth open," she said, and he obliged; "not as wide as that, yes, better. An opened mouth tips the head upward, makes it more of a feature. And I want the eyes open too, can you do that? Can you do that without blinking? Think glass eyes. Think your eyes are glass, that you're dead, and we've taken out your eyes, and we've put glass beads inside the sockets."

She didn't say anything else for a long while; then, a little impatiently, "I finished the inspection ten minutes ago, you may as well get up." So he did. She told him that he was hired, and said well done.

"I'm not going to pretend there won't be a little pain," she said. "I'm not going to pretend that you won't get stepped on. Obviously, we will try to minimise that, but accidents will happen, there'll be a lot of guests at the party, and people get clumsy when they're drunk. It is *imperative* when they step on you that you do not cry out. It would destroy the illusion. And, it goes without saying, getting up and remonstrating with them is *completely* out of order." He said that he understood. "But there might be something I can give you to help," she went on. "Bend over."

She opened a bottle of rubbing alcohol, and splashed a little of its contents on his back, on his arse, the backs of his legs. She massaged it hard into his skin. He felt her bare hands kneading away for all they were worth. She grunted as she worked, she really put some effort into it, Alex felt curiously pleased. Her hands were surprisingly smooth, or was that just the alcohol? "I'm not really sure this'll do any good," she said, "but if nothing else, it smells nice."

And then she turned him round so they were face to face—and he thought, wouldn't it have been simpler for her to have walked around to me?—but no, she'd taken him by the shoulders and swivelled him about and he'd swung as easily as if he were on a pivot. And she was looking into his eyes again, and once more she held his gaze so strongly. "I want you to understand," she said. "This isn't for me. This is for my husband. Do you see? All of it, it's for my husband." Was this it, then? That twinge of embarrassment he'd been looking for? And he fumbled to start the reassuring speech he'd been taught, but if she'd wanted to hear it it was too late, she had moved away now and was putting the rubbing alcohol away, the moment had been lost.

"There's nothing more to say, is there?" she said—again, to herself. "I don't think so. It's an easy job, I think. Easy, compared to what some of us have to do. You're lucky. Remember that."

"Thank you," he said. "For the opportunity."

She nodded. "Come on then."

"Now?"

"Of course now. The party's already started."

He took in as much of the room as he could. He supposed he wouldn't be in a position to see it again for a long while. It looked moneyed, but not especially ornate; he had an impression of rich browns on the walls and furniture; it was smaller than he was expecting.

"There's a position for you," she said, "right here." And he was to be the centrepiece of the room, lying down on the very middle of the carpet. To one side there was a tiger rug, to the other a grizzly bear. Their fur looked so soft and glossy, their glass eyes stared sightlessly out into the distance. "Do you want me to do that thing with the mouth?" he said. Because they were so fierce, their teeth white and sharp, they looked ready to bite.

"Let's not get too ambitious," the woman said.

He lay down between the two other rugs, and, mouth excepted, imitated their posture as best he could. And for a moment her cool reserve was broken, he heard her giggle and even give a little clap.

"Oh, you're just perfect!" she said. "The tiger's stripes, the brown of the bear—and you, in the middle, so pasty white! What a contrast! What fun!"

She left the room then—or, at least, Alex suspected she left. There was silence for a while. He was not uncomfortable, the carpet beneath him was warm. The rubbing alcohol made him feel sticky; he thought he smelled sweet as a toffee apple. He breathed shallowly through his open mouth, trying his best to make sure that his body stayed flat and still. He was glad she hadn't wanted his mouth in a roar position, it was an effort to keep it open as it was. He kept his eyes fixed on nothing in particular, let them blur. He thought of glass eyes, hardened them like glass.

And then there was a rumble behind him, not too distant, not as distant as he would have liked—and he didn't know at first what it could be, and it was footsteps, and chatter, and laughter, and then party guests were entering the room—the performance was starting, he was on!—and his body tensed, and he felt a flush of panic, and he nearly gulped, scratched, turned his head, he nearly did everything that would lose his composure.

The guests talked with such excitement, with so much emphatic animation, you'd have thought they'd never talked before, that talking was some exquisite treat they had to make the most of. The men were loud, the women shrill. And already they sounded to Alex so vague and inhuman somehow, but he managed to pick out the odd snatch of conversation. The men talked of cars and cigars and the stock market and the weather. The women talked of shoes and hair and the weather. Some of them trod upon his hand. Some of them dropped cigarette ash on him.

He wondered if any of the guests admired him, had stopped to comment upon the exquisite new rug at their feet. He supposed some might have done. The words all sounded strange and silly. The men talked of tough measures and hard truths, the women talked of riots in the street. Alex decided to ignore them all.

He just hoped he looked good next to the tiger and the bear. Not as ferocious, maybe, but just as proud. That it'd seem he too had been hunted once, on the savannah, or wherever tigers and bears come from—that he'd been thought *worth* hunting. That someone had pursued him because he had a good pelt. And the tiger and the bear—there was no shame for them lying next to him, they'd been *kings* of their domain, they'd been untamed Nature, and Man had fought them fair and square and they'd lost bravely and here they were now as rugs upon the carpet but that wasn't humiliation, it was *commemoration*, they were displayed as noble savages in all their wild dignity, there was honour to the fact that they were here at this party for the great and the good, it raised them above the rest of their kind, this was as much their party as anyone else's. And Alex knew he couldn't compete with that, not really, not at all. He was no tiger. He could never be a bear. But he hoped nonetheless that when they looked down at him the guests would think there was honour to him too, that they'd think he belonged.

Someone dropped a canapé right in front of Alex's face. He didn't let it break his concentration. He didn't let his eyes change focus. The canapé was warm, and there was pastry around it, and Alex thought he could smell chicken.

The men talked of shoes, the women talked of cars, they both talked of all the executions, and how they laughed.

Alex didn't know how long this went on for. And then there was a new sound, breaking down the wall of chatter, a gong. "Dinner is served!" called a voice, it must have been the woman who hired him—"Dinner is served, come along, bring your drinks, come along!" And it seemed to Alex as if all the guests abandoned all pretence of polite decorum, they stampeded to the door, maybe they were very hungry, maybe they hadn't eaten dinner for a long while.

The door was closed. The sudden silence made Alex's head throb, he felt a little sick.

He stretched, and every one of his muscles groaned.

"Don't move," said the bear.

And it was the bear, Alex was sitting up and rubbing life back into his legs, he was looking straight at the bear when it spoke.

"I'm sorry?" said Alex.

"Don't move," said the bear. "Get back into position. They could be back at any moment."

"Leave him be," said the tiger. "It's obviously his first time."

"The pack is only as strong as its weakest link," said the bear. "And he is clearly our weakest link. Back into position now, little man, or I'll rip your fucking head off."

Alex lay back down again. Arms spread, chin on floor. He wished he hadn't moved in the first place, the muscles had woken up and couldn't believe he was proposing to subject them to the same ordeal all over again.

"I'm sorry," whispered Alex. "So, what, are you guys dressed up as wild animals? Or. Or, are you a real bear and tiger? Or what?"

They ignored him, or they didn't break character—they didn't answer him at any rate. And after a while Alex began to doubt he'd even heard the animals speak to him at all, maybe he was asleep, could he fall asleep with his eyes wide open? Because his eyes were hard and staring, he was still thinking of glass, they were glass beads in dead sockets.

The bear had been too cautious. The guests were gone a long time. How long could it take to eat a dinner? Even if it were a banquet, and Alex thought it may have been a banquet, maybe it had seven courses and coffees and mints for afters—even so, why was everyone gone so long? Alex became certain the party was over. The job was done, and he'd been left here on the floor, forgotten, the joke was on him—and maybe the woman was standing over him now, laughing silently at his unquestioning obedience, this was a test. He should get up, get up right now and demand to be paid. And yet still he stared ahead, and still his mouth hung open, and his mouth felt so dry, he felt his tongue was hard and cracked, his tongue was draped over the bottom teeth like it was a rug and there was no life to it any more and it wouldn't move now even if Alex tried—I'm going to get up, he thought, I'm going to get up, I'm getting up. Up I get.

And then, before he could flex that first joint, before he could stir that first muscle, the doors were flung open, and the guests were back, and the party was resumed.

So this was the way it would be—every few hours the party would be interrupted by the gong. The guests would file out to enjoy their dinner. But they'd be back sooner or later, and the drinking and the chatter would begin again. People would stand about and make jokes and talk of nothing and stand on his hand and let ash drop on to his bare back. Were they different guests each time? Were they the same ones as before?—breaking from dinner only to let their food go down, all this socialising was just something to fill in time whilst their stomachs made space for the next bout of food, they would glut themselves on it—and Alex imagined them all as fat and shiny, that by now their swollen bellies were breaking out of their trousers and dresses. He couldn't see them. He didn't know.

During the dinners, during the periods of silence, he might try speaking to the bear and the tiger. There was never a word from either of them. He whispered, he didn't want to upset the bear's professionalism. And then, in time, he'd try to provoke the bear, he told the bear its fur was mangy, that he'd seen grizzlier things at the petting zoo, that it was barely a bear at all. He dared it to rip his head off then and there if it thought it was hard enough. Still, never a word, never a single movement from its rug fur body. Though Alex thought he detected growing disdain from the bear, from the tiger a sighed disappointment.

Alex kept going, he fixed his thoughts on what he was doing the job for. Mainly, for his family. For his wife and kids. He tried to remember when he'd last seen his wife. Probably about the same time he'd seen the kids, that made sense. It was quite a long time ago. He must make sure he saw them all again soon. Otherwise, what was the point? He'd see his wife again soon, he'd go visit, right after this new job was over. He'd see the kids. He tried to remember how many kids he had. He stopped counting at seven. He might well have more now, whenever he went to see her his wife was pregnant, he didn't know how she managed that. He didn't quite like to ask.

And he thought of his eyes, he thought they were glass beads. He knew they were glass now. He could have prodded them with his fingers just to be sure, he could jab at them with his fingernails and he wouldn't even blink. He'd have done it too, just for fun—but that would have meant moving his body, and he wasn't ever going to move again.

The half-eaten canapé was still on the carpet just in front of his face. It had long cooled. The guests had trodden all over Alex, but somehow they had always missed the canapé. The pastry hadn't even flaked, it looked firm and plump.

One day, after she'd sounded the dinner gong, and all her guests had gone, the woman knelt down beside Alex and fed him the canapé.

"It's all right," she said. "You can eat this." She broke the canapé into little pieces, and one by one put them into his open mouth. They melted on his tongue. She stroked the back of his neck as they did so.

"Thank you," he whispered.

"Ssh," she said, still stroking him.

"How much longer?" he asked.

She stopped stroking him, got up, and left.

He liked to think he was her favourite, though Alex had to admit there was very little evidence for that. She fed the other rugs too from time to time—vol au vents, sausage rolls, whatever came to hand. Once she sat with the tiger and fed him an entire bowl of crisps, gently putting them into his mouth one at a time and waiting for the crunch before moving on to another. That took perseverance. Still, Alex thought he was the favourite anyway, because he was the one she had fed first.

And one day she left the dinner table and came to see them, and nuzzled their heads one by one, and then she said, "Come on." And Alex thought maybe she was talking to him, but no, it was to the bear, to the bear.

"Come on," she said, her voice a little harder. "I shan't tell you again."

Alex had turned his head and was sitting up on his haunches, and he was watching, and he knew that was bad—and he only felt a little better when he realised the tiger was on his haunches watching too.

And the bear rug seemed to shiver, and it looked like a sigh. Then it heaved itself up to its feet, slowly, painfully. It teetered a little, trying to get balance, it hadn't been on its feet for such a long time. It steadied. It stood a full eight foot tall, and dwarfed the woman who waited fearlessly by its side.

The woman turned, and went to the door. The bear sighed once more, slumped its awful brute shoulders in resignation, shuffled after her.

The woman closed the door behind them.

"What was that about?" said Alex.

But the tiger just shook its head, settled back into position. Alex did the same.

It wasn't ten minutes before the door opened again. And the bear was back. Its gait was still unsteady. It grabbed on to a cocktail table for purchase, it looked as if it were in shock.

"What happened?" hissed the tiger.

"I don't want to talk about it," said the bear.

"Was it, you know? Sexy stuff?"

"I said," repeated the bear, "I don't want to talk about it." He fell to his knees. For all his bulk he did it so gently, the bear rug was so soft, he hardly made a sound. He spread himself flat on to the floor. He opened his mouth in an impotent roar.

"Oh God," said the tiger. "Oh God. I'm going to be next." And he began to cry.

Alex wanted to console the tiger, but he didn't know what to say. He wanted to roll over and give the tiger a hug, but even tiger rugs are pretty dangerous things, and he wasn't sure his comfort would have been appreciated. And, in time, the snuffling stopped, and the tiger fell silent.

The tiger didn't have to wait too long. A couple more parties, a couple more dinners, and then the woman was back.

She nuzzled them all, but she spent most of her time with the tiger, and the tiger was shaking with fear at all the attention. And then she put a finger upon his head, just the one, very deliberately, and pressed it down firmly. "Come on," she said.

"I don't want to," said the tiger, but the woman gave no reaction to this at all—maybe she couldn't hear him, maybe she couldn't speak tiger. The tiger staggered up on to its four legs—and then, awkwardly, up on to just two. The woman left. The tiger said, "Think of me, won't you?" And it might have been to the bear, or to Alex, or to both of them, but neither replied. The tiger waited for a response, anything—

then he shook his head, and still on hind legs, tottered out after the woman.

Alex expected that when the tiger came back it'd be crying. It wasn't crying. It was beyond tears. It lay down upon the carpet, covered its face with its paws. "Oh God," it said, "oh God, oh God." Over and over, all bloody night.

And then, suddenly, the bear spoke up. "I've had enough of this."

"What are you doing?" said the tiger.

"What do you think?" said the bear.

"You can't just leave," said the tiger.

The bear said, "I can do anything I bloody well want."

It was up on its feet. Eight foot tall, and this time not bent over in defeat, standing as proud as could be.

"You won't get paid," said the tiger.

"You two share my money," said the bear. "I don't want it. I don't want anything she can give me." And he shambled across the room, fiddled about at the door knob with his claw, opened it, and shut the door gently behind him.

"Do you think he's coming back?" said Alex.

And the tiger said, "Fuck it. He's right. I'm worth more than this. I can take the pain and the discomfort. But I'm not going to be *humiliated*." He got to his feet too, but now on all fours, the way tigers are supposed to, and he looked good that way, he looked *sleek*.

"I'm a tiger," the tiger said. "I should be doing, I don't know, what tigers do. Killing antelopes, and chasing gazelles, and shit."

"You can't just leave me here alone," said Alex.

"Watch me," said the tiger. And went.

When the party resumed, Alex thought someone might raise the alarm that the bear and the tiger had gone. Two wild beasts had taken to the streets of Kensington, savage, unpaid, and pissed off. No one seemed to notice. The woman didn't even care.

"The animals left," Alex whispered to her later, next time they were alone.

"Yes, yes," she said.

"They said I could have their pay."

"Hush now," she said, and put a cheese pasty in his mouth.

She would come for him now, Alex was certain. The way she had for the bear and the tiger. And that frightened him at first. But as the days went by, and the days bled into weeks, Alex felt a certain resolve—that he wouldn't let the side down the way the animals had. A pack was only as strong as its weakest link, and he would be as strong as he could be, damn it—mistreat an animal and sooner or later it'll turn on you and bite, but what dignifies mankind is its inexhaustible capacity to take whatever shit it's given, and put up with it, and like it, and say thank you. To remain loyal to the persecutor, no matter what, that was the human way—steadfast patience against all logic and sense. He was a man, wasn't he, he was better than a beast, and he would show her, whatever it was she wanted of him he wouldn't let her down, he would prove himself. He would prove he was worthy of her love. And she would see, yes—that he belonged in Kensington too.

Every day she came to him, and she nuzzled his head, and stroked his white pasty skin, and his heart beat faster in anticipation. He waited for that fingertip on his forehead that would tell him it was time to face the test she had in mind, sometimes he strained his head against her hand to force it.

He writhed to her touch now. No more pretence that he was an object without thought or feeling—they were on their own, he broke character, she never seemed to mind. Even her breath upon his skin made him roll into a little ball, or he'd stretch, or he'd twist and show her his belly. And the weeks turned into months, and he knew he must be her favourite now, she hadn't replaced the tiger or the bear, there was no one else left.

"How much longer?" he'd ask, and each time she'd ignore him.

"How much longer?" he asked, and one day she said, "Come on."

He got to his feet, he stood up nice and tall in front of her. He inched up on his toes, just to look a bit taller. He even flexed his muscles a little. She smiled. "No, no," she said. And she picked him up, and draped him over her shoulder. They left the room then, his feet dragging limply against the floor—and he thought, but the animals were allowed to walk out all by themselves! And he thought, she's touching me, I'm hers. And he wasn't sure whether he was being punished or honoured.

She took him into the party, and the guests were all around—and they were staring at him, and some were cooing, and some were laughing—but he had no time for them, he was looking at the middle of the room, he was the centrepiece, he expected to be laid out prominently with all the rites a centrepiece deserved—and there was no room for a rug in the middle of the room, because there was a bed in it, a big four poster bed, and the bed looked so much softer and luxurious than a simple rug could ever be, and its sheets were folded over enticingly.

She let Alex down from her shoulders then, he pooled on to the floor. She took her clothes off.

And Alex worried he wouldn't be able to perform. Oh, he could perform all right, if just lying back on your stomach with your mouth open and eyes out front was your idea of performance—but he wasn't sure he had anything more to offer than that. He was limp. And she was naked now. And no, not beautiful, never beautiful—but attractive, oh yes, he felt all the hairs on his body prick up, as if her attraction was actually magnetic, his body now covered with its own thin coat of fur. She was so white. Her skin was so dazzling white. It wasn't pasty white, it was thick like milk.

One or two of the guests gave wolf whistles, but she ignored them.

Alex tried to get on his feet, he wanted to take her in his arms.

"No," she said.

And from the crowd she pulled out two people, a man and a woman. Both were rather elderly, and one was his father, and the other, coincidentally, the other was his mother. Alex was rather surprised to see them. He hadn't expected them to have invitations to a party like this. They were rather letting themselves down, too, couldn't they have found some clothes to wear? He hadn't seen them in ages, even longer ago than he'd seen his wife and kids—and hang on, wasn't one of them dead? At least one of them, Alex was fairly sure he'd read that somewhere.

The woman smiled, and turned the full force of that smile on Alex's parents, and she gestured towards the bed. Mum and Dad were smiling too, they couldn't resist, but they turned to each other, and they looked confused and frightened. Dad went first. That was right, too, Mum had always deferred to him.

The woman fucked Alex's father, right in front of Alex, and all the guests were cheering, they were clapping their hands and beating their feet to keep time. Dad did his best, though he looked somewhat winded by the experience, maybe he was the one who'd died? And then, when she was spent, the woman pushed Dad off the bed. He collapsed into a heap, and squirmed there, then stopped. The woman pulled Mum down beside her, and then she fucked her too.

Alex knew his mouth was hung open, not too wide, not in a roar. And he felt water prick behind his glass bead eyes, but the water couldn't find a way of leaking out.

And as the woman rode high upon Alex's mother, as she pressed her bottom ever harder against Alex's mother's face, so that Alex thought he could hear the nose crack—as she rode high upon the party guests' applause, she cried out—

"This is for you, my darling husband! Are you watching, my love? Can you see? This is all for you!"

And it was so hard for Alex to turn his head now, and all he wanted was to turn his head, just so he didn't have to see his father in tears, so he didn't have to see his mother as her face bled—Alex turned his head and looked behind him, looked to where the woman was shrieking, looked to see her husband.

He was an old man. Alex couldn't tell how old. He could have been as young as seventy. It wouldn't have surprised Alex if he'd been a thousand. He was on the wall. He was nailed to the wall, upside down, legs splayed—the rug of her husband's skin was stretched out so wide and taut you could see through it. His mouth was open too, in what looked like leery astonishment, his eyes stared hungrily out at his wife's escapades. He may have been laughing, or was that just the way his face hung, was that just a gurgle coming down his throat? And his arms, his arms were swinging from side to side, and when the hands collided they made a little clap—he was clapping to see such sport.

"All for you, darling," the woman said, more gently. She climbed off Alex's mother, idly kicked her body off the bed. There was a catch in her voice, and Alex couldn't tell whether it was vengeance, or love, or something far stranger than either.

She stood in front of Alex.

"You can go now," she said. "Or, stay and get paid. It's up to you."

She held his gaze still, just for a moment, and then she turned her head, and she never looked at him again.

The guests had cleared a path for Alex to leave the room. He took it.

Alex went back to his room. It felt like his room now, he had earned it. He lay down upon the carpet. He took up the position.

It was nice and dark in his room. He liked the dark.

The bear and the tiger had gone. They had summoned up all the little dignity they'd had left, they had got to their feet and walked out. They didn't *want* the money, they had their pride.

Alex had his pride too. He thought of leaving. He knew no one would stop him.

But it did seem rather silly to have come this far—to have seen so much, and suffered so long—and not to get paid for it.

He waited for the woman to come back.

He decided he wouldn't make it easy for the woman. When she gave him his money, he wouldn't accept it politely. He'd take it out of her hands with all the contempt within him. He wouldn't say thank you. He wouldn't even say it sarcastically.

He waited for the woman to come back.

He might even *refuse* the money. That would show her. That would prove he wasn't to be disrespected. She'd offer him the money, and he'd say no. He wouldn't even *say* no, he'd just shake his head. He'd stay here, and wait, just so she could see his dignity couldn't be bought.

It would depend on how much money.

He wouldn't refuse the money.

He waited for the woman to come back.

He got to his feet. Whatever else, he didn't have to wait lying on the floor. He didn't have to be a rug. If he were to take the humiliation, he would do it standing, he'd take it like a man.

He waited and waited.

There were some champagne glasses about the room that hadn't been cleared away. He took one, sipped at it, and it tasted good.

He waited, and waited some more. He could go, but where would he go? What was outside? Nothing, nothing but a broken marriage and more children than he could count and riots on the streets and all around Kensington, all around and everywhere, Kensington, bloody Kensington.

He tried to cry again, but the water still was jammed fast behind his eyeballs, he could imagine the water building up behind them like a dam, he could imagine soon his head might burst.

He waited. And, at last, the party resumed.

A moment of panic. He should get back on to the carpet. But no, not this time, he'd stand his ground. His white pasty body shook at his bravery.

A rumble of footsteps—and here they were, with their chatter, and their laughter, and they were holding glasses in one hand and cigarettes in the other, and how they talked, they talked so merrily! And they replenished his glass with champagne, "Enjoy, enjoy!" they said. "But I'm just the rug," he tried to say, and he held up his remaining hand in protest, and they chuckled, and they shoved a cigarette between his fingers.

They stood about him, and they smiled warmly enough, but Alex thought there was desperation to their smiles, and their eyes, all their eyes glinted like glass. They chattered about cars and cigars, about shoes and the weather. They chattered about the impending revolution, it must come soon, please God, be soon. Alex chattered back, it wasn't hard. He fed their lines back at them, and he drank, and he smoked, and he laughed. He talked to all the men in suits and all the women in dresses, he talked to the bears and the tigers and the naked fools in pasty white skin. He looked for the hostess, and she was there, but always out of reach, no matter how many conversations he abandoned he could never get close enough to say hello. And he felt strangely happy anyway, and a little drunk, and very very scared, and all the creatures in the room waited and waited and waited and waited for someone to ring the gong to call them to dinner so they could eat.

And the old woman says:

- *Rugs are perfectly imperfect and precisely imprecise—so the Persians say. Discover how they can be the means to appease God in* **The Disappointing Story in the Book** *(story 6, page 85).*
- *If you enjoy parties, and want to go to another, take your bathing costume to* **The Swimming Pool Party** *(story 15, page 251).*
- *Is this a revenge story? Is the woman who hosts the party punishing her husband or titillating him? If you think it is the former, turn to* **Alice Through the Plastic Sheet** *(story 43, page 707).*
- *Bears and tigers are all very well—but let's face it, pigs are best. If you agree, turn to* **Oink** *(story 65, page 1113).*
- *Someone else who struggles with cocktail parties is an old queen who has run out of tales to tell. Find out why in* **Scheherazade's Last Story** *(story 100, page 1687).*

THE WORDS IN THIS BOOK HAVE
YOU OUTNUMBERED 650,000 TO ONE.

IMAGINE WHAT WOULD HAPPEN IF
THEY EVER WORKED OUT HOW
VULNERABLE YOU ARE, READING THIS,
ALL ALONE.

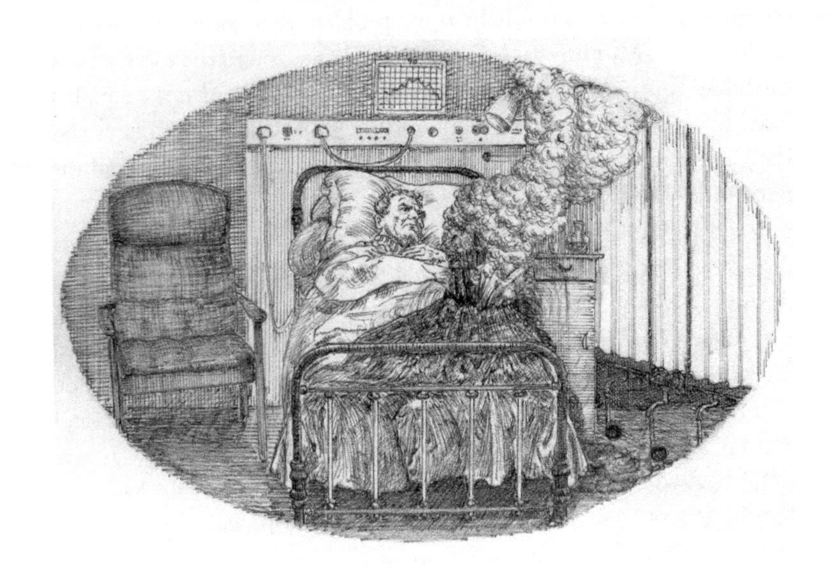

70
ERUPTION

FOR HIS EIGHTH BIRTHDAY Liam Copsey had asked for a volcano. Miss Dexter had taught him all about volcanoes and showed the class diagrams and video footage and everything, and he'd asked when he could see a real life volcano erupting all for himself, and Miss Dexter had said there'd been no volcanic activity in Britain for fifty-five million years. It seemed an awfully long time. It seemed to Liam that a new volcano was long overdue.

His brother and sister had got what they wanted for their birthdays. He'd been told his brother had got to go to a theme park, and his sister had thrown a disco party and invited all her friends from school. But Liam didn't have friends, and rollercoasters made him feel sick. He said he wanted a volcano for his birthday, please, or nothing at all.

Liam Copsey tried his very best to like things. But things were complex, and there was usually some problem that got in the way and spoiled them. Mummy said, "I thought I'd take you to the zoo for your birthday. You liked the zoo last year, didn't you?" And no, he hadn't liked the zoo. He'd liked the lions and the bears and the monkeys and the giraffe, and he'd liked the bats, and he'd liked the penguins and the parrots. But he hadn't liked the reptiles, the reptile house had been too hot and he hadn't liked their reptile eyes. He didn't like zoos, but he did like volcanoes. There was nothing not to like about volcanoes. His favourite volcano, of course, was a stratovolcano, because they were the biggest and the best and they were very loud and destroyed everything in their path—Krakatoa was a stratovolcano, and when that had gone off it had made the loudest noise every recorded, as loud as four atom bombs! But he wasn't a greedy child, he knew it was unfair to expect a stratovolcano for his birthday, so he told Mummy he would be happy with a cinder cone volcano instead, which would be nice and tall but have slower moving lava and would probably kill fewer people.

"I'll have a word with your father," Mummy had said.

Liam tried to like people, too, but they were just as difficult as things. Mummy told him he had to try harder with people, and it wasn't fair that he should hate them because one little irritation might get in the way—and Liam wanted to explain that they weren't little irritations, it was a zero sum situation, whereby any multiplication would be reduced to nothing if at some point you multiplied it by zero. You could have pages and pages of calculations and you could build up some really big numbers in the process, and then all you had to do was throw in a 'times by zero' and the whole edifice of digits would come crashing down. He'd tried doing it for himself, he had made one sum last over five full sheets of paper! And then he'd sneaked in that 'times by zero', he'd done it on the fourth page, and from that point on the calculation was entirely void. It was quite funny, really, but he didn't tell Mummy this, because she didn't like it when he talked that way, and he wasn't an unkind boy, and he really *did* try liking people: with people he tried to isolate all the 'times by zero' bits and put them into some separate sum elsewhere in his head. So, for example, he liked Miss Dexter at school because she was nice and told him stories and said he was clever—and he chose to hate an entirely different Miss Dexter whose perfume made his skin feel prickly. He tried to like his (sort-of) brother and his (sort-of) sister—he knew they were only sort-of, but he was told to refer to them as brother and sister, and he did the 'sort-of's silently in his head. He tried to like his (sort-of) Aunt Sharon, although he was fairly sure she didn't like him very much.

He tried hard to like his father too.

He found his father hard to read. His father would always say he was happy to see Liam, and he smiled at him a lot, but he never tried to hug him. And Liam didn't like being hugged much, so that was a good thing, wasn't it? Liam didn't see his father very often. He didn't know whether his sort-of brother and his sort-of sister and his sort-of aunt got to see more of him than Liam did, but he thought that was probably the case since they lived with him. Liam's father had never lived with him the way other fathers with other children got to do—and this was a good thing too, because Liam didn't like the idea of anyone even visiting his home, a third body inside the house made everything so much more cramped, and they'd be using up an extra third of the air supply. All of these things were good—his father's absence, his not wanting to touch him, his not wanting to talk to him too much when he had nothing to say, because Liam never quite knew how to respond when people did that, and that's when Mummy told him he was being rude. But, still. He had to work hard trying to like his father, it was a real effort for him to squeeze all the things that seemed wrong into a separate sum, and he couldn't work out why.

Three days before his birthday Liam found his mummy crying in the kitchen. She tried to smile when she caught him standing in the doorway, she tried to pretend she hadn't been crying at all. And Liam told her she needn't worry about getting him a volcano if it were proving too difficult for her. He'd known it *would* be difficult, there must have been a logical reason there hadn't been one in Britain for fifty-five million years. He could do without. And he was being very brave, he told her, because he really *did* want his volcano, more than anything. And he suddenly knew this was how life was always going to be, cruel and unfair, whatever he'd asked for Mummy had always provided, but he knew that at some point he'd ask for too much and she'd stop even trying, and it was his fault. He told her all this, and now she was crying again, but it was different crying this time, she seemed so moved by his plight—he wished he could cry too, but he'd often tried, and never find the knack. She hugged him close, and he didn't mind, and she assured him she loved him very much and she would never stop trying to look after him, not ever.

His birthday at last—and when Liam woke up he knew he was a whole year older, and Mummy asked him if he felt any different, and he really did.

They got into the car, and Mummy asked him whether he'd like to ride in the back or ride in the front like a grown-up, and Liam usually preferred riding in the back because he had so much more space, but this time he chose the front. He didn't know where she was driving him, but he trusted her, he knew it wouldn't be anywhere nasty like the doctor's or the dentist's or the zoo. After a while he recognised the route—"We're going to Daddy's house!" he said, and from that he worked it all out, every little detail—"That means I'm going to get my volcano after all!" Liam didn't get to see Daddy's house very often, it was only on very special days. Mummy told him to hush now about the volcanoes, and Liam shut up, but he was so happy, he couldn't help but grin the whole way there.

His father was waiting to answer the front door when they rang the bell. "Happy birthday, Liam!" he said. He was smiling. He didn't hug him. Aunt Sharon was there too, and his brother. His sister wasn't, she was out playing with friends. They led Liam through to the sitting room, and there was a mound of presents there waiting for him to unwrap. "Jump right in, Liam," said his father, and Mummy nodded. He got a computer game and a nice pocket calculator and a book about Romans. They were good presents. He kept looking about him for the volcano. "Where's the volcano?" he eventually had to ask. His father frowned. "What do you mean, Liam?" he said. Mummy said "Now, Liam, don't start." And Liam wondered whether this was all part of a joke, and at any moment Daddy or Mummy would wink at him and tell him they were only teasing, and out they would wheel his volcano. And then he realised his father never joked about anything, and he felt sad.

And then—there it was, the wink! His father winked at Mummy, and Mummy winked back, and they began to laugh, and Liam laughed too, in relief, although he didn't dare believe everything was going to be all right, not yet. "We can't keep it from you any longer," said Father, and Mummy told Liam he had been *such* a good boy this last year. "Come out back," said Father, and Liam thought, of course, it's in the garden, you wouldn't put a volcano in the sitting room, would you? They went out the French windows, and stood on the nice patio his father had made, and there it was, the volcano, standing on the lawn.

"We couldn't wrap it for you," said his father. "I hope you understand."

"Your father had to apply for planning permission to build it," said Mummy.

"I've been out here, every weekend, constructing the thing," said his father. "I do hope you like it."

It wasn't a very big volcano, not in the scheme of things. But if Liam was anything, he was a realist, he knew that to have expected a full size volcano on the lawn would have been unfair. It still rose some sixty feet into the air, though, and the base perimeter took up the entire lawn—Liam was impressed by how steep the sides were, tapering at last towards the open mouth at the peak. He could hear the magma inside spit and seethe. It was a classically designed cinder cone volcano, and really, what more could a boy ask for? Like it? He loved it. And when he said so, his father broke into a huge grin that at last seemed unforced and entirely natural.

"Will it erupt?" asked Liam. But he already knew his answer. "It can only erupt when the tectonic plates collide."

"You let me take care of that," said his still grinning father. "Shaz, put on the garden lights, it'll help the mood. Now, watch this." He took a spade, and beat it hard against the grass. Once, twice. On the third time there was a crack, they all felt a sudden lurch under their feet. "That's got it!" said his father. The ground rumbled like a big dozy giant being stirred from its sleep. His brother and his aunt laughed, and held on to each other. His mummy looked nervous, so Liam held on to her too.

The rumble was getting louder now, and it was making his feet tingle. "Here it comes!" cheered his father, "Everybody look!" Clear white smoke was billowing out of the cone; then, firing straight up into the air were these little balls of lava, one after the other, phut-phut-phut, they sailed upwards, and all the family craned their necks to follow them; they flew so high that when they popped apart they looked like shooting stars.

Everyone relaxed and watched the show. Some of the lava balls made loud bangs and big technicolour patterns; others zizzed around like mosquitoes and made Liam laugh. Liam liked best the ones that rocketed up, up into the clouds—when they exploded they seemed to decorate the whole sky. "You might want to stand back on the patio, Liam," said his father. "The lava flow is getting pretty close now, I don't want you getting your feet burned."

And they were all so happy, and Mummy and Daddy didn't seem weird or angry with each other, and Liam knew he was right to have wanted a volcano for his birthday present, really, a volcano was something everyone could enjoy.

"Thank you," said Liam, and he'd never felt the urge to hug his father before, and had he stopped to think about it he'd have been frightened by that, but he didn't think, he hugged him. And his father was surprised. And his father hugged him back. "You're a good boy, Liam", he said. "You're a good boy, don't you ever forget, I like you very much."

They stayed outside with the volcano until the lava was all spent and the cone little more than a smoking stump of ash and rock.

Liam Copsey never made a conscious decision to lose touch with his father. He thought that his mother probably did. One day she said to him, "Liam, you're an adult now, and how much you want to know that bastard is up to you." It excited him a little, that he got to make his own decisions about people, because people were complex things—but it also made him a little sad. He felt guilty. He knew that it was because of him that his father had never wanted to live with them in the first place, it was his fault. He told his mother. She laughed in a way Liam hadn't liked. "On the contrary," she said. "If you hadn't come along, he'd have been out of my life years ago."

He used to think back to that birthday with the volcano rather a lot. Whenever he felt confused about his father, he only had to remind himself of all the effort that had gone into the volcano, and the evidence of the love behind it made him secure again. Liam supposed, in his memory, he may have exaggerated its size and destructive force, but not by much, not much, surely? When he met up with his father, for months afterwards, he would thank him for the volcano. His father had seemed quite happy at first, but as time had gone by, had become ever more taciturn and irritable. "For God's sake, can you stop going on about that bloody volcano? Haven't you got anything else to talk about?"

When at last he left home, his mummy was concerned that Liam wouldn't adjust to the real world outside. But Liam was clever, and he adjusted extraordinarily well. He soon learned how to do the smile that everyone expected of him. He still didn't like being hugged, but he got better at hugging, and at time he would feel an urge for physical contact with others that was almost desperate, he would hate all the sensations it would force on him, the way their skin smelled, the way that skin stuck against his own—but he couldn't stop the urge, he *needed* it, it was like prodding at a tooth until it hurt or scratching at his arms until they bled. He had relationships. His partners would leave him eventually, they'd say he'd grown too cold—and they didn't know the half of it, the coldness was all there had ever been, the coldness and a meticulous act he had at last decided to drop. At work he excelled, and managed a team of fifty employees, all of them liked him and respected him. He adjusted. It wasn't hard. Adjusting isn't hard. It's finding a reason to keep the adjustments in place that is the tricky part.

He receives a letter in the post, and that is unusual in itself, he prefers email, getting information he can read, process, then delete. The letter is handwritten, which seems almost offensively personal. It is from a man calling himself Simon Copsey, and it takes him a moment to work out who that can be. The letter says that their father is very ill. He'd had cancer a couple of years before and had fought it off successfully, at the cost of part of a lung, but now the cancer is back. The prognosis is not good. If Liam wants to say goodbye to his father, now is the time to do it—and there are details of the hospital, and the ward he is in, and the name of the attending doctor. Liam reads the letter several times, trying to determine whether he can consider any part of it a rebuke for his years of silence. He decides, at last, that he can.

When he gives his name at reception, he half-expects more of that rebuke, that a nurse may ask him where the hell he has been. Nothing, of course—and he is relieved, and he is disappointed. The ward is on the third floor. Can he see where the lift is? Yes? Good.

He hopes someone will show him which is his father's bed, because he isn't sure after all these years he will recognise him, and how embarrassing will that be? He walks slowly down the ward, looking left and right, scanning the names on the progress charts as much as the faces. His father is on the right, third from the end, and of course he knows him at once. He is smaller than he remembers, and so frail, and his arms are as thin as tracing paper. But the face—as old as it is, the face is Liam's own.

Right away he knows that this is a mistake. His father's eyes are shut. He can turn around and leave. What will the nurses think of him?—why care about that? His father's eyes open. It's still a mistake. He can still leave. What will his father think of him? Why care about that?

He sits down beside his father.

"Do you know who I am?" he asks. "Hello, Daddy." He never graduated from calling him Daddy into something less childish. Whose fault is that? He's already spoiled things. This old man is nobody's daddy.

His father nods, tries to smile. Tries to speak, but it's indistinct. Liam sees there aren't many teeth left in his father's head.

"How are you?" asks Liam. His face burns with shame. He tries to remember all the tricks and turn of social conversation he's learned over the years, and none of them help him now.

He doesn't wait for an answer. Instead, he tells his father how *he* is. He doesn't give him any details, just broad strokes—and realises with each new fact that the context is missing, he needs to reach further into his past to explain how he became associate director, and then how he got into business in the first place, and how well he did at college. All the while, his father nodding, smiling, egging him on.

What is the point of any of this?—even his mother barely knows what he is up to these days.

"Daddy," he says at last. "Father. Tell me. Is there anything, I don't know. Is there anything I can do for you?"

His father tries to say something. Liam leans forward to listen, and Daddy takes him by the hand. Liam hates the feel of it, the skin so frail he fancies he's directly touching blood and bone. "Volcano," says his father. "I want a volcano."

Liam finds the nurse and tells her what he needs. He likes the nurse for her starched uniform, her height, and her kind eyes. He dislikes the nurse for her provincial accent and the small tattoo on her wrist that looks like a smudge of dirt. She is wary at first. "But we mustn't disturb the other patients." He knows he can charm her, he has been charming people like her for years. He promises her he'll keep the noise and smoke to a minimum, and that they can pull the curtains around his father's bed to give the eruption full privacy. In the end she not only agrees, she says she'll check in supplies for some of the gases and raw materials he'll need.

He builds the volcano on his father's bed. He constructs the basic shape of it with soil he's gathered from the hospital garden; it's been baked hard in the summer heat. He works hard at the magma chambers, and makes sure that the conduits from them to the throat of the cone will allow the free flow of molten gas and lava. The volcano climbs higher and higher, he has to work fast, he knows soon it will be the end of visiting hours. It is only as it nudges the ceiling that he realises he too has built a classic cinder cone volcano, and he feels a stab of nostalgic affection for that.

He pours in all the superheated water, the steam stings his eyes. His father has fallen asleep, he has to wake him to he can see what's been built for him.

"Bring your knees together," he tells his father, "And that will simulate the collision of the tectonic plates." But his father is too weak to move his legs, or in too much pain, or simply doesn't understand—and Liam fights down a flare of angry impatience, who was this volcano for in the first place, can't he help a little bit? "Don't worry, Daddy, I've got it," he says, and he slams hard against the base of the volcano with his hand, and the eruption is triggered.

Only now does Liam realise he's made a mistake—the volcano is so tall that in his supine position his father cannot hope to see the lava coming out. It dribbles down the side, but as much as his father twists his neck, he can only see it as it congeals thickly around the base. The smoke that billows out of the crater is too wispy—it disperses into the ward as soon as it is expelled—and the volcano is so *slow*, Liam wanted it to be belching out fire and ash, and instead it releases its innards in a way that seems almost insultingly desultory, less like an elemental force of nature, more like tomato ketchup from a bottle.

It's almost too much for Liam to bear and only now he cries, and he's never cried in front of his father not *ever*—his mummy used to say that if he cried when his father visited it might make him not want to come again, his father didn't like a fuss, his father would be embarrassed by it. His father would be embarrassed by *him*—"I'm sorry, I'm sorry," Liam says, and he's apologising at first for the crappy volcano, but he's also crying for his own tears, and he's crying that his father is dying and soon won't care about his tears anyway—"I'm sorry," he says, and his face is streaming, it's streaming far better than his volcano could. It hurts to cry like this. It hurts, it makes him feel his entire face is breaking apart. "I'm sorry, Daddy, don't go!" and his father catches him by the hand, and looks up at his son and he smiles, and whispers "Thank you."

He phones his mother on an impulse—he knows if he *decides* to do it he'll find a reason not to, so he waits until he can catch his brain unawares. "Hello, Mummy," he says. "I'm sorry." He isn't sure whether he really *is* sorry, or whether he just knows he ought to be—but he doesn't suppose it matters much either way.

"Liam?" she says. "Oh God. Is that really you? Oh God. Oh God."

It is not a long conversation; neither of them can bear it. But he promises he will come and see her. And the third time he tries to do so, he succeeds.

They have tea. She has been out, she has bought a cake. He doesn't like the idea of her going out to the shops to buy cakes, she looks nearly as frail as his father was, and he comes very close to making a promise to do her shopping from now on that would be terribly inconvenient for him.

He tells her that his father is dead, and that his sort-of brother Simon has written, and that they are both invited to the funeral.

"Oh, God," she says. "No. No, I don't want to go."

He asks her why not.

"You don't understand people, Liam," she says. "You think because you had one moment of connection with your father, that it changes everything. It doesn't. It doesn't change who he was. And it doesn't change who you are."

He says he understands. She's right, of course. It's like a sum which has 'times by zero' in it, and his father has timesed it by zero many times over. He won't go to the funeral either.

He writes to Simon, and thanks him for the invitation, and tells him that neither he nor his mother will be able to attend the service, and offers him his condolences.

He tells the office he won't be in to work on Monday, it's the day of his father's funeral. In itself it's a fact—he doesn't tell them he won't be going. He gets up that morning, and he puts on his best clothes, he makes himself look as smart as he can be. He waits until noon. Noon is the time his father is to be cremated, or then abouts—he doesn't know precisely when, noon is a decent estimate. At noon he leaves the house, and goes out to the park. His father never took him to a park, he wasn't a man who much bothered with parks, or not as far as Liam was concerned—but it's a nice park, it's as good a place as any.

That day he saw his father at the hospital, he didn't know why he kept the remains of the volcano, why he didn't just throw them away. He knows now. He stands still in the centre of the green, and he reaches into the bag of ash, and he feels it run between his fingers. "Goodbye," he says. He thinks there should be something better to say, but really, what is there? He pours out the ash, and watches it blow away in the wind. And he waits to see if he'll feel anything, whether his tectonic plates will shift.

And the old woman says:

- *Young Liam doesn't enjoy zoos, because just one single animal he dislikes taints the whole. Judge what he might have thought of the inhabitants of the ark in* **The Monogamy of Wild Beasts** *(story 26, page 437).*
- *You can't choose your families, and families can't choose you. Sometimes it even seems that they come from an entirely different race or culture. If you are lucky enough to have a family you understand and respect, congratulations. And turn to* **Death to the French** *(story 29, page 473).*
- *Being able to harness the power of a great natural disaster like a volcanic eruption is quite an achievement—but it's nothing to how the apocalypse is exploited in* **Dig Deep** *(story 38, page 633).*
- *If you too weigh the pleasures of life with numbers and zero sum calculations, consider* **Digits** *(story 44, page 741).*
- *The love between a father and his son is one of the greatest love stories of all. Read more about love in* **101 Heartbeats** *(story 101, page 1695).*

71
The Shadow Mother

THEY NEVER BELIEVE IT when they find out I'm the son of David Forbes. And yes, *that* David Forbes, the famous one. There's no resemblance. And he had such a distinctive face—the sharp eyes, the jet black smear of a moustache (which I happen to know he dyed regularly, oh, you would be surprised by the affectations my father had), that chin. It's a striking face. It's strong and determined, and so iconic that it's hard to believe it wasn't always there, that there was a time it didn't represent our nation, when those craggy confident features weren't common property, like Big Ben, the Queen, William Shakespeare, fish and chips. But of course there must have been.

No, I take after my mother.

So they don't believe me to start with—and I don't care two hoots, you can bet your life I wasn't the one who brought the thing up in the first place. But then they'll look impressed, even act a little shy with me, as if a fraction of my father's greatness may have been passed down, and then maybe they'll shake my hand, as if a fraction of that fraction might be passed on to them. And they ask, inevitably—what was he like? By which they mean, what was *it* like, growing up in a household with David Forbes, where you got to see David Forbes every day, where you got to walk about on David Forbes' carpets, and eat off David Forbes' plates? Breathing David Forbes' very air, to know him, actually *know* him, what was it like?

And I always say. My childhood was perfectly ordinary—or so it seemed to me. It wasn't as if I had any other childhood to compare it with. And at that they'll nod thoughtfully, they'll accept that, they can see the logic of that. "Yes," they'll say, "oh yes."

It's nonsense. My childhood wasn't ordinary. Of course I could see the difference between my father and the fathers of friends at school. For Christ's sake, my father was David Forbes! And their fathers were nobodies, posterity wouldn't remember them, there wouldn't be statues erected or statutes passed in their names. My father the inventor, the war hero, the statesman, the philanthropist. And their fathers, who knows? Who cares?

"My childhood was perfectly ordinary." And they might look a little annoyed then, these people who didn't believe I was his son at all at first, who now do believe but feel let down. Because I am not as remarkable as my father was. As if I, an unremarkable man, am trading off my father's good name. At least I have my own name. Not like Davey, my elder brother—thank Christ my father could name only one son after him, that even his egotism had its limits.

At last the conversation dries up. They're so effusive, but I won't be as effusive in turn. I accept their gratitude for my father's life, but I won't feed it. "Well," they'll say, "it was a pleasure to meet you," or some such, and at that they'll go; sometimes they'll ask for an autograph first, and I carry a pen with me everywhere just in case. They get out their wallets. They take out their twenty pound notes. On the one side the Queen, on the other, my father; there he is, the eyes, moustache, chin. I scribble my name all over his face. They tell me they'll frame it. I suppose most of them do.

It gets a little chilly in my father's shadow. But I wouldn't mind that.

I'd be proud even, proud like they expect me to be. If I had only liked him a little better. Oh, I accept he was a great man. I don't dispute that, the good he has done for our country, and for scientific progress, and for modern thinking. He averted, so they say, at least one world war—that's clearly a good thing. But he was a shit, he was a bastard, an unutterable bastard, and there's not a day that goes by I'm not pleased he's dead.

Naturally, there have been many movies featuring my father, and when at first I hear there's to be yet another I take little interest. But then there is a lot of fuss made that this is going to be the first film to examine David Forbes the *man*, in matters not just political but domestic. The centenary of my father's birth is fast approaching, they want something to commemorate that, or take advantage of it at any rate. The producers make play about how this will be a truly authentic portrayal of the great man, and they write to me and Davey offering a consultancy fee. It goes without saying they don't want to consult us in any practical sense, the script is already written, but cooperation from the Forbes family is something they can use in the publicity. I phone my brother's wife, and of course they are accepting the offer—the money will help pay Davey's hospice bills. I go to see my solicitor. I ask whether there's any way we can stop the film being made. He says there isn't, that a life as public as my father's can hardly be copyrighted—that if the screenplay were to depict my father negatively we could block it on grounds of slander, but of course it'll be yet another hagiography. He suggests I take the cash.

They send me the script. I skim it. For all their lofty claims, it doesn't seem especially domestic—there's the inevitable section set in the prisoner of war camp, and most of the second half takes place at Whitehall. I appear in just two scenes—the first, as a young child in the background at a Christmas party, the other, as a slightly older child watching my father get presented with the Victoria Cross. At least, I presume the child is me; the movie has simplified things somewhat and given Father only the one son, so I suppose it may well be Davey.

I don't expect to hear from the producers again, save maybe for a complimentary ticket to the premiere. I am surprised when some months later I receive an invitation to the set to see the actors at work. I write back quite politely saying I have no interest in doing that. Their response is charming, but rather forceful: it's pointed out that I am obliged to attend at least one day's shooting as per the terms of my contract. I wasn't aware I even had a contract. I call my solicitor, who tells me that I have indeed agreed to make myself available for minor publicity duties; no doubt they want nothing more onerous than a couple of photographs with the cast. I promise myself I will change solicitors when all this is over.

I have to give my name to a security guard, and he doesn't seem to react when I use the name 'Forbes'. Very soon an excitable young girl comes to greet me. "I'm sorry, I'm sorry," she says, "we're running behind!" She tells me she will be looking after me for the day. I ask if she's the director. She says she isn't.

"Such an honour," she says. "I get to meet a lot of actors, but you get used to actors, don't you? Your father was a great man."

I wonder whether I am going to have to sign a twenty pound note for her. "Quite so," I say.

She takes me onto the soundstage. There there's a facsimile of the room I had dined in as a child. The same large round table, the chairs with those ornate head rests. The attention to detail is remarkable—but I suppose it has to be, my father's old manor house is so familiar to the general public. I feel a strange chill standing there. I haven't been back to the family home since the National Trust started charging admission in the seventies.

Up comes the director, all smiles, and he's barely older than the young girl he's assigned to chaperone me. Up comes the lead actor, I don't recognise him, but I'm made to gather he's very famous. He tells me it's an honour to play my father. He tells me this will be a new direction for his career, he's got typecast playing action heroes. He tells me that my father was a great man. "Quite so," I say, again. I think he's good casting—he's grown the moustache, and his eyes burn with the same sort of ambitious intensity. There is nothing to be done about the chin. We shake hands, fictional father and real life son, and I'm half-blinded by all the camera flashes.

I feel tired. I've done my bit. I want to go home. "Would you like to stay and watch a scene?" asks the girl, and I say I would be delighted.

They bring on my mother. She's a nice looking girl in her twenties. I can see that they've dressed her according to the fashion of the times, and have echoed one of the more famous photographs of my father—

the one where he acknowledges the applause of a grateful crowd, and my mother's standing next to him, her hand held up in an awkward wave, her eyes squinting a little in the light—or maybe because she never got used to the cameras the way Father had—and they're both smiling, and Mother's smiling wider, perhaps to compensate for everything else, who knows? They haven't bothered to cast an actress who looks very much like my mother. She's nice looking, though, I'll give them that.

It's a simple scene. There's not much dialogue. My father and mother are at breakfast. My mother eats eggs solemnly. My father is reading a newspaper, the headline says, 'Country in Crisis'. At length he sighs, and gets to his feet. He announces that he will be home late that evening, there is work to be done. He kisses my mother on the top of her head. My mother doesn't get a line.

They shoot the scene. The director talks quietly to his cameramen, to the man who's doing the sound. He says that they shall go again.

My father looks troubled by what he reads in the newspaper—troubled, but resolute and strong. My mother looks loving and concerned. And she looks grateful too, as if she knows how lucky she is to be eating eggs in the presence of a great man, as if she knows he'll win through against the odds. He kisses her head. The scene ends. And her smile fades, and just for a moment I see her flash at her husband a look of hateful contempt. I know it's for the actor and not for my father, but I like her for it all the same.

They get ready to shoot a third time. They uncrease my father's newspaper, and reset my mother's eggs. My chaperone asks if I'm enjoying myself.

"But there's something wrong," I say. Perhaps a little too loudly, at my age it's hard to judge.

My father hears. "What's that?" he says.

"Kissing her on the head," I explain. "He would never have done that."

"In this scene," the director tells me, "we would like him to kiss her on the head, because it shows the affection between them."

"I like it," says my father, "because there's all this war brewing, yeah? But he still has time to love his wife."

"I understand," I say. "But it's not what he'd have done."

"Well, what *would* he have done?"

"Nothing. He'd have just left. He probably wouldn't have had breakfast with her in the first place."

"That's interesting," said the director. "And I thank you, Mr Forbes. But, you know, this isn't a very important scene. This is just an establishing scene."

"Wouldn't it be better if what you established was right?"

My father looks thoughtful. My mother smirks. The director glares at my mother—she isn't important enough a character to smirk.

The director says, "This scene is set before you're even *born*. So how would you know whether your father back *then*, in *those* days, kissed your mother or not?"

"She would have told me," I said. And it's hardly credible, but it's true.

"I don't have to do the kiss," says the actor. "Gerry? I don't like the kiss anyway. How about I, I don't know? How about I touch her shoulder or something?"

"Would you rather touch her shoulder?"

"I'd like to touch her shoulder. I don't know, I could do it with inner weariness."

"Okay," says the director. "Go for the shoulder. Let's get on with this, please."

My father reads his newspaper. My mother eats her eggs. My father gets to his feet, tells my mother he won't be home early. My father touches my mother's shoulder, my mother visibly recoils.

"What the hell was that?" says the director.

"Sorry," says my mother, and it's the first time I've heard her voice, and it's beautiful. "I wasn't psyched for the shoulder touch. I'll be psyched next time."

The next time it's a wrap.

The director comes to see me. He is all smiles once more. "Well," he says. "And that's what it's like on a movie set! I hope you've enjoyed your day. And I promise you, we're doing our very best to bring your father's story to the screen. He's an inspiration to us all."

He shakes my hand and politely intimates we should never meet again.

They call me a cab. I wait outside.

"Oh, hello," says my mother, and for a moment I don't recognise her; her wig is off, and her hair is blonde and cropped. She's smoking a cigarette, and that's something my real mother did only very infrequently.

"You were very good," I say.

"Oh, really? Thanks! I didn't do anything. I mean, not in that scene. I do plenty in some other scenes. It's not just a minor supporting part."

"No," I say.

"I liked what you said in there," she says, her voice dropping to a whisper. I can't help it, I lean in close to hear her. "Sometimes there's so much bullshit in this job, you know? Sometimes people need to be reminded of that." She takes a puff of her cigarette, blows the smoke away from me, nice and respectful. "I like playing your mother. She seems lovely."

"Quite so," I say. "I mean. Yes. She was."

She smiles, and I smile, and we shake hands. Her hand is very cool and smooth. She tells me her name is Mary, and I tell her it's the same name my mother had, and she laughs and says she knows! And I wonder whether it's why she got the part.

Davey inherited not only my father's name but his looks too, and that was his misfortune. I took after Mother, and I suppose that was mine. She was not a plain woman, I must stress that. But there was nothing striking about her either; when she was younger her hair was an undistinguished mousey brown, and as she aged it turned into an undistinguished mousey grey. Her face was a little too flat somehow, and she didn't know how to smile properly, it always came out lopsided. Were she just anybody's wife none of this would have mattered; but her husband had a bearing that would one day be featured on currency, and he eclipsed her entirely. Had the great diplomat Mr Forbes been a funny little scruff of a man, and Mother the raving beauty by his side, then that would have been apt—and, indeed, I once attended an international conference with my father and looking at the other politicians I could see this was often exactly the case. But my father had the brains and the looks, my mother neither. Even as a little boy, that never seemed fair to me.

Maybe it was because of her plainness that she had such wonderful jewellery. Kings and presidents all around the globe were always giving presents to my father of jewellery, of pendants and tiaras ringed with diamonds. Father accepted these gifts as a matter of high honour. I rather wondered whether it was more that everyone wanted to pretty his wife up a bit. Father used to say that the contents of Mother's jewellery box were worth more than the rest of the contents of the house combined, and I think he was exaggerating, but maybe not by much. And when Mother had to be displayed as his consort on would go the pearls, and they did do something to transform her—you were so drawn to the shining jewelled earrings accenting her face you never needed to think about the bland pink mass that lay between. But at home she never wore jewellery. She never, I think, in her whole life even had her ears pierced. At home she was Mother.

I wonder where all that good jewellery went to. We didn't get to keep it after she died. I suppose it was returned to the nations that had gifted it—but then, that wouldn't make it a gift, would it, more of a loan? I've got a few little trinkets of hers, simple things, stuff she'd inherited from her mother. Worthless.

I like to think I was her favourite. She never showed I was her favourite, she was always completely fair. She made sure she gave as much attention to Davey as she did me, that we got the same amount of toys and sweets. "Don't tell your father," she'd say to us, and she'd wink, to suggest giving us treats wasn't so naughty really, if Father found out he might not have minded after all. And for years too, yes, that's right, she would pretend to be the tooth fairy, and leave us shillings if we put our baby teeth under the pillow. I never believed in the tooth fairy, not even at the start, I always knew it was Mother, that this was a game we were playing. Davey was two years older—but still thought there was some sort of force that magically invaded our house, got past the policemen stationed at the front door, and removed bits of our bodies for cash. But because I knew it was Mother, and she knew I knew, it always felt like our own private secret; it was the tooth fairy leaving shillings for Davey, but Mother leaving them for me.

It all came to an end, of course, and so abruptly: there was one time Davey lost a tooth, and he decided he would try to catch the fairy in the act. He pretended to be fast asleep, and poor trusting Mother fell for it. Davey felt so betrayed that he screamed the house down. Father was awoken, and one never woke up Father unless it were urgent. He said he would punish both of us. He told us, very sternly, that the tooth fairy game would go on no longer. If we were old enough to question the fantasies of childhood, then that was well and good—but that meant we were too old to reap the profits of childhood either. Mother tried to object, and she *never* did that, and Father told her she mustn't interfere. He then reached into the drawer of his desk, and I had no idea what he might produce—a cane, maybe—he never beat us, but maybe that was because we had been children, maybe that was one of the profits from which we were now disqualified—and he took out not a cane, he took out six bright shillings. "Three shillings each," he said, and explained that this was a settlement against any further teeth we may yet lose, but it was a single one-off payment, after this there was nothing more to be had. We took the money. We had never owned so much money before. Davey's tears dried up at the sight of it, he couldn't believe such a prize. And I stood there in my pyjamas, and I felt the cold shillings in my palm, and knew that something precious had been lost.

I said to Mother, years later, "But what did you want the teeth *for*?" And she looked surprised, and said, "Because they're you, darling. Because they're part of you."

I say again, my father never beat us. It would have been easier if he had. If behind closed doors he had taken off that mask of methodical statesmanship, and set about us all with his belt. But that wasn't his way at all. I knew it *was* a mask, but it never came off—try as hard as I might to find a crack, it sat there snugly on his face whether in front of the camera or behind the dining table. When I'd done something wrong, I was summoned to his study—and he never so much as raised his voice. He would sigh, and put aside his work, as if this appointment was an unnecessary drain upon his time and resources, as if the minutes he wasted disciplining me would disrupt delicate negotiations on an international scale. And that famous face would sag a bit, he would *let* it sag, never think that any of this wasn't calculated—his sharp eyes would dull, he'd stroke at that chin thoughtfully, and he'd tell me I had disappointed him. That was it. That was enough. I might be in tears now, just for that—and as I got older, and was summoned to his study all the more often, I would tell myself this time I wouldn't cry, I mustn't cry, but I always did. He would lower his head and return to his papers. He wouldn't look up at me as I bawled away like a baby. I was dismissed.

Davey would do anything to avoid causing disappointment. I remember back when we were small, I can't even guess how old he would have been. Five or six? I can't even guess. And the family were all together, my mother too, and Father was asking us what we wanted to be when we grew up. He asked Davey first.

"I want to be a train driver," said Davey.

My father chuckled at that. And he said that was a perfectly reasonable dream for a little boy. But when Davey grew up he would realise that being a train driver wasn't all it was cracked up to be. You wouldn't be in charge of where you went, or when you set off, you would have to follow a strict timetable. And wouldn't it be better to run the trains instead, to be the one who drew up that timetable? And Davey looked confused, and nodded, and he didn't seem sure whether he was being told off or not.

I was furious. Because it wasn't Davey who wanted to be the train driver, it was me. He'd just stolen my dream so he would have something to say. Couldn't my father remember, I was the one who'd got the train set for my birthday? And now I couldn't say I wanted to be a train driver, my father would just think I was apeing my brother, and it turned out wanting to be a train driver wouldn't have impressed him much anyway. "And what do you want to be?" my father said, turning at last towards me.

"Nothing," I said.

"Nothing?"

"I don't know. I don't want to be anything."

My father sighed, he put on his disappointed face. "Oh, boys," he said. "Now, you listen to me. You have to have ambition. Without ambition, what use are we? We're no better than animals. I've had ambition all my life. Still so much, it'll never be fulfilled. But it's what keeps me alive. It's all I have to live for."

This was for both his sons' benefit, but it was directed at me. And I looked across to Mother, I thought she would defend me, but she was nodding. Nodding sadly—perhaps like me, she'd hoped that what Father lived for was us.

My father hadn't finished. "You are in a position of extraordinary privilege. Do you understand? You start out higher than most men will ever be allowed to reach. Whatever ambitions you find, however lofty, you're already closer to them than anybody else. So make the ambitions worthwhile. Be great. Be as great as you can be."

I was angry, as I say, but I was also inspired. I remember thinking this might be a pivotal moment in my life—I was always on the lookout for them. How silly to think that when I was so young, but it was true! I felt suddenly like an adult. I went upstairs to my bedroom. I put away all my railway engines, dismantled the yards and yards of track. I cast them aside. It was time to think of higher things, the way my father wanted.

But try as I might, I could never find anything to think about.

My brother won a place at Oxford University, at my father's old college. I no longer recall what it was he studied, it wasn't much, I'm sure. When my time came I said I didn't want to go to Oxford. I wanted to do it my way. I applied to read classics at Cambridge. I hoped my father would be proud of me for going it alone, and maybe he was, but he never said. The application was rejected. I don't know why. Maybe I didn't interview well enough, maybe I should have dropped my father's name a little more. I was distraught. Even at eighteen years old, when I went to my father's study to inform him that Cambridge didn't want me, I was shaking with fear. For once he didn't seem disappointed. He told me it would be all right, and I was so grateful for that rare show of comfort. Later that day he summoned me, and gave me the good news: I would be going to his old college at Oxford, just as he had always hoped, I had been accepted sight unseen.

Father only visited me at Oxford the once. As a fresher I joined the debating society, and had some success. The college invited him to watch me compete in the finals, and to my surprise, he accepted. He drove up with Mother. When he entered the hall everyone rose to their feet and gave him a round of applause. He made a speech to introduce the debates that spoke of his own happy days at Oxford, and how we could all achieve as much as him if we put our backs into it. My team lost the debate. I don't know quite what we were debating now, but it was something political—we took a controversial stance, for fun's sake, something about Government policy, something that wouldn't be expected from a Forbes. Afterwards my father shook my hand and said well done, but told me that it was right I had lost. "You chose the wrong issue," he said, "and in everything, no matter how well one speaks, the issue must triumph over the speaker." Even my father's congratulations had a moral lesson to them. I thanked him. He and my mother couldn't stay for dinner, they had to hurry back to London. My mother gave me a hug. Father said, "Make me proud."

But Mother came to Oxford many times, she would visit at least once a term, and maybe two or three times in the summer when the weather was warm. She was always so relaxed away from Father. No, that's not true—Mother was never properly relaxed, there was always a nervousness to her, a sense that she was on show. But she would at least speak more freely, she would smile a lot more. I would take her for scones and tea. I would take her punting. In truth, I learned how to punt especially. I lost my virginity to a girl after taking her for a punt, and had told her I had taken it up to impress her. But that wasn't true. It was for Mother.

And we might go out to the pub, and she would say to me, "Just don't tell your father!" As if he might be scandalised to find his wife drinking a port and lemon in public. It was with me that she would smoke her cigarettes. She would lie back in the punt, all laid out like Cleopatra on her barge, and she'd light up. "Don't tell your father," she'd say, and she'd smoke ever so shyly, take shallow little puffs then turn her head away so I wouldn't be bothered by it, and that was silly, because I smoked like a chimney by this stage—"Don't tell him, he wouldn't like it," and as soon as she'd finish she'd drop her butt overboard as if to drown the evidence, and she'd pop a mint into her mouth in case Father turned up on a rival punt alongside and caught a whiff of her breath.

And we had an agreement. We would not mention Father at all. We could talk about anything else, but never him. In truth, we never talked very much. Conversation with Mother was very sporadic; I wouldn't ask her about home life in case it encroached upon the taboo subject, and she wouldn't ask about Oxford because she said she'd never understand my answers. No talking then—we'd drink, and smoke, punt and eat scones, and it was nice to be in the company of a woman to whom I didn't need to seem clever. Sometimes I forgot she was my mother altogether. When I booked her a room in the hotel, I never used Forbes, I always used her maiden name.

Incidentally, I had never stopped giving Mother my teeth. After my father had paid for them in advance, it made no difference to me—whenever one fell out, I'd secrete it away carefully, I'd keep it hidden until I could pass it to her later. I didn't want anything for them, I felt they belonged to her. I'd wait until we were on our own, strictly on our own, and then I'd present her with her latest jewel. "Thank you," she'd whisper, in case anyone might hear, and then she'd wrap up my tooth in a handkerchief and steal it away. I never knew where she kept them. That was her business, not mine.

I regretted, as an adult, that I had no more teeth to give. I would have to give her other things. Whatever she might want. Whatever Father wouldn't provide.

It turns out my new mother's name is Kathleen E Jackson, but I don't know what the E stands for. She is five foot five inches tall, her hair is dark blonde, and she has a playing age between twenty-five and thirty-five. She can speak in a variety of accents: RP, Liverpool, Scots, American. She is trained in fencing and horse riding, and piano up to grade three. I feel a burst of strange pride for her when I learn all this, that Mother is so accomplished.

Her CV on Spotlight also lists some of the roles she has taken earlier in her career. She has done a bit of Shakespeare at some theatres I haven't heard of, and some corporate videos (whatever they might be). She has had a part in BBC TV's 'Holby City', and I don't know whether it was a big part or not, I'm guessing she was a patient, my old mother never looked the sort who could have had a medical degree and nor does Kathleen E Jackson. She has also appeared in two feature films. I order copies of them both online. The DVDs are with me by the end of the week.

In her first film she is credited merely as 'waitress', and I assume the waitress is not a leading character, and I am right. The film seems to be some sort of romantic comedy, one of those moronic ones that suggest people ever find true love; I may be a tad too harsh, I don't know how it turns out, after a while I put it on fast forward and look for any scenes set in cafés or restaurants. And, at last, there she is! She stands over the lead actress, coffee pot in hand, and asks whether she would like a refill. She tells her that the special of the day is meatloaf. Even though I know Kathleen E Jackson is British, she has the American accent down pat—or, at least, she sounds authentic to me. I speed on through the movie, and there are a couple more scenes in cafés later on, but none of them feature Kathleen E Jackson, and that seems rather a wasted opportunity. I rewind to her big moment, I watch it again, and again, and again. I am excited to see her there, serving coffee in a diner in New York—I am fairly certain my mother never had to serve coffee for money, but she *could* have done, that had been a possibility, it was a life choice that marriage to my father had cruelly denied her.

The second movie is British, and cheap, and rather nasty. It's some sort of gangster film. Everyone swears a lot, and most of the cast get shot. It's not a lead part for Kathleen E Jackson, but I can't afford to fast forward—whilst everybody around her is getting gunned down left, right and centre, she somehow manages to stay alive all the way to the end credits. There's a sex scene. If I pause the DVD at just the right moment I can freeze still both of her naked breasts.

I find on the internet only two interviews with Kathleen E Jackson. The first is taken soon after she has left drama school, and she talks about her dream to work in the theatre, that one day she might play Viola or the Duchess of Malfi. The second is publicity for the gangster film, and all she talks about is Hollywood. Different interviews, different contexts? Or did she just change her mind?

It's her smallest role, I know, but my favourite of Kathleen E Jackson's oeuvre is that first film, when she works in a café. She looks so happy there. Kathleen E Jackson has taken this unnamed waitress and fleshed her out and given her a background, she's decided that she's a very happy waitress indeed, that serving coffee is what she's always wanted to do. Yes, she's in the background, but that's all right—she's being overshadowed by her co-stars, but she knows her place and she doesn't kick against it. And perhaps my mother was like that once? Because she must have known what she was getting into, mustn't she? When she married my father, a man of greatness, a man whose genius rang out loud and clear, did she think she *wouldn't* be in the background? "Would you like a refill, hon?" "Our special today is meatloaf!" So charmingly, my father's companion, his faithful friend, always there with what he needed, as wife and as aide and as servant. Look how contented Kathleen E Jackson is! Look how contented my mother might have been, if she'd just *let* herself be content, if she had accepted my father's status, and her mediocrity in contrast to it. "What do you want to be when *you* grow up?" "I don't know. Nothing. Nothing at all."

I watch that café scene a lot, I watch it dozens of times a day. And if you divorce it from the rest of the movie, if you watch the scene and nothing else, then my mother doesn't have such a small role after all.

She's still not the lead, no one could say she was the lead. But she's essential.

I wonder what it would have been like to have seen Kathleen's movies as they were intended, on a huge cinema screen—me, sitting in the dark, with popcorn maybe, all alone, so small—and there ahead of me, towering as high as a double decker bus, my mother—my mother the giant, looking down at me and telling me about meatloaf, she could pick me up and crush me in her fist if she would want to but why would she want to?—all the audience staring at my mother, at last the centre of attention and as spectacular as she always deserved to be, coffee pot in one hand, bare tit in the other.

One night I have a bad dream. I dream that I have forgotten what my mother looks like. It isn't that I think she's now got Kathleen E Jackson's face, but I still know this is something Kathleen E Jackson has done to her. And done deliberately—this, I realise, is how my mother will be remembered, looking like an imposter, with a voice that's RP or American depending on Kathleen E Jackson's whim. My father will never be supplanted, if you want to see his features you can just gawp at a twenty pound note, but his wife is changed into someone else forever. And in the dream I get ever more frantic, I search through my memories of her—but she's always turned away. She lies flat on her stomach in the punt, she enjoys her scones and tea at another table. And on her death bed, as I stare down at her, as I watch the shadows take her, still, still, she manages to twist her face aside from me. In that famous photograph, the one of my father where she's caught by surprise, I can see the squinted eyes but not the face surrounding them, I can see the hand raised in a wave but it's not attached to a body.

I wake up, and I still can't remember. And I go to the shelves, I grab at the history books. All the pictures of my father, that black moustache still black even as the hair on his scalp turns grey. And there at last, Mother, and Mother's face—and I am so scared that for a moment I'm not sure it's right, is it right, do I really recognise her, has she been replaced? My mother looks nothing like an actress. She is so plain, her teeth are crooked, her eyes ugly, that squint has nothing to do with the sunshine. Oh, Mum.

Enough is enough. This has become an obsession, I have quite forgot myself. My parents would be ashamed—both of them. I take the movies of Kathleen E Jackson, I throw them into the bin. I try to snap the discs into two, but I'm not strong enough, and besides, that may be somewhat melodramatic. I tear up the CV I had printed out. I take down the photograph I had Blu-tacked to my bedroom wall.

And as I do so the phone rings. I am still so frantic, it takes a couple of rings before I decide it's real. I steady my breath, answer it.

"Hello?"

"Hello? Is that Mr Forbes?"

"Speaking. Who is this?"

"I'm sorry to disturb you at home. I don't know if you remember me! My name's Kathleen Jackson."

I should know that voice, but it's curiously normal, without any trace of artificial accent.

"I play your mother in the movie." A pause. "Hello?"

"Yes, yes, hello," I say.

She explains how she got my number, some call sheet or something. She apologises again for calling me at home. She knows it's unorthodox. She resumes shooting on the movie next week, and she's having trouble getting a handle on my mother. She's a tough nut to crack, she says. She needs to find a way in. Is there anything I can do to help? Can we meet, maybe, and discuss it?

"Hello?" she says one last time.

"Hello," I say again. "Yes. Yes, that would be all right. Yes. Why don't you come over? You could come over for supper. I could cook you supper, if you like."

She agrees, and I'm so excited I hang up before she can change her mind. She has to call back to find out what my address is.

When my father died everyone wanted to give him a state funeral. The Government wanted it, the people wanted it. I didn't want it, and, to be fair to him, neither did my father: he didn't approve of the waste of public money or the unnecessary hoopla. His will stated that he wanted as little fuss as possible. The Government said they would respect my father's wishes. It wasn't a state funeral, then, but it was still pretty big: Westminster Abbey was packed out, the Prime Minister was there, and so was the Queen.

When my mother died, Father summoned me and Davey to Whitehall to see him. "This is a very sad thing," he said to us. "I think it should be a quiet service, just family and friends. I think that's what Kathleen would have wanted." Everyone was very sorry for Father, the secretary who brought in our tea was wearing black and looked as if she had been crying; "Thank you, Claire," said Father, and Claire nodded and left. We all sipped our tea. "A quiet service, then," declared Father. "Are we in agreement?"

She hadn't been ill for long, and there was a mercy to that. Father had telephoned with the news. That he hadn't designated the task meant I knew the illness had to be pretty serious. "She's got a shadow on her brain," he said. And that seemed such a stupid thing to be ill from—what was a shadow? A shadow wasn't anything, that was the whole *point* of a shadow. We'd lived in Father's shadow for years, and none of us more than poor Mother, if there was anyone who knew how trivial a shadow was it would be us. "There's nothing to be done to remove the shadow," Father went on, "and the shadow seems to be spreading." I asked him if Mother was going to die. I didn't want him to be political with me, or give it any spin, just come out and say it. "Yes." Bastard. And there was nothing to be done, really? He couldn't chivvy along a cure, he couldn't pull a few strings? "No." Then what good was he? What was he for?

I hadn't seen Mother in the longest time. We would talk on the telephone every couple of months or so, and she would scold me for this, it wasn't enough, she pointed out we only saw each other at Christmas, and then only fleetingly. The scolding would be gentle. She said she knew I was busy, she said it was doubtless her fault as much as mine—but could we see each other again soon? She would then go on and on about those happy days in Oxford, where we could just be ourselves, couldn't we have another day out on the punt? And I would remind her I had graduated from Oxford thirty years ago, I didn't live there any more. If I tried to punt her now, I'd probably drown her. "Oh yes," she'd say, remembering.

"Then I'm coming to see you," she said one day.

"What?"

"I'm getting the train. I want to see you. I'm coming to see you on Wednesday."

"Mother, I'm busy on Wednesday."

"Thursday then. I'm coming. We can talk, we can go out for scones and tea. Can you pick me up from the station?"

There were no places in town that served scones and tea. It wasn't that sort of town. I took her to a shop that sold carrot cake, it would just have to do.

She sat down, lit a cigarette, puffed the smoke away from me.

"What is it, Mother? Is something wrong?"

"No," she said. "Everything's good. Everything's wonderful." She smiled, reached forward, and took my hand. "Darling, I want you to know. I'm having an affair."

"What?"

"Just don't tell your father." She sat back, smoked. "Or, you can tell him if you want. I don't care."

She told me that she had met this man, and he loved her, and she loved him. She told me he wasn't handsome, but he was nice and made her happy. They had sex sometimes in the afternoon in hotel rooms, and he was gentle.

"Oh, darling, I feel so alive again!"

"Mother," I said. "Aren't you a little old? How old are you, anyway?"

She ignored that. I asked her whether life with Father was really so bad. I asked her if she didn't love him any more. Was she going to leave him, think of the damage she'd do, the scandal!

"There's no need to be so silly," she said. "I'm not going to bring down the Government. I shan't embarrass anyone. I'm discreet. I'm just happy, that's all, and I haven't been happy in a long while, and I wanted to tell someone. And I chose you. You're the one I chose. Is that all right I chose you? Be happy for me, can't you?"

I told her I was happy. We changed the subject, but as always there wasn't really a subject to change to, so we sat in silence for a while. We ate our cakes. We drank our tea.

"Is there anything else you want to do, Mother? There's no punting here, of course. But I've taken the day off. We could go to the cinema, I suppose."

"No," she said. "I don't like the cinema." So I took her back to the train station.

"It would be nice if you could meet him some time." We were staring at the platform, and the train was delayed, it was taking a bloody age for it to arrive. "I think you'd like him."

"I'm sure I would."

"He makes me feel special, for me. I deserve that, don't I?"

I said, "And are you sure he's not just using you to get close to Father?" It seems cruel now that I said this, but I don't think it was unreasonable. Ingrid only married me because of who my father was, she'd made that very plain.

And Mother didn't seem offended. She took the question at face value, frowned, and gave it proper consideration. "I don't think so," she said at last. "I don't know. I'll ask him."

I never did get to meet him, of course. I never even found out what his name was, and I'm sorry for that, I'm sure Mother would have told me had I ever asked. I alluded to her affair on the telephone a couple of times, I asked her cryptically if she were happy, she would answer cryptically that she was. And then we just stopped doing even that, I supposed it was either all over or she was so blissed out she didn't need to share any news. We made no mention of it when we met at Christmas. And then, what, there was another Christmas, and the next time I saw her was after she'd been taken ill.

I was there at the very end. Father's personal secretary called to say I should get to the hospital immediately. As soon as I arrived I was shown in to Mother's private room. Father was there, and so were a few of his staff, for a moment it was hard to see Mother through the crowd. I was shocked; every time I had visited she'd looked more and more frail, as if she were shrinking into herself rather—but now she was nothing more substantial than an overgrown doll, and her skin was so thin and waxy I could see right through it.

"Oh, Kathy," said my father fondly. "Oh, my poor dear. You've stood by me all these years, haven't you? You've been my little soldier, fighting beside me. You do know I couldn't have done it without you, don't you? I couldn't have achieved half so much." He stroked her forehead, I saw her gulp at his touch, but she didn't open her eyes.

We all stood there for a while. Father would occasionally give further tribute to his wife, it was like each time was a revised draft, and the words were smarter, more honed. At length a man in a suit came in and muttered something to him quietly. Father nodded. He turned to me directly, perhaps for the first time.

"I'll be a few minutes, I have to deal with this. Stay here."

With my father gone, I think I saw Mother relax. It might have been my imagination. She sighed, and her body deflated slightly, became even more tiny and precious. And she opened her eyes to me. And she winked.

And for one delightful instant I thought it had all been a joke, let's get out of here, but don't tell your father!—And then the other eye winked, then they blinked, then the first one winked again. She was looking straight at me. I wondered if she remembered my face.

I began to tell her I loved her. By which I mean I drew the breath with which I could say it. By which I mean I thought of the words, and realised I'd need to draw some breath.

And I swear this is what happened. It makes no proper sense, but this is what I know. I saw that shadow in her brain. I saw her face darken with it. I saw a cloud pass over, and for a moment her skin was in thick shade. And then down from her face I saw the shadow steal over her, down her night dress, down her spindly little arms, down her body and beneath the sheets. I saw my mother disappear into the shadows, and she sighed once more, and she shut her eyes, and then she was gone.

And now she's gone, there are so many questions I want to ask her, and I've lost the chance, I never shall. Not profound questions, silly questions. The information dies with her—what was the name of her childhood pet? Did she have a favourite colour? What did she think about things, oh, all sorts of things? And where oh where did she keep all those baby teeth of mine?

Father returned eventually. He stared down at his dead wife. "Oh God," he said. He turned to his aides. "Get out of here, please!" They scurried away. He looked back at his wife. "Oh God. I wasn't even here."

I said to him, "She wouldn't have known. She didn't wake up. There was nothing you could have done." And he smiled at me so gratefully, and he took my hand and squeezed it, and I wondered how long I should let him do that for, a few seconds later I pulled away.

So, a quiet service. We were in agreement. I told my father I would like to give the eulogy. He looked concerned. "Are you sure?" Yes, I said, I'm quite bloody sure, actually. Is there a problem? "All right," said Father.

My mother's death was in all the newspapers. On the covers, pictures of my father.

I wrote the eulogy. I wanted to talk about the times we spent together, our private times alone. I learned it all by heart so I'd sound spontaneous.

The day of her funeral.

I get into my black suit. Ingrid is there to help me. Our marriage is in its final stages, but just now she is being so kind. She lost her own mother a while back, she says she knows what I am going through. She has no idea.

Everyone in black, looking so smart. My mother's favourite hymn. I hadn't known she had one.

I get up before them all. All these people, friends and family only he said, I don't recognise them. And not for the first time she seems to me so far away and unknowable. I want to talk of our times in Oxford, but they seem so pointless now, is that what a life adds up to? I wonder if one of these strangers staring at me is her lover. I wonder whether he was even invited.

I look at my father. Eyes bright, jet black moustache matching the jet black of his mourning suit. "I can't," I say. "I can't. I'm sorry."

And my father is up on his feet and coming towards me. Looking so sad. His arms are out. I think he is going to hug me. In front of all these people, I would allow it. I wouldn't feel the slightest shame. He puts his hands on my shoulders, gently. He steers me slowly back to my pew.

The eulogy my father gives is beautiful, and everyone cries, and I cry too in spite of myself. He is so *good,* we all love Father, and I love Father. I love Father so much, and I wish he were the one who were dead, I wish he was the one in the coffin.

Shit.

I go to the supermarket. The shelves are *packed* with food, there's so much choice, what would she like? I decide on chicken. Everyone likes chicken. I wonder how best to cook chicken, it has been years since I tried to seduce someone, is there a way of preparing poultry that is especially seductive? I pay for the chicken. I take the chicken home. Everyone likes chicken. Unless they're vegetarian. A lot of people are vegetarian these days. Can you seduce someone with vegetables? I go back to the supermarket, I buy some salad too.

She arrives late. She's five minutes late, and by the time she rings the doorbell I'm sure she won't be coming.

"Hello!" she says. She looks nice. She hasn't made a special effort, but she's nice, she's definitely nice. She's brought a bottle of wine. "Oh, wine!" I say. "How lovely!" I show her into the house. "You needn't have brought wine, that's lovely!" I'm making too much fuss of the wine. It's a cheap Merlot, it won't go with the chicken, but why should that matter? "You sit down, and I'll go and open the wine, that's lovely." I bring out from the kitchen two glasses of wine, I wonder whether I can sit on the sofa beside her, I choose the armchair to the side. "Wine, what a treat!" I say. The wine is pretty tart. Even she can't sip the stuff without wincing. I should have opened another bottle of wine, let her think she'd bought something decent, that would have been flattering. Too late now.

"It's good of you to see me," she says. "I was at the end of my tether!"

"It'll be all right now."

"We start shooting my big scenes on Tuesday, I don't know what to do!"

"It'll be all right."

It'll be all right. When she came in she looked nothing like my mother, and that was a bit disappointing. But now it's there, the awkwardness, the self-doubt. I want to protect her. I'll do anything I can to make it better. "I'm quite certain," I say, "that no one would be able to depict my mother better than you."

"Really?"

"Oh yes. And I knew her quite well."

She laughs at that, as if it were a joke. I laugh too. Perhaps it *was* a joke, a little one.

"I shouldn't really be here," she says. "Don't tell Tony."

"Tony?"

"Don't tell your father. The actor who's playing your father."

"We're having chicken," I tell her. "Do you like chicken?" She says she does. That's a relief.

"If you can give me any insight," and she takes out a notebook and a pen, God bless her. "If I could just find something to latch on to, you know? I mean, I'm a very instinctive sort of actor. I can build a character out of any little thing, if I can just find a way in. But your mother. She's so bland."

"Yes."

"Sorry, I don't mean your *mother* is bland! But the script. She doesn't *do* anything. She's just sort of *there*. She never gets angry, she never seems especially pleased either. That bit where your dad is imprisoned by the Nazis, she doesn't get worried, everyone else is worried, but she's just so confident he'll be all right. She's so bloody *serene*, it does my nut in!"

"Well, some people *are* serene."

"Sorry. Yes. But there are always cracks. Aren't there? I need a crack, to worm my way into a crack. Do you have any cracks for me?" Kathleen E Jackson sips at her wine, looks at me with such hope. "I mean, if she had a stammer or something, I could work on a stammer..."

"She didn't stammer."

"Or some sort of nervous tic..."

"I don't think so."

"Oh."

"Some people just don't have much to offer," I say. "Some people just stay in the shadows." I want her. I want to put down my glass of wine, and go to her, and kiss her on the lips. I want to take her to the bedroom. The bedroom is only a few metres away, we could be there in just a minute. "I loved you," I say. "I loved you, erm, very much. In that film you did."

"Oh!" She looks so pleased. "Oh, thank you!"

"Asking if they wanted a refill. Talking about the meatloaf."

"Oh, *that* film?" And she's frowning. "The waitress?"

"I thought you were very good."

"I'm surprised you even spotted me in it." The frown is deep now, it's like a shadow upon her face. I don't like it, the shadow is getting bigger. I've got to do something to stop the shadow.

"Are you ready for chicken?" I ask. "And there's some salad too."

"Not much for me. I'm on a diet."

I give her a little bit of chicken, pour her a Sauvignon Blanc. We eat and drink. My Sauvignon Blanc is quite excellent.

I ask her how she became an actress. I already know the basics from her interviews, but she likes talking about herself, I can tell.

"Your parents must be very proud," I say.

"You'd have thought so, wouldn't you? I mean, they're okay with it. They paid for drama school, I suppose. But they never say the right things. Dad's always asking when I'm getting a proper job. My mum didn't even bother seeing my Duchess of Malfi."

I smile politely.

"I think this might be the job to impress them," she says finally. "I mean, this is a big feature film, isn't it? About someone famous. Not that I'm the famous one, but you know what I mean!"

"Well, let's find some way to make them proud." I pretend to give it some thought, and my young little mother looks at me so innocently, and I'll do anything to help her, I don't say anything for a while, I elongate the moment.

"All right," I say. "Well, there are some little things. But I don't talk about my mother much, this is private…"

"Oh yes," she says. "And thank you!"

"If you're going to portray these things in the film, I must ask you to do so with great delicacy…"

"Delicacy, yes, of course!"

"Well now. Well." I take a bite of chicken. The chicken is good, it's not as good as my wine. "She did have a nervous tic of sorts, I suppose. It came out at times of stress. She used to scratch a lot."

"She'd scratch? Where would she scratch?"

"All over. She'd itch so badly, you see, and she'd just dig in her nails and scratch away. It could get quite manic."

"God."

"She used to have to wear thick gloves," I say. "So she wouldn't bleed everywhere."

She scribbles down the information. "How horrible for her."

"And there *was* a stammer too, come to think of it."

"There wasn't? Really, there wasn't! Was there?" She looks delighted. "The researchers didn't come up with a stammer!"

"She never spoke in public. They wouldn't have known. This was behind closed doors."

"Of course."

"She used to stammer something chronic," I say, "on the letter D."

I can see her make a quick calculation. "I say lots of things beginning with D!"

"Well, there you are."

"Your father's name, that begins with D."

"So it does."

There's no shadow now. She is happy, I've beaten off the shadows forever.

"Oh, Mr Forbes!" she says. "Thanks, this is exactly what I need! Oh, I could kiss you!"

"You could, if you liked!"

She laughs, and doesn't.

The chicken is eaten. She says she should be leaving soon. I ask her to stay for another glass of wine, she can do that, surely? We can adjourn to the sitting room and drink our wine together in comfort. This time I sit next to her on the sofa.

"Well then," I say. And she smiles. And we both make little stabs at conversation, but they never lead anywhere interesting, and I wish my mother were here, I wish we could just hold a silence and not feel bad about it, my mother was a woman who understood how to make silence work.

"You must miss him," she says, suddenly.

"Who?"

"Your father."

"I loved him," I say.

"We all loved him. Sorry, but for you. It must be different."

"I loved him very, very much." And I'm crying, what the hell am I crying about?

"Hey," she says. "I'm sorry. I'm sorry. Hey." And suddenly her arms are around me. Not tight, but it's better than nothing. I put my head on her chest. I put my head on her tit. I think, hello, tit, I've seen you before.

"What does the E stand for?" I ask the tit.

"Sorry?"

"Your name. Kathleen E Jackson."

"Oh!" She moves away so she can answer me. "It doesn't stand for anything. There was already a Kathleen Jackson in the actors' union. You can't have two Kathleen Jacksons, so I added an E."

"Maybe they should have cast the real Kathleen Jackson," I say. "Maybe she'd have played my mother better!" The joke doesn't quite work, and I don't think she takes offence, but she moves her tit even further away from me, and I realise it's lost to me forever.

"I should go."

"No. Wait. I want you to have something."

"I need to get going. Thank you for dinner."

"Wait, please. I'll just be a moment."

She looks annoyed, I've annoyed her for the first time, but I've had such a good idea.

It takes me a few minutes to find the box, and by the time I come back she's got her coat on and is clearly angry.

"Thank you for your time, Mr Forbes, but I want to go now, please."

"I'll let you go, I'll let you go, but first, please, look at this, please."

I open the jewellery box for her.

"This was against my real mother's skin," I say. "And this hung from my real mother's ear. And this, around my real mother's neck." And in wonder she is picking through it, so deliberately, as if afraid they'll break. With such reverence too—as if a fraction of my father's greatness may have rubbed off on them, as if a fraction of that fraction might rub on to her.

"Kathleen," I say. "I want you to have them."

"What?"

"What am I going to do with them? She would have wanted you to have them. Kathleen, my mother would have liked you. My mother would have *loved* you. She would have wanted to look after you, she would have been so proud."

"I can't," she says. "You see that I can't."

"Just a single bracelet, then," I say. "Just a pair of earrings. Please," I say. "Please, put a tiny bit of my mother up there upon the screen."

I think she's going to refuse again. But she looks down at the box. She takes out some earrings, the simplest of the lot. She looks at me for confirmation. I nod.

"Thank you," I say.

Advance reviews for the movie are respectful, but hardly enthusiastic. A recurring criticism is that at nearly three hours' running time the film is just too damn *long*. The director gives an interview in which he says that that's a necessary problem with detailing a life as full and complex as that of David Forbes—the implication being, therefore, that it was my father's fault for having achieved so much.

It goes on to receive only two Oscar nominations, one for film editing, and one for its score. It wins neither.

One journalist suggests that the poor box office reception marks the first time in my father's career that he can ever be said to have failed.

I am invited to the premiere. I plead sickness. The rest of my family,

I gather, all make an appearance on the red carpet. They even break Davey out of the hospice for it. He is interviewed on live TV, they ask him to describe his pride at seeing his father's life honoured on the big screen, and the pride of being a Forbes. There must have been something good in his meds, he makes a surprisingly good fist of it.

Kathleen E Jackson is mentioned in a couple of the reviews, but in addendum. No one passes judgment on either her stammering or her scratching, so I assume that the director dissuaded her, or left those scenes on the cutting room floor.

The movie plays at my local cinema for two weeks, but I do not go. It is released on DVD, but I do not buy it. That Christmas it plays on television—not on Christmas Day itself, in the dead time before New Year. I do not watch it. I don't want to see it. I don't want to hear of it again.

When in the New Year the Bank of England decides to change the twenty pound note, and to replace my father's face with that of the economist Adam Smith, no one seems to object.

And one day I receive a parcel. Inside there is a little box for jewellery, and a letter. The letter is handwritten, and none too neat. I have to work hard to translate it.

I'm sorry, it says. *I tried my best, and I'm sorry if I let you down. But sometimes the best simply isn't good enough, not when there are people beside you who are better.*—I had no idea her performance was so poor. I'm especially pleased I didn't see it now.

She didn't need to send the earrings back. I am rather hurt. It's true, Kathleen E Jackson may not have deserved them. But it made me feel better there was a little piece of my mother somewhere out in the world. And that maybe those earrings would have gone on to feature in other films, any films Kathleen E Jackson appeared in—as a waitress, maybe.

I take the little jewellery box, and go to put its contents with the rest of Mother's things. But when I open the box I find there are no earrings inside after all. They sparkle out at me, white and pure. Fat little baby teeth, catching the light.

I go back to find the letter, but I can't find it, I've lost it, as if it were never there at all, as if it's been taken back by the shadows.

And the old woman says:

- *It stirs up complex feelings to visit your childhood home, even as a replica built on a soundstage. It's more complex still if when you get there you find yourself usurped. Consider* **Unfurnished** *(story 19, page 321).*
- *A father and son work hard on resolving their differences in* **Thumbsucker** *(story 34, page 557).*
- *The punting tradition in Oxford is to steer from the front, whilst in Cambridge it is always from the back. The rivalry between the two great universities extends even to how you stick poles in a river.* **Master of the Macabre** *(story 89, page 1511) features the Cambridge version; judge for yourself which you prefer.*
- *To play darker children's games than these, turn to* **Yesyes** *(story 80, page 1385).*
- *In* **The Curtain Falls** *(story 98, page 1661), an actor finds himself recast in the story of his life. Consider how he deals with this indignity.*

72
72 VIRGINS

MICHAEL BELL DIED, and went to Heaven, and was told by the man on the front desk where he could collect his seventy-two virgins. “Oh,” said Michael, much surprised, “I don’t think I’m entitled to… There’s been a mistake… I mean, I’m not a Muslim,” and the man on the desk looked cross and said that if Michael had any complaints could he please take them up with someone else, it was a busy day, and he had a lot of corpses to process. So Michael apologised, signed the register, took his room key, and set forth into the afterlife.

He had been assigned his own apartment. They called it an apartment, but it was more like a mansion, really—there was a garden with a swimming pool in it, and a billiard room, and a study, and a kitchen full of all the latest mod cons, and a basement with a swimming pool in it. It would have been too big for Michael all on his own, so at first he was rather pleased there were seventy-two virgins to help fill it.

Some of the seventy-two virgins were useless. He could see that in an instant. Eleven of them were babies. Eighteen of them were men. Four of them weren't even human; he'd been given two virgin cats, one virgin goldfish, and a virgin grey squirrel. But that still left him with thirty-nine virginal women—young (mostly), ripe (he supposed), and his for the taking. "Hello," he said to the throng, a little shyly, "my name's Michael, but, uh, why not call me Mike?" He asked them their names. "Goodness," said Michael, "I'll never remember all those. Maybe you should all wear name badges?" So, for a while, they did.

He told them they should feel free to use all the facilities. The swimming pools were at their disposal, and if anyone ever wanted to join him in a game of billiards, all they had to do was ask. None of the virgins like swimming, apparently. And no one fancied billiards. They would instead crowd into the sitting room around the widescreen television set. They would squabble for space on the single sofa that was there, and shush each other when the ad breaks came to an end. Michael sometimes watched TV with them, but they never seemed to want to watch any of the programmes he liked, and besides, he was never fast enough to get a spot on the sofa. Sometimes he'd hang out in the kitchen and make himself toast. He couldn't work out how to use most of the mod cons, but the toaster was nice and easy. Or he'd go to the billiard room, and he'd roll all the balls from one end of the table to the other, and then walk to the other side, and roll them all back again.

He got to know Eliza quite well. Eliza was fond of toast, and would sometimes come into the kitchen when Michael was making some. She wouldn't say much, but her fingers and his fingers might collide taking slices of bread out of the bread basket.

Michael began to think about Eliza a lot. He wondered if she ever thought of him too. One day he asked her why she didn't watch TV with all the other virgins, and she blushed, and said she didn't like TV much, and that besides, she'd rather be with him. She wasn't especially pretty, but she looked as if she were in her teens, and Michael was pushing seventy, and he felt guilty for flirting with her until she told him she'd died of scarlet fever in the 1860s and was therefore older than his grandmother.

He asked her whether she'd like to be his girlfriend, and steeled himself for a rejection, and she kissed him gently on the cheek and said that that'd be quite all right.

He was intimidated by his own bedroom. Sweet incense and crushed silks and pillows that were fleshy—he couldn't sleep like that. He'd kicked the pillows on to the floor. Before they got into bed together, Eliza stacked the pillows high again.

She said, "I'm scared. Is that silly?"

He said, "Of course it's not silly."

She said, "You won't hurt me?"

He said, "I promise."

"Tell me," she said. "What it was like. Your first time. Were you scared?"

"No," he said, wanting to be brave for her sake, but he had been terrified. He could remember the circumstances now, and the basic sequence of events that had got the girl from the dance floor to the car seat, but there were events missing, the bits that linked a to b to c. He remembered now only the urgency, the desperate urgency, the need to be a man and abandon his childhood as fast as could be, and that he wasn't sure during the whole thing whether he was in the right hole or not, the girl seemed to have grown holes all over the place, was she going to laugh at him?—and then afterwards the dull realisation that the world hadn't changed, everything was just the same, he may now be a man but nobody cared.

"But it was nice?" she said.

"It was very nice," he said.

They had sex then, and it had been so long since he'd done it with Barbara that frankly he felt just like a virgin too.

And after he was out of breath and was sweaty and his heart was going like the clappers, and he wondered whether he might be having a heart attack but supposed he couldn't die twice. He stroked at Eliza's hair, kissed her softly. He asked her if her first time had been all right.

"It was very nice."

He fell asleep then, with Eliza in his arms, and he dreamed of Barbara, and he hadn't dreamed of Barbara in ages, really not much since the divorce at all. And there were some bad things in the dream, inevitably, but it wasn't quite bad enough to be a nightmare.

When he woke in the morning Eliza wasn't there. He thought she might be making some toast. She wasn't.

He asked the other virgins if they had seen her. They were watching *The Jeremy Kyle Show*, they didn't want to be disturbed.

Michael went back to the man on the front desk. He explained the situation. The man didn't look very sympathetic, he spoke to Michael as if he were an idiot. "You get seventy-two *virgins*," he said. "She's not a virgin now, is she? She's gone." Michael could see the logic of that. But he asked whether he could have Eliza's address. Even if they couldn't be anything more, and why should she want to be, with an old man like him, he'd be a fool even to think it—even so, he hoped they could still be friends. He'd like to see her still, as a friend. The man rolled his eyes. "When I say gone, I mean *gone*. That's it. One bang, and she's gone forever."

From the remaining seventy-one virgins there came one morning a deputation of ambassadors to his bedroom. "We want you to get rid of Cheryl," they said.

Cheryl was big and blousy and so fat she took up space for two upon the sofa. She talked too loud during the programmes and had an annoying laugh and would fight for the remote control, and, moreover, was an utter bitch.

They brought Cheryl to his bedroom later that evening. There was a sack upon her head. There was some evidence of a struggle, her legs were bleeding, and she had had to be dragged to him. But she was quiet now, accepting. They pushed her into Michael's arms, and shut the door on them.

Michael pulled the sack off her, asked her to sit down, tried to be as nice as he could. "It's all right," he said. "We don't have to do this, you know."

"No," she said. "I suppose I'm going to have to pop my cherry sooner or later, may as well be with you."

They both got undressed in silence. He tried not to look at her, all drooping bust and tummy. She had no such qualms. She stared at him, grimly, as if staring at an execution block.

"I'm sorry," he said. "I know I'm not much to look at."

She shook her head.

"So, what?" she said. "You get killed in a war, or something?"

"Me? No."

"To get all us virgins."

"No."

"But you did something heroic, right?"

"No." Michael's death hadn't been especially heroic. Up to the end in that hospital pleading for even one more day of life, and all of the nurses trying to reassure him that it was going to be okay—and he'd felt, he really had felt, that they had never seen this happen before, that he was the very first man in the world who was going to die, that he was special. "I didn't go to war. There wasn't any war on."

Cheryl sniffed. "There's always some war on somewhere, if you just look."

"I suppose I was too scared."

She nodded at that, seemed to accept it. She got into bed. She seemed resigned now, not too nervous, neither of the loss of her virginity, nor of the oblivion that would happen afterwards.

She kissed him on the lips, almost by way of experiment. He kissed back. It was nice. She kissed at his neck then, and he nibbled at her ear, and he'd never thought to be a nibbler before, not ever, not even when he and Barbara had been happy. She moaned a bit, and he was worried for her, but she said it was a good moan.

"You're wonderful, Cheryl," he told her. "Do you know that? You're wonderful."

And she smiled at him, and she cried a little.

"I'm going to make the very best love to you that I possibly can," he said, and she thanked him, and true to his word he did his best.

He tried to remember the last time he and Barbara had slept with each other, but there hadn't been a last time, not as such, but then, there had to have been a last, surely? But it had been nothing momentous. It hadn't been so bad that it had caused either one of them to have been banished to the spare bedroom, there had been no tears or anger. One night he and his wife had had sex, and, as it turned out, they'd never bothered to try it again.

In the same way, nothing specific had ever caused the divorce. Looking back, he couldn't even decide which one of them had brought the matter up. No, it had been her, definitely her. Still.

One night as he dreamed of Barbara he realised he'd given her Cheryl's face. And try as he might, he couldn't recall what Barbara had looked like. And one night, whilst he dreamed, he realised he couldn't recall Cheryl's face either.

He killed Eunice quite by accident. She'd suggested they just fool around for a bit, and Michael had never been much good at foreplay, he just told her he'd follow her lead. They didn't do anything worse than kiss and squeeze at the other's genitals, and yet in the morning she was gone, and there was no way of getting her back.

And Natalie was unhappy, she had attempted suicide any number of times, she had tried drowning herself in the swimming pools, she had stuck a fork into the toaster. Nothing had worked. Before she impaled herself upon him, Michael asked her what she was so upset about, and the poor woman had burst into tears—"It's my babies, I miss my little babies." Michael asked her why she had ever been given to him, she wasn't a virgin at all then, surely? And Natalie shrugged, she really wasn't interested in discussing the finer points of her employment contract, not now—and she flung herself upon him, all lactating breasts and crude stretch marks, and she was gone.

The other virgins kept their distance. Michael didn't blame them. It wasn't that they were afraid of death, it was simply that they didn't like him very much. Even the squirrel gave him a wide berth.

And in the summer the eighteen young men lay out in the garden and sunbathed, and they bronzed there naked, and their muscled limbs gleamed golden in the heat, and their tackle looked thick and firm like barbecued meat, and Michael thought he had never looked as good as that, not when he'd been young, not his entire life.

One day he came up from the billiard room to find all the virgins were having an orgy. To be fair, they asked him if he wanted to join in, but he could see they were just being polite. There was a lot of sucking and suckling and squelching, everybody was trying to find ways of inserting themselves into another so that they became some writhing wall of flesh, even the goldfish was throwing herself into it—and as they did so the virgins began to break apart and pop like soap bubbles. Michael went and hid in his room for a while. When he came out later, he was entirely alone.

Michael didn't see anyone for quite a while. He ran out of bread to toast, and moved on to cereal.

They came for him one night, put a sack over his head. They said, "You've been reassigned, handsome."

He was taken with seventy-one other virgins to a new, bigger apartment. They called it an apartment, but really, it was more like a palace, it had everything, Jacuzzis and saunas and an entire beauty salon. The virgins were mostly young men, but there were a few girls thrown in, and some babies, and half a dozen squirrels. Michael said, "There's been a mistake... I mean, I've already had sex, really I have." They told him to shut up.

And Barbara arrived, and inspected her entourage, and seemed pleased by the young men, and bemused by the squirrels—and when she reached Michael in the line she just stopped, and stared, and swore. Michael said, "I'm sorry." "Just keep away from me," she hissed, "and I'm sure it'll be fine."

Michael could never get a seat on the sofa, let alone get close to the remote control. But Barbara cut a swathe through her virgins, showing a sexual voracity now she was dead she'd never hinted at when she'd been alive. She got through all the boys, then the girls, then the babies, then the squirrels, and she didn't so much as glance at her ex-husband. Michael was a little hurt, but soon enough he was able to stretch out wide and comfy upon the sofa and watch whichever channels he liked.

They muddled along amiably for a while. They'd potter about in separate rooms during the day, in the evening they'd sit together silently and watch television. Then they'd say good night, and go to different bedrooms. It was very safe, very familiar.

One evening Barbara turned off the television. Michael looked up at her in surprise. It had been *Coronation Street*, it was one of her favourites. She went without a word to the kitchen, returned with two glasses and a bottle of rose wine.

"We're going to have sex," she said. She poured two glasses, both to the very brim. "Whatever it takes."

They drank three bottles before Barbara was in the mood. She fell off the sofa flat on to her arse, which she found hugely funny. "Sod it," she said. "Too much wine. I'll know better tomorrow."

The next day they drank only the one bottle, Barbara was strict about that. They drank it very slowly, and Barbara said they would have to wait for it to take full effect. Some half an hour after the last dregs were drained, Barbara nodded primly, said, "It's time," pulled Michael up from the sofa, pulled him into the bedroom.

The sex was quite nice, and their bodies sort of fitted together in all the right places, and Michael wondered why they'd ever stopped doing it all those years ago.

Afterwards she looked at him intently, and Michael wondered whether she was wanting to say something loving. Then realised she was just waiting to see if he would pop.

"How do you feel?" she said.

"Fine."

"No, I mean, how do you…?"

"No, I know, fine, fine."

"Okay."

They lay there for a bit. He said, "Would you like some toast?" She nodded. He got out of bed. She watched him carefully, as if to see whether his weight upon the carpet would be too much for him, whether at last his structural integrity would break. It didn't. He brought her in some toast. He'd buttered it thick, the way she'd always liked it. She munched upon it gratefully.

"What are you going to do today, then?" he asked her. She didn't know.

They got up eventually. He sat down on the sofa, watched afternoon television. She stared at him for a bit, then went off to the kitchen to wash up his breakfast things, clear up the mess he always made.

She went out shopping later. Before she went she kissed him on the cheek, said goodbye, just in case he wasn't there when she got home. When she returned she looked annoyed by his continued existence—but as Michael helped her put away the groceries, he noticed she'd bought ready meals for two.

That evening they watched television. And she sighed, and said, "One more try. Okay?"

"Okay," he agreed.

She fetched the wine. She seemed somewhat impatient this time, they barely had more than a glass each.

They got undressed. This time they watched each other. They'd not bothered before—either they'd been too drunk, or too disinterested, or both.

He said to her, "I'm going to make the very best love to you I possibly can." And at those words a faint memory of Cheryl stirred, it's true. But Barbara didn't know.

"I'm going to miss you," Barbara said.

They made love very gently this time, hoping against hope they wouldn't damage the other.

"Are you done?" Michael asked her, and she smiled, and said yes. He didn't pull out. He thought he'd wait.

And he felt something for her that was a little like love—but it wasn't love, was it? It was relief. And it soared inside, he felt it fill his body up, he filled up like a balloon. He looked at her, and she was still smiling, and he could see that she felt the very same thing. And they both held on to each other, and waited, to see which of them would burst first.

And the old woman says:

- *Michael does not deserve his heavenly gift of seventy-two virgins. He is not a hero. To read of true heroism, with no expectation of eternal harems, turn to* **The All New Adventures of Robin Hood** *(story 11, page 187).*
- *Another couple find a more practical means of filling the gaps in their conversation in* **Unfurnished** *(story 19, page 321).*
- *If even Heaven isn't what it's cracked up to be, what's the point in putting in so much effort to go there? May as well* **Send Me to Hell** *(story 64, page 1103).*
- *It is a galling thing to forget the face of someone you once loved. In* **Jonas Rust** *(story 62, page 1053), a man is parted from his wife and sees her face everywhere.*
- *I would never want to be given my virginity back. Not after I fought so hard to lose it in the first place. But consider how much simpler life was back then, and turn to* **Mummy's Little Miracle** *(story 86, page 1477).*

If you read this book at
the rate of one word per hour,
it will take you
seventy-three years to finish it.
Read faster.

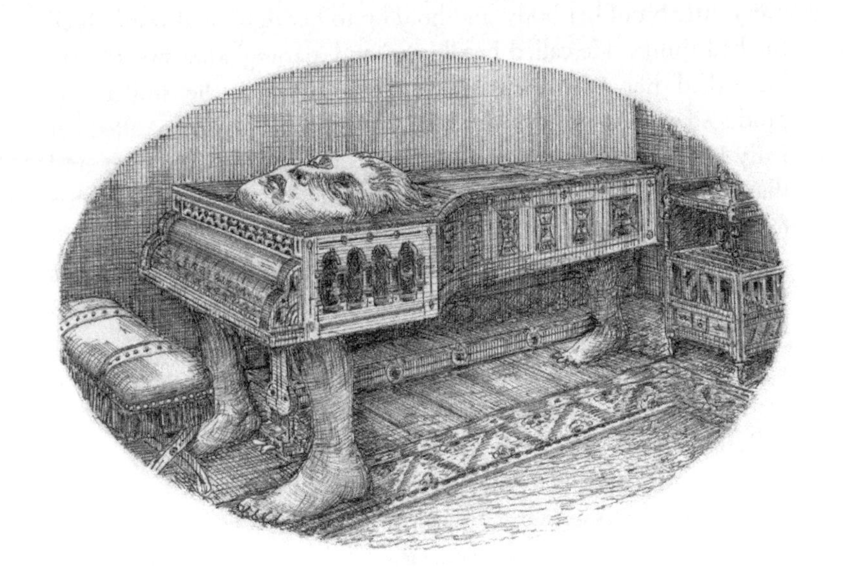

73
PAGE TURNER

HE CALLED HER HIS *grande dame*, his grand lassie, Miss Grandiosity—and it was sort of a joke, because she was really rather short, when she turned the pages for him the audience could barely see her lurking behind the piano, in some theatres they worried that the rake of the stage would prevent her from reaching the pages at all, in one of them they had to fetch her a box to stand on!—but it also wasn't a joke, because she produced such grand emotion within him, he said he felt his love for her as a roar inside, and so it was; and for all her size she was such a whirlwind, when she was happy it was infectious and he felt so happy too, and his problems seemed unimportant and the sunshine brighter and the music he played sweeter, even when it wasn't sweet at all; when she was unhappy he wanted to put his arms around her, wrapping up every little bit of her body, and hold on to her tight, and ward off all the bad things. He called her 'kitten' and 'darling' and 'sweetheart'. He called her Mrs Dimpleface, because when she smiled she produced dimples he thought were just adorable—and he called her Lady High Dimpleface when she was being bossy or stuck up, and that happened sometimes, or when she was cross with him, and that happened a lot—and it never failed, it made her smile, and within moments Lady High would have left the building and she'd be his Mrs Dimpleface again. He called her his 'dearest dear', his 'own', his 'world'. He called her 'love'.

She called him Maestro—but then, everybody called him Maestro—but then, she alone really meant it.

Both of them had prayed for this, in their own ways.

Louis had prayed to God to make him a musician. He hadn't even thought about music before the age of fifteen, when he had reluctantly accompanied his mother to a concert, and there he had heard Bach. It was, he later recognised, an indifferent performance at best, but it didn't matter, it was as if a light had been turned on in his head, and he wondered how he'd lived so long without realising his purpose. His mother made discreet enquiries, and all the tutors said he was too old to start if he wanted to do it seriously—it could be a hobby, they suggested, something nice, something fun. But Louis stamped his foot, this was now going to be his life, and he was going to be the greatest musician of his age, and he would show his genius before the crowned heads of Europe. His father was having none of it; Louis may have been too old to be a musician, but he was certainly too young to *decide* to be a musician; at the very reminder of his son's ambitions Father would fly into one of his tempers—"My son wants to be a performing monkey!" he said. He'd planned for him to be in the army, or in the church, or in law. "An entertainer?" he said. "Over my dead body!" And Louis prayed, and over his dead body it was—his father suffered a sudden heart attack during one particularly contemptuous rant against tunemerchants and singsongsmiths and hurdygurdyists, and dropped dead right there on the spot—and Louis went to church and gave thanks to God. He didn't even know what instrument he wanted to play. He tried the violin, the trumpet, even the harp—and he was glad the harp didn't take, because it really was most cumbersome, and a bit effeminate, he never thought he'd find himself a woman while hugging onto a harp. The piano seemed the natural fit. It was sturdy. It was solid. It wasn't a bit sissyish, not if he banged on the keys hard enough. So a pianist he became.

And Lizbeth too had prayed. She prayed for Louis to notice her. She had been to five of his concerts, each night, one after each other, and she'd sat in the front row, hoping that he would catch her eye. But he looked only at the piano, at his piano and nothing else. And on the sixth night she could bear it no longer. It was his last night in Edinburgh, then the tour would continue to other cities far away, and Lizbeth would never see him again, and she couldn't bear that—she'd never seen a man she had wanted more, she felt it deep in her belly, a desire, a yearning, an actual yearning, and she'd never felt such things before, she was a little shocked at herself, and she didn't know if it was because he produced such beautiful music or that he looked so very dapper in his coat and tails. Before the performance she found her way backstage. She knocked at his door. He looked a little scandalised to see her, and she liked that—in coat and tails he was intimidating, but now with that shy and awkward face he looked like a little boy. "Mademoiselle," he said, "you should know I am a married man!" Married, yes, she knew that; and twenty years older; and French; and Jewish; oh, Mother would never approve. "I want to be of help to you, Sir," she said. "I could be your page turner." He told her he already had a page turner for the night—the theatre supplied one—but she said, "Not tonight, for every night." He looked at the clock. "I have to get ready," he said, lamely—"I'll give you an audition, but we'll have to be quick." He played some Chopin, one of the nocturnes. And she stood so close to him as his fingers slid across the keys, and her heart was beating so fast, she thought it might distract him, it might put him off the music—he would say, "Mademoiselle, I cannot play the piano with all that drum accompaniment!"—but she turned the pages, she kept up with him—and she knew the Chopin, it was very famous, and she supposed very pretty, but she'd never properly listened to it before, and it made sense to her now, it wasn't just melody, it was full of life and such sweet passion. She kept pace, turned the pages cleanly, and he never had to pause, the entire piece ran as smooth as could be, she wanted to say, don't let's stop, never stop, let's drag it out to a full symphony! And she didn't tell him she'd lied. Didn't dare tell him until months later. On their wedding night, and she was still afraid he'd be angry at the deception, but he just laughed and kissed her and then they made love once more. She'd lied, she'd never turned pages for other pianists as she'd claimed; she couldn't even read music, the notes on the page were just black smudges to her; she didn't know why it was the right time to turn the page, it just was, it was an answered prayer, it was Louis, it was her, it was the togetherness of them both, they were *simpatico*. He told her she must now leave the dressing room. He had to perform to his audience. But she would be watching, wouldn't she? She'd be in the front row? And she was, and this time as he played he didn't just look at the piano. And never again in her lifetime did she watch him from the stalls, from this point on she would always stand up there with him, turning his pages, and standing so close with her heart beating—but this was maybe her favourite performance, watching him as he watched her, hearing the nocturne, hearing him make little stumbles when he caught her smiling at him. And from that moment she loved Chopin, and from that moment she loved Louis, and she called him Maestro.

He divorced his wife, an atonal double bass of a woman. And they went on tour, and that tour merged into another tour, and then another; the tours went on for years. And he never played before the crowned heads of Europe, not even one of the minor ones. And he never played to a full auditorium. But he'd never played better either. And sometimes they'd both wonder if they'd prayed for the wrong things. He wondered whether he should have asked God to make him not just a musician, but a *great* musician; and she wondered whether she'd held him back, that her love for him had been a selfish thing that had stunted his talent and stopped him from being the Maestro he ought to have been. But then they'd put those thoughts right from their heads. They loved each other. They'd got what they'd prayed for, and so much more. They couldn't complain.

On they toured, and he played Bach, and Brahms, and Mendelssohn, and Schubert, all for the thinning crowds; and when he played Chopin, he played it for her.

The tuberculosis took Lizbeth fast—and she was too young, and that was unfair, no, it was *obscene*—but it took her fast, and there was some mercy to that—it took her fast enough she didn't much suffer, but slowly too so there was time to prepare. She arranged the next touring dates for after she'd gone, when he'd be on his own; she'd always arranged the tours, she was the practical one. She told him to hire a new page turner, and he'd said no, and she'd pressed the point, and he'd said no, adamantly no, the theatres would have to provide, just as in the old days, and on this matter at least he won. And he said to her, "I don't want you to go," and "I can't bear it if you go," and she'd say, "Oh, love," and she'd say, "Love, I know." And he'd pray that she wouldn't die, and that was too much to ask. And he'd pray that she wouldn't feel any pain, and that too, it was just too much, God doesn't answer prayers like that. And he'd pray, at least let us be together, let us always be together. And he had no right to expect an answer to that either, hadn't they been given enough already? But God listened.

One day she woke and she was smiling, and it wasn't one of the brave smiles he'd grown used to, it was a smile broad enough to make her cheeks dimple. She told him that the pain was gone. He could hardly believe it. He began to hope. Though as he looked at her she still seemed so pale and thin, still, he let himself hope. She felt a little numbness on her back, and when he turned her over, he saw that it had turned to wood. A brown, rich wood, he thought it might be mahogany; it was mahogany, he knew it from the grand piano they owned in the drawing room. He pressed against it gently, she said he could press harder—he asked if she could feel him and she said she could, but he mustn't worry, it was a nice sensation; it seemed somehow *solid*, if a sensation can be solid. He rapped his fingers against her and she smiled—and he kissed her on the wood, and there was something familiar and earthy about that taste, as if the wood had just this day grown out of the soil—and he kissed her again, not on the wood now, on the mouth, and she kissed him too, and he could taste the blood there, and the sickness, and death.

The wood grew. She was such a little woman, and so she remained; the illness made her shrink into herself, if anything. But her back now stood proud and tall, like a great sturdy frame. He stroked it. "Oh, my love," she said. Her feet narrowed, then they doubled, then they turned to brass. She opened her mouth in her widest smile, and her teeth filled an entire keyboard with dazzling white ivory; on her hands her fingernails blackened, and it was a rich black, a deep black, and they smoothed, and they swelled, and they dotted between the ivories as the sharps and flats. "I love you," she told him, and he loved her too; he loved her as her two eyelids merged into one heavier lid altogether, the one that locked the keyboard away and kept it safe; he loved her as her lungs, her kidneys, the heart itself, as they all stretched themselves taut as strings; as one single eye became a knot in the wood just above the rack on which he kept his sheets of music, so now, when he sat at his wife and played on her and had his fingers tease at her and thrilled to the strange music she made, he gazed at the eye and it gazed at him, it wouldn't wink, it wouldn't blink, it held him, so wide, so sure, telling him that it was all right, everything was going to be all right. He played for hours, and no matter the tune, no matter how jaunty or light, each time it made him cry. "I love you," she told him, "I love you, and you're the best of me, and you always have been, and you always will."

And in the drawing room the grand piano softened into a mass of pale and melting flesh, and it coughed blood, hawking thick black gobs of it on to its own chin, and there was pain there, and something rather worse than pain, but it was only a piano, it was only an instrument, it didn't cry out, it didn't complain, it didn't say a word.

And when the doctor came it was the piano he examined, not the wife; and Louis thought him rather a fool not to notice; and he shook his head and led Louis away from the piano's earshot with warnings to expect the worst. But Louis knew there was no worst, his wife was alive and well and getting so much better, no longer turning the pages of his music but producing all the music herself—he couldn't even pretend it was him any longer, it all came from her, the music flowed straight from her, and when his fingers danced upon her teeth it was just to help let her genius out. And the piano died, it gave one splutter one morning and just slipped away; and it was the piano they took away, the undertaker and his crew all muttering condolences, and Louis was glad to be rid of it, it looked like a poor faded corpse, like a spent thing, like something broken, something that could never have made music, what music could there be in something so sad? And they buried it. And Louis could hardly stop himself from laughing, but he knew for form's sake he must be seen to grieve—and yet it was a trick, he'd still got Lizbeth, his dearest dear, he'd still got her and would never lose her and he could tickle her ivories and make her chest thrum, he'd got her, he'd never let her go.

All the stories say that he went back on tour and took his own piano with him. And he performed in his dear wife's memory, and whilst he never found great success, he was happy. But not one can agree on the ending. Here are just a few of those endings.

In one story Louis dies onstage. He's an old man, but he's still performing—and it's his birthday, it's his hundredth birthday, no, that sounds a bit too neat, let's say he's one hundred and one. He bows before the audience and dedicates the evening, as he always does, to Lizbeth—who was the best of him, always has been, always will. And it isn't a full house—even sentiment can only go so far in this tale, he'd never have sold that many tickets, a hundred-and-one-year-old has-been like him! But though it's only of modest size, the crowd is appreciative. It gives him a standing ovation at the end. And Louis cannot stand to acknowledge it, because he's dead, he's had a heart attack, so sudden and so profound he wouldn't have felt a thing, there was one great thrum in his chest and that was it. Louis dies proud. And they can't prise his fingers off the piano keys, and they can't prise his foot off the pedal. It's as if he's become fused to the piano itself. There's no join where the piano ends and the man begins—there is ivory as far as his knuckles, brass spread over his foot. And his back has become wood, all the best mahogany. They're buried together, the grand maestro and his grand piano.

And, in another story, the Nazis get him. He lives to be an old man, but it's no good, history catches up with him. The Nazis break down the front door to his house. They find Louis in the drawing room, sitting at the piano. Maybe he's playing. Maybe he's just caressing it, like he does every day—because that's enough now—there's no more performance left in him, but if he caresses the piano and strokes the wood and kisses at the keyboard there's still music of a sort. He doesn't rise for them. He doesn't even turn around. The soldiers jab the old Jew with their guns, and laugh, and tell the music man to play them something good—something patriotic—*Deutschland über Alles*! Louis doesn't play that, of course. Maybe he even tries to, but Lizbeth won't let him. Whatever his fingers tell the keys to do, the piano will only play Chopin. And no matter the shouts of anger, the threats, Louis won't even change the tempo, this is a calm Chopin, something sweet to be savoured, he won't be rushed or panicked. They shoot him. Or maybe they're so overcome by the music's beauty, and the dignity of the old man and his darling piano, maybe they leave in shame. No, they shoot him, clean, in the back of the head, and then, and then the piano keeps on playing. The Chopin won't stop. The love just won't stop, not for them, not because *they* say so, not because *they* will it, it's more powerful than anything they will ever feel in their uniforms and jackboots, this is his *grande dame* playing, his grand lassie, Miss Grandiosity, in tribute to the man she adored. The piano plays until in rage the soldiers chop it into firewood.

Or, in one last story. And this one seems real to me. This one true. Because what more magic can Louis and Lizbeth expect? In a lifetime that has given them such miracles already?

Louis falls in love again. He doesn't mean to. Oh, don't blame him, he doesn't want to. He tells the woman this. He says, I can't do this, and she says she'll be patient, and she is, and it's all right.—And he's been lonely enough, surely? Hasn't he had his fill of suffering?

And when she smiles her face doesn't dimple. But her face does entirely new things he couldn't even have guessed at.

On their wedding day he feels as if he's inviting a curse upon his head. But nothing happens. He toasts his new love, and she toasts him, and everyone applauds, and is happy for them as they cut the cake and kiss and dance their first dance as husband and wife.

He doesn't tour again. That part of his life is over, and besides, his new wife doesn't love him for his music. This doesn't make her a bad person. She loves him for other things. But he keeps the piano. He keeps it, and he buries it under a rug, and he locks it away upstairs, and keeps the key hidden.

They have a daughter. He loves his daughter. At this late stage in his life, Louis has at last created a work of art all of his own.

He indulges the girl, but he won't spoil her. If she wants to ride a horse, he'll find the money for riding lessons. If she wants a new toy, a new dress, a pet dog, a pet parakeet even, that's all right, she can have them. But he won't let her learn the piano. No more music. Enough.

And one day he hears it. He has been out walking with his darling wife, they've walked hand in hand through the parks of Paris as they like to do, they've smelled the flowers in bloom, they've kissed. But it begins to rain, and they hurry home.

And though the locked room is right at the very top of the house, really so very far away, he hears it immediately. Fingers bashing at keys, not knowing how hard or light to be, and the notes straining in protest. All that discordant music. All that ugly din.

He races up the stairs as fast as he can. He has never been so angry. He can feel his heart pounding in his chest, and he thinks of his father, and how angry he always was, and he thinks, is this it? Will I kill myself with my anger too? But he keeps running, and below him he hears his wife distraught, Louis, she cries, go easy on her, Louis, come back!

She's beating away at the piano so loudly she doesn't even hear him until he bursts into the room. She's lifted the rug from the piano lid, but most of the piano is still smothered, it looks now like something old and dead—it looks like something embarrassing. And her hands are dirty, he sees, she hasn't even washed them, she'll be smearing her fingerprints all over those gleaming white keys, she hasn't even put on *gloves*—and as she hits the keys, *plink plonk plunk*, in any order, she keeps time by kicking at the wood—sitting on the stool and so short she can't even reach the floor, her legs dangling in mid-air and scuffing the side of the piano as she finds some sort of rhythm.

She turns around now, and she still doesn't know, still doesn't see he's angry. She smiles at him, as if she's been clever, as if she's just uncovered a big secret—there's music in the world! And her smile is so big, and no, the cheeks don't dimple for her either—but that smile certainly has something good about it.

"Papa," she says. "Teach me! Teach me how to do it!"

When he puts his hands on her he still doesn't know what he's going to do. But he lifts her off the stool gently, ever so gently, and she laughs. He sets her down safely on the floor. He pulls the rug off the piano, it comes off in one hard tug, and the piano doesn't look dead any more, or embarrassing—it's *old*, certainly, but that's all right, he's old too. And he sits down upon the stool. And lifts little Lizbeth up on to his knee. And begins to play for her.

And the old woman says:

- *In* **The Grand Adventure** *(story 1, page 19) a man discovers his dying wife has turned into something sweeter, dearer and more heartbreaking than a mere piano. Find out what it is.*
- *But I imagine there are worse things to be metamorphosed into than a piano. At least someone might still tickle your ivories. Turn to* **Suffer Little Children** *(story 35, page 575) to read of a transformation of a more terrible nature.*
- *It is unusual for God to answer prayers—perhaps it's hard to reach him when he lives so far away. Perhaps we might have more success if we knew his exact address. Find out where he lives in* **Lo! He Abhors Not the Virgin's Womb** *(story 91, page 1541).*
- *There are two types of love stories: ones about loss, and ones about reconciliation. In* **Jonas Rust** *(story 62, page 1053) a man quests across the world to get his wife back. See whether or not he succeeds.*
- *And if you think that's wrong, that there are as many types of love stories as there are lovers on Earth—then turn to* **101 Heartbeats** *(story 101, page 1695). And perhaps you are right.*

74
PLEASE ME

SOME PEOPLE TALK OF LOVE at first sight, and I've never had that, but from the moment I laid eyes on Paul Lindblad I knew he was the one I wanted to take my virginity. Afterwards Nanny asked me why, and I said it was because of his fingers, and that I'd felt mesmerised watching them play across the keyboard. But that was a lie, his fingers were neither here nor there to me. I never quite knew why I had settled upon Paul Lindblad, I didn't know then, and all these years later I certainly can't tell now—not even when nostalgic reminiscence has lent him a certain charm I somehow suspect he never actually possessed—oh, I was so young back then, and I was given to such romantic exaggeration, really, who could have blamed me? But the choice didn't feel random, it felt instinctively correct. I saw Paul across the mezzanine of that hotel in C____ , and playing at his piano with such dismissive confidence, and I knew I liked him, and I was going to be the object of his every wicked desire.

We had just come in from dinner. I had had the duck, so Nanny had had the duck too. We ate alone that night, I remember Mother had gone to bed early with one of her headaches. Nanny was expecting us to retire as well, and she was making those little yawns designed to make me think I was drowsy—she'd been using them on me since I was in the cradle, I think, and sometimes they worked and sometimes they didn't. There was a white piano in the lounge, and though the hotel was out of season the room was quite crowded, and most of the chairs occupied—wives sat with their sherries, husbands with brandies and cigars. I have never liked crowds, and Nanny knew that, of course, so she was surprised when I said I wanted to stay and listen. The music was all very gentle—there was some Chopin, some Schumann, a little Liszt, and I noticed that the pianist put in a few extra trills when the original wasn't florid enough for his audience's taste, and he played upon the keys with a self-conscious flourish. Each time he finished a piece he acknowledged our applause with an unsmiling nod—the applause was polite but sincere, and his appreciation of it showed similar restraint. Nanny made a few more of her little yawns, and then gave up, and resigned herself to watching the rest of the performance with me.

Was Paul Lindblad a good pianist? I do not know. I told him later he was, of course. I think he was tolerably good. Like his fingers, his music was neither here nor there to me.

I knew it was high time I had an adventure. My sister Nerys had had her adventure three years ago, in B______ , with a Swiss waiter. It had kept her busy the whole two months we were staying there. She had asked me to be her confidante—by which, I supposed, she wanted me to listen as she boasted of her sexual exploits in increasingly lurid detail. I hadn't liked Marcel—he was handsome, I could see that, but he was also *smooth*, and he looked so comfortable with himself, as if he had had many such dalliances with the upper classes. As if, moreover, Nerys was *his* lover as much as he was hers, as if he had some control. And, yes, perhaps that's the reason I was drawn to Paul Lindblad. Because he was never a man who was going to be well-versed in carnal matters, because any adventure he took me upon would be an adventure for him too. I wanted to matter to him in a way that Nerys could never have mattered to Marcel. Is that so wrong? I would be Paul Lindblad's goddess.

He was not an attractive man. He was very short. Even seated at the piano, his diminutive stature could not be disguised. I discovered later that Uncle John referred to him as 'the dwarf,' which was a tad unfair—he stood by my reckoning at about five foot tall—but, still, there was something strangely dwarfish about him. His features didn't seem properly proportioned to his frame, his head too large, his hands, his fingers. He was never ugly to me. I never thought of him as ugly. But I could see why others would—he certainly looked very unusual. And dressed in his coat and tails, he was a bit like a child at fancy dress.

I make no pretence that I am a beautiful woman. Not even then—when I was a girl, and had dresses, and had deportment, and had Nanny to do my hair. I accepted there was a limit to what could be done to make me socially presentable. Mother, I knew, was disappointed. Mother would study me sometimes, and sigh, and say that maybe I'd grow into myself when I was older—but it seemed to me that the problem was I had already grown out too much. Of course Nerys could attract a man like Marcel—she was petite, and had fine skin.

I remember that night so well—that was the night I became an adult, I think, not with the sexual act itself but with the decision to have one. I watched Paul play, and already I determined quite coolly I would have to keep our affair a secret. Nerys' affair was a secret of sorts—but of course Mother knew about it, and Uncle John knew, and the chambermaids knew—Mother even gave tacit support, and told Nerys after it was all over that if she were going to practise sexual relations on hotel employees she had at least selected one of the better ones. I knew Mother would never think Paul Lindblad was one of the better ones. He would have to be a *proper* secret, and details of my progress in seduction would be restricted to Nanny and essential staff. And I felt pleased for the first time that Nerys was not staying at the hotel with us. I did not like Nerys very much. She was a rather spiteful sister. But she had been company, and I had missed her. Now she was newly married, to an American stockbroker called Donald, and it might be years before she'd had her children and would be allowed to go holidaying with me again.

I knew I would be married too eventually. That I would be next. But that night, seeing Paul for the first time, all of that seemed very far away: I was fifteen, and I had selected a lover. I was happy, I was blissfully happy—and at that moment, in the realisation of it, I felt I could cry. I reached for Nanny's hand and squeezed it. Nanny misinterpreted the signal, and hurried me upstairs to our suite before I could dissuade her otherwise.

And as Nanny undressed me for bed I told her of what had passed, and of the adventure that now lay before me. "Why the pianist?" she asked. I came up with the long fingers reason. She told me I'd made a good choice. She'd heard it said that men with long fingers make good lovers. She'd heard it said that men with long fingers had big cocks. She kissed me on the head, and tucked me in and turned off the lamp, and told me we'd speak more of the matter in the morning.

I lay there in the dark, and cuddled my pillow close, and pretended it was my little hotel pianist. And I thought of how, when the affair was done, it would be my turn to boast. I would tell Nerys that Paul Lindblad was handsome. I would instruct Nanny to say the same. Nerys need never find out the truth. She need never find out what Paul really looked like. After all, it wasn't as if I planned to take photographs.

By the time Nanny woke me the next morning, she had already made enquiries about Paul Lindblad. She told me everything as she brushed my hair. She now knew his name, of course, and his age—which was thirty-four years old. That was a good age for a first love, she told me, her own had been pushing sixty and that had been a shame. Paul had only been employed at the hotel a few months, so there wasn't much gossip about him yet—and he was said to be a somewhat remote man who kept to himself, and had never yet been found drunk or necessitated any disciplinary action. He was a Frenchie, or possibly a Croat, or possibly a Turk.

I was grateful to Nanny for those little titbits, but I reprimanded her anyway—I told her that I had wanted to find out all about my new love by myself, that would have been the more romantic thing. I did ask her, though, whether Paul was seeing any other woman. I asked it very casually, but Nanny saw through my pretence of indifference, and she teased me. I was not in the mood for teasing before I had been properly breakfasted. I threw the hairbrush across the room. Nanny assured me there was no other woman in Paul's life—"Not that it would matter in the long run," she said, "But it makes it simpler, don't it?"

And Nanny was so excited, she was practically skipping around the room, she said it was all going to be *such* an adventure for us. And I felt guilty, I think, that I hadn't been as eager an accomplice to Nerys, this was probably just the sort of encouragement she had wanted. Nanny's enthusiasm was infectious. But, I told her sternly, we had to be discreet—discretion was of the utmost importance. Nanny said, "Oh yes, discretion!", and put her finger to her lips, and giggled.

Nanny had found out that Paul gave two piano engagements a day: one in the late evening after dinner, as we had already observed—and one to accompany afternoon tea. This, Nanny reasoned, would be the best time to confront him; the earlier performance was rarely well-attended, and it would be more proper to affect an introduction in the daylight. I agreed on all particulars except one—Nanny proposed that *she* should be the one to approach Paul on my behalf. This was not what I wanted. I explained that I wanted to seduce the man myself. She said that I would have all the latitude to seduce him in any way I pleased, once she had brokered the conditions of that seduction first. I was cross; I was adamant; I'm afraid I threw the hairbrush again. "Well, well," said Nanny, "I'm sure we can try it your way." And she suggested that we spend the next few hours bathing me and primping me so I would be as pretty as a picture.

We went down. I wore my favourite dress, and Nanny had managed to coax my hair into ringlets. We ordered cucumber sandwiches and tea and as I waited for my lover to arrive I confess I felt such dreadful nerves—not that I would turn back now, for I have always been headstrong, just like Nerys, just like Mother—but because I could feel my childhood years slipping away, and my time as a woman about to begin. I held my teacup the way I had always been taught, with my finger crooked, and sipped at it most genteelly, and I suddenly *knew* what I looked like, I was a grown up like all the others. And that seemed like a such a wondrous thing, and yet also deliciously sad.

At three o'clock precisely Paul Lindblad made his entrance. He really was very short. I could feel Nanny's eyes on me—are you sure, are you sure? I didn't look at her. I sipped at my tea, let the warm liquid sit for a little while on my tongue. I was sure.

The medley of music was the same as he had played the night before. The order may have been a little different, I couldn't tell. I watched those long fingers. I watched his mouth.

He only looked to the audience when we applauded, and even then I could see that he looked through us. He looked through me. And it didn't annoy me. I was amused. He would know me so very soon.

And after he'd polished off an especially trite sonata by Schumann, he got to his feet, and assayed a little formal bow. He turned from the piano, didn't look back at it, didn't look back at us, and marched from the room. And I got to my feet too.

I felt Nanny's hand on my arm. This wasn't the end of the recital, just a short break. I didn't care, I wasn't waiting any longer.

He had no idea that a woman was following him, tripping over herself to catch up. Into the lobby, through the doors marked 'Staff', into the corridor behind.

My first impressions were not of him—it was of the corridor itself, and how suddenly bleak it looked, and how dirty, and it seemed so strange that one thin door was all that divided the gilt opulence I was used to from this dinge. Paul was leaning against the wall, he was smoking a roll-up cigarette. At last he saw me—he looked confused, and he made to put his cigarette out.

I tried to reassure him. "*Non, non,*" I said. "*Nyet.*"

He seemed to understand that. He smoked. And I just stood, fixed to the spot. He turned away, as if pretending I wasn't there, or as if not to embarrass me by looking at me without permission—there was such a collision of deference and contempt, and I couldn't work out which was the greater, and I thrilled to it, and it made me bold.

"*Excusez-moi,*" I said. He looked at me. I nodded at the cigarette. "Do you have? May I have?" From a pocket he took a little tin, he gave me one of his cigarettes. It was thin, and dripping tobacco. I put it in my mouth, and bent closer so he could light it. I touched his hand as he brought the match to me.

Mother was teaching me how to smoke, and had bought me a short stubby holder for that purpose. I hadn't got used to the taste yet, but Mother said I was getting better at blowing the smoke out, I was becoming properly ladylike. I tried to hold it the way she had shown me, hand raised over shoulder, cigarette pointing upwards, but it was so small and sorry it disappeared between my fingers; I tried to be ladylike with the smoke, but the taste was so strong it made me cough.

And he laughed. He actually laughed at me—and then looked afraid that he had done so, so I laughed too, to show him that there was nothing to worry about, though I didn't feel like laughing at all, not really.

I leaned into him, to be close the way we had been only seconds ago, when he had lit my dreadful cigarette. And my heart was beating so fast now, and I thought, I have never been so close to a man before, surely, a man who wasn't family—and for all his borrowed finery, for all he dressed like an artist, he smelled of sweat.

"Please," he said. "Please." What did that 'please' mean? And what was the accent, it didn't sound French to me. It sounded like nothing I had heard before.

"Please," I said back. "Please, I want you to…please, I want you."

And I was blushing, I'm sure, I blush now as I recall it—but I didn't want him thinking I was embarrassed, I held his gaze fearless and direct, I wasn't going to stop looking at him.

He was the one who broke eye contact, he turned his head, looked up and down the corridor to see if anyone were watching. And I realised how incongruous a pair we looked, this shabby pianist next to such an elegant young woman, and how I towered over him, I was a head taller at least.

I took a deep breath. I spoke again. He turned back to me. "I want you to come to my suite. It is at the top of the hotel, it is room number 414. I want you to take this key." The key was in my hand. Then the key was in his.

"Please." That *please* again, what was it? "Please. No. Please." He'd taken my hand within his. I felt his fingers. I wanted him to squeeze my hand. I wanted him to squeeze it tight. "No," he said again. Pressing the key back into my own palm. And I looked at him, and wanted to know what this was—did he think he was unworthy of me? Was it modesty? He was smiling. He was smiling up at me, and he looked so *kind*. It was pity. He pitied me.

My face was burning again. I pulled away. I fled.

I didn't cry. I refused to cry. I ran straight into the lobby. If other people saw me, I don't know. I ran for the elevator. I didn't want to wait for it. If I'd had to wait for it I would surely have been unable to hold back any longer—I was lucky—I got in. The bell hop made as if to speak to me; he changed his mind. He knew to take me to the private floor. He knew me. They all knew me. In every hotel I stayed in, all of them, they were trained to know my family name.

I made it back to my suite. I fumbled at the lock with the key. The key he had rejected—oh! I fell into the room. I fell onto my bed.

I don't know how long it took Nanny to come upstairs to join me. It wasn't long.

"My darling child," she said.

"I want to die."

"You made a little exhibition of yourself down there," she said. "But I don't think your mother will find out." She smiled to show she wasn't scolding me. She was giving me pertinent information, like a good accomplice should.

"I will never love again."

"My poor, dear, darling child." She stroked my hair, and she sang to me a little, and I slept.

By the time she shook me awake it was already dark. She sounded sterner now. More businesslike. "You need to get ready for dinner. And change your dress, you've crumpled it."

"I don't want dinner. I'm not well."

"Your mother has given instruction that you join her. Hurry, darling."

Mother had the salmon, so I had the salmon too. I wished Nanny were with me, but Nanny was only required to be my chaperone when family were not about. Instead there was Uncle John. Uncle John had a face that reminded me of Father's—it was a little wider, more jowly maybe. Uncle John had a steak that was rare and bloody, and he chewed it intently, it seemed to me, as a distraction from listening to Mother. Mother talked about how bored she was with the dreary mountains, and the dreary mountain air, and the sort of dreary people who frequented mountain hotels. She said the boredom of it all brought on her headaches, and that Uncle John was going to take her away for medicinal reasons and that they might be gone a few weeks. I was to stay at the hotel with Nanny, and amuse myself the best I could. "Why aren't you eating?" she asked. I said I wasn't hungry. I asked if I could be excused. I wanted to return to my room, I wanted to be there safe before the piano started playing in the lounge. Mother said "No."

It took ages for Mother to eat her salmon and for Uncle John to smoke his cigar. And then they were up—Mother kissed me on top of the head, "Behave yourself whilst we're away," and they were gone.

I knew Nanny was waiting for me upstairs. I felt a certain freedom in being on my own, just for a little while. I heard the piano even before I left the dining room. I would not go to see him. I would not watch him play. I would not give him the satisfaction of seeing me there. The room was crowded, but not so badly as the night before—there was a chair near the front—I took it.

He was nearing the end of his Mendelssohn, it was the third time I had heard him play it now. He did not see I was there. I knew soon that he would stop, turn his head to acknowledge the applause. He would see me then. I hoped it would give him a little start, even hurt him, just a bit.

And the music ended, and I set my face into something hard and cold and disinterested, and he turned to it and his face was as hard and cold as my own, and he gave a little nod—but not to me, never to me, to everyone else there but not to me. And then, then he went back to his piano.

I got to my feet. And this time, with dignity, I walked away.

By the time I was back in the suite I was in tears.

I only ever saw Nanny be angry twice—properly angry, not like when I was a child. She was angry now. "No more of this," she said. "Wait here. I shall be back presently."

I got changed back into my favourite dress; Nanny had ironed it for me.

When Nanny returned, she said to me, "Last chance. You're sure this is the man you want?" I said that it was. "Come in," she called.

Paul Lindblad was still in his coat and tails. I was so happy to see him there, at last, in my bedroom. And he looked down at the ground, and he seemed so sorry, and my heart opened out to him, I forgave him at once.

But I didn't want him to know that. Not when he had pitied me.

"Take off your clothes," I said.

I told Nanny to stay and watch.

When I was small, I once asked Nanny what her background was. She laughed, and said she'd been created specially by the elves to look after me. I knew even then it wasn't true—but still, I accepted it. There were certain things not to be spoken of until I was older—Cook's pregnancy, Mother's gentlemen friends, money. I always imagined I'd have time to ask Nanny about it again when I *was* older. And there was time, wasn't there? More than time enough. But somehow I never got around to it.

Mother said, "Ordinary people don't have backgrounds. That's what makes them ordinary." Mother had a background. Her family had a coat of arms. Mother had it embossed upon her writing paper. Father had no background, she was always keen to tell us she had married beneath her. But Father had money; he was a 'self-made man', even though I never really understood what it was he had done to make himself. I think Mother appreciated the money, and I think she loved Father too, in her own way—we saw him only a couple of months of the year, at Christmas and in the early spring, he was too busy at work to accompany us on our travels. His brother John was a self-made man too; after the war had left so much of Europe in ruins, Uncle John had bought up old hotels at deflated prices and turned them into luxury resorts. He had hotels in M___, in N___, in B_____, in P____; he had, of course, the hotel in C___ where I met Paul Lindblad. Mother would say that Uncle John was a grubby opportunist, but she said it with some admiration. She couldn't have found his grubbiness too off-putting, she never hid the fact they were lovers. And that's what we would do, Mother, Nerys, and I—we would spend most of the year living in the suites of my uncle's hotels, out of season, always out of season. Mother didn't enjoy the crowds any more than I did. We would stay only for six to eight weeks, maybe, then travel on when the season changed, or the hotel got busy once more, or Mother got bored. We chased the dying days of summer, it seemed to me, and the sunshine was a little too ripe and the sunsets always just past their best.

Lying together in the afternoons, I might ask Paul Lindblad of his background. I had decided that afternoon visits were the most suitable. Sometimes I let him visit me after his evening performance too, but at night time I was tired and fractious, and I didn't want him *sleeping* in my bed, that felt wrong somehow. After we made love Paul would hold me, as I asked, or stroke my skin, or stroke my hair—I might say, but tell me about yourself. Tell me who you are. Nanny one day said that I should stop. It was odd, because I had never known her take Paul's side before, she was always the one who reminded me I should see him as a servant and nothing else—and it was obvious Paul had appealed to her, and I was angry he had gone behind my back. She said to me, I shouldn't ask to know too much of Paul. I mustn't tease him. I mustn't belittle him. Even the humblest man needs to retain some dignity.

But I wasn't teasing Paul. I genuinely was curious to know all about him. I wanted to lap him up. And I didn't mind if the stories of his poverty were shocking—indeed, the more shocking the better!

"Do you love me?" I asked him.

"I am not permitted to love a woman such as you." In that funny accent of his.

"It's all right," I would say. "You can tell me the truth. We're equals now, just for a little while. Do you love me?"

"Yes."

And I loved Paul too. Though I sometimes wished I had chosen a more experienced lover after all. One time, I remember, I asked him to kiss me. When he came up to my suite, sometimes I didn't just want to start with the sex, occasionally I wanted something more affectionate. I said, "Kiss me as if you're aching for me." But he wasn't any good at it, he didn't know what I was talking about. I had to call Nanny for help.

"Nanny," I said. "Show Paul how to kiss me."

"What's he doing wrong?" she asked.

"I don't know," I replied. "Everything. Just make him do it *nice*."

I watched as Nanny taught him. She showed him how to use the tongue, how to nip very gently with the teeth. Paul seemed to sulk throughout the lesson, I was almost very cross with him. But at last Nanny nodded, and said he was ready, and he took me in his arms and put his mouth against mine, his mouth *inside* mine, and Nanny was right, really, Paul had come on in leaps and bounds.

The sex was good. The sex was satisfactory. He worked hard to satisfy me. It's true, even then, I realised the sex was not perfect. I went on to have better sex with other men later—even now, I have better sex sometimes—well, sometimes it is worse and sometimes it is better. But I realised quickly that my relationship with Paul Lindblad was not predicated solely upon the quality of the sex he offered. I had wanted a man to take my virginity, but I wanted so much more besides—I wanted someone who would romance me, who would light my cigarettes and drink champagne from my shoe. Who would give me flowers—I had to ask him to bring flowers, but once he'd been given the initiative he brought them to every subsequent assignation without fail. I wanted someone, yes, who would play the piano for me. I would go and watch his evening performance after dinner, I would sit at the very front, and I would look at those long fingers dancing upon the keys and I would think how only hours before they had been dancing upon *me*, how they had been inside me and exploring every inch of me, exploring wherever I told them to go. And I didn't care that I had heard the Chopin before, or the Schumann, or the Mendelssohn, I didn't care a stuff. Because at the end of every piece, when the audience applauded and he made that darling little nod, I knew now that nod was for me.

That first night, when he came to my room. "Take off your clothes," I said.

He'd been looking at the floor. He raised his head then. Raised it to me. He didn't seem surprised. I wanted him to look a little surprised. It seemed impertinent somehow that he wasn't.

"Please stay," I said to Nanny. She nodded silently.

Paul Lindblad unbuttoned his shirt. He took off his jacket. He took off his trousers. He stood there, naked, awaiting my appraisal.

I didn't want to be too harsh. "It's very good," I said. "Nanny, isn't it good?"

"It'll be fine," she said.

"Please," I said. "I don't want you to be afraid. It's all right. I won't hurt you. I want you to like me."

"Please," he said too. And that was it.

"Come to bed," I said. He seemed to want encouragement. I reached for his hand.

We made love, and as I say, it wasn't perfect. But it was gentle, and brief, and I think that's all I needed right then. I thought his skin would be hairy, but his body was smooth, and as I helped him on top of me, he seemed small and sweet, I felt so tender and loving towards him. He knew what to do, but he struggled for a while—it wasn't until Nanny lost patience and helped guide him inside me with her hand that he seemed to relax into it.

"And we can do this every day!" I told him. "We can do this every single day if you like!"

After he had left, Nanny and I drank to the occasion with a glass of wine. And I said to Nanny, because I was no fool—what had she said to change his mind? Had she offered him money?

She said she hadn't, and I asked her again, and this time she didn't respond.

"Don't give him money again," I told her. "Do you understand? You won't need to any more. Not now he knows me. He's not my gigolo. He's not my whore. He's my lover. And I want him to love me for *me*."

I had already had a glass of wine at dinner with Mother. I shouldn't have had a second, they always made me squiffy.

I had invited Paul Lindblad to join me in my suite for the evening. I had been unsettled all day, and I hadn't been sure whether that would act as provocation for my headache or my libido—the libido won out. Paul asked whether he had to bring another bunch of flowers, and I told him that one a day was sufficient.

We made love, and afterwards I still wasn't tired. "Play me the piano," I said.

"It is not permitted. The lounge will be shut."

"I'm sure we can open it."

So we got dressed, and we went downstairs. It was past one o'clock, and there were no guests to be seen, only hotel staff that ignored us discreetly. The lounge was completely empty. I sat on the piano stool. "I want you to teach me," I said.

"I am not a teacher."

"Please."

He pulled a chair beside me. He made me fan out my fingers, placed them directly on to the keys. I realised still, for all that I was taller, his fingers were so much longer than mine. He told me to play the scales, each note in ascending then descending order. "Again," he said.

I loved the sensation that I was the one making these notes ring out, even though it wasn't music, this wasn't music yet. "I want to be as good as you," I said.

"You will never be as good as me."

"I want you to teach me every night. After we make love, I want us to come downstairs, and sit here, and you can teach me the piano until morning."

"I do not want to teach you the piano," he said. "The piano is mine. This belongs to me."

"I am only joking," I said. "Don't sulk." I did the scales again, faster this time. I thought that would please him. "Forgive me," he murmured.

"Sit in my lap," I said.

"That is not the way to learn the piano." He sat in my lap. His coat tails felt rough and starchy against the skin of my thighs. I decided not to mind. "I can't reach the keyboard," he said.

"I'll lower the stool." I hoped he would soon stop complaining. He spread his fingers across the keyboard, just as he had taught me. And very gently, very lightly, I placed my fingers on top of his.

"Now," I said, "When you play, I can make believe it is me."

"What," he asked slowly, "Would you like us to play?"

"One of your favourites."

He thought about this, then gave a little nod. He started to play. It was slow, but sometimes his hand would escape mine, I had to chase them. I didn't recognise the tune. His left hand tapped out a gentle pulse, it offset the melody he played with the right. It sounded wistful, somehow. A little sad. Soft.

He finished. He took his hands away from the piano. My own, now orphaned, flailed a little, they didn't know what to do. He didn't say anything. Nor, for a while, did I.

"That was beautiful," I said.

I think he smiled.

"You should put that in your repertoire."

"I do not believe," he said, "the hotel would approve."

"I love you," I said.

Again, silence—I think I felt his body tense.

"I want you to marry me," I said.

I had no idea that I was going to say such a thing—I honestly had never even considered it before. And as soon as the words were out of my mouth I knew that they were stupid, and then, I thought, why stupid? Why?

"I want to be your wife," I went on. "I love you, I want you for ever. I will tell Mother, she'll be back from her travels soon. She won't be pleased, but she'll come round. She married beneath her, and Nerys married beneath her. When you're as high up as we are, you have to go beneath, where else can you go?"

"Please," he said.

"And if Mother *doesn't* come round. Why, then. Why, it doesn't matter. I don't want to be rich. You think it's easy being rich? I can be poor, like you. We can be poor together. You can play the piano, and I can cook for you, maybe, and Nanny will help me."

"Please," he said. "No. Please."

"I love you."

He told me he didn't understand. This was not what he'd been promised. If he didn't come to me we'd said we would tell my family and he'd be dismissed from service. He didn't want to be dismissed, he didn't want to go back to his village, I could have no idea. Now I was saying that I *would* tell my family anyway, but this was what he had been threatened with. And he was crying. I could feel his little body shaking with tears as he sat there on my lap, I hugged him and hushed him and told him it would be all right. I said I *knew* all that. I knew we'd had to threaten him a bit. But it was different now. Because I loved him, and once I told Mother, he would be free.

"No," he said.

And I knew. I think maybe I had always known. Nanny had not lied to me, she had said there was no woman in his life.

I said, "What is his name?"

"Leave him be."

"What is his name?"

"Nils."

"Nils? What sort of name is that?"

"I do not know."

"Where does he work?"

"He is in the kitchens. Please."

"I want to meet him."

"Now?"

Not *now*, I hadn't meant now, I didn't know when, I was hurting, I didn't know anything. "Yes, now. Of course, now. Go and wake him. Bring him here. No. Bring him to my suite. Bring him straight there."

"Please," he said. I think, for the last time.

"Go."

He scrabbled off my lap, he almost fell over in his hurry. He ran from the room.

I just sat there for a little while on the stool. At last I closed the piano lid. I went back to my room. Paul was not there yet. I went to wake Nanny. Nanny was not pleased to be woken up, she told me she needed her sleep, she wasn't as young as I was. I told her to shut up. I told her I knew about Nils. Nanny said, "I didn't want you to get hurt, my poor little darling girl."

There was a knock at the door. Paul hadn't needed to knock for weeks. Nanny opened up. Paul and Nils came in. I had half-expected Nils to be another dwarf, but he was as normal as anyone else.

"Paul," I said. "I love you. Don't be frightened. I love you."

Paul was starting to cry again. Even Nils looked a little embarrassed.

"You can have your toy," I said. "I'll let you have your toy. But I want you to show me. Play with your toy for me."

Paul and Nils looked at each other.

"You heard her," said Nanny. "Strip."

They did so. They stood there, both shivering, though it wasn't cold. I told them to get onto the bed. They did. I told them to pretend they were alone. To pretend I wasn't watching. I did watch. I watched everything.

I said, "We'll get married, Paul. We'll go away. And you can take Nils with you, I don't mind. And I'll take Nanny. We'll all go away together." And that was the new plan, and we all agreed it was a good one.

The afternoons were mine, and mine alone. The night times for Paul to do whatever he wished. All that I asked was that I was present to observe. That he did it in my room. That he thanked me at the end, that they *both* thank me—though I didn't care about Nils, to me his gratitude was neither here nor there. One night Paul came alone, and I said, "Where's the toy?"

"He's tired," said Paul. "He's unwell. But you and I could be together."

"That's no good at all," I said, and I sent Nanny out to fetch him.

It was simpler that they stayed in my suite, and at last that's how it was arranged—the bed was big enough for all three of us, and after they'd made love, Paul and Nils were usually very tired, and I could sleep beside Paul, I didn't want to sleep beside Nils, I didn't want to touch Nils, Paul had to sleep in the middle.

"Do you love me?" I'd ask Paul.

"Yes," he'd reply.

I still went to his piano recitals, every single one of them, sitting in the front row. Really, for the whole day, Paul Lindblad was very rarely out of my sight. We used to joke about that.

I am not unaware as I tell you all this that I come badly out of this narrative—I seem selfish, of course, and capricious, and maybe a little insensitive. I do not want you to think I am not truly sorry for any mistake that I have made, and I ask you to understand that these were the follies of youth. I was so young back then, and given to such an exaggerated idea of romance, who could blame me? What I will say is this—that I made Paul happy. I know I made Paul happy. And I believe too, that my actions in that hotel in C___ that summer saved his life. That is very clear to me. Whatever guilt I feel, that is some consolation.

Nanny's job was to bring us all breakfast on a tray—a pot of coffee, and brioches, and smoked salmon. But one morning she came in and slapped at Paul and Nils, and shooed them away. "Your mother has returned, darling, and she wants to see you immediately. Get dressed, hurry now!"

I went to her suite, and sitting behind a desk was Uncle John. "Where's Mother?" I asked.

"Your Mother has a headache," he said. "So I said I'd handle this." He suggested that I sit down. "Now," he went on, offering me some coffee, offering me a cigarette, "Is there anything you want to tell me about?"

"No," I said.

"You don't have any grand statements or demands?"

"I don't think so."

He raised an eyebrow at that, which was his way of showing me he was amused. Uncle John never smiled, the eyebrows was the best you could hope for. "We have already spoken to Aleksandra," he said. "We understand you have had a little adventure."

It took me a moment to work out who Aleksandra was. "Yes," I said. "A very little one."

"Now, don't be cross with Aleksandra. She was under strict instructions to keep an eye on you. She answers to your mother, not to you." I said I wasn't cross with Nanny, and I wasn't. "It's perfectly alright you have had an adventure. But it's time for it to end now. Your mother wants a change of scenery altogether, she says she doesn't want mountains, she wants the sea. We'll leave for the coast tomorrow."

"Yes," I said. "I'm ready to go." And I was. It was a funny thing—it seemed like a weight had been lifted from my shoulders. I had thought something really very serious indeed had been going on, but that was just the game, wasn't it? Everything was safe now. I could be a little girl again. I was ready to be a little girl, adulthood had been exhausting.

Uncle John said, "The usual outcome of one of these adventures is I have to sack someone. This Lindblad fellow, the dwarf. Now, I'm perfectly willing to dismiss him right away..."

"No, don't!" I said. I was annoyed at how desperate I sounded. "No, don't get rid of him. None of this was his fault."

"Of course not. Well then. All right."

"But," I said. "You can get rid of Nils."

Uncle John just looked at me. "Very well," he said.

He poured himself another cup of coffee, and I had the strongest sensation that I was dismissed.

I went back to my suite. Inside, Nanny was already packing. "All right?" she asked me. Was there a slight challenge in that? I think there was. I said I was perfectly all right, and smiled, and she smiled too, and squeezed my hand before she returned to filling the suitcases.

I didn't go down to see Paul Lindblad perform that afternoon—and nor did he come up to see me afterwards, and that was perfectly fine.

That night I had dinner with Mother and Uncle John. Mother had the sea bass, and I had the sea bass, and Uncle John had his steak. Mother was excited about our journey to the coast the next morning; we would travel by train, and be there by nightfall. "I can almost hear the sea already!" she said. "And smell the salt in the air. The sea is so much more enervating! Scientists say we came from the sea, didn't we? That's our background, and I can well believe it, I always feel better when I'm there, I feel home. And the men are more handsome." Mother told me I was looking very pretty, and she even winked at me—it was odd to see her in such a rare good mood.

I heard the piano play in the lounge. "Excuse me," I said, and got up and left.

My chair in the front row was empty, of course—I don't know whether the hotel guests had all colluded in my affair with Paul somehow, but they all seemed to realise that only I could sit in it. I didn't want it. I didn't want to get too close. I wanted to apologise to Paul, to make some sort of explanation—I *did* love him, as I'd promised, but all those plans we had made for a future were just pipe dreams, weren't they? I hoped he would understand that. I'm sure he understood—God knows, the lower classes are more practical than I am. I still wanted to say goodbye. I wanted him to know it meant something. And at the same time, I just wanted to keep well away. I stood at the back, where I was sure he could not see me.

His Chopin done, he turned from the piano into the applause. Taking the crowd in, and yet rejecting it at the same time—looking at us all, and seeing none of us.

Back to the piano, and he seemed to hesitate. Then he spread his long fingers across the keyboard.

Softly, so softly, his left hand tapped out that mournful pulse, the right hand the gentle melody on top. His favourite, private tune—and I knew that he had seen me after all, somehow, though I was being so very discreet.

Only for a few seconds. He seemed to change his mind. He stopped.

There was silence for a while. The audience began to mutter. He ignored them. He stared down at the piano as if it were something he barely recognised. And then he got to his feet.

His right hand still on the keys, his left reached for the piano lid. And he slammed the lid down, hard.

He lifted the lid again, and the audience didn't know how to respond—all that blood, his hand now a mangled mess, it must be a magic act, surely, a joke? Because people don't do such things. Because blood was something they paid good money to avoid.

Paul Lindblad slammed the piano lid down upon the fingers of his right hand three more times before the screams started, and got another slam in before hotel staff pulled him away, and now he was howling too, in pain of course, and I think in despair.

They hanged Nanny in the end, of course. She didn't even get to wear a hood, the old-fashioned way, she was strung up from a lamp post. They said I had to watch. They assigned a woman to take me to the execution, she had such a sour face. Nanny looked so old.

She didn't look frightened. She looked angry. I didn't see her drop. At the last moment the sour-faced woman took pity on me, she shielded my face from it. That was kind of her. You learn to treasure acts of kindness.

They hanged Nanny because she was a collaborator. They hated us aristocrats, but they hated the collaborators more, the ones they felt had betrayed the working people. They didn't want to kill the aristocrats, they prefer to humiliate us. Though they shot Uncle John in the face, but they said that was an accident, they hadn't meant to do that. Me, they sent to a labour camp. Mother, they sent to a labour camp.

Nerys got away scot free, of course, living in America with her stockbroker. God bless America. I doubt I will ever see Nerys again. I don't think I much care. I'm not sure we have much in common any longer. I'm not sure what I would say to her.

My little adventure with Paul Lindblad, that was just two years before the Purge. It all started when we were in C___ again, it was in that very hotel that we were arrested. We hadn't been there since, and I admit I was uncomfortable being back there. I knew Paul would be gone, he'd been dismissed the moment he'd destroyed his hand—but, still. I didn't ever stay after dinner long enough to see the replacement, even the sight of that white piano standing untouched in the lounge made me feel sick. All told, I almost welcomed the arrival of the revolutionary guard. It seemed to break the tension.

I believe that I saved Paul Lindblad's life. Had he still been employed at the hotel, they'd have hanged him like they did Nanny. He was a collaborator. He was a pianist of degenerate music. He was a sexual deviant. They would have hanged him three times over. My actions now may seem to you cruel and manipulative and destructive, I may have cost him his job and cost him his music. But unknowingly I engineered his salvation.

You ask me now how I could have lived in those times, and been so unaware of the revolution that was coming. It seems to you now so inevitable. You think it's another sign of my decadence, that I could be surprised when the whole world turned upside down. I do not know. Maybe you're right. I was blind. I was a girl who loved to be in love.

It has been nearly twenty years since the revolution. I have spent longer working in the linen factory than I ever spent living as an aristo.

So when does this become my revolution? When does this become my country?

And that music Paul played for me that night on the piano—it is everywhere now, like an anthem. There are lyrics to it. He was right, the hotel would not have approved. But still, every little while, I think of that song as our song. And I hear it, and I think of us, and I am happy.

I think I saw Paul Lindblad once more. I think, though I cannot be certain. Walking down the pavement in a flannel coat, and it was raining, and he was brisk, this was a man with somewhere to go! He was a little taller than I remembered, but what of that? And his right hand had been replaced by a stump. He looked happy. He looked full of purpose. He looked like a man who had found *his* country, at least, and had found *his* revolution. I called out to him, but I'm glad now he didn't hear me. I think it was Paul. I think so. And I knew too, finally, what it was like to fall in love at first sight after all.

And the old woman says:

- *For a closer look at the brave new world the revolution has created, turn to* **Sympathy for the Shorn** *(story 3, page 43).*
- *There is some doubt about Paul Lindblad's Turkish background. There is no ambiguity at all about the credentials of the Turks who affected the fall of the Byzantine Empire. To read of them, turn to* **The Constantinople Archives** *(story 21, page 345).*
- *Our heroine in this tale is learning how to smoke in a ladylike fashion. Turn to* **That Tiny Flutter of the Heart I Used to Call Love** *(story 22, page 355) to find a man who is cursed with the same unmanly style.*
- *To read another tale of piano playing under duress, turn to* **Page Turner** *(story 73, page 1269).*
- *Throughout this story there is some confusion from our narrator whether she has ever been in love or not. If you think she has, then turn to* **101 Heartbeats** *(story 101, page 1695).*

75
TASTE ME

I

THE THING TO REMEMBER is this—there was a time when Edith Tipper had been slim. Or, not slim, not slim exactly, but average—you know, perfectly average; she hadn't always been defined by her weight, there had been a time when, had you been asked to identify her in a bar, you wouldn't have said, Edith, yes, she's the *lardass* in the corner, she's that *porker* over there. There was a time, and not that long ago, not so long ago it can't be remembered. That's the thing to remember—Edith Tipper had not always, even in her own mind's eye, pictured herself as a heaving fat sow.

Not now, of course. No, now she was fat, absolutely and definitively. Her first husband had said, this was Glyn, Glyn had said—I don't want my wife to work. I want her to stay at home, and sit on her arse, and eat all the food. And there had been so much food to eat, because Glyn worked hard, didn't he, and he could afford lots of food, couldn't he, and it seemed almost criminal to waste it. I'm the breadwinner, he'd said, and had it just been bread that might have been all right, but there was cake and biscuits and crinkle cut potato chips, one was never enough, once you popped you just couldn't stop. Glyn had been her first husband—he didn't stay long—one day he had come home from work, looking so sad, and he'd said, "I'm leaving you, Edie. I'm sorry. It's not you. It's me. I've found a younger woman, and I'm running off with her. I don't know why, I'm just shallow that way, I guess." And Edith had said, "Is it because I'm overweight?"—and he'd replied, "Well, yes, it is a bit."

If Glyn didn't want her then that was fine, there were plenty more fish in the sea—and pretty soon Alan had swum along. And Alan didn't seem put off by the fact she had eaten really an awful lot of doughnuts since Glyn had divorced her. And they married, and had a child, and they've been together now for what, nearly twenty years? Nineteen years, give or take. Alan isn't very interesting, and he isn't especially attractive, and their sex life isn't very good, but you can't have everything. And yet the memory of what Glyn had done to her is always there, eating away inside her brain, and sometimes she'll say to Alan, "But don't you mind that I'm so big?" Sometimes—usually in bed, usually after he's made another excuse not to come anywhere near her. And he'll tell her, "No. No. I don't mind you look like an engorged balloon. I don't mind your puffed-out face, your tree-trunk thighs, the lakes of sweat that gather and pool beneath your sagging tits. It makes no difference to me that you get out of breath when you walk, and when you walk you fart, and when you fart it smells like warm fat. You know what, I love it. And I love you." And that is very nice to hear—but still, still she isn't wholly reassured.

She doesn't like the way she wheezes in the dark as she lies in bed. She doesn't like the way it's counting the wheezes that makes her drowsy, as if she were counting sheep. No one should grow too dependent on bronchial obstruction to get a good night's rest.

And if she can't sleep, then she might get out of bed and go downstairs. Gently, very gently, because she wouldn't want to disturb Alan as he sleeps beside her, though he has jammed plugs hard into his ears against her snores, and he's grown not to notice the way the mattress buckles whenever she shifts her bulk. Downstairs she goes—

to the photo album on the shelf in the sitting room, and she looks at her wedding pictures. Not the wedding to Alan—she was already so fat then, no—no, the one to Glyn, all those years ago. And how she looked in that white wedding dress, and with such pride her face shone—and she supposes the pride wasn't so much she was getting married but that she could fit into a dress like that in the first place. The dress *flowed*, and she *flowed*, and she had hips, she had poise! She had been slim. Or, not slim, but average—she had been blissfully average. When she can't sleep, Edith stares at her younger self, and takes such care not to touch her image in the picture in case she pops the bubble of her long-lost beauty, in case she crushes herself beneath her clumsy fat fingers and makes her a greasy smear. She stares at the Edith she was and weeps a little.

There was a time when Edith Tipper hadn't been fat. It's hard to imagine now, but believe it—and remember.

ii

Yvonne has come to visit. Yvonne, that's her daughter, and she doesn't visit often, to what does Edith owe this pleasure? Yvonne sits at the kitchen table, and Edith has poured some chocolate shortbread biscuits on to a plate in front of her, the best chocolate shortbread biscuits too, you have to look after your guests. Yvonne's fingers dance over the biscuits, then she pounces, she plucks one off the plate and rams it into her mouth. Yvonne's fingers are already a bit chunky, and she's still so young, Edith thinks she should keep an eye on that. Yvonne begins to talk, about her job, about her flat, about her boyfriend—the truth is, thinks Edith, she doesn't like her daughter very much; the truth is, she's a little bit *frightened* of her.

Yvonne says, "I've got something important to tell you," and Edith winces, because that's never a good thing to hear—like the time she got caught smoking at school, or was suspended for bullying, or failed all her exams, or got herself preggers and wanted Mummy and Daddy to get rid of the baby growing inside. "I've got something important to tell you," she'd say, and look so innocent, and her problems would be made to vanish. "This is a *good* something," says Yvonne, "don't look so worried! I'm getting married! To Steve, yes, because we were round at Dan and Sharon's, and he just got down on one knee and gave me a ring, and I thought he was drunk at first! Aren't you happy for me?

Tell me you're happy!" Edith tells her daughter she is happy; she urges her to have another chocolate shortbread biscuit. Yvonne's fat fingers flutter over the plate, then pull away. "No," she says. "No, I want to make myself slim for the big day, I'm going on a diet! I'm going to look amazing, you'll see! Maybe you should do the same?"

After Yvonne has left, Edith goes upstairs to the bathroom and looks in the mirror. She tries not to look in the mirror too hard or too often—when she brushes her teeth she does it so shyly, with her head tilted sideways on so she won't see. Now she stares at herself, properly stares. Her face stares right back at her, with big scared eyes, it looks as if it wants to run away. She gives herself an encouraging smile, it makes her look almost pretty. "I can lose weight," she says. "I can lose weight in time for the wedding. I can do it. Really, this is an opportunity. Really, this is the best thing that could happen to me." She smiles even wider, and that overdoes the effect a bit, now her face distorts into a maze of grooves and trenches. "Starting right now," she says. "Yes."

She goes back to the kitchen, and tips the uneaten chocolate shortbread biscuits into the bin.

Half an hour later her heart is beating too fast and she feels so hot and she's so short of breath, and she's on the phone to Yvonne. "Darling, I was wondering if you'd mind if I don't *come* to the wedding?... I just think I might be busy... I just think, just thought... No, don't shout... I'll be there, please, please don't be angry. I'll be there, I promise!"

iii

Alan is as supportive as ever. "I don't care if you get thin," he says, with an easy smile, "or stay as fat and grotesque as a brick shit-house. I'll still love you!"

In the supermarket Edith discovers to her delight there is so much food she can buy that is both delicious and healthy. Salt crackers, and carrot sticks, and as much fruit as she can handle. (Except for bananas—it turns out bananas are *very* fattening, a word to the wise!) She loads everything into her shopping trolley, as much as she can wheel to the checkout. The girl at the till is impressed by just how much she's buying: "Wow," she says, "someone must be hungry!" Edith laughs, and explains that she is on a diet, and she's going to lose so much weight. "Well, don't eat it all at once," jokes the girl with a kindly wink, "or you'll end up even fatter than you are now, porky!"

She forces herself on to the bathroom scales, and that's a real effort of will, she hasn't dared even guess how much she weighs in years. The number displayed is terrifyingly huge, of course, but it's all right, she tells herself, that's the heaviest she's ever going to be. Really, it's good to be so heavy, it'll mean her weight loss will be all the greater an achievement. She knows that the kilos will just start peeling off, at the very moment she's tottering upon the scales she's gnawing on a carrot stick like she's Bugs Bunny.

Edith gets out the calculator and does some sums and works out that so long as she loses a kilo every other day she'll reach her target weight in time for the wedding.

The next day she weighs herself again, and the numbers haven't budged.

She goes to the gym. She thinks about becoming a member. She likes the look of the gym, all the treadmills and barbells and fitness bicycles look like overgrown toys for children. Cimbing on to one of the bikes alone leaves her winded, she can't muster the strength to turn the pedals. "Do you like cake?" asks an instructor with tight skin and big biceps, and Edith admits that she does. "When we're finished with you, you'll never look at a slice of cake ever again!" Edith waddles out of the gym in as much haste as her bulk can manage.

And still the weight won't shift. The numbers remain stubbornly huge and depressing. She makes an appointment to see the doctor. The doctor is slim, she's what you might call *pert*, Edith doubts the doctor has ever had cause to diet her entire life. The doctor says, "You are morbidly obese. Do you know what that means?" Edith says that she thinks she does. She'd like to be made slim, please—or, if not slim, at least average. And if average isn't possible, she'll settle for obese without the morbidly part: how much does the doctor think she can lose before the wedding? The doctor all but shouts at her. "You don't even want to get better! You just want a quick fix! There is no quick fix!"

Edith returns to the supermarket. There's nothing she can buy. It's all too fattening. The salt crackers have far too many calories, even the carrots have too many calories. All the fruit has been rubbing up against the side of the bananas, it might have been infected. She's got a big shopping trolley and she wants to put *something* inside it, but there's nothing she's allowed to eat, and she mustn't stay in the supermarket a moment longer, because even the smell of the hot sausage rolls wafting across from the delicatessen counter is bombarding her with tiny molecules that will swell up inside her nostrils and make her huge. She flings aside the trolley, she runs.

In the department store now, looking through all the dresses. Figure hugging and how they'll *flow* on her, show her hips, her poise. She can't get a white dress, she mustn't compete with the bride, but this one's nice, what is it, a sort of cream, that's only white-ish. A sort of silky cream, the cream is sweet and thick, she grabs hold of the dress and wraps it round her body and hugs on to it tightly—as if she's trying to make it stick, as if trying to suck it in. "Madam, Madam . . ." "Leave me alone!" "Madam, we don't have it in your size. Let's see what is in your size." "Leave me alone! This dress is mine, do you understand? It's for me!" Sitting on the floor, with everyone around, and she hasn't even got the breath to get to her feet.

iv

She finds the quick fix quite by accident in the newspaper the next morning. Edith is sitting at the kitchen table, and has had her breakfast—a single cup of coffee, without any sugar in it, or milk, or very much coffee—and she's trying to ignore the angry growling in her stomach by looking through the headlines. Idly glancing at pictures of people from all around the world who may well be suffering terribly but who, come what may, are resolutely less fat than she is.

She can see it's a quick fix immediately; it's the very words that grab her attention, 'QUICK FIX!' On an otherwise entirely blank sheet of newspaper, right in the very middle, in a tiny box, is an advertisement. 'QUICK FIX!' it says, in small writing. And then, in even smaller writing, 'CHANGE YOUR BODY THE EASY WAY. EAT WHAT YOU WANT, WHEN YOU WANT'. And then, in writing so small it hurts her eyes to squint at it, 'NO REFUNDS'.

That's all. Edith turns the page over, but on the other side there's some usual guff about war and famine and horoscopes. She turns the page back, stares hard at the ad. 'QUICK FIX!' it says again, and even the type seems quick, so hot off the presses the ink looks wet. But now there's different text underneath. It's tiny. She needs to read it with a magnifying glass.

It says: 'No Fee! No Fee Required! Or, Rather, There is a Fee. If You Think There Should Be. Do You Think There Should? What Do You Want With Money, What's Money Worth Over Health And Happiness? Send What Money You Like To Box 1865. Send All You Can Spare! Send More Than You Can Spare! Send It All, Now, Offer Only Good For Today. Now! Now! Now!!!'

And then: 'Only one transaction necessary'.

It's really a very bad advertisement indeed, and Edith isn't taken in by it for a second. She only goes back to look at it again a couple of hours later because there's nothing good to watch on the television—and only once more a couple of hours after that because she's bored.

She's no fool. She puts ten pounds in an envelope, no more than that, addresses it to Box 1865, stamps it, and takes it down to the post office. And when she gets home she feels bad that it was only ten pounds—no, she's no fool, but she's not mean either; she puts a hundred pounds in a second envelope, addresses that to Box 1865 as well, stamps it, and returns to the post office. After all, what's money over health and happiness? She read that somewhere once, and it's very true.

Edith is surprised that the very next morning there's a package waiting for her on the doormat. She knows it's from the Quick Fix people at once, her address has been printed in such very small writing, and when she touches it the ink smears under her thumb. She has no idea what the quick fix might be. A self-help book? Some fitness gizmo? Appetite suppressant pills?

Inside the envelope is a little bottle, and tied around the neck of the bottle is a paper label with the words 'DRINK ME' beautifully printed on it in large letters.

Edith checks the envelope for any other instructions, but there are none. Drink me before or after food? Drink me but do not operate heavy machinery? Drink me only as part of a calorie controlled diet? Nothing.

"I'll just take a sip," says Edith. "I don't how long I have to make it last." And she pulls off the stopper, and puts the bottle to her lips, and the taste is very nice. It tastes of cherry tart and custard and turkey and hot buttered toast. "Can't be good for the diet," says Edith. Nevertheless, it's so nice that before she knows it she has finished the whole thing.

"You don't get much for a hundred pounds," she says out loud, and she begins to think she's something of a fool after all, and that there are a whole gang of people packing up bottles at Box 1865 and that even now they are laughing at the gullibility of Edith Tipper. But the aftertaste is very pleasant, and it's given her a warm cosy feeling in her stomach, so she decides to forgive them.

V

And it works! She can hardly believe her eyes! The next morning she climbs upon the bathroom scales prepared to accept the daily crush of disappointment—but no, no, the needle flickers! The needle itself seems confused, it's got so used to damning the fat woman with proof of her morbid obesity—who is standing on the scales, it seems to say, is this someone *new*? Someone *slimmer*? The needle tries to give her bad news, it does its level best to drag itself on to the larger number, but it can't quite get the grip—it gives in, it shows Edith that she's lost an entire kilo overnight!

Edith phones Alan at work to tell him, and he is, of course, delighted for her. She phones Yvonne to tell her not to postpone the wedding, just in case she had secretly been planning to do so. It's going to be all right. It's all going to be all right! And she treats herself to a *full* cup of coffee today, she drowns it with the creamiest of milks and the whitest of sugar.

She wonders whether she ought to order any more of that wonderful medicine.

She tries to find yesterday's newspaper, but it has gone. She feels a burst of panic that quite takes her breath away—she empties all the dustbins, searches the kitchen from top to toe, then searches all the other rooms she knows for certain the newspaper was never even taken into. She looks for the newspaper for hours, and at last she gives up, lying panting on the floor with the realisation that she is still very overweight and has such a long way to go.

'Only one transaction necessary,' the ad had promised. She hopes that's true.

The next morning she hasn't lost an *entire* kilo, but she's well on the way. The morning after that, as if to make up for it, she's lost another kilo and a half.

She wishes now she could find the newspaper—not to order new medicine, but to write a thank you, and apologise for her scepticism, and offer some more money. She knows she has bought her salvation very cheaply, and she feels bad about that; although she is a very large woman, you could never say of Edith Tipper that she is greedy.

vi

The dreams start that night.

And it's not the actual events in the dreams that shock her—at least, not at first. It's the detail. She can smell the flowers, feel the heat of the summer day upon her skin. She can feel the tightness of the frock that is just a little too small for her.

She's sitting on the grass, next to her sister. And that is a surprise, because she doesn't have a sister. But in spite of this, a sister is, clearly and indisputably, there.

Her sister is a pretty little girl, with blonde hair down her back and smooth skin and perfect bow lips. She wears a blue dress, and through her hair there's a black band tied to a bow.

Edith is also wearing the same blue dress. She puts a hand to her head, and feels a band there too. She wonders whether she looks quite as pretty as her sister. She assumes not. She assumes that she's also a little girl—and younger, probably.

She wants to look at her sister, but doesn't dare—she can sense the hostility from her. She wonders what her sister's name is. She wonders whether there's a way of asking without sounding strange.

She won't look at her sister, and so needs something else to look at. Fortunately there's an open book in her lap. She stares down at it. She can't make head nor sense of it, the words are so very long and blur into one another. And there are no pictures, and there are no conversations. What's the point of a book without pictures or conversations in it? There's not even a man nearby, who does she think she's trying to impress?

She has to look at her sister, it's like scratching an itch. Her sister stares back, coolly, implacably. I wonder why, thinks Edith, my sister hates me so? What did I ever do?

And then she starts, because her sister opens her mouth to reply, and Edith hadn't realised her thoughts were so loud.

"Because," the sister begins, and this is the moment she could be wise, she has a wise face; she could say because they're *sisters*, and sisters are meant to hate each other sometimes when they're young, but one day they'll realise there's such a bond that unites them deeper than love because nobody on Earth will ever understand them the way they do—not the daughters they will produce, not the husbands they'll marry. But the sister, sadly, doesn't say any of that. Instead—"Because you are so *fat*."

Edith nods at the fairness of this. Then she frowns. But I'm not fat. I'm not slim, but I'm average.

The sister laughs unkindly. "Not fat yet, but one day soon you'll be a tub of fucking lard."

Edith is quite surprised to hear her sister swear—especially since she looks so nice in her blue frock and her black band with a bow.

And she's sure she could give a clever riposte, if only she had the time, or the intelligence, or the wit—if only she wasn't such a silly young child—but suddenly her sister is up on her feet. What is it? And now she's running, fast, across the field and into the woods.

Edith doesn't know what she should do about that, and so she shrugs, and turns back to her boring book. And the words in the book say, "Follow Her, You Fool!" And just the thought of running makes Fat Edith sweat, but she remembers this is a dream and she hasn't destroyed her body yet—and she springs to her feet and makes chase as if she is as light as air.

It seems she runs for hours, but she has never run for hours her whole life, but she is young now and the world is before her and it's a world unspoiled by age or by compromise, so who knows, who knows? She chases her sister this way and that through the trees, and she runs so fast that the breeze whips past her face, and she whoops with joy, and at times her sister whoops for joy too. And she realises her sister is chasing something of her own. It's a rabbit. It's a white rabbit. A rabbit in a waistcoat that keeps anxiously checking a fobwatch, and from some angles the rabbit looks just like a rabbit, and that's the way you expect a rabbit to look—and from other angles it seems to be the size of a man.

And at last, and so abruptly, the chase comes to an end—the rabbit dives into a hole in the grass, plop! The sister turns back to Edith, and her face is wild and glowing, and the black band in her hair is askew, and she's grinning—and in that moment Edith loves her, for all the cruelty she's shown, for all she doesn't know her name, she's her sister and always will be.

The sister says, "Follow me if you dare." Then she turns her back on Edith, finally, deliberately. She jumps down the hole after the rabbit.

Edith stumbles her way towards the hole. And now at last she can admit she's tired—and look, her thighs are swelling, and look, her belly is popping out. She's on her knees, the fat girl drags herself to the rim. She peers over the edge. The hole is dark, and so deep. Edith can't see there's a bottom to it.

"Hello?" she calls. "Hello, are you all right?" Her voice echoes weirdly; there is no reply.

What should she do? (What *can* she do?) Because she's not an adult yet, and it's not *fair* that any of this should be her responsibility. Her head starts to thrum. Can she fetch help? Can she fetch her parents? (Does she have parents? If so, where do they live? If so, do they love her?) "Hello?" she calls again, but quieter this time, because the sound of her own voice is making her head hurt so bad, her head is *thumping* now, she grips it between her hands and screws her eyes tight shut, the pain is all too much and she thinks her head is going to split right open…

And when her eyes open it's dark. It's dark—and she's lying down—and the ground beneath her is soft, and that's because it's a bed—she's in bed and everything is all right. Except it isn't all right, because the pain is still there, she's brought her headache with her from the dream world and it makes her want to *scream.* And for a moment she believes that's what she'll do, she wants to be like the little girl she was only moments before and scream out loud for help, scream the entire house down—but Alan is next to her, she mustn't wake Alan, it would be unfair. So, as carefully as she can, she gets out of the bed—and the movement causes a fresh bolt of pain, it's like another steel bolt driven through her forehead, and she stumbles, she falls, she falls hard against the wardrobe. And it doesn't wake Alan. Nothing wakes Alan. His earplugs are in good and tight and the bastard will not be stirred.

Staggers into the bathroom. Fumbles for the light. Painkillers in the cabinet, she thinks, find them. Stares into the bathroom mirror. Through the looking glass she sees the truth.

The first thing is—she's not losing weight from her belly, or her thighs, or her arms, or her hips, or her face. She's just as fat as she ever was. She's just as ugly and just as embarrassing.

The second thing—it's the head that is shrinking. Only her head is getting smaller.

It hurts so much when her eyes are wide open, but she can't help but stare. The cheeks are just as puffy as before, the jowls still hang loose—but the skull itself is taut and squat. On top of her broad shoulders it looks deflated; it isn't the head of a grown adult (a grown adult who has grown too much, and that's a fact)—it's the size of a little girl's.

And maybe she's imagining it, because there are specks dancing in front of her eyes, and she feels sick, and she begins to sway, she thinks she might pass out—maybe it's just imaginary, but the head seems to be bulging. Ever so slightly. Something rippling under the surface of the forehead. The skull is getting smaller, but the brain inside is the same size as before. She can feel it now. The brain pushing for every last scrap of space as it's crammed beyond endurance; the skull crushing it tight and holding it fast and squashing it down. There's no room for her brain any longer. She thinks suddenly of battery hens, hemmed in on all sides and waiting to die—the brain is trapped inside her head, and it's frightened, and it's shrieking.

So she's kneading the sides of her head with her fingers. Uselessly trying to stretch it just a little wider.

She begins to cry. There's no room for the water to be inside her head anyway—the eyes are distorted and spit out hard little globules of teardrops like bullets. And now she's pounding the side of her head, hard, harder, with her fists.

That's how she pops her head open.

She's so surprised that for a moment she stops crying, she stops even feeling the pain.

The scalp has swung upwards, just above the forehead, as if the catch fastening it shut has given way.

Very timidly, Edith reaches out for the lid of her head, and raises it. The hair falls over the entrance—she pulls it apart like a bead curtain so she can see inside.

She can't see much of the brain, and perhaps that's a good thing. But some of it does bulge out in relief at the extra space. The head still aches, but it seems to recognise at once that some of the pressure has been released, and the pain dulls down a little in gratitude.

She strokes at the bit of now exposed brain. It's softer than she expected. When she presses in her fingers it yields easily, and she can see the indentations left behind. It seems to respond to the stroking—it likes it—she can feel it tickling, and it's strange, because it feels so distant, it feels as if she's being caressed by someone else a very long way away.

She plays with the brain for five minutes or more. Her fingers find the brain comfy and warm. The brain finds the fingers soothing and cool.

"All right," she coos softly, as if to calm a wounded animal. "It's going to be all right." The headache has faded, it's just the memory of it that still aches. It's time to go back to bed, time to shut up the head once again. She takes hold of the top of the scalp. She thinks it's like the swing-top bin in the kitchen, and if she presses it down it'll find its catch with a click.

She's going to have to tuck the extraneous bits of brain back inside the skull just so she can get it shut.

She tries to do so very gently—with one hand she pats the brain down into place, then she lowers the scalp back over it with the other. The brain gives a little yelp of betrayed surprise. Then the pain is immediate, it's as if she's stabbed at her head with a fork, it almost blinds her. She releases the scalp, lets it swing wide open—the pain stops.

She stares at the brain, pooling out of the skull once more. She doesn't know what to do.

The exposed brain breaks off surprisingly easily. She thinks the operation might hurt, but it comes away in her hands as if she's shedding dead skin. Now it's free from the head altogether, and it runs thick and sticky between her fingers.

She thinks she's removed enough. She lowers the scalp back into position, and there's plenty of room for what's left of the brain, she can feel it settle into position perfectly cosily.

She looks back at the brain bit in her hand, oozing there like jam. She thinks she should wipe it away with tissue paper, flush it down the toilet. But that seems almost rude, somehow. And who knows what memories might be imprinted upon it? How can she be sure she won't need it later?

It's had no ill effect, it seems, this impromptu piece of lobotomy. She checks that she still knows her name, where she lives, the lyrics to the national anthem and the name of the Prime Minister. She tilts her head from side to side, raises one knee then the other. Her movement is fine.

She read somewhere once that we only use about ten per cent of our brain anyway. And what's making her fingers sticky isn't even as much as that, it's probably no more than two per cent, or four. Did she read that, was it in a book? Or did she hear it on television? Oh, she can't remember.

Edith reaches right beneath the sink and smears the brain parts on the underside by the drainpipe. Like a kid sticking chewing gum under a bus seat—and it hangs there quite readily. At least this way she knows where it is, and it's not as if Alan will ever find it, he never cleans the bathroom.

vii

She says to Alan, "Do you think I look different?" And he says, "Totally! You look totally different, well done!"

And she says, "Where do I look different?"

And he says, "Just different, all over really. You're doing so well, well done."

And she says, "I need you to look at me really hard. Tell me where. Where, how do I look different?"

And he says, "I don't want to look hard. Edie, I just don't want to. Edie, what's the point? There's no point."

She goes out to the shops and no one gawps at her or stares, or at least no more than they normally would at a fat woman daring to be seen in public; no one points at her now curiously diminished head. And if she touches it with her hands it feels normal to her too—yet it *is* smaller, it *is*, when she gets home she goes up to the bathroom and inspects herself in the mirror, and it makes her gasp. It's shrunken further than last night, surely? She thinks it has. She fetches a tape measure.

The headache is back by the afternoon. She tries to ignore it for a while, and pretends it isn't the same headache. It's good that Alan isn't home, when she can stand the pain no longer she screams loud and shrill without shame. Back to the bathroom, and her eyes look wild and bloodshot. She reaches for the catch that will release the pressure in her head, and she can't find it, where was it, was it above the hairline, she can't remember? And she prods everywhere looking for it, hard, all over the skull, she jabs her nails into her ears, her eye, and she's so desperate that when at last her twitching fingers throw the catch and her head pops open wide she can't but help laugh out loud with the relief.

The pieces of brain matter that are released look red and angry, and Edith thinks hard about what she should do, and she sees the effort of it fizz across the surface as electrical charge.

Do understand—she doesn't just rip out bits of her brain. She doesn't tear out gobbets of it and stick the pieces under the sink. It's not so crass, that would be disgusting. She is gentle—so gentle. She rubs her fingers over the brain with tender care, and it is smooth like pâté, and lifts off easily, she digs her nails through the tissue of the cerebral cortex and scoops it out in soft chunks. And when she does stick it under the sink, she does so respectfully.

And at last she asks—is that enough? She thinks that may be enough. That must be about a quarter of the brain gone, maybe even a little more. That should give the surviving lump plenty of room to swim about inside her shrunken cranium—and still have space to spare if it shrinks a little further.

The pain has gone, and she feels fine. She sees the colour green as grey now, but what of that? And she can't remember when her birthday is, but she's sure Alan will tell her when it's relevant, it might even make it a nice surprise.

In the kitchen her crackers and her carrot sticks have no taste at all—but did they ever have, really?

That night she's woken up by her headache at one o'clock, and at half past five, and a little after dawn. Each time she pulls out just a little bit more of her brain, she doesn't want to get carried away, she worries she's removed too much already. Just enough to give her some respite from the pain, enough so she can get a few more hours' sleep until the pain starts over. Green has turned grey, yellow has turned grey too. She thinks she can smell burning tyres everywhere, but it's not unpleasant, merely distracting—burning tyres, flowers, and fish. She smears all her fresh excavations on to the growing mound of brain now hardening by the drainpipe.

And onwards through the day. It gets to the point where she thinks it would just save time to leave her scalp ajar—but in truth she likes the sound it makes when she pops the head open. She keeps on popping it, even when the headache has gone and there's really no need to rummage inside her skull for a while. Pop, pop, it's fun—up and down the scalp rises and falls, pop, pop.

She decides that if she's bent upon this course of self-lobotimisation, she should go to the library and learn the facts about it. It would be as well only to take out the bits of her brain she doesn't really *need*: for example, the part that would help her speak French can go, she's never going to France. But she has some vague understanding that the brain does lots more useful things (didn't she read that, or was it on the television?)—it wouldn't do to cut out the bit of gunk that keeps her heart beating. She gets on the bus, but then has to turn back when she realises she's still in her nightie. She reaches the library, and asks the man on the desk for help, and she's not so very good at finding the words to express her needs, she has to keep pointing at her head to get the message across. At last he fetches her a huge tome on neuroscience. She turns over the pages, and really puts every focus of her concentration into understanding what's written there. The book tells her that the brain doesn't remotely work the way she thinks it does, and it isn't like a buffet where you can choose the bits you want and leave the rest, and by now she should be dead, or worse. And she doesn't think the book should tell her such awful things, and she has *rights*, she shouldn't be spoken to like that, she's pretty sure she has *rights* (was that on the television, or did she read that once?). She puts the book down. She puts the book right away from her. She *throws* the book, actually. She doesn't want to read any more of the book. Just in case it starts to tell her she should be dead all over again, and it convinces her, and she will be.

(She turns over the pages, and there are no pictures or conversation, and what's the point of a book without pictures or conversation?)

Green has turned grey, and yellow has turned grey, every single bloody colour has turned grey—except grey, for some reason. Grey now seems to her a peculiarly oily shade of black.

She gets on to the bathroom scales and the needle is haphazard, it can't decide *what* to make of her! The fat still piling round her body, but the head so small and neat. She likes her head, it's perfectly round and hard like a sucked gobstopper.

She keeps measuring the head to see how fast it's shrinking, but it's silly because she always forgets the previous results.

Pop, pop goes the head—pop, pop—she does it on the bus, but everyone ignores her. Pop, pop, once you pop, you just can't stop.

"Do I look different?" she says to Alan. "Do I? Do I look different? Tell me how. Tell me how I look different. Tell me if I look different, you bastard. You shit. Do I? Do I look different? Do I? Do I?" Sometimes she punches him, raining her fists down upon his arms, his chest, anything, sometimes she needs to hurt him, but he doesn't even seem to notice, he's an unobservant sod. One day she removes the part of the brain that remembers how to stop drooling, so now there's always a trickle of it running out the side of her mouth and down her chin. It's around this time that Alan decides to sleep in the spare room.

The wodge of brain under the sink is getting so big now, was it ever supposed to be this big, however could it have fitted inside her head to begin with? It hangs heavy and distended, and two long icicles of cerebral matter inch their way towards the carpet.

And she's lost so many memories, she's sure she must have—though once you've lost them, does it matter? Because how would you ever know? Hey, answer me that! Once they're gone, it was as if they were never there! So, no matter! No matter.

There's just one memory left that is hard and fixed, and nothing can eat away at it. On the contrary—it seems to emerge from the growing fog in her mind with ever greater clarity, and the more the memories surrounding it get detached and lost the more it stands out. Just this one memory—and Edith knows it must be a very significant one, and she hopes it'll be an *entertaining* one, and she looks forward to losing more of her other cognitive powers so it'll be pulled into even sharper focus. She thinks it may be the only thing in her head of any consequence, the most important thing in the entire world.

Alan says to her, "I think you're different."

She says nothing.

He says, "Do you think you're different? Don't you think you've changed?"

She says nothing. She's concentrating upon making some perfect bubble of spit come out the side of her mouth, and it's not an easy thing to do, and she doesn't need this distraction.

He says, "Edie?"

Still, she says nothing. She's lost the bubble. Bugger. Pop, and once it pops you can't stop. It takes some effort to remember who this man speaking to her is. That's the nice thing about having your head shrink—you can let go of all the useless things.

He says, "Edie, I'm leaving you. I'm sorry. It's not you, it's me. No, that's not true. It's you. It's definitely you."

His voice has an angry drone to it, and she wonders whether that's a perceptual change caused by removing some of the auditory capabilities of her brain, or whether it's because her husband is a prick. A prick! She likes that! Once you prick, you just can't stick!

After her second husband walks out on her, Edith decides to give up on the diet altogether, and eats her way through an entire cream cake. She can feel the calories pile on, and her fat is fair rippling with the acceptance of it. The cake tastes good. Cake tastes good. It's not a complex thing. How else is cake supposed to taste?

viii

She's relieved that the diet is over. That she's let go of the woman she was trying to be. She'd pictured herself walking into Yvonne's wedding, quite resplendent in her new cream dress, and how everyone would have gawped, all eyes would have been upon her—and for *good* reasons for once, do you understand? And some men would have said they couldn't believe she was Yvonne's mother, she must be her sister surely (or her daughter!—is that going too far? Perhaps a little too far) —some men would have said, let's ditch this stupid wedding, let's you and I get married instead. And how proud she'd have felt of her brand new identity, this completely different Edith—and from this point on everything New Edith would do would be *exactly* right, no more mistakes, no more compromises, no more binges of comfort eating cheese in the middle of the night.

But now—she could still be a brand new Edith, still she could reinvent herself. Who she was, and how she behaved, she wouldn't ever again need to care what anyone thought of her. Fat, who cared if she were fat—oh, she'd give them something to stare at, she'd go out in her dressing gown every day, and a dressing gown stained from last night's feeding frenzy—she would go out *naked* if she wanted, her breasts sagging down and farting every step she walked, she'd be shameless, she'd be without fear. Because she'd torn shame and fear from out of her skull where it had poisoned her life, and now it was dripping down the underside of the bathroom sink. With her baby-sized head bouncing on top of her burly shoulders, oh she'd give them nightmares, she'd make them all *scream*. This would be who Edith Tipper was from now on, with dead air between her ears—stupid, maybe, but defiantly stupid, fat as fuck without even the sense to notice.

So many years thinking she could transform her life just by making her body the shape men wanted—and all she'd ever had to was remove her brain.

ix

She doesn't remember the name of her daughter, or her parents, or her childhood pet, or whether she had a childhood pet. She doesn't remember how to boil an egg. Tying her shoelaces is now a mystery to her, and she's long ago given up trying to plumb its depths—she walks around with her laces loose underfoot and she has to take care they don't trip her up. And when she gets her headaches she doesn't remember it's because her head is shrinking, and she'll go into the bathroom to extract a portion of her brain as if it's the first time, and she'll see her reflection in the mirror and she'll scream.

This may all disturb her—but for most of the time she doesn't remember to be disturbed, and that in itself is a blessing.

But there's that one memory that's constant—and it bobs around in her mind like a giant iceberg whilst everything else around it melts away. And she's not even sure it's *her* memory, because she seems to be wearing clothes from the olden days, it's like something in a book—but she's remembered it so many times now, it's like a memory of a memory, and that still counts as hers, doesn't it? That's still worth something?

She doesn't have to be asleep any more, the memory will burst upon her quite suddenly and it's more startlingly vivid than any mere dream; the grass is greener, the summer's day warms every inch of her body—and she has to sit down, wherever she is, right at that moment, so she isn't totally overwhelmed in the rush of it. Sit down, catch her breath, and *remember.* The green grass, the summer heat, there's a book in her lap, and her sister beside her with her blonde hair and her blue dress and her neat little headband.

Why can't she love me like a sister should? (And what is her *name*?)

"Because," says the sister, "you're so fat."

Why should that matter? What difference does it make to anyone else what her own body looks like?

"You make it bad for the rest of us," the sister says. "Look at me. No, *look* at me. Study me hard. I'm beautiful. I'm slim. I'm perfectly contoured. And a whole life of possibility stretches out before me. I can be an actress. I can be a model. I can be a lawyer, or a company executive, or a personal assistant to a rich banker and fly around the world on private jets and have slim, contoured personal assistants of my very own. I can be a *wife.* I can be some man's *dream.* But you. You, fatty. You hold yourself back, and you hold the rest of us back too, and that's why we despise you, while your sisters are out there trying to make something of ourselves, to get noticed in this man's world. You, with your jowls and your thighs, what sort of role model are you? Whoever will aspire to be *you*? Your children will dislike you and your husbands will divorce you and any love you are ever given will be so fleeting, the stuff and nonsense of Wonderland."

And Edith does look at her sister, and she does study her hard, and she knows this is exactly how it's always going to be—the pretty girls will be the ones who get on the television screens, on the cover of fashion magazines, setting the tone for what women will have to be. Telling all the average women and all the ugly women and all the *fat* women the doctors will label morbidly obese. That they're worthless, holding them down and keeping them in check.

That's when Edith hits her. And she doesn't mean to use her nails, but the single blow draws blood, it sprays over the sister's perfect cream-smooth skin, and that looks so *good.*

Edith flinches against a return blow. There isn't one.

"You can do what you want," says Alice. "But my scars will heal by morning. And you'll still wake up a droopy-titted cunt."

All in all, this is the least opportune moment for the white rabbit to appear. But that's exactly what the white rabbit does, wearing its stupid waistcoat and checking its stupid fobwatch and, like Alan, looking like a prick. And Alice is up on her feet and is chasing the rabbit towards the forest—and Edith at last knows who her sister was, and what happened to her, and how it was all her fault—and she's on her feet too, she's fast in pursuit.

Too slow. The rabbit has made it to its hole, and jumped through.

Alice prepares to do the same. Edith cries, "No! No!" And she doesn't know whether she means, "Don't jump!" or "Don't leave me behind!" Alice turns, and looks at her sister one last time—and she's right, there's no trace of blood on her cheeks, her face is perfect once again. Alice doesn't say a word. For a moment Edith thinks it's going to be all right. And then Alice contorts her beautiful face into a sneer, and she slowly raises her hand, and in the most unladylike way imaginable gives her little sister the finger.

Then she too jumps, and she is gone forever.

"Help!" shouts Edith. "Help!" Who's she asking help from, the missing grown-ups in this story, any other white rabbits that might be around? She stares down into the pitch black of the rabbit hole. She even reaches down inside, and quickly pulls them out because there's a strange warmth that is not altogether pleasing—"Are you all right?" she calls into the darkness, and she's going to add her sister's name at the end of that but she's forgotten it once again—"I'm going to get help!"—but she can no longer even picture what her sister looked like. There was a headband, what colour? There was hair, how long? She was pretty, but lots of girls are pretty, aren't they? Lots of girls are so very very pretty.

Edith gets to her feet, straightens herself down, and doesn't call out any more.

It doesn't take her long to bury the hole. She gathers loose soil, big clumps of it, and tips it into the void. She knows she can't fill the hole, but she can make sure that nothing that ever falls down will ever come back. She finds bracken and sticks, she heaves a log over the opening. It's soon as if there was never a hole there at all.

She goes home. She doesn't know what to tell her parents. Father is mutton-chopped and Mother wears petticoats, Edith hadn't realised quite how Victorian they both looked. She keeps on expecting them to ask, "But where is your sister? Weren't you playing with your sister?" She sits through dinner in silence, hoping she won't be asked to explain herself. And she's in luck, it's an age when children are seen and nor heard. "Eat up!" her parents say. "Eat up till you're nice and round! You are our only child now, so we'll overcompensate!"

That night she retires to the bedroom she has all her life shared with her sister, and there is only the one bed in it, and there only ever has been. Mother comes in to ensure Edith says her prayers and is in no way surprised by the sleeping arrangements.

Edith kneels by her bed. "God bless Mother and Father," she says. She wants to say a prayer for her sister too, but she's not sure Mother would approve. She gets into bed and Mother blows out the candle; in the darkness she resolves she alone will never forget her sister even if the rest of the world does—but she is so very drowsy, and her thoughts get so very muddled! "How many sisters do I have? Do cats eat bats? Do bats eat cats?" And she has lost whatever it was she was trying to hold on to, but it doesn't matter, she is asleep now, and if it were important she's quite sure she'll remember in the morning.

This is the memory she has left herself; she remembers that she didn't remember. And the guilt of it is almost too much to bear, until another headache helps to blot it out, and she goes up to the bathroom to open up her head and edit out more of the fear and the shame.

x

And that night Edith can't sleep, so she gets out of bed and goes downstairs. Gently, very gently—even though she has no sister to sleep in her room, and no husband either—but it's good to be gentle, isn't it? Downstairs to the photo album on the shelf in the sitting room, and she looks at the wedding pictures. She runs her fingers over all the faces, trying to work out who they are, as if by touch alone they might reveal themselves. She pauses at the woman in the wedding dress—this very average looking woman, with her wonderfully average sized head; she runs her fingers over her face too, she stabs down at the face, she tries to stamp it out. She doesn't know her at all. She doesn't know her. And when she tears the photograph into small pieces, when she tears up all the photographs in the album and flings the pieces high into the air so they rain down upon her, she doesn't know why it is she's crying either.

xi

Sometimes Alan will phone, and he'll say he's worried about her, and maybe he should move back home and look after her? And Edith thinks that sounds very nice. But some of these times she won't remember who Alan is, and others she'll remember Alan but won't remember the ability to frame words with her mouth, and still others she'll remember Alan and she'll remember how to speak but she'll also remember his betrayal, and she'll tell him that the whole point of love is that you stand by someone during the bad times, that he should fuck right off. It's such a pity! With all the remembering and all the forgetting, it's so hard to get them into sync!

Sometimes Yvonne will phone, and she always sounds so angry.

One morning the headache is so blinding Edith doesn't think she will make it to the bathroom before passing out. She manages to stagger inside; she pops her head open; she stares through the looking glass. And, "No," she says, out loud. "No. No more. No more. Enough." Because the brain she has got left is such a miserably small chunk of meat, it's barely bigger than a chicken nugget—and she won't rip out another atom of it, she's lost too much as it is.

And instead she reaches round the sink and pulls out a handful of brain from the mass that's been collecting there; she sticks it into her open skull, presses it down. Even though there's no room for it, but she doesn't care, she'll squeeze as much as she can inside somehow. The pain is excruciating, but she's had lots of pain before, there's nothing left for pain to frighten her with. She doesn't stop, though the agony is now so intense and concentrated she wonders if her entire head is about to explode—and with every new bit of brain she recovers enough sense to see that the cranial matter she's wedging so higgledy-piggledy into her skull has grown mould, there are hard white specks mottled across the surface, and bits of it are a dull green.

She thinks at first the ringing sound is also inside her skull, but it happens again, and again, and she realises it's the doorbell. With one hand she balances the brain on top of her head, and as far as she is able she prevents the softer parts from dripping down her face; with the other hand, she grips on to the banister rail and feels her way down the stairs.

By the time she opens the front door there is no one there—but there is a small parcel left upon the mat. She picks it up, as best she can.

She recognises the handwriting instantly, though it seems like such a long time since she first saw it. The print is so very tiny.

She rips the package open. Inside, there is a small ebony box; inside *that*, a very small cake, by which lies a card with the words 'EAT ME' beautifully inscribed in large letters.

Edith likes cake. She had forgotten she likes cake so much. In her excitement she forgets to hold her brain intact, and some of it splashes on to the carpet.

EAT ME, it says. But should she? Wasn't she supposed to be on a diet, once?

EAT ME. Well, it does seem very insistent about it.

She doesn't know whether the cake is bitter, or sweet, or sour, or salty, she's lost the complicated distinctions of taste buds ages ago. But it must be said, it feels so good to be biting into a nice piece of cake again!

Edith wonders now whether her head will grow back. And she wonders whether it will grow back quite all the way, or whether it'll still end up a bit on the small side. She won't complain if it's just a little bit too small. And she wonders whether it'll tickle as it grows.

She sits down upon the floor to wait. She's very patient.

There's not much to do whilst she waits. She stares at the walls. She stares at the ceiling. She stares at the rabbit hole that is growing in the carpet. She stares at the ceiling. She stares at the walls.

The white rabbit says, "I'm late! I'm late!" There he is, in his waistcoat and holding a watch, and really, he *still* looks such a prick.

"Have you ever wanted to visit Wonderland?" the white rabbit asks her. Edith says she hasn't given much thought to it, really, but she supposes that would be all right.

"No," says the white rabbit. "No, you have to really *want* it. You have to really *believe*. Try again. Do you want to go to Wonderland?"

Okay.

"Do you want to see Wonderland, right now?"

Yes, all right. Yes!

"Well," says the rabbit. "The pity of that is, you'll never see Wonderland. You'll never fit down the hole, Fatso."

And with that the white rabbit kicks her over the edge! Head first! And Edith thinks, the white rabbit is wrong, I'm plenty slim enough to fit down the rabbit hole! All that dieting must have really paid off. And it gets darker and darker, and the air gets thinner and thinner, and there's a strange warmth that is not altogether pleasing. And still she falls—she thinks, I wonder whether anyone on the surface will remember me! Remember the *real* me, as I once was, I mean! I *do* hope they remember me, at least a little bit! Down, down—and it's so dark now that it's hurting her eyes, and the little air that's left cuts into her throat. And then, suddenly!—stop. Have I reached the bottom at last? thinks Edith, and she tries to wriggle, and she realises she's jammed fast. She's stuck! The white rabbit was right after all, she's just a fat loser.

She tries to flex her arms—first one, then the other. There's no give at all. She's tight as a cork in a bottle. As a raspberry in a jar of raspberry jam. As a, as a, as a brick in the wall of a brick shithouse. And she can feel now clumps of soil raining down on her from high above —small at first, but getting bigger. The rabbit is filling the hole in! He's going to bury her alive! "I'm still down here," calls Edith, as politely as possible. "Don't forget, it's still me inside!" But she doesn't think she can be heard amongst the crush of the dirt, of the bracken, of the sticks. And as she opens her mouth further to protest, some of the soil crumbles its way in. More and more, in it pours. I *do* hope it isn't too fattening, Edith thinks, I am trying to lose a little weight!—and then all is dark, and all is quiet, and maybe that's a blessing of sorts, and maybe it really truly isn't.

xii

The car is booked for noon. It is a special car. "So we should be ready for half past eleven," says Alan, "and we should get you up at nine o'clock. Because it's a big day!" But at nine o'clock Edith doesn't want to get up. She's been having such a wonderful dream where she was warm, and safe, and free.

Alan takes Edith into the bathroom, and strips her naked. He helps her to sit in the tub. Then he turns the shower on her. "Not too warm? Not too cold?" No, it is neither too warm nor too cold. Good old Alan. Now she's wet all over he lathers soap on her. It takes a while, because there's so much of her, and some of it gets hidden beneath the folds of fat. It takes even longer to get her dry. Alan was right to get her up at nine o'clock.

By half past eleven she's in her lovely new dress. By five minutes past noon the special car still hasn't arrived. "Where is it?" fumes Alan. "I don't fucking need this, not today." But the special car arrives at ten past noon, and Alan is immediately all smiles once more. "No, you're not too late!" he says to the driver. "Plenty of time!" The driver helps Alan get Edith and her wheelchair into the back.

And now they're in a church, and Edith hasn't been inside a church for a long time, and it certainly wasn't this church. So she has many questions: what? why? how? where? And Alan has to keep whispering to her, asking her to be quiet. "It's all right," he says. "I promise you, it's all right. This is happy! It's a happy thing!" He squeezes her hand, and doesn't let it go for ages. I'm still down here, she thinks. Don't forget, it's still me inside.

After the service Yvonne wants photographs outside the church; she wants pictures of her with her dad, and one with Mum too. "Cheese!" says the photographer. He says, "cheese," a lot, he has to take lots of the same photograph over and over, perhaps he isn't very good at his job. And cheese is bad, cheese is fattening. "Thanks for everything, Dad," says Yvonne, "thanks for *all* of this," and she flaps her hand about to take everything in, and everything seems to include her mum. Yvonne looks nice in her white dress, has she lost weight? "My pleasure," says Alan. "My absolute pleasure." Edith's dress is nice too—it is not the cream dress, it's a sort of turquoise, which is nearly the same thing.

And then they're somewhere else, somewhere new. So many people. So much food. Edith doesn't think she should be allowed near the food, but she can't think why. "It's a special day, it's special, eat up!" It *is* special, isn't it? And why it's special? Well, she's pretty sure it's something to do with her. She rocks backwards and forwards in her wheelchair in appreciation. Alan makes some sort of speech, and everyone listens, and some people laugh, and Edith isn't entirely sure what he's talking about but she knows it's all about her and how much he loves her and how he'll always stand by her.

"A toast!" someone calls. So everyone raises their glasses, and Alan has to help her, and she holds the glass up high. And the glass is so clear, it's like a looking glass. She can see her true reflection, she thinks—and yes, she's fat, and yes, she's drooling, and yes, her head is now the size of a withered melon. But she's beautiful. She's really beautiful. And when she dissolves into floods of tears, only she knows it's because she's so happy.

And the old woman says:

- *Aren't all weddings a disappointment? Especially if they're not your own. As you're relegated to spectator to someone else's happiness, someone else's demonstration of love. Turn to* **The Disappointing Story in the Book** *(story 6, page 85).*
- *Of all the great powers of the human brain, the most extraordinary must surely be the way we understand language—that all the different grunts and noises made by six billion people can be identified and interpreted. Consider what would happen if that understanding was altered, in* **Mond** *(story 54, page 911).*
- *Fish is a good dietary food. Full of proteins, and high in Omega-3. If you need to lose weight, go on a fishing trip with the boys in* **Shelter from the Storm** *(story 58, page 985).*
- *Popcorn, though, is no good at all. Especially the bad tasteless sort you'll find only at* **The Circus of the Incuriously Drab** *(story 68, page 1187). Only visit if you can afford the calories.*
- *Read how another woman escapes from the children's fantasies that bind her and makes them her own. Turn to* **Scheherazade's Last Story** *(story 100, page 1687).*

HAVEN'T YOU BEEN HERE BEFORE?

76
Slow Handclap for the Moronic Horde

I REMEMBER THE VERY first time I was taken to the theatre. My father didn't want me to go. He looked unhappy about it. It was my mother's idea—she said, "Dickie, you have to take him to the theatre sooner or later," and my father stared down at me critically, the way he would analyse everything, not blinking, not moving his head, giving me a once-over assessment. And I stood up straight and tried to look well-behaved, and adult, and whatever else he might want me to be. He then nodded curtly, and said that my perspective as a seven-year-old might come in useful. And I had to put on my best clothes, the ones I only ever wore when Grandma came round; he put on, as always, his work clothes—that brown tie, those brown trousers, that tweed jacket he liked.

There was a certain allure to the theatre even then. This was where my father went to work, and it seemed to me that therefore this would be a place rather like him, quiet, a bit forbidding, and very mysterious. And I knew that it involved people dressing up in funny clothes and saying things that weren't true, but that they hardly ever got told off for it. If anyone ever told them off, it was my father; at this stage he was the third most senior drama critic on *The Sunday Times*—which wasn't terribly senior, really, and meant he rarely got to review any of the top West End shows but instead the lesser things on the fringe or in the provinces. Still, he took it all very seriously, and once in a while, when one of his critiques was published, he would present the newspaper to me and my mother at the breakfast table. "Look at that," he'd say, and we'd see his name at the top of the article, RICHARD HARDY, and in a thick font, and that was exciting—my father was famous, he was almost as famous as the actors he was criticising!—and then he'd proceed to explain why this particular evening at the theatre had been joyless or disappointing or starved of all cultural merit. Showing us his reviews were the only times that I ever saw him properly smile. He told me he loved theatre. "Theatre is the life-blood of any healthy society," he said. "That's why it has to show the very highest of aspirations. That's why I have to complain when it's found wanting." And he ruffled my hair as he said this, a rare sign of affection, as if I'd been admitted to a secret important truth, as if now, like him, I was one of an elite.

There was no hair ruffling that first day we went to the theatre together. I'd never seen before how tense my father would get before a performance started, as he settled down grimly in the auditorium with his notebook and pen at the ready, as if the pressure was on *him*, as if he would be the one required to declaim a speech or break into song. There were children all around us, calling out to each other, spilling out of their seats, and my father said he hoped they wouldn't make too much noise during the play itself. They were all drinking lemonade and eating Maltesers, and I asked my father if I could have lemonade and Maltesers too, and he said no. "Now, hush," he said to me, as the house lights went down.

It's impossible for me now to appreciate how good, bad, or indifferent that production of *Aladdin and His Magic Lamp* really was. Probably it was all a bit passé—in retrospect I certainly don't recall anything original being done with the source material, and I suspect the costumes and set design were gaudy and cheap. But it seemed fresh to me, so *new*, that there were all these strangers on a stage and I was allowed to stare at them and keep right on staring and that it wasn't rude—and that they were talking to each other, but they were also sort of talking to *me*. The plot was easy to follow, and the songs simple enough so that all the kids could join in when required. At one point Wishy-Washy threw some sweets into the audience, and I got some Maltesers after all.

And throughout my father would tut, and shake his head, and scribble things down in his notebook.

Afterwards, my father asked me if I had enjoyed myself, and I said I had. And he did that assessment thing on me—he stared down at me unblinking and unmoving. "Why?" he said. And I suppose the main reason was that I was with him, I was with my father for once, we were doing something together—but I couldn't tell him that, that wasn't what he wanted to hear. I told him I'd thought the show was funny. And what it really was, I think, was that there was such a sense of community in that auditorium—that when the panto was working, there were two thousand eyes all trained in the exact same direction, and we all held our breath as one, and laughed as one. And at the end we all applauded as one, Aladdin and all his friends came out to take a curtain call, and everyone in the audience clapped—even my father clapped—and I didn't really know what clapping was, but it seemed like the right thing to do, it was fun to be a part of that barrage of noise offering thanks and approval for the evening's entertainment. And the curtains came down and the lights came up and we all filed out of the theatre as strangers once more—but for a couple of hours in the dark it was as if we'd all been family, all been one, sharing the same thing.

My father's review took my reaction into account. He damned the direction and the acting and the script and the stagecraft. But he also wrote, "It may be engaging enough for children without discernment." And he pointed out the review to me, and it was the first time I'd been mentioned in a newspaper, even tangentially, and I felt so proud.

And that's the reason I became a playwright, I think. That first taste of the theatre had given me the desire to tap into that community I'd felt, I too wanted to make an audience bond together like that. And I suppose, too, I wanted to create a piece of theatre that my father would like. Something that would make him write a good review. Something that'd make him ruffle my hair again, and smile.

The greatest casualty of the zombie apocalypse was the arts. It's typical that in times of national crisis arts funding is always the first to be slashed, and that's because we live in a philistinic society which sees culture as essentially bourgeois, and irrelevant to the needs of the ordinary man. It quite makes me fume. The government pumped all their money into the emergency services, of course, into the police and the hospitals—and I don't pretend there wasn't a need for them, but let's be honest, from this vantage point, where we can see quite clearly that there was no cure to be found for the plague that turned the population into undead monsters, and that there was no law enforcement strong enough to resist the ravening hordes, all that money seems to have been rather wasted, doesn't it? We might as well have had a few million siphoned off towards the galleries that proposed an exhibition of new sculptures and multimedia tableaux inspired by the outbreak, or towards some questing agit prop theatre productions that would have inspired thought and debate.

What my father said was true. Theatre is the lifeblood of a healthy society. And by closing the theatres we denied that blood a chance to flow. It happened with Oliver Cromwell, it happened with World War II. It's happening now, and I tell you, the consequences will be devastating. Let's face it, what we're seeing on the streets of London is one of the greatest social upheavals since the Industrial Revolution or the Poll Tax riots. It's my job as a playwright to document it, and the tools with which I can do so have been taken from me.

I'm not arguing this for my own sake. Revolutions in theatre occur every twenty years or so, and I think that's essential—believe me, if the zombies were espousing some new artistic movement of their own that would render mine outmoded and quaint, I would welcome it with open arms. Any true artist will be prepared to tear down to the foundations the tired structures of the now, so he can build something in its place more urgent and inspiring. But all I see going on is a lot of tearing down. The zombies don't seem interested in expressing themselves, just in killing people and eating their brains. And here in my garret at night I hear them out on the street keening at each other, and I try to detect in it the signs of music—but I think instead it's probably just wails of hunger.

I knew that the zombies would come for me eventually. I was holed up in Chiswick, and it seemed so far I'd been lucky—I'd look out of the window and see that neighbouring houses and shops were being gutted, but that they were leaving my block of flats alone. One night I heard screams from the floors below, and I knew then that the end would only be a matter of time. They took the family from across the hall, and the woman in the flat above went two nights later. And when at last they battered down my door I was almost relieved. I'd been living off baked beans for weeks, and my supply was running out. And I had put in a strong box under the bed all twenty-six of my plays (seven produced, nineteen pending), in the hope that future generations might discover them and commit them to posterity. I was ready.

There were three of them; a man, and a woman, and something too rotted for me quite to tell. And they looked so hungry, and I couldn't help it, I felt a wave of such pity for them, it seemed to me that all the brains in the world wouldn't be enough to feed those poor souls. I hoped the woman would be the one to get me, she looked the best of the bunch, and I moved closer towards her to give her first dibs. But she didn't step forward; neither of her partners did. Instead they flapped their arms at me, gesturing at the door. I couldn't work out what they wanted at first. "Should I follow you?" I asked, loud and clear, as if to infants, as if to the OAPs in the dress circle seats on Thursday matinees, and they nodded; and they looked so *unhappy* about it, as if the only thing they really wanted was to tear chunks out of me, and the woman in particular gazed at me so longingly, and her mouth drooled. Anyway, they kept on flapping their arms like that for a while, it was quite clear they weren't going to leave without me. "Hang on," I said, "I'll get my coat."

There was a sea of zombies on the streets below, and when I reached ground level I was quite sure they would attack me—now, en masse, I could hear their keening as a constant thing, their teeth were chattering with the need for food, and their lips smacked thick and wet. But as I walked they fanned away from me, and I began to feel like a prophet, like the waves were parting for Moses—or a bit like a pariah, actually, it was like when all the actors avoided me at the party after that particularly poor press night.

They took me to their leader. There was nothing special about the leader, nothing about him that suggested charisma or statesmanship. He dared to come quite close to me, and I could see that it was a real effort, he so obviously wanted to give in to his primal instincts and chow down.

"You write us play," he said.

I had no idea that zombies could talk. It came out slow, as if language was something he had to remember, as if all that was very far away.

Bearing this in mind, it seemed cruel that I said, "I beg your pardon?" and forced him through the effort of saying it again. A look of very human irritation passed over his face as he did so.

"Of course," I said. Because you should never say no to a commission. "What sort of play? I have lots of plays."

"Celebrate. Victory."

Well, I could see why the zombies might want that. They'd done so well, and now they wanted to kick back and relax and enjoy themselves with a show. I asked about cast size, and box office forecasts, and how long an interval he wanted, and he just sort of glared at me as if these were matters of great irrelevance.

"Friday," he said.

"You want me to deliver a draft this week?" Because that wasn't my method at all. I liked to workshop scenes with the cast first, see if anything helpful came out of improv.

"Performance. Friday," he said. And that was that. I should have realised. Zombies are all about hunger, the need for immediate satisfaction. Why would it be different whether they wanted fresh brains or a three act light comedy?

I was allowed to choose the venue. I had always wanted a play at the National Theatre. They had rejected my manuscripts too many times. I said I'd need paper, and I was promised it. I said I'd need more food. I was given all the baked-bean tins I could carry.

"You'll get your play," I said. "But what do I get in return?"

He didn't say I'd get my life. I was glad of that, because I knew it wouldn't be true. He didn't insult me with a lie. He said, "Your father."

I went home right away, and set to work.

I am an experienced dramatist. Indeed, I am probably the most experienced dramatist working in Britain today. And so I can tell you that one of the greatest traps you can fall into when writing a new script is to anticipate your audience too much. Who are these people, 'the audience'? You don't know them. You don't know their particular concerns, their likes or dislikes. They arrive at the theatre to see your play from a thousand different lives, they're as disparate a group as can be. And your job as writer is to find some unifying factor amongst them and play upon that—rather, your job is to celebrate their diversity and channel it for your own ends. They should come to the show a random ragbag, and leave bonded by the clarity of your vision, your single vision, your vision as author and artist.

But in the case of zombies. Well. It's different. They all seem to have one specific thing on their minds from the outset. And I think it's perfectly possible to second guess that and write for them directly.

And that's where I first went wrong. I looked at my zombie producers, and decided that they wouldn't understand the innovations of modern drama technique, they wouldn't appreciate what I had learned from new wave productions in Eastern Europe, or the little moues I liked to make towards the nouveau avant garde. I looked at my zombies, and I patronised them. I admit that now.

I decided upon a plot. I decided upon a love story. Everyone loved love stories. Everyone could get that.

Two star-crossed lovers. One boy, one girl (no need to challenge sexual orthodoxy). Brought up on different sides of the tracks. He's a zombie, she's a living human being. Both families disapprove. Oh, it's *Romeo and Juliet*. It's *West Side Story*. It's intimate, but also epic. It's perfect.

It took me hours to come up with names for them. Any writer worth their salt will tell you that you can't rush into these things, names are important. At last I fixed on Sally and Steve. Sally and Steve sounded good. And then I decided I'd written enough for one day—if there weren't any words actually on paper yet, I was sure they would flow tomorrow. And I went to bed.

I couldn't sleep. I made the mistake of thinking of my father.

Because suddenly the audience wouldn't be anonymous at all. There would be one man there I knew I had to impress. Assessing my words in that cool emotionless way, all brown and tweed. What would he think of Steve? Was the name too populist? Would he think its combination with Sally too alliterative, not alliterative enough?

I had realised long ago that my parents must be dead. It wasn't that we hadn't spoken since the zombie apocalypse. The truth was, we hadn't spoken for years—and I realise now that was my fault, it had all been my fault. Every Christmas, every birthday, I had thought of giving them a phone call, to see how they were, to see whether I could maybe apologise and put things back the way they should have been. And when the news of the zombies came out, and it was clear so quickly that there was no hope, no way of beating them back, our civilisation was being swept aside and the reign of mankind was over and a new order of undead had begun—I thought, this is it, this is my last chance—I must make peace with my mother and father, and I must do it now, before it's all too late—because what do old feuds matter, we're family, we're family, there is more that connects us than keeps us apart, and it has always been that way, and I've been too proud and too stupid to admit it—call them now—I must call them now, and we can say our goodbyes. I knew my father would never run from the zombies. He wouldn't hide away, as I had, like a rat. He had too much dignity. And Mother—my mother wouldn't fight a zombie, she wouldn't fight anyone, if a zombie came to the door she'd invite it in and offer it cake. Both of them would be amongst the first to fall, as the zombies advanced they would stand their ground and face their fates with equanimity. As the crisis spread, as reports filtered in that entire swathes of Britain were being wiped out, I knew that every moment I hesitated to find my parents would cost me dear.

And I hesitated. I admit it.

The play I offered my father would have to be worthy of him, and make up for the silence of the last eight or nine years. I needed his forgiveness. No, I needed his pride. I needed this play to be a masterpiece, something bold and true, and I couldn't worry about what any other zombies in the audience might make of it.

Steve and Sally and their little romantic entanglements seemed so trivial to me now.

I got up from bed, and went to the window.

Outside I saw the zombies thronging the streets. Indefatigable in their search for food. Unsleeping, tireless, pushing on as one single body of men, an *army*, a beautiful army—and I thought, that's it, *there's* the unity I've always tried to inspire in my audiences, there's your *community* theatre, and it's there beneath my feet—these are people who aren't held back by ego or neuroses or father issues—these are people better than I am, more determined, focused—these are the victors—how dare I patronise them, how dare I even think of that.

And if they could work all through the night, then so could I.

I sat down and wrote the first act. It was the best writing I had ever done. It poured out of me, my hopes, my love for a better world, my new belief in undead superiority. I took a break then, a single half-hour break, and cooked myself some baked beans. Then I wrote act two. Act two was even better still. Act two was soaring and majestic, it was a triumph. Sally and Steve conquered all in the name of love, and their fathers at last accepted their love, they embraced it. Living and undead came together as one, forever more, accepting and constant.

Exhausted, I collapsed upon my bed. And I could still hear outside the march of the zombies, their feet slouching in an unending rhythm that sent me soon to sleep.

When I woke up, Sir Andrew Lloyd Webber was leering over me. And it still looked like Sir Andrew Lloyd Webber. There was a pallor to the skin, and the eyes were whitened a little, and not quite looking in the same direction maybe. But he looked reasonably fresh for all that. Maybe he'd only recently been turned. Or maybe, even in death, he'd got the cash to keep his corpse nicely manicured. There was an expensive sheen to his rotting flesh, and the bits of skin that were drooping off his face did so with a monied languor.

I'd never liked Sir Andrew Lloyd Webber. His populist approach to theatre went against everything I'd held dear. Not that I'd ever seen a production of his, mind. "It's an honour to meet you," I babbled.

Sir Andrew held up one withered hand to shut me up. "I've come for the script," he said. So I gave it to him.

He began to read it. Slowly at first, but then with ever increasing and disdainful speed. "Where's the music?" he said.

"There isn't any."

"No music! But I have a cast ready. I have an orchestra. I have my dancers. What will they do without music?"

I told him that the story of Steve and Sally wasn't a musical, it was a vibrant and soulful exploration of themes of identity and social…

"Yes, yes," he said. "Like *Phantom of the Opera*. But it has to have music. There has to be a melody to the dialogue. With melody you can find emotion, no matter the banality of the storyline itself."

I refused to accept my story was banal; Sir Andrew raised one dead eyebrow at that, most ironically, and a part of his forehead snapped off.

He made me read my dialogue aloud. It sounded clumsy and awkward. I told him it was the clumsiness and awkwardness of real living people. He told me that no one wanted that; they didn't want *truth*, they wanted something that was better than truth.

He told me that there were precious few real living people out there anyway.

"We must do rewrites," he said.

So we sat down, the two of us. He showed me how to soften the dialogue, how to make sure that Steve and Sally no longer hid what they were feeling but spoke it out good and loud and clear. It wasn't subtle, but, by God, you knew what was going on. Once in a while I made a rhyme, and Lloyd Webber seemed to smile approvingly. I wrote the lyrics, he wrote the music, lots of it—all quite catchy, but none of it exactly memorable. We worked through the day. I was fuelled by my baked beans, he by a packed lunch of raw kidney and lung.

It was long dark when Sir Andrew Lloyd Webber said, "At last." And it was done, and I had written a new script, and it was covered with staves and treble clefs. "We must get this to the theatre at once so rehearsals can begin!"

We went to the National Theatre in his limousine. Even undead, Sir Andrew still employed a chauffeur.

When we entered the rehearsal room, the zombie cast shuffled to some sort of attention. Some were dressed as cats, some as steam trains, a handful of them hippy Biblical characters. They gathered around for a readthrough. Most of the actors couldn't speak at all, and those that could delivered my lines in a slurred monotone. Then Sir Andrew got them all up on their feet, and they improvised a dance, and quite a few of them fell over.

Sir Andrew said, "I know a hit when I see one!" And then said that this was in no way a hit. "It's a disaster! The show opens on Friday, and the singers can't sing, the actors can't act, the dancers can't stand up!" A couple of his cast had collapsed and never got up again; their fellow thespians devoured them.

Privately Sir Andrew said to me, "I've seen a lot worse. You should have been here for the first few weeks of *Cats*!" And he smiled, and offered me his hand. I had never touched a zombie before, and I was afraid that the merest contact would turn me into some diseased brain-munching fiend. But it didn't, and though his skin was leathery, it was warm and surprisingly soft. "It's a pleasure working with you," he said.

And in the morning there were three more zombies standing over my bed.

"We've come for your script," said one, in an Irish brogue. I explained my script was finished, and had been approved, and was now in the swing of rehearsals. "We'll be the judge of that," said another, and his accent was Irish too.

The tallest of the corpses was George Bernard Shaw. Even sixty years dead he was a formidable figure; he had a beard so thick that he was not so much wearing it as it was wearing him—it was matted and mildewed, but it masked how much of Shaw's upper torso was decomposing, so was therefore clearly a good thing. He scoffed at my script. "It's all about the heart, but there's nothing for the *brain.*" He kept breaking off from his stentorian admonishments to nibble at a brain of his own that he had brought along; an outspoken vegetarian in life, he was addicted to brain in all its forms now. "I don't care how your characters *feel* about being dead," he said. "I want to hear them reason it through in intellectual discourse!"

"Poppycock," said Oscar Wilde. Of the three zombies his body was in the worst state; everything he said was delivered with ironic detachment, no doubt accentuated by the fact most of his face had ironically detached, and his mouth was fixed in a mocking grin. "What your script needs is to be lighter, more trivial. 'We should treat all the trivial things of life seriously, and all the serious things of life with serious and studied triviality'."

"What's that even supposed to mean, you dilettante?" snapped Shaw.

"You great big bloody bore," grinned back Wilde.

Shaw bit a chunk out of Wilde's leg. Wilde clawed at Shaw's face with long nails and produced blood and white gunk.

I had to separate them. It was agreed that Shaw would stay in the kitchen and rewrite act one. Wilde, meanwhile, would be sequestered in the bedroom and inject some frivolity into act two. Shaw produced long aching speeches of social conscience. Wilde put in jokes about handbags.

For all this time the third zombie hadn't said a word. I thought maybe he couldn't speak at all, that in death his tongue had atrophied. But when at last he talked, his voice was clear and authoritative. I asked him who he was. He took a long pause, and thought about the question, and said, "Harold Pinter."

"And what does your work stand for, Harold Pinter?"

And he took an even longer pause, and thought about the question harder still, and said, "Mind your own fucking business."

And when Shaw and Wilde had delivered their rewrites, Pinter looked the script over, crossed out anything which looked like an explanation, and stuck a few long pauses in.

I took the new script over to Sir Andrew in rehearsal. "Thanks," he said. He'd got most of the cast on rollerskates now; some of them were doing acrobatics, and some of these acrobats were even able to keep all their limbs intact. "Got to have spectacle," he said to me, "and by God, this is going to be *spectacular.*"

The last time I saw my parents was the opening night of my first play. I lie; it wasn't my first play, it was my eleventh; I mean it was my first play anyone had wanted to produce. I'd been sending scripts out all over the country, to big power houses like the RSC and the National, to the repertory theatres, to the touring companies. This new play was received most enthusiastically by a small troupe I'd never seen but had heard good things about. It'd be put on in a fringe theatre in London, right above a pub, and there wouldn't be any money—the cast were getting travel expenses only, and I was asked if I could contribute something towards that. It was one of the well-respected venues, though; they didn't put on any old rubbish.

By this stage my father had long since lost his job at *The Sunday Times*. He was still writing reviews, but doing them on spec; he'd buy a seat for any play that took his fancy, and write a crit, and send it around on the hope that someone might find his disapproval worth publishing. Nine times out of ten they didn't. I felt sorry for my father, but I was pleased in a way too—I thought this meant we were both in the same boat, I thought this would bring us closer together. It didn't, somehow.

We had an awful dress rehearsal. Some of the actors kept forgetting their lines, and then laughing because they'd forgotten their lines, and this made the other actors laugh too, even if they were the ones who *hadn't* forgotten their lines. The pace was sluggish. The lighting cues were all mistimed, the one sound cue I'd wanted didn't happen at all. We had scant hours before we let the audience in for the first performance, and I felt sick. The director bought me a pint and told me that a bad dress rehearsal always meant a good opening night. I couldn't quite see why that should work. But then the girl from box office found us, and she said there was a sudden rush on ticket sales, it was unbelievable, she'd never seen anything like it! There was a sudden new buzz in the air, and I went to the auditorium, and almost all the seats were filled, it was a miracle! Forty people, there must have been at least forty people in there. And in there, too, I saw my father and mother. My mother wearing her best clothes, frills and bows, as if she were at a wedding, and looking so proud. My father in his theatre critic garb.

I couldn't sit with them. I couldn't sit at all, in fact—adrenalin kept me out of my seat, I spent the entire evening pacing up and down in the wings! And I think it was adrenalin that got us all through. The performances that had been so flabby at the dress now seemed sharp and precise—the actors hit their lines exactly. There was laughter, too, but at all the bits the audience were *supposed* to be laughing at. And the director gave me the thumbs up, and I thought—this is *good*, I'm not pretending this is *great* theatre, but it's *good*, everyone out there is enjoying themselves and no one has walked out or heckled or died. This is the beginning of something, this is what I want to do for the rest of my life. And at the curtain call the audience applauded—and it's hard to get a fringe audience applauding for very long, by God, it's cold and lonely out there, but the cast had to take bows *twice*! "Author! Author!" called the director, and "Author!" came from a few members of the audience too; "Go on, then," said the director, and laughed, and he pushed me out on stage. And the lights felt so warm on my face, and the audience were all in shadow but I could see on the front row that everybody seemed smiling and sincere, and I enjoyed the moment as the clapping built at my arrival, and I took a bow too.

I bought my parents a drink, and thanked them for coming.

"Oh, darling, it was so good," said Mother. "Though I'm not sure I understood all of it."

"Yeah, it's not really meant to be understood. What did you think, Dad?"

And my father stared down at me. Then, slowly, he took his notebook from his tweed jacket pocket, cleared his throat, and began to read.

"The greatest pleasure afforded any theatre critic is to be at the debut of a new writer of talent," he said.

I blushed, I think, and thanked him.

"But not every maiden voyage can be destined for success. And, sadly, Richard Hardy Jr is to theatrical flair what J Bruce Ismay was to the *Titanic*."

I appreciate now what he was saying, of course. And, too, that by refusing to flatter me, by treating me not as his son but as any other professional playwright, my father was paying me the very greatest of compliments. And looking back I know it hadn't been a good play, and it hadn't been a good evening, and no one really had enjoyed themselves after all, and my father had been spot on. But I'm afraid I didn't see it that way at the time. And I'm rather afraid I punched him.

I wish I had had the door to my flat fixed, but I dare say the zombies would only have broken it down again. The next morning I had Richard Brinsley Sheridan turn up, full of advice about how to turn my play into a copy of his eighteenth century smash hit, *The Rivals*. Later in the afternoon a whole gaggle of Restoration comedians arrived—I thought Sir John Vanbrugh was there, and maybe George Etheredge, and I only know because I looked them up afterwards in an encyclopaedia—but they didn't have faces left at all, and they had no conversation either; they put into my script lots of crossdressing, and Steve was left spending most of act one wearing a large floppy hat.

When on the Friday I woke to find yet another corpse in the bedroom with me, I wasn't horrified, just annoyed. "That's enough," I said. "No more rewrites. For God's sake, the play opens this evening!" And I turned on the light.

I didn't think it was even a man at first. This was the remains of an animal, a bottled spider—there was a skull balanced on top of a skeletal frame, but most of the bones supporting it had long since decayed, and so the skull wobbled precariously as the zombie moved towards me—I kept thinking it would soon snap and fall off. The merest sliver of a heart quivered away behind the ribs, like a startled budgie in a cage.

"Are you Shakespeare?" I said. Because, impossibly, for all that the skin had long since melted away, the creature was wearing an Elizabethan ruff.

"Ack," said Shakespeare. He didn't say it, in fact—the bottom half of his face was missing. But he found that noise inside him, somewhere, somehow, and let it out.

"Did you want to see my script?" I asked him. And I handed him the latest draft, covered as it was with the handwriting of a dozen different dead playwrights. He looked it over for a few moments, his one remaining eyeball rolling over the pages. And then he threw up over it. I don't know where the effluence came from, but it didn't matter, it was dark green and it stank, and it was now all over act one, scene two.

He let back his head and gave an ack of frustration.

"It's all right," I said. "It's okay." I took the script back, and wiped the pages clean. "I bet you want me to rewrite it all in iambic pentameter, don't you? And put in the odd sword fight. Of course you do. Well, that's fine. You can watch me if you like. You can watch."

And I scribbled away for a few minutes. Shakespeare's eye never settled on me. Once in a while he squawked another ack. They sounded increasingly plaintive.

"Are you hungry?" I said. "Of course you're hungry. I'm sorry. I'm sorry. I've nothing to feed you." He could have had me, he could have taken me, I would have let him too. But how he was going to chew, this little stunted genius, there wasn't enough of a mouth left to bite, there wasn't a throat with which he could swallow.

And he took my hand. William Shakespeare took my hand.

The eyes rolled one last time, the little bird in the ribcage stopped moving and was still.

I held William Shakespeare close. "I'm sorry," I said, I put my arms tight around my poor broken bard, and I don't know why, I cried.

"Where have you been? We have a crisis!" And Sir Andrew Lloyd Webber's face looked as hungry as I have ever seen it, there was spittle at his mouth when he spoke, and his eyes were bright and feral. And I backed away, I couldn't help it, I thought he was about to go for my throat—and then I realised this was not his hunger for flesh, but a hunger for the thrill of theatre.

"What sort of crisis?" I asked, and I admit, I was weary, there was not an ounce of adrenalin in my body. I had spent the afternoon burying Shakespeare's body in the garden, and if I had had my way I would have skipped this opening night altogether and gone straight to bed. Would have done so, too, had I not been sure that the zombies would have dragged me to the show regardless.

"Most of the actors can't talk," said Lloyd Webber. "I pushed them too far in dress rehearsal, most of their mouths broke."

"And?" I said, but I could already see what was coming. And Lloyd Webber said I would have to be the one to speak the lines for them. I would stand in the wings, miked up, and the actors would lip synch. Those of them, at least, that had lips to synch.

Sir Andrew busied himself with the orchestra, threw into the pit from buckets assorted chunks of flesh and organs to keep the musicians happy during the show. I peered out at the audience as they entered the auditorium. It was a huge space, one thousand seats, and at least two thousand zombies sitting in them, crawling over each other's laps, wedging themselves into every spare crevice—it was like looking out at a wall of dead meat.

I had never played to such a large audience before. The most had been a hundred, tops. And now I wondered what was wrong, why this felt different, why for all those bodies crowding every last inch of the stalls and the dress circle this suddenly struck me as smaller and more inconsequential. And I realised it was because they were silent. There was not the slightest murmur of anticipation. Not the scrunch of a single Maltesers bag.

I could see no sign of my father anywhere.

The lights went down. The actor playing Steve stepped out on to the stage. He looked the part, the zombies in the wardrobe department had clearly thrown themselves into the costume store with something like enthusiasm. But this close up I could see that Steve had barely got a jaw left at all, presumably I'd just given him too many lines to say and the effort had caused his entire chin to cave in. I would have to be his voice. I would be all the voices of the dead.

Steve spoke of his passion for Sally. His love of being a zombie. I put in more energy to his twin declarations of joy than he ever could have. He did a little zombie dance, and sang a little zombie song, and made some jokes about handbags.

There was not a sound from the audience. They were just concentrating, that's what I told myself. But I knew that was rubbish. Hushed quiet in a theatre is always a good thing. Stone silence never is.

But the silence gave me a new confidence. A confidence I hadn't felt in ages. Not since the apocalypse, for sure. Not since my first play had opened, and I'd hit my father, and the police had been called.

I had the confidence of knowing that, in that silence, there was no one listening, and no one cared.

I began to edit the script. I could clear away all the rewrites I hadn't approved of. No more Pinteresque pauses, no more Sheridan quips, no more songs. I began to reinstate my original lines. The play was the better for it. Why couldn't the dead just stop interfering? Why couldn't the dead accept that their time was done, and the living would be so much better off without them? They'd made their mistakes already. Now let us make ours.

And I realised that I was beginning to say this sort of stuff out loud. And no one could stop me. I took my script, my stupid compromised script, and threw it aside. I wouldn't need anything from those pages any more. I felt inspiration.

What did I talk about? I don't know. I talked about my father. I remember that. I talked about how much I missed my father. I talked about how much I loved him, in spite of all, no matter how much I really deeply couldn't stand the miserable old bastard.

And the actors on stage just sort of stopped, really, they didn't even bother to mouth this stuff. And the orchestra got bored, and began gnawing at their oboes and clarinets, then began gnawing at each other. And Sir Andrew Lloyd Webber just stared out into the wings at me with a look of utter hurt, as if I'd betrayed him, as if I'd stabbed him in the back. But, Andrew, if I stabbed you in the back, you wouldn't feel a thing, you walking sack of death. I think I may have said this out loud too. I think I'm pretty sure I did.

I talked about the brave new world I had dreamed of for them, a bold civilisation of the undead just waiting to happen. And how they'd never achieve it. Because they were dead inside, and if they had any capacity for sense or feeling they wouldn't be sitting so placidly in their seats watching my play, no, they'd be standing up and jeering and throwing things on to the stage and tearing up the seats, because my play was really a piece of shit. It was shit. This was shit. They didn't deserve a brave new world. Not if they meekly accepted such mediocre entertainment.

There was a unity in the theatre that night. And I had always wanted to inspire a unity. But this wasn't a unity I understood, and I wanted no part of it.

And still they wouldn't boo, still they wouldn't shout at me to shut up or get off or to bring the singers back on so they could listen to more plinky-plonky tunes from Sir Andrew Lloyd Webber's stale back-catalogue. And so I stepped out onto the stage. I stepped out, knowing their zombie celebrations were in tatters, that I was walking to my death. That at the sight of me thousands of hungry mouths would tear me apart.

I went out for my curtain call.

And stood there. The zombie actors really didn't know what to do with me there. They hadn't rehearsed this. They looked confused. They shuffled to one side, a bit embarrassed.

I stared out at the audience. I couldn't see them for the bright lighting. They were still so silent, deathly silent of course, but I could feel those eyes all staring back. "Come on!" I cried out. I tried to strike as defiant a pose as possible. I stuck out my arms, as if I'd just given them a showstopper musical number. I imagine I looked pretty silly.

My eyes began to adjust, and at last I could see them, all the dead. And all they'd wanted was a good night out.

They began to applaud.

Wild, proper applause. I had never heard anything like it. If they didn't have hands to clap with, they used other parts of their bodies. And once their own bodies were tired, once their rotting flesh had taken all the slapping it could take, they turned to their neighbours in the seats beside them, they began beating upon them, beating out their appreciation, eagerly, desperately, they weren't going to stop, they *couldn't* stop—and the sharp staccato of the applause began to sound wetter somehow, as they beat past the skin and at the vital organs underneath, the clapping began to splash.

And I enjoyed it, in spite of myself—this applause, for *me*—nothing polite about it this time, nothing middle-class and safe and slightly equivocal (because they hadn't liked the set, or the jokes, or the twist in the second act, because the seats had been too hard, because the drinks in the interval had cost too much, because the play had been too long or hadn't been long enough, because they didn't frankly like theatre in the first fucking place and had been dragged there by their wives)—this was the sound of madness, the sound of frenzied animals. I couldn't help it, I even took a bow. But then. But then, somehow. Somehow the clapping just never stopped, and it became more ordered, and then they were clapping in unison, all of them, every last one of them, never missing a beat. And not a face was smiling. They all wore the same expressions, and not a one had anything that resembled a smile.

"Is my father here?" I shouted out. "Where's my father?"

At first I thought nothing was happening, that after all my rewrite hell the walking dead had still cheated me. And then I saw a figure stand up. And walk towards me. And up on to the stage. And into the lights.

And he was wearing tweed.

My father stared at me. He alone, in that amphitheatre, wasn't clapping.

And I knew what had to happen then. That he had to forgive me. That he had to accept me, and consume me, and eat me down.

"I'm yours, Dad," I said. "You must be so hungry."

He continued to stare. His dead eyes narrowed in assessment. Then he made a little noise of contempt, just a pff!—and he turned around.

"Hey!" I said. "Hey!"

He started to walk away.

"Don't turn your back on me! Get back here. Eat me, you shit!"

But he wasn't having any of it. He didn't want me.

That was when I leaped upon him. That's when I forced his mouth wide open—with one hand I grabbed at his nostrils and pulled upwards, with the other I took his chin and yanked down—and I felt something give—and I heard a splitting sound, a ripping, as his face was torn open, and his mouth was so *big* now, and my entire head could fit inside a mouth like that, I could put it in and he could bite down and he could eat me whole and I would be like him, I would be like my daddy, it would be over, at last I would be like them all.

And they jumped me, I was dragged off before I could force a bite, and I was howling at them to let me go, please let me go, please, just give me the end I deserved, but they weren't listening—they weren't listening, their bastard ears were dead to me. And still all about me, still, the clapping went on.

They've brought me baked beans again, and some writing paper. I told them I don't want them. And the zombies smile, because what I want has really very little to do with anything.

They said that they liked my play. It was quite good; *very* good, actually, well done. Everyone was most amused. Especially once all that silly romance stuff had stopped. So, more like that, please. They would expect another production within the week.

And they were sorry about the clapping. They'd been out of practice. They'd get that right next time.

Noel Coward and Terence Rattigan sometimes drop by. But not to offer me advice on my script. The mere idea! A playwright like me doesn't need advice, they say, not after my last show, I am world class. They just visit as fellow men of the stage, and share with me theatrical anecdotes. I hate them, I wish their dead bones would turn to dust. I tell them this sometimes, and they just grin. I ask them to eat me, and they laugh, as if I've made the very wittiest of jokes. "You should write that down," trills Noel. "You could use that!"

I'm the zombie laureate. "Why can't you write your own bloody plays?" I say. But they don't reply to that.

"What do I get in return?" I ask. "I write you some plays, what do I get out of it?" And they don't tell me they'll kill me, because that would be a lie.

"We'll keep your father away," the leader promises. And he rolls his rotted eyes, and he shrugs his rotted shoulders, as if he hopes that'll be enough. And I suppose it is.

So I eat my baked beans, and I set to work on a new play. And, feeding and writing, I wish I had something meatier to get my teeth into.

And the old woman says:

- *I would never want to eat my fellow man. Not for any moral reason, and not because I am revolted by the idea of chewing on human flesh—but I went to enough nightclubs in my youth to believe that my stomach deserves a better quality cut of meat. Consider* **Peckish** *(story 52, page 877).*
- *If you're the sort of person that actually enjoys pantomimes, then really, give yourself a stern talking to, and turn to* **The Eighth** *(story 8, page 127).*
- *Poor William Shakespeare. To see the bard in better shape, turn to* **Canon Fodder** *(story 12, page 199).*
- *The reason why I believe Art must always be celebrated is because of that shared unity it offers. Maybe it's a false unity, I don't know—maybe no one leaves the auditorium truly any closer to understanding their neighbour. But at the moment we all clap I believe in the possibility of it. See an entire nation unified by the work of one artist in* **The Girl from Ipanema** *(story 63, page 1071).*
- *The great betrayal a father lays upon his children is that he is, in the end, just an ordinary, flawed man. Consider* **Ground Beef** *(story 93, page 1573).*

77
The Ineffectual Photoscopy of Cats

One basic problem with early photography was its inability to hold the image of cats. Nicephore Niepce's process of taking a metal plate coated with bitumen and bombarding it with light was quite the discovery, of course, and the further pioneering efforts by Daguerre and Talbot to develop this technique were of huge influence. For the first time in history there really was the sense that a moment could be frozen forever, that people and places and events were to be preserved accurately. It gave us a glimpse of something godlike, something immortal. We drew a blank with cats, though.

Dogs were all right. There was something so essentially noble and straightforward about a dog, it would have been an offence to the sensibilities had dogs not been photographed. And, although it took a bit of fiddling with the lenses, by the late 1870s it had become increasingly easy to capture the likeness of horses as well. But no one had successfully managed to hold a cat upon film; there were various (unsubstantiated) reports from experimental 'graphers that they had done it (and on the continent, always on the continent!)—only for a little while, and blurred maybe, but feline, quite definitely feline. But the image never held long enough for anyone to verify these claims, the cats faded away from the pictures within seconds.

Some said it was because the cat had no soul. Others, that it was simply too minor a lifeform, too low down upon the table of creation for the camera to recognise it. And some people—the ones who actually *owned* cats, who knew what they were about, knew their moods and their characters, said that the cats were doing it deliberately. Cats had no interest in their images being preserved on paper via a collusion of light and oil. What was in it for them?

For the sake of simplicity we had long claimed that the photography of cats was impossible, but that didn't mean we thought it was actually, genuinely, *impossible*; no one believed that, I think, except perhaps Gerard Pomfrey, but his fustian ideas about the photosciences had long since been discredited. I was certain that the solution was out there. It would be a long voyage of discovery for someone. That someone was not going to be me. I don't like cats. I was not prepared to devote my hard-earned photoscopic skills on them.

I still don't know why it was me that Simon Harries contacted. We had both studied at Oxford together, and I remember that back then his views on the inconstancy of calotypes from silver salt solutions were regarded as mildly controversial. But Harries was not the man for controversy, he had neither the charisma nor the gall to carry it off. I had had respect for Harries, I could see there was talent within him, and I think maybe I was the closest he had to a friend—but, still, we were *not* friends, not by any stretch of the definition, and I had neither heard from him nor of him since we'd graduated fifteen years before. I can hardly describe the surprise I felt when I received a telegram from him, let alone my surprise at the contents of that message.

He asked me to visit him at his house in South London that very evening—promptly, at half past eleven. He had something of vital importance to show me. There was no hint in his words that we had had no communication for so long, there was no greeting or attempt at reintroduction, it was as if we had been working side by side in the same laboratory every day. I was half-inclined to ignore the thing, but for the urgency of the final sentence. He urged me to come alone, and to tell no one—and I confess, I was intrigued.

I had a light supper, and then caught a hansom cab to Streatham. I hadn't been south of the Thames for a while, I don't know how man can live in such slum conditions. Still, I was surprised by the poverty of the place when the cab dropped me off, the driver himself looking eager to get back to the civilising areas of the city and only too relieved when I told him he had no reason to wait. I had thought that Harries must have found some decent lodgings here, however cheap; but this was not a house, this was a garret, there wasn't even a doorknocker, I had to beat on the door with my fists. Photography was a science studied by gentlemen; this was not a place where a gentleman could live; what had happened to Harries to bring him so low?

Harries opened the door and showed me in. I would not have recognised him. He had aged. His hair was grey. He had not shaven. His cravat was askew. "What is all this about, Harries?" I asked. I felt I had the right to be a little abrupt.

His eyes wouldn't settle on me, they darted about nervously. "You came alone?"

"As you can see."

"And you have spoken to no one?"

"You try my patience, man."

"Forgive me," he said, and he smiled, and he grasped my hands in his, and shook them briefly, and he began to giggle. "I see so few people nowadays. Oh! but I have done it. I have done it! It is the discovery of the age!"

He lived in one room, I could see, and that a small one; over the floor were papers; over the papers were sheets of acetate, broken or chipped lenses, dyes, gels, scraps of stale food. "I have 'graphed a cat," he whispered to me, eyes shining.

I felt no personal affection for Harries, but I was nonetheless sorry that a man of his potential had gone down such a scientific blind alley. He could see the disappointment on my face; I confess, I did not try to disguise it; he grabbed on to my arm, tight. He said, "I've done it, I tell you!"

"Then let me see," I said.

And then he was smiling again, a crafty little smile, I did not like that smile much. "Oho, not yet! Not yet! Not until midnight! The cats only come out at the witching hour, you'll see, you'll see." And he cleared the debris off the only chair, and invited me to sit down.

A little before twelve, he fetched for me a 'graph. He'd taken a picture of the room. He had taken it from the chair, I think, from the exact place I was sitting. The books were in slightly different positions, maybe, I saw a pile of photoscientific treatises that had since then toppled over. "There's nothing here," I said—"Not yet, not yet," he insisted, "I tell you, midnight!" And I looked hard at the picture, and so did he, and that's how we spent the next few minutes. I felt ridiculous.

The clock struck. Loud, too loud. "Sorry, sorry," said Harries, "I wind it up tight to ensure I never sleep through it. But look, look, on the 'graph!" And I was looking at the photograph, and of course, I expected to see nothing, and there would be an end to this. I even opened my mouth to say so; I shut it again.

For wasn't there something swimming into focus? Wasn't there a blur?—and the blur was taking on a more rigid outline, and then a solid shape. "My God," I said, and I apologise, but I was that surprised. Because there, looking out of the picture, indubitably, was a cat. Looking out at *me*. It appeared to be as shocked as I was. Its eyes were wide in the flash light, its ears were pricked, its fur was standing on edge.

"But it must be a trick," I said. "Harries? Is this not some small child you have dressed up as a cat, or…?"

"I have the proof!" he laughed. "Ha ha, I have *proof*!" And at that he threw aside a few more papers, and lifted from the floor the cat itself. He picked it up by the tail. Its face was set in the exact same expression I saw in the 'graph, its fur still set fast and rigid.

"Dead," I said, uselessly.

"Dead, yes, ha ha, it always kills 'em, don't know why!" said Harries. "Normally they just die, ha ha, and there's nothing to show for it. But this time I set the exposure right! I got the picture! The cat didn't die in vain!"

"And how long have you been doing this?" I asked.

He waved his hand as if it were a matter of utter irrelevance; and, I suppose, to him it was. "There are lots of cats on the streets, sniffing around the waste is a good place to find 'em. Sometimes they claw and bite," and I could see now, yes, there were marks all over his arms, little scars on his cheeks, "but I'm bigger than 'em, ha ha, they're no match for me! I take 'em here, and I 'graph 'em, and I get rid of 'em, and their bodies end up so frozen hard they sink straight to the bottom of the river! But I kept this one, he's my little pet, my little boy. I'm proud of him. He's made me a success, yes, he has, he's made me all proper and worthwhile." And he actually stroked at the dead cat's stiffened fur.

"And what do you want of me?" I asked. And I felt a chill, as if I thought he might want to take *my* photograph, he would rob the life from me and set me down on film—but that was silly, no harm had ever come to a human being from being 'graphed, I was not an animal.

"You have a Reputation," said Harries, and he said it like that, with a capital R. "You are a good man. People will listen to you. I charge you to bring my discovery to the world."

"No," I said. I didn't even know I was going to refuse him until I spoke, but the refusal came out immediately, as if all my instincts were revolting against him, my intellect knew I wanted no part of this before my mouth did.

"Why not?" he said, and for a second he scrunched his hands into fists and something dark passed over his face—then he relaxed, his face slumped back into the same failed despondency I had known from Oxford. "Why not?" he said again, meek and defeated.

"I am a man of science," I said, "and I duly believe that the purpose of science is to better mankind. And I can see no betterment that comes from the photography of cats, not whether they are alive, or dead, or some state inbetween, confound you."

I did not want to leave on such a terse note, and so endeavoured to make some light talk with Harries about his health and the weather, but neither of our hearts were in it, and I soon gave up and took a cab home.

Three weeks later Simon Harries was dead. The police came to my house and asked whether I could help them with their enquiries, and at first I thought they meant I was implicated, and I was fully prepared to get quite angry about the matter. But they assured me that wasn't the case, and made apologies, and spoke to me with such due deference that I fetched my coat and my hat and agreed to go with them.

They took me to Harries' lodgings. In the middle of the room, spread over his papers, was a body, I presumed Harries', covered with a sheet. I recoiled at that, but not at the sight of death, just at the insensitive way in which I'd been allowed to see it.

"Sorry, Sir," said the constable on duty. "We've tried to move it, but it weighs a ton, and that's a fact." He showed me a box. He told me it had been left for me, and indeed, it had my name and address written upon the side.

"Would you like me to open this?" I asked, and the policeman said it would be a blessing for 'em if I didn't mind.

I could not imagine why Harries would leave me anything. Inside the box I found his camera, and a dozen or so photographs. The camera was old and outmoded, I dare say he'd never had the funds to purchase a better one; I had no need of it, I had several cameras of my own at home. The photographs were an odd mix; some of them, I assume, had been taken by Harries; some of them, like the portrait of Queen Victoria, no doubt rescued from a newspaper, definitely weren't.

At the bottom of the box I found an envelope. I opened it.

"Can't Stop Them Now," was all it said.

It was an unhelpful note, one of vagueness and imprecision, and unworthy of an Oxford graduate. And I understood why Simon Harries had managed no better than a lower second.

The constable said, "Begging your pardon, would you look at the body, Sir? It's got us properly stumped, and you're a man of science and all." I pointed out that my science was photography not medicine, but accepted after further pleading that I was still the best qualified scientist there, and permitted them to present me the corpse.

The sheet was removed. In death Harries looked larger, swollen somehow, as if he'd been the victim of drowning—though his body, naturally enough, was perfectly dry. That he was peculiarly bloated was not the most disturbing thing about him—it was more that his mouth was open, wide open, opened wider than I thought a mouth could stretch.

"For Heaven's sake," I said, "give the man some dignity. At least shut the mouth!" And the constable said to me his men had tried to do just that, but the mouth *wouldn't* shut; "The jaws have got stuck somehow, Sir." So I had a go. I put on my gloves, and reached out to Harries' face. I saw as I neared it there were fresh scratches upon his cheeks. I pulled on the chin, but it was indeed stiff. For a moment I thought his body had frozen hard like the carcass of the cat he had shown me—but no, I pulled harder, and I could feel some give—I admit, I was none too gentle about it, and at last the hinges of the jaws gave way to my bidding and the mouth snapped tight shut.

"Thanking you, Sir," said the constable.

"That's all I can do, I'm afraid," I said. "This death goes beyond the knowledge afforded me by photoscopic theory. I'd say he didn't die easily, though. Poor devil."

Back home I perused the contents of the box once more. There was nothing new to be gleaned from the enigmatic letter, so I destroyed it. I checked the camera; it had no film. I left it in the kitchen. It was junk, but I thought I might cannibalise it for parts.

I took the photographs up to my study. I sat in my favourite chair, drank a brandy.

Yes, some of them had clearly been taken by Harries. Two of them were of his own lodgings for a start, and I assumed they were failures from his cat experiments. But others were not of his hand at all, the style was wrong, the composition. There were pictures of empty anonymous streets. Of famous London landmarks, the one of St Paul's Cathedral at dusk was especially striking. There was a man and a woman outside a church, all dressed up in their best—was it their wedding day? They looked uncomfortable, was that at the prospect of spending the rest of their lives together, or that someone was aiming a camera at them and stealing the moment and freezing it for his own ends and committing it to film and making it possible that strangers like me could finger at it and paw at it and stare at it without shame? There was Queen Victoria. She didn't seem amused.

I could see nothing to connect the pictures whatsoever. I tried to puzzle it over, but not too seriously; it wasn't my mystery, after all, I didn't have to care. I felt drowsy. I raised a glass to Harries, and toasted him. I meant it respectfully enough, but quite see it may have come out wrong.

I dozed.

And when I woke, the fire was nearly out, and there was a crick in my neck, and I'd dropped the photographs all over the floor. I looked at the time—and it was on the verge of midnight—and then, soon enough, the grandfather clock downstairs began to chime.

The top photograph was of Harries' room. And I stared at it. I didn't *want* to stare at it. I didn't want to see a dead cat shimmer into view. But I couldn't take my eyes off it—and yes—yes—there it was, the outline, then filling in with more clarity, more depth—there was the cat, sure enough, its 'graph taken at the very point of death. The previous cat had looked merely surprised. This one was angry.

And it wasn't alone.

Because the picture continued to blur, now all around the fringes of it, I could see the blurring ripple beneath my fingers and I all but dropped the photograph, it buzzed to the touch. And there was a sound to it now, a whispering? A hissing. And more cats began to appear.

How many cats had Harries squeezed into his studio? What had he done?

There were a dozen—then there were more—then the picture was *full* of them, a hundred cats, a hundred and one, who could say?—big cats, kittens too, and all spilling out over each other, jostling for space, cramming themselves into every last crevice of space the picture could afford, blotting out the background of the room until all that could be seen was wall-to-wall cat.

And even though the picture was full, I could see that the 'graph was blurring still, and the hissing was louder now, it was a *seething*—and there were yet more cats being born, but there was no space for them, they were crushing the other cats now, they were bending themselves out of shape too, they were distorting, they were making themselves anew.

And still, still, the cats wouldn't stop. And there was no light to the picture now, it was all just a mass of black, and the black was crying out, I knew that black wasn't a void, it was anything but, it was the weight of all the cats in the world stuffed into an area no larger than a few inches square, and still, still the cats wouldn't stop.

And the other pictures.

There were cats piled up as high as St Paul's Cathedral, they were choking up the River Thames. There were cats in the wedding dress, there were cats perched on top of the bridegroom's hat, and pouring out from under his hat, and pouring out from under *him*. There was Queen Victoria, regal, unsmiling, and the cats were prodding at her face, they were prodding at her cheeks, they were trying to force a smile whether she liked it or not.

And I knew they were here. That the world was full of ghosts, crammed together tight, and that we couldn't see. But the camera could see. The camera could see the cats, at least. At least it could only see the cats.

I wanted to throw the photographs from me, get them away as far as I could. But I couldn't move. And I felt something so heavy on my chest—and I knew they were there, all of them, all the cats who had ever died, all of them were sitting on me and crawling over me and trying to find somewhere warm to shelter safe from the cold of extinction. I couldn't breathe. I thought I couldn't breathe. Then, then I forced myself to my feet. And, of course, there was nothing pinning me down, of course there was no weight to shift—and, of course, nothing kicked and wailed and howled as it scattered to the floor.

I lit a candle. I went downstairs.

I had to get to the camera. To destroy it? I don't know. To take pictures, lots of pictures, to fill the world with cats, say to everybody, look! look! this is where the dead go!

Film that doesn't show us what is really there, that gives us stories and fantasies instead, what use could that ever be?

And as I went down the stairs I thought the ghost cats beneath my feet would trip me up, and I held on to the banister rail so tightly. And I imagined my stepping on their tails, my treading down on their backs, the crunch of their phantom bones breaking underfoot, the howls, the mews, the pitiful mews.

I entered the kitchen.

The camera was where I'd left it, on the table.

Wrapped around it—licking it, even?—was a cat. The fattest cat I had ever seen. Greasy too, its fur looked slick and oily and wet.

It bared its teeth at me.

"Get away!" I cried. "Get out of here!"

It wouldn't take its eyes off me. It wouldn't move from the camera.

"Didn't you hear what I said? What do you want? Tell me what you want!" I was ready to bargain with a cat. And I threw the candle at it.

I didn't aim at the cat directly. I think it knew that. I think that's why it didn't even flinch. The candlestick passed harmlessly overhead.

"Get out!" I said, and I mimed throwing something else, although

I had nothing left to throw, and of course the cat could see that. But it yawned, it stretched. It gave me a look that I can only describe as reproachful. And then, slowly, in its own time, it slunk away from the camera. It dropped off the table, and for all its bulk landed lightly on its feet.

"You get away!" I said. But it was ignoring me now. I backed away from it as it trotted towards me, out of the door, out of the room.

I looked for it in the corridor, but it was dark now without the candle. I couldn't see it.

I went to the camera.

I was going to destroy it. But now I picked it up, I felt the urge to take photographs with it. What else is a camera for? No, I was going to destroy it. I was going to smash it down upon the table, now, hard, the glass would shatter, and all the ghosts would be locked away forever somewhere we couldn't see.

And I saw there was film in it. There hadn't been film earlier. I had checked. Who had put the film in?

I hesitated.

I took out the film, and had it developed.

I haven't destroyed the camera.

I've told Cook to keep it in the kitchen. And if the cats get in, and sometimes they do, she is to remove them from the house. But she must be gentle with them. She must give them milk first, and treat them with respect.

I haven't used the camera, either. Though one night I woke up, and I was downstairs, in the kitchen, and I was holding the camera with both hands. And I had never walked in my sleep before. I woke up in time, I went back upstairs, I locked my bedroom door. I keep the door locked every night now.

Maybe I'll destroy the camera anyway. One day. We'll see. I just don't think that would make the cats very happy.

There are African tribes I've heard of, savages really, who don't like the white man photographing them. They fear that it takes their souls. But I worry that the reverse may be true. What if the camera brings a dead soul back? What if every picture confers a little immortality, and the world simply cannot support the weight of all those never-to-be-forgotten memories?

I burned the photograph that I had found in the camera. No one else need ever see that. For my part, though, it might as well still exist. I might as well have framed it, and hung it over my bed. It's not as if I'll ever forget what was in that photograph, not one single detail of it.

The picture was of Simon Harries. And I now know how he died. And I now know why his mouth was open so unnaturally wide, because there was something forcing the bulk of its entire body in. It knew what it was doing, too—the photograph had caught a little jaunty wave of the tail. And I don't think it was the first cat that had crawled inside his mouth, I think that Harries' bloated body was full of them.

And I remember how I had forced his jaws shut, and the resistance I felt, and I think I must have had that ghost body bitten clean through.

I'll destroy the camera one day. I will. But for now, I treat all cats well, and I sleep with the door locked, and my mouth taped up.

No one can take photographs of babies either. Babies have no souls. But no one wants a picture of a baby.

And the old woman says:

- *If your favourite cats are the ones to be found in a Lloyd Webber musical, turn to* **Slow Handclap for the Moronic Horde** *(story 76, page 1329).*
- *Science has given us great things. The toaster, lightning rods, penicillin and the selfie stick—and I know I'm forever indebted to the invention of gravity because I'm scared of heights and would hate to be bouncing about all over the sky. Consider the breakthroughs offered in* **The Constantinople Archives** *(story 21, page 345).*
- *It's hard to judge how much the cats in Harries' experiments suffered. Maybe animal cruelty can be justified if the benefit to Mankind is great enough. If you believe this, turn to* **The Monogamy of Wild Beasts** *(story 26, page 437).*
- *Do you believe in the concept of souls? Can we really be nothing more than animated hunks of meat? Consider, then turn to* **The March** *(story 28, page 463).*
- *To read of another man who is frozen stiff, turn to* **Shelter from the Storm** *(story 58, page 985).*

78
FAMOUS LAST WORDS

PHILIP BROWN'S LAST words were staggering—so profound that everyone who heard them felt the very breath catch in their throats, and the lifting of something inside, deep inside, where even the crassest parts of us appreciate true wisdom. Within those words there was nothing morbid, just an acceptance that this is what life should be, fleeting, and yet beautiful for being so fleeting, a dash of colour against the darkness of an eternity in which we would no longer exist but had once existed and by dint of that had once *mattered*; there was a summation, then, a sense that within an ending one could look back and get full perspective on all that had gone before; in death we had at last achieved a completeness, and that was a blessing, a gift—because all that seeming randomness we had lived through now *was* connected, *had* purpose, fairly *burst* with meaning. Philip Brown was not a man given to profundity, and the people who overheard him at that moment—his wife, his teenage children, a few lone customers and the check-out girl at the supermarket—could in no way have anticipated that his final statement would have had such power. It made them want to applaud, frankly. It made them want to give him a standing ovation.

And the only false note struck was that as Philip Brown uttered these last words he was reasonably healthy. He was forty-four years old, and a little overweight maybe, but the doctor was happy with his cholesterol levels and said his blood pressure was so precisely normal it was almost text book. He was about as far away from death as any averagely unspectacular middle-aged man could hope to be.

Philip Brown looked as surprised as anybody else that these words had popped out of him. He chewed at the air for a moment, as if trying to get his mouth back into the right shape for the sort of forgettable nonsense he would usually come out with. And then he opened up wide, and he took a breath, and he was going to speak, he was going to spoil everything—and his wife actually clapped her hand to his face to stop him. "Don't," she said, "you're never going to top that."

Pretty soon they weren't just last words, they were famous last words. One of the customers at the supermarket had sold the story to the newspapers—or maybe it was that check-out girl, there had been something nakedly acquisitive about her features. Even though Philip's words had suggested that the pursuit of money was a futile exercise, and that true wealth could only be found through spiritual endeavour. A reporter came to the Brown house. He rang the doorbell. Mrs Brown answered. The reporter asked what Mrs Brown's impression was of the last words, and Mrs Brown said she thought they'd been very nice. The reporter asked whether they might form the epitaph for her husband's gravestone, and Mrs Brown said that was a good idea—though there were rather a lot of them, she might just use edited highlights. The reporter concluded by expressing his condolences for Mrs Brown's loss, and Mrs Brown said there was no need—not now—not yet anyway—Mr Brown was in the sitting room watching the snooker on television. But, thank you anyway, she said; when the time came, his condolences would make her husband's passing easier to bear.

Philip Brown had not spoken since, of course. Hadn't been to work, where the requirement to talk about sales figures for gardening equipment could only have been seen as a crashing anticlimax. He had reached his apogee, and now he was there he could do nothing but shut up and accept it. He had no more words to add, his greatness stood for itself without need for embellishment or elaboration. And though his family felt new respect, there was a smugness about him now that was decidedly off-putting. He was given charge of the remote control, and would change the television channels without warning, and that could be irksome; he would let them know when he was hungry by clapping his hands or stamping his feet or by any method of slamming his body parts audibly against a standing object to get their attention; he would tell them what he wanted to eat by getting out tins from the kitchen cupboard and pointing. His wife and children still talked around him, naturally enough; they were only in the presence of greatness, they weren't great themselves; they hadn't yet said anything sufficiently meaningful, they had nothing left to aim for. But conversation always felt a bit forced, no sooner were words out of their mouths than they would somehow stutter and wither and die, it was as if there was a black hole in the room sucking every syllable into silence.

His words were printed in magazines in every country around the world; choice phrases were quoted on mugs and ashtrays and T-shirts. And along came the copycats, of course. A fourteen-year-old boy in Wisconsin tried to better Brown, came up with famous last words of his own. The words won their admirers, but most agreed that they were too practised, the boy had written them down in advance and that seemed a bit like cheating, and when their utterance was over and the child had thrown himself off the freeway bridge to gory death below the general consensus was that they were a little too gauche to be taken seriously. The power of Philip Brown was that his words had been given to the world quite freely, there was no pretension to them, they were the complex sentiments of a simple man. And that's what inspired everybody. The teenage American was soon forgotten by all but his parents and a few of his more impressionable high-school classmates. Whereas Philip Brown just lived on.

He was given a memorial service. The people insisted. A cathedral was hired for the event—one of the smaller cathedrals, anything larger would have shown an ostentation at odds with the basic tenets of Brown's teachings. Tickets were sold. His famous last words were recited by a well-respected actor; the actor managed to bring such artistry to his performance, mining from Brown's words both the triumph of life everlasting and the dread of inevitable loss, and Brown himself could never have said them so well, not with his monotone and his mumbling and his flat vowels, not if he'd rehearsed his dying message for weeks. The congregation was moved; one woman cried out, "Love you forever, Philly!", though she'd never met Philip, though she'd never known him, though Philip hadn't been called Philly since he was twelve and hadn't liked being called Philly since seven. Philip Brown himself was present. He sat near the back, he couldn't afford the more expensive seats—or maybe that was down to his characteristic humility, yes, it would have been the humility. Philip Brown thought the service went off rather well. But he couldn't express his satisfaction verbally. He gave little smiles and nods, that was how his family registered his approval. They were happy for him. And they mourned him, too.

Mrs Brown hoped that grief would bring her family together. After the service she gave both her children a big hug—and they looked so smart, dressed in their best, she said she was so proud of them and that their father would have been proud too—and then she hugged their father as well, though that was something of an afterthought. She told them that she loved them all, and that the times ahead were going to be hard but that she knew they would weather them, that if they just held tight they would come out stronger.

The children went to see a counsellor on Thursdays. The daughter overcame her initial reticence, and soon let out her feelings about her father quite volubly and without inhibition. She was angry she'd lost him. She was angry he was gone before she'd taken the chance to get to know him properly. The counsellor suggested she could take some comfort in his famous last words—death was not an end, it was a new beginning—or maybe it was a continuation, it was sometimes hard to work out exactly what her father had meant, but it was all very uplifting nonetheless, didn't the girl think so too? Couldn't the girl be happy that her father had been a great man and that his words had inspired so many? And the girl said it made it worse, so much worse.

Because she didn't recognise from those words the man who had watched *Top Gear* and had drunk lager in front of the telly and belched and farted and whose stares had embarrassed her friends. That if death merely robbed you of a future with a person then that was bad enough—but death did more than that, it took from you the past as well, it sentimentalised the deceased, it made them seem more kindly and more interesting and more profound, it changed your memories and left you with someone strange and unknowable. Death was such shit. Death was such a lying piece of shit.

The son was much less affected by the loss; he said he wasn't bothered at all; he soon stopped going to counselling altogether, and that was all right, the counselling was expensive. And then he was busy, staying out late and getting drunk and committing acts of petty vandalism, knocking over lamp posts and setting fire to cats. And it was perfectly possible this had nothing to do with his father. He might well have been doing all that stuff anyway. Both Mr and Mrs Brown thought there was every chance this was just a harmless phase of ordinary teenage hijinks.

As for Mrs Brown, she was lonely. She had never spoken enough to her husband, and she regretted that, but she refused to be bitter. She just knew that if she ever met another man she'd have to try harder and seize every moment and never take him for granted. She met a man at church. He began visiting after service on Sundays. And then he began visiting her during afternoons whilst the kids were at school. One day she took him to her bedroom, and he started to get undressed, and she froze up, and cried. She said that she couldn't go through with it, it was disrespectful to her husband, why, his body was still warm! And the man said her husband had been a great man, but she was still young, her whole life was stretching out before her, Philip wouldn't have wanted her to grieve forever. And at this they both looked across to Philip, who looked frankly non-committal, but now at least moved to the far side of the bed to give them more space. She said he could never be the equal of her husband, and he agreed, too easily. So then she accused him of sleeping with her just because of her famous husband, it wasn't for her at all—and he admitted it, he wanted to touch where greatness had touched, he wanted to go deep inside her and see whether he too might be inspired to find words of grace and wisdom and genius. She let him take her then; she let him take her clothes off, and climb on top of her, and go as deep inside as he wanted—and she held back her tears, she knew his passion didn't belong to her, this wasn't the expression of earthly lust but an appeal for something spiritual. "Oh God," said the man as he shot his load, "oh God, oh God, oh shit, oh *God.*" And Mr and Mrs Brown exchanged glances at that, and neither was much impressed by the words the man had found. And Mrs Brown got up from the bed and put back on her clothes and redid her make-up, and supposed she should refuse to see him again. But she managed to keep some sort of relationship with him going for the next nine months; and when they broke up, she found someone else.

The children grew up and went away. They said they would come back and visit, and to be fair, they sometimes did.

Mrs Brown got old. Her hair turned grey, then white, then fell out altogether. She put on weight, the flesh just spread out every which way—and then, just as suddenly, retracted again, leaving her thinner than she'd ever been before. She found it hard to walk. She found it hard to breathe. She'd wake up some mornings and there was a pain inside, thrumming away, and she couldn't work out which part of the body it came from.

And one day she went to the hospital, and she knew she wasn't going to see her home ever again.

Philip Brown went to see his wife. He brought her some flowers, and the nurse cooed and put them in a vase. He nodded his thanks to the nurse silently, then sat beside his wife's bed and took her hand.

"I love you," she said, "I love you," and it may have been the medicine talking, or maybe it was fear, or maybe the cool reality that comes over us before death. "Do you have any words of comfort for me?" And he smiled, and she smiled back; of course he didn't; of course not.

"Will you stay with me?" she asked. "Will you make love to me, one last time?" So he climbed into bed with her, and he took it very slow and soft and made sure he didn't give her a heart attack.

He stayed with her for the next few days, right beside her, right close, and no one seemed to mind, after a while the doctors and nurses seemed to pretend he wasn't there. And he was with her at the end. She suddenly gripped his hand, her eyes were wide open, wider than they had been in years, wide like a child's."Oh God," she said. "I think this is it. Oh God, oh shit, oh God." She winced then, screwed those child eyes up tight so she couldn't see what was coming for her. "God, it hurts, it hurts, you said it would be kind, oh God, you lied to me, you lied to me, you fuck." As last words went they weren't profound, and they would never be famous, but they were sincere at least, and that must count for something.

The grip on his hand slackened. He let go of her. He stroked his wife's dead forehead. He kissed it. He kissed her lips.

She opened her eyes. She sat up. She smiled.

And now she kissed him back, and her lips weren't dry and cracked with age, they were so smooth they slid right off his own lips and on to the chin, on to the face, all over the face.

No words. No words left. Nothing to say any more.

He offered her his arm, and she got out of bed. And, dressed in her nightie, she left the ward, together they walked right out of the hospital and into the world to see what it had to say for itself.

And the old woman says:

- *For most people, of course, the only last words that are left are their names engraved on to a tombstone. Consider* **The War Artist** *(story 10, page 149).*
- *Some of us manage without words. Some of us can command entire crowds with our very silence. Turn to* **Dumb Lucy** *(story 46, page 771).*
- *Maybe we attach too much importance to words. The words aren't the real thing—they're just totems holding in place the feelings that inspired them. But where do you draw the line? At what point when your language is taken away from you should you resist? Consider* **Death to the French** *(story 29, page 473).*
- *It must be galling to realise you've reached the climax to your life several years too early. Turn to* **The Pillow Menu** *(story 48, page 799).*
- *If you too enjoy watching snooker on TV, turn to* **Unfurnished** *(story 19, page 321).*

There are almost four times
as many words in this book as
there are words defined in
the Oxford English Dictionary.
And yet still I didn't make
room for your favourite.

79
THE SMELL OF BURNT ORANGE

HELLO, LITTLE MAN. They tell me you're in pain. I can see it's true, your face screwed up like that, but you're not crying, you're a brave boy. Perhaps you've already worked it out—crying doesn't help the pain go away, it just makes your face wetter. If you have, then you may be the wisest man I know. You'd have thought pain gets easier with age, but it doesn't. I so much as stub my toe, I holler.

You're teething, and that sounds like an exquisite sort of torture. I can't imagine what you're going through. If I get toothache at least I know it's because I've eaten too much sugar, it's self-inflicted. I have no one to blame but myself. But your teeth are hurting and you haven't even used them yet. To be in pain because your body hasn't finished growing yet, could anything be more cruel?

It was different in my day. I don't say this to gloat. We had it easier than you.

I have things to tell you, and you alone. I have kept them a secret for so many years. And it's not been hard living a lie. I love your mother very much, but lying to her has been particularly easy. The false name, the made-up history of my life—she's believed in it all so readily, frankly she's complicit. She made it possible for me to believe it too, most of the time. The times when she was cursing my grandfather, and I happily joined in.

So don't think my telling you the truth now is some sort of compulsion. Something bottled up inside me that has to come out—no. The truth is, I'm telling you because you're eighteen months old. If you were even a little bit older, I wouldn't risk it. And also because you're my son, and I think you deserve to be told. My shame is your shame, sorry. There is that. But, really, it's mostly the first reason, I'm telling you because you won't understand.

I came close to telling your mother once. Late one night, and we'd been married for a while, and you were on the way. We lay together in bed, and held each other, and we just talked. I felt I could tell her anything. I said to her, "What did you smell? What did you smell, my darling, when your body was dying? Back in the days you knew you were sick by smell alone." I hadn't dared ask it before, I knew it was a dangerous area. She told me it was stewed apricots, and I said, that made sense, because they always said that those who smelled fruit were the sweetest people in the world. I think that's maybe what put me off saying any more. That it was fruit, and that she was so good, so much better than I deserved, I didn't want to ruin it all. If she'd said she smelled, I don't know, cat shit, I might have carried on and confessed everything.

For me, it was aniseed. God, even now, the slightest whiff and I want to gag. That's why I won't ever allow liquorice in the house. When your teeth have grown, little man, I'll give you all the sweets to rot them that you like, but I draw the line at liquorice. My grandfather smelled burnt orange. That's fruit too, of course. People would be surprised, he was far sweeter than they gave him credit.

When you grow up you're going to hear a lot about your great-grandfather, and it's important you don't try to defend him. There's a reason the family changed its name. People are still very angry. Maybe one day they'll forgive him, I think they will. When my generation dies out, and there's no one around to remember what it was like in the old days. Your generation may forgive and forget, when they've nothing to compare their lives with. But whilst anyone who lived through the better times can hear, I tell you, keep our family secrets to yourself.

As far as anyone can tell, my grandfather was the first man in the history of the world to have died at the age of seventy-nine. Certainly he is the first in *established* history—I think there may have been a couple in the Bible, but you have to take those ages with a pinch of salt. What he did has made a lot of people very unhappy, of course, and I can't blame them for hating him. But I do disagree when they start banging on about how he was evil and responsible for more deaths and atrocities than Stalin, Hitler, or Genghis Khan—because, yes, a lot of people have died, and a lot of people *will* die, but they would have died anyway, wouldn't they? Isn't that the point? And to claim my grandfather was some sort of genius mastermind hell bent on causing worldwide suffering is so wide of the mark it beggars belief. I knew him. I knew him, and I promise you, he was no monster. He was no more a monster than I am.

The story goes, God was once very angry with the people of the Earth, and caused a flood to wipe them out. And to the survivors he said he was sorry, and promised he would never again try to murder us all, and gave us a rainbow as a sign of good faith. And to make the covenant even better he promised too that there would be years of our lives safe from death and strife, for he recognised that Man's lot was a hard and painful one. That's what it says in the Bible anyway, I had to learn that at school. I don't know that I much believe in God. Don't tell your mother.

Whatever the reason, this was the outcome. That no one would ever die if their age was a prime number. They wouldn't even feel pain. It isn't that we wouldn't know death or pain at other ages, that would be absurd. But we would all have years of respite from it. And it was fair. Babies have so much to learn about the dangers of the world—that fire burns, that knives cut, that falling headlong and hard to the ground is rarely advisable. But they could learn what these dangers were without getting killed in the process, and surely that was right, it seems very wrong that a baby should be punished in the great game of life before it's had a chance to work out the rules. A child was born, and so long as it had the wit to make it to its first birthday, then it'd be safe.

And say a baby did put its hand into the flames, as any curious child might do. The body would send out an alarm cry to tell them it was a bad idea—but that alarm wouldn't be anything cruel, like pain. It would assign the alarm a certain smell, something it would know that particular baby wouldn't like. Aniseed for me, stewed apricots for your mother. You're one year old now, you wouldn't be suffering toothache like this, you'd be smelling strong mint or sour lemon or sulphur. A gentle rebuke to let you know something is wrong.

One, two, three—those ages were safe. Four was the first danger year, the first time your invulnerability was turned off. But even so I remember a certain excitement when I turned four, and I'd be allowed to experience pain for real, like a proper grown-up would. My parents supervised my first pain together, with the whole family gathered around, they pulled back my finger till it nearly broke—a lot of families would do that, it was a rite of passage, showing your child what suffering could be with all his loved ones there for reassurance. And if a lot of children went on to die at four, they'd still be burning themselves or cutting themselves or falling from great heights, the general feeling was they'd had three years to take the lessons of what was safe and what wasn't, and if they hadn't worked it out by then they were probably too stupid to make it to adulthood anyway. Being four was exciting but scary, but you knew you had five just around the corner and then you could take a breather. Six, another dangerous year, but hard followed by seven. We realised that even ages were always hard, and odd ages were safe—or safer, at any rate, because before long there'd be multiples of three and five and seven getting in the way. But that was good too—the older you got, the fewer prime ages there'd be, and that's because we were becoming adults, we were taking our places in a world that had gently prepared us for the realities of mortality and adversity, we could at last enjoy life without the training wheels. We could be proud of that.

Prime birthdays were still the best, though. It wasn't just the day that was special, the entire year ahead was special as well—and I remember my eleventh birthday well, my parents threw me a party and we had a clown and a bouncy castle and lots and lots of cake, and I could eat as much cake as I liked and know it wouldn't give me tummy ache. And it's the first time I properly remember my grandfather too—he'd always been around, of course, but I mean as a separate individual, standing apart from all my other elderly relatives. He smoked thin cigars, he was always smoking them; my mother disapproved but he didn't notice or didn't care. And when we were on our own he held out his cigar to me and said, "Go on, birthday boy, take a puff." And I hesitated, and he laughed and said I was eleven years old now, it couldn't do me any harm. So I took it and put it in my mouth and the smoke made me cough, and I couldn't be sure how much the aniseed taste was part of the cigar itself.

Grandfather smoked his entire life, so it was hardly surprising when he was diagnosed with cancer. The doctors gave him six months to live. He was seventy-five; his next prime age was seventy-nine, years away. But against all the odds he defied the prognosis, and he didn't succumb to the cancer for a long while—he was still out and about and smoking away on his seventy-sixth birthday, and then on his seventy-seventh. He even outlived Granny, who had been perfectly healthy, and had never smoked once, and drank only in moderation at Christmas, and who just keeled over unexpectedly one day at the age of seventy-four. Being widowed took its toll on Grandfather—he looked sadder, he didn't eat so well. The cancer began to win the battle. He was taken into hospital a month before birthday number seventy-eight. We were told he wouldn't last long.

We went to see him on his birthday. He was propped up on his bed, and the nurses had put his birthday cards on display, and there was a lone balloon attached to the headboard. He looked so small, as if the pain had shrunk him down to a hard nut. I asked him if it hurt much, and he smiled and lied and said he was all right. None of us knew what to say, really, and we were all quite relieved when the visiting hour was up, my grandfather, I think, included. I said goodbye to him, and couldn't help but wonder if it were for the last time—it was as if Grandfather knew I thought that, because he took hold of my hand, and his eyes twinkled, and he said to me, "I'm not giving up yet!"

And still, he continued to live. Three more months, then six more months. The doctors said to my parents, "You mustn't start believing he'll make it to his seventy-ninth birthday, that's too much to ask." But we did start to believe it, and the nurses too—when we visited they'd say to us he was their little mascot! Grandfather no longer had the strength to speak, and his skin was so thin you could see through it. The nurses had to feed him by hand, and he wasn't able even to suck in the stray crumbs into his mouth, he kept dribbling down his chin. "If he slips into a coma, it may not be kind to keep him alive artificially." But Grandfather didn't slip into a coma.

On the morning of his seventy-ninth birthday my grandfather woke up and breathed easily and felt strong. The doctors reminded him he wasn't cured—he now had a year's reprieve, but the moment he passed out of a prime age he'd collapse to his previous state. He had exactly one more year of life—he should make the most of it. And that he should get out of bed, because there was a whole slew of seventy-eight and eighty-year-olds who needed it more than he did.

For a while Grandfather seemed to enjoy his new lease of life. He travelled the world, he went to see the Northern Lights and Macchu Picchu and Angkor Wat. He took up ski-ing and scuba diving. He read Proust. Back from his Caribbean cruise, I went to see him. His skin was still see-through and his body was still shrunken, but he stood up straight and gave me a hug. I asked him how he was. He shrugged, and lit a cigar. "I'm bored," he told me. "There are lots of wonders in the world, I know, but once you've seen half a dozen of them, they all start to look the same. And I'm seeing them without your gran." I didn't know what to say—my parents were annoyed enough he was spending so much of their inheritance, if they had any idea he wasn't even enjoying himself they'd have been furious. "And all I smell is burnt orange," he said. "Breathing in, breathing out, standing, walking, anything at all. Burnt orange everywhere, Christ, I'm drowning in it."

It was at Christmas, when the family were all together, that he told us all what he had planned. He'd bought us all expensive presents, so everyone was happy, he said it was his last opportunity to buy us anything so he wanted to do us proud. He didn't eat his turkey with much enthusiasm, and I supposed the burnt orange was spoiling the taste somewhat. And then he said he wanted to make an announcement, and so we all dutifully paid attention as he leaped to his feet and began to talk. He thanked my mother for the dinner she had cooked, and my family for a lifetime of love. "But I've had enough of it now," he said. "I've crammed these last few months with all the pleasures I can, and I realise there's only one thing left that'll give me any satisfaction. I want to die."

He took refuge in our spare room. And for a few days it was almost a joke. We'd knock on his door and ask him how he was—"Are you dead yet, Grandad?" "Go away." "Still in the land of the living?" "Leave me alone." And we'd go in anyway, and we'd find him sitting on the floor in the corner of the room, with his eyes closed. Concentrating. Willing himself to death.

I was the one who found his body. I had gone upstairs to bring him his tea. He was still sitting in the corner, and it was only when I touched his shoulder to get his attention that I discovered he was rigid and cold. I was seventeen, I was in a prime age of my own.

No one could quite believe that he'd managed to do it, that he'd actually found a way to die. Even at the funeral we half-expected to find out it was some macabre joke, that my grandfather would suddenly leap out of the coffin and tell us it was just a bit of fun. And when we burned him, the smell of burnt orange was so powerful we all had to leave.

The press got hold of the story, of course. And we were idiots, we couldn't see the implications of what Grandfather had done—we spoke to the journalists quite freely. Most people thought it had to be a scam of some sort, that we were telling this impossible story of life over death to make money or get famous. A few people said that maybe it *was* true—but if so, Grandfather had denied the grace of God, and thrown his mercy back in his face. We should all despise him, even pity him a little—we shouldn't waste any more time on him, though. And then that changed, when the body count started to climb.

There were reports of a woman in China who'd died at the age of eighty-three. No one took it too seriously—China was a very long way away. But then a seventy-one-year-old was found dead in Germany, and there was another death closer to home, an eighty-seven-year-old man from London. All of them were elderly, of course, and had been very sick—maybe they too had had enough of life, maybe these deaths were blessings from God, miracles of relief? The President of the United States had a stroke at the age of sixty-seven when he was playing golf. He refused to believe he was in pain, and with tears in his eyes, and wincing through gritted teeth, he told reporters that he was perfectly all right and there was nothing to worry about—and when he jumped to his feet on a live telecast to demonstrate this to the stock markets he triggered a second stroke that polished him off altogether.

That's when the panic started. There were countless suicides—but were they really suicides? Weren't they just people unable to believe that the natural order of life had shifted, and wanting to check for themselves? There were murders—but again, how genuinely murderous were they, these men who killed their wives, these wives who killed their husbands, these parents who killed their children?—killing everyone they had ever loved in utter incredulity that this was what they could now do. My mother was out shopping when she saw a fifty-three-year-old woman in a frenzy drinking bleach in the supermarket. "I can't smell it," she was screaming, "I can *feel* it!" Outside our house a thirteen-year-old boy was knocked off his bike by a car, and he didn't get up again.

And I remember how I locked myself in my bedroom and I took out the sharpest knife from my mother's best dinner collection, and I was seventeen so I knew it shouldn't hurt, it mustn't hurt—and how I drew the blade across the palm of my hand and the blood ran out, and just for a moment I thought there was no pain, I felt no pain at all, and somehow I had fixed the world and put everything right again and I could smell aniseed.

It's been twenty years since my grandfather died, since he triggered the plague of ordinary deaths all around the world. The plague has never stopped, really—but the authorities have stopped calling it one, and the panic has calmed, and there's an acceptance of sorts. Life has changed its parameters and its meaning, and we can never get the old world back again, no matter how much we pray. We had something magical and precious, and perhaps we took it for granted—and the slender thread that had sustained it had been wilfully and selfishly snapped by one elderly man who wasn't able to appreciate life and the riches it offered. They looked for scapegoats. Thank God my family fled in time. We changed our names, and ran to all the corners of the globe, and we haven't spoken since. It's safer there's no contact, just in case someone spots a link between us and works out who we are. I don't know what my sister or my father or my mother are called now. I don't know whether they are still alive.

For a while I couldn't get close to anyone. I got a job, and I kept to myself. I lived in a bedsit and I ate and I slept and I went to work and like my grandfather I wished that I were dead, but I never quite wished hard enough. And then one day I met your mother, and she rescued me, she gave me a reason to live. And we got married and we had you, and now I have two reasons to live—two reasons, that's twice as much as some people! She held our brand new baby to her breast and I asked her whether giving birth had hurt, and she said, no, no, it had been a miracle. And we both looked at you and you were so very small and vulnerable, and it seemed that anything out there could seize you in its jaws and tear at you and kill you, and we knew that one day something would. My wife, the best and sweetest woman in the world, the one who'd smelled stewed apricots when she was a little girl, said that she hated that old bastard who had changed the world and condemned our child to a life of suffering, and she prayed he was burning in Hell. And I agreed. How could I not?

I sometimes like to pretend that life is better now. That God granted us a gift, but he hadn't stopped to think whether any of us wanted it or not. Whether my grandfather had wanted it. And that even to be living in a paradise is a kind of tyranny, if it isn't a paradise you're allowed to destroy. You're in pain now, little man, and I'm sorry. But at least you know the truth. That this pain is all there is, that you won't get time off for good behaviour—you'll suffer this year, and you'll suffer the next, and you'll just go on suffering more and more and worse and worse until everything stops. There's a freedom to that, isn't there? And a consistency that's reassuring.

They used to say that when our bodies had no more things to smell, that we'd go to Heaven. And that Heaven was a wonderful place where we would be happy forever more, and there'd be no more death or hurt, just warmth and serenity. Except, of course, on our prime ages. On our prime ages we would be inflicted with all the agonies of Hell everlasting.

I don't know that I much believe in God. (Don't tell your mother.) But if Grandfather broke the world down here, maybe it got broken up there too. I can but hope.

The last time I saw Grandfather alive—I've never told anyone this. Not even my family ever knew.

I went up to bring him his tea. I didn't bother to knock, he never answered anyway. He was sitting in the corner of his room, his eyes closed. "Still alive, Grandad?" I asked—because I loved Grandfather, but I was seventeen and cocky. I touched his shoulder, and he wasn't rigid, and he wasn't cold. He opened his eyes and he looked at me.

"Please make it stop," he said. He *croaked.* "The burnt orange. I could live forever, I could take as much life as God wants. If it weren't for the burnt orange." He was crying. He was actually crying. You know that crying doesn't help the orange go away, little man. It just makes your face wetter.

"Please," he said. "For pity's sake." So I helped him, for the sake of pity. My grandfather didn't will his life to stop. He hadn't the strength for it. He was just a weak old man stinking of fruit. But I was young, and I was strong, and what fear does death have when it's so very far away? I willed it to stop. I willed it all to stop. And it did.

There will come a time, little man, and it won't be so very long off in the scheme of things. When you'll be strong, and I'll be weak, and I'll need your pity and your love, and your courage to look death in the face for me. For me, and for your mother too. And you'll have finished teething, your teeth will be grown full size and they'll be sharp like daggers.

I love you. You'll get used to the pain, I promise.

And the old woman says:

- *Prime numbers are safe. The seven times table is considerably more dangerous. Find out why in* **Suffer Little Children** *(story 35, page 575).*
- *Come celebrate another little boy's birthday at* **The Swimming Pool Party** *(story 15, page 251).*
- *The people who kill themselves in this story do so to test the limits of natural order. For a man who has to face the full reality of suicide and the impact it makes, turn to* **Ice in the Bedroom** *(story 7, page 101).*
- *I don't like burnt orange. If the taste of cherry tart and custard and turkey and hot buttered toast sound more appealing to you, drink deep at* **Taste Me** *(story 75, page 1301).*
- *Watch the laws that govern our world shift once more in* **Dumb Lucy** *(story 46, page 771). Maybe they'll become something you like.*

80
YESYES

THE CHILDREN ARE PLAYING on the yesyes board again. It's the only explanation. It's true, it has been getting darker in the afternoons, but never this dark, and never this early. And there's a thickness to the dark too, something that the streetlamps can't penetrate. It seems to hang off the windows rather, it seems to stick there fast.

Mrs Burgess promised she'd speak to the children. She didn't promise she'd stop them. She said she's had a word, so they could at least give us fair warning, so we could lock up tight and be on guard. It even worked a couple of times. A scrap of paper under the door, and the words scrawled there, blunt and untidy: "They're coming."—Well, what do you expect, they're not ones for writing much, they're only kids after all. But no warning today. Mrs Burgess has failed us. Not that Mrs Burgess should have any influence. She's only the caretaker. It's not like she's their mother.

There was a new tenant a month or two back, he turned up to the residents' meeting we have on Monday nights. He was from the second floor, I think, that's where they tend to house the newbies, you can't get much further from the children than that. But even he had heard the children, racing down the corridors at all hours, he thought at first they were rats until he heard their laughter and their nursery rhymes and their skipping rope games. And he asked, who *is* their mother then, is there anyone in authority we can complain to? It wasn't his fault, poor man, he wasn't to know—but we couldn't help but smile! He didn't like that. He said the children needed discipline. He said that if their own parents wouldn't give them discipline, then he would. I think he was showing off in front of his wife—yes, she was there too, and it's rare for us to have couples living in these apartments. I think they were newlyweds, it was rather sweet to see how close they sat together, how much they were in love—sweet and only a little bit nauseating. Anyway, Mrs Burgess advised him not to go looking for the children. She said no good would come of it. But he refused to listen. He was firm and manly, and his wife squeezed his arm and looked so proud. We never saw him again. Look, it doesn't mean anything bad happened to him, he could simply have moved to another tenement block. It happens. His wife, though, she still comes to the Monday night meetings. She sits at the back all alone. She never says much.

Yes, it's a yesyes night, for definite now, no fooling. The signs are all there. The darkness is like black liquid now, waves of it rolling and splashing against the window. Every few seconds a thump as another surge breaks against the glass. And the electrics are fizzing. It's not a good fizzing, like, I don't know, champagne on a summer's evening. It's bad fizzing, like a housefly spinning round on its back, a giant housefly, desperate and dying. I didn't used to like the fizzing, but you can get used to anything. The lights flicker, it's too hard to read; I could put on the radio but when the children are playing, all the songs that come out are sad. I sit in my armchair, I close my eyes. The thump at the window, the fizzing all around, it's quite soothing if you let it be. Close my eyes tight enough, I can pretend it's nice.

Sometimes I get jealous of the couples. That one we used to have on the second floor, and there's an elderly couple a few doors down from me, I think, I can sometimes hear them talking to each other, and I heard there was another couple somewhere who are gay or something, but that may just be a rumour. Sometimes I get jealous, it would be nice to have someone to talk to. Someone to reassure me when the nights are so black. But then I think—what if *he* were the one who needed reassuring? That would be annoying. A relationship, I think, what it comes down to, is someone needing to make the other feel better, and you've only got a fifty-fifty chance the one who's going to be sucked dry won't be you. It would be nice to be with someone now. It would be nice to have someone to touch. But maybe they would persuade me there's something wrong with the electrics fizzing, they'd make me realise I'm scared after all. I'm better off lonely. I'm better off like this forever.

I'm beginning to doze off, to think that with my eyes this tight I might sleep through the whole of yesyes night after all—and then there's a knock at the door, and for a moment I hope I might have dreamed it, but no, there it is again, unmistakable, there is someone wanting me to open up, and in a moment I'm alert, and the sudden tensing of my body makes my head spin. "Who is it?" I ask. And I think, is it one of the other residents, have they not made it back to their own apartment in time, do they need shelter? In which case there's only one neighbourly thing to do—and I think, but is it something *else*, something that's been summoned by the yesyes board, isn't that just why we keep our doors locked? And my neck begins to itch, just like it always does when I'm really frightened. "Who is it?" I ask again, but if they weren't going to answer before there's no reason they should answer now, and sure enough, they don't; "Who is it?" I try one last time, and my neck is prickling now with hives, it's all I can do not to scratch but I know once I start scratching the itch gets worse than ever.

There's no answer. There's no sound. There's no more knocking. And maybe they've gone, maybe the danger has passed. I walk to the door, I walk on tiptoes so that they can't hear I'm in, and that's silly because I realise I've just been calling out to them. But it feels good to be quiet, ever so hushed now, not a noise—I put my eye to the spyglass, but not too close, just in case something can reach through the wooden door and pull me through. And there's nothing to be seen.

The empty corridor. The lights flickering out there too, the stained wallpaper of the corridor wall lit up every other second before being winked back into darkness once more.

I'll open the door. I'll check. If I open the door, it'll only take a moment and it'll prove there's nothing to be afraid of. If I don't open the door, I'll believe there might be—I'll never be able to relax, I'll never relax *again*, quite probably—not for years and years and years. I'll open the door. I'll open the door. I fumble at the upper bolt. And then the lower bolt too, good. I'll open the door, it'll only be for a moment, and I'll even pop my head out into the corridor and look up and down it just to make extra certain. I can do that, and it might elongate the moment, but it still won't take *too* long, and that way I'll know for sure. All three bolts are free now, there's just the chain, and that's the chain off, and there's the key, and that's it, that's the key turned. And I ignore the burning of my neck, after this I'll put on some camomile lotion, that'll cool it down. And I put my hand to the doorknob and I'm about to pull it open—there's another knock, the other side, just like before.

And I've come this far, and there's no going back now. I open the door.

The moment I open it the lights in the corridor wink out again, and it's only for a few seconds, but it means I can't right away see who's there. And maybe that's a good thing. Maybe those few seconds' grace allow me to hold my nerve. Because I'm telling you, if I were confronted by a figure that very moment, regardless of who it might be, I think I'd have a heart attack—I'm not breathing right, the air's going in normally, but I'm not remembering how to puff it back out. Just a few seconds of blackness for me to adjust, to prepare, to get myself together.

The child is very short, it's no wonder I couldn't see him through the spy glass. Blond hair, blue eyes, fat ruddy cheeks, actually I can't tell whether it's a boy or a girl. "What do you want?" I say, perhaps a little too gruffly, I instantly regret it—maybe the child's frightened, even children can be frightened I expect. But it doesn't seem to take offence. It breaks into a smile, a nice warming smile, and shows me a mouth full of perfectly white teeth. "I don't know what you want," I say, and I think then the child is going to reply, it opens its mouth wider—but all that comes out is a little yawn, as if it's up long past its bedtime. And I don't know, there's something about that yawn, about how light and carefree it is, how very *innocent*, that makes me feel better. The child smiles. I smile back. It offers me its hand. I don't hesitate for long. I give my hand in return. I feel skin against skin for the first time in—I don't know how long, have I ever been touched before, I can't remember? It's smooth. And the child's delicate little hand is lost within the clumsy meat of my own.

The child smiles wider. And pulls me out into the corridor.

And I wonder whether I could resist. It should be easy, to tear my big hand away from that little one—but I don't want to resist, skin against skin is such a wonderful sensation, and I'll go wherever this child is taking me—moving so fast now, for all the fact its legs are so short I still struggle to keep up—and the child is giggling now, it's excited and so am I. And maybe I could pull loose, and maybe I couldn't—because now as I try to think of it I can't tell where my hand stops and the child's hand begins, it's buried deep within my palm and I might as well try to pull off one of my own fingers. And I don't care. I don't even care when we reach the stairway, and the child pulls me upwards. I have never gone upwards before. I have never wanted to go upwards, I live on the eighteenth floor (I think, or it may even be the nineteenth)—whichever, it's high in the sky, it's high enough for me, and yet the child wants me to go up, and we go up together.

Up and up, and round and round—the lights fizzing all the time, flicking on and off so fast that when I look at the child it doesn't seem to be moving at all, it's a series of still photographs one after the other—and I'm in all these photographs too, I'm not moving either, I can feel only a sense of static moments one after the other, I'm not moving, I'm not *going* anywhere, I have already *been*. And yet there's giggling still from both of us. Even though I feel so nauseous and I can't tell whether it's the altitude making me dizzy, or that the staircase is spiralling so wild, and getting more *narrow* too, surely; the walls are now hemming us in on all sides, and I can see why the children live up here, only a child can fit through these cramped spaces. And I'm going to tell the child I can't go any further, I'm too big, I'll get stuck—I begin to panic—I'll get wedged here, unable to go forward or go back, I'll be stuck fast like a cork in a bottle and I'll never pop out, I'll die here and no one will be able to get past until my body rots. But the child squeezes my hand, the child is with me, and there's a promise made, if I die I won't die alone—and on I push. And I think of Mrs Burgess, who claimed she spoke to the children—Mrs Burgess with her fat hips, she's such a liar, she could never have made it up here! I'll never trust Mrs Burgess again—but I have to laugh, Mrs Burgess is such a sweet old lady, she always has a smile for everyone, I can't stay cross with her for long.

And then—free. My body groaning with relief at all the sudden space it can find—so much space, for arms and legs to move in, for a head to turn, whatever will I do with it all! And I breathe out again, and I hadn't realised I'd been sucking in my stomach quite so much or how good it can feel to let it go.

I am in an apartment—it is furnished the same as mine, one armchair, one table, toilet in the corner, one window looking out at nothing. Here the children live, and there are half a dozen of them, I think, or maybe a couple more—they don't even bother with the electrics up here, and though there are candles dotted about the place I can't yet make an accurate count. The children turn to look at me; all of them, I think, though it's hard to be sure; they are wide-eyed and apprehensive, as if they've been caught by a grown-up doing something naughty.

"Now, now," I say, "What have you all been up to? Wouldn't your parents be ashamed?" And I'm not sure what I say has the right impact, so I lift my free hand and wag a finger at them.

Silence. Then, one of the children speaks. A thin, reedy voice. I still can't tell whether it's made by a boy or a girl.

"There's a message for you."

And with that he—she?—moves to one side. And reveals there on the table framed by four candles, one at each corner, the yesyes board.

I want to scratch at my neck so very much. "But I don't know anyone dead! I've never met anyone who's dead!" Though I wonder if that's an exaggeration—are my parents dead yet? Or my grandparents, even? I can't remember.

At this the boy shrugs. I *think* it's a boy. The eyes are wide and soft like a girl's but there are bristles on the chin, it makes this child look a little older than the others. "There's a message," he says again, and he invites me to sit at the table.

I shake my head. I turn to go. But I can't see how to leave—there's no door, I can't see the door. I turn around again, back to the table, there's the yesyes board on it, and it's waiting for me—all the letters around the edge, the little glass planchette and I cannot, I will not touch it. And then I feel my child by my side, and he's stroking at my fingers with his, he's soothing me gently like a lover, and I look at him, and he smiles bravely, and I smile too. My other hand is taken, and I turn my head and see that another child is hanging on to it, and for a moment I feel only resentment, I don't know this child, it's not *mine*—but it too is smiling, and so I love it with all my heart.

All the children join hands. We form a ring, and it's like a big game, and I'm the only adult sticking out, tall and awkward. All the children, save for the little boy with the stubble who sits at the table in my place.

"He's coming," he tells me.

He flutters his fingers for a moment, like a concert pianist about to launch into a concerto. And then, with a delicacy that is heartbreaking, he puts the tip of his forefinger against the planchette. A momentary jerk, like an old car juddering at ignition—and then the planchette is away, sliding across to the letters with practised ease, as if the boy has done this a thousand times before. I suppose he has.

"Adam," he says.

"I don't know an Adam."

"Adam Purcell."

"I don't know an Adam Purcell."

"Adam Purcell, your husband."

And yes, of course, *that* Adam Purcell. I was married to an Adam Purcell, wasn't I? He was alive, I'm pretty sure, and then—what, I suppose he died. Died of cancer, yes. Or died in a car crash. Or died falling from a horse. How easy a thing life is, and how easy it can end.

"What does he want?"

The boy spells out the words with no expression, with no anticipation of what might come next, or what they might mean. "I still love you," he says.

I lick my lips. They're so dry. I want to scratch at my neck, but my hands are taken, lip licking is the best I can do. "I love you too," I say, and in a moment it's true, it's as if something is unlocked inside me somewhere—

—And I can see Adam Purcell. It's a jumble of memories, I assume they're memories—I remember our wedding day, and everyone dressed for the rain and carrying umbrellas, but at the last moment it was sunny after all—and I remember our first meeting, approaching me across a crowded room and telling me I was beautiful—and I suppose these memories must be in the wrong order, because that ought to have happened before the wedding surely? And little memories, breakfasts in bed, supermarket runs and watching TV, holidays in the Cotswolds, giving him a thick woollen scarf for Christmas, kissing, some disastrous barbecue, kissing again, touching, making love.

And his death, what was it? Died in a fire. Died in a freak yachting accident. Died after an unsuccessful trapeze act.

I don't want this. I want to go. And I don't know why. I love this man, this man on the end of the yesyes board, I know I love him and I know I want to run away. I pull at my left hand, at my right, and the children hold on to me firm.

"I'm sorry," says the boy. "If I made you unhappy."

"You didn't make me unhappy," I tell my husband.

"I'm sorry," says the boy. "I wanted to join you. But I couldn't."

"Of course," I say. And I don't know what he means.

"It's been hard," says the boy. "Without you."

"Yes," I whisper, and I can feel I'm crying.

"Forgive me. I have fallen in love again."

I don't know what to say to that. So I say nothing.

"Helen?" says the boy, and I don't know who Helen is, and then I do.

"Yes," I say.

"I want to move on," says the boy. "I need to move on."

"Yes."

"Give me your blessing."

"Yes."

"Thank you."

"Yes."

And this isn't how it was meant to be. The tears are streaming now, and if it weren't for the children holding me up I'm sure I would collapse, but they're hanging on, they're stronger than they look. Stronger than me. Stronger than I ever was—and I've only just remembered him but I can't let my husband go so easily, can I? My husband who was there to reassure me, to make me feel better—my life, my love, my saviour. Though he didn't save me in the end.

And still, still, I can't remember how he died. Did he hang himself with a rope? Did he hang himself with that thick woollen scarf?

My neck flares again, and I can't bear it, the itch is so great. And I pull my hands free at last, and I think there's a tearing sound as skin breaks from skin, I think I feel pain, and the children to my sides shriek. But I've no thoughts for that—there's only the itching, and I dig my nails into the deep groove around my throat and I scratch so hard and there's a relief.

The circle is broken. The children look confused. They put thumbs in their mouths, they stare about scared and wild-eyed. The little boy at the table is weeping. I elbow him aside. I put my finger on the planchette.

"Don't go," I spell out.

And there's nothing in response, am I too late?

Has my saying don't go *made* him go, that would be petty, wouldn't it, was I married to a petty man? Who knows?

"Tell me," and I'm saying it out loud. "Tell me you love me. Tell me you needed me. Tell me," and I'm trying to remember so hard, and it's hurting my head, I'm sifting through all the memories I never knew I had, and wondering how I could have done without them so long.

I whisper, "Tell me. Did we have children? Did we ever have a little boy or girl?"

There's no movement from the planchette, and I realise I should have moved it with my fingers, that wherever he is Adam cannot hear my voice. And he's not there, he's not there, and this is stupid, you can't talk to *ghosts*. And then, slowly, the planchette stutters back into life, it drags itself slowly over to the letters.

"You're not Helen," it spells.

I stare at the yesyes board. And I can feel the cold hostility coming off it. And then, spelling out the letters one final time.

"Helen," it says, "would know."

And the wooden board is just a wooden board, and it has nothing more to tell me.

I look across at the children, hoping for some comfort, maybe a little sympathy even? But there's only one child left. The boy with the stubbly chin, and I can see how handsome he is, what a fine man he was intended to be.

I gaze at him, and he holds my gaze, fearless but I think in no way accusing. And there's a name to that face, if I could just recall it. And I look away, I look away, I actually do that, I take my eyes off my child again, and it's only for a split second. And he's gone. And the name has gone too.

I sit on my own in the room for an hour or two. Maybe much, much longer. There is no sound. I wish there were some fizzing from the electrics, it'd keep me company.

I look out of the window at last, and the darkness is thinning, and the night is done. Outside, rows and rows of tenement blocks—all dark and grey, all the same, stretching on as far as I can see.

It's time to move on. My husband has managed it. My son, I can only hope, he has done it too. And out there, maybe, there's someone I can touch, there's someone who can make this cold world feel just a little warmer.

I pack away the children's game into its box, neatly. I blow out the candles. I don't own much to take—a coat, my shoes, a long scarf to keep away the chill. I go downstairs, all the way down, as far as I can go, and step out into the lifting dawn.

And the old woman says:

- *Dying from an unsuccessful trapeze act sounds like a very spectacular way to go. Turn to* **Clown Envy** *(story 41, page 685).*
- *To read how to curb the excitement of naughty children, turn to* **The Eighth** *(story 8, page 127).*
- *And if they require corporal punishment, consider* **Suffer Little Children** *(story 35, page 575).*
- *Grief is a form of obstinacy, it's a refusal to let go. Consider this, and turn to* **Good Grief** *(story 39, page 647).*
- *If, try as you might, you can't let go—if your love is just too strong—turn to* **101 Heartbeats** *(story 101, page 1695).*

There is a map to this maze
hidden somewhere
in the book.
Finding it would make
everything so much simpler.

81
DETACHED

I DON'T USUALLY GET TO work on kids. I don't know why. Kids are just as fragile as their parents, after all—even more so, maybe, the way they fling themselves at the world so hard as if nothing is going to break them.

I suppose, with kids, it's harder to be dispassionate. Adults, I think, generally respond well to frank honesty, even when the news is bad, *especially* when the news is bad. Because when they're faced with mortality, they don't want it clouded by hysteria. They don't want my sympathy. I'll say 'I'm sorry', but it's a matter of form, it acts as a sort of verbal stepping stone between the verdict and the inevitable questions that follow: the how long untils, the will it hurts, the is there anything to be dones? And there's panic, I'm sure, but all that comes after, that's nothing to do with me; if I'm calm, then they're calm, and I believe that they're grateful for that, and the moment I pass judgment and sentence them to death I treat them like equals, I give them the illusion we're all in this together. And in that togetherness, as we seem to collude against the illness and the suffering to come, I've surprised them, I've shown them how dignified they can be. And that dignity is something they can look back on and aspire to in the darker days ahead.

Kids don't do that. Kids are unpredictable. Some cry, some call for their parents (because their parents can fix everything), some ignore me altogether and stare out of the window, stare down at their socks. Sometimes they laugh. They even laugh. What's up with that?

I know people who say there is no greater tragedy than the death of a child, and some of them are even quite intelligent, some even quite good doctors. They talk about all that wasted potential. I, respectfully, disagree. I see only people who haven't done anything yet. I would far rather mourn an elderly man, say, who has spent a lifetime learning through experience and achievement—just think how much further he could have gone! The cure for cancer isn't going to be discovered by a twelve-year-old, it'll be discovered by an adult long in the tooth with the weight of years on his shoulders, by an adult lucky enough to get as clever as he can be and not be felled by some silly disease or another along the way. I suppose it's just a different way of looking at it. I can't mourn a child. It'd be like mourning an embryo or a pupa.

I don't mourn the elderly either. I don't mourn anyone. But if I had to mourn, it'd be the elderly, I think, in principle.

And when I first met Steve Herbert I saw nothing to be impressed by. He had flung himself hard against the world, he'd had an accident on his bicycle, or scooter, or some such thing, and the accident no doubt had been his fault, and there he was in the emergency room grinning from ear to ear like it was all some big adventure. I suppose it was, at that; his whole body had been X-rayed to check for broken bones, and I imagine the sort of kid who gets his kicks from scooters is probably one who'd get kicks from X-ray machines too. There were no bones broken, he'd escaped with bruising. I didn't know why I'd been called in to look. Nurse Johnson showed me the X-rays; she didn't tell me what else they had found during the examination, she said she'd let me see for myself. And then she looked on, hopefully, as if I would tell her that she was wrong, as if my second opinion could make everything bad go away.

At first I didn't think it was a real cockroach. For a start, cockroaches aren't as big as that—certainly not in this country, at any rate. And secondly, how had it got inside? The kid couldn't have swallowed it, he'd have choked. I assumed it must be some strange growth on the heart that just looked like a cockroach. But then I checked against successive X-rays and I could see that the wings had moved, that the mandibles had flexed somewhat—this was a giant cockroach, about the size of my fist, and it was clinging on hard to the boy's pericardium, its wings obscuring the whole of the right auricle, its pincers piercing both of the atria deep. And it was alive.

I asked the boy whether he'd noticed any discomfort in his chest. He told me he didn't, much; sometimes, if he went running, he'd get out of breath, he'd start wheezing; recently, if he lay in bed on one side for too long, he'd have the same problem. But there was no discomfort, really; certainly, no pain. I told him I was surprised. That there was a large hostile parasite fixed fast to his insides that was lacerating his vital organs. That I had never seen such a thing before, and wasn't sure there was much I could do about it, and the chances were he was going to die.

He didn't cry. I'll give him that. He didn't ignore me, and he didn't laugh. Nurse Johnson said his parents had been called for, and I asked Steve Herbert whether he'd rather wait until they got to the hospital before we discussed the matter further, and he thought about it, and he said that he would.

As I say, I don't usually get to work on kids.

His parents were dreadful. The calm frankness didn't work on them at all, it was tears and pleading right from the start. I knew the type; had I been telling them they were the ones about to die, they'd have been as dignified as could be, they'd have kept all that fear bottled up for form's sake. But for their child, though, they just couldn't rein the emotions in. The mother began to sob, and it was quiet enough, but somehow all the more irritating for that, all the more embarrassing—and the father kept on saying, "But why Steve? It should be one of us! Why isn't it one of us?" And, privately, I agreed. If only it had been, everything would have been so much less dramatic.

I admired the boy. He was patient with them both. He took his mother's hand and held it. To his father he said, "I'm sure the doctor will do his very best." I said I would.

The parents calmed down enough so that I could run them through the various options available. We could put Steve on a course of radiotherapy, and try to kill the cockroach with radiation. Or there were various drugs we could administer with chemo. Both treatments would have side effects, of course—we could attack the cells of the invading pest, but inevitably some healthy cells belonging to the patient would be destroyed as well. Or we could try direct surgery, but I pointed out that there were severe risks to that—from the pictures we could see that the roach had punctured the heart in several places and the tissue had actually grown over it, and that pulling the creature free might cause extensive damage, that ironically it might be the very presence of the insect keeping Steve alive, blocking his wounds, keeping the heart beating—"Rip it out of him!" the mother positively snarled, "just get that fucking thing out of my son!" And the father nodded, and the boy shrugged assent, and that was that.

Before the operation I read up on insect anatomy, and it didn't take long; they really are remarkably simple creatures. I had removed all sorts of lumps and bumps from inside people's chests, but I had never performed a dictyoptectomy before—I saw no reason to tell the Herbert family that. We opened up the chest, and there was the cockroach, bigger than I'd even expected, it had wrapped itself right around the heart and now that it was exposed to the light it unfurled itself, and opened its wings wide, and quivered. I had no desire to harm the cockroach, but it wasn't my patient. I cut through its legs with a laser scalpel, until I felt the insect had loosened its grip sufficiently so I could lift off the bulk of it without much force—still, though, it found a way to cling firm, it hugged into the heart with an obstinacy that seemed almost possessive, and when at last I managed to pull it free it came out with a sick sucking sound. Then I had to remove the leg stumps that were still embedded in the myocardial layer; I had not appreciated how deeply the cockroach had punctured the heart until I pulled that first stump with a pair of forceps—out it came, long and sharp and wet, and quivering still, as if there was life in it yet, as if this weren't just some reflex action. The holes that had been gouged in the heart now seemed big and black, but there was no blood, and for all the tissue damage I hoped that they might heal and that young Steve might affect a full recovery.

Steve was very proud of the new stitches on his chest. He said he couldn't wait to show them off to his friends at school. The skin was swollen and inflamed, and I could tell it must be sore, but the boy was having none of it, he told me he felt fine, he thanked me for all my hard work. The parents demanded to know whether their son was cured now, whether he was going to be all right, and I told them I didn't know. He'd have to come back in a week so we could X-ray him and find out. The parents looked sulky and betrayed. Steve gave me a smile and said he would look forward to it.

I was annoyed that Steve brought his parents back for the consultation, but he was only twelve, and I suppose he needed someone to drive him. I showed them all the X-ray. "This," I said, "is what I was hoping not to see." I explained that we had tried to remove the whole cockroach, but it seemed we'd been unsuccessful—part of the insect had been left behind. And now the pictures clearly showed that what looked like hairy twigs were poking out of the gashes in Steve's heart; one of the legs had grown back so fast that it had even begun to taper out at the end into some sort of carapace. In only a week we could see that the cockroach was rebuilding itself, and at this speed I didn't doubt it'd be at its full size once more by the end of the month.

I pointed out the positives. The heart was still basically healthy; if it weren't, the cockroach would have no means for sustaining itself. The shock of the operation alone would have caused a weaker heart to fail, but Steve's was strong, and that could only be a good thing for the long battle ahead of us. Mrs Herbert cried again, of course; she didn't like the use of that word, 'battle'.

We bombarded the cockroach with radiation, but if anything it seemed to thrive beneath it; it grew at still greater speed, and even under X-ray I could see how its body glowed with a new smooth sheen. I had read, of course, that a roach could outsit a nuclear war, but I had still hoped that a concentrated blast would have been too much for it. We pumped it full of poisons, some of them highly experimental, and the roach seemed only to get fatter. It seemed to me that with each X-ray it gazed out with even greater triumph; it was fine; it was sitting pretty; it would squat in its home forever. Steve wasn't doing as well. His hair fell out, and his skin got pasty and paper thin. I asked him if he was in much pain, and he would smile at me, and I could see that his gums were bleeding, and he assured me it was nothing he couldn't handle. I could see it wasn't true. He'd make jokes with me, one time he said his veins must be more acid now than blood, and he laughed, and when he did so he couldn't help it, I saw he winced terribly with the effort. He told me, when I pressed him, that he threw up a lot. That was the worst thing, he said. He hated all that throwing up. He hated all the mess. He hated being a burden on his parents. They had enough to worry about already.

One day I had to tell Steve that we'd failed. There was nothing more I could do for him. We would have to let nature take its course. The parents wept, both of them this time; both got angry. Steve hugged them, and told them it was going to be all right. He told them that he'd grown to love his cockroach. When he tried to sleep at night he could hear it hissing to him, deep inside; he thought it was trying to encourage him on, or just trying to communicate; he thought maybe it was lonely too, and confused, and just wanted to have a friend. He said it was all right. The cockroach was a part of him now, and he called it Tony. Steve said, "Please, I want to speak to the doctor alone." His parents left.

He said to me, "Don't feel too bad, Doc." And I wanted to tell him he was mistaken, I didn't feel bad at all, this was the sort of thing I did every day. But my eyes were brimming with tears. I told him I was so sorry. Had it been a giant housefly on his heart, or some sort of woodlouse perhaps, then we'd have beaten the bugger, I was sure. But cockroaches are such tenacious beasts. He said, "We did our best, didn't we?" And he offered me his hand, and kids never offer you their hand, and I accepted it, and he shook mine, strong and hard. "You take care now," he said to me.

I never saw Steve Herbert again. And I like to think that maybe he's still all right. Maybe he found a way to coexist with that cockroach perfectly happily. Maybe the two of them are out there, and both thriving. I suppose that's unlikely.

I went back home that night, and my wife said to me, what's wrong? She can read me like a book. And I said that nothing was wrong, on the contrary. I told her that I'd been thinking it through, and I'd decided we should have a kid. I wanted to have a kid. I wanted a kid who was just like Steve Herbert, who was the bravest kid I'd ever known. I thought my wife would be happy. When we'd first got married it was the biggest hurdle, for a while I thought she'd divorce me over it. She'd wanted a baby, I didn't. I didn't see the point of them. "I see the point of them now," I said. But she told me it was too late. She'd got used to the marriage we had already, she'd grown to like the compromise, she had made it work for her. I couldn't now just come along and open up wounds that had healed over. She told me, you can't meet one brave child and assume all children are going to be brave, it doesn't work like that. Any more than it had when I'd met children I'd despised, and had assumed ours would be a child I would despise, that was the excuse I had given her. That's not what people are, she said, you can't predict them. I begged. I actually begged. "Please let me have a brave little boy," I said. And she said she was too old now, anyway; she was forty-five; I was a doctor, didn't I know that the chance of birth defects rose substantially in older mothers? And she missed the point, as she does so often—that's what I *wanted*. I wanted a child with birth defects. I wanted my wife to drink a lot whilst pregnant, and smoke, even though she didn't smoke already, maybe she could start? I wanted a child who would be brave. I wanted a child who would grow up needing to be brave.

I said I never saw Steve Herbert again, and that's true. I did phone his house a couple of times. He didn't answer, once it was his mother, the other his dad. I didn't want to ask how their son was, I thought that would be impertinent, it wouldn't suggest quite the right level of dispassion, I didn't say anything and waited until they got cross and hung up, and then I'd put the phone down. Oh, and one time I parked outside his house. I was a little drunk, I think, and I sat in the car and waited to see whether he'd come out. And then I realised it was late and he'd probably be asleep, he was only a little kid, so I thought I'd wait there till morning, I'd wait until he left the house to go to school. I just wanted to make sure he was all right. I wouldn't have even spoken to him, probably. But I stayed there till gone noon, and he never emerged. And that doesn't mean anything, he might not have had school that day, it might have been the holidays, kids are always on holidays it seems to me, how should I know when school holidays are?

Over the couple of years I had three more patients who had cockroaches on their hearts. They were all adults, they'd lived their lives, one of them was an old man, what was he still hanging on for? They were all very upset when I broke the news. None of them had cockroaches even half the size of Steve Herbert's cockroach. I told them, what they had was *nothing*; I'd once met a twelve-year-old with a cockroach who was twice as brave as them! They didn't take much comfort from this, they were scared like little babies, and, to be fair to them, they had reason to be, not a one of them survived surgery.

My time will come. Of course it will, and for all my experience, I have no idea what to expect. I'll be there with some doctor, and he'll ask me to sit down because it's always better to hear about death if you're sitting down, and he'll be the one to break the news to me. He'll show me the X-ray, and maybe I'll look at my own cankered innards with the same dispassion I felt for everybody else's, maybe I'll assess my own chances for survival with calm frankness. I now know how to behave. I'll behave like Steve Herbert. Steve Herbert has shown me the way. And I want a cockroach. No, I want two cockroaches. I want to do better than Steve Herbert. He was only a little boy, I have to be better. I want two cockroaches, and they'll be nestled around my heart, one each side, my heart will be enveloped between their embrace, maybe they'll be spooning? No. I want an egg, I want to see on the X-ray a big white egg, my heart has gone altogether and what's hanging there is just this egg, and it's starting to crack, you can see it's already hatching, and maybe, maybe, from the crack you can glimpse the odd leg wriggle out towards life and freedom. I want to hatch a dozen cockroaches, more. I'll be a father after all. And I'll listen to the doctor deliver the judgment with detachment, always such detachment, and I'll thank him, and explain to him why I think in this instance further treatment would be unnecessary. And I'll phone my wife, and tell her the good news.

And the old woman says:

- *All brave little boys deserve a trip to the circus. Turn to* **Clown Envy** *(story 41, page 685).*
- *Sometimes it's not the patient who needs to be brave, it's the loved one who's left behind. Turn to* **The Grand Adventure** *(story 1, page 19).*
- *But is it really brave to have a stoical acceptance of death? Isn't it just another form of denial, of making it feel safe and comfortable? Consider* **The Death Room** *(story 27, page 453).*
- *I think bravery is overrated. Why not rail against the injustice of pain, of disease, of mortality? There is a very frightened little girl in* **The Bathtub** *(story 61, page 1037). Find out all the things that upset her.*
- *The parents in* **The Urn** *(story 30, page 485) try their very hardest to be brave. See how well they do.*

82
Bobbo

I'M NOT SAYING I'M A better writer than Robert Aickman, but when you read my horror stories you at least can tell what's going on. If I say it's a vampire story, you'll have no doubt who the vampire is; if it's set in a haunted house, you'll be guaranteed spooks and ghouls aplenty. When I first read Aickman, many years ago now, I didn't even realise it *was* horror to start with. A friend at school had got hold of one of his collections, and he'd read the book and loved it, and was so desperate for me to read the book too that he actually stood over me as I did so, he was literally bouncing from foot to foot and studying my face for a reaction. "Isn't he brilliant?" he asked, every time I paused to turn over yet another page of unedifying prose. "Isn't he the best writer ever?"

I'd never suggest ambiguity in horror writing isn't a useful tool. You don't want to tip the nod to the reader too soon, or else how are you going to surprise them with your twist ending? There should always be a twist ending. Like a joke, every good horror story needs a punchline—preferably one that's macabre, and even a little gory. You need a smattering of ambiguity to pull that off, it's a necessary ingredient for the generation of suspense. But a story can't *just* be ambiguous. At some point you're going to have to turn the lights on and show your monster. The suspense has to *go* somewhere, or else it becomes ridiculous. Not knowing how to interpret what's happening around you—to me, I don't know, that's not entertainment, that's just ordinary life.

So often I've tried to enjoy Aickman. Other writers in the horror community adore his work, and they seem to do so without irony—I'm sure some of them are just jumping on the Aickman bandwagon but I have no reason to believe that every single one of them is faking it. This time, I'll tell myself, I'm going to see what the fuss is about. I pick up my Aickman. Even without opening it, the book already feels too weighty in my hands. I choose a story to read at random. All those words stare up at me. I go to the first paragraph, I take a deep breath, I jump in. Over the course of just one story I have to take so many deep breaths it's a wonder I don't hyperventilate.

Maybe the fault is mine. I do accept that possibility. Maybe I'm just not sophisticated enough to appreciate his clever-clever stories, maybe I'm just a moron and don't deserve Robert Aickman. And I'm fairly sure that Aickman and I would never have been friends; when I wade through his stuff, and God, it's like wading through treacle, I can imagine him, standing there, with his arms folded maybe, and he's *judging* me, and all his cronies are sneering at his side and pointing and having a good laugh. Aickman clearly took the horror story very seriously. He wrote: "(It) does seem to derive its power from what is most deep and what is most permanent. It is allied to poetry." What an arsehole.

I wouldn't want you thinking I was obsessed with Aickman, and I hadn't thought of Aickman for weeks that time our paths crossed so meaningfully as I was staying in Bath. I was in Bath on what you might call a working holiday. Sometimes I like to go away when I'm writing, I'll find some nice town and go to a decent hotel, I'll clear my mind and turn the job into something akin to fun. It takes the stress out of a fast deadline. This story I was writing was a *very* fast deadline. I'd been asked to contribute to a new werewolf anthology called *Scary and Hairy: All New Tales of Lycanthropy*; I think someone else had failed to deliver, and the editor had written me a very flattering letter, he needed someone reliable to fill the gap with a no-nonsense piece of about seven thousand words. I like to think I have a reputation—if you need a quick story when your first choice lets you down, I'm your man. Literary writers like Aickman can't do quick, they can't handle the pressure. They couldn't write a solid werewolf story either, I'll be bound—but I digress.

I'd never been to Bath before, but I'd heard it was pretty, and it was. I spent that first day walking around the Georgian lanes, thinking about wolf-men and then turning those thoughts into good thick lurid prose. I'd had a good start at the story, I'd got through nearly two thousand words and there had already been an evisceration I was rather proud of. I decided to reward myself with a nice meal at the hotel. I placed my order at the bar, bought a pint, and sat in the lounge. The lounge was made up of soft plastic armchairs, but the tasteful sort, and there was an electric fireplace, and all over the walls were shelves of books. I looked at the books with only mild curiosity. There were a couple of Jackie Collins, some paperbacks from the seventies, a few hardback *Reader's Digests*. And then I saw a book that made me start in surprise.

You might well imagine that I couldn't have cared less about finding a Robert Aickman book. But Aickman is hard to find—yes, you can track him down easily enough on the convention circuit, but I'm not sure I'd ever seen a copy of Aickman 'in the wild', so to speak. It was a copy of *Dark Entries*, his first solo collection of short stories. I took it off the shelf. It seemed thin, even apologetic—it didn't know how rare it was. Was it first edition? Of course it was, when did Aickman ever sell enough to run to second editions? The purple dust jacket was a little faded with age, maybe, but it was in perfectly good nick, there was not a tear to be seen. Inside the book there was an inscription. *'To my dear darling Wendy. My love and inspiration. Yours forever, Bobbo'.* I wondered if the inscription reduced its value. I supposed it wouldn't matter.

I had no idea how much it was worth, but I was thinking hundreds of pounds. Could it be worth a thousand? It might. I turned the pages very carefully, making sure only to touch the edges, and not a one had a blemish. It was ridiculous that a book this rare should be sitting here on public display, where just anyone could read it. The streets of Bath seemed littered with children—children of tourists who could get into the hotel lounge with sticky fingers and drool and, yes, *crayons*, didn't children like to draw with crayons over everything? It made me shudder. It was really a wonder the book was still intact at all.

Of course I wanted the Aickman. I'd be doing it a favour. I would liberate it. I would keep it from harm. It wasn't the money. I had friends, good friends, friends who loved Aickman's work and would treat this book with the care it deserved. They would be so excited I had discovered it, the book would make someone an astonishing present. And if that was too generous, and of course it was too generous, I could at least sell it to one of them. Or I could just keep the book for myself. It would only appreciate in value over the years. Should I display it on the 'special shelf', the one under the mantelpiece? Yes, it would look good. I could imagine my friends' faces going green with envy when they saw it there. "But you don't even like Aickman!" they'd cry, and I'd just shrug and smile.

I wondered if I could just steal it. Or not steal it, not exactly—I would replace it with some other book. No one would mind. They'd probably prefer it, how many people who came to Bath would want to read Robert Aickman? I'd pick them up a Jane Austen, that'd be more suitable. Just take it now, why not? And I looked around, and I'd missed my chance—the barman was coming over to me with my steak and chips, and he'd seen me holding the book, he'd seen me stare at it in such wonder.

"Here you are, Sir," he said, and put the plate down hard upon the table. "Help yourself to ketchup, it's on the side there."

"Thank you," I said.

"You a reader?" he asked.

I could tell he wasn't a reader. His face had no character to it. "I am actually a writer," I said. He seemed nonplussed by that. "I wonder," I went on, and I tried to keep my tone neutral, "I wonder, about these books? Are any of them for sale?"

"They're just for decoration," he said. "They look nice."

"They do look nice," I said. "But a couple of them tickled my fancy. This one, for instance. This one here. Do you think I could buy it? Would that be all right?" And he was reaching out for it, he wanted to put his fat fingers all over it, and I had to let him take it, it wasn't my book, it was his and he could smear his fingers on it to his heart's content.

"I don't think so," said the barman. He was opening the book now. Too wide, he'd break the spine. "They don't belong to me. They belong to Miss Shaffer. She's the one who owns the place."

"Do you think you could ask her if…?"

"I don't think so," he said. He was riffling through the pages now, I wanted to punch him. "They're not for sale."

"I'll be honest," I said. "I'll tell you what it is. That book, that little book there. It's very valuable."

"Is it?"

"Not in money terms," I said. "Nothing like that. But the writer, you see the name? Robert Aickman. Well. I knew him. In fact, he was my uncle."

"Oh."

"Yes. The family, we knew he'd written some books, but they never sold well, do you see? They probably weren't very good! But my mother. That'd be Robert Aickman's sister. I just know how much she would want to have a copy of this. Her brother's book. For sentimental reasons."

"I don't know," said the barman.

"And she's dying."

"Oh," he said. "Oh."

"Yes."

"Oh. Well. In that case."

"Yes?"

"If you're family."

"I really, really am."

"Then I suppose. Well, you could just have it."

He even offered the book to me, he was going to get those fat fingers off it, but I was so surprised by his generosity I didn't take it. "I couldn't," I said. "No, no, I'll pay."

The barman shrugged. "It isn't my book," he said. "I wouldn't know what to charge for it. And if you're family, it's yours already, really, isn't it? I'm sure Miss Shaffer would want you to have it."

"Well," I said. "That's very kind." I now reached out my hand for the book. "Well. Thank you." He didn't let go. I gave it a gentle tug. "Thanks." He released it.

"Enjoy your meal."

"I will." Though I didn't want the meal any more. I ate it as quickly as possible, I wanted to get away from that barman and up to my room before he could change his mind. I'd hide the book, no, I'd *pack* the book straight away, right at the bottom of my suitcase, I'd wrap a shirt around it for protection. I'd check out first thing tomorrow. I was in Bath for the whole week, but I'd find another hotel, that would be best.

When I made it to my room I quickly locked the door. I took a shower, but I kept on imagining that someone might break in and take the book, so I cut it short. I got into my pyjamas. I picked up the book. It didn't feel so grimly solemn as the Aickman I had at home, this volume hadn't been republished in the small press by reverential enthusiasts, it had been released into the world fifty years ago with no more fanfare than a young writer's hope. It felt humble. It felt normal. I wondered if this time, at last, I might enjoy it. I began reading one of the stories. It began comprehensibly enough, with talk about church bells and honeymoons, but pretty soon I couldn't tell which of the characters were alive or dead or somewhere in between, and that annoyed me. I nodded off.

I was woken by a knock at the door. The knock didn't seem angry, it wasn't the knock of someone who thought their hotel had been swindled. But it was insistent, and it wasn't going to go away. "Yes," I called out. "Who is it?"

There came a woman's voice. "It's the manager, Sir. May I come in?"

"I'm in my pyjamas," I said. The book was on the bed. I should have packed it in the suitcase as I'd first intended. I put it in the bedside drawer.

"I don't mind," she said.

I put on a dressing gown, and opened the door.

"I'm sorry to disturb you," said the woman, though she didn't sound very sorry. "Your light was on, or I wouldn't have knocked." And then, without invitation, she came in.

I've never found it very easy to describe women. There aren't an awful lot of women in my stories, and they tend not to live long. She was quite old, I suppose, but not unattractive. She wasn't fat the way old women tend to get. Her face was nice. Her breasts were nice. Her hair was dark brown and glossy, and it didn't look quite right sitting there, I was pretty sure it was a wig. "Do you mind if I sit down?" she asked, and she perched upon the end of my bed.

I offered her a drink, and then felt silly, all I had were the sachets of cheap instant coffee she herself had provided. She thanked me, and said no.

And all the while she was looking around the room, her eyes were darting every which way—her nostrils were flaring too, it seemed as if she were trying to sniff out the book. Then she reached across, and opened the drawer, and took it out, and smiled at me. There was nothing accusing in that smile, and the look of triumph was measured, as if she'd done nothing more than found her car keys. "I see you have the book," she said.

"I do." And then, because I thought I should say so, "It's very good."

"It is very good. His first collection, of course, and I do feel there's more emotional complexity to be found in his later work. But there's something very wonderful about a first book, isn't there? Knowing that it's the foundation for so much more to come."

Oh God, I hadn't thought she might be an Aickman devotee. How dull. How alarming, too—this was going to make things difficult. She'd know how much the book was worth for a start. "I wasn't just going to take it," I said. "I did offer to pay."

She waved her hand at that. "Oh, never mind about the book. Keep it with my blessing. Bobbo gave me lots of copies, I don't need them all." And I remembered the inscription.

"Are you Wendy?" I asked.

She nodded. "Gwendoline Shaffer," she said. "Is the name familiar?"

"No."

"Are you sure?" she asked.

"Yes."

"Oh," she said. She looked so disappointed.

"Though it might ring a bell," I said. She brightened at that.

"When Bobbo signed that book for me," she said, "we had only just become lovers. He would come to visit me at this very hotel, this was back when my father ran the establishment. Father didn't like me to sleep with the clientele, but he turned a blind eye where Bobbo was concerned. After all, Bobbo was a writer, and Father always respected the arts. I would bring up Bobbo breakfast in bed, and we'd make love, and afterwards we'd lie under the sheets together, and he might read me some of his stories."

"God," I said. "Did you understand any of them?"

She ignored that. "I always wondered. Whether he mentioned me to his family. Whether I was important enough. You're his nephew. Did he ever tell you my name? Did he ever talk about me at all?"

I frowned hard, as if trying to remember. "Well, maybe," I said. "But I wasn't close to my uncle. To Uncle Bobbo."

"He was a bit of a recluse," she said, with a sad smile. "Poor Bobbo." And she was looking straight at me, but she seemed to be talking to herself. "I know I was important. I was important. But was I important *enough*?"

I stood there, and I think I was smiling, and I hope it was a sympathetic smile. I felt cold in my dressing gown, and I hoped she'd now put my book down and leave. But instead she opened the book, and she started to read, she relaxed and made herself comfortable. I wasn't sure what to say. She turned a page, carried on reading, completely absorbed by the story. And still I was standing, and I knew the sympathetic smile had long faded, I cleared my throat but she didn't react. I thought she'd forgotten I was there at all, so when she spoke again I almost jumped. "Poor Bobbo," she said again. "What's your mother's name? Which of the Aickman sisters is she?"

Now, I didn't even know that Robert Aickman had had any sisters. I somehow had imagined he was an only child. His work seemed so chilly and isolated, his stories the product of a little boy who had no one at home to play with.

My mother's name is Daphne. I toyed with Daphne in my head. Did Daphne Aickman have a credible rhythm to it, was there any chance Robert Aickman would have had a sister called Daphne? No, I didn't think so, Daphne Aickman sounded dreadful and lumpen. But then, I tried a few other girls' names, and they all sounded lumpen—that was the problem, Aickman was just a lumpen name, it just got in the way and ruined everything. "Sue," I said, at last. "Sue Aickman. More of a half-sister, really."

"Sue," said Miss Shaffer. "Yes, of course. I heard Bobbo talk about Sue often. Perhaps you could pass on my best wishes to Sue."

"Of course I will," I said.

"He was so good at sex," she said. "There's such forceful control in his work, don't you think? As if he's pounding the words hard right on to the page. He used to stroke my skin, he said I had the most beautiful skin, he'd kiss my shoulders, and then my neck, and then he'd work all the way down. And afterwards he'd hold me, he liked to hold me, and out would flow the stories. His beautiful stories." I had the urge to pull her hair, I was certain the wig would come straight off.

"You must miss him very much," I said.

She nodded. "And yet his work lives on."

"Yes! In a way. I suppose."

"We had a son," said Wendy Shaffer.

"You had what, sorry?"

"We didn't tell his family."

"God."

"He works here at the hotel."

"God." I thought hard. "It isn't the barman, is it?"

"Steve? No, that's Steve. It isn't Steve."

"No."

"Steve is an idiot."

"I was going to say."

"No, when I say he works here, I mean this is where he writes his stories. He's a writer. Just like his father. Just like you."

"That's nice," I said. "So. What, what sort of stories does he write?"

"Would you like to meet him?"

"Well, I..."

"You are his cousin. Would you like to meet your cousin? I know *he* would like to meet *his* cousin."

"Yes," I said. "Yes. I would love to meet him."

"Come on then," she said, lightly. And she offered me her hand for some reason, and for some reason I took it.

Still in my dressing gown, barefooted, she led me out of my room, down the corridor, and through a door saying 'Staff Only'. We climbed the stairs. We climbed them for quite a while, I had no idea the hotel was so tall.

At the top of the stairs we stopped outside a wooden door. It was as bland and functional as any other hotel room door, but this one didn't have a number on it. "Now," she said, her voice dropping to a whisper. "No loud noises. He doesn't like loud noises."

"All right," I said.

"And you have to be careful," she said. "It's very dark in there. He's photosensitive. Light hurts him. Too much light, he'll die."

"I understand," I said.

"And you've got to keep your hands to yourself, that's most important of all. You mustn't touch him, until I say it's safe to do otherwise."

She smiled then, and took a key from her pocket, and unlocked the door. She looked at me, a little impatiently. "In you go, then."

I stepped inside the room. It was pitch black. Suddenly the darkness seemed to swallow me up, the light from the corridor seemed a world away. I could see nothing. And in a moment I knew this was a trap. I knew that the landlady would slam the door behind me, and lock it, and I'd be left in the dark. And no matter how much I begged her she would never let me out. And that there was something here in the dark with me, and that it would find me, and that it would take its time.

Instead, she followed me directly. So I was wrong about that.

"There now," she said, and she closed the door gently behind us. "Here we are."

I listened. I thought I could hear breathing, shallow and uncertain. I thought it might just be me.

"Bobbo?" she said, gently. "Bobbo Junior? I've brought you a visitor."

The breathing wasn't mine. I heard it catch, it seemed to splutter in acknowledgement.

"This is your cousin," she said. "Sue's boy. You've heard me talk about Sue, haven't you?"

Nothing.

"What's your name?" she said to me. I wasn't going to give her my real name. "Adrian," she said. "You've heard me talk about Adrian."

"Ick ick ick," said the man in the darkness. It wasn't a noise, this wasn't further spluttering from his throat. These were his words, exactly as he said them. "Ick ick ick," he said again, and they seemed deliberate and articulated.

"I'll just check his straps are secure," said Miss Shaffer. "Sometimes he gets excited and pulls them loose, and we don't want him hurting himself. There now, that's nice, that's comfy. You can step forward. Adrian? Adrian, I'm talking to you."

I shuffled on. Something touched my hand. I gasped, but it was just Miss Shaffer again.

"Here I am. That's good. Do you want to say hello to your cousin?"

"Hello, Bobbo," I whispered.

"Tell him you're happy to see him."

I couldn't see him, not at all. "It's nice to meet you at last," I said. "I've heard so much about you."

"Tell him what your favourite Robert Aickman story is," said Miss Shaffer. "He does so love literary discussion of his father's work."

"That would have to be the one about the church bells and honeymoons," I said. "It's got great ambiguity."

"Ick ick ick," said Robert Aickman Junior.

"He likes you," said Robert Aickman Junior's mother. "He likes you a lot. You can stroke him if you like."

"What?"

"Come on," she said. "Don't be afraid. It's nice to stroke him."

So I stretched out my hand, lowered it down towards where the bed might be. And what I touched was warm and wet. I thought that I must have put my hand in Bobbo's mouth by mistake—"Sorry," I said—and I moved my hand, but it was everywhere, the warm and wet was all there was.

"He's an excellent writer," said Miss Shaffer. "But what can you expect with his genes? He's a prodigious talent. I come up here, and I stroke him, and he tells me all his stories, and some of them are beautiful, and some of them are shocking. And then I go and write them down. Would you like to read them, Adrian?"

"I would," I said.

"I bet you would," she said. "But you can't. They're all mine, and nobody else's."

We said goodbye to Bobbo shortly after that, but he didn't say anything back. I thought perhaps he had fallen asleep. His breathing sounded good and regular. We made our way to the door, and Miss Shaffer opened it, and we stepped out into the light.

"That was nice," said Miss Shaffer. "He was on good form." Discreetly I wiped my wet hand on the wallpaper.

She led me back to my room.

"Well," I said, "thank you. Thank you very much. It was good to meet my cousin. And it was good to meet you too."

She didn't leave. "Do you really want the book?"

"Yes," I said.

She followed me into the room. She took off her clothes, and she told me to take off mine. We got on to the bed, and she climbed on top of me. I've never found it very easy to describe sex. There's not an awful lot of it in my stories, and as a rule it gets brutally interrupted before I have to come up with any embarrassing bits. She was not, as I say, unattractive. I had that urge once again to pull off her wig, but I couldn't reach it. We banged around a bit, and I must admit, I felt some pride during penetration that I was following in Robert Aickman's footsteps, and I knew that when I told them my friends would be proud too. And then, when it was over, or when Miss Shaffer decided it was over, she climbed off me, got up, and lit a cigarette.

She picked up my writing notebook, and opened it.

"Is this your story?" she asked. I said it was.

She blew smoke at it. "I'll read it tonight," she said. "I'll tell you what I think."

She got dressed and left me. I locked the door behind her.

And I slept for a while, but I was disturbed by the sound of the doorknob being turned. Someone was trying to get in. And I assumed it was Wendy Shaffer, she wanted more sex perhaps, and I didn't want any sex now, I was sleepy, but she struck me as a woman who wouldn't take no for an answer. I got up, I went to the door, I fumbled at the lock. "Just a moment," I said. *Ick ick ick*. I froze. *Ick ick ick.* "Bobbo?" I said. "Is that you?" The doorknob swung backwards and forwards, more violently each time. Then the doorknob was abandoned, and there was a scratching at the door. With fingernails, I supposed, did Bobbo even have fingernails? *Ick ick ick*, he said to me. "Go back to bed, Bobbo!" I said. "Go back to bed this instant!" And I pressed my hands against the door, as if that was ever going to stop him. But he wasn't going to stop, was he? Because I could hear the door cracking, the wood splintering, I could feel the warm wetness soaking through. "Bobbo!" I said, as sternly as possible. "I'll turn the lights on and hurt you. I'll turn *all* the lights on, and *kill* you. Go back to bed!" Could he even understand me? Or hear me properly, because stupidly I was still whispering, I didn't want to cause him any pain. *Ick ick ick*, he said, and it didn't seem contrite and it didn't seem obliging—but the scratching stopped, and there was a silence I took to be hesitation, and then I heard a figure slouch wetly away.

In the morning I checked the door, and it was dry enough, and the grooves in the wood weren't nearly as deep as I'd imagined, I don't suppose I'd been in any danger at all.

I wanted to leave at once. I put the Aickman book in my bag without any qualms whatsoever, by now I'd earned the bloody thing. It was dawn, I could just sneak away. The one thing that held me back was that Miss Shaffer had my notebook—two thousand words of werewolf action. I even considered abandoning it. I could buy another notebook. I could write it all again.

And I'd almost made up my mind to do that, I was going to leave. I opened the door. And standing in the corridor was Miss Shaffer. I wondered vaguely how long she'd been there.

"I'm checking out," I said, and patted at my suitcase by way of demonstration. I thought she might be offended, but she nodded blithely.

"I read your story," she said. She handed me back my notebook. "Or, I suppose, your work in progress."

"Yes?"

"Your prose style is fine. It's a little overdone at times, but a good editor can fix that. You're clearly not without talent."

"Well," I said. "Thank you."

She sighed. "But Adrian, what is it all about? Your writing is so empty, isn't it? Writing ought to have a bit of depth to it. There's so many stories in the world already, why add to the sum total unless you've got something to say? There's no meaning to this. There's no point."

"I haven't finished it yet," I said. "Maybe the meaning will come later." But she was smiling sadly, and shaking her head. "Well," I said. "Well. I never said I was a better writer than Robert Aickman."

"I like to collect writers," she said. "But I don't think I'll be collecting you." And it was odd—at that very moment that's all in the world I wanted, to be collected by Wendy Shaffer. To write stories for her, to try to impress her with each and every one, to make her my muse. I would plead with her to change her mind. I would get down on my knees, and beg. But it was just a moment, a passing moment, and then it was gone.

"Fine," I said. And then, I think because I wanted to hurt her, just a little bit, "And thank you for last night. I do hope you don't regret it, now that you know I'm a writer with no depth."

She looked straight at me then, she blinked in surprise. It made her look suddenly young. It made me want her after all. "Oh, there's no depth to fucking," she said. "A fuck's just a fuck, isn't it?" And then she went.

I would like to say that my encounter with Robert Aickman made a profound difference to me. That I became the sort of writer he might have respected. For a while, I really tried. I destroyed my werewolf story, Wendy Shaffer was right about it. I started something new. For a week or two I felt the whole world open up to me, starting now I could be profound, starting now I could *matter.* I poured meaning into my work, and point, and such great depth. It was awful. Even I couldn't read it. I couldn't imagine why anyone else would bother. I'd looked inside myself, I'd searched hard to find some part of me that wasn't trivial or shallow, that had something to offer the world. And there wasn't anything. There wasn't. And what shames me is I wasn't even ashamed.

I went back to my old style. I'm not saying I'm better than anyone else, but when you read my stuff at least you can tell what's going on. And fuck the rest of them. Fuck Robert Aickman.

I put the signed first edition of Robert Aickman's *Dark Entries* on Ebay, and sold it for nearly four hundred pounds. I could have got a lot more if I'd gone to a dealer, but I'm not greedy.

And the old woman says:

- *Do you prefer your horror stories ambiguous or traditional?* **The Sixteenth Step** *(story 16, page 273) is a tale about a haunted house. Judge for yourself which category it falls into.*
- *'Ick-ick-ick' is such a strange thing to want to say. It's the calling cry of one particular species of beast. Can you guess which one? Turn to* **Angels in Australia** *(story 59, page 995).*
- *Literary jealousy is bad enough, but it's nothing to the jealousy one feels when your friend has a father who gets a job at a circus. Turn to* **Clown Envy** *(story 41, page 685).*
- *Robert Aickman's horror stories are rich and sophisticated, and so only very rarely feature societies of children transforming into fruit. Find out if he was missing a trick, and turn to* **Pumpkin Kids** *(story 84, page 1431).*
- *I used to dream of books, and nothing but books—I wanted to be able to live long enough that I could read every single book in the world. Now I have read them all, and still I am hungry. Turn to* **The Censor's Report** *(story 99, page 1679).*

Isn't this starting to look familiar?

83
THE MASTERWORK

THE FIRST BOOK HADN'T sold many copies, but the reviews had been kind. "An absurdist take on the creation of the world, with imagination to spare," said *The Times*. "Fantasy hokum it may be, but it's hokum told with wit and heart," said *The Guardian*. *The Daily Mail* said, "I loved the bit with the talking snake."

And there was an unmistakeable buzz about the sequel, that this would be the break-out novel. The settings were more exotic, the action more intense: there were big battles, and chase sequences, and bushes that burned inexplicably, and not just one plague but ten! Hollywood had already taken out an option on it, even before it had hit the book stores. Rumour was that Christian Bale had signed up to take the lead. Richard Unwin, it was generally agreed, was a writer who was going places.

The book launch went down a treat. Unwin had been so nervous beforehand—What if nobody came? What if people came, but nobody cared?—he'd never liked parties, or crowds, or even much talking to people one on one, that's why he'd turned to writing in the first place. But the room was packed, and the audience well happy on their free wine and quiche, and as he shuffled onto the stage shyly he looked so endearing, and they laughed with enthusiasm at his reading, even at the bits that weren't supposed to be funny, even when he put in one or two many 'begat's. He had to sign a lot of books that night, and it began to hurt his wrist the number of times he wrote his name, but it was a good pain, he rather began to enjoy himself. "You'd better get used to this," said his new agent, and he nodded happily, and had a glass of wine, and relaxed.

The very next day his publishers called him into a meeting. "We're going to give you a three book deal!" the publisher exclaimed. "Anything you want to write, whatever comes out of that noggin of yours!" "All right," said Unwin. "We're going to make you huge! *Rowling* huge!" "All right." And, fired up, Unwin went home, set to work. He wrote all day and all night, letting the words take over, and he didn't hold back this time, there was no doubt, he was *good*, he knew he was. Within three months he had three novels finished, just like that. The publishers were so amazed they doubled his advance. The first book he called *Leviticus*, the second *Numbers*. He couldn't think of a title for the third for ages, he had to take a long bath, until at last it just rolled off his mind. "Deuteronomy," he liked saying it out loud, "Deu-ter-on-om-y." He looked it up in the dictionary, found out that it meant 'second law', and yet that didn't put him off.

Reviews for the new trilogy were complimentary, if a little cautious. He was the critics' new darling, and they weren't prepared to stamp him down, not just yet. *The Times* called *Leviticus* 'brave and fearless... taking the risks we must expect of modern literature.' *The Guardian* decided to trumpet *Numbers* as a 'return to form': 'Those of us who felt after the disappointment of *Leviticus* that Unwin's career was *numbered* will have to think again!" *The Daily Mail* said of *Deuteronomy* that they hadn't liked the last two books much, but this was one was better, and they liked the bit with the haemorrhoid curses.

But you can't fool the reading public. And the talking donkey in *Numbers* just didn't catch the imagination the way the talking snake had.

Still, Richard Unwin was a publishing phenomenon. If not necessarily for the popularity of his books, at least for the speed at which he churned them out—*Joshua, Judges, Samuel, Ruth*. Maybe it was just too much for the public to keep up with. Certainly the critics stopped reviewing them all; they'd say, quite rightly, that if they missed Unwin's latest there'd be another one along in a minute. They were undoubtedly good books, put a compendium of them together you could call it the Good Book. But privately they all agreed Unwin's work had got a little *preachy*. 'A return to form!' every new review would say, but no one could quite identify exactly when Unwin had gone *off* form, when suddenly, without people noticing, his readers had stopped believing in him.

Unwin was still on the convention circuit, pimping his books to his dwindling fan base. After one especially unenlightening panel he shared with Martin Amis and Dan Brown about the death of the novel he was signing autographs in the hotel lounge. There was a young woman, surely no more than eighteen, twenty at the most?—and she came up to him, and passed him a copy of his latest, *Ecclesiastes*, and asked him to sign it to her. "I love your work," she said, and shoved her breasts in his face. Unwin took the lid off his special autographing pen, the first time the lid had come off all day. "Well," he said. "Well. Who shall I make it out to?" "Just write down your room number," said the girl. "Okay," said Unwin.

She made love to him with a tenderness that made him cry. He apologised for the crying, but she said it hadn't put her off. They lay back in bed together, and she smiled at him, and he smiled at her, and he didn't know what to say. "So, you like my work?" he asked, and she said she did. "That's nice," he said, "thank you, would you like me to give you a reading?" "All right," she said. And so, propped up high on the pillows, all naked, still sweaty, and just a little bit blissed out, he began to read: "Saith the Preacher, vanity of vanities, all is vanity." The girl frowned; "Can you read me some of your earlier stuff? I love the earlier stuff. Can you read me the bit with the talking snake?" So Unwin agreed; she had a copy of *Genesis* in her bag, he read about the naughty serpent, and as he did so she reached between his legs and kneaded away, and he rather wished he'd made his serpent talk for just a little bit longer.

He wrote her a book, in the frenzy of his passion. He called it *Song of Solomon*. He sent it to her over email. She didn't reply. He wrote to her again, asking if she'd received his attachment; he'd got a book for her, it was all for her, he loved her so much. She wrote back that he was very sweet. But she didn't love the man, she loved the writer. You know, there was a difference. Unwin apologised. He didn't email her again. He went back to work on the *Book of Job*.

And still he wrote, because he was a writer, wasn't he, what else was he good for? But he began rather to hate the writer he had been, for whom it had all seemed so effortless, who had had so many ideas, and *good* ideas, why couldn't he get ideas like that any more? And now he'd sit in front of a blank computer screen, and he'd struggle to fill it with words, with any words, without making them sound lumpen or gauche or passé, reading the words back as he imagined the critics would read them back, hearing their sneering judgement before he'd even finished the sentence, sneering right along beside them, "This is shit," he'd say out loud as he typed, "this is shit, this is shit." It was around this time that he started to drink.

And whilst he was drunk he might look back through his earlier books, the popular books, the ones he could no longer remember writing, he couldn't remember being that young. He'd scribble in the margins. Against a paragraph in which he asserted that the world had been created in six days, he wrote, "What about the dinosaurs?" Next to the sequence about Noah's ark, he scrawled, "Drown them all, drown every last one of the bastards." He read and reread the story of the Tower of Babel, and how in man's arrogance he had tried to climb to Heaven, and before that there'd been just one language and everyone could understand each other—and he wished that someone would understand *him*, for all he wrote no one ever seemed to take in a blind word he said.

His agent died. Some say he'd committed suicide, but surely not—and surely it was nothing to do with the fact he was found with a copy of Unwin's latest manuscript on his bedside table with all the pills. The new agent was a young firebrand, and had capped teeth. He called Unwin into a meeting. "You've lost your way," he said, plopping Unwin's latest books on to the table, "no one cares about Habakkuk or Malachi, no one cares what shit those guys are into. You need to come up with a hero. Someone we can relate to. Someone we can all root for." Unwin said he didn't believe in heroes. "I advise you to try," said his agent.

So Unwin set to work on a new novel. About a man who was just very, very nice. He went fishing, told his friends stories, did lovely bits of carpentry. Unwin pushed it further. He could walk on lakes, he turned water into wine. "Oh, he's just too good to be true!" said Unwin, and crossed it out—but then he started drinking again, and giggled, and put it all back in. He cast devils from people, he brought back the dead, he turned the other cheek. Unwin was pissed out of his skull when he emailed over the finished manuscript. The agent called him the next day. "It's brilliant!" he said. "It's genius! This is going to sell like hot cakes!" There was even a nice twist ending, apparently, something involving a cross and a resurrection, Unwin couldn't even recall writing that part. "Do what you want with it," said Unwin, "it's sod all to do with me." The one thing he insisted upon was that it retained its title. The agent wanted to call it, *Jesus Christ—Demon Slayer!* Unwin called it *The Book of Matthew*, he named it after his pet dog.

"We need a sequel!" said the agent. It was only a few months later, and the phone call cut nastily through one of Unwin's morning hangovers. "The world wants *Jesus II*!" "Can't do it," said Unwin, "I killed him off, remember?" "Oh, that won't matter," said the agent, "just write the same thing again, the readers'll never notice." And they didn't. *Mark* was even more successful than *Matthew*, and *Luke* headlined both the Oprah Winfrey and the Richard and Judy book clubs. For the release of *John*—dubbed 'The Christ Chronicles IV—he's back again, with all your favourite parables!'—Unwin was on every chat show, he was flown to New York and LA, he was guest host on *Saturday Night Live*. He would take back eighteen-year-old girls to his hotel suites, and he'd do so without shame, and in each bedside drawer the hotel staff had thoughtfully placed a collection of his complete works; they called it the *Gideon Bible*, named after some minor character in his seventh book.

And then there were all the spin-offs—unauthorised, so Unwin didn't get a penny. Concordances to the Bible, and dictionaries of the Bible, and comparative studies of the Old and New Testament—all these books telling people how to read *his* books, when the best answer, surely, would have been just to read his book in the first place. And all the fan fiction on the internet—the further adventures of Jesus, or the crossover fic, in which Jesus teamed up with Muhammed and Buddha and Batman and together they'd fight crime and defeat monsters and convene synods, or the slashfic, in which Jesus copped off with Mary Magdalene and Lazarus and each and every one of his apostles. And secretly Unwin thought these stories were better than his, they had a bit more vigour to them. And then there was all the merchandise, the John the Baptist bendy toy, the Judas Iscariot horror mask, the crucifixes, all those endless crucifixes.

And sometimes he'd dream that maybe all stories were true. That he really did live in a world where there was something to live for, to fight for, to die for; that if you prayed at night there would be someone who'd listen; that there was meaning. The dreams would seem so real, he'd wake from them and he'd lie in bed and for moments—not for long, just moments, but so precious those moments—he'd believe that the world he'd conjured up in his head was the true one.

And sometimes he'd think that maybe all the stories *were* true. Each and every one of them. And that the events he catalogued had really happened, all of them, from the poisoned apple in the magical garden onwards. Not just fairy tales, but true history. Something real. Real, right up to the point when he wrote it down. Right up to the point when he turned it into novels. That in the instant he put pen to paper the very truths of the world became fiction. That he took the only meaning there was, the only meaning there could ever be—and in his hands it'd be transformed, he'd turn it all into gaudy adventure stories with giant whales and burning bushes and magic fingers writing curses on the wall, he'd trivialise it into a series of silly laws and commandments that could only ever be misconstrued, he'd reduce the ineffable oneness of the universe into a straight narrative with beginnings, middles and ends, when there could be no beginnings or ends, all of this was all there ever was or ever should be, and there could be no middles, how could the infinite have a middle?

He'd realise he was destroying God with his stories. The stories only became mere stories when he made them so, and the world of those stories was so much duller and paler than the world he was erasing. And the more he tried to describe the world, the more he tried to preserve it on paper, even an essence of it, the quicker that erasure happened.

And he thought he was the God that he so often wrote about, and that God was an idiot.

He would read his first book. He'd think about Babel.

One night he broke into his publisher's warehouse. And there he found his books, waiting to be shipped around the world, stacked up in crates, wrapped up in plastic. Leatherbound editions, hardbacks with colour pictures, children's easy reading versions with the sex removed and the gore made more emphatic. So many words. So many trees.

He wondered if he should set fire to the lot of them.

And instead, without yet knowing why, he took one book, and set it down gently in the middle of the floor. He looked down at it. It seemed suddenly such a small thing, his life's work, there on its own.

And he took another copy, and placed it carefully on top. And then a third. And then a fourth.

By the time he'd stacked twenty, he'd made himself a nice little tower. By the time he'd stacked a hundred, the tower was beginning to wobble. But it wouldn't fall over, he mustn't believe it could fall over, he had faith. And still he kept building.

He thought that if he stacked all the Bibles of the world on top of each other, neat and flush, it'd make the tallest tower in the world. He wondered if it would reach all the way up to Heaven. And, with that thought, he began to climb.

And the old woman says:

- *Talking animals are always good for a laugh. Turn to* **The Fall of Troy** *(story 4, page 57).*
- *To read of a particular fan of 'The Book of Ecclesiastes', turn to* **It Flows from the Mouth** *(story 85, page 1459).*
- *If the author of the Bible can no longer make a commercial success of his work, he should stop moaning about it, and do what the rest of us do—teach creative writing at some half-arsed university somewhere. If you agree, turn to* **Petty Vengeance** *(story 25, page 409).*
- *One thing can always be relied upon—wherever someone feels a creative urge, there'll be a critic waiting to explain where it'll go wrong. Turn to* **Slow Handclap for the Moronic Horde** *(story 76, page 1329).*
- *The problem with The Bible is that it doesn't have the common touch, it doesn't speak to the man on the street. It's pure escapism—all the exotic locations, the deserts and mountains, give it the feel of a James Bond movie. It's never set anywhere recognisable we know from the daytime soaps. Consider, then turn to* **Angels in Australia** *(story 59, page 995).*

84
Pumpkin Kids

1

MY PARENTS DESPISED me, of course, and with good reason. But they didn't *hate* me, and I need you to understand that. They were good people. They fed me and they clothed me and they kept a roof over my head—and no, they didn't tuck me in at night, and they didn't read me bedtime stories, but I didn't need tucking and I didn't need stories; they taught me right from wrong, they instilled within me some sense of morality, and isn't that more important? In these difficult days, when everything has turned so topsy-turvy. They gave me an upbringing. And the fact that I have lived this long and have done so many Questionable Things, and yet have never been arrested nor put on trial nor sentenced to any sort of Christ-witnessed punishment can only be testament to the quality of that upbringing. I was lucky.

Or rather—my da didn't hate me. He wasn't a man who had much hate within him. Momma was another matter. I like to think that what she felt for me wasn't hatred in the strictest sense—but when she got angry or frustrated or just plain fed up there was a vein in her forehead that used to bulge, and the bulge used to alarm me, and sometimes I was reading a book or playing with my toy and just minding my own business and then I'd realise she was staring at me and I didn't know why she was staring at me and I could see she had a full bulge on, and I didn't know what I had done other than just *being* there. Other than simply existing. So I tried not to be there very much, I tried not to exist when Momma was about—but the house was small, and there weren't many places to hide, and so she got angry quite a bit.

Momma only told me she hated me on two occasions, and considering I lived with her until my sixteenth year, that is hardly excessive. The first time I was five, maybe six—either way, I was old enough to have known better. And it was Momma's birthday, and I had spent *ages* making her a birthday card; well, it felt like ages, but it was probably no more than a couple of months. I'd drawn it myself, and I'd decorated it with lots of sticky sparkles, and I'd tried to draw *her*, but smiling, with a great big smiley face. And in the morning I gave it to her, and she looked at the card and she seemed bemused, I think she even seemed a little pleased, she said a thank you and everything. But that night, when I was in bed, she suddenly stormed into my room and snapped on the lights. I had never seen her so furious, her entire face was a bulge. "Can't you understand how much I hate you?" she screamed. "Why don't you just *die*?" And she tore up the birthday card and threw it at me. "I'd curse you," she said. "I'd curse you, if only curses worked, but they don't, so what's the point?" And she was right, I've tried cursing many times, I've done them proper the way the Bible tells us, and they do no good at all.

I don't want to talk about the second occasion. Not yet, anyway.

Don't you go thinking bad of Momma. The reason this is such a particular memory is because it was out of the usual. If she'd frequently screamed at me and flung birthday cards at me, I'd have nothing to remember, would I? In a way, this only shows how patient she was with me every other day of my childhood. It should only define her in your head as a strong and worthy mother. But that said, at the time my feelings were hurt and I was picking up sticky sparkles from my bed for weeks.

Just as my parents did, I spent a lot of time thinking about the Pumpkin Kids. About what I might have been. Should have been. How I'd been cheated out of my birthright—but there was no one to blame but myself, I had done the cheating: right from the moment I was born I had fucked things up royally and I would *never* be special and I would *never* be of any use. Sometimes I got angry too. They say that when I was a baby I used to lie in my cot and rant and kick and yell, and I had to be injected with a sedative the doctors had prescribed just so my poor parents could get some rest.

But the awful truth is this—some days I wouldn't mind I'd not been born a Pumpkin Kid. I'd even feel relieved. Some days, and more and more as I got older. I would always be an also-ran, and that was better. And I despised myself for that, just as my parents despised me, just as the neighbours did, and the school teachers, and Pastor Lewis. How feeble I was, that I *embraced* failure. Maybe that was the point? That I didn't feel strong enough to be a Pumpkin Kid, to be born with all that responsibility, to know that I'd have a Christ-witnessed purpose to live up to, that would justify my life and the lives of the parents who had spawned me, forever and ever and ever, amen. Oh, easier not to bother. Easier to hide in the shadows, if you can find shadows big enough to hide in—and stay still, and be quiet, and do nothing.

I suppose if I *had* been born a Pumpkin Kid, I would have been born with that Pumpkin Kid strength, and I wouldn't have had these doubts. But then, I wouldn't have been me.

Half an hour after Momma left there was a knock at my bedroom door. "Are you asleep?" It was my da. I wasn't asleep, I couldn't have slept, right at that moment I wasn't sure I'd ever be able to sleep again. Da came in and sat on my bed—which he never did—and he stroked my head—which he never did neither. "Momma was drunk," he whispered. "Or she wouldn't have said such things." He didn't tell me he was sorry, and he didn't tell me Momma hadn't meant it, and that was good, falsehoods are doorways to the Devil. He didn't say anything else for a while, and I just lay there and I closed my eyes, and I tried to keep them open too so I could enjoy my father being there—and I make believed that for all the hate my mother felt for me my father felt the same amount of love. And he said eventually, "This day of the year, it's hard to be around you. It was on her birthday, when she'd been drinking, I got her into bed with me. It was on this day that you were conceived, and everything in our lives went wrong."

I miss my da. He died only a short while later. I came home from school and Momma told me he was in the bathroom hanging from a rope. I asked if I could go and look, and she said no. "With Heaven's favour, we'll see him again soon." But we haven't yet.

So I gather, this is what happened.

I was expected on the last day of October, some time early afternoon. There was no reason to anticipate any problems with that—the pregnancy had gone without a hitch, my mother had been strong and healthy throughout, she hadn't even suffered so much as a twinge of morning sickness. But there are never problems with Pumpkin Kid pregnancies—all other children are conceived in sin and guilt, and the struggle to bring them into the world only reflects that; Pumpkin Kids are pure. And my parents were pure too, I knew they were, and this was the pregnancy they deserved, because they loved Jesus with all their might.

They were admitted into their own private suite in the hospital, paid for by the Council. From now on, and for the rest of their lives, everything would be paid for by the Council—we honour those who create miracles. Doctors and nurses all came in to pay their respects, and asked if there was anything they could do to make my mother more comfortable. There wasn't. She was serene.

It was only as afternoon passed into evening that Momma began to show any concern. And the doctors tried to reassure her that the timing of birth is never an exact science—little miracles must be allowed a degree of wilfulness! Baby would come out when Baby was ready. But my mother was right—and as the hours ticked by she began to get so distressed there was nothing anyone could say to calm her down. "Why won't it come out?" she cried. "What's the matter with it?" And she battered at her swollen belly with her fists, clawed at it with her nails as if to prise it open. "What bloody game does it think it's playing in there?"

Past eleven o'clock, and still no sign of contractions, my mother begged the doctors to induce the birth. But they refused—they couldn't intervene with a miracle, God would see. Halloween wasn't over yet, they told her. The baby could still come out in good time.

And you can imagine that the doctors must have been panicking too—Pumpkin Kids were *never* born late, this wasn't how God willed it. Forty-five minutes. Thirty. Ten. At five minutes to midnight my mother let out a groan so profound that for a moment the medical staff assumed the baby must have finally given up the fight and popped out—but no, my mother could feel all she had ever wanted and all she had ever dreamed of slipping away from her and she'd given a cry of heartbroken despair: her child would be nothing, she was nothing, there was nothing to hold on to any longer. At midnight the nurses helped my mother up out of bed, and supporting her by the shoulders moved her from the luxury of her suite and into a public ward.

I was born on November the first, a little after four o'clock in the morning. "I don't want it," my mother said. "I don't want it." But there I was.

Pastor Lewis was by her side. He'd been in attendance thinking to bless the arrival of a miracle; now he was on hand to offer good counsel. My mother wouldn't look at him as he spoke, numbed with shock she turned to the wall. "You're still a young woman," Pastor Lewis said, "and you're still fertile. You have a Pumpkin Child in you yet, I know it. You mustn't be discouraged by this near miss. Go to it again. Go to it, and breed us all something outstanding."

But my parents didn't breed again. I remained their only child. I don't know why they didn't, Pastor Lewis was right, they were clearly capable—and the sin was mine, it wasn't on their heads, was it? Was it?—and yet all my life I remember them only sleeping in separate beds, at opposite sides of the room, as far away from each other as they could get. I never saw them kiss, or hug, or touch.

One Sunday I decided to stay after church and talk to Pastor Lewis. I liked church. I liked the way that I felt part of a community. I could sing the hymns along with everyone else, and pray, and nod my head and say amen—and just for a little while I didn't stand out and nobody judged me.

And I liked the way that when we lined up before the altar, and Pastor Lewis gave us a sip of wine, how it turned coppery and thick when it turned into the blood of Christ. I liked how those little wafers of bread became fat hunks of raw flesh. I felt awe that something so simple could be transformed by the grace of God, I dared to hope that through that grace I too could be transformed.

Pastor Lewis glared as I approached him. Of course he did. He raised an eyebrow as I told him I needed his help. "I want to be a Pumpkin Child."

"Indeed?"

"I'm very nearly a Pumpkin Child already. I was very close."

He sighed, and began collecting up hymn books. "You can't *nearly* be a Pumpkin Child, any more than I can nearly be Jesus Christ. You either are, or you're not."

And I started to cry, because I knew it was true, but up until that moment I had allowed myself a little hope. That if I repented hard enough, if I'd really really tried to earn forgiveness, then it might still all be put right. I didn't want to cry—I'd quickly learned that my crying just irritated people—and I expected the pastor would be irritated too. Instead he put the books down, and turned to me with an expression that seemed almost sympathetic.

"Look at me," said the pastor. "Can you guess when I was born? I was born on April the sixteenth. More years ago than you can imagine. I could never have been born a Pumpkin Child, that was never my destiny. But I determined to do my best with the limitations I had, and I became a priest. It's all we can do. We take what God has given us, and make the best of it."

"Yes," I whispered.

"But you," he said. And he wasn't trying to be cruel, but he couldn't help it, his lip twisted into a sneer. "God offered you everything. He *chose* you. All you had to do, was lie back and relax and get born. And you wouldn't do it. You decided not to. What little slice of evil was already in you, boy, so to take God's bounty and fling it in His face?"

"I'm sorry," I said. "I didn't mean to."

He reached out his hand, and cupped my chin, and stared right into me—and I flinched, because no one ever touched me, and because his fingers were bony and sharp. "I don't know," he said. "Could it be that you're not wicked at all, but clumsy and indolent?"

"Yes, that's it," I said, too eagerly, and my chin waggled in his grip. "Clumsy and indolent! I'm clumsy and indolent!"

He nodded at this. "Then it's not impossible. Maybe there's a little pumpkin inside you after all. Shall we go and see?"

I'd never been in the vestry before. It smelled of old books and pipe smoke. He went to his desk, opened a drawer, and took out a knife.

"This is my pumpkin knife," he said. I had honestly thought it would be a lot bigger.

"Now," he said, "every year, before it's Halloween, I go and visit all the little Pumpkin Kids, and find out whether they're ripe or not. You've got to check! Jesus only wants the ripe ones! We can't expect much, but I could apply the same procedure to you, see if I recognise any familiar signs..."

No one had ever been quite this nice to me my entire life. "Yes, please!"

"Keep your head still," he said. "This won't hurt a bit." That wasn't true. It did. He made a slice at my neck. "Now, now!" he chuckled. "Don't cry out, that's not the way proper Pumpkin Children behave! We have to make a second notch across it, so it's the sign of the cross." And he cut at me again, and I could feel the blood running down my skin, and this time I clenched my teeth tight and it didn't hurt so much.

I asked if I were now a Pumpkin Kid, and he laughed. "I can't tell just by *looking* at the blood," he said. "What do you think I am? I tell by taste." And that's when he pressed his lips against my neck, and his tongue was lapping away at the gash there, and the stubble on his chin was rough and tickling me but it wasn't the sort of tickle that makes you want to laugh. I wanted to pull away but didn't for fear of spoiling the magic.

"Well?" I asked when at last he stopped. I dared to hope.

Pastor Lewis frowned. He smacked his lips a few times as if he was appreciating a fine wine, then sighed, and wiped the blood from his mouth and chin away with the back of his hand. "I'm afraid," he said gravely, "I can't taste any pumpkin in you at all. No, more than that. I'd say there was *less* pumpkin in you than an ordinary person." He passed me a paper towel. "Clean yourself up."

And I wanted to cry again, and my neck was smarting, and I felt crushed, and also betrayed somehow. Yes, betrayed—as if everything that could have made me good and decent and worthwhile was just arbitrary, and God didn't care, and Pastor Lewis didn't care either. But I didn't cry, and I wasn't going to cry, not ever again, not for anyone. I would be like a proper Pumpkin Kid, I would be patient and unfeeling and I would never say a word. I turned to leave, and then the pastor said, "Of course, it could just be that you've not ripened yet.

We could try again. If you want to. If you ever feel a little riper, come back and see me." And I didn't thank him, and I didn't say yes or no, I just left the vestry and closed the door behind me.

When I got home my parents didn't notice the cuts upon my neck, or the blood upon my shirt, or maybe they did, and just didn't say anything. And every week I'd go back to church, and sometimes Pastor Lewis might catch my eye, and give a subtle nod towards the vestry door. Had I ripened? Had I turned pumpkin yet? And sometimes I stayed behind to see him, and sometimes I didn't.

2

It wasn't until Momma brought one home in the trunk of her car, gagged and all trussed-up like a turkey, that I had the chance to see an unripened Pumpkin Kid up close. They didn't go to school like the rest of us, they don't need to learn the stuff we do, and they were mostly kept at home under lock and key away from prying eyes—after all, we'll get to see them properly all in good time, we don't want to spoil the Halloween treat! But once in a while you might see one out on the streets, always flanked by two chaperones, one at each side, and you never want to stare, you never wanted to show too much curiosity, that would be rude. Rude and *ungrateful*. We'll mutter a "Thank you for your service," look down, and hurry past.

I looked out of my bedroom window to see that Momma had come home from her job at the supermarket. I waited for her to get out of the car, bring in the bags of food she would cook for us. But she just sat there—she didn't move. Her hands were gripped tight upon the steering wheel, and I thought she must be very angry with me that she didn't even want to come indoors, I thought there'd be a big bulge upon her face. There wasn't. There was nothing there at all.

And I knew as I hurried down to find her that something was very wrong. I thought she might be dying, having a heart attack maybe. And I was frightened, yes—but mostly I think I was excited.

I rapped on the car window. I didn't expect Momma to look around. She did.

"What have I done?" she said.

"Momma?"

Her voice was muffled behind the glass. "I don't know," she said, "what I've done." And then it was as if she recognised me at last, her face came back to life, and hardened. "In the trunk," she said. "Open it. Carefully."

I did so. I looked inside. Then I lowered the lid, and went back to my Momma.

"Do you see it?" she said, and I nodded. "Is he still breathing?" I didn't know, so I went back to check. She had stuffed some plastic bags from the supermarket in his mouth as a gag, but his nostrils kept flaring inwards and outwards, and I took that as a good sign. I closed the lid again, and went back to tell her the good news.

We waited until the coast was clear, and then we lifted the kid out of the trunk, taking one arm each and yanking on him until he was out in the open. Then we staggered with him up to the house. The kid didn't help at all, but he wasn't just being difficult, Momma had tied his legs together with tow rope, so it really wasn't his fault.

It wasn't until the front door closed behind us and we let the kid drop to the floor that either of us dared catch our breath.

"I just saw him there on the street," Momma said. "A Pumpkin Kid, large as life. And so I took him."

"Where were his chaperones?"

"He didn't have any."

"Did anyone see you?"

"I don't know."

"Someone must have seen you, Momma. His chaperones."

"I told you, he didn't have any. He was just staggering about on his own. I thought at first he was a drunk, until I realised he was wearing the orange smock. Wearing the smock, and it's not even Halloween, anyone could have seen him! He was lucky. Anyone could have seen him, anyone could have coshed him over the head, and stuck him in the trunk of their car. He was lucky it was me."

I don't know whether the kid realised he'd been lucky. He was still lying on the floor, his head jammed against the skirting board, and he was twitching a little. We sat him up so he might be more comfortable. His eyes began to take in his new home slowly and incuriously.

"He was just *there*," said Momma. "I don't know why I did it. But if I hadn't done it, if I'd let this one chance just slip through my fingers, to get myself a real life Pumpkin Kid…I don't know. I would have regretted it the whole of my life. Do you understand?"

Of course I didn't. "What are you going to do with him?"

"Let's put him in your room." That wasn't quite what I had meant, but I didn't push the point further.

"We aren't going to hurt you," I said to the kid, though I didn't really know whether that were true. We laid him on the bed, on his back, so he was staring right up at the ceiling.

I asked if we could take out the gag, and Momma thought about it for a bit, and then said that we could. I pulled it out from his mouth, and Momma had pushed those plastic bags in pretty deep, I'm surprised he hadn't choked. I then asked her if we could take off the ropes that were holding his arms and legs in check, and Momma thought about that too, and then said, no, best not—we'd already taken out the gag, we mustn't get carried away.

What did he look like? He didn't look much like a pumpkin, really. Maybe there was a wet sheen to his skin, and his face was a bit fat. But if he hadn't been in his orange smock, really, you wouldn't have known he was part vegetable at all. He was just a kid. Younger than me, maybe twelve or thirteen. His orange smock was dirty. His feet were bare and bruised.

I knew, of course, that what Momma had done was a Questionable Thing. I'm not sure it was even Questionable; it might even have been a proper unambiguous Crime. And I knew too that we were going to get caught. You can get away with a few Questionable Things here and there and everyone will turn a blind eye—Pastor Lewis had told me every time we'd met in his vestry. But no one was going to accept the disappearance of anything so precious as a Pumpkin Kid. They were going to hunt us down, and catch us, and then they'd be really mad.

"We could just take him back," I said. "No one would know. We could just leave him somewhere on the side of the road, what's he going to say, he isn't going to say anything."

And I think for a moment Momma may even have been considering it. We wouldn't have to destroy our lives over this. We could just sink back into the quiet misery of before. But then, as if to call me a liar, the Pumpkin Kid began to open his mouth. We heard the lips pull apart, we heard the jaws creak as they stretched like taffy.

"He's going to speak!" Momma said, and she was so excited, because the words of Pumpkin Kids are rare blessings. And we put our ears close to listen.

He didn't speak. Instead out from his mouth rolled a ball of vegetable pulp. It was wet and it was warm, and it fell upon my mattress. And then the kid closed its mouth, and smiled at us for the first time, big and wide, as if he'd done something extraordinarily clever.

"He's mine," said Momma. "And I'm not giving him back, not ever." And she smiled too, which only made the kid smile wider still, as if his only possible purpose was to please her—and there they were for a while, the two of them, grinning at each other. And I saw that vein in her face give a satisfied bulge, and I knew nothing now could dissuade her.

I'd lost my bedroom to the Pumpkin Kid, and so I tried to make the downstairs sofa as comfortable as could be.

But it was hard to sleep, knowing there was another body in the house. For so long it had just been me and Momma, and now someone else was breathing our air, and it sounds stupid but I suddenly resented that, we only had so much air to go round and here was some stranger making free with it and sucking it into his body and wasting it—and then I thought I could hear him upstairs, a third heart in the house beating away and making the night that much louder—and I knew he couldn't stay here, he didn't belong—and I thought that if I opened my eyes I would see him, he'd be in the room, he'd be looking at me. And I didn't want to open my eyes and find out it was true, I wanted to be asleep, why couldn't I just be asleep? I wasn't going to open my eyes, I refused to do it, and then I did it anyway, I opened them, and he *was* there, he *was* in the room, he was standing in the doorway and looking at me.

He didn't say anything. "What are you doing here?" I managed to get out—but no, nothing—and then as if in answer he took a step forward. And I could see his face more clearly in the moonlight. His head seemed more swollen than before, and in my terror I could see it was starting to crack, his face was splitting and juice was bubbling to the surface.

And he was smiling in that strange vacant way he had, as if the smile wasn't triggered by anything, it was just the shape into which his mouth had been carved. His teeth were jagged, his nose a cavity. And those eyes.

I closed mine. I squeezed them tight, and lay back down on the bed, and turned my body towards the wall. And I promised myself I wouldn't open them again until I had to, not until he touched me—when he touched me I would have no choice, I would have to do something, I would run or I would fight, I didn't have to decide just yet. Not until he touched me. But right now I was safe, I was safe for just a few precious moments longer and I wasn't going to spoil them by worrying. And I waited. I waited a long time. I began to feel impatient. I counted in my head, and when I reached one hundred I felt brave enough to turn around and see what the Pumpkin Kid was doing.

He was gone.

I got up from my bed. I went upstairs. I didn't want to look.

I went into my old bedroom. And there he was. Still tied up upon the mattress, face up towards the ceiling. Still nothing more frightening than an ordinary little boy. I tiptoed to his side, I didn't want to wake him—and then I realised he wasn't asleep. His eyes were wide. It made me jump—but he didn't even flinch, he looked straight through me, he didn't care, I was nothing to him.

And slumped in the chair by the bed, there was Momma. She was fast asleep, and she was smiling. I shook her gently by the shoulder; she stirred. "Come on," I said. I helped her to her feet, and she let me lead from the room, across the landing, into her own bedroom. I laid her down, and she folded into her pillow and began to snore gently. "Good night, Momma," I said, and kissed her.

I went back to the Pumpkin Kid. I stood in *his* doorway, I stared at *him*. Let him have the nightmares about me. Because I could do anything to him that I wanted. And I went up to him, close, closer than I thought I could dare. I lifted a finger. I put it on top of his forehead. Resting it there so it was just skimming the surface—and then pressing down, pressing down hard. I took my finger away. I had left a mark. Only a little indentation, but it was there. And was there a bit of juice bleeding from it? I think there was. I said, "Good night, Pumpkin Kid," and went back downstairs to the sofa.

I felt calmer than I had in a very long time, and I slept soundly.

There are tales about the awful fates awaiting those that defy the Pumpkin Kids. We learned them at school. One of the best had been about a group of naughty little boys who had been jealous of a Pumpkin Kid and his special relationship with God and Death, and had vowed to do him harm. This would have been, I don't know, hundreds of years ago—there were lots of versions of this particular tale, and you could read about it in pop-up picture books, or see it acted out in puppet shows or pantomimes; it had given me nightmares as a little boy, but rather delicious nightmares, because you knew you would never be in danger yourself, this would never happen to you, you would never do anything so stupid as to harm a miracle child that was under the protection of Christ! And in this tale the boys lured the Pumpkin Kid into the forest, and there they killed him. They kicked him, or they stoned him, or they trapped him in a deep pit and left him to starve. But God punished them all. He destroyed the naughty boys, one by one. He wiped them off the face of the Earth—and their parents, and their brothers and their sisters, and all of their friends, every single one of them, were turned into pillars of salt.

And as those first weeks went by, it became clear—I wasn't going to be turned into a pillar of salt, and nor was Momma. And neither did the police come by (which, I supposed, seemed more likely.) I couldn't work out why not. I thought at first that the disappearance of our Pumpkin Kid hadn't been reported yet—maybe the chaperones were ashamed to come forward. (Because where had the chaperones been? Why hadn't they been doing their Christ-witnessed jobs? Wasn't their carelessness enough to turn them into pillars of salt?) Our town safeguarded its store of precious Pumpkin Kids to the very best of its ability; had the theft of one become public knowledge it would have caused widespread outrage, if not actual panic. But it could only be a matter of time. Soon, surely, the disappearance would be noticed, and then an investigation would begin, and someone would point the finger at Momma. And our lives would be over, and I guess at least then so would be all the waiting.

But no one came. And as a new month began, and then another, and *still* no one came, I realised that somehow, incredibly, we must have gotten away with it. Every last Pumpkin in the town was accounted for. It was as if nothing had really happened, and there wasn't a spare one, large as life, tied up in my bedroom after all.

And some days that's precisely how Momma acted. She pretended that there was nothing untoward, that life was just the same as it had always been. She wouldn't so much as mention our special guest, let alone go to see him or ask how he was. She would go to her job at the supermarket and come back from her job at the supermarket and that was the full extent of all she was prepared to think about, thank you—her face was set as hard as stone and I knew there was no point in talking to her. But other days she was a different person. She would go to his bedside and spend all her time there, she would forget to eat or go into work. She'd stare at him in wonder, and maybe stroke his body, stroke his face. "He's beautiful," she'd say. And, "Why can't you be this beautiful?" And, "I wasn't sure I believed in God. But look at him! Now I know it's all true."

Sometimes she'd close the door on me, and I had to put my ear to the keyhole to hear her whisper to him. "Are you in there, my poor dear Da?" she'd ask. "And Momma too? I love you both. I love you, and I miss you so very much!"

But I was the one who had to look after him, who cleaned him and fed him. I would moisten a towel with water and rub it against his skin, and yet it never lost that shiny oily glow. "Where have you come from? Was it another town?" But the nearest town was a hundred miles away or more, I didn't know quite how far, but it was impossible to believe a barefooted boy could have walked that distance on his own. "Why did you come here? Tell me that at least!" He wouldn't chew his food, so I had to pour soup into his mouth, then hold my hands over his face so that it wouldn't all run out—and sometimes I made the soup piping hot and I hoped that it would burn him. "Do you think you're better than me?" And he'd never reply, he'd never so much as grunt a word, he'd stare up at me, and smirk that little smile. Of course he was better. He didn't need to answer.

The first time I cut into the Pumpkin Kid's neck I was nervous. I did it just the way I'd been shown, two nicks in the sign of the cross. But it wasn't as if I were blessed like Pastor Lewis was, I wasn't a man of God—if anything, I know, I was a sick failure who had denied his blessing. Still, the Pumpkin Kid didn't seem to mind—he actually nodded as I approached with the knife, and smiled a little wider, and stuck out his fat pulpy tongue in encouragement. I made the cuts, and I sipped at his blood. I don't know what signs I was looking for—Pastor Lewis had always been frustratingly vague about what a ripening child should taste like—but it seemed to me a little sweeter than the Christ blood I drank in church. That first time I tested him was hard, but it got easier after that—after a while I wouldn't even bother to bandage the gash, and I'd sip at the pumpkin juice until no more flowed out and I was full.

One day I stayed behind after church, just like old times. Pastor Lewis looked surprised to see me, and a little nervous too. He licked his fat lips. "It's been a while," he said. "I didn't think you liked me any more." We went back into the vestry, and it still smelled of pipe smoke, but I also detected a heavy tang of body odour. He cut into my neck, and I refused to flinch, I had seen how bravely a real Pumpkin could take it. He guzzled at my neck for a little while, and there was the familiar not-funny tickle from his stubble, and when he pulled away his face was flushed. "Yes," he said. "Interesting. I mean, you're not ripe quite yet, but there's a little bit of pumpkin in there."

I kissed him on the lips then, and he was very surprised, and he responded, and I stuck my tongue into his mouth and felt around for a bit, but I didn't know what he was talking about, I couldn't taste any pumpkin there at all.

We had to lie down for a while after that. I spoke to him, really just to make conversation, the silence was embarrassing. I asked him how the Halloween preparations were going.

"Well, I think, yes, yes," he said. "Couple of months to go yet, but I think we're on track, some of this year's batch are ripening nicely!"

And I asked him what would happen if you had a Pumpkin Kid who was ripe and ready, and yet was somehow missed out of the ceremony. And he looked aghast, and said, "I have never missed out a child, not once." But I persisted, what would actually happen? "It's a ridiculous question," he said. "It'd be like Jesus Christ turning up late for his own crucifixion. This is what Pumpkin Children are born for. This is their purpose."

He looked quite offended, and began to get up. "I love you," I said. "I love you with all my heart, more than I have ever loved anybody." It was fun to say it, fun to see how embarrassed it made him.

"Look," Pastor Lewis said. "I'm not sure we should meet any more. Obviously, you're welcome to come to church, and take part in the holy sacrament. I'm not going to excommunicate you or anything, ha! But all this... this other stuff... You don't taste of pumpkin. Let me be straight with you. You don't taste of pumpkin, and you never have. I was just being kind. I didn't mind being kind to you, when you were younger. I liked it, when you were younger."

I said I quite understood. I got up, and I went home. Momma was still in her Sunday best, and she was standing at our Pumpkin Kid's bedside, and she was holding on to his hand, and her eyes were shining. She looked up as I came in to the room, and she smiled. She smiled, and she reached out to me, and I was too surprised to resist, I let her take me by the hand too. And we held that pose for a little while, as if someone was about to take a picture, but no one was going to take a picture—hand in hand in hand, like a human chain, and Momma in the middle of it all, and she looked at me, and she said, more gently than I had ever heard her, "We're a proper family at last. This is perfect. Whatever else might happen, this is perfect, right here and now."

One night the Pumpkin Kid came for me again. I was drifting off to sleep on the sofa when I saw his outline framed in the doorway. "Come closer," I said.

His face was fatter and pulpy, and the cracks in his skin were deep, and now sheer gobbets of juice were running down his cheeks and his chin. And his face was also that of a little boy and his cheeks were smooth like a baby's and his eyes were wide with confusion and fear.

I got up. And as I approached his boy face twisted nervously, and his pumpkin face broke into an ever wider smile. "What do you want?" I asked.

He went to the front door. He turned the handle, and the door fell open, though I was sure it had been locked. He stepped outside into the dark night. He didn't even bother to turn his head to see if I would follow. I did.

And I thought how funny he looked as he marched along—barefoot, and dressed only in that orange smock—and then I realised I was barefoot too and in silly striped pyjamas, I guess I looked funny too.

I expected to feel the cold, and that the hard pavement would cut my feet, but I felt nothing.

I caught him up, and we walked side by side. And though we didn't talk, and he never turned to look at me, I was proud that we were together, that I'd found a friend. That I *belonged*—and the town was deserted, and the lights in every house were dark, and it wasn't just that everyone was asleep, it was as if they were all missing, or vanished, or dead. Gone for good, leaving everything for us to play with, just for us and no one else.

We turned up a side street, and then another. And soon I was in uncharted territory, I had never been to this part of the town before. The houses looked colder and more forbidding, and that was silly, because they all looked just the same as my own house, the one I had just abandoned for no good reason in the middle of the night—the one I knew I would never be able to find again unless the Pumpkin Kid helped me back, I was lost, I was lost forever. All alone, and the houses getting more densely packed and crushing in on us. And then I realised with a sudden chill that we were *not* alone—that in the distance were more children in their orange smocks—and coming at us from the left—and now from the right, from all directions—and the orange looked brown and filthy in the moonlight. Dozens of them now, and some were older teenagers like me, and some were infants. A baby was doing its best to match his pumpkin fellows stride for stride even though its legs were embarrassingly short.

We all converged in front of one of those anonymous houses. My Pumpkin Kid gave no sign of welcome to the others, he stood still and waited until everyone was ready. And I stood with him, but now I felt out of place—and at any moment one of the children would challenge me for crashing a party to which I had clearly not been invited. I even thought then of running away, but where would I have gone? The streets would have drowned me, and I'd never be heard of again.

All together now, all the Pumpkin Kids and me. And they turned towards the house—and I turned with them. Inside the house, as if on cue, a single downstairs light switched on.

We marched up to the front door. We stepped inside.

The sitting room was much the same as at my house; the carpet was a different sort of beige.

A man sat on a hard chair, staring down at the floor. He looked up when all the children came in, maybe there was just a flicker of surprise?

"We all die alone, destined to be forgotten," he said. "Save those who choose to die, and die in good faith." I wanted to say the amen afterwards, but my throat was too dry, and when I opened my mouth

I couldn't speak. I thought I'd seen this man in church, but I couldn't be sure, lots of people went to church.

The man hung the rope from the ceiling. We waited. None of us tried to help. Then he climbed on to the chair, and put his head through the noose. "Well," he said to us all, "I guess this is it."

He didn't kill himself right away. I began to get bored. I think maybe some of the Pumpkin Kids did too, though their faces never changed expression; one of the Pumpkin Infants sat down on the floor, it was way past her bedtime. "I've changed my mind!" he said suddenly. "I can do that, can't I? I don't have enough faith!" Still, he kicked away the chair in the end, and he just hung there for a while, and he writhed, and his feet spun around like he thought he was riding a bicycle, and his eyes were wide and wild.

He couldn't speak, but he reached out towards us, it looked like he wanted some help. And so two of the Pumpkin Kids came forward, each took a leg, and gave one single yank downwards with all their might. There was a snap, and the man was still. It was beautiful, really.

Some of the older Pumpkin Kids extricated the man from the noose, and gently lowered him to the floor.

Then, one by one, the Kids came forward, and bent down in front of him. They touched his face. I thought at first they were paying their respects, but it was too meticulous for that. They prodded at his lips, his nose; they squeezed his jowls so that all the fat got bunched up; they traced the contours of his chin, his cheekbones, eye sockets.

And when my own Pumpkin Kid had taken his turn, he looked at me, and nodded his head.

"Oh," I said. "No, I'm good, thanks." But all the Pumpkin Kids were watching, and they were patient, and it soon became clear that until I took my part in their ritual no one was going anywhere. So I stooped down beside the corpse, and rather gingerly I wiped my hand over his face.

And at once I knew the dimensions of his skull, how to measure the gap between his eyes, the particular curvature of his jaw. I understood the span of his face fully and practically, I learned it all—and I didn't know why.

We had all now examined the man's head, and committed its exact size and shape to memory. I thought we would leave him there upon the floor, or put a sheet over his head or something. Instead we hoisted him back into the noose, and set him swinging, all ready to be found by his family the next morning.

It was over. I wanted to thank the Pumpkin Kids, for letting me share their evening with them. But I wasn't sure that was appropriate. So I nodded at them, and gave them big smiles, and they gave me big smiles in return. But to be fair, the smiles were already etched upon their faces and I couldn't be sure they were for me.

We all went our separate ways then, the children in their orange smocks fanning out across the streets as they headed home. And I went back to my own home with my own Pumpkin Kid, and as we reached the house the sun was starting to rise and the world to wake. "We don't have to go to bed just yet," I told him. "Stay with me. I'm not tired." But perhaps he *was* tired, or perhaps he just didn't fancy it—he gave me a farewell nod, then went upstairs.

In the morning I went to see him, and fed him his soup, and as usual most of it dribbled out of his mouth and on to the bed. And he was lying on his back as always, and his eyes stared at me without recognition. But I knew we had had an adventure together, and I gave his hand a friendly squeeze.

In the local newspaper the suicide was reported, and the article gave thanks that his Christ-witnessed death had passed cleanly and without complication.

3

October the first. And out comes the bunting, I watch as the banners are hung across the streets. "Happy Halloween," say some, and "Holy Halloween," say others, and there are streamers everywhere, and there's tinsel and coloured lights, and in the shop windows there are pictures of Jack-o-Lanterns and quotations from the Bible, all the best bits where Jesus mentions pumpkins.

October the sixth, and 'tis the season, so I go out to buy a Halloween tree. I set it up in the sitting room, and it's a tall one this year, it nearly reaches the ceiling! Momma usually helps me with the decorations, but she's too busy upstairs, and so I do it all myself: and when I'm finished there are bright orange bulbs hanging from every branch, and on top an angel stares down in solemn judgment.

October the tenth, and Momma calls out to me, she sounds so excited. "Look at him!" she cries. "I think he's ripening! I think he's nearly done!" The Kid won't tell; he grins at us, and the heavy slat of ribbed flesh growing over his eye makes it seem like he's winking. He opens his mouth and another ball of vegetable pulp plops out.

The eleventh, and the papers report there's been another suicide. I feed the Pumpkin Kid his morning soup. "I guess you were busy out with your friends last night!" I say. "But next time, if you like, I'd be happy to come along too. If I wouldn't get in the way!"

The fifteenth. We get visited by the trick or treaters and the carol singers on the same night. The first take all our sweets, the second our spare change.

The sixteenth, and Momma says, "I'm not going to let him go. He's my miracle, and he'll stay with me forever." And then she bursts into tears, because we both know that can't be true.

The eighteenth. There have been three more suicides; there's always a rush on them as people get ready to celebrate Halloween. I feed the Pumpkin Kid. "Was it some sort of test?" I ask. "Didn't I do it right? I'm sorry. Let me try again. I know I didn't do it right, I'll do better next time."

The twenty-fourth, and with one week to go, Pastor Lewis tells us all in church that he has completed his inspections, and that this year there are no fewer than seven—seven!—Pumpkin Children ripe and ready. That's a bumper crop, it's going to be the best Halloween ever. And then he tells us of Mrs Prentiss who lives on the high street, and Mrs Watkins who lives by the common, and a couple more mothers aside, and how their pregnancies are all set for completion on October the thirty-first, and we all pray for the health of their babies and say amen. Because this is the cycle of life, and God always provides new pumpkins to replenish the bounty.

The twenty-ninth. The pumpkin we have been allocated this year is waiting on our doorstep. I think it is a little knobblier than usual, it's hard to make it mimic a human head. But I do my best—I cut out a lid from the top, and pull out all the flesh within. I make sure it's good and hollow. I make the face, two triangular holes for eyes, another for the nose, and a mouth of jagged teeth opened wide in a smile. And as always, I try to think of Da. I dredge up every happy memory I have of Da, and put them into my handiwork, and though it looks nothing like him, I pretend that this head might be his. When I have finished I kiss it on the forehead, and bless it with the proper words. And I give thanks to God that he has shown us how to triumph over death, so long as we have enough faith, and are brave enough to be cruel.

I go upstairs to the Pumpkin Kid. There have been eight more suicides, one of them was our next door neighbour. "Fuck you," I tell him.

The thirtieth, and it is a day of curfew and of fasting. I remember how as a child I would gobble as much as I could the evening before in preparation, but I'm not hungry this year, and nor is Momma. I guess I'm as grown-up as she is now. And at the end of the day, as we slide into another Halloween, she calls out for me, and she's lying on her bed in the dark, and when I make to turn the lights on she asks me not to.

I sit by her bed, and I listen to her breathing, and she doesn't say anything for a long while.

"Give me your hand," she says, at last. And so I do.

"I've said goodbye to our Pumpkin Child," she tells me. "We really ought to have given him a name, don't you think? That would have been nice." I agree, so right there and then we kick around a few possibilities and at last we come up with a really good one.

"I was so angry," she says, "when your father died."

"I know."

"Because we were supposed to die together."

"Yes."

"That was the dream. Matching nooses, hand in hand. Nice."

I think she's forgotten I'm still holding her hand, and I don't know what to do, I don't think I should squeeze it because that might get mistaken for sympathy. So I let it rest in mine like a dead weight.

"He couldn't wait. He had such faith. Oh, I used to envy him that faith. But I think he also felt. I don't know. That if he left us, didn't get in our way, that we'd be better together. Love each other even, I don't know. I don't know. I'm not," she says, "I'm not going to the Halloween ceremony tomorrow."

"No."

"I've had quite enough of magic. Come closer." Her voice has dropped to a whisper.

"Yes, Momma."

"Are you closer?"

"Yes, Momma."

She says, ever so gently, "I hate you." And she sounds so sad about it, so I can't even blame her.

I wait until she's asleep, and I say goodbye, and kiss her on the forehead just as I had my pumpkin-headed da.

I go next door to see the Pumpkin Kid. He is shining. He is beautiful. "We've given you a name," I say, but I don't tell him what it is.

I undo his bonds at last, and only now do I see how tight they've been. They've cut into his skin, and the grooves they've left are wet with pus. "Go on," I say. "Go away. You're free. Get out of here while you can."

And his head twitches, and I don't know whether that's a shake or a nod, and his mouth creaks open wider. And I expect that from the mouth will slither another turd of vegetable pulp—but then there's a hiss, and I think it's a whisper, and I think I hear words.

I put my head close to the pumpkin mouth, and he tells me what I have to do.

Jesus always makes it rain at Halloween, it's part of the celebration. And this year it's particularly celebratory—it pisses down, and batters hard against the windows. I put on my best Halloween clothes, and a pair of galoshes. I go to see Momma, it's the respectful thing to do. "I hope to see you later, Momma," I say, and who knows? Maybe this year I even might.

I pick up the pumpkin I've carved. I light its candle, and leave for church, cupping the pumpkin under my coat to protect it from the rain.

The church is full. Usually everyone sits away from me, but there's no choice in the matter, and the family that I squeeze next to on the pew grit their teeth and grip their pumpkins and stare ahead refusing to look at me.

For my part, I grip on to a pumpkin of my own. It seems to me a sorry thing compared to the others in the church—some people have carved into theirs expressions of real personality. They've been made with great love and craft, and I can see that the eyes I've gouged aren't straight and the mouth doesn't have enough teeth. It looks nothing like my da. It looks nothing like Momma either, come to that.

And we fall quiet as Pastor Lewis emerges from the vestry, and takes his place before us all. He opens his arms wide, as if embracing us. "Welcome," he says, "on this most hallowed of days, a time of transformation and resurrection, a time when we can all truly be one." His surplice is gleaming white; I see he's shaved off all of his stubble.

"Before we start, some good news. All the pregnancies are going well, and there's no reason not to believe that by the end of the day there'll be four more little miracles in our town. There *can* be errors, of course, but . . ." And at that I am certain he looks at me, and the family next to me clearly think so, they glare and bristle with contempt. "But for now," says the pastor, "let's focus upon *this* year and the harvest it provides."

He pauses, licks his lips, enjoying the moment. Then, "Bring forth your offerings."

We file up the aisle then, one by one, and we place our pumpkins at the front of the church. By the time it's my turn there's a wall six pumpkins high, and it rings around the altar like a fortress, and all the candles inside the pumpkin heads shine bright and pure. I kneel, and Pastor Lewis gives me a sip of wine and places a wafer upon my tongue. "Only the best quality on this holiest of days," he tells us, and the blood is thick and its copper taste so rich, the body of Christ is fleshy and packed with flavour.

When all the pumpkins have been offered, and Christ has been completely devoured, and we are sitting back on our pews, Pastor Lewis begins the litany. We all know the words and mutter amens in the right places. But somehow this year the words sound more magical, and I listen to them as though they're brand new.

"For we who are still living are of the dead. And we will soon be dead, and this gasp of life will seem as a fleeting dream. And Jesus said, "Yea, I say unto you, you that eat of the pumpkin fruit shall this very evening dine at my father's table. Amen. Blessed are the children of the pumpkins, for they will be both the quick and the dead, and we see death through a glass darkly and yea they are that glass. Jesus wept, amen. And God said unto Abraham, "Take your child to the top of a mountain and slay him, for I am thy Lord and he is thy pumpkin." Jesus wept. For the children must suffer so we elders can be free. And we sacrifice but a scrap of our future so we can hold on to our past. Amen. Abraham wept, and slew his son, and the Lord said, "Yea, that's the idea." For Moses said, "Die, but be not forgotten!" Amen. "Die, but return by grace of God, and grace of the Pumpkin Children." Moses wept. I show you life eternal in a handful of pumpkin seeds, and those that take their lives in true faith never die alone. Amen, they wept, they all wept, we all weep forever."

"Amen," we say again.

Pastor Lewis grins then, his eyes twinkle. "Bring forth the children," he says. "Oh, I think you'll like this, they're an especially nice batch this year."

And in come the Pumpkin Kids, walking up the aisle.

There are seven of them. Do I recognise any from that night at the hanging? I cannot say for sure. When they reach the front and look out at us, I wonder whether they might recognise *me*, I feel the absurd urge to wave and get their attention. Barefoot of course, and in orange smocks that look grubby beside the Pastor's surplice—and I think that's maybe the point, we are supposed to honour them but we don't want to *admire* them, they're not heroes, they're lambs to the slaughter. Pastor Lewis inspects them with the pride of a doting father, and that's perhaps just how he sees himself—and there's a little girl that can be no older than twelve, and she's standing a bit lopsided, and the Pastor gets her to straighten up, and then gives us all a wink, and there's a ripple of laughter from the congregation—yes, how we love the cute little girls, the ones who *never* stand up straight!

The kids look pasty, their heads seem swollen. Are they ripe? I guess so, it's hard to tell. And the Pastor says:

"The children are the future. And we disdain the future. It is a world we yet know not of."

The children file behind the pumpkin wall, and take hands, and face us. They close their eyes.

For a while, nothing. It doesn't look as if the Pumpkin Kids are even trying. There's no effort at all. We have to be patient. And then, you can see it—some of the children are clenching their teeth. The little girl begins to shake, just a bit—then the others start to shake too.

But we shouldn't be watching the children. We should be watching the pumpkins. And then someone cries out, "Look!" One of the pumpkins is beginning to change; the carved face is blurring and taking on real features—real skin, real eyes and teeth, hair. And there in the wall of the pumpkin fort there's now a fully formed human head, blinking, looking around the church for its family.

I don't know the woman who's been resurrected, but there's no need to waste time on her. Because other pumpkins are starting to follow suit. Another shimmers and resolves itself into the form of Mr Pattern, who taught me math in school; and now there's one of my neighbours; there's Mrs Thornhill from the chemist; there's that man I helped to hang.

My pumpkin at last begins to shimmer, and I hope it will be Da, or maybe even Momma, but it turns into someone I've never seen before, and that can happen sometimes. The congregation are crying out now to all those they had lost, who have made it back from the dead for this special occasion—"I love you!" "I miss you!" "Darling, I think of you every day!" They jump up upon the pews, waving to get the attention of the pumpkins they know; they aren't allowed to embrace the heads, this is a Christ-witnessed festival of deep solemnity; and the heads can't reply, they have big burning candles wedged tight inside their skulls.

And the Pumpkin Kids have done it again, and we all praise the Lord, because death *isn't* the end, because the Pumpkin Kids prove it—that we get to see the dead, or at least some of them, those with faith, those brave enough to take the noose—and death looks like such a jolly thing, just see how merry the heads are, twitching and blinking and winking, just imagine what stories they might tell if only they could speak!

You might expect that the little girl would be the one to falter first. She looks so very fragile. In fact it's one of the boys, and his head suddenly cracks open. He rains juice down upon the church floor, and his body slumps forward—and the Pumpkin Kids holding his hands either side grasp tight so they won't break the chain. But we know it's the beginning of the end, the time of resurrection will soon be over—as one we call our goodbyes, each desperate for our message of love to be heard over the others. "Take care!" "Remember me!" "See you next year!" "Remember me, please remember!" The little girl breaks next, her head dissolves in a plume of orange pulp, and seconds later another boy comes apart. "Goodbye! Goodbye! Goodbye!" And we wave at the heads like cretins, and it's not as if they can wave back, and I'm waving too and I don't have anyone to wave to.

It's done. It's done. The heads freeze, they flicker. They're pumpkins once more. And the children? Pumpkins too—but their faces haven't been carved into the side, and there's no candle within. They're just pumpkins, the innards spilling out and rotting.

Pastor Lewis was right; it *was* a good Halloween, and those seven children gave us nearly two whole minutes with the dead. And for the moment there's still that buzz of celebration in the air. "Did you see Gramma?" "Did you see Poppa?" And then the disappointment; Halloween really is, finally, over. The miracle is spent. And right now we're as far from the next Halloween as it's possible to be, it'll be another long year before we get to glimpse our families again. Yet we all still sit in our pews. No one quite wants to admit there's nothing more to look forward to, that it's time to go home and get on with our lives.

Then I stand up. And even as I do so, I'm not yet sure I won't do the simple thing and leave the church and go home. I think I decide I will. But still, in spite of all, I walk up the aisle to the altar.

For a moment Pastor Lewis doesn't even register me. And then he looks baffled, he can't work this out. "What are you doing?" he hisses, as I walk through the fort of pumpkins, as I take my rightful place. As I make my announcement.

"I am a Pumpkin Kid."

The congregation doesn't know how to react. Maybe not all of them even recognise me? Then some laugh, catcall. "I am a Pumpkin Kid," I say again, "and I am ripe to bursting," and I stand my ground.

I close my eyes, and wait for something to happen. I concentrate with all my might. And I don't know how to do this, I can't just make myself special at a moment's notice. Not just because I decide I am, not just because I've had enough. And there's more laughter, and I can feel someone grab at my arm, and from the smell I guess it's Pastor Lewis.

I have no other children to hold hands with, but at the touch of the Pastor my hands ball into fists, and then with all my strength I *push.* Down, deep into the rotten pumpkins, the ones that were kids just like me.

I can feel them, and I'm not alone, and I never was alone.

I realise I'm shaking quite a lot, but it doesn't hurt. I can feel the sweat running down my face, and it's sweet, and it's sticky.

I dare to open my eyes. To find out why the people are screaming.

And every pumpkin is my da. Here he is, and it's good to see him, and I've missed him. But now he's here, he's just a dead man, isn't he? What use is his stupid dead face to me now? And every pumpkin is my momma, and now I think every person I have ever known, and now every person I have *never* known. All the dead stare at me and howl out their pain and their fear, and for all their cries their breath is weak and won't blow their candles out. And then they're me, all the pumpkins are me, everyone is me.

And I look at Pastor Lewis, still grabbing my arm, it's like he's paralysed, he can't let go—he's got my face, he's me. And those in the front row, and everyone at the back, yes, they're all screaming out of my mouth.

Pastor Lewis' head pops like a balloon, he was alive one moment and not the next. And doesn't it seem funny that life can become death so suddenly, all that fuss and fear and it's easy peasy, here's death in an instant! Balloons are popping all over the church, it sounds like fireworks, it sounds like a proper celebration. And yes, I guess I shall pop as well sooner or later. I wonder what it will feel like. I wonder how long it will take. And then there's silence. There are no more balloons to burst, and I'm still here, and a part of me is disappointed.

After it's all over I'm too tired to move for quite a while, and I sit right down on the cold church floor. And I am so hungry, and there's pumpkin pulp everywhere, and so I eat some. I'm not proud of it.

The town is empty, it's so quiet. When I get home, Momma has vanished from her noose, and I guess that's a good thing. I go upstairs to see the Pumpkin Kid and wonder whether he's popped too. He isn't there, but I find no trace of him, so maybe he got away. And he's left his orange smock on the bed, all folded up neatly and ready for use.

I sleep that night in my own bed, for the first time in ages, and for the last time in my life. The next morning I put on the orange smock, and go downstairs, and out of the front door, and out of the house. I've been told all the things I have to do, and there are lots of them, and some of them are Questionable, but what of that? I get started. It's a long walk to the next town, especially barefoot. But I'm happy. The rain has gone, and the sun is shining, and it's my birthday.

And the old woman says:

- *Where would you rather face your monsters?*
- *In the sea? Turn to* **The Beast at World's Edge** *(story 92, page 1561).*
- *In the air? Turn to* **Turbulence** *(story 53, page 895).*
- *At home? Turn to* **Tom is in the Attic** *(story 32, page 521).*
- *Or in the nightmares of an innocent child? Turn to* **Bedtime Stories for Yasmin** *(story 5, page 71).*
- *If, on balance, you'd really rather not face monsters at all, there's a rather sweet story about a kindly alchemist and some numbers called* **Digits** *(story 44, page 741). You could always turn to that instead.*

85

It Flows from the Mouth

I'D BEEN FLATTERED WHEN asked to be the godfather of little Ian Wheeler, of course, but I'd had certain misgivings. When I'd met up with Dan in the pub, something we'd liked to do regularly back then, I'd tried to explain at least part of the problem. "Oh, don't worry about the whole spiritual adviser nonsense," said Dan. "Lisa's no more religious than I am, this is just to keep her parents happy." So I caved in, and went along to the christening, and watched Ian get dipped into a font, and afterwards posed for photographs in which I must admit I passed myself off quite successfully as someone just as proud and doting as the actual father and mother.

But my real concern had nothing to do with any religious aspect, and more with the discomfort of shackling myself for life to a person I had no reason to believe I would ever necessarily like. I'd had enough problems when Dan started dating Lisa—Dan and I had been inseparable since school, and now suddenly I was supposed to welcome Lisa into the gang, and want to spend time with her, and chat to her, and buy lager and lime for her—and it wasn't that I *disliked* Lisa, not as such, though she was a bit dull and she wore too much perfume and I had nothing to talk to her about and she had a face as dozy as a stupefied cow. It was more that she had barged her way into a special friendship, with full expectation that I'd not only tolerate the intrusion but welcome it. She never asked if I minded. She never apologised.

And so it was with little Ian. I'm not saying he was a bad child. It was simply that he was a child at all. I've never been wild about children, not even when I was one, and I had always been under the impression that Dan had felt the same, and I'd been somewhat surprised that he wanted one. Surprised and, yes, disappointed. But then, Dan had done lots of things that had surprised me since he'd met Lisa. And my worst fears came to be realised. On the few occasions I went to visit, I would be presented before Ian as if he were a prince, and every little new thing about him was pointed out to me as if I should be entranced—that he had teeth, or that he could walk, that he'd grown an inch taller—sometimes I was under the impression I was supposed to give the kid a round of applause, as if there was anything on display I myself hadn't mastered with greater skill years ago! I just couldn't warm to my godson. It seemed to me that he was constantly demanding attention. And I could put up with that if it was only his mother he was bothering, but all too often he'd pull the same stunts on Dan. Still, I tried to be dutiful, and at Christmas and on birthdays I would send Ian a present. But is it any wonder he made me uncomfortable?—this infant who had crept into my life, though his birth was none of my doing, though his existence wasn't my fault. With his strangely fat face and his cheeks always puffed out as if he were getting ready to cry. I played godfather the best I could, but I felt a fraud.

When Ian was killed at the age of three, knocked down by a car (and safely within the speed limit, so the driver could hardly be blamed), I was, of course, horrified. The death of a child is a terrible thing, and I'm not a monster. But if a child was going to have to die, then I'm glad it was Ian.

Dan and I had always been rather unlikely friends, or so I was told: at school he was more popular than I was, more sporty, more outgoing. I suspect people thought he was good for me, that's what my mother said, and I resented that—I'd point out that, in spite of appearances, he was the one who had sought me out, who wanted to sit next to me in class, who waited to walk home with me. I'd been there for him when he failed his French O-levels, when he got dumped by the cricket first XI, when he first smoked, drank, snogged. I'd been best man at his wedding to Lisa, and I'd arranged a very nice stag night in a Greek restaurant, and given at the reception a speech that made everybody laugh. And I tried to be there for Dan when Ian died. We met up at the pub, at first it was just like the good old days! And I got in a round. How was he feeling? "Not so good, matey," he said, and stared into the bottom of his pint. "Not so good."

We drifted apart. And I'm sorry. I would have been a good friend if he had wanted me to be. But he didn't want me to be.

Dan and Lisa sold their house and moved up north. We exchanged Christmas cards for a couple of years. In the last one, Dan told me they were moving again, this time overseas. He promised he would write to me with his new address. He didn't.

One evening I was at home reading in my study when there was a phone call. "Hello? Is that you, John?" The number was withheld, and so I'm afraid I gave a rather stiff affirmation. "It's Dan. You remember, your old friend Dan? Don't you recognise me?"

And I did recognise him then, of course; and he sounded like the old Dan, the one who'd call me every evening and ask for help with his homework, the one who always had a trace of laughter in his voice.

He told me he was down in the city for a 'work thing', and the firm had given him a hotel for the night. "Would you like to meet up on Thursday?" he said. "We could go to the pub. No problem if it's too short notice. But we could go to the pub."

It was rather short notice, to be fair, but I didn't want to let Dan down.

The pub was heaving with businessmen, it was just after the banks had shut, and the pub Dan had chosen was right in the financial district. And I felt a sudden stab of discomfort—what if I couldn't remember what Dan looked like? What if I couldn't tell him apart from all these other smart suits? (What if he couldn't remember me?)

But he'd arrived first, and he was guarding a small table in the corner, and I knew him at once, he really hadn't changed a bit. He was standing up, and laughing, and gesticulating wildly to catch my attention. No, I was wrong—he *had* changed, a bit, just a bit, actually—as I got closer I could see he'd put on some weight, and his hair was grey. But I'm sure just the same could be said of me, I'm not as young as I was, though I try to keep myself trim, you know? I stuck out my hand for him to shake, and he laughed at that, he was laughing at everything. And he pulled me into a hug, and that was nice.

"What are you drinking?" was the first thing he said. "My round, I'll get the drinks."

We stayed rather late that night, and we had a lot of beer, and I suppose we got quite drunk. But that was all right. For a while we had to shout over the crowd to make ourselves heard, and that was a bit awkward, but pretty soon all the bankers began to go home to their wives and left us in peace. He asked me what I was up to these days, and I explained it the best I could, and my answers seemed to delight him and he laughed even more. I asked him how long he would be in England.

"Oh, we've moved back now," he said. "Mum's dying, I wanted to be close. Well, not too close. But the same country is good. Back over last year, sorry, should have been in touch."

I told him that it didn't matter, he was home now, he'd found me now—and I expressed some sympathy for his mother, I remember quite liking her, when I went to Dan's house she'd give me biscuits.

"We've got this lovely house in the countryside," Dan said. "A mansion, really. Almost a mansion. And the garden's fantastic. Lisa has been designing that, but of course, no surprises there!" I wondered why it was no surprise, I wondered whether Lisa was famous for designing gardens, I supposed she might have been. It was the first time he'd mentioned Lisa, and I said I was glad they were still married.

We shared anecdotes about our schooldays, some of the ones Dan told me I had no memory of whatsoever, so they were quite fresh and exciting. I asked him how Lisa was, and he said she was well. I didn't bring up Ian at all, and I felt a bit bad about that—but then, Dan didn't bring up Ian either, the evening was mercifully free of dead children.

I said I'd walk him back to his hotel.

"You should come and stay," he said to me as we walked the streets. He hung on to my arm. It was raining, and Dan didn't seem to notice, and I didn't care. "Come and stay this weekend. It'd be lovely to see you properly. And I know Lisa would just love to have you." Before I knew it he was all over me with practical details—the best train I could catch, that they'd pick me up from the station. I said I wasn't available the next weekend, I was too busy—I wasn't as it happens, but I still didn't want him to think he could just swan his way back into my life and be instantly forgiven. I promised to come up the weekend after.

Now, I am aware that I don't come out of the following story too well. I can't pretend I understand more than a fraction of what happened when I visited Dan, so I'll just tell it the best I can, warts and all. And I think you'll accept that the circumstances were very strange, and perhaps, to an extent, extenuating.

Dan met me at the station in his car. I asked if it were a new car, and he smiled, and said it was. Then we drove to his house through the rolling countryside, and he talked about his new car all the way. He'd said that he lived somewhere conveniently situated for occasional commutes into London, but I was glad I hadn't got a taxi, the drive was half an hour at least.

Lisa was standing in the driveway to welcome us. I wondered how long she had been standing there. I had been concerned she might remember that I had often shown her a very slight resentment, but she gave no indication of it. She smiled widely enough when I got out of the car, she opened her arms a little in what might have been the beginnings of a hug. I didn't risk it, I offered her my hand. She accepted the hand, laid hers in mine like it was a delicacy, gave a little curtsey, tittered. I still didn't like her very much.

I had to admit, she looked better than I'd expected. Some women grow into their faces, do you know what I mean? They just age well, their eyes take on a certain wisdom, maybe, they just look a bit more dignified. (Whereas I have never known that to be true of men—we just get older: flabbier or bonier, it's never better.) I had always likened Lisa to a cow, and it wasn't as if she had totally thrown off that bovine quality, but the fleshier parts of her face that I had once dismissed as pure farmyard now had a certain lustre. She was beautiful. There was a beauty to her. That's what it was, and I was surprised to see it.

At first I couldn't see why Dan had referred to his house as a mansion. It wasn't especially grand at all—bigger than my house in the city, of course, but you'd expect that in the sticks. They showed me their kitchen, and the stone Aga that took up a whole half of the space. They showed me the lounge, the too-big dining table, the too-big fireplace. I made the right sort of approving noises, and Dan beamed with pride as if I were his favourite schoolmaster giving him a good report card.

"Let me show John the garden!" said Lisa. "Quickly, before the light fades!" And she was excited, impatient.

And now I understood why Dan had used the word 'mansion'. Because though the house was unremarkable, the gardens at the back were huge. "It's just shy of two acres," boasted Dan, and I could well believe it, it seemed to stretch off into the distance, I couldn't see an end to it. But it wasn't merely the size that was impressive—on its own, the size was an anomaly, a vast tract of land that had no business attaching itself to a house so small, like tiny Britain owning the whole of India. What struck me was the design of the thing, that it truly was *designed*, there was honest to God method in the placing of all those shrubs and hedges, the garden was laid out before us like a fully composed work of art. Even in the winter, the flowers not yet in bloom and the grass looking somewhat sorry for itself, the sight still took my breath away.

"I did all the landscaping myself," said Lisa. "It was a hobby." We walked on pebbled paths underneath archways of green fern. One day the paths would lead to big beds of flowers—"I've planted three thousand bulbs of grape hyacinth," Lisa told me, "and, behind that, three thousand of species tulips—so, in the spring, there'll be this sea of blue crashing onto a shore of yellows, and reds, and greens! You'll have to come back in the spring." And every archway opened out to another little garden, different flowers seeded, but placed in ever-winding patterns; there was topiary, there was even a faux maze: the design was intricate enough, I could see, but the hedges were still four feet tall, only a little child could have got lost in there.

And then, through another archway, and Lisa and Dan led me to a pond. There was no water in the pond yet, this was still a work in progress. And, standing in the middle of the pond, raised high on a plinth, a statue of an angel—grey, stone, a fountain spout sticking out of its open mouth.

The wings were furled, somewhat apologetically even, as if the angel wasn't sure how to use them. Its face was of a young cherub, and I stared at it, trying to identify it—it seemed familiar, and I wondered which painting I'd seen that had inspired it, was it Raphael, maybe, or Michelangelo?

"It's Ian," said Dan helpfully. And I had a bit of a shock at that. But now I could see it, of course—the infant hands, body, feet; the strangely fat face; those puffed out cheeks he had always had, now puffed out in anticipation he'd be gushing forth a jet of water.

"We gave a photograph of him to a sculptor," said Lisa. "Local man. Charming man. Excellent craftsman. Can you see the detail in that?"

"This way," said Dan, "it's like Ian is always here, watching over us."

I said I could see the effect they were aiming for. And I couldn't help it, I actually laughed, just for a moment—I remembered that nasty, sulky godson of mine, and thought how unlikely an angel he would have made. If there's an afterlife, and I have no reason to believe in one, God wouldn't have made Ian Wheeler an angel, he wouldn't have wasted the feathers on him. And I thought too of how, had he lived, he'd be a teenager, or nearly a teenager?—if he were still about by now he'd be even nastier and sulkier. Instead here he was, preserved as a three-year-old, forever in stone, with wings sprouting from under his armpits.

I apologised for laughing. "No, no, it's good," said Lisa. "The fountain of remembrance is supposed to make you happy."

We went back to the house. Lisa had prepared us a stew. "Only peasant fare, I'm afraid!" she said. The meat was excellent, and I complimented her on it. She told me it was venison. We opened the bottle of wine I had brought, and disposed of it quickly; then Dan got up and fetched another bottle that was, I have to admit, rather better.

After we had eaten we settled ourselves comfortably in the lounge. Dan took the armchair, which left me and Lisa rubbing arms together on the sofa. Dan smiled, stretched lazily. "I like being the lord of the manor!" he said.

"It suits you very well!" said Lisa, and I agreed.

They placed another log on the fire, and we felt safely protected from the winter outside. But I thought there was still not much warmth to the room. It felt impersonal somehow, as if it were the waiting room for an expensive doctor, or the lobby of a hotel. It was neat and ordered, but there were no knick-knacks to suggest anyone actually lived there. No photographs on the mantelpiece.

There were more anecdotes of our childhood, and Lisa listened politely, and sometimes even managed to insinuate herself into them as if she had been part of our story all along. The wine was making me drowsy, so I didn't mind too much.

I said how happy I was they were back in England.

"Oh, so are we!" said Dan, quite fervently. "Australia was all well and good, you know, but it's not like home. You can only run away from your past for so long." It was the only time Dan had ever suggested he had run away at all, and Lisa frowned at him; he noticed, and winked, quite benignly, and the subject was changed.

"It's a lovely community," said Lisa. "There are village shops only ten minutes walk from here, they have everything you really need. The church is just over the hill. And the local people are so kind, and so very like-minded."

At length Dan did his lord of the manor stretch again, and smiled, and said that he had to go to bed soon. "Church tomorrow," he said, "got to be up nice and early."

"Dan does the readings," said Lisa. "He's very good. He has such a lovely reading voice. What is it tomorrow, darling?"

"Ecclesiastes."

"I like the way you do Ecclesiastes."

I expressed some surprise that Dan had found religion.

"Oh, all things lead to God," said Dan. "It was hard, but I found my way back to His care."

"Maybe you could come with us in the morning, John?" said Lisa. "You don't have to believe or anything, but it's a nice service, and the church is fourteenth century."

"And my Ecclesiastes is second to none," added Dan, and laughed.

I said that would be very nice, I was sure.

"I'll show you upstairs," said Dan. "Darling, can you tidy up down here? I'll show John to bed."

"Of course," said Lisa.

I thanked Lisa once again for a lovely meal, and she nodded. "A proper peasant breakfast in the morning, too!" she promised. "You wait!"

"We've put you in Ian's room," said Dan. "I hope you enjoy it."

I must admit, the sound of that sobered me up a little bit. And as

Dan led me up the stairs, I wondered what Ian's room could be—would it still have his toys in, teddy bears and games and little soldiers? Would it still have that sort of manic wallpaper always inflicted upon infants? And then I remembered that Ian had never lived in this house at all, he'd died years ago—so how could he have a bedroom? Was this something kept in memorial of him? And I had a sudden dread as we stood outside the door, as Dan was turning the handle and smiling and laughing and ushering me in, I didn't want to go in there, I wanted nothing more to do with his dead son.

But I did go in, of course. And it was a perfectly ordinary room—there was nothing of Ian in there at all as far as I could see. Empty cupboards, an empty wardrobe, a little washbasin in the corner. Large bay windows opened out on to the garden, and there was an appealing double bed. My suitcase was already lying upon it, it had been opened for me in preparation, and I couldn't remember when Lisa or Dan had left me alone long enough to take it upstairs.

"It makes us happy to have you here," said Dan. "I can't begin to tell you." His eyes watered with the sentiment of it all, and he opened his arms for another hug, and I gave him one. "Sleep well," he said. "And enjoy yourself." And he was gone.

I went to draw the curtains, and I saw, perhaps, why this was called Ian's room. I looked out directly upon the garden. And from the angle the room offered I could see that all the random charm of it was not so random at all—that all the winding paths, the flowerbeds, the arches, all of them pointed towards a centrepiece, and that centrepiece was the pond, and in the centre of that, the fountain. Ian stared out in the cold, naked with only bare feathers to protect him, his mouth fixed open in that silly round 'o'.

I pulled the curtains on him, got into my pyjamas, brushed my teeth, got into bed. I read for a little while, and then I turned off the light.

I felt very warm and comfortable beneath the sheets. My thoughts began to drift. The distant sound of running water was pleasantly soporific.

I vaguely wondered whether it were raining, but the water was too regular for that. And then I remembered the fountain in the garden, and that reassured me. I listened to it for a while, I felt that it was singing me to sleep.

I opened my eyes only when I remembered that the pond was dry, that the fountain wasn't on.

Even now I don't want to give the impression that I was alarmed. It wasn't alarm. I didn't feel threatened by the sound of the water, anything but that. But it was a puzzle, and my brain doggedly tried to solve it, and its vain attempts to make sense of what it could hear but what it knew couldn't be there began to wake me up. I don't like to sleep at night without all things put into regular order, I like to start each day as a blank new slate with nothing unresolved from the day before. And I recommend that to you all, as the best way to keep your mind healthy and your purpose resolute.

Had Dan or Lisa left a bath running? Could that be it?

I turned on my bedside lamp, huffed, got out of bed. I stood in the middle of the room, stock still, as if this would make it easier to identify where the sound was coming from. It was outside the house. Definitely outside.

I pulled open the curtains, looked back on to the garden.

And, of course, all was as it should have been. There were a few flakes of snow falling, but nothing that could account for that sound of flowing water. And poor dead Ian still stood steadfast in the pond, cold I'm sure, but dry as a bone.

I was fully prepared to give up on the mystery altogether. It didn't matter. It wouldn't keep me awake—far from it, now that I focused on it, the sound seemed even more relaxing. And I turned around to pull closed the curtain, and went back to bed.

If I had turned the other way, I know I would have missed it.

The window was made up of eight square panes of glass. I had been looking at the garden, naturally enough, through one of the central panes. But as I turned, I glanced outside through another pane, the pane at the far bottom left, and something caught my eye.

There was a certain brightness coming from it, that was all. A trick of the light. But it seemed as if the moon was reflecting off the pebbles on the path—but not the whole path, it was illuminating the most direct route from the house to the memorial pond. The pebbles winked and glowed like cat's eyes caught in the headlamps of a motor vehicle.

And there, at the end of that trail of light, at the very centre of the garden, there was the fountain. And now the fountain was on. Water was gushing out of Ian's stone mouth, thick and steady; I could see now how his posture had been so designed, with his little hands bunched up and pressed tight against his chest, to suggest that he was *forcing* out the water, as if his insides were a water balloon and he was trying to squeeze out every single last drop.

There was nothing even now so very untoward about that. If the fountain was on, so it was on. But I changed the direction of my gaze, I looked out at the garden through the central pane again—and there the fountain was dry once more, the garden still, the pathways impossible to discern in the dark.

I'm afraid I must have stayed there for a few minutes, moving my head back and forth, looking through one pane and then through another. Trying to work out what the trick was. How a piece of the window could show one view, another, something else. I'm afraid I would have looked rather like an idiot.

And I tried to open the window. I wanted to see the garden without the prism of the glass to distract me, I wanted to know what was real and what was not. The catch wouldn't give. It seemed to freeze beneath my fingers.

Then there was a knock at my door.

It brought me back to myself, rather; it wasn't until then that I realised it, that I was on the verge of hysteria, or panic at the very least. I don't know whether I had cried out. I thought I had been silent all this while, but perhaps I had cried out. I had woken the house. I was ashamed. I forced myself to turn from the window, and as I did so, with it at my back, I felt like myself again. I smoothed down my pyjamas. I went to open the door. I prepared to apologise.

Lisa was outside in a white nightdress. She came in without my inviting her to do so, smiled, sat upon my bed.

"Hello, John," she whispered.

I said hello back at her.

"Did you never want children of your own? I'm curious."

She began unbuttoning her nightdress then. I decided I really shouldn't look at what she was doing, but I didn't want to look through the window again either, so I settled on a compromise, I stared at a wholly inoffensive wardrobe door. I said something about not really liking children, and that the opportunity to discover otherwise was never much likely to present itself. I was aware, too, that something was very odd about her arrival and the ensuing conversation, but you must understand, it still seemed like a welcome respite from the absurdities I had glimpsed through my bedroom window.

She seemed to accept my answer, and then said, "Would you help me, please?" Her head disappeared into the neck of the nightdress, its now loose arms were flailing. I gave it a tug and pulled the dress off over her head. "Thank you," she said. She smiled, turned, pointed these two big bare breasts straight at me.

"What do you think?" she asked. "Are they better than you were expecting?" I endeavoured to explain that I had had no expectations of her breasts at all. She tittered at that, just as she had when she'd curtseyed to me in the driveway, it was a silly sound. "They're new," she said, and I supposed that made sense, they seemed too mirror perfect to be real, they seemed *sculpted*. And they didn't yet match the colour of her chest, they were white and pristine.

I wanted to ask her about the view through the window, but it seemed suddenly rather impolite to change the subject. What I did ask, though, was whether she was quite sure she had the right bedroom? Didn't she want the one with her husband in it? And at this her face fell.

"Dan hasn't told you, has he?"

I said that he hadn't, no.

"Oh God," she said. "Bloody Dan. This is what we... This is why. God. He's supposed to tell. Why else do you think he brought you here?"

I said that we were old friends, and at that she screwed up her face in contempt, and it made her rather ugly. I suggested that maybe he wanted to show me the house and the garden.

"Dan hates the fucking house and garden," said Lisa. "He'd leave it all tomorrow if he could." She grabbed at her nightdress, struggled with it. "Bloody Dan. I'm very sorry. We have an agreement. I don't know what he's playing at. This is the way *I* cope." She couldn't get her arms in the right holes, she began to cry.

I said I was sorry. I asked her whether she could hear running water anywhere, was it just me?

"I've always liked you, John," she said. "Can't you like me just a little bit?"

I said I did like her, a little bit. More than, even.

"Can't you like me for one night?"

I tried asking her about Dan, but she just shook her head, and now she was smiling through the tears. "This is the way we cope. Can't you help me out?" I said I was puzzled by the fountain outside, but by this stage the nightdress was back over her head again, maybe she couldn't hear.

She said, "Now, don't you worry. I'm not going to do anything you won't like." Then she climbed on top of me and gripped me hard between her thighs. She let her long hair fall across my face, then she whispered in my ear. I expected her to say something romantic. She said, "I won't get pregnant, I've been thoroughly sterilised."

Now, I have no objection to sex, but I hadn't touched a woman in years. Not since I was at school, not since Dan had discovered girls, and had started touching them, and I had touched them too so he wouldn't leave me out.

But even accepting my unfamiliarity with the whole enterprise, I don't think I did an especially good job. To be honest, I let Lisa do all of the work, the most I contributed was a couple of hands on her back so that she wouldn't fall off and sprain herself. And I listened to the sound of the fountain outside; sometimes the mechanical grunts of Lisa would drown it out, and I'd think maybe it was over, but then she'd have to pause for breath, or she'd be gnawing at my neck with her lips, or she'd be sitting tall and gritting her teeth hard and screwing her eyes tight and being ever so quiet, and I could hear the fountain just as before.

At length she rolled off, and thanked me, and kissed me on the mouth. The kiss was nice. I grant you that, the kiss was nice. She curled up beside me and went to sleep. Then she turned away from me altogether and I felt alone, so alone.

The curtains were still open, but there was no light spilling into the room, it was just black and bleak out there. And from my position I couldn't crane my head to see whether there was any light coming through the pane on the bottom left.

I didn't want to wake Lisa. I got out of bed very gently. It was cold. My pyjama trousers had got lost somewhere. I'd have had to have turned on the bedside lamp to find them. I wasn't going to turn on the bedside lamp.

I went straight to the pane, I looked out.

As before, the pathway to the centre was lit by sparkling pebbles. But this time the snow was falling in droves, big clumps of it, and every flake seemed to catch the moon, and each one of them was like a little lamp lighting up the whole garden. The flowers were in bloom. It was ridiculous, but the flowers were in bloom—the blanket of red and white roses was thick and warm, and the snow fell upon it, and the roses didn't care, the roses knew they could melt that snow, they had nothing to fear from it. I looked out at where Lisa had planted the hyacinths and the tulips—it was, as she'd said, like a wave of blue breaking upon a brightly coloured shore.

And at the fountain itself. Ian was throwing up all the water he had inside him, and he had so *much* water, he was never going to run out, was he? But I would have thought his face would have been distressed—it was not distressed. The worst you could say about the expression he wore was that it was resigned. Ian Wheeler had a job to do, and he was going to do it. It wasn't a pleasant job, but he wasn't one to complain, he'd just do the very best he could. And the flowers were growing around him too, and vines were twisting up his body and tightening around his neck.

Over the sound of the fountain I heard another noise now. Less regular. The sound of something dragging over loose stone. Something heavy, but determined; it seemed that every lurch across the stone was done with great weariness, but it wasn't going to stop—it might be *slow*, but it wasn't going to stop. And I can't tell you why, but I suddenly felt a cold terror icing down my body, so cold that it froze my body still and I could do nothing but watch.

And into view at last shuffled Dan. He was naked. And the snow was falling all around him, and I could see that it was falling fast and drenching him when it melted against his skin, but he didn't notice, he was like the roses, he didn't care, he didn't stop. Forcing himself forward, but calmly, so deliberately, each step an effort but an effort he was equal to. Further up the path, following the trail of sparkling pebbles to the fountain. Following the yellow brick road.

I tried looking through the other panes. Nothing but darkness, and the snow falling so much more gently. I only wanted to look at that garden, at that reality. But I could hear the sound from the other garden so much more clearly, I couldn't *not* hear it, the agonised heave of Dan's body up the path. The flow of running water, the way it gushed and spilled, all that noise, all of it, it was pulling him along. I had to look. I did.

Once in a while the bends of the path would turn Dan around so that he was facing me. And I could see that dead face—no, not dead, not vacant even, it was filled with purpose, but it wasn't a purpose I understood and it had nothing to do with the Dan I had loved for so many years. I could see his skin turning blue with the cold. I could see his penis had shrunk away almost to nothing.

And now, too soon—he had reached the statue of his dead son. At last he stopped, as if to contemplate it. As if to study the workmanship!—his head tilted to one side. And maybe his son contemplated him in return, but if he did, he still never stopped spewing forth all that water, all the water there was in the world. Then—Dan was moving again, he was using his last reserves of energy, he was stepping into the freezing pond, he was wading over to the stone angel, raising an arm, then both arms, he was reaching out to it. And I thought I could hear him howling. He was, he was howling.

I battered at the window. I tried again to open it. The catch wouldn't lift, the catch was so cold it hurt.

But Dan had his son in his arms now, wrapping his arms about him tightly, he was hugging him for dear life, and he was crying out—he was screaming with such love and such despair. And then, then, he fell silent, and that was more terrible still—and he put his mouth to his son's, he opened his mouth wide and pressed it against those stone lips, and the water splashed against his face and against his chest, and yet he kissed his son closer, he plugged the flow of water, he took it all inside and swallowed it down.

The window gave. The rush of cold air winded me. I called out. "Dan!" I shouted. "Dan!" But there was nothing to be seen now the window was open, nothing but dead space, dead air, blackness.

"Darling," said Lisa.

I turned around. She was awake.

"Darling," she said. "Darling, close the window. Come back to bed." She patted the mattress beside her in a manner I assumed was enticing.

I closed the window. I looked through the pane once more, I looked through every pane, and there was nothing to make out, the moon was behind the clouds, the darkness was full and unyielding. I went back to bed. I did as I was told.

I had fully intended to go to church the next morning. I had made a promise, and I keep my promises. But when I woke up the house was empty. Dan and Lisa had gone without me. I made myself a cup of tea, and waited for them to come back. Eventually, of course, they did. All smiles, both looking so smart, Dan in particular was very handsome in his suit. "Sorry, matey," said Dan. "I popped my head around your door, but you looked like you needed the extra sleep! Hope you don't mind!" And Lisa just smiled.

Neither of them said a word about the adventures of the night before, and neither treated me any differently. Lisa had told me she'd cook a big peasant's breakfast, and she was as good as her word—bacon, eggs, and sausages she said were from pigs freshly slaughtered by a farmer friend she'd made. Then we settled down in the lounge, and shared the Sunday newspaper, each reading different sections then swapping when we were done. It was nice.

Some time early afternoon, though, Dan looked at the clock, and said, "Best you get back home, John! I've things that need doing!" And I hugged Lisa goodbye, and Dan drove me to the railway station, and we hugged too, and I thanked him for the weekend.

We drifted apart. I don't know who drifted from whom, I doubt it was anything very deliberate. No, wait, I sent them a Christmas card, and they didn't respond. So they're the ones who drifted. They drifted, and I stayed where I was, exactly the same.

That would be the end of the story. I had heard from an old school friend that a couple of years later Dan and Lisa had separated. It was just gossip, and I didn't know whether it was true or not, and I felt sorry for them just the same.

That was maybe six months ago. Recently I received a letter.

Dear John,

You may have heard that Dan and I have gone our different ways! It was quite sad at the time, but it was very amicable, and I'm sure one day we will be good friends.

But sometimes when something has died, you just have to accept it, and move on.

I still have the house. Dan was very generous, to be fair. All he wanted was half of the money, and the fountain from the garden. We had to dig it up, and I'm afraid it has made the garden a bit of an eyesore! I tried to tell

Dan it won't work, it was specially designed to fit with all our underground piping, but as you know, there's no talking to Dan!

I'm going to rethink the garden. I'm sure I can make it even better.

All the locals have been very nice, and they're attentive as ever in their own way. But I don't know. I think perhaps they liked Dan more than they ever liked me.

If you would like to stay again, that would make me very happy.

Maybe I shouldn't say this. But that night we spent together was very special. It was a special night. And I think of you often. Sometimes I think you're the one who could save me. Sometimes I think you could give me meaning.

But regardless. Thank you for always being such a good friend to me and Dan, and for being best man at the wedding, and any other duties you took on.

Best regards,

Lisa Howell (once Wheeler).

I haven't written back yet. I might.

And the old woman says:

- *In horror stories I'm not frightened by vampires, or zombies, or ghosts with clanking chains. I'm not frightened by monsters. What unnerves me is dissonance. There's absurdity to the world just out of the corner of my eye. Seeing a different view of the same garden through two panes on a window—the certain sense that life has been bent out of shape, and at any moment I might get lost through the cracks that's caused. Consider* **The Sixteenth Step** *(story 16, page 273).*
- *When you were young, your parents' friends were never very pleasant, were they? There's a perfect shocker in* **Bedtime Stories for Yasmin** *(story 5, page 71).*
- *A whole statue as memorial to just one little boy seems very ostentatious. Turn to* **The War Artist** *(story 10, page 149) for something more economical.*
- *Angels deserve better than being frozen stiff as hunks of marble. They should be free to range around the wide open plains. Turn to* **Angels in Australia** *(story 59, page 995).*
- *To see a family do something really special with their garden, turn to* **Something in the Soil** *(page 47, page 789)*

86
MUMMY'S LITTLE MIRACLE

MY DAUGHTER LAURA is pregnant. I wouldn't mind, but she's only two years old. Her little girl stomach is distended with the weight of her baby inside; she only started to walk nine months ago, and now she's having to prop herself up clinging to the walls, otherwise that big bulge in her tummy will topple her over. My wife is so happy about it. She's over the moon. She'd always wanted a child, she told me that clearly on our very first date—I'd asked what she was interested in, expecting her to come out with a hobby or her favourite TV programme, and she said just one thing—"Breeding." And now she gets to have a grandchild too, and she's already knitting it socks and booties. "I'm going to be a nanna," she says, "I'll be the best nanna in the world. It's a blessing." I'm not so sure. I wonder whether a family can be just a little too blessed.

My wife had loved being pregnant. She would show off about it to all her friends, and wear clothes that emphasised her swelling bump. And she was fascinated by the way her body would change daily; I'd come home from work sometimes and she'd be waiting for me, standing in the hallway, naked, all the better to show the latest instances of her metamorphosis, she'd point out the darkening of the areolas around her nipple, or the way her belly button had pushed out. And she'd delight in her glow; "Look, darling," she'd say, "I'm glowing, can you see how much I'm glowing?" Laura hasn't got the vocabulary to express herself properly yet, but it's clear she's not enjoying her pregnancy quite so much. She sighs as she heaves her bulk around her little playroom, sometimes she's in tears. My wife tries to be supportive, and is full of good advice about what to expect in the third trimester, and ways Laura can best nurture the foetus—but for all her good intentions, she often loses patience. "You don't know how lucky you are!" she snaps at her. "Why, all around the world now there are women just *begging* to conceive, they're trying all sorts of unnatural methods with frozen sperm and sieves. And here you are, and it's fallen into your lap. And look at how you glow!" Sometimes my wife gets so angry with Laura she won't speak to her for days. Once I even saw her slap her. It wasn't too hard, though, and it was only across the face—she wouldn't do anything that might hurt that little baby within.

We didn't realise Laura was pregnant for a while. Try as hard as we can, we're not expert parents, and when at first our little daughter ballooned in weight we just thought we were feeding her too much. It wasn't until the morning sickness took hold of her that my wife recognised the symptoms; she had been taken exactly the same way, daily vomiting both loud and copious, and how she'd gloried in it, her face rising up from that toilet bowl at me all full of smiles, "Darling, you're going to be a daddy!" Laura would wake up each morning and have to toddle to the bathroom and throw up, and her mother would be there, pulling her hair back so it wouldn't get caught in the effluence, and telling her that she was going to be all right, and telling her how lucky she was. I'd suggested we take Laura to a doctor, because when all is said and done, falling pregnant at two years old is decidedly unusual. But my wife was dead set against that—they'd want to run lots of tests on Laura like a lab rat, they'd take her away from us. "And this is *our* miracle," said my wife, "this is all ours." We hid Laura away. It wasn't as if it were that hard. Laura attended playgroup on Thursday mornings, and we cancelled it. And it wasn't as if anyone ever visited, it wasn't as if we had many friends left, most of them had got bored with us when my wife had been expecting.

I did sometimes wonder who the father might be. After all, it wasn't as if Laura had much of a social life, I couldn't see there could be that many contenders. Certainly, I loved Laura; when I saw my daughter for the first time—in that hospital bed—all bald and squalling—oh, I felt such a sudden rush of love for her, and I just wanted to pick her up in my arms, and the nurse gave her to me to hold, and I was terrified I'd break her, fragile little thing like that, and the nurse laughed and said she was stronger than she looked. And I'd held her tight then, and I've held her tight since, whenever that rush of love came over me I'd lift her out of her cot and give her the biggest cuddle—had I made her pregnant doing that? Had my love been too much? My wife thought it was unlikely, but I couldn't help worrying about it. The only alternative I could see was that it might have happened at the playgroup. There was a woman in charge of the playgroup, and all the assistants at the playgroup were women too, and only mothers ever collected their children from the playgroup, fathers were too busy—really, it was wall-to-wall women at the Shillingthorpe Nursery, I can assure you. But some of the toddlers left in care were boys, and I was a boy myself once, I know what naughty tricks boys can get up to. And I went along to the nursery one morning. I stood outside and watched them secretly through the window. None of the little boys seemed sexually boisterous, but I suppose you never can tell. I wondered whether Laura had led them on a bit, had she been flirty, had she flaunted herself, had she been a bit of a tramp?

But my wife had another, better explanation. "It'll be a virgin birth," she said. "You know, like that one in the Bible." And it was funny, because she'd never been a religious person before, we'd got married at a registry office at her insistence. And there was that time my mother came over, and all she'd done was ask whether we were going to get Laura christened, and the way my wife had shouted at her, had told her to mind her own business, it had reduced my mother to tears. But now my wife would study the Bible, looking for some way to make sense of this unexpected blessing bestowed upon us. "It stands to reason," she told me. "The first virgin birth was a grown woman, in the sequel God would want to make it harder."

And one of the great joys of my wife's pregnancy had been choosing Laura's name together. We'd lie side by side in bed, and try different ones out for size, and we'd laugh at them all, we'd laugh so much back then. And we chose Laura in the end, because Laura was the name of my wife's late mother, and my wife's mother had died very young and my wife had never known her well but she was certain she'd loved my wife very much, and she wanted her mother to be commemorated somehow because she thought it'd have meant the world to her. And because it was the name of the very prettiest of my ex-girlfriends. Though I didn't share that information with my wife. And, no, we didn't christen her, but how proud I was when we signed her name on the birth certificate, that name somehow made her real, it turned her into a person. And I had hoped that now there was a new baby in our lives we could do the same thing; we'd lie in bed, we'd say names, we'd laugh. But my wife wasn't having any of it. "He already has a name," she told me. "He's Jesus." And that did solemnify the mood somewhat, it was hard to laugh in bed when you knew that the messiah was growing inside your infant daughter's belly in the room just across the hall.

I wouldn't want to give you the impression that my wife wasn't kind to Laura, because she was, quite often; and she's the one who had to spend all day with her, after all, I got to go to the office, I got some escape from it. And Laura does moan too much. The way she complains about her cramps, you'd think no one had ever been pregnant before! You'd think her own mother herself hadn't been pregnant, and she'd had the cramps too, she was bent double with them. But I feel sometimes that my wife doesn't talk to Laura very much, she just talks to the foetus inside her—and even when she addresses Laura by name, tells her to clean her teeth or pick up her toys, it's the bump she's looking at. And me too—I still pick her up, I still hold her in my arms, but I feel I'm faking it, I no longer quite get that rush of love, I try to, I look for it, but it's just out of reach. I hold Laura in my arms, and I can feel her little heart beating, but now I think, is that *her* heart? Or is it Jesus's? And it troubles me. Laura cries so much, and my wife feels no sympathy, she tells her she should be grateful to be the vessel of the Living Lord. And I admit it, I can't feel much sympathy either. Because I know she's my little girl, and I know she's hurting, and I know I wouldn't want her hurting for the whole wide world—but deep down I wonder whether she might have brought this on herself, that she might just be a cheap slapper.

The cramps were so bad this morning. Laura came to our room, and she was crawling along the floor, it was as if she'd regressed all the way back to a one-year-old. And there was blood. I insisted we take her to the hospital, and at first my wife refused, but I could tell she was scared, and I was able to convince her to do the right thing. And the doctor inspected Laura. He took X-rays. And even then I wondered whether we'd got the symptoms wrong, that Laura wasn't pregnant, that our daughter was merely a fat kid who threw up. But no, he was amazed; he said he'd never seen anything like it; "Mr and Mrs Marshall, your little girl is with child." "Yes, yes," snapped my wife, "but what of the baby, is He all right, is He going to be okay?" The doctor smiled through his medical bemusement. "Everything's all right," he assured us, "the baby's fine. You're going to have a healthy granddaughter."

My wife didn't say much in the car, and Laura didn't either, she could tell her mother was cross. I tried to be cheerful. I said that maybe it'd be okay, or maybe the doctor had made a mistake. Until my wife retorted, "It's not going to be okay, Jesus wouldn't come back as a *girl*, would He? That's just ridiculous." So I said nothing for a bit. I then said, that maybe if the baby wasn't Jesus, we could all have some fun thinking up another name for it instead? But my wife said she didn't care, and Laura was still being quiet, and I had to admit I couldn't think of anything appropriate.

When we got home there was a message on the answering machine. It was the doctor. And he sounded excited, and that wasn't a surprise, he'd sounded excited from the start, he hadn't had the time to get fed up with the pregnancy like we had. I nearly turned the message off, but my wife stopped me. And the doctor said they'd examined the X-rays of the foetus. And it was incredible. It was incredible, there was no other words for it. Because she was pregnant. Not Laura—well, yes, Laura, but not just Laura—the foetus, the foetus inside her. The foetus was pregnant. Inside that little lump of life growing inside our daughter was another living lump littler still, not even a lump, no more than a speck, but it was thriving, and it was getting bigger, and it was human. And the doctor said he couldn't tell the gender of the speck for sure, but he thought it might have a penis. A new baby. A new miracle. And my wife standing there listening to the news, and tears rolling down her cheeks—and my daughter, feeling at her stomach involuntarily, tears streaming too. I have to be honest, even I felt a bit emotional.

Laura's still cramping badly, but we've given her painkillers, and we've closed the bedroom door so we can't hear her. And my wife and I are alone. And my wife has put on perfume, and she never wears perfume, not now. She's come to me, and she's smiling again, and I see the smile is made of lipstick. The smile is meant to be seductive, or maybe it's trying to be happy, or maybe it's just trying to look shy and awkward, and shy and awkward is its best bet. "I love you," she says. "I love you." And she kisses me, and we haven't kissed for a long time, and I'm a bit taken aback, I don't think of her as anything other than a mother any more. "We've still got it, baby, haven't we?" comes the whisper in my ear. "We've still got it?" And she asks me to make love to her. "Fill me with your baby juice, we can be special too, can't we, we can be special too, tell me we can be special." And it seems wrong, that we're competing with our own daughter like this, but my wife wants a baby of her own, and whatever she wants, that's what I try to give. And I do my best. I really do. I strain inside her and try to think baby thoughts, I try to will something new to life. But I keep thinking of my grandchild on her way, and of my great-grandchild too, and all the descendants that may be following after, and I'm sad to say, I can't help it, I droop a little, I droop, I feel so very old.

And the old woman says:

- *The image of poor Laura and her pregnant child is rather like a Russian doll. To see some unfortunate dolls face the firing squad, turn to* **That Tiny Flutter of the Heart I Used to Call Love** *(story 22, page 355).*
- *To read another tale of miracles, turn to* **Something in the Soil** *(story 47, page 789).*
- *The Virgin birth part of the Bible is one of the very best bits. To see its writer at work, turn to* **The Masterwork** *(story 83, page 1423).*
- *We would do anything to prevent our children from suffering. What if you could live in a world where they couldn't die, and couldn't feel pain? Discover the rules behind* **The Smell of Burnt Orange** *(story 79, page 1373).*
- *Giving birth to new life should be the greatest of all love stories. If you have ever experienced the process—either as parent or as offspring—turn to* **101 Heartbeats** *(story 101, page 1695).*

87
Shalt Not

IN LATER YEARS, GOD would consider his greatest mistake not to be disease, or suffering, or engendering a warlike impulse in Man; it was not the pips that ruin the satsuma, or the stones that compromise the pleasure of the plum; it was not the way that Winter can be far too cold and Summer is frequently much too hot. God's greatest mistake was opening his heart to Kevin Collins. Really, he should have taken one look at Kevin Collins and started running.

It was all so much simpler back in the olden days. The peoples of Earth either obeyed God, or they didn't. Those that didn't were liable to be turned into piles of ash or pillars of salt, drowned in big floods or plagued by locusts. Those that did were sometimes rewarded with manna. There was none of this problem with faith, none of the not-believing-in-God thing. Everybody believed in God. Why wouldn't they? Once every couple of months or so they'd get to see God; he'd make a spot check on them, and they'd all have to march past him in single file whilst God looked them all over and up and down and every which way he chose.

The chief of the peoples was called Moses, and so it was that when God decided he ought to set down some commandments in stone, Moses was the one who traipsed up the side of Mount Sinai every morning to record them. God told Moses that he really didn't have to do all the secretarial work—"Haven't you heard of delegation?" he asked—but Moses just said this was an important job and as team leader he wanted to make sure it was done right. They'd work from nine in the morning till five in the afternoon, with a lunch break never to exceed sixty minutes in duration, and God would impart to Moses the laws by which Mankind was now to live, and Moses would chip them down into marble with a hammer and chisel. Moses never passed comment upon any of the commandments, not even God's really good ones, the ones God thought were truly inspired and that he had taken all night to come up with. They didn't fraternise. In the lunch hour God ate alone in his office; Moses had usually packed sandwiches and had them at his desk.

One day Moses didn't show up for work. Instead, with slab of marble at the ready, was Kevin Collins.

"Where's Moses?" asked God.

"Off sick," said Kevin. "Think it's a cold or something. Anyway. I'm Kevin. I'm the temp."

God wasn't very good with faces, but he could tell immediately that Kevin looked very different to Moses. He didn't look quite as respectful, somehow, and that irked God—he'd dart a look at him every now and again to catch any hint of insubordination, but there was nothing, really—the eyes were livelier, maybe, they twinkled a bit, and God wondered whether there was something ironic in that twinkle when he was called 'Lord' or 'Sir'—his skin seemed finer than Moses' skin, his beard was shorter—wait, Kevin didn't even have a beard—that was it, that was the problem, this Kevin was *young*. "I hope you realise the great importance of what we're doing," growled God, and Kevin said he did, and grinned. But Kevin was just as good a worker as Moses; if anything, Kevin was rather better. The younger man could hold up the marble slab for longer before getting tired, and the handwriting seemed neater and more confident, there had been a wobble to Moses' own style that possibly came from the fact his hands shook so much in awe.

In the afternoon, Kevin said, "Got to say, I loved the one about not coveting your neighbour's ass. That was brilliant."

"Oh, thank you," said God, surprised. "Thanks." He thought for a bit. "Why?"

"Well, you know. It's an ass."

"Yes?" said God.

"Asses are funny, aren't they?"

"Oh. Yes. Yes," said God. "I suppose they are."

Kevin chuckled at the thought of asses, and of anyone fool enough to covet asses, for a moment longer. "Brilliant," he said to himself.

They worked in silence for the rest of the afternoon, though God felt something had happened, the mood had lightened somewhat. And he wondered what Kevin would make of the next commandment he'd got up his sleeve, the one about honouring fathers and mothers, he wondered whether Kevin would think that was brilliant too.

At five o'clock God said, "That's it for the day," and Kevin nodded, stretched, and laid down his chisel, nearly halfway through carving a 'shalt'.

Kevin got his things together. "Well, g'night then," he said.

"Good night," said God.

"And what are you up to this evening?"

"What?"

"You've got nothing planned? Going to stay in, take it easy, yeah? Brilliant."

No one had ever asked God before what he might be up to of an evening, not any evening, not ever. "Oh," said God. "Well. I might work on some more commandments."

"Yeah?"

"Might come up with some new ones. You know."

"Okay," said Kevin. "Well, don't you work too hard, eh? You know what they say. All work and no play, and all that."

"No," said God. "What do they say?"

"You know. Makes you dull or something."

"You think your Lord and God is *dull*?" And there was just a hint of thunder in God's voice, there was a distant rumble and the skies blackened somewhat.

If Kevin had noticed he didn't show it. "Nah," he said. "I mean, come on. You're the guy who came up with the ass, right?" And he grinned. And God couldn't help it, he grinned right back, and the clouds parted, and there was sunshine.

God thought about Kevin that night. He went back to the first draft he'd made of his ass commandment, the one which said, "Thou shalt not covet thy neighbour's ass, or anything else belonging to the neighbour, or any ass belonging to anyone not your neighbour, or anything else belonging to anyone else," and wondered whether that had been even funnier.

The next day Kevin came to work again. He was twenty minutes late. "Sorry, sorry," said Kevin. "I overslept, yeah? I'll make up for it in the lunch hour, yeah?" And he grinned again.

"You'll have to," said God.

"Sure. And how are you today, God? You get up to any fun last night?"

"I think," pronounced God, "we should get started, shouldn't we? There's a lot to do, and enough time has been wasted already."

"You're the boss," said Kevin amiably, and finished off last night's 'shalt' with cheery gusto. He began to whistle as he worked, and God didn't like whistling. But he hadn't the heart to tell Kevin off, it was just a little whistle, quiet through the front teeth, and besides, it was quite a nice tune, God thought it was quite nice.

Good progress was made that morning, and at lunchtime God told Kevin that he could take his full hour's break after all, and Kevin smiled, and said, "Sure." God said, "And I'm perfectly fine, thank you for asking."

Kevin didn't seem surprised it had taken God so long to answer his question. "That's good," he said. "Because, you know, I'd have thought it must get a bit lonely, up here on your own."

"Oh no," said God. "No. No, no."

"No?"

"No. I don't have time to get lonely. There's so much to do. There's always so very much to do."

Kevin nodded, and agreed that there must be, yeah.

God decided he wouldn't eat his lunch shut in his office today, he stayed out with Kevin. God ate some manna, and Kevin ate a sausage sandwich, and God rather liked the look of that sausage sandwich, and

Kevin asked whether he'd like one, and God said that'd be lovely if Kevin didn't mind, and Kevin didn't, so God took a sausage sandwich, and asked Kevin whether he'd like some of his manna, and Kevin said no, he was okay.

Around half past four, God cleared his throat, and said, "So, what are you up to this evening?"

"Well," Kevin said, "it's Friday night, isn't it? Friday nights I go down the pub with the lads. Gary, Barry, and Stew, Stew talks such shit, he's brilliant, he's mental. Have a few beers, it's a laugh. Hey, you could come with us if you like."

"Me?" said God. "Oh, no, I couldn't do that."

"Why not? The lads won't mind."

"But it wouldn't be. Well. It wouldn't be professional. Would it? If I were seen to, you know. I have to maintain a certain authority, I wouldn't want to be recognised, I wouldn't want to be seen, I...I'm God, I'm your lord and master."

"No one's lord of anyone on a Friday night," said Kevin. "But it's up to you."

Around quarter to five, God cleared his throat again. Said, "I do get a bit lonely, actually." And Kevin said, "You could wear a hat." And that was the matter sorted.

And so, disguised in a blue baseball cap, God followed Kevin into the pub. There were butterflies in his stomach, he hadn't felt this nervous since he'd triggered the Big Bang—but maybe nerves were a *good* thing, maybe they made him feel *alive*. He was introduced to Gary, Barry and Stew. "This is Norman," said Kevin, "I know him from work;" "All right, Norm?" Gary, Barry and Stew each said, but they didn't seem especially interested in the answer. The pub was full to heaving, crushed with the bodies of all God's followers let loose at week's end with a pay cheque, and it was very loud, and to hear what Gary, Barry and Stew had to say God had to huddle closer to them than he really felt comfortable with. "I'll get the first round," said Kevin, and God said he'd go with him to the bar and help carry the pints back, he didn't want to be left alone with the lads, he'd already run out of things to say to them. "They're just the lads," Kevin reassured God as they waited to get served, "they're brilliant, they're nothing to worry about." Kevin ordered five pints of lager, and together they steered the glasses back to the table. God had never tasted lager before, and discovered it got better the more he swallowed—by the end it wasn't horrid at all. The lads all talked about girls, and how much they liked girls, and whether certain girls were up for it or not, and how the ones who weren't up for it were ugly anyway, ugly or lesbian—and God felt quite proud, he'd been the one who'd created girls in the first place, girls were really his whole idea, he was rather inclined to tell the lads and take the credit. But that would give away his identity, and even four pints down he still wasn't able to lose that many of his inhibitions. Barry knocked his glass on to the table, mock accidentally, and said, "Just as well my glass were empty," and the lads all laughed, and looked at God pointedly, and Kevin had to tell him it was his round. And God blushed bright red and said sorry—and he went to the bar and to make up for it, he ordered *ten* pints of lager, yeah, and five packets of crisps whilst you're at it, and peanuts too, no, I don't mind, salted, dry roasted, what's easier—he didn't want the lads to think he was mean. "You shouldn't try so hard," Kevin hissed at him, but the lads didn't seem to mind, they cheered him as he necked one pint and then the other and they tried to match him for speed. And Gary tried to say something funny but the words didn't come out right, but that didn't matter, that was quite funny anyway, and Stew – well, Stew talked such shit all right, he made God laugh so hard with all that shit, he was mental, he was brilliant, the lads were *all* brilliant, God liked making new friends.

A bell was rung, and the barman called time, and the lads groaned and said they weren't done yet. There was this club nearby that was open all night, Barry said, although it may have been Gary—a cover charge to get in, but drinks till dawn. So they went down there, and there was a huge queue to get inside, and the lads kept on saying it wasn't worth it, they should just give up and go home, it wasn't fucking worth it—and then suddenly they were at the front of the queue, so that was all right. A man on the door the size of Goliath told God he couldn't come in wearing his baseball cap, and God said he wouldn't take it off, and Goliath said he wouldn't be let in then—and God said, "I'm keeping my baseball cap on, *and* I'm coming in, no feat is too impossible for your Lord," and it wasn't clear what happened, it was as if Goliath just gave up, he sort of shrugged, and sighed, and waved them all in. God had thought that the pub was busy, but the club was just wall to wall flesh, he hadn't realised he'd created quite this many people, he began to wonder whether it'd be time soon for another cull. And the noise was loud, you had to shout to hear yourself heard, the bass music got into everything, it got into your very bones. Gary and Barry and Stew were soon lost within the crowd, and God never saw any of them again, except for Stew a couple of hours later who seemed to bob to the surface like some stray piece of flotsam only to be pulled back under again—God called out to Stew then, but Stew didn't seem to recognise God, maybe he was too pissed, maybe he just didn't care. God grabbed on to Kevin's arm—"Don't you leave me, don't leave me on my own," and Kevin promised he wouldn't.

A couple more pints later Kevin shouted to God, "I think those girls are eyeing us up. Which do you prefer, the blonde or the brunette?" And God opened his mouth to say that he thought he should get home now, he was tired and he had to write more commandments in the morning, but what came out was, "The blonde! The blonde! The blonde!", and Kevin laughed. The blonde shouted her name was Cheryl. The brunette shouted her name was Cheryl too. "That must be handy!" shouted Kevin, and the girls laughed, they shouted back that it was handy, they were inseparable, the two Cheryls, they were like sisters, like. Kevin took his Cheryl on to the dance floor. The blonde Cheryl said to God, "I like your baseball cap!" And God said, "I like your…hair. I like your hair. Your hair." She pulled him on to the dance floor too. She didn't seem interested in dancing, she just gyrated her body against God's irrespective of the music's rhythm, and God tried to gyrate back but found it just made the room spin. Cheryl gave him a pill, and he swallowed it, and he told her he now wanted to create entire new worlds, entire new planets from scratch, he could do it too—but she wasn't listening. She put her tongue in his mouth and God tasted fags and booze and sweet fruit, the fruit was ever so sweet. God told her he loved her, or started to tell her he loved her, or only mumbled it so she didn't hear, or only thought it so no one would ever hear, and then he panicked, he couldn't see Kevin anywhere, he thought he'd lost Kevin—but then he saw Kevin, it was all right, and Kevin was snogging too, and then Kevin caught God's eye, raised a thumb and grinned, and God wasn't sure what that meant—but then Kevin was leading his girl out to the back, and God supposed he ought to do the same. In the alley outside the sudden cold hit him, and he could now see Cheryl more clearly, and he didn't think she was a real blonde. Kevin was leaning against a wall and was back to the snogging, and God thought he'd copy some of his moves. And then Cheryl said, really very politely, "Do excuse me, I'm about to be sick." And she was, and God was relieved, frankly, it could so easily have been him who'd been sick first.

"I am your lord and master!" said God. He began to shout it rather a lot. "All bow down and worship me!" He told Kevin he wanted to go home now. Kevin told him he was quite busy. "Don't leave me," said God, "you said you wouldn't leave me." And Kevin sighed, looked at the brunette, who was so obviously gagging for it, then looked back at God, who was his mate. "All right," he said. And he took God off to find a taxi. "Take him to Mount Sinai," Kevin said to the driver, "take care of him, yeah?" And God said, no, no, not to Mount Sinai! It made it obvious who he was! No one should know who he was! The lord and master!—and Kevin took hold of God by the shoulders, very gently, and it seemed that there were two Kevins dancing in front of God's eyes – "No one cares who you are," Kevin said. Just a truth, a truth told by a mate. "Do you hear me, God? No one cares."

The next morning God rolled out of bed early to start work as usual, and his head was swimming, and he had the most peculiar bad taste in his mouth. So he commanded that no one should work on the Sabbath, got back into bed, pulled the covers over his face, and went to sleep.

God didn't know what he was going to say to Kevin, and he rehearsed many different openings leading to many different outcomes. But Kevin didn't come to work on Monday. Moses was there, the same long beard, the same respectful expression, those eyes that never twinkled. "I'm feeling better now," he said. God didn't know whether to be disappointed or relieved.

At length God said to Moses, "Your replacement. Kevin Collins, I think that was his name."

"Yes, Lord?"

"I don't want him working for me any more."

"Yes, Lord. Do you want him stoned, or crucified, or…?"

"No, no!" said God. "Can't we just sack him? Can't we just let him go?"

"Yes, Lord."

"Without necessarily killing him in any way? I just… Look. I don't want to see him ever again. All right? Does that make sense?"

"Yes, Lord."

God then said, as an afterthought, "And I want you to tell him. Um. It wasn't him. All right? It was me."

And later he said, as another afterthought, "And. If he wants any references. You know. Tell him they'll be excellent."

Moses worked diligently that day, but he wasn't as fast as Kevin had been, his writing really *was* more quavery, and he didn't whistle. God felt the urge to make up a really stupid commandment, just to see if Moses would react. But he knew he probably wouldn't.

Five o'clock, time for Moses to go home. He got up to leave without a word.

"Just a second," said God, and Moses stopped. He turned back towards God, but didn't look him in the face, he never looked God in the face, what was all that about? "Moses, my commandment about the neighbour's ass. I was wondering. What do you think if it?"

Moses stood up straight and tall, as if he were on parade. "Thou shalt not covet thy neighbour's ass, Sir!" he barked.

God thought about that for a moment. "That's it, Moses, that's right," he said, and sighed, and he felt something light fall from his shoulders, and something heavy as stone take its place, and that was right, that was just, that was Godly. "Well done."

God had had such plans for the commandments. He'd thought at first he might write a million of them! But his appetite for the project had gone. After he'd dictated the tenth, he said to Moses, "Well, I reckon that's your lot." God thanked Moses for his sterling work, shook him by the hand, and told him they wouldn't be meeting again.

And once he was on his own, he stretched out Mount Sinai, good and long, some seven and a half thousand feet into the air, so no one would want to climb it. And he locked his doors.

One evening, listlessly going through his pockets, he found a scrap of paper with a phone number on it. It was written in lipstick. He couldn't be sure who it belonged to, but he had his suspicions. "Hello, is that Cheryl?" he asked, when a young woman answered. He wondered if it were the right Cheryl. Cheryl was polite, but he thought she didn't remember who he was. "I'm Kevin's friend," he said at last. At that he could hear her voice lighten. "Oh, Kevin's friend, yes, hello!" They arranged to meet for a drink, but at the last moment God didn't bother to go.

He threw out his baseball cap. Then retrieved it from the rubbish. He threw it out quite often, usually in the dead of night, usually if he'd been drinking. It was always waiting for him in the morning.

And many years later, God received a Christmas card from Kevin. It was the very first Christmas, in fact, Kevin wanted to send his congratulations. 'Congratulations', was all the card said, there wasn't even an exclamation mark that might make it sound softer or warmer or more jolly, and God wondered whether the message was ironic. When God thought back on Kevin Collins, he often wondered whether all of that, that spark of friendship, had been meant ironically.

God mulled over the card for a few days, then decided to reply. He used a really nice Christmas card, one of the expensive ones, not a jokey one with reindeer on but something fancy with his son in a manger and angels all around. And he wrote a long letter to Kevin inside. He said he was sorry. He said he hadn't been a good friend to Kevin, he wasn't very good at handling that sort of thing, maybe he had something broken inside. He said he was still lonely. He said he missed him.

Of course, he didn't send it. But it helped him to write it all out. It helped, for a while.

God hadn't been to a party in ages, God didn't like parties, but this was Baal's party, and God always felt it best to attend parties thrown by the minor deities, he didn't want to seem grand and stand-offish. And it was there that he saw Kevin Collins, and he didn't recognise him at first—he'd put on weight, his skin was sagging, he had a long white Moses beard, he was *old*.

God's first instincts were to turn and run, and then he thought, why should I run? I'm God. I'm God, and what is he? He's nothing. And he put on a big smile, the one he kept for popes and martyrs, and stepped forward to greet him.

"Kevin, isn't it?" he said. "Kevin, how are you? You're looking good." No, not merely old, this man was *decaying*!

"Thanks, I'm fine," said Kevin Collins, a little stiffly.

"So! So, you got a job working with Baal, then? Glad things worked out okay."

"Yes, I got a job. Eventually I got a job. Even without a reference. If you'll excuse me." And Kevin turned to go.

And God actually felt the blood drain from his face. "No, wait," he said. "Wait, Kevin, that isn't fair. I gave you a reference. I told Moses. I said, give him a reference."

"If you say so."

"No, please." And he was holding on to Kevin's arm. "I can't have you thinking that... Christ, no. You don't mean to say you didn't get it? It was a good reference. Kevin, I promise you. The *best* reference. You have to believe me."

"Okay," said Kevin. "You sent a reference, okay."

"No, but it's important," said God, and his fingers were digging into Kevin's arm tight. "I can't bear the idea that you have spent, what? All this time, millennia now, thinking I didn't give you a good reference? Tell me you believe me. I'm a good guy. I wouldn't have done that to you."

"All right."

"Tell me you believe me."

"Please, let me go."

"First, tell me you believe me."

"I believe you, sure."

"I'm a good guy."

"You're a good guy."

"Good. Because I did, Kevin, send that reference. I know I didn't treat you... I know mistakes were... But I would never, ever, have held you back. I'm not a vengeful god."

"Okay."

"Okay," said God. "Brilliant! And look, this is silly. We should catch up. We should definitely do that, and have a drink some time. Would you like that? We should definitely exchange phone numbers. Have you got a phone number?"

"Sure."

"Can you write it down for me? If I, if I let go of your arm..."

"Sure," said Kevin. "There. We'll have a drink. Now, if you'll excuse me..."

"Sure," said God.

"It's the boss's party, I have to mingle..."

"Sure," said God.

God thought that maybe they'd have that drink. But Kevin's eyes hadn't twinkled much. Maybe that meant he wasn't being sincere. Or maybe with age his eyes didn't twinkle any more.

The music got louder, there was dancing. And drinking, oh, and God remembered he *did* like parties, why did he always forget? Parties were brilliant. God and Kevin didn't speak again all night, but once in a while their eyes would catch, and God would smile, and Kevin smiled back. So that was a good thing. That was a good thing. Probably.

The blonde girl was at God's arm suddenly. "I like the baseball cap," she said. She smelled of fags and booze and blood.

"Thanks," he said. He was glad, actually, he wasn't talking to Kevin much, the old man would have cramped his style. "I'm God, and you are...?"

"Impressed," the girl finished. "I know who you are. Everyone knows who you are." She leaned into him, suggested something in his ear.

"Yes," said God. "Yes, I would like that." And he let her take him by the hand, she knew where she was going, he'd let her be the boss. And they went somewhere private.

And the old woman says:

- *When you consider the limitless bounds of human imagination, the Biblical God—in both his Old and New Testament portrayals—is a curiously two-dimensional sort of deity. Do you agree? If so, turn to* **The Disappointing Story in the Book** *(story 6, page 85).*
- *If God came up with the Ten Commandments, who came up with the idea of God coming up with the Ten Commandments? Unravel your way round that, and turn to* **The Masterwork** *(story 83, page 1423).*
- *If there's one thing more heartwarming than a bromance, it's the innocent passion of first love. Feel nostalgic, and turn to* **The Family Picnic** *(story 31, page 501).*
- *I like to picture God perched high at the top of his mountain. When people go on mountain holidays, is it really for the ski-ing, or that they fancy themselves being closer to Heaven? Consider, and turn to* **Please Me** *(story 74, page 1279).*
- *God is love, so they say. It's a nice story. For other nice stories about love, turn to* **101 Heartbeats** *(story 101, page 1695).*

88
Memories of Cravings Long Gone

NO ONE EVER SAW HER smile. But hers was a face you wouldn't want to smile—something as hard and as sour as that wasn't made for smiling, and the contorted effort of it would surely have been too much, it would have given nightmares to the children. The children were already frightened of her, she was what parents threatened them with to get them to behave: "You calm down, or we'll take you to Frau Loecherbach. We'll give you to Frau Loecherbach, and she'll make sausages of you!" But it was a *good* fear; the children followed her around the market, and sniggered, they'd call her a witch, a troll, they'd say she was in league with the Devil—but never to her face, and only in fun, just fun. A good fear, a healthy and exciting fear, full of adventure and the possibility of magic.

She wasn't the public face of the restaurant. Charm, clearly, was not her thing. Her husband Alois served the tables, and he was amiable enough, he would joke with the guests as he took their orders and recommended the specials of the day. And her three sons, Franz, Hans, and little Johann, they would help out too, they would bring out the food from the kitchens—great steaming plates of it, of Knödel and Schweinshaxe and roasted Rindswurst. Frau Loecherbach would stick to the kitchens. No one doubted the genius of her culinary skills. But that didn't mean anyone wanted to look at her.

When you ate one of Frau Loecherbach's meals, you didn't want to like it all that much. Because the cook was so displeasing a human being, you wanted her pancakes and her borscht to reflect that. But it wasn't possible to resist. The food was good. She could do miraculous tricks with a chicken, she could make it fizz with flavour, no matter how dubious the quality of your average chicken to be found on sale in that market square. Her breads tasted light as air. Her soups were rich and thick like steak, and spiced with something you couldn't quite identify but seemed as familiar as nostalgia itself. To eat at Loecherbach's was expensive. And these were hard times, and the townsfolk resented the expense. They resented the expense, and they resented Julia Loecherbach, strutting around the town with her hard face and her tight bosom as if she owned the place. But still they came back. And still they wanted not to like her food that they paid for dearly. And still they couldn't help themselves.

No one knew how she had managed to snare herself a husband like Alois. And people wondered why her three sons didn't leave home. They weren't exactly handsome lads, Franz, Hans and little Johann, but they were strong, the girls of the town could net themselves worse, no one quite understood why they didn't cut themselves free of their ugly mother's apron strings and set out to find futures of their own. But Julia Loecherbach kept her men close. The gossip said she must have put a spell on them. It wasn't just the children who thought there was a spot of devilry to her.

By the time the news reached the town that they were at war, the war was nearly over. Still, the garrisons demanded that every man fit enough to wave a sword must join their number. The army would continue its march towards the front the next morning; the town was expected to give up its men to them then. It didn't look much like an army. The soldiers seemed like children wearing adult clothes, all baring their teeth with adult disdain, smoking and spitting and swearing the way adults do; there were old men, too, squeezed into uniforms too small for them, their white beards now tapered towards sharp martial points. They carried mostly cudgels and sticks. But they were very insistent—they *were* an army, really they were—and the leading officer carried some sort of seal, and said that it gave him authority direct from the emperor of Austria himself, so that was that.

Franz, Hans and little Johann prepared to go to war. They put their favourite belongings into knapsacks; little Johann took a toy boat his father had carved out of wood for him when he was a child. They all seemed very excited. Alois prepared for war too. He took out the greatcoat his father had worn the day *he* had been called to war; Alois now mostly wore it when the weather turned fierce in the winter, and sometimes killed the chickens in it—but nevertheless it had been part of a uniform, and Alois was rightly proud of it. Julia watched her men busy themselves with men's things, how they laughed, how they swaggered, how they jabbed at each other with sticks and pretended to kill and pretended to die. And she said not a word. And went to the kitchen to prepare dinner.

Frau Loecherbach let it be known that there would be a special dinner at her restaurant that night, and all were invited. People need only pay what they wanted. This was to be a celebration feast. There would be room for all—there would be tables lined up the streets, everyone would be able to eat at Loecherbach's, man, woman, child. And, as one, the town came.

"Do you want me to wait tables, liebchen?" asked Alois. And Alois was standing in his greatcoat, and already stroking at the places where he imagined his medals might hang. And his wife told him no; no, tonight he too would be a customer, tonight he would be able to sit back in their restaurant and relax and eat his fill. And the same was true for her sons; tonight would be a busy night, the busiest night of her life thus far, but still she would manage all by herself.

There was no menu. And there was no wine. Instead, the town took their seats and waited, hungry and sober, for dinner to be served. And there was palpable disappointment when at last Frau Loecherbach brought forth nothing more spectacular than a single tureen full of stew, and began ladelling it into bowls. There were catcalls. Some men beat against the tables, and they were laughing, but it was an angry laughter, they were soldiers already and feeling warlike and oh so fierce. "Hush," said Frau Loecherbach, and she didn't raise her voice, but the sound carried to all of the tables, and everyone fell silent. "You shall eat what you are given, and no more," she told them, "and you will like it."

The stew looked unappealing. Thin and watery, and a little bit brown; it seemed to have been made from the dregs of whatever had been in the Loecherbach larder. In one bowl there might float a discoloured lettuce leaf; in another, a chunk of carrot seemed to have drowned itself in despair. And here was Frau Loecherbach splashing the liquid into the bowls, still not smiling, still so sour, and warning the townsfolk not to eat until everyone was ready. It quite took people's appetites away. No one much wanted to like Frau Loecherbach's food, and for once this was going to be easy.

"Now, eat," she said, and they did.

And they tasted their childhoods.

They might taste the memory of the first pie they had ever eaten, the balance between pastry and meat being just right that first and only time. They might taste the apples they had scrumped when they were teenagers, then lying back on the grass on long summer days that seemed to stretch out before them and promised, faithlessly, never to end. They might taste sauerkraut, or stollen, or schnitzel, they might taste Butterkuchen the way they remembered their mothers making it. They ate not only their favourite meals. They ate the recollections of their favourite meals, the best they had ever been, better than they had ever been, the happiest they had ever felt—when, in spite of all, the world had been so full of possibility, when, in spite of all, they had been in *love*. Long-married couples, grown bored and resentful of each other, tasted again their own wedding cake, and how sweet it had been, and how it had crumbled upon their tongues—and how afterwards they had kissed each other, now husband and wife, now so proud and so grown-up, and had gone to bed, and how together they had made those tongues dance.

They were the best meals, and they were as good as they had ever been, and they were better than they had ever been. Spicier, sweeter, and the portions so much bigger.

Customers begged Frau Loecherbach for seconds. "Fill our bowls again!" they pleaded. She refused—"What you are given, and no more," she said. She asked them to settle the bill. And the townsfolk paid all the money they had.

Tonight the women take their husbands to bed, and they make love. And their lovemaking is as sweet as memory too. And, for now, their bellies are full, and warm, and they hold each other all night, and they feel as one—and nothing can separate them, not time, not space, not war certainly—and there is a recognition that if there had once been better times, then there can be better times again. Surely. Surely that makes sense. Surely that is *just*. And when at last they fall asleep there lingers the taste of Knipp on their lips and Apfelwein on their breaths and the salt sweat of honest passion on their skin. And the next morning the men get up and go to war.

A few weeks later an army came to town. It was a different army, and the schoolboys and old men wore uniforms of a different colour.

The commander was one of the old men, and on his cheek was a deep scar that he displayed with pride a little too obviously. He told the town that the war was over. There were still pockets of resistance, of course, one must expect that, but the resistance would be quashed, the war was over as far as the townsfolk need be concerned. They had all been liberated from the rule of a tyrannical emperor who did not love them, and they were now under the rule of another sort of emperor altogether. They were part of Prussia, as they should always have been.

He said too that his soldiers would be billeted at the houses of the conquered townsfolk. And that, in respect of his position, he himself would be billeted at the wealthiest of those houses. That house, of course, belonged to Frau Loecherbach.

Away from the crowds, away from the soldiers protecting him with muskets and swords, the commander looked younger and more awkward. He politely told Frau Loecherbach that he regretted the inconvenience he was putting her to, and that he would do his level best not to get in her way. And he fingered at that scar of his nervously.

"Do you have anyone in the war?" he asked.

Frau Loecherbach told him that indeed she had four men in the army, one husband and three sons, all fighting for their country.

The commander attempted a consolatory smile. "God speed an ending to this damned war," he said, "and that your family will be restored to you, and then we can all live in peace."

Frau Loecherbach didn't smile back. Frau Loecherbach didn't ever smile. Instead Frau Loecherbach gave a nod, just the one. She then said that she was prepared to let the commander stay in her house, and did so with great gravity, as if she'd ever had a choice. But she said that she would not be cooking for him.

"I understand," said the commander.

The commander issued instructions to his troops moreover that they must treat the women whose houses they were occupying with all respect and civility, and any reports of lewd behaviour, up to and including rape, would be punished severely. And he was a good commander, and his men listened to him, and most of them even obeyed.

It was believed that because the commander was staying with Frau Loecherbach that he must be giving her special attention. Money, favours, more besides. On the days she went to market the people wouldn't look at her. Under their breaths they muttered the word 'traitor'.

The commander would buy a chicken each week, and roast it on the Sunday. Frau Loecherbach could tell from the smell coming from her kitchen that he had found a way to render it devoid of all juice or flavour. But she kept to her room away from him.

When the first snap of winter came on, the commander went outside, wearing his greatcoat for warmth, and chopped wood. From the sound Julia could almost believe that Alois had returned to her—or that Franz, Hans or even little Johann was making logs for the fire. She asked the commander to stop, but he laughed amiably and told her that the exercise alone kept him warm! That it was his pleasure, and his privilege, to make the house a comfort to them both, to do what he could for her. And when Frau Loecherbach went to market that week, her neighbours called her whore and spat at her.

"You don't ask me my name," said the commander one night, as they sat by the fire.

"I don't need to know your name," she said.

"You should ask me something," he said. "It would be polite. You don't ask if I have a wife."

"Do you have a wife?"

"Yes," he said. "Yes, I do. And I miss her."

The winter wore on. The snow began to fall. Log chopping was no longer so much fun, and the commander ordered his soldiers to the task instead. Many of them had been chopping logs for *their* women, but the commander was having none of that, they would chop for Frau Loecherbach or for no one at all. Frau Loecherbach stopped going to market altogether. And the commander sent his men to market, and they brought back only the best food.

The commander asked if he could cook for Frau Loecherbach. Frau Loecherbach was surprised. No one had ever cooked for her since she was a child.

He served her a red wine that he'd been saving for a special occasion. He said tonight was that occasion. He said that the wine was the emperor's favourite. He said that he hoped it was special to her, that this was all special to him, and he fingered at that scar of his a lot. Frau Loecherbach accepted the wine was better than the stuff she had served in her restaurant, but she still had the power to make hers taste richer, fruitier, darker. He served her Knödel, and Schweinshaxe, and roasted Rindswurst in a wine sauce.

"Do you like it?" he asked. Still touching at that scar.

"Your food is terrible," said Frau Loecherbach.

"Oh."

"It's the worst I have ever tasted."

"Oh."

"You do not care about the food. You do not bother to find anything *inside* the food that is good or special or dear. To you it's not food, it's just something to chew, then swallow, then shit."

"Oh." And then the commander said, and he sounded confused, "Well, what else should food be?"

And so she got up, went to the kitchen, and showed him.

It was a harsh night, and the fire in the hearth made no impression upon the freezing cold, and the snow outside was falling so thick and so fast that it felt to Frau Loecherbach as if the house would be lost, buried behind walls of white forever and the world would never be able to get in and see them and judge them.

"I love you," he said. "I don't know why."

"No," she said. "I don't know why either."

And he suggested he take her to his bed. And when she refused he nodded sadly. And she told him that she'd take him to *her* bed instead, and his face lit up in surprise and he no longer looked like an old man but a delighted little boy.

"We will marry one day," the commander said to her. "My wife will die. She'll die eventually. And your husband too, maybe he'll never come back from the war."

And Julia lay in his arms, and she fingered his scar with the tips of her fingers so lightly, and she said nothing to that at all.

With the spring came the news that the fighting was done. The fighting was done, there would be no more death, and peace would last forever more. The soldiers were no longer soldiers, and the townsfolk no longer hostiles under martial law; they were men, and they were women, let them be friends, let them be one people, one nation united. And in announcement of this, a dozen engagements were announced between the women and the soldiers billeted to them on the spot.

No one seemed to wonder where the men from the town had got to, or whether they would be home soon. They all *had* men, didn't they, *new* men? Who needed the old?

Frau Loecherbach suggested that maybe the commander could now return to his wife. The commander said his wife was a world away, his wife was in Prussia of all places. Frau Loecherbach asked—but weren't they in Prussia too now, wasn't all the world a Prussia? And the commander said he didn't care.

"I love you," he said. "You have bewitched me."

And he told her that Alois wouldn't be coming home. Neither would her sons. Neither would any man from the town. That only a week after they had left for war they had been routed by the Prussian army, and they had all been executed. All of them, and little Johann too. "I was waiting for the right time to tell you," said the commander. "When we were no longer enemies, and could just be lovers."

Frau Loecherbach complimented him on his delicacy.

"I'm sorry about your children. But I'm still strong, and you're young enough, I think we can have children of our own. This poor town, and all it has suffered, it needs to move on now, we need to forget the past, what good will the past do us? We need to live, and to love, and can't you hear it? Can't you hear all that love out there? And so soon, I promise you, this war will be forgotten, and the town will be full of babies, the sound of all our babies crying in joy."

It sounded sincere enough. It sounded like a reason for celebration. Frau Loecherbach let it be known that there would be a special dinner that night at her restaurant, and all were invited.

Tables were once more set out on the street. And women sat with their soldier lovers, holding their hands, gazing into their eyes—who had conquered not only their land but their very hearts—and they were all so *hungry*, they wanted this meal so badly, and that after all this time of bitter war and bitter cold there could be now some reason to go on, some reminder that at the end of the day they were all just people with appetites, surely, and what was wrong with that, what could be the harm? And the commander asked if he could help Julia, and she said no, tonight he too could be a customer, tonight he could sit back and eat his fill.

She brought out the stew. The winter had been hard, and there weren't many dregs in Julia's larder to fill it. No discoloured lettuce, not a suicidal carrot to be seen.

They ate. And they tasted their memories.

And the women cried for the loved ones they had lost, the sons they had weaned for no bloody purpose now, the husbands with whom they had promised to share a life, a whole life, an entire life.

And the men cried, because they thought of their mothers, and that their mothers would be ashamed of what they had become.

It was the best food they had ever tasted.

"Fill our bowls again!" they both pleaded, the men and the women. "Just a little more!" begged the commander, who had not been able to stop his tears from flowing the moment the spoon had entered his mouth.

"Oh, as much as you like," said Julia. "As much as your bellies can take."

And they were eating more—eating their first sweets, fed to them by hand by indulgent parents, and how they'd laughed to see their child's eyes bulge at all that *taste*, and how the child had laughed too without even knowing why, but the child knew it was a good thing, it was good to hear Mummy and Daddy happy. And they were eating with their baby teeth, and they were so much softer than their adult ones, and they remembered how different everything seemed when your little teeth wobble so, little teeth in little heads, little heads on little bodies, such very little bodies. And then they were sucking at their mother's breasts, all that milk and they could never have too much, and oh my God, Mother, long since dead, or maybe just dying, or maybe just old and ignored—does she still love us, could she possibly love us now we've grown so old and hard and cold, and so unlike the little babies guzzling away like tiny animals, all innocent, not knowing anything, not remembering anything, because there's nothing to remember, nothing's happened yet, you're at the beginning, you're back at the very beginning.

Julia steps through the crowd of babies, and goes into the kitchen for her knife.

And she bends to pick up the commander. No longer in a position to command anything, looking faintly surprised to be sitting in this pool of clothes, the uniform of a man he could surely never dream of becoming. Eyes wide and so blue, smooth skin, smooth lips, looking at Julia in utter trust as she scoops him up into her arms.

Julia holds the knife to his throat. The commander blinks. Then smiles at her.

And then she does something that only the baby ever sees. She smiles back. She smiles. And there's a magic in that smile—and maybe that's where all her magic ever came from and no one ever saw it to know. Or maybe it came from somewhere else entirely, who can tell, who can ever really tell.

She doesn't kill him.

Into his cheek she traces his scar. It's quick, it's as if she's cutting up a chicken, it's no more cruel than that. And the commander is too surprised to howl out in pain. One quick gulp, then that's it. And then she has forgiven him.

She kisses him on the cheek, and her lips come away red, but the wound is already healing, and now the bleeding has stopped, look.

The other babies look around at each other in some confusion—what do they do now? Where do they go from here? But that's up to them, that's not Julia Loecherbach's problem. And the commander is so light in her arms, like bread, like her freshly baked bread, and he's no weight at all, and she can walk on with him forever, and she walks straight out of the town.

And the old woman says:

- *Nostalgia isn't a concern to a woman forced to live through the echoes of a dead marriage in* **A View From the Clifftop** *(story 20, page 327).*
- *If you're the sort to find banquets rather too grand, the relaxed charms of* **The Family Picnic** *(story 31, page 501) may appeal.*
- *To read of a much more melodious metamorphosis, turn to* **Page Turner** *(story 73, page 1269).*
- *Sometimes there's nothing supernatural about finding pure nostalgia in a meal. Consider* **Ground Beef** *(story 93, page 1573).*
- *In his dying moments, as his life flashes before his eyes, an actor discovers his memories are not what they are supposed to be, in* **The Curtain Falls** *(story 98, page 1661).*

89
MASTER OF THE MACABRE

THE EDITORS OF THIS VOLUME have asked me to give a brief introduction to the life and works of E G Wolverson, and I shall say at the outset that I have misgivings about the enterprise. The enterprise being not merely the introduction itself, but the very publication of this collection. I do not think Wolverson would have wanted to have seen his books back in print; indeed, I am quite sure not. And I do not think that the motives behind their reissue are of the best either; the letter I received this morning urging me once again to reconsider and to write about Wolverson speak—and I quote—of 'the public's fascination and appetite for the "Master of the Macabre".' I put it to you that the fascination is not with the stories themselves, which I suspect to be no better than the rest of their genre, but with the author himself, and a rather prurient curiosity about the manner of his death. I put it to you, too, the reader, holding this book in your hands, that the aforementioned appetite is sensationalism of the worst kind, and I say, shame on you, Sir, shame on you.

But nonetheless, and much to my surprise, I find myself writing. There is a storm outside; there is a draught in my study that I cannot locate nor still; the very candle by which I work is guttering. And I am not without a sense of humour, no matter what my students claim, and I can see the irony of a night like this, the very setting of so much of Wolverson's work, a setting which lets the mind fancy about ghosts and witches and wendigoes. So, here I put this before you, if not with my blessing. And this way I may at least hope, with the book on sale, that Margaret may be given some money.

I do not say that Wolverson's interest in writing supernatural fiction was beneath him. Every man must have a hobby. I myself am quite a keen golfer, with a handicap of sixteen above par, and I take great pleasure in that, but would also venture that it in no way intrudes upon my academic reputation. The same was not true of Wolverson, and that was his curse. He was a scholar of some undeniable merit, and although many critics would claim that his analysis of fourteenth century poetry yielded little fresh insight, I've never heard anyone suggest that his research was anything less than thorough and his theories anything less than cogent. But there is surely no question that whatever his academic prowess, in the last few years of his life all the renown he had won was for his ghost stories. It wasn't even as if he had published that many; he wrote one a year, as I understood it, always performed on Christmas Eve during the university celebrations. This was the sum total of his literary fame, or shall I say, notoriety: no more than three thousand words per year, and all three thousand of them wasted on melodramatic mumbo-jumbo.

I attended his final ghost story reading. There was an excitement in the air, and I allowed myself to enjoy that excitement in spite of myself. The undergraduates were all dressed in their gowns, and were drinking wine and ale, and eating pork and steak, and singing Christmas carols and songs of an altogether more secular nature. Wolverson sat up on high table, of course, and looked shrunken in on himself, not conversing, not eating, barely taking part in the festivities at all—but then, when the sherries were served, and cigars were lit, the lights were lowered, and Wolverson got to his feet—and it seemed to me that he was suddenly *transformed.* He seemed much taller, much younger, and at once the room fell silent in ready anticipation. And Wolverson read, and we all shivered in the hope of something chilling that would set our nerves jangling and let reel our darkest imaginings. I do not think Wolverson was a natural actor. Even as a lecturer he had a propensity to mumble, and as a reader, merely reading the words in front of him, he was inclined toward halting monotone. And I do not think that the story was a good one, even by his standards: the tale of a ghost in a hotel preying upon the residents within seemed to me rather stale and obvious, and painfully lacking in theme or subtext. But what could not be argued was the *authority* with which Wolverson spoke, the way there was no other sound to be heard save his voice for the full half-hour, in a hall large enough to fit five hundred (and had done so, easily, to bursting) and had only so recently rung loud with the unfettered boisterousness of youth. As Wolverson read of his ghosts and demons, there was a change in the atmosphere. It seemed to grow colder. It seemed to grow darker. There was an almost preternatural stillness to the air, I fancied that time itself had stopped, or at least *slowed*, that I would look outside the window and the branches would only be inching in the wind and the snow would fall at half-speed. And by the time he had finished, the world seemed more mysterious, and unsettling, an altogether more *remarkable* place to live.

I only discussed his horror writing with Wolverson on two occasions, many years apart. And his answers were contradictory, but I like to think that the first time was the *correct* answer nonetheless—back before he'd made a name for himself, even so, back before he'd been defined and limited by his own peculiar imagination. I asked him, simply enough, why it was he put such focus upon his tales of the uncanny, and I asked, I think without judgement—and he blushed (as well he might) and told me that it was really all about trying to make people *laugh*. That was it. He thought that within his flights of fancy there was something so absurd that it would amuse people, that delight could be taken in the dissonance between what they expected and what they received, like the way a child giggles in a hall of mirrors seeing himself fat or tall. But something always went wrong with the punchlines to his jokes, he said. What he'd hoped would elicit a chuckle would instead produce a gasp; the tightrope, he argued, between comedy and horror was really very narrow, and his problem was he just kept falling off it. As a little boy his attempts to make his parents laugh only made them recoil; he gave his sisters nightmares with the jolly adventures he'd dream up for their dolls. And pretty soon he realised that if he couldn't win anyone's heart with ready wit, he wouldn't try; he'd let that dissonant way he looked at the world—a way that deep inside still would make him chortle, he alone still found full of jest—be as unnerving and twisted as one could wish. If he couldn't make them love him, he'd make them fear him a little. And at this he blushed even deeper, and of course I knew the reason why.

The reason why was Margaret. Of course he loved Margaret, just as I did; she was an outsider. We were all of us outsiders there, at a university which was based upon privilege and rank, where most students could trace back their family's college attendance as far as their great grandfathers. Wolverson was the first person in his family to go to university; so was I; his father was in trade; so was mine. And it sounds an unlikely contrivance now that we met on our first day there, but it was true; it was as if we wore badges telling the other undergraduates that we didn't belong, they smelled out we were frauds at once, and the way they so blatantly excluded us made it all the easier for us to find each other.

We became firm friends immediately.

And very soon, once we'd found the nerves to speak to her, Margaret joined our group – a female student, back in the times before that became a point of fashion, and from the middle classes as well. Wolverson was very shy of her, I recall, and it was hard for him to introduce himself, as soon as he even got close he'd wring his hands and start to stammer so he looked less like a first class academic in the making than a babbling simpleton—I was, I think, much smoother with her, I was able to say hello and tell her my name and comment upon the weather and ask her the time. But to his credit it was Wolverson who invited her to go punting with us—he came back to the halls one day, and threw himself down on the chaise, and he looked so red I thought he was having a seizure. "I've done it," he said, "I've asked her out. She'll go punting with us on Sunday afternoon at two o'clock sharp." I pointed out to him that I didn't know how to punt, and nor did he; at this he turned even more red, he hadn't thought of that. So for the next four days we neglected our studies, we spent our time on the river trying to master how on Earth one can steer a wooden boat with a pole. I fancy by the time Sunday came both of us had achieved a certain halting proficiency; we had stopped falling in, at any rate; and we both had the blisters on our hands to prove it. But when Margaret came to join us, all of Wolverson's training went in an instant, he didn't know what to do with that pole, whether to push it or pull it or wave it about like an idiot—and I must admit, I too, I was tired and the weather was warm and I was not at my best. Margaret watched us struggle with the pole; we were both getting irritable with it, and with each other. "May I?" she asked, ever so gently, and we stepped aside, and she took the pole, and *she* took control, and Wolverson and I sat in the back and enjoyed the afternoon as she punted us up and down and all over the river.

I would say, where Wolverson and I were concerned, that I was the more attractive. I was more confident; I was taller; I had dark hair, where Wolverson's was wispy and blond like a girl's; I was specialising in John Milton, who is the greatest poet of the English language, and Wolverson's interest lay in Geoffrey Chaucer, who had palpable talent, of course, but was rather too inclined towards bodily function jokes. It was understandable that it was me that Margaret fell in love with. But this in no way affected our friendship with Wolverson—and indeed, we became an inseparable trio; Margaret and I would walk the streets of the city hand in hand, and Wolverson would bound about us good-naturedly like an amiable dog trying to amuse. It worked. Margaret called us 'the Three Musketeers'—and I didn't like that, I thought that as students of English literature we should really avoid a reference to Dumas and concentrate instead upon our own heroes. I suggested we be called 'the Three Metaphysicals', after the great poets, Donne, Herbert and Marvell; but it didn't catch on; no one could agree which one was Donne, which one was Herbert, which one was Marvell; after a while I gave up trying to persuade them and let Margaret and Wolverson have their way.

It occurs to me now I can't recall which poet was Margaret's own area of specialist interest. I'm sure it was one that I didn't disapprove of, however; I would remember.

Later that term we celebrated our first Christmas together. There was a formal dinner on the Christmas Eve, and we wore our gowns, and ate, and drank, and looked quite the picture of academia, I should think. And Margaret had had an idea; that we should have our own private party afterwards, in her room, and each person would bring along an entertainment to perform. There was wine, and I think it was where I smoked my first cigar; I'm pretty sure it was Wolverson's first cigar, and he cried through the smoke, and we laughed; it was Margaret's first cigar too, and she puffed away quite proficiently, and I felt very proud of her, I remember thinking that she was my girl. There was a dozen of us in all; Margaret's social circle was rather wider than ours. One student sang a ballad, another played his violin really very reasonably indeed. I read aloud my own translation of one of Virgil's Eclogues, and it went down well, and afterwards I was given a round of applause, and I remember making a little bow. It was Wolverson's turn. "I'm going to read a story I've written," he said. "Can we have the lights off, please?" Someone laughed and pointed out that if it was dark he wouldn't be able to see to read; he hadn't thought it through! Wolverson said quietly that he'd rehearsed it thoroughly, he knew his story by heart.

And I remember how different everything felt in the darkness. Some of our number made jokes, but they were uneasy jokes, and Margaret called for silence. And Wolverson began. As I've said, he was not a natural performer, but I think his nervousness did something to lighten his shy monotone, it gave the piece a wavery inflection. "What stuff is this!" said one student, Baines, halfway through, and Margaret rounded on him; she told him bluntly that he had to shut up or leave. Baines' interruption had sounded scornful, of course, but I knew where it had come from; a desire to break the atmosphere, to emphasise that what we were listening to was really just nonsense, there was nothing to be afraid of. And Baines didn't leave, he couldn't leave, none of us could.

I can't recall the details of the story now, and I see it isn't one that Wolverson ever collected for publication. Quite possibly it lacked the sheen of the more practised stories he would later write; quite probably he lost it. The plot naturally enough sounds ridiculous, as most plots do when boiled down to synopsis: even Milton can't escape that. It was something about an old curse, and a man who awakens it by reading a book, and the book (I think) was found in a crack in a wall of an abandoned church, or an abandoned monastery. And the hapless man is pursued by a ghost who drives him to suicide, setting himself on fire. Wolverson was the last person to perform that night, because after the lights were turned back on no one was quite willing to continue; I was just glad I'd got my eclogue out first. Wolverson apologised. He could quite see he'd destroyed the party. He hadn't meant to.

It had hardly been an auspicious debut, but it was astonishing how its reputation spread. By the beginning of the Trinity term, Wolverson was being approached by students who had never deigned to speak to us before. They were asking whether he would perform it again. I knew Wolverson didn't want to. He was, as I say, a naturally shy man. But he found it hard to say no, especially when it seemed that friendship (or, at least, acceptance) was being offered to him at last. He asked Margaret what he should do, and my girlfriend said she thought he should try once more—and if it would make him feel better, she would be there too to support him. At this he agreed. He performed the story another four times, I think, and then he added another story, and then a third, and it was a cold winter that took its time to thaw, and everybody seemed to be in the mood for something dark and creeping. And Wolverson's name became something that was known on campus—even though, as I warned him, it was for his frivolous fictions alone; his Middle English prowess, by anyone's standards, left much to be desired. By the time Baines killed himself Wolverson had an identity—and, as his best friend, so had I.

Student suicide was a fairly common phenomenon around examination times, but what made Baines' one unusual was that it occurred in March, and mid-term at that; with fewer opportunities to distract us, his death occasioned no little interest. He left no note. His friends said they were quite surprised, because he hadn't even hinted taking his life was under consideration. And it was the manner of the death that really caused comment. Most students liked to hang themselves, or took poison, or, if they were of an especial melodramatic bent, threw themselves off the bridge. Baines had set fire to himself.

It was clear where he'd got the idea from, of course. And Wolverson was appalled. He came to me one night, and he was shaking, so Margaret and I didn't turn him away, although I must confess I was a little put out. He asked us whether we thought he should write to Baines' parents to apologise. (We said no.) He asked whether he should confess his involvement to the police. (Definitely not.) He asked whether he should stop his ghost stories—and at this Margaret and I disagreed; I felt it'd be inappropriate for Wolverson to write any more of them, even ones that didn't involve self-immolation of some kind or another. In truth, I was rather tired of having a reputation based upon my knowing a spook writer—I felt it was high time I found a reputation all of my own.

It was around this point that Margaret and I broke up. Wolverson came to me and asked if he could step out with her instead. His hands were wringing and he was stammering, he looked as pathetic as he had when I'd first met him, he was that frightened. And I told him that he was welcome to try his hand. That I'd had enough of her. That I'd used her up. But I suggested he might not have much luck knocking against that particular door. "Oh, no, you don't understand," he said, and he looked truly wretched. "Margaret's asked *me* out. I just wanted to make sure you didn't mind."

I didn't see much of Wolverson or Margaret after that. It really wasn't personal, and I still regarded them as friends. But I don't think they were quite as subtle in their love as they might have been; on a Sunday you could see them kissing on a punt, and I thought that lacked a certain class. And at Christmas Wolverson was asked by the senior staff whether he would perform a ghost story. No longer something hidden behind the doors of drunken undergraduates, but as a part of the formal celebrations. I can only imagine how terrified he was. I imagine Margaret got him through it. I wasn't in attendance at the revels that year, I agreed to go home and spend the holiday with my family.

We rubbed alongside each other quite comfortably over the next few years. Whenever we met, we would greet each other affectionately enough, with protestations that it had been far too long, that we should all get together again soon, the Three Musketeers forever, that we were still all so close and dear. And when I had an invitation to the wedding, I genuinely considered going. But of course I'd found new friends, and I no longer needed Wolverson or his girlfriend, his fiancée, his happy little wife. I won a first class honours for my degree, of course, and was offered any place I wanted to go and study for my doctorate and teach: I chose Oxford. Wolverson got his first just barely, I understand, and was kept on right where he was. I think they took some pity on him. I think they liked his Christmas ghost stories. And there was no need for us to meet again. He was fourteenth century, I was seventeenth; we were kept apart by entire centuries of difference.

I didn't speak to Wolverson again for a very long time. There were the Christmas cards for a while, of course, but I rather think he stopped writing to me before I stopped writing to him. It was fifteen years before I had a letter marked 'Wolverson' again—and that was surprise enough, before I realised it was initialled M J, not E G. I still didn't think of Margaret having a surname like that. I couldn't.

Margaret told me she was passing through Oxford the following week; would it be possible to have lunch with me for old time's sake? I wrote back at once, and assured her it would; and I followed her request that I should be discreet, not to mark the envelope so that it was clear it had been sent by me, and I would normally have found such fuss rather irritating, but I decided to indulge her. It led me to believe, of course, all sorts of idiotic things. That for fifteen years Margaret had loved me, and only me. That finally she had worked up the courage to say so. None of this chimed with the Margaret I knew, of course, the woman who had taught us how to punt, how to smoke cigars, how to (yes) love. But it was a happy fantasy all the same.

We agreed to meet on a Thursday, in a cake and tea shop that one of my undergraduates recommended, somewhere quiet. I was shocked when I saw her. She hadn't aged well. I could see the resemblance to the girl I'd known, but it was a resemblance one would find in a *mother*—she had always had a fleshy figure, with cheeks so plump they dimpled when she smiled, but now she'd thinned, and it made her look hard and plain, and when she smiled the smile had nowhere to grow. Her eyes were dead. We had tea. I asked her how she was. She said she was well. I asked her how Wolverson was, and at this she sighed. She said he was well too, she believed. She stressed the 'believed', as if there were some cause for doubt, as if she might not be the best person to judge. I asked her why she had come. I told her I did not believe she was passing through to anywhere, and I was right. She told me that Wolverson was a different man. I asked her if he hurt her in any way, and at this she looked rather offended. She said that he had days of mistemper, but the mistemper was always with *himself*; he was remote; he seemed, if anything, and she picked the word carefully, haunted. I laughed and told her that would seem appropriate for those little spine chillers of his, and she attempted a laugh back. And all the while she wouldn't look me in the face, and at first I thought this was out of shame, that she wanted to apologise, and my heart went out to her, her embarrassment was apology enough. But as our time together wore on, and she still wouldn't look at me, and she still wouldn't tell me she regretted the way we had parted, I rather decided I wanted a spoken apology after all. "Could you go and see him?" she asked. "He wants to see you. He needs an old friend. And he's too proud to ask." I told her that I would think about it.

But that was in August, and I had a new term's lecturing to prepare, and a new paper to complete. In December I received my annual invitation to the high dinner on Christmas Eve at my alma mater, and as always I threw it into the dustbin. But something made me pull it out and reconsider.

I saw Wolverson perform that last time. I didn't recognise him at first. If Margaret had aged, that was nothing to her husband. He was a man in his late thirties now, but he didn't look a day under sixty. And a badly worn sixty at that—his hair had greyed, he wore a drooping beard that did nothing to hide how his face sagged. And he was hunched—as he sat at dinner, he seemed bowed over the food, as if in some grim obeisance towards it. I didn't let him see me, of course. I kept my distance.

And I decided that this was all a mistake. That I should get out before I was identified. Get out before Margaret saw me, and made it impossible for me to leave. But no one looked at me, and I searched the room for her, I looked hard, and Margaret wasn't there. And then Wolverson read his ghost story. He performed. As I say, I don't think he performed it well. I don't think it was a good story. But the world seemed to shift, and I decided I had to explore what this new world was before I got back on the train to Oxford and lost myself once again within the old one.

It was strange. After the impact his story had made I would have expected Wolverson to have been flooded with well-wishers, students and academics alike congratulating him. That had certainly been the way when he was an undergraduate performing his ghost stories for the first time—and how shyly he had received those compliments, how he had blushed. But now, though he was a bona fide celebrity, everyone ignored him. The lights were turned back to full, he sat down morosely, stared at his food, prodded at some vegetable matter with a fork.

I went to see him.

"My God," he said. "Is it you? Is it really you?" And his face lit up, and years fell off it in an instant—not enough, I should add, he was still pushing sixty, but it was an improvement. "Did you like my story?"

"I'm afraid I arrived too late to hear it," I said. And at that his face fell so glumly, and I wished I could call back the lie. I wanted to reassure him, I promised I'd come to the next year's.

He indicated I should lean in, he wanted to say something to me in confidence. "There won't be another year's," he said. "I'm getting out of it. I'm getting out of the ghost story racket."

I told him I was pleased to hear it, and he nodded seriously.

"Can we talk in private?" he said. "Can you come to my rooms?"

And I said yes.

He seemed properly affectionate to me as he showed me in. As if all the years of silence hadn't mattered a jot. He showed me around his study, waited for my approval.

"More than serviceable," I said.

"I'm sure your rooms in Oxford must be..."

"Well, yes," I said. "But that's Oxford."

He nodded.

I told him that academia would be delighted he was giving up his spook stories, that he had become something of a laughing stock. And he smiled and said, "Indeed, indeed!" and nodded, like a crusty old don, like the crusty old don he'd become, wanting to make a good impression on his bright young pupil.

"I should have listened to you in the first place," he said. "That's the truth of it."

I asked him why he'd written horror stories in the first place. And I expected the same answer he'd given me so many years ago. But it was different.

"Because," he said, "horror has to find a way out into the world."

I didn't quite know what to say to that. He looked apologetic. Wine, would I like some wine? To ease the mood, I said I would. A cigar? Why not, I said. We lit cigars, and as always, he never looked comfortable with a cigar, it looked ridiculous jutting out of his mouth like that, his eyes watering all the while. "This is good," he said, "this is fine, having you here again, yes, yes." I asked him how he was, generally. Like Margaret, he said he was well. I asked him how Margaret was. Well, he believed. I said I was pleased.

"They're not stories," he said suddenly.

I asked him to repeat himself.

"They're not stories," he said. "They're all true."

I scoffed at that. Asked him whether some sort of ghoul scaring hapless hotel patrons was *true*.

"No," he said. "I'm not saying it happened. But it's true all the same." He poured me another glass of wine. "But," he said, "I'm stopping that now. Before it's too late. And there's nothing they can do to me worse than what I've done to myself and to Margaret."

He asked how I was. I said I was well. He asked if I had a wife, was she well? I said I didn't have a wife, but if I had one, I'm sure she would be well, well. I told him to explain what was going on, I told him to stop dancing around the matter like a student who hasn't prepared his tutorial.

"The stories don't die," he said.

Wait, I asked, his ghost stories? I understood the print run had been rather small.

"Any stories. Do you know why Chaucer wrote? Do you know why Milton wrote?"

I said I'd spent an entire lifetime discussing why Milton wrote.

Wolverson grinned at me then, and he showed all his teeth, and at that moment I had a flash of fear, I had the most certain knowledge that my old friend was quite mad.

"They're kept alive in the books," he said. "In *all* the books, they live on. And they come to me, you know. They stand over me. They stand over me at night, when I'm alone."

I asked him whether Chaucer came to him, and he said he did. I asked him whether he could talk to Chaucer, and he said he could. I told him that must be useful for a lecturer in Chaucerian studies, he could ask him for all sorts of tips. But Wolverson wasn't listening to me, and couldn't be chivvied along by my good humour.

"They're all trapped in the books," he said. "And they've had enough. They want to die. I've got to set them free. Posterity just isn't what it's cracked up to be."

I asked him then about Margaret. He told me he didn't see much of Margaret any more, he slept alone in his rooms. I asked him how Margaret felt about that. He said it didn't matter, he had to help the ghosts, they wouldn't come unless he slept alone.

"The stories make you write them," he said. "They tell you they want to be let out into the world. Let them out, and they promise they'll leave you alone. That's what they told Chaucer, and Milton, and the rest of them, that's what they tell me. But they're liars. There are always more of them. Always more, filling your head, blocking out the light."

But I reminded him he only wrote one story every Christmas.

And he gripped my hand, and I recoiled at the touch, it felt like old man's skin, it felt like thin paper. "I write one *every day*," he said. "I write a new story *every single day*."

He asked me where I was sleeping that night, and I told him I had a hotel in town. He said I should stay with him and Margaret, and I replied that I wouldn't want to put them out at Christmas. He made me promise I would visit him the next day, and I said I would.

I went then and got on the next train back to Oxford. It was a long wait, and it was snowing. But I felt better for it.

As I left him, and wished him a happy Christmas, he said to me again, "I should have listened to you. I should always have listened to you. You were my best, my dearest friend."

And he said, "I'll do my best to last as long as I can."

Wolverson didn't even last the year. 'Ghost Writer Dies in Blaze', said the newspaper of December 29th. It went on to report that the 'Master of the Macabre', E G Wolverson, had burned to death in the great libraries of the university where he had made his home. They suggested it was suicide, that he had set fire to himself whilst gazing out on all the great works of literature he held in such high regard. There was no note. The article went on to say that he is survived by his wife, Margaret, and two children, John and Abigail. I never knew he had children.

The article of course doesn't explain many things. Why kindling was found all around the library itself, as if he'd wanted to set fire to the whole collection. (Not a single book was even scorched. The university reported that this was a stroke of luck.) Nor did it explain why, had Wolverson wanted to kill himself, he'd not doused his body with a flammable agent like alcohol or gasoline first, that might have hastened the process. Self-immolation otherwise would be such a slow and painful way to go.

I wasn't invited to the funeral. I wrote to Margaret offering my condolences. I told her in the kindest of terms that she would be welcome to visit me in Oxford, at any time, for tea and cake. She hasn't written back yet.

There has been renewed interest in Wolverson's fiction. I understand why the publishers have wanted to get his complete ghost stories back into print, in one easy volume like this one. As I say, I am not sure it is what the author would have wanted.

And I had said no. I wouldn't write this introduction. For that reason, and more. Because although Wolverson called me his best and dearest friend, he was wrong, as he was about so very many things.

But the publisher keeps writing to me. They won't take no for an answer. Every day I receive a new letter, longer, more insistent than the last. I have never heard of the publisher before. I do not even know where I can send this introduction. They have not furnished me with a return address.

I can only hope that now I have written this out, that they'll keep their promise, and will leave me alone.

Wolverson suggested to me he had hundreds more stories he'd written secretly. No one in the press has made mention of them, so I'm assuming they were not found amongst his personal effects. Maybe Wolverson managed to destroy them in time. Maybe he never wrote them at all. Maybe, as I suspect, they are hidden—and for his sake, they should remain hidden. For pity's sake, leave the man alone, let him rest in peace.

As for these, now back in print—I'm sorry, Edward. I'm truly sorry.

And the old woman says:

- *Reading is in itself a reassuring experience—and so the trick of really good horror is to subvert that. There should be the suggestion that merely by turning the pages you are releasing a curse. Do you find horror stories relaxing or confrontational? Consider, then turn to* **Bedtime Stories for Yasmin** *(story 5, page 71).*
- *Many horror stories exert their hold by playing upon our fear of death. If the threat of it were taken away, so that you knew you couldn't die, or even suffer, could the horror still work? Try the events of* **The Smell of Burnt Orange** *(story 79, page 1373).*
- *There's no riper time for reading horror than at Halloween. If it's October, or thereabouts, and you have a taste for it, turn to* **Pumpkin Kids** *(story 84, page 1431).*
- *This story is written as a tribute to the great ghost writer of the nineteenth century, M R James. Turn to* **Bobbo** *(story 82, page 1407) if you want to read a tribute to the great ghost writer of the twentieth.*
- *It's the height of arrogance to suggest that your stories won't die, when the sad truth is most will make barely any impact at all. Consider the failed career at the heart of* **This is Why We Can't Have Nice Things** *(story 90, page 1527)—and ask, but nevertheless, is this writer better off?*

90
This is Why We Can't Have Nice Things

EDWYN ARNOLD WAS NOT, by any standard criteria, an unsuccessful man. He had been married for nigh-on thirty years to a woman he still loved, and who still loved him. He had three children who were healthy and happy, and each of them seemed now to be navigating adulthood in a manner that made him proud. He enjoyed his job as a schoolteacher—geography, history and some basic mathematics—and he had never had reason to doubt that any of the thousands of pupils who had passed through his care hadn't to some small degree been bettered by the association. In short, he was a man who had treated his life with respect, and life had paid him back with interest. It didn't matter that his success had been won more by luck than by judgement—or, to be fair, by calm patience rather than anything particularly profound or inspirational; it was success of a sort, and Mr Arnold deserved every last scrap of it.

But in his youth he had also been a published writer, and there at least success had eluded him. His only novel had had disappointing reviews and even more disappointing sales. Some writers rally against harsh criticism, are even spurred on by it; others buckle beneath and never find the necessary arrogance to put pen to paper again. Mr Arnold had been neither encouraged nor confounded: he had read all the reviews, considered what they said rationally and honestly, and concluded that they were perfectly justified. He simply wasn't a very good writer. He showed some ability with the broad mechanics of it, the putting down of words one after the other in comprehensible order. What he lacked was an imagination—the critics were right, he simply had nothing to say. Edwyn Arnold had dreamed of being a great writer, but he shrugged off that dream—it was ridiculous, and there was no point in entertaining it further. And he had never turned his hand to writing again.

He kept a pristine copy of his novel on a bookshelf in his study, but he never felt the slightest urge to read it. It was a part of his past he had no reason to deny, but even less reason to advertise: it seemed of very little consequence to the man he had become. Even by the time he met the future Mrs Arnold, only a couple of years after publication, he hadn't thought it worth mentioning to her. The honest truth was Mrs Arnold had at first found Mr Arnold to be courteous but a little dull, and new information that he'd once harboured artistic longings would have hastened the whole courtship considerably: even so, she managed at last to put aside her qualms and fall in love with him regardless. She only found out on their wedding day, when the novel and its failed fortunes were alluded to by the best man, in that part of the speech usually reserved for jokes about embarrassments with ex-girlfriends. Mrs Arnold took Mr Arnold's hand and whispered, "I didn't know you'd written a book, how awfully clever! I shall have to read it!" And Mr Arnold had smiled benignly, and told her she was welcome to try, but even the *Daily Mail* had said it was thin gruel. "No, I will," she insisted—and she'd meant it at the time—and had even once or twice determined to fetch it down from the study bookshelf and open it—and she'd never quite got round to doing so.

Mr Arnold hadn't even thought about his novel in several years when he saw it in the hands of the man seated opposite him on the

16.47 train from C___. Mr Arnold always caught the 16.47—were he to leave the staffroom promptly he had time to catch the 16.17, but only if he put a sprint on, and Mr Arnold didn't like to put a sprint on after a solid day's teaching. The 16.47 would get him into S___ at 17.14 and the short walk from the station guaranteed he'd be back home at half past five with Mrs Arnold for tea. He knew by sight most of the people who travelled on the 16.47, they were a rarefied bunch. He didn't recognise the man who took the seat facing his, opened up his briefcase, took from it Mr Arnold's novel, and started to read it blatantly for all the world to see.

And at first he didn't even realise it was his own book. "How funny," mused Mr Arnold, "I wrote a book with that very title once!" And as his eyes travelled down the front cover, he added to himself, "Funnier still, the author has the same name as mine too!" He thought the coincidence would be something he could tell Mrs Arnold when he got home, they could chuckle at it over supper. When it finally dawned on him that the book with the same title and the same author as his own book *was* his own book Mr Arnold wasn't distressed, but for a moment his head swam and he felt a little nauseous. He looked at the design on the dust-jacket. Was that the design on his dust-jacket, sitting on the bookshelf at home? He supposed it was. How dreary and old-fashioned it looked.

"Excuse me," said Mr Arnold. "I say, excuse me!" But the man didn't look up from the book; maybe Mr Arnold had spoken too gently to be heard above the locomotive engines. And he considered raising his voice, and then decided not to, as he hadn't worked out what he wanted to say. For his first reaction was that it seemed impertinent this complete stranger should be flaunting Mr Arnold's novel in public—and he had to remind himself that it was no such thing, that if the man had purchased the volume fair and square he had every right to expose it on any train he wished. And then, in contrast, Mr Arnold felt the absurd urge to thank him—that of all the books that existed in the world, it was Mr Arnold's that this man had chosen to read. He wanted to ask him what he thought of it, how much he was enjoying it. He wanted this man to be his new best friend.

Though, was the man enjoying it? It was hard to tell. The man wasn't smiling. But then, Mr Arnold reasoned, he could no longer remember whether there was anything in his novel to smile at. He couldn't be properly sure, but he had the idea his book had been rather high-minded and serious. In which case, it was probably just as well that the man wasn't smiling; thank God, moreover, that he wasn't *laughing*, that would be very bad indeed. The man did not have a face that looked like it had ever laughed. Several adjectives popped unbidden into Mr Arnold's head. Saturnine. Swarthy. Sinister. Mr Arnold hadn't had any adjectives pop into his head for quite some considerable time, and now they were there he didn't know what to do with them. He vaguely wished he had a piece of paper so he could jot a description of the man down.

The more Mr Arnold looked at the face of his reader, the more relieved he felt that he hadn't attracted his attention and he resolved he wouldn't try to speak to him again. After all, what if the man didn't like the novel? Or what if he had editorial queries about it, or asked Mr Arnold to justify certain passages?—Mr Arnold wouldn't know where to put himself. What if the man demanded his money back? Mr Arnold was reasonably sure a reader had no legal case to claim financial compensation from a badly written book, but it would still be highly irksome and might cause a scene. He was getting ahead of himself—the man was unsmiling, but he showed no other signs of censure, certainly nothing forceful enough to suggest he'd seek remuneration—the face was passive, wholly passive, there was nothing there at all. The words were going in, but whatever effect they were having on the inside wasn't reflected on the external features. That, when Mr Arnold thought about it, had disappointments of its own. And yet, he noted, the man was about halfway through the book—he hadn't given up on it, that had to be some indication of approval.

At 17.14 the train reached S___, and Mr Arnold prepared to get up from his seat, because he had to get up from his seat if he wanted to go home to Mrs Arnold and to the supper she'd have made for him. But he knew that if he left now he would never see this man again. And though he dared not speak to him, he suddenly wanted to know everything about him—who he was, where he lived, what other books he enjoyed. Mr Arnold stayed put. The train moved on B_____, to D___, and then to P___. Mr Arnold knew that by B_____ his wife would be pouring him a glass of sherry, by D___ she'd be wondering why he was late, by P___ she'd be getting worried. And yet he couldn't tear his eyes from the man opposite him—and the man opposite him never once took his eyes from the book.

Mr Arnold didn't think the man was going to get off at R___, but at the last moment he lifted his eyes from the book, placed it back into his briefcase, stood up, and followed the commuters off the train.

Mr Arnold had never been to R___. He pursued his reader through the ticket gates and R___ opened up before him, and it looked grey and unwelcoming. The street was lined with rows of dirty semi-detached houses, and all the commuters seemed to fan out towards them and were absorbed by them. There was only one beacon of light, a small café on the crossroads. The reader went inside. Mr Arnold hesitated for a moment, then he went inside too. A jolly little bell above the door announced his arrival.

The café was mostly empty. There were only a handful of customers, all sitting alone and joylessly sipping their teas. Mr Arnold was glad they were there, they gave him some cover. The reader took a table at the back of the café; Mr Arnold selected one far enough away it wouldn't attract suspicion but kept the man in his sights. The man retrieved the book from his briefcase and resumed reading; he didn't even look up as the waitress put down a pot of tea beside him. She knew what he wanted, he had been there before. The waitress then came to Mr Arnold. She was sour and lumpen and blocked Mr Arnold's view. "Pot of tea?" she asked, and Mr Arnold was courteous and said that would be very nice. "Sticky bun?" she went on, and Mr Arnold wished the fat sow would get out of the way—he thought briefly of Mrs Arnold with his supper all ready, and then put her from his mind; yes, yes, he'd have a sticky bun, go, please go, I need to see.

The tea was hot and tasteless. Mr Arnold broke off little pieces of the sticky bun, and chewed them slowly. The reader never touched his tea, he was too gripped by his book and Mr Arnold watched as the steam rose from the pot, thinned, then evaporated.

There was something very wrong with the reader. Was it that passivity?—because as the hour went on, and then the next, at no point did his face ever change expression. And maybe it was because Mr Arnold was staring at it too long, in the same way that if you stare at it on a piece of paper hard enough even the most ordinary word starts to look distorted and alien—but it seemed to Mr Arnold not just still, but *slack*, as if the skin was just hanging there and was too heavy to move. No movement at all—except for the eyes, always moving, the eyes darting backwards and forwards as they reached one margin of the page and returned to start another. And yes, that was wrong, that all felt wrong—but there was something worse, and Mr Arnold couldn't quite put his finger on what it was.

The waitress brought Mr Arnold another pot of tea, another sticky bun. He hadn't asked for them. He hadn't realised he'd finished the last lot. He scowled as once more she blocked his view, even though only briefly, he wasn't going to waste any patience on her any longer; he mechanically lifted the cup back to his mouth and nibbled at the bun. The tea was hot once more, but this time he thought he could detect some taste to it after all, a sweetness that was subtle and distant, it was reaching him from some place very far away. The sticky bun made his fingers fix fast together, they turned his hand into a hoof. And as he sipped and swallowed and chewed and swallowed and smeared his fingers against his lips and against his cheeks and against his entire face he suddenly realised what it was that didn't make sense about the man reading the book, what it was in the pit of his stomach that made him so afraid.

And it was as if the very realisation of it triggered something. As if he'd cried out, but he hadn't made a sound, had he? He hadn't even dared to gasp—but it didn't matter, because all the other customers got to their feet, put on their coats, picked up their briefcases. And left the café.

Don't leave me! Mr Arnold wanted to plead, but he couldn't—either out of embarrassment, or because he discovered that his tongue was still and dead in his mouth, he couldn't budge it. Don't leave me! He shouted at them in his head, but they couldn't hear, or didn't want to hear—either way, not a one of them even deigned to look at him. Just a single customer remaining—and, of course, it was the man at the back, and of course he was still reading the book.

But was he reading it, really? The eyes darting back and forth over the words, yes. But he'd never turned the page. He'd never turned the page. Not on the train, not in the café, not in these last few hours. He'd never turned the page.

Mr Arnold tried to get up, but it wasn't just his tongue that was lifeless. He willed his body to heave itself out of his chair, but it was no good, as if caught in a spider's web the strain only seemed to hold him there the faster. He couldn't even turn his head, now frozen towards the man with the book—he wanted to look away, he'd have done anything now to be able to look away—but he'd done this to himself, hadn't he, hadn't he chosen the seat with the perfect view? Nothing able to move now except his own eyes, darting back and forth, back and forth.

The waitress fetched her coat. She didn't say anything to Mr Arnold, but she deliberately stepped into his field of vision and gave him a smile he thought was sympathetic. That was nice of her. She pulled down the window blinds. She turned off the lights. As she left the café, the door rang its jolly little bell; she locked the door behind her.

For the longest time they sat apart in the dark, the author and his paying public. Mr Arnold could only make out the shape of the man, and his arms were still out, and his head was tilted in the same position, and Arnold presumed he was still staring at the book, though now there wasn't enough light for the pretence he was reading it. And did Mr Arnold try to work out why he'd been lured into this trap? Why it was he who'd be singled out for punishment, when there are so many writers, and so much worse than him, who have written such greater guff undeterred by bad reviews and reader apathy? Of course he did.

Mr Arnold made himself believe he would be all right so long as the man kept staring at the book. That in spite of all, he might forget Mr Arnold was even there, so long as he remained fixed by that single page he'd been studying. And he was allowed to believe that for a long time.

When the man finally lowered the book, and pulled back his chair, and got to his feet, and walked to Mr Arnold, he did so with a sigh that might have been of reader satisfaction.

He stood over Mr Arnold, and Mr Arnold could see him closely now, and his eyes were still darting even though he no longer had anything to read. And he held out the book to Arnold, and just for a bewildered moment, Mr Arnold thought the man wanted an autograph. He could not reach out for the book, of course. He could barely even breathe, as if his lungs too had been glued fast by the sticky bun, and as he fought for air he thought, is this how I die? And he thought of Mrs Arnold and his three happy, healthy children, and he was sorry.

The man stuck out his tongue, slowly and deliberately, and extended it towards Mr Arnold. And Arnold thought that was rather rude of him, and that he could still feel a flare of irritation surprised him.

The tongue may have been just a little too long, it was hard to tell in the light. The man raised the book up to his face, and brought the dusk jacket against the tongue. He began to lick. At first with the respectful delicacy due even a failed work of literature, but then with increasing speed, and increasing passion, he was slathering it all over, every inch of it. Like it was a lover, and he closed his eyes, and his face was no longer passive, it was ecstatic—how Mr Arnold wished he'd been able to write something that had unlocked that face to release expressions like that.

He'd finished. The cover was dripping a little, small beads of spit clung to the corners and then fell off. The man held up the book so Mr Arnold could see the dust jacket clearly. And it was bare—no old-fashioned and dreary design, no title. No mention of Edwyn Arnold's name as proud author. The man had licked it clean.

Mr Arnold wanted to apologise, and he didn't know why. He tried to open his mouth to do so, he very nearly managed it. The man shook his head, and put a finger to Mr Arnold's lips, ssh, it was all right, it's all perfectly all right.

And he drove his finger in between those lips, and the finger became a whole fist, and it forced Mr Arnold's mouth wide open, and Mr Arnold thought how cold his hands were, he should have drunk his hot tea after all, and the man took hold of Mr Arnold's inert tongue. Very gently he pulled Mr Arnold's tongue out of his mouth, as far as it could go.

So Mr Arnold sat there with his tongue pointing directly at the man and he thought that now he was the one being rude. He tried to flex it, and there was a little life returning to it, he could just about waggle the tip.

The man opened the book, and held the first page of the first chapter close to Mr Arnold's face. Still Mr Arnold didn't know what he wanted, and the man grunted a little impatiently, and waggled his own tongue by way of demonstration. And Arnold understood, and set to work.

There was no taste to his novel.

And every minute or two, once a page had been erased to the man's satisfaction, he would turn over so Mr Arnold could continue.

The man had the hardest job, really, holding out the book and keeping it straight. All Mr Arnold had to do was sit there and lick. But nevertheless, he felt they made quite a team.

Mr Arnold's novel hadn't been particularly long, but it was still nearly dawn by the time they'd finished. He was grateful he hadn't turned out a *War and Peace*, they'd have been there for weeks. And when the book was over, Arnold felt that the pair of them had really achieved something. "Thank you," he said. "Thank you." And then he realised he could move his jaw again, and turn his head too, he was pleased.

The man didn't acknowledge the thanks, and Mr Arnold thought that was rather a shame. He flicked through the book, and confirmed that not a page had been missed. And he put it, still dribbling Mr Arnold's spit, back into his briefcase. Without a word or a glance he unlocked the door to the café and went.

It was another half-hour before Arnold got the feeling back in his legs. Everything was pins and needles. He stumbled outside into the morning air, and took deep breaths. He felt clean somehow, even pure. It was still too early for the train, so he began the walk back to S___. By the time he reached home the sun was shining. His wife had spent the night on the sofa waiting for him, and was fast asleep. He kissed her on the forehead, put his arms around her, and took her up to bed.

Sometimes Edwyn Arnold could feel the novel inside his head. It was big and heavy and had sharp edges. He knew if he weren't careful his passing thoughts would cut themselves on it. But he *was* careful—it was a part of him, after all. It had always been a part of him, and he couldn't quite believe he had let himself forget that. And at night he would lower the part of his head that contained his novel gently on the pillow, and he'd feel it lurch into a new position, and it was a comfort.

He felt happier—younger. His novel had been born out of ambition and youthful self-belief. And heady excess—never one word when three would do! Though he recognised it wasn't very good, the clumsy innocence of it was a tonic. In class he surprised his pupils by being witty. He even managed to inspire a few.

He wanted to revel in their youth to show them they weren't so very different—he wanted to tell them all about his novel. But he wasn't sure they'd enjoy it, and held his tongue.

He liked chapter four best. Chapter four had been composed in a rush of such disarming naiveté than it brought tears to his eyes. "We should have the kids round for dinner," he told his wife one day. She was astonished—said he never wanted to be bothered with that—said he hadn't even referred to them as 'the kids' in years. "Well, why not? They *are* our kids, after all!" And the next Sunday they were all together, and it was the first time in years, since the funeral of some dead aunt or another, and his kids brought their own kids, and he felt like a kid too, and there was such laughter, it was a house of kids spanning three generations.

Mr Arnold wanted to tell his family about his novel, but he thought they might not understand it.

Mrs Arnold bought herself a new dress one day. She showed it off to him when he came home from school. "I don't know why," she said, "something just came over me. You don't mind?" And she looked so beautiful suddenly—and so nervous too, fearing he might no longer find her so. He kissed her, and it was a real kiss, and they hadn't kissed in such a long while. And then they went to bed and made love, and they hadn't done that in even longer.

She lay in his arms, and she told him she loved him, and all he wanted to do was tell her about his novel, his novel.

"I don't think we've ever been happier," she said.

"I don't think we have either," Mr Arnold replied.

The next morning he went into the study and took his novel down from the bookshelf. The pages were bare and soggy. He put it into his briefcase. Mrs Arnold said, "Have a good day at school!" and he thanked her, and she said, "Supper at the usual time?" and he said he was looking forward to it. Then he said goodbye and walked out of the house forever.

He crossed over from his usual platform and caught the train to R___ instead. On the journey he prodded at the novel in his head and it cried like a little baby.

The café was mostly empty. There were only a handful of customers, all sitting alone and joylessly sipping their teas. Each one of them was working on a manuscript. Mr Arnold took a seat. The waitress put down a pot of tea in front of him—she knew what he wanted, he had been there before. Mr Arnold took out his own manuscript, and began to write.

It was hard to make an impression upon the paper, it was still so damp with spit. Still, he persevered. He drank tea and nibbled at buns, he consumed each and every thing the waitress gave him, but he didn't look up, he had no time to look up, he was busy. Every so often she would pull down the blinds and turn out the lights and lock up the café and he carried on regardless, he wrote by moonlight. All the words he had written before—and yes, he could have changed some, and for the better, he was older now and maybe wiser too and he could see exactly where his novel could be improved. But Mr Arnold didn't think that was fair somehow. And at last, one day, he reached the end, and there it was in front of him amongst the empty tea cups and the crumbs of a thousand sticky buns, there was his first novel reborn—wet, and fresh, and unique and utterly utterly dreadful. Mr Arnold stroked at the pages fondly for a moment, he couldn't help himself. And then he got up from his seat, walked over to the counter, and dropped the book into the bin.

There was a cavity in his brain from where the novel had been torn; his head throbbed. And he felt sadder and lonelier than he ever had before.

The waitress said, "Pot of tea?" And he said yes, a pot of tea, please, and some paper. She brought him the tea, and she brought him the paper, and Edwyn Arnold took a deep breath and set to work on his second novel.

And the old woman says:

- *Edwyn Arnold's novel is not very good. But it may still be better than* **The Disappointing Story in the Book** *(story 6, page 85).*
- *The novels in Edwyn's head could crack his skull open. Consider whether that would depreciate its market value in* **Brand New Shiny Shiny** *(story 94, page 1585).*
- *Another, more famous writer finds a tale growing inside her head in* **Scheherazade's Last Story** *(story 100, page 1687).*
- *The legacy of a more famous writer still is explored in* **Canon Fodder** *(story 12, page 199).*
- *Beyond the point of death, a man falls in love with reading books in* **Unfinished** *(story 18, page 311).*

Have you found the map yet?

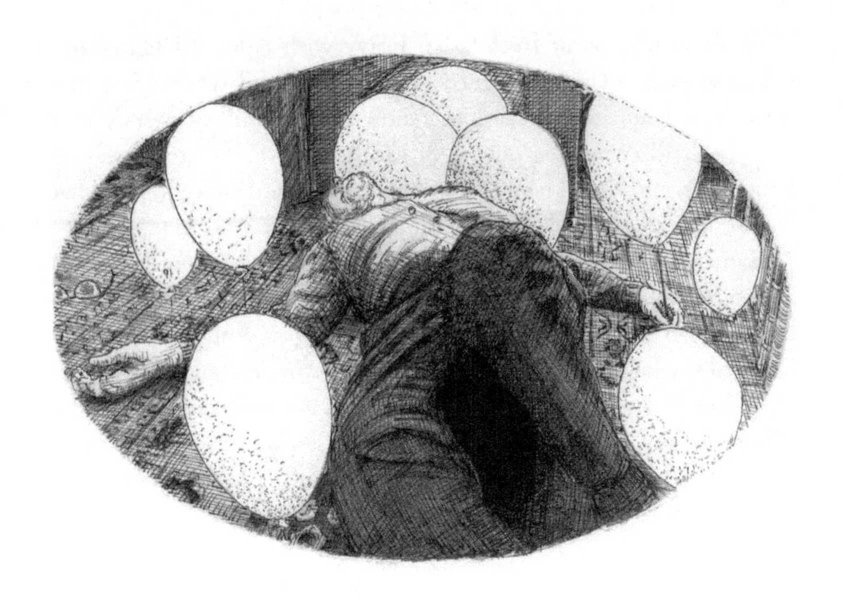

91
Lo! He Abhors Not the Virgin's Womb

CAMERON MASON WAS just old enough to remember a time when the balloons floated. He knew there was more to Christmas than balloons, of course. He'd learned about Christmas in history class. There'd been a Santa Claus who'd flown about the world on a sleigh, there'd been carol singers, and cards, and crackers, and they said that when you ate the turkey it had tasted like meat and not like ash. And so it was easy to pass off the balloons as a false memory—something Cameron had heard about at school, or seen in the family photographs—because the photo album had been brought out every now and then, oh yes, whenever his parents were feeling nostalgic, and they would berate themselves for it afterwards, and they'd pray to God for forgiveness, though nostalgia seemed to Cameron really a very minor sin: "Look," Mother would say, and she'd show photos of trees laden heavy with coloured lights and coloured balls, of men sculpted out of snow (and what a feat that must have been, to persuade the snow to keep still in exactly that shape!)—and there'd be photos of Mother and Father too, wearing paper hats, and they'd be *smiling*, and that was odd enough, but what was odder still, they'd both be smiling at *the exact same time.*

Cameron knew that he'd lived through the times of indoor trees and snow beings, and of magic men in sleighs. He *knew* it, but he couldn't feel it, he had no real recollection of it. And that's why he believed the balloons had to be real memories, not things he'd picked up from anecdotes or books: so bright they'd been, so colourful, all the colours of the rainbow (and more besides!), and the balloons were these perfect spheres, and they floated upwards into the air, not too fast, they were in no hurry, they had all the time in the world—up they went, right up as high as the ceiling! And they weren't being held there by anything, there were no strings attached, they weren't fixed on hooks, these balloons defied gravity! And there against the ceiling they would bounce away for a bit, blindly trying to find a way onwards, and Father said (maybe it was Father) that the balloons would go on all the way up to Heaven if we hadn't invented ceilings to stop them. And when they couldn't break past the ceiling, when they realised there was nowhere higher for them to reach, then the balloons would bob back down to head height, right in front of Cameron's face, and they quivered with expectation, as if Awaiting Further Instructions—and they'd follow Cameron around the house all Christmas long to keep him company, they'd be his friends, they'd play games with him and never get tired of him and never get cross with him if Cameron went through one of his Black Moods—they'd stand guard over his bedside as he slept and be there for him when he woke up. And he wanted to hug them—but Father said (or maybe this time it was Mother) that if he hugged the balloons too tight they wouldn't like it, they'd burst with a bang, they'd burst themselves to death. There were just some things you had to learn to love from afar.

So that was his first memory, and there are worse first memories to have. Cameron could only have been two years old at the most, he accepted that the memory might be a little inaccurate. He didn't know what had happened to his balloon friends, why they had gone away.

But he was happy with even only half a memory. The balloons were his. They were there in his head when he needed them. And sometimes, even now he was fourteen and all grown up, if he wanted to cheer himself and find a reason to keep going, he'd think how they floated! They could have floated forever.

Floating balloons were part of the old times. And Cameron knew that the old times were bad, that they were times of ignorance, and ignorance was bad, and they were times of doubt, and doubt too was bad. And the only balloons you could buy nowadays were grey, each and every one as grey as granite. And when you blew into them they seemed to resist your breath, they seemed to find it an imposition, you could feel the disapproval coming off—and they didn't float, they'd crash straight to the ground like rocks. Because they were heavier than air, and they obeyed the stern laws of gravity.

The taxi driver didn't say a word when he put Cameron's suitcase into the car, nor when Cameron gave him the piece of paper on which he had carefully written his grandfather's address. And so for a while Cameron wondered whether the driver could even speak at all. But at one junction another car swerved in front of the taxi, and the taxi driver hadn't liked that, and had said something very rude—so Cameron now knew that the driver wasn't mute but simply refused to speak to him. The driver must have been angry. Cameron wondered why, and whether he should apologise. But he didn't want to apologise. And the reason for not apologising was this, so:

The taxi had been arranged to pick Cameron up from the train station, and it wasn't Cameron's fault that the train was so very late. And any sensible person would have expected the train to be late—it was Christmas Eve, and there were always delays on the lines at Christmas. Especially since the state hadn't ruled against people throwing themselves on the tracks—they hadn't actually *condoned* it, but they'd only made illegal any suicides that endangered the lives of others. And no one could claim, surely, that throwing yourself into the path of an oncoming train was going to cause damage to any of the passengers onboard, the train was so *very very* heavy and mere flesh and bone so very weak. Everyone knew that the train drivers were under instructions to plough on through the bodies, stopping every time there was a fatality would cause ridiculous inconvenience. But there had to be a limit to how many bodies a train could plough through, surely? And at some points on the journey it had seemed to Cameron that the bodies were lying on top of each other in piles, it'd be like asking the train to drive over a wall! Christmas was always such a popular time for the suicides. If that's why the taxi driver was so angry, it wasn't fair: it wasn't Cameron's fault there were suicides, no more than it was his fault it was Christmas.

The taxi pulled into a street. Houses lined the road on both sides, jammed tight together, they looked clean, tidy, aggressively neat. The taxi stopped outside one of these houses. The driver waited, then turned to look at Cameron. Cameron didn't recognise the house, it had been years since he had seen his grandfather, but the number on the door conformed to the number he had on the address, so he got out of the car.

And before he'd even fetched his suitcase the front door of the house opened, and out came his grandfather. He was smiling, and his arms were wide, and it looked as if he were coming at Cameron for a hug, but at the last moment he changed his mind. "Well!" he said. Cameron's grandfather had a white beard, and that ought to have made him look like Santa Claus, but the beard wasn't long and flowing, it was short and clipped, and it made him look like his headmaster instead, or maybe one of Father's friends from the bank.

Grandfather tried to pay the driver. The driver wanted more money. Grandfather said that he wanted to pay the price they had agreed. The driver said being out on the streets this close to Christmas was dangerous, he should be paid extra. Grandfather said that there were still hours left before Christmas, that the driver would be able to get home in plenty of time. "You don't know where I live!" screamed the driver. "You don't know where I live!"—and he seemed to Cameron to be on the verge of laughter, maybe this was hysteria? Father had accused Mother of being hysterical quite a lot over the last few months, but she'd not sounded remotely like that. Grandfather gave the driver some more money. The driver sped away.

Then, back to Cameron. Back with the smile. "Well," said Grandfather again. Another move for a hug, this time it was Cameron who blocked it. "So. Was your journey all right?"

Cameron said it was.

"How's your mum? How's your dad?"

"I don't know."

"You don't know?"

"They're fine. They're stable."

"And your little brother? Billy, is it?"

"He's stable."

"And your sister?"

"Stable," said Cameron, "too."

"That's good. That's fine. Well." And Grandfather was reaching out again, and this time Cameron might have accepted the hug after all, but Grandfather was taking the suitcase out of his hands, now *he* had the suitcase, so.

"Shall we go inside?" asked Grandfather, and it wasn't really a question, so why ask it? They went indoors, and straight away Cameron thought the house smelled like old people, and Grandfather closed the front door behind them, and the winter and the darkness were shut fast out, and that was all that was left now, the old people smell.

"Welcome," said Grandfather, rather stiffly. "I hope you'll be very happy here."

"Should we do a prayer?" asked Cameron.

"Yes," said Grandfather. "All right."

They both got down on to their knees, it took Grandfather a little longer because he was so horribly old.

"God," said Grandfather, "if you're listening. Thank you for the safe arrival of little Cameron, and that this year I shan't be spending my Christmas alone."

"O Lord," said Cameron, "if you are listening. Thank you for getting me to Grandfather's house, and that the taxi wasn't *too* badly delayed." Cameron was good at prayer, it never made him nervous to speak to God the way it did some of the other children, and he liked saying 'O Lord' rather than just 'Lord', it had a nice ring to it. At school Cameron was an average student at best, and he didn't play well with the others, but he was top of his class in prayer practice.

"Would you like to eat?" said Grandfather. "I've got some food prepared. I don't think it's very nice. It won't have much taste this close to Christmas, but it's better than nothing." Cameron said he wasn't hungry. "Would you like to sleep? I can show you to your room, you can get in a few hours' rest before midnight." Cameron said he wasn't tired, but yes, he'd like to go to his room and be on his own.

Cameron's room was small, the bed looked hard. There were a few pictures on the dresser, Cameron didn't know who they were of and didn't want to ask. "I'll leave you to it, then," said Grandfather. "Call me if you need anything." Cameron knew he wouldn't need anything. He heard his grandfather trudge his way back down the stairs, and only when he couldn't hear him any more did he get on to the bed, still fully clothed, put his head on to the pillow, and stare up at the ceiling. The bed wasn't as hard as it looked. That was good.

He didn't think he would ever commit suicide by throwing himself under a train. He could see the appeal, he was sure it was quite painless. Lots of the bodies he'd seen on the tracks had had big smiles. But Cameron thought that death should be a private thing. No, when the time for suicide came, he'd do it discreetly behind closed doors. He used to think that poison would be a good method, but the events of the last few days had shown it wasn't efficient. No, he'd probably now use a blade.

He wondered if the taxi driver would commit suicide. "You don't know where I live!" he'd screamed. Cameron hoped the taxi driver was all right. He hadn't liked him very much, but nevertheless he hoped he made it home safe in time for Christmas.

Cameron dozed.

He didn't know how long he slept for, but he felt hardly rested when his grandfather was at his side, gently shaking his shoulder. "Do you want to see the snow?" Grandfather asked, and Cameron said that he did. He got to his feet, and the room seemed to spin, the last few days had hit him more than he had expected, and he was strangely pleased by that, he'd worried that his reactions hadn't been normal. He knew the feeling wouldn't last. He knew come midnight he wouldn't feel much of anything any longer.

Grandfather led him downstairs. "This is the best window!" Grandfather promised. "You can see everything from here!" The night sky hung heavy, the darkness seemed to bulge down to them. Grandfather checked his watch. "Forty seconds to go!" Was he actually excited, or just trying too hard?

Midnight—Christmas Day—and there, on cue, the first flakes twirling down. Then, within seconds, a whole army of them, streaming down from the heavens, fast, hard. A billion white specks, they burned white. They singed the very air.

"We're dreaming of a white Christmas," muttered Grandfather.

"We're praying for a white Christmas," said Cameron, and he tried to keep the correction out of his voice.

"Amen," they both said together.

And Grandfather found Cameron's hand and squeezed it, but already the numbness was creeping over Cameron's body, Cameron could see his grandfather was touching him but it felt so very far off, and he looked back out of the window at the blazing snow and when Grandfather took his hand away Cameron didn't notice.

"The television's on," said Grandfather. Of course the television was on. Today there might at last be an announcement.

That the Second Coming had taken place on Christmas Day had been apt, but some maintained it was a coincidence. They pointed out that Christmas had never been the birthday of Christ, it was really something to do with Pagan ceremonies and the Winter Solstice. But the majority argued that that surely was hardly the point—Jesus would have known that December the twenty-fifth had become the day adopted to celebrate the nativity, did the doubters think that the Son of God wouldn't have availed himself of a decent calendar and checked to see when the holiday season started? Whatever the truth behind the scheduling, Jesus himself wasn't available for comment.

That it was really Jesus, this time there had been no doubt. No ambiguity, no is-he or isn't-he guessing games around a crucifixion site, no more listen-to-my-parable nonsense. At the moment that Christ had returned to Earth, that Christmas evening twelve years before, the world had collectively stopped in its tracks; the ineffable truth of his divine presence was seared into the forefront of everyone's minds, and there it would burn, and it could never be extinguished now, not ever. The world had changed in an instant—and now a line had been drawn, there was only *then*, the time of ignorance, and *now*, an unending now, in which the single essential fact was there for all to know. Or rather, as some preferred, the world *hadn't* changed, not in the slightest—because this was the world as it had always been, but we had been too vain and too dumb and too evil to see it, the most important thing we had ever been required to accept had been standing before us all in plain sight but we had obscured it with the inconsequential babble of our daily lives, with sex and money and the ever pointless staving off of death, and now the irrelevant guff had been cleared away, and now we could see at last, we could see, and we would never stop seeing now, not even if we ripped our eyes out.

The first thing Jesus did was to build himself a palace. It took only a moment. He plonked it down right in the middle of Florida, where there's sunshine three hundred days a year, Jesus was no fool. The second thing he did was to go inside his palace and shut the door. There was one single message given: Await Further Instructions.

So the peoples of the world awaited. They prepared their questions. They wanted a resolution on border disputes, on the economy. They wanted his thoughts on women priests and gay marriage and all the contradictory bits raised by the *Book of Deuteronomy*. They hoped, principally, for an explanation. It didn't have to be a complex one. Just something that broadly told them they were doing all right, and maybe of the little areas where they were doing wrong, and an easy way they could resolve the two.

The weeks went by. Then months. The message from the palace never changed. Those further instructions were still to be awaited.

Some wars stopped, because no one could be quite sure what they were fighting for any longer. Other wars started, as new convictions took hold. Roughly the same number of atrocities were committed after the return of Jesus as before. The weather didn't get any better. There were still traffic jams.

And at last it neared Christmas once more. No longer commemorating the birth of Jesus Christ but his glorious return. There was even a sense of relief—it all made sense, we hadn't been abandoned, we'd been given a little time to adjust and think things through, and that was perfectly right of Jesus, and actually very wise, wasn't it? But now a year was up, and this is what we had been waiting for—that on the anniversary of his second coming, Jesus would surely emerge from his palace and deliver some statement to the world.

The moment Christmas Day began snow began to fall from the sky. It fell upon every nation on the planet. It fell in the Arctic, it fell in the deserts, it fell right on the middle of oceans where only the fish could see. There was no more pain: the sick and the diseased, to their wonder, found that they could rise from their beds, their limbs were lithe and supple and they felt so *free*. There was no death—no man nor woman died that Christmas Day, and no beast either, no four-legged creatures nor birds in the sky, nor things that crept upon their bellies. There was an end to suffering. It was a miracle. It was the greatest gift God could bestow. And everyone settled down happily by their television sets, the cameras trained upon the doors of the palace, full certain that at any moment they would be flung wide open and out would step Jesus, arms wide, all smiles, and his smile would be so dazzling, we would be blinded by the brilliance of that smile and we wouldn't even care, the blinding couldn't hurt us, nothing could hurt us any longer.

The doors stayed closed. Obstinately closed, even. And, at midnight, the snow stopped abruptly, as if it had been turned off at a tap. The sick who had been prancing gaily around their beds collapsed once more. And there was so much death, twice as much death, as all those who would have died on December 26th anyway were joined by those postponed from December 25th, the mortuaries were crammed full to bursting.

And still, still that message. Await Further Instructions. We hadn't received them yet, but they were on their way, and soon. We just had to be patient.

A second Christmas passed. A third, the fourth. And on Christmas Day, and on Christmas Day alone, there was no death and no pain—but there was no taste either, and not much smell, there really was barely a sensation to be felt at all. The colours of the world drained to monochrome that second Christmas, and when they came back the next day they seemed a little duller than before. And the snow, that snow that fell from up above, surely direct from God himself, the snow burned.

Grandfather and Cameron had been sitting by the television for over an hour. They stared at the great wooden doors to Jesus' palace.

"I think I saw something," said Grandfather.

"Where?" said Cameron.

"My mistake," said Grandfather. "The screen flickered. It's really a very old television."

It was the twelfth Christmas since the Second Coming. There was a lot of hope for the twelfth, twelve was a significant number. The twelve tribes of Israel. The twelve apostles (before one of them turned bad). Twelve, surely, would be the year.

At last Grandfather sighed, stretched. "Come on," he said to Cameron. "There's something I want to show you."

"It's down here," said Grandfather. He unlocked the door to the basement with a key. The wooden steps downwards looked uneven, and there was a blast of cold air that pricked at Cameron's numbed skin. "Down here, where no one else can see."

Cameron asked, "Can't God see down there?"

"God probably can see it," Grandfather conceded. "But I'm hoping that he'll be too busy to bother with us today."

Cameron suggested they should offer him a prayer before going down, and Grandfather thought that was a good idea, they hadn't prayed to God for at least half an hour. Then they got up from their knees, and made their way into the darkness of the basement. Cameron asked if they could turn the lights on, but Grandfather said no, it would spoil the surprise. "You go first!" he said. "It's exciting!"

And at last Cameron could go down no further, the stairs had come to an end, and he stopped dead, and Grandfather bumped into him. "Sorry!" laughed Grandfather. "Sorry! Yes, all right, I should turn on the lights!" And he spent the next minute or two feeling around the walls for the switch.

In the dark the numbness of Cameron's body was absolute. It hardly felt as if he were still alive. He wondered if this was what the dead felt. He wondered if it was because of this calm that the suicides on the railway tracks had been smiling. When the lights were turned on he was surprised, a little surprised—and the shock of that sensation, as muted as it was, was enough to take his breath away.

"This," said Grandfather, "is all for you, Cam. All for you. Christmas, just like in the old days."

Because the walls were studded with coloured balls, and streamers hung down from the ceiling. There were ornaments of snow men, and smiling angels, there was a big Santa Claus and lots of little Santa Clauses, the big one had reindeer, the little ones carried sacks. And there was a tree, a tree indoors, the insanity of it—and the tree was wearing fairy lights and tinsel like cheap jewellery, too much jewellery, like a little girl playing dress-up, like the whore of Babylon—and under the tree were lots and lots of parcels wrapped up in shiny paper, of all shapes and sizes.

The tree wasn't happy to have been disturbed. It writhed within its tub from side to side, it thrashed its branches at them angrily. It tried to shake off its fairy lights.

"Is it suffering?" asked Cameron.

"Nothing suffers on Christmas Day!" said Grandfather. "I expect. No, no, he's probably just pleased to see you!" But even so, Cameron decided not to get too close.

Cameron didn't say anything for a while. Instead he looked around the room, at all the colour and festivity. The basement was cold and damp; he could see water trickling down the wall in one corner, it dripped on to a gleeful reindeer head. "Isn't this against the rules?" he asked at last.

"No."

"Didn't they come and take all this stuff away?"

"You can see they didn't."

"But isn't this from the old times?"

"I want to give you a merry Christmas!" said Grandfather, and he forced a chuckle. He stroked at his white beard, as if he too wished it were long and flowing. "Do you like it? I just thought. After what you've been through. After so much *shit*. I thought. Do you like it? Tell me you do."

"I like it," said Cameron. And Grandfather beamed.

"I've got you presents," said Grandfather. "You know, we all used to give each other presents at Christmas? All those presents, every single one, they're all for you. Get them from under the tree, ha, have at them!" But Cameron didn't want to go under the tree, so Grandfather fished them out himself. And whenever the tree swiped at him with one of his branches, he'd laugh as if it were a game.

Cameron unwrapped his gifts. There was a kettle, a tin of beans, an interestingly shaped pebble. "They're not very good," admitted Grandfather. "I just wanted you to have the fun of opening something. They're just things I found around the house. But they're yours, all yours."

"Thank you," said Cameron.

"And next year. If there is a next year. In the wider scheme of things, assuming a new year comes to pass. And on a different scheme, ah, assuming you want to see me again. I can maybe find you fun things to unwrap. Things you might actually enjoy."

"Yes," said Cameron. "That would be nice."

Grandfather sung *Away in a Manger* then, all the words that he could remember. Even the tree stopped thrashing and listened, maybe in shock.

"I want to make this your best Christmas ever," said Grandfather. "I know I've not been there for you. For you, or your dad, and it's too late for him now. Well, we'll see. But I'll try hard. I'm trying my best. Truly. I don't know how to love you. But we'll work it out, okay?"

"Let's do a prayer," said Cameron.

"If you like."

"O Lord," said Cameron, "if you are listening. Thank you for all the glorious bounty with which you have provided me."

"Yes," said Grandfather. "Thanks."

He got up from his knees, and suggested that perhaps it was time they went to eat.

Upstairs the television was still playing. It showed the same image as before, the tightly sealed doors of the palace.

Grandfather asked Cameron if he would like to carve the turkey. Cameron said he'd never carved the turkey before, his father had always done it. Grandfather said that this year Cameron could be the man of the house, he was a grown-up now. Would he like to carve? Grandfather would be there to help. Grandfather would be right beside him in case he got into any trouble. Cameron said he'd give it a try.

The turkey was well cooked, it was brown and looked so very moist, and the thought alone of how it might have smelled caused Cameron to salivate a little. It took both him and his grandfather to get it out of the oven—the turkey kicked at them with its one remaining leg, there was quite a force to it for all that it was so tender and crispy, and it wouldn't relent until Grandfather had seized hold and wrenched it off. Even then, the turkey still put up quite a struggle. The headless bird wouldn't stop fidgeting upon the plate, and as Cameron sliced at its breast Grandfather had to keep the rest of the body pinned down with a fork. Cameron poured a little gravy over the hunk of meat he had cut for himself, but the meat shook itself dry and went to quiver by the vegetables sullenly. Grandfather and Cameron ate. Once in a while they would be forced to stab at the turkey remains and tell them to settle down.

As always, the turkey tasted like ash. Everything tasted of ash at Christmas. But it was a good quality ash, Grandfather was quite pleased. "If I do say so myself, I'm quite the chef," he said.

There was a cry from outside. A woman's voice. Nothing coherent, but sounding with such despair. Grandfather left the table and went to the window. Cameron finished chewing his mouthful, neatly lay down his knife and fork, then got up to join him.

In the next door garden there was a man. He seemed to be dancing—and yet it wasn't dancing, because there was no rhythm to it, or it was the rhythm to a mad music only he could hear. He jerked his body from side to side, then spun it around completely. His arms were raised high. His head was tilted back, and he was staring joyfully up at the sky. The cry hadn't come from him—there was a smaller figure in the garden too, closer to the house, and it was protecting itself under a big grey coat. And this figure was reaching out to the dancing man—it was appealing to it, pleading—though Cameron couldn't hear what it was saying, the snow was falling so thickly now and it seemed to be smothering sound itself. It seemed that the dancing man couldn't hear either, he ignored the figure altogether, and yet there was no anger to that, he continued to beam beatifically up at the heavens. Then—"Come, Jesus, take me to your palace!" he shouted—that much was clear, anyway—and that was followed by another incoherent cry from the figure protected by the coat, it *was* a woman, was it his wife?

"Do you know them?" asked Cameron.

"Not by name," said Grandfather. "But by sight, I think, a little."

Oh, the coat wasn't protecting her. It wasn't protecting her. It snowed just as hard on her as it snowed on him. The snow was burning the coat. The coat was sparking, each little flake caused it to flash, look! And on the man's face. The snow burning through his skin. You could see it, his cheeks just craters now, and getting ever deeper as the snow melted away his features. The snow fell into his eyes. The snow fell into his mouth. And still, in spite of the fact his tongue was burning, that lick of flame was surely his tongue, still he sang out to the night sky: "Take me, Jesus!"

The woman beneath the coat slumped to the ground, the coat fell away.

The man stopped dancing. He didn't fall. He didn't die. He couldn't die, not today. Nothing can be dead on Christmas Day—and he twitched a little as his skull smouldered. His arms still held out high—in supplication? a welcome hello to death? looking for a divine hug?

The woman lay there sobbing.

"Let's have some giblets," said Grandfather. "Would you like some giblets?"

They ate giblets. The turkey didn't like it, but at midnight Christmas would end and at last it could be dead.

Grandfather turned off the television set. "Nothing's going to happen," he said. "Nothing is ever going to change."

Await further instructions. But some of us get tired of waiting. We turn our impatience into a virtue. We say that faith should never be a passive thing—to believe in God, steadfastly and without doubt, in spite of all the pressures from science and philosophy and common sense, has always required committed action. Jesus has come down to *us*. He has travelled so very far already. Shouldn't we be prepared to take the final few steps?

Cameron and his grandfather drank whisky. Cameron didn't usually like the taste of whisky, but today it was just ash, and all it could do was warm his throat a little.

Grandfather drank his whisky more quickly than Cameron could manage.

"Your grandmother didn't kill herself. I know that seems quaint now. But it used to be quite common in the old days. Do you remember your grandmother? I don't see how you can. She died so long ago, you were so very young. It wasn't an easy end. She suffered. She fought against death, you know, she didn't want to leave me. I think that's true, that she fought for my sake. And when Jesus came back. Well, I know lots of people were pleased. They thought they'd get an answer. To why there's death, why there has to be suffering. But I didn't want that. I thought I already knew. Watching Barbara, those last dreadful weeks, I thought I worked it out. Because there has to be an end, I see that. Because if it all goes on forever, it isn't worth a damn. And so ends shouldn't be easy. There should be suffering, or you won't care that you're letting go, and if you don't care then was it worth having in the first place? I don't think so. I don't think it could be. So, when Jesus came back. And showed us that maybe after all there was life beyond. That there's eternity. That I might see my Barbara again, in some heavenly place, who knows? And that final goodbye I gave to her, when I kissed her on the cheek before she went to sleep, that it wasn't a goodbye at all. Well. I just thought that ruined everything. Is that all right? Is it all right that I think that?"

Cameron finished his glass of whisky at last. This is what he said.

"I don't see why they left me behind. My father and my mother and my brother and my sister. They poisoned themselves so they could get to the palace. They poisoned themselves so they could see Jesus. Why didn't they want me with them? Why? Why am I not good enough?"

Grandfather said, "I don't know."

They didn't speak for a while.

Grandfather said, "He botched the job, didn't he? Too much poison, or too little. He botched the job, your father can't do anything right. They didn't die. They're stable. You told me they're stable. If you want to know, you can go and ask them."

Silence.

Grandfather said, "Or sometimes we don't really want answers."

"Can I have another whisky?" asked Cameron.

"No," said Grandfather. "We're getting maudlin. We can't get maudlin at Christmas. Let's go back to the basement."

Cameron didn't want to go back to the basement. He hated the decorations. He hated the presents, he hated the tree. It was cold, and, worse, it was too colourful, and he couldn't make sense of the colours, and the water that dripped down the walls probably smelled like old people just like everything else.

"But I have other treats for you. I do. Things I've kept from years ago. Christmas crackers that go bang and have jokes in. Board games. We could play games, lots of games. Balloons. Do you hear me, Cameron? I have balloons."

Cameron held the empty balloon in the palm of his hand, and it seemed such a small and shrivelled thing.

Grandfather smiled, and took it from him. He put the end to his mouth and he blew. As he did so, he pulled a face, he puffed out his cheeks and rolled his eyes with pretend effort—but Cameron didn't laugh, so he soon stopped that. The balloon quickly swelled up. It was yellow, and it looked like the sun. "This is the fiddly bit, tying the knot," said Grandfather. "Ah. Got it. Here. Catch."

And he tossed it to Cameron. Cameron flinched, he'd been told not to touch the balloons by his father, and now he couldn't avoid it—the bright yellow sphere punted harmlessly off his chest, and then bounced higher into the air. Cameron giggled as if he were just a silly child, he couldn't help it. The balloon slowly floated to the ground.

"Doesn't it go up?" he said.

"It did go up."

"Doesn't it keep going up?"

"I don't think so."

"I'm pretty sure they're meant to keep going up."

Grandfather stooped, picked up the balloon, once more tossed it to Cameron. This time Cameron caught it. He held on to it gingerly, his fingers gripping the sides. He threw it high into the air. It floated up lazily. It floated downwards lazily. It was going to be subject to laws of force and gravity, but it wasn't going to be too fussed by them.

"Are you disappointed?"

"A little."

"Well, it's only my breath in there," said Grandfather. "And I'm just an old man. Maybe we need better quality breath."

"Do you have other balloons we could try?"

"Oh yes," said Grandfather. "Lots."

Cameron blew up his first balloon. Grandfather was right, it was hard to tie the knot, and the first few times he tried he fumbled and let go, and the balloon spat out all the breath he'd put inside and flew around the room farting. After that, Cameron decided he would have to be much stricter with his balloon friends—he loved them, but they needed discipline, and he held on to them much more tightly.

The first balloon Cameron gave life to floated well enough, but it didn't defy any laws of gravity. Nor did the second, or the third. He burst the fourth, he was careless, he was too impatient—and Cameron was shocked, but Grandfather laughed at the loud bang it made, and so Cameron laughed too.

And Grandfather kept blowing up balloons as well—faster than Cameron, for all his old breath, he'd tie the ends then drop them then move on to another. And none of his tried to float to Heaven either. But pretty soon the entire basement floor was covered with balloons, bobbing up and down and jockeying for position—they weren't able to keep still, they were alive, but they weren't in distress like the tree was or the turkey had been, they were little innocents clustered about Cameron's feet and staring up at him and hoping he might play with them.

"That's enough balloons for now," said Grandfather. "I'm all out of puff." He waved some balloons out of the way, off they scurried as he sank down to the ground.

"No," said Cameron. "There must be a balloon here that'll do what I want. I just have to find it."

His grandfather didn't say anything. Cameron blew up three more balloons in quick succession, each as useless as the last. And at the end of that time his grandfather still hadn't spoken, and Cameron went to his side.

"But you can't die," said Cameron. "Not now. It's Christmas."

"I was wrong," said Grandfather. "Seems there's change after all."

"Does it hurt?"

"It's exactly what it should be."

It seemed to Cameron that the balloons were full of his grandfather's breath, and that if he only gathered them all up and untied the knots, then Grandfather would get it back. But he was clumsy, and he was starting to panic, he was starting to have one of his Black Moods, and he kept on bursting them. One after the other, popping under his fingers, and spraying Grandfather's breath uselessly into the air. Cameron was beginning to feel something, the numbness was fading, and instead he felt hot and frightened. He began to cry. "Don't," said Grandfather. "Don't." So Cameron stopped crying, and he stopped popping the balloons, and he sat down beside his grandfather, and his grandfather died.

Cameron got on his knees to pray. "O Lord," he said. "O Lord," he said again. "O Lord." He wanted to thank God for his grandfather, but he couldn't find the words. And God waited, and God stopped listening, Cameron could feel it, God got bored and went to listen to someone else better at prayer practice than him. But Cameron stayed there on his knees for ten minutes before giving up and getting to his feet.

He went back upstairs. He turned on the television set. The doors to the palace still hadn't opened. The commentators were trying to put a brave spin upon it. Twelve wasn't that important a number. Now, forty, that's important. In the Bible there's lots about forty days and forty nights. Forty is the keeper, we just have to wait till year forty. We just have to be patient.

Cameron stayed up until midnight. He watched as the snow stopped falling, and as it melted harmlessly into the ground. Then he went to the kitchen, and saw that the turkey was now at peace. Then to the basement, and he locked the door, leaving his grandfather and the balloons together in the dark.

A taxi driver came by the next morning to take Cameron to the railway station. It wasn't *the* taxi driver, it was just *a* taxi driver, and Cameron wondered whether that meant that *the* taxi driver had died after all, and he supposed it didn't.

This taxi driver tried to be chatty. He asked where Cameron was going, and Cameron lied, and pretended that he knew.

He took the last pack of balloons from his pocket. He took one out, it was another yellow, but the colour was already fading, this could never be a sun. He played with it idly, he stretched it between his fingers. He blew it up, tied a knot in the end.

He unwound the window of the taxi, and released the balloon to the world.

"Hey, kid," said the driver. "Don't do that."

Cameron ignored him. He blew up another balloon. This one was already monochrome. This too went out of the window.

"Do you hear me?" said the driver. "You can't throw rubbish out on to the streets. Aren't you ashamed? Jesus sees. Jesus sees everything."

The next balloon burst, and that made Cameron laugh. But the next one—maybe it was the wind, maybe it was a freak air current getting underneath it, but the balloon just sailed into the sky, and as it did so it caught the dull sunlight and it seemed suddenly a bright and fiery red, it soared higher and higher, upwards, ever upwards, as if nothing was ever going to stop it.

And the old woman says:

- *If balloons don't float, what use can they have? An answer may be provided deep within* **The Popping Fields** *(story 14, page 227). Go and see.*
- *Do you like turkey? If you're more impressed by the country than the meat, turn to* **The Constantinople Archives** *(story 21, page 345).*
- *To play with snow of a softer and more caring disposition, turn to* **The Rainman** *(story 36, page 603).*
- *A man tries to understand the work of his genius grandfather in* **A Short History of Tall Buildings** *(story 33, page 539).*
- *Unappealing as it may sound, if everything tasted of ash then going on a diet would be considerably less painful. Turn to* **Taste Me** *(story 75, page 1301) if you need to lose some weight.*

92
The Beast At World's Edge

NO ONE SAW THE captain die. For the first few hours that he'd clung to the wall he'd called out to them, "Hold tight, lads!", and "Stay brave, lads, for king and country!"—calling them *lads*, yes, as if they were all in this together and had always been, as if this foolhardy expedition hadn't been his idea from the start—as if, by God, adversity had made them friends. They were not friends. The captain had stuck to his quarters for most of the voyage, issuing orders through his first mate (now dead, of course, like so many others), coming up on deck only to check the progress of the day, check the weather, check when a man was flogged that it was done to his satisfaction. After a while the captain's cries lost their authority—"It'll be all right, won't it, lads? Tell me, lads, that we'll pull through!"—and then he'd stopped crying out altogether, though sometimes Wright believed he heard the captain mumbling to himself on the breeze—and at some point he shut up altogether, he must have given up, he must have let go.

They all saw the cook die, however. For everyone else it took all their strength just to hold on. But not the cook—he wouldn't be beaten, not by mere gravity—and they heard him too, grunting with effort and pain as he pulled himself higher and higher up the sheer cliff face of dark blue, finding footholds in the lulls of waves, jamming his fingers into the crevices of that hard ocean wall and refusing to let go. He climbed for over an hour, and they all looked up at him, craning their necks straight upright—and it'd be dizzying to do that, it hurt Wright's neck, it made his head swim—but still he had to watch the cook climb, because if the cook could find the power to survive then just maybe Wright could too. And at last the cook reached the top. He reached the very summit of the ocean wall, and Wright heard him give one whoop of joy—this cook who had been so sullen throughout the voyage, who had given them their slops without a word, and whose face was as unyielding as rock. Wright had never liked the cook, but he felt the cook's victory was his victory as well. And the cook tried to swing himself up onto the flat plateau of the charted seas—and he couldn't. He couldn't because there was nowhere else to climb. The sky was a roof. The sky was a roof, something thick and solid, and no matter how much he heaved his shoulders up against it the sky would not budge—he'd climbed all that way for nothing, the cook was wedged into that tiny corner where the sea met the sky and there was no give to either. And Wright could see him there panting for a bit, he thought it was panting anyway, the cook's body was heaving—maybe he was crying, maybe he was praying to God—and then the cook threw himself into space, down he plummeted to his death. Wright thought there was something almost noble in it. That as he leaped into the great unknown he refused to make a sound. Even if in his fall he hit the boatswain and knocked him off his perch; as he killed himself, he killed his shipmate too.

The captain had said he'd wanted to discover new lands—but now they knew the truth, didn't they? There were no new lands to discover, there was an end to the world, as Wright had known there must have been—as there's an end to life, an end to love. But still he had signed up—and on they'd sailed, off the maps, and the captain told them they would just keep going forward whatever the cost. They hadn't seen anything but ocean for over a month, and the crew had begun to mutter of mutiny, they'd wanted to go back; Wright hadn't been one of them, he was curious to see just what the edge of the world would look like. And now he knew. The boy in the crow's nest gave no warning, but it wasn't his fault, they had come upon it so suddenly, it was hardly as if there'd been a signpost; the horizontal of the seas had just finished, and pitched forward into a sheer vertical drop, and for maybe half a minute the bulk of the ship was teetering on its very precipice, could they stop themselves going over the side and dropping into oblivion, could they yet save themselves? But no—no, the captain had said forward, always forward—and that's what happened, forward they went, the ship tipped over and fell down prow first into empty space. And most of the sailors hadn't had time to jump free, and most of them probably knew nothing about it. A hundred and fifty souls on that vessel, and only a dozen survivors, holding on to the side of the world for dear life, scrabbling on to the sea wall as it flowed over their bodies straight down. A dozen survivors—at least, to begin with.

Richard Wright hadn't jumped. He alone had been thrown free. He'd thrashed out instinctively, grabbed on to anything that might save him. Though had he been given choice in the matter he might well not have bothered. But here he was now, surviving—against all odds—he'd grasped hold of a wave that was jutting out of the cliff face, it was liquid and yet it was hard and it gave him purchase, and he could feel it ripple as if thrilling to his touch.

He knew he couldn't hold on forever. He hadn't the strength. He hadn't even the inclination. But he would choose when to drop. And he pitied the men around him as they gibbered with fear, as they realised they couldn't save themselves from death, that all they'd done was to postpone the inevitable. He pitied them, and despised them a little. Hadn't they realised that this had always been the case? That when they'd first set foot upon the ship, all the way back in Portsmouth, at some point the sea would claim them? You can't tramp down on the sea like a public highway without provoking it sooner or later. It had only been a matter of time.

The men cried out, and asked Wright to sing with them. But all they knew were sea shanties and hymns. And Wright didn't want to sing to the seas, not now they'd finally beaten him and taken his life—

he wasn't bitter, but still thought that serenading his murderer was a tad too much to ask of him. And he didn't believe that hymns would work here. They were off the world. They were off the world, and here there was no sense, no point, and no God.

But even here at the edge of existence the sun could set, and soon it was night. And Wright began to drowse, he could feel his very muscles turn to soft jelly, his body began to shut down. And the waves he clung to were now softer than any pillow, the foam trembling against his face and lulling his eyes shut. "I'm going to fall asleep," said Wright, "and when I do that I shall let go, and when I let go I shall die." And saying it out loud was something to keep himself awake, to give his brain a task to perform and keep it alert, but he didn't reach the end of the sentence, and soon he was snoring.

He dreamed of oceans that night, as he did every night; of unending blue without hint of green land or brown earth. And he tried to push away from it, as he did every night too—but still, still, in spite of all, he held on, because that's what he was, he was a sailor, and that's all he was. And when he awoke the next morning he was amazed to find himself yet alive, his arms still wrapped fast about the waves, his feet still balanced on tiptoe upon a shelf of current. There were only two other survivors left. He could see them both, slightly above him; one called out, "Hallo-o!" to him. "Hallo-o!" they all called back, "Hallo-o-o!" they sung out to each other, to prove they were not dead yet, that they were fighting on. They stopped calling after a while, there was really very little else to say. And there was a gnawing in Wright's belly, he was hungry and so thirsty, and the sun was at a strange angle here at the edge of the world, it was no longer high in the air above him but somewhat to his side, it beat hard upon him regardless and made him feel faint. He stuck his head deep within the wave, just to escape the heat, and whilst he was there he couldn't but help gulp at the water—and it was cool and refreshing, it ran fast over him and washed away all his sleep and exhaustion. He drank deep, and there wasn't even a hint of salt to it, he filled his stomach. And the stomach cried out for something solid, it cramped with the very desire of it, but he chose not to think of food, not right now.

And soon after that the mermaids came.

He thought of them as mermaids anyway; though they didn't have the sultry faces of repute, they didn't have long flowing hair, there were no breasts. And there was none of that half-fish nonsense—they had long legs like an octopus, there was jelly where their fins should have been. But they had faces. And they could speak. They could whisper close in his ear.

Hargreaves didn't last long. He turned to his mermaid, and he looked so happy—Wright wished he could have ever felt happy like that. And Hargreaves put his arms around the mermaid, and he fell right through her, he passed through her body and straight out the other side—but it was *slow,* it was as if he were sinking into thick treacle, and Wright could see his face as he fell, and he never stopped smiling, his face shone with something like ecstasy.

The mermaid hadn't even spoken to Hargreaves; he'd let her win without a struggle.

Wright could now see the mermaids turn to Frayn. And Frayn closed his eyes, he tried to push himself even deeper into the sea wall. He begged them to go away. He screamed at them to stop. Wright couldn't hear what the mermaids told him. He could only see the effect, the way Frayn's arms slackened, the way he didn't choose to let go but just *did,* as if he hadn't even noticed he was dropping into void.

Then they came for Wright.

The first mermaid looked like his wife. Of course it did. And it was his wife as he'd first met her, and loved her, and married her, when he'd thought that love was an undying thing, when he'd thought it could remake the whole world. He looked into that face, the hard bitterness he was now used to smoothed back to teenage innocence. And he'd wondered, he'd wondered. Whether all those years of disappointment had tainted the memories he had of her, whether if he saw his wife again as she'd once been he could forgive her. And now he knew.

"Come with me, darling," she said; and Wright said, "No. I went to sea to get away from you. And I shall not, in my final hour, be with you again."

The second looked like his mother. And he hadn't even thought of his mother for such a while, he hadn't dared—and at the sight of her he felt his eyes prick with unmanly tears, and his heart grow soft, and his heart wasn't used to that, it groaned in protest. He remembered how she had used to sit him on her knee when he was a boy—and he remembered too how she had grown old and her skin had turned thin as paper and the marks on it had looked like ink. He remembered how she'd taught him to read and write, and the stories of fairy she'd shared with him—and he remembered too how she'd sickened so very fast, how the coughing had taken her, how there'd been so much blood. Her telling him she loved him, and always would, the sheer bloody lie of that—because he also remembered having to bury her, digging the grave himself, all that soil shoved aside so that she could be hidden from sight forever more. I'll always love you, she'd said; but she hadn't, she'd gone—and how when the sickness was at its worst she'd cursed him, the words she'd used, she'd forgotten even who he was.

"You're going to die soon," she said; and he said, "Well, old mother, you would know."

And the last looked like his daughter. So beautiful—prettier than his mother had ever been, prettier than his wife, she was the best of all of them. And she didn't say anything to him, she just giggled girlishly and waited. And he shed tears at the sight of her, and wondered how old she must be now, and whether back in England she ever thought of him, and whether she hated him so very much. He said, "I never wanted a child," he said, "I could never want you, don't you know you're why I left? That this is all because of you!" he said, "You're so beautiful, I knew you couldn't be mine, you're so very perfect,"—and he cried some more, and told her how he loved her, and he spat at her, his throat was parched once more from heat and from strain but he still found enough venom in his mouth to spit.

So the mermaids left. After that, he was alone, for a while.

And once more night stole upon him, he began to feel drowsy. This time he didn't think he'd fall off the waves in his sleep. His arms had grown so numb now, and he fancied they'd somehow fused to the side of the cliff face—he couldn't let go even if he'd wanted to. For a moment he thought he'd even try. He would tear himself away from the wall, and prove his theory, that he was rock; or, if not rock, safe; or, if not safe, he wouldn't fall anyhow—and he decided to do it, then decided he'd go to sleep first and *then* do it, he'd just shut his eyes for a while instead and dream.

He dreamed of oceans that night, as he did every night; but tonight he dreamed that in the distance he spied land. And he swam to it with powerful strokes. But when he reached it he realised it wasn't a land of green and brown, it was blue, it was still *blue*; the ground was wet to walk on, the houses made of foam and spray, men and women looked like puddle reflections of people he couldn't quite discern, and when he tried to love these men and women, when he'd take them to bed and put his arms about them, why then, they'd break apart in his grasp, they'd splash out in all directions, and he'd be left on a mattress of water beneath water sheets hugging on to water, the only solid person left in a universe of liquid.

He woke to feel something tugging at his leg. And he looked down to see.

There was a fat yellow snake gripped around his ankle. Jerking every now and then, as if to say, hallo-a! Hallo-a! Would you like to play? It wasn't a snake—the head stretched away from him and straight down the side of the ocean wall. It was a tentacle. It was a tentacle, getting tighter now, and trying to pull him to his doom—and it was part of a creature so vast it *filled* the edge of the world, how hadn't he seen it before, and now every spare inch of the void seemed crushed full with the beast, there was more beast than air, how was he going to breathe? —it was a writhing mass of legs and fins and jelly, and so many eyes, what could it want with so many eyes, what was there to see now the world had come to a stop?—and each one of those eyes were turned upon him. Not as grand as a tentacle, to the scale of the beast this was little more than a stray hair, a *filament*—and here it was again, squeezing its grip and jerking at him again, it wanted him and it wasn't going to let go—and here came another filament, now circling his waist, and still another, wrapping around his head. Held tight in position, his eyelids jammed open—looking straight down at the beast —and he saw all the mermaids swimming through it and popping out in little bubbles and waving up and smiling, and then breaking back on to the side of the monster and becoming part of it once more.

He would have screamed, but his throat was too dry, and the creature was in his mouth now, he felt it pull across his lips as it tightened its grasp, he could taste it, it tasted like rope, like wet rope. He gagged. The creature didn't care.

It tugged at him again. He slid down the waves. The waves cut into his skin. They were sharp like razors. So clean the cut he could barely feel it, just saw the blood.

He was going to be eaten, he supposed, and that was the way of it, and it seemed churlish to kick against the fact of it, and say it was unfair—but it *was* unfair, there was no justice to it when he was the one that was so hungry. His stomach growled again. His stomach wanted feeding.

He bit down. He bit into that writhing rope. His stomach revolted at the thought of it, but still he bit through the skin, and he could taste something salted and coppery—but maybe he only imagined the copper part, because this had to be blood, it was the beast's blood, wasn't it? And he chewed, and he chewed, he swallowed the meat down.

The creature stopped tugging. The filaments stayed coiled around him, but they loosened, turned baggy. He felt the beast slump. His hands were free. Now he could grab at the beast, he was tearing off bits of its flesh, jamming them into his mouth. The beast raised a querulous eye towards him. He tore off the eye too, and it seemed to splash open as he crushed it between his teeth, the eye tasted sweet as fruit.

He ate his fill. He licked at the blood to quench his thirst. His own hands no longer were sore, he felt good, he felt strong. And he felt comforted too—he looked down at the beast and it was as his mother to him now, he was sitting on her knee, and she was feeding him with her own body, she was keeping him safe and warm.

He slept again.

And he dreamed of oceans. The oceans were all about him, lapping away at every bit of his body, oh, they wanted *in.* So, he let them in. He opened his mouth as wide as it would go, and in they poured. His head poked just above the surface, and his eyes were large with wonder as he watched the waters rush towards him. Swirling round and round and down the plughole, and he was the plug! And he could feel his body swell with the weight of all the water in the world—he thought after one ocean had been consumed there'd be no room for any more, but no, look, that was just the Atlantic, here comes the Indian, save space for dessert! All that blue inside him now. And he thought, well, if I drink up all the oceans, sooner or later I must find land! Land will be whatever's left over! He liked the thought of that, so he *sucked* at the water now, greedily; he pursed up his lips so they could be a straw, and his body heaved with the impatient effort of it, got to drink every last bit, chug chug chug! And he imagined his body swelling as some vast balloon now, the waters rushing down his throat, then coming to a stop. Because that was it. Because there was no more water left. All the water was gone. And he felt a little irked by that, he was still thirsty, he hadn't done drinking yet! And he looked about for the land that should have been left behind, all the greens and browns. But it wasn't there. All was blackness. He began to panic. He'd swallowed up all the land too without realising! That's what he must have done. He had to find it, rescue it. He reached into his mouth, put his hands in deep, and started to rummage about. Up to his very elbows, his fingers itching for something to grab on to, something solid he could yank out from between his teeth, and say, this is Australia, or the Americas, these are the West Indies! These lands can be my home! But all there was to touch was water, that's all there was, and he cried, a grown man he may have been but he was crying with frustration, a little tear eking out the side of his eye, one single speck of water released to fill the gaping void of the world.

He woke, and there was nothing in his mouth, and he smacked at his lips, and in spite of all he felt quite thirsty. He turned his head to drink the blood of the beast, but the beast was no longer there.

Once more, he was all alone. But there was an aftertaste in his mouth that was a little like salted meat and a little like squid, and he knew he had eaten every last morsel.

And he thought, I am the beast at world's edge. I am the monster beyond the far flung seas.

He laughed at that. And he let go of the walls.

He didn't fall. Though he had expected to.

He walked on the vertical surface of the world. He walked on the hard glass waters. He kicked idly at the waves.

He turned to where the sun was beating down on him, and he didn't like the way it beat. So he reached out and grabbed it between his fingers, because he saw now it was really no bigger than a ship's biscuit. And he tossed it high into the air.

He thought, I can remake the world.

He went back to the very waves he had clung to all those days. They were stained with his blood. He realised how hard he had grabbed on to life, his hands were now in shreds. He decided to forgive the waves for hurting him. They knew not what they did.

He turned to the great wall of ocean, the water swinging upwards towards a flat solid sky. And he pushed at it.

He felt it resist him. Are you sure, said the world, that this is what you want to do?

Yes, he told it. I want to tear your walls down. I want to start all over again.

He pushed harder. The walls shifting.

The oceans gurgling with the force of it. Teetering, then starting to fall.

And, oh, the spray, as the seas toppled in on themselves! And oh, how Wright laughed, how he rode the surf, the foaming water in his face, his eyes, his throat, and he remembered how much he loved the seas, why he'd set out to explore them in the first place.

There was a splash, the greatest splash the world had ever felt, and now the seas were flat, the waters ran now from left to right and not from up to down, and there was a horizon worth the naming, and the sun was perched high in the sky above it.

Richard Wright bobbed around in the seas for a while, and the waves supported him, he didn't have to hold on to anything.

He scanned that new horizon. There was no land to be seen. There was probably no land within hundreds of miles.

He was going to drown. He knew it. He could only swim so far, even with all his strength, before the seas would claim him.

He'd changed the world, he'd given other ships and other sailors new lands to discover. But he was done for. Those lands, he wouldn't see any of them.

But he'd held on to life this long. And he was the beast at world's edge. And he still had some little strength left. And he had a daughter out there somewhere that he didn't yet know.

He felt a weight lift from him, he felt *light,* and it might have been the swell of the salt seas raising him afloat, it might have just been that.

He smiled. He wondered in what direction he should swim. He made a choice. And struck out for shore.

And the old woman says:

- *What can be worse than abandoning your child? The feeling when a child abandons you. Consider* **The Popping Fields** *(story 14, page 227).*
- *Do you fancy another meal of raw meat, but this time with better décor and table service? Then turn to* **Blood** *(story 24, page 383).*
- *Hanging off a cliff edge at the very edge of the world is a very natural time to contemplate the inevitability of death. If you would like to ensure your own demise is taken care of, why not install* **The Death Room** *(story 27, page 453)?*
- *The ocean is a vast unfeeling bastard. Turn to* **And This is Where We Falter** *(story 49, page 811).*
- *You don't want to end your days on the Wall. Either clinging to it, or building it. See a man get a better job offer in* **The Censor's Report** *(story 98, page 1661).*

93
Ground Beef

My kids won't believe it, but there was a time when there was only one Burger King in London. The kids take Burger King for granted now, of course. My two don't even go down there for the food, they just like to hang out there with their friends at weekends. Even Sonia, and Sonia's a vegetarian, or so she says; she goes mad if I put animal products on the same shelf as her food in the fridge. I ask Sonia what she does at Burger King, and she says she just hangs and chills, and besides, the beanburgers are all right. And I ask Sonia whether she's worried that the beanburgers are cooking around all that dead cow, and she shrugs and says it doesn't matter.

I suppose you get too much of anything good in this world, and you start taking it for granted. Health. Family. Fast food restaurants.

I don't remember the first time I was taken to a Burger King, no more than I can remember any specific childhood Christmases or birthdays or days we broke up from school—all those good times just roll into one. But I do remember the first time I heard about Burger King, because Dad was so excited. Dad had occasional business meetings in London and went there on the train, his London trips always seemed to me like great expeditions for which he'd have to pack properly (with his special suitcase) and dress nicely (with his special ties), and I'd hope he'd bring me back some sort of toy. This particular time he came home from London and his eyes were shining, I can see his beaming face in my mind's eye now quite distinctly, and he told the whole family of this wonderful new restaurant he'd discovered. Even the name was royal. And it had, he said, the most delicious food he'd ever tasted. And it was so good that he was going to take us all there, this very weekend, which was as soon as Tabby and me had free time from school and Mum had free time from the shop. Mum objected—we couldn't just go all the way to the capital city of England for *dinner*, that was such a waste of money, that was just too long a journey and Tabby and me would get all tired out—but Dad put his foot down, and said this was a once in a lifetime treat, and for our own sakes he wasn't going to allow us to miss it. And Dad didn't put his foot down too often. No. Looking back, poor sod, I don't think he often got his way.

London's first Burger King stood just outside Victoria railway station. Or, at least, it was the first one we knew about, and for several years that was the one we visited. We used to do it on special occasions, like my birthday, and Tabby's birthday too—though I've spoken to Tabby about it since, and she claims it was never such a big deal for her, it was more my treat than hers. We'd go there by train, and that was exciting in itself—from the moment Dad went to the ticket office to pay our fares—always to 'the city', he never even needed to say London!—the adventure had begun. And on the train we'd choose what we were going to eat that night, because there was always a choice, especially with the flavoured milkshake we'd have as dessert. I always chose a Whopper with cheese, and fries; I don't think that I dared eat anything else from the menu just in case it didn't live up to the Whopper with cheese, and fries; to come all that way and order something else and for it not to have been as good as the Whopper with cheese, and fries, would have been tragically disappointing.

And what I remember is how *bright* the restaurant was. And that was so unusual back then, most restaurants were just cafés with more expensive food, and the light was just the same as the light at home, and they smelled like ordinary things, Grandma's front room, school. But Burger King had a special light, everything so yellow, and so *happy*; and the smell was of meat and of salt and of special sauce. And by the time we arrived my anticipation was at fever pitch, but we didn't even have to wait for the food—in most restaurants it'd be so boring, you'd sit down and wait ages for someone to come and take your order, and then you'd have to wait more ages for someone to come and deliver it, and you'd wait so long you waited yourself right out of being hungry. Not at Burger King—we'd get into queues, and within a minute Dad would be telling the server how many Whoppers with cheese he wanted, and the server was *smiling* because serving us was such a pleasure, and you didn't see many smiles in the early 1980s. And the meat had a tang I'd never tasted before, and even the chips were special, specially thin, with that special name. And we'd be done in five minutes, usually, and then we were ready to go home again.

"It's because it's American," Dad would say. "The Americans know how to do things properly." He and Mum had been to America once, before Tabby and I were born—it had been a work thing, they'd gone over on a ship and stayed for nearly a *year*. America seemed like somewhere impossible to me, with its skyscrapers and its film stars and its cool lazy accents—oh, and it had Disneyland there too. But Burger King offered me a little slice of America, just off Buckingham Palace Road.

Many years later I asked Dad how often he'd taken us up to that first Burger King outside Victoria station. He said he didn't know—maybe three or four times? But he's wrong. We went far more often than that. Every one of my birthdays until I was a teenager, at least, and Tabby's birthdays, and sometimes when school ended for Christmas or the summer break. I don't want to exaggerate. I'm not pretending I *lived* for our family Burger King expeditions or anything like that. But I always looked forward to them. They were always there, in the back of my mind, something to get excited about.

I've been to America now, several times. I nearly went with my first 'proper' boyfriend when I was nineteen, we got this close to buying the tickets, and then he broke up with me. I've always thought that if we had bought the tickets we'd probably have stuck together, the fares were too expensive to waste. And maybe if we'd gone America would have fixed us, and we'd be married now. Well. But. But that put me off going to America for a while.

Eventually I went with Frank, and we treated it like a honeymoon, though we'd been married over a year by then, and I was already expecting. When I went round to see Mum and Dad, a week or so before the trip, Dad said he had a present to give me. It was a guidebook he had bought for that time *he* had been over; he said I'd find it very useful. The book was about New York, and I told Dad we were going to Florida, remember, they were two entirely different places. He got a bit irritable at that. Told me he knew they were different, but there were some parts of the book that were still relevant; information about the currency, or the electrical voltage, or the change of time zone. And about the Americans themselves, the phrases they used, the expectations they had, how they carried themselves. "They're not the same as us," said Dad.

When Mum fell ill, Dad tried to look after her at home for as long as possible. But he was ten years older than she was, and besides, for so long now she'd been the one who'd cooked for him and cleaned after him. Dad did his very best. He did a good job. But it wasn't good enough for Mum, who was used to things being 'just so'. One day she threw her dinner against the wall, because it wasn't fit for eating, she said the food was 'shit' and she never used the 'shit' word—if I hadn't been over there to hear it for myself I'd never have believed it—and this woman who had been so houseproud, who'd been a tyrant with the vacuum cleaner, didn't mind that the baked beans were now running down the wall. "Leave it," she told me when I tried to sponge them away, "no, I said, leave it! The place is a sty anyway, your father can't clean for shit, what difference does it make?" She said, "Just because I have cancer, he doesn't think I deserve anything decent!" And sometimes I'd visit and he'd have these bruises on his arm. He told me everything gave him bruises. It wasn't as bad as it looked. But I agreed with social services when they recommended that the best care Mum could receive was in the hospice.

I went to see her every now and again. Truth to tell, I didn't visit her very often, because it was all a bit depressing. And each time I'd see her she'd aged another ten years, she'd become this ancient thing. And she'd got thinner, and her face was sallow, and her hair had fallen out.

Dad was always there. He was always pleased to see me.

And this one time, near the end, he asked if I had to hurry back home so soon. And I said I did, really, I wanted to get back on the train before the rush hour. And he said it'd just be nice, really nice, if we could spend a little time together, we could go into town, have a spot to eat? I could hardly say no, I said, so long as it didn't take too long.

We walked through the shopping centre, and it was probably October or November, there were a few Christmas decorations out, and that late in the afternoon it was already getting dark. But it wasn't too cold, actually. And Dad and I spoke about this and that, actually anything except Mum. And then he plucked at my sleeve, and he was grinning, and pointing. There was a Burger King. "I haven't been in one of these for years!"

There was some sort of music playing in there, and it may have been Christmas music too. We got into a queue. "What are you going to have?" I asked. I said I wasn't hungry, I'd just have a coffee. "No, no," he laughed, "a Whopper and cheese, we'll both have that, yes?" We reached the counter. He began to tell the server that he and his daughter had been coming to Burger King all our lives, and we always had Whoppers with cheese, and the server looked bored, and I interrupted and made the order. "I'll get this," said Dad, and he began looking through his pocket for the money—I already had my purse out—"No, no, this is my treat," said Dad, but he was taking too long, and the server was starting to look cross, and I paid. Dad looked upset at this, until I told him it was all right, he could get the next one; "We'll do this again?" he asked, "Really?" and I said, sure.

I carried the tray of food over to a plastic table, and Dad and I sat opposite each other on plastic chairs. I chose the plastic table which had the least lettuce on it.

I took the grease-proof paper wrapping off my Whopper, and bit into it, and spilled onions and tomato sauce everywhere. Dad asked about Frank, about Sonia and Jackie. And then he was asking whether Sonia and Jackie were going to visit Mum at any point, and Mum was mentioned, and it was all about Mum.

"How do you think she was today?" Dad asked, and I said I thought she was a bit brighter. "She always looks brighter when you're there," said Dad. "She likes it when you visit. I think she gets bored with me." I said that I wasn't always sure Mum cared, she'd long ago stopped talking to me, and he said no, no, no, she did; I should see how bored she got when it was Dad on his own; the way she didn't talk to me was completely different to the way she didn't talk to him.

Dad played with his fries a bit.

"I've tried my hardest, you know," he said.

"I know you have."

"It's not easy sometimes."

"I bet."

"And she'll be gone soon, I suppose. The doctors don't know when, they keep changing their minds. One young chap says she might live for years, she'll outlive me! But she's already gone, really."

I didn't know what to say. I tried to think of something to say. I said, "Yes."

"I don't love her," he said.

He tried to open a sachet of ketchup, but his fingers were too thick. I took the sachet from him, tore it open with my teeth. I passed it to him, and it was bleeding ketchup everywhere. "Thanks," he said.

"I can see," I said, "how it must be difficult," I said.

"I used to love her," he said. "I'm pretty sure of that. But now she's gone, you can see she's gone. And I don't miss her at all. I mean, I've nothing against your mother. She had her faults, but who doesn't? Who doesn't?"

I pushed away my Whopper with cheese. It was too big, and its innards kept spilling out.

"When we were in New York," he said, "she was the one who wanted to do everything. Go up the Empire State Building. Go to a Broadway show. I didn't, I just wanted to stay at the hotel. I was there to work. And she said to me, David, for God's sake, live a little! Make the most of this moment. It won't last forever. Do you think we'll be in America forever?" He sighed. "I sometimes wonder why she stuck with me."

He ate his Whopper with cheese in big bites. He was hungry. "Do you want some of mine?" I asked. "Don't you like it?" he asked. "I told you I only wanted a cup of coffee," I said. "These burgers are good, aren't they?" he said, and then he said, "I should have burgers more often," and then he said, "I'm sorry."

"That's okay."

"When your mother dies, I'm going away. I'm going back to New York. I'm going right across America. Nothing will hold me back this time. Not when there's so much out there. I'll do it in her name."

"Okay," I said.

"I love you," he told me.

"Yeah, I know."

He nodded at that.

"I think that's when we were in love," he said. "When we were in America. Even though I didn't do America well, even though I only let her down there. I was in love then, and only then, and I've never been in love again since."

He didn't seem to realise that America was before I was born, before Tabby was born. "I've got to go to the toilet," I said.

When I came back, Dad was in hearty conversation with the man who had come to take our tray away. "I used to come to Burger King with my family. So many years ago now, before you were born!" The teenager looked embarrassed, and a little resentful. "Come on, Dad," I said, and Dad got to his feet. "Nice talking to you," he said to the kid, smiling all the while.

There was some talk about Dad coming to live with either of us, Tabby or me. Neither of us liked the idea of him rattling around the house on his own now that Mum was gone. Tabby didn't have a husband any more, and she'd never had children, and her house was almost as big as mine, so she seemed to me the perfect choice. But Tabby disagreed. Frank said Dad should live with us, and Sonia and Jackie said they didn't mind. And I told Sonia and Jackie that having Dad would be a big commitment, that they'd have to share the television with him, that they couldn't come and go so late at the weekends because they might disturb him now he was old. And Sonia, Sonia might find Dad putting meat next to her vegetables in the fridge, he was old, that's what might happen. I said that, as a family, we should all take a vote on it, and that no one should feel bad if they decided that having my Dad live with us was too much to bear. Frank voted yes, the two girls no. I abstained. I didn't think my vote would be entirely fair.

Dad never went to America again. I think he intended to, properly, at least for a while. He went out and bought a fresh guide book. But after a little research he was put off by things like visa waiver forms. He said he'd wait until all the complicated stuff like that went away.

My father woke me up one night. He was standing by the side of my bed, and shaking my shoulder gently, and calling me by name. Frank was sleeping next to me, he didn't want to disturb him. For a moment I thought maybe Dad *had* come to live with us after all, and then I remembered he hadn't, and that I was pleased he hadn't—this was precisely the reason it would be difficult, he'd be in my bedroom at all hours of the night shaking me awake because he wanted the toilet or something. And I knew this was a dream then, and it was a relief.

"What do you want, Dad?" I hissed, and I tried to sound nice because I knew he was imaginary and so there were extenuating circumstances—but I was still a little annoyed with him.

"I have a treat for you," he said. "Get dressed. Get dressed up nice and smart." And so I did, I went along with it. Dad waited downstairs for me, and I decided I'd go for the full evening dress, why not. He nodded approvingly at me, and I saw only now that he was in a tuxedo himself, I'd made the right choice.

It didn't feel like a dream, the way the evening dress was a little too tight around my waist. I thought, shouldn't dreams feel more comfortable than this? Dad took my arm, though, as if I were still the daintiest thing ever, and we left the house. We got a train, the railway station was parked right next door to the house. And within minutes we were at Victoria station.

The original Burger King, I knew, had long gone. Nowadays there are tons of Burger Kings all over Victoria, around the station concourse and spilling out on to the road, none as grand as the first Burger King, all fast and unfussy. I wasn't surprised, of course, that Dad was taking me to *our* Burger King, the one that had belonged to *us*. The familiar logo shone in bright lights like it was some glitzy West End theatre show.

The lighting was bright and friendly, but still subtle somehow. They knew us by name, of course. We didn't have to queue. "Ah yes, Monsieur Bishop," said the maitre d', "we have your special table reserved for you." The maitre d' was all smiles and pleasing unction, and he led us somewhere discreet, close enough to the pianist so we could enjoy the music, far enough away so we could talk. "The usual, Pierre," said my father, and there was a certain amused smugness to that, and he winked at me, look how I know a French waiter by name! (Except he wasn't French, he was American, wasn't he? And wore a cowboy hat?) "*Très bien*, Monsieur," said Pierre, "howdy howdy!"—and within seconds he was back again, there were Whoppers with cheese on bone china plates, and there were gleaming steak knives to cut them with, and the fries came in a golden tureen. He poured our milkshakes into champagne glasses; I asked for banana, and I'm not sure Burger King even sell banana, and Dad had tutti frutti, and I'm quite certain they don't have that. "Bon appétit, and have a nice day!" said Pierre. He made a formal little bow, and went; we unwrapped our burgers from the grease-proof paper and we set to work.

The burgers were really good.

And I tried, then, telling my Dad I was sorry. And he shushed me.

"I'm proud of you," he said. I told him I couldn't see why. And he said nothing to that, instead he raised a glass of tutti frutti to me, and I clinked it.

"I love you," I said.

"Oh, darling," he said. "Of course you do."

The dream might have ended there, but it played out properly, it was a full date. Just the two of us, and chatting more and more easily, and laughing at God knows what, and Pierre kept on appearing and topping up our glasses—"No, any more, I'll turn into a tutti frutti!" said Dad, and then he winked, and said, "Go on, then, just another one!"

We caught the train home. He said goodbye to me on the doorstep.

"Thanks, Dad," I said, and he smiled, and kissed me on the cheek. And I went inside, and went back to bed, and in the morning when I woke up I didn't doubt it was a dream, but I still felt full and satisfied.

If this were a story, then that would be the night my father died. But it wasn't. Or it would be the means by which we became better friends. And that wasn't true either, though we did speak on the phone more often. I only saw him four more times, I think, and none of the meetings were bad ones, but I think we always did better on the phone.

That very next day I gave him a call. I thought I'd tell him about the dream. I thought he might find it funny. But, as it happens, we found lots else to talk about, and I never quite got round to it. And maybe that's just as well. What would his reaction have been, after all? He might have suggested we go out for a *real* meal together, and I didn't want that. I really didn't want that.

If this were a story, I suppose I would find a proper ending. But endings are difficult. When things start out, they're all so simple and clean, and there's a sort of purity to them—and then they get corrupted somehow, or if not corrupted, complicated. And it's silly to mind too much, to rail against what we can't change. We just have to be grateful for those beginnings, and treasure the memory of them. And I went to the very first Burger King in London, and it was a nice restaurant, and the food was good, and we were all happy there.

And the old woman says:

- *I love America. I fear America. Its confidence and its sense of self—and the height of it, do they need all those skyscrapers, isn't the country big enough already? Turn to* **A Short History of Tall Buildings** *(story 33, page 539) to see how skyscrapers changed the world.*
- *Though sometimes I think the best thing to come out of New York is the cheesecake. Turn to* **Mond** *(story 54, page 911).*
- *Some of my favourite books are travel guides—they just brim over with optimism, full of such wonders you have never seen. And phrase books too, they're even better—they're like the keys to those wonders, with just these secret codes you can unlock the doors to an entire new culture. Turn to* **Unfinished** *(story 18, page 311) to see a man who enjoys a particularly fine phrase book in French.*
- *Another father attempts to bond with his child, without the benefit of fast food, in* **Eruption** *(story 70, page 1217).*
- *This story has no ending. Does that leave you frustrated? If so, consider* **Page Turner** *(story 73, page 1269), which has far too many endings. Read, and take your pick.*

94
BRAND NEW SHINY SHINY

RICHARD MARKLEW HAD a skull which was cracked across the top, forming a gash that ran from the roof of the scalp right down to the middle of the forehead. In the right light the crack seemed to yawn open most invitingly, and Marklew took pains to enhance this effect, always positioning the skull near candlelight or flickering lamp. And sometimes when Marklew hosted a dinner party (and, sometimes, when he merely attended someone else's), he would present his skull at the table after the meal was done, and he'd dare the ladies to put their fingers into the crack, deep down, as deep as they could go.

Most of the ladies shrank away, of course, but he could usually persuade one or two to give it a try. These bolder women weren't necessarily the most attractive, but that didn't matter; to Marklew, beauty was rarely skin deep.

That night the first woman to accept the challenge was Mrs Alice Powell, and she was a somewhat unlikely candidate—Marklew had written her off as too mousey, too timid, to be of any interest to him. She too seemed surprised at her own daring, and now that she was standing up seemed only to want to sit straight back down again—but everyone's eyes were upon her, and she wavered, uncertain what would frighten her the most: to touch Marklew's skull, or to suffer the humiliation of changing her mind. She looked back to her husband, but Mr Powell was no help at all—he nodded and smiled, he actively seemed to be encouraging her. "It won't bite," said Marklew, kindly enough, he thought—and there was a ripple of laughter, and Mrs Alice Powell blushed bright red. She stretched out one finger, daintily, and let it brush against the skull—not at the crack, nowhere near the crack. And because that was clearly not enough, she touched it again, gave it an actual prod this time, and she shuddered, and laughed as she shuddered.

"But, Mr Marklew," she said. "How can you ever sleep, with such a fearful thing in the house?" And her eyes were big and round, and Marklew knew she wouldn't be sharing his bed that night.

"I want to try," said Lady Constance suddenly, and rose from her chair, and there was nothing for it but for Mrs Powell to retreat to her own, dismissed. Lady Constance was the sort of woman that could be termed handsome. Marklew thought there was something bovine about her, as if her blue-blooded ancestors had bred with cattle.

"How old did you say this was?" she asked, and Marklew hadn't, and told her it was not so very old, it dated back maybe to the sixteenth century. Lady Constance nodded at that, as if that were an answer she approved of, as if she had been checking the skull had a decent vintage. And then she plunged her fingers into the crack.

There was silence for a few seconds as she began to explore.

Then one of the husbands said, with a slightly embarrassed cough, "And how many of these skulls have you collected, Marklew?" But Marklew ignored that, it was a typical question from the gentry, how many, how big, how much is it worth? Another man asked what had caused the crack, had it been in battle? And Marklew said, yes, in battle, or perhaps in ritual sacrifice—although of course it was a battle wound, but he liked talking of ritual sacrifice, the women always thrilled to it, it gave them such a frisson. All the time Marklew looked only at Lady Constance, into the crack now up to her knuckles. And she said, softly, "Do you give the skull a name?"

"I do not," said Marklew. "But you can correct my omission. You can name the skull for me." He thought she would like that. She did.

"Very well," she said. "Then I shall name him Oswald."

And there was some amusement at that. It was an open secret that Lady Constance was having an affair with Oswald Lutyens, the artist, and the rumours were that she was tiring of him.

"Oswald it is," said Marklew.

"It's all so smooth," she said. "Do you think we're all so smooth, beneath the skin?" Marklew said, very probably; he knew the reason the bone was so smooth was that he had the servants polish it each week with linseed oil.

"And to think," Lady Constance breathed, her eyes no longer on the skull, eyes only on Marklew, but her fingers were still stroking at the bone, stroking away. "That this man lived hundreds of years ago. He lived, and he died, and now you *own* him. He's *yours*, and you have the power to do whatever you like to him. He cannot resist. He has no rights. He's like your personal dead slave."

"Yes," said Marklew.

And at this the maids brought in liqueurs, and Lady Constance returned to her chair, and the conversation was changed. And Marklew put Oswald away—Oswald, or James, or Sylvester; the skull had been at so many dinner parties, and had been given so many names.

After his other guests had retired for the evening, Marklew took Lady Constance on a private tour of his collection of *memento mori*. He showed her fully articulated skeleton puppets operated by gossamer thin strings; they stood ten feet tall, and came from Mexico. There were canopic jars from ancient Egypt, death masks from Renaissance Europe; there were iron markers from children's graves, dug up in Austria a hundred years before. Lady Constance cooed over the beauty of the jewelled clasps he had collected, and he told her that each of them had been worn by grieving widows and contained locks of hair from their dead husband's heads. And there were more skulls, of course there were; he had skulls from Saxon times, from Norman times, he had skulls from Africa and Asia and the most obscure island tribes in the South Pacific. And they all looked the same to Lady

Constance. But Richard Marklew knew the differences between each and every one of them, and he loved them all.

He showed her an erotic portrait of two cavorting corpses, and Lady Constance reached for his hand and squeezed it.

"What a display!" she said. "Well, well. You must feel you have triumphed over death!" But that wasn't it at all.

As he showed her all the pieces he had, gathered over so many years, the little memorabilia, the knick-knacks, the shards of bone and cartilage, Marklew felt a growing pride. And she seemed still to regard it all as some flirtatious game, as the exotic hobby of a wealthy man who had nothing better to do with his time. Something flippant, something trivial—with every fresh *objet d'art* he expected less and less from her reaction, and he really rather hated her for that.

He took her finally to his bedroom. He showed her the bed.

"Is it something wickedly sinister?" she asked. "Has it been constructed from the skeletal remains of torture victims?"

"No," he said.

He pushed her on to the bed, and he fucked her. They fucked twice, and then he was tired, and he suggested she should return to her own room so that he might sleep.

Marklew did not expect to be understood by Lady Constance and her ilk; and, truth be told, he wouldn't have much wanted to have been. They saw at best a random assemblage of curios—interesting, certainly, maybe even a little macabre, but without proper form or intent. Whereas Marklew knew that each item he owned had been specifically hand-picked, that the entire collection was a single piece of art, that it was a summation of something, that it was a summation of *him*. Yes, it was an expression of self, and by now, at the age of fifty-five, he knew himself quite perfectly, everything he set his mind to accomplish, he did; and everything he did was something he had set out to do, quite deliberately. And whilst the collection grew each year, he also edited out earlier acquisitions—pieces he felt now symbolised a younger man he no longer was and did not want to be again; he would throw out skulls that he judged to be naive, entire skeletons that he'd once loved but in his maturity had outgrown. Had Lady Constance seen his collection for what it was he would have been irked, maybe even a little frightened; what man wants to be so easily decoded, his real and complex self to be exposed? Richard Marklew thought he was deep—Richard Marklew *knew* he was deep. He was a man who had depths all over him, he alone could guess how many depths he had.

No, if Marklew wanted appreciation for his life's work, he would find it at the convention. The convention was attended by the like-minded: enthusiasts, scholars, and collectors of the arcane. Membership was offered by invitation only, and was reassuringly rigid in its selection: you could not apply for it, or ask others to make applications on your behalf, and any member found colluding in any such practice would face summary expulsion. Membership was also, needless to say, extremely expensive.

Marklew remembered the first time he had received an invitation. It had arrived by some special delivery, the envelope was small and plain and had no stamps upon it. Inside had been a card informing Marklew of the location of that year's convention, and that his attendance would be permitted. It had not said so, but Marklew had known instinctively that had he turned the invitation down, no more would ever be forthcoming. Marklew had then been only twenty-four, and his collection was only small, and, by his later standards, mostly worthless; certainly, by the time he'd reached his thirties, he had disposed of the majority of it. He had heard that such a convention existed, of course. Sometimes the dealers he bought from would allude to it—but only in jokes, as if it were a myth none of them quite believed in. Marklew did not know how the convention had heard of him. He never asked.

That year it had been in Istanbul. He later learned that the convention was never held in the same place twice, and that Istanbul was amongst the least exotic of the hosting cities. But this had been in the days of the Great War, and Turkey had not only got itself caught up in the middle of the damned thing, but had ended up on the wrong side. To go to the convention would have all but bankrupted Marklew; he had never been a poor man, but these were still the days in which he could hardly have been described as rich. Nevertheless, he went.

To be in the company of other men who explored so fully the passions he was only starting to feel—that itself made the adventure worthwhile. Marklew had tried to talk to these men, and they'd accepted his drinks, they had even been polite, but they had never encouraged any friendly intimacy. Now, so many years later, Marklew himself understood why—and it sometimes made him wince to think of his younger self, still wet behind the ears and knowing nothing, worth nothing, wanting to impose his presence upon others. He marvelled in retrospect at the senior members' patience with him. He wouldn't have shown any. Indeed, if Marklew was now approached by any such novice he refused even to acknowledge him—there were always new members every year, and it was something the old crowd may have to tolerate, but didn't need to indulge.

If you wanted to be invited back to the convention, you quickly learned: these men were closer to you than family, but that didn't mean they were your friends. To be amongst your peers, the only people to whom you would never have to explain yourself—that was enough.

Richard Marklew liked to hold a dinner party on the eve of a convention. The contrast amused him.

By the time he awoke in the morning, Lady Constance and her chattering friends had gone. He was taken by cab to a private airfield; from there, by chartered plane he flew to Bogota. Marklew didn't know Bogota. By the end of the weekend he still wouldn't; he was met at the airfield by an arranged driver, who took him to the hotel in a limousine with windows so black he could barely see out of them. The hotel was maybe a two hours' drive away; it was small and anonymous. It could have been anywhere in the world—which Marklew always supposed was entirely the point. He was shown to his room. It was spotlessly clean and luxuriously appointed. The bed was large and hard, as to his stated preference.

He unpacked. It did not take long. There was little that he'd needed to bring. And then he went downstairs to the bar, where the other members of the convention had started to gather. He sat down in an armchair, at a table on his own, ordered an Old Fashioned, and pretended to read a newspaper. He allowed himself to be seen.

The centre piece of the weekend's events was the auction on the Sunday afternoon. It was always fully attended, although Marklew knew that there were never more than the same dozen serious bidders. There was someone from China, someone from France, someone from one of the Indies, Marklew didn't know which, it may even have been India itself. Several Americans, of course, no doubt trying to seize hold of a history they had never had. The majority were British, which was as it should be.

Marklew knew the names of his rivals, and over the years had learned something of their reputations. Most were reserved to the point of fanaticism, and would not speak to one another at all—it was as if the auction were some grand poker game, and revealing any part of themselves would be a strategic weakness. Marklew could understand the sense of that, although he didn't take it so very seriously. He wouldn't talk to the other bidders either, but mostly because he didn't like them very much.

None of the lots were ever announced in advance; it was understood that any expert in the room should understand their significance without preparation. And Marklew preferred that. He enjoyed the palpable excitement it lent the proceedings; there were usually a few real surprises to look forward to. He had learned one golden rule. Whenever a fresh lot was introduced, he made a snap judgement upon whether it would enhance his collection or not. If it wouldn't, no matter how interesting a piece it might be on its own terms, no matter whether it might be a bargain, he would let it go. And if he *did* want it, he would automatically decide upon an upper limit he would be prepared to pay. That, and not a penny more. It wasn't a question of what he could *afford*—he could afford so very many things. It was instead what he would be *seen* to pay. People mustn't think he overestimated the value of anything, offering ten thousand pounds for an Etruscan skeleton when it was really worth no more than eight. He had a reputation to uphold.

The auction at Bogota offered, it must be said, slim pickings. Lots usually came from deceased members, collections lovingly assembled over a lifetime now broken up and divvied out piecemeal; or, maybe, new discoveries would be presented from fresh archaeological excavations. In the year before Bogota no one had died—or no one, at least, of any great significance; there had been excavations aplenty, but little of interest had been found. There had evidently been lots to tell us about how the Sumerians had lived, but precious little about how they'd died.

So, Richard Marklew bid upon a pair of guillotine blades used in the French Revolution, and an entire coffin lacquered with real bone—and he did indeed actively want them for his collection, and won them both at a reasonable price—but moments after the bidding was over he felt a tinge of regret that he'd even bothered, he knew that they already bored him. Not every year could be successful. It didn't matter. Marklew resigned himself to classifying Bogota as an honourable failure. And then the auctioneer announced the final lot.

There was some laughter, naturally—from the younger members, probably, who knew no better. Mostly there were tuts of exasperation, angry mutterings. The auction was not a joke, a sense of humour was not appreciated. But the auctioneer remained deadpan, there was not even the hint of a smile upon his face.

Some wag asked about the lot's provenance, and still the man refused to smile. He stood tall, presented himself proud. "The provenance is me," he said. "Self-evidently. I cannot talk of the mother, I did not know her well. But the boy has my looks. Now," he said again, louder, "may we start the bidding, please, upon the skull of my son?"

For the first time Marklew looked at the auctioneer, properly examined him. He'd never really thought to look at any of the auctioneers over the years, what they were presenting was far more important. The man was some Colombian, Marklew thought, with some surprise—he'd have assumed the convention would have flown an expert in, that they wouldn't have got some local. The man spoke well enough, it was true. He even looked quite dapper in his suit. But Marklew could now see something too dark in the man's face, too swarthy, too foreign.

Another voice—cooler, stiffer—"May we see the lot?"

At this the auctioneer gave a nod. And on to the stage stepped a little boy, no more than four feet tall. Marklew had never spent much time around children, but he supposed the specimen might be about six or seven years old. There was indeed, as the auctioneer had said, a family resemblance, a thick-set swarthiness that made the boy's face hang heavy and look older than it was.

If the boy seemed alarmed or surprised that his father was preparing to sell him, he did not show it—Marklew wondered whether he might have been drugged. "I say once more, gentlemen, I offer this boy's skull. After he is dead, the flesh will be stripped, and the skull boiled and bleached, and it will be packed up nicely in a box and sent to you. I cannot tell when that death may occur exactly, but if you look at him, you can see he doesn't look well, it cannot be long."

That cool, stiff voice once more—"Just the skull?"

"The skull alone, down to the top of his cervical vertebrae. Everything beneath, that belongs to me. May I start the bidding? Do I hear five hundred pounds?"

For a moment, silence. The threat of renewed laughter, even. And then, that stiff voice: "Five hundred then."

"Six hundred," said Marklew.

He hadn't intended to make a bid. Maybe he was intrigued. Maybe there was something about that little child's face he imagined would fit neatly into his collection at Richmond Park. Or maybe it was something about the voice of his rival bidder, something in it that felt out of place at the convention and that he wanted to challenge.

If the auctioneer were surprised he'd attracted a single bid at all, he didn't show it; he waited expectantly to see if there would be a counter offer. And at Marklew's bid the little boy's face had come to life. He beamed happily out at the audience, at Marklew specifically. He clapped his hands, just the once, in joy.

"Any more bids?" asked the auctioneer, at length. "For this fine piece by my side." And the little boy loved that, he clapped his hands again, he began to jiggle about in excitement.

"Seven hundred pounds," said the stiff man.

"One thousand," said Marklew, and right then and there he decided that he'd reached the upper limit he'd pay; what was this anyway, what was it for, he collected skulls of antiquity, not skulls of dago stock, this was just an anecdote to impress the ladies at dinner—no, one thousand pounds, and no more, no more surely?

"One thousand five hundred," returned the stiff man promptly, and at last Marklew turned in his seat to find him. There he was, to the side, a few rows behind; as Marklew had suspected, he didn't recognise him, he must be one of those new members, those nouveau riche upstarts who didn't yet know there were rules to this place, that a certain respect should be accorded the practice of auction, a certain respect should be accorded *him*; but no, he didn't look like a young man at all—no, pale, thin, with a face so bland it seemed that all expression had been smoothed out deliberately, and wearing a suit—an undistinguished sort of suit, the suit a solicitor might wear—this man wasn't even a member Marklew realised, he was here as an *agent* for someone else, and didn't that contravene the rules of the convention? If not, it should! If not, it was at least highly irregular!

And he turned back, and he realised that all eyes were upon him, waiting to see whether he would make a higher bid. The auctioneer waited patiently; less patiently, the son, he was now almost frenzied with anticipation, he was shaking and jumping about on the spot. He was sticking out his tongue. He was *stretching* out his tongue, and licking at his face, he was sliding great gobs of saliva over his chin as if to make it look shinier.

"Two thousand," said Marklew. He didn't dare turn to look behind at the solicitor—somehow he didn't want to see that man angry, somehow he couldn't bear the idea of that, what such anger might be. But when the rival bid came, seconds later, it was done without emotion, nothing but cool calculating self-assurance—"Three thousand."

And at this the boy could no longer contain himself. He broke rank altogether, he began to *dance*, he waved his arms high above his head, fingers pointing downwards—it's me, this is me, hear how much I'm worth! If the auctioneer was annoyed by his son's antics he didn't show it. And then, so suddenly, the boy was off the stage—he jumped high, higher than should have been possible, surely, and Marklew could only think in that moment of a frog, or maybe a grasshopper—and the boy landed nimbly and soundlessly upon his feet.

Then rushing towards Marklew, as if to a new prospective father, so eager he was clambering over chairs to get to him—and he was squealing with excitement, the squeals so shrill, and the tongue was still out, and still licking away, but it was so fast now, and so *long*—it stretched down past the chin, it reached up high to tickle his nose, and higher—slathering away, with spit as thick as soup, and with such force it seemed as if he were trying to strip the flesh off to expose what was beneath, and where he slathered it did indeed seem to leave a sheen behind, it did indeed allow Marklew to picture that head as a skull with all the skin removed, just white gleaming bone, just bone, displayed in pride of place in his collection.

"Fifty thousand," said Marklew. He spoke softly—for a wonderful moment he thought it was so soft no one had heard him—but it was out of his mouth, and at the sound of it the hushed room fell more hushed still. It was done now, it was done. "Fifty thousand pounds," he said again, louder now, because why not? If he'd already made the bid, do it with pride! Trying to put into his quavering voice the self-confidence for which he was renowned.

The hush held. And the solicitor stirred. Marklew could see him out of the corner of his eye, he half-turned in his seat—and he didn't want him to make a rival bid, but oh, he so wanted him to make a rival bid—this cool stiff man could win the living skull and Marklew would bid no higher, and there would be an end to this nonsense, Marklew would be off scot free with his integrity intact. He thought he saw the solicitor open his mouth. But no, maybe he was just setting his jaw. The solicitor got to his feet, carelessly smoothed down his cheap suit; he turned, and unhurriedly walked out of the hall.

Marklew turned back to the auctioneer. There he was, banging down his gavel. And there, next to him, stood his son—calm, as if he'd never left the stage—still, slumped, as if he were already close to death.

In the bar afterwards Richard Marklew was the centre of attention. All the young men gathering around, pressing drinks into his hand, even slapping him on the back as if he'd given them the most wonderful sport. As if he'd perpetrated a joke—and all for their especial amusement! Not one of them asked about the guillotine blades he had bought. He soon made his excuses, and retired for the night.

He did not sleep well. He usually found the hardness of a bed reassuring, but now it jabbed and prodded at him accusingly. It seemed to him he woke every other hour or so. One time he awoke and became convinced there was a figure sitting in the chair by the dressing table. His heart lurched terribly at that, and then he realised he'd left his clothes there, his jacket and waistcoat on the chair back, the trouser legs drooping down towards the floor. He even laughed at himself.

Then the figure said, "If you're awake, Mr Marklew, then may we discuss business?"

Marklew was at the bedside lamp in an instant. The solicitor was still cool, still stiff. There was not even the pretence of apology in that too-bland face for breaking into Marklew's room and watching him as he'd slept.

Marklew wanted to shout at him, demand to know what the hell the man was playing at—and yet the self-composure that had defined him for so long kicked into play. Forcing down the fear in his stomach, forcing his face into a mask of non-committal reserve, Marklew heard himself ask, "What may I do for you?"

The man said, "That last item you won. My client has instructed me to make you a further offer."

Over the years many buyers had approached him once he'd made a win. Sometimes the money they offered was fully twice what Marklew himself had just paid. He always refused to negotiate. He'd say that he was a collector, not a shopkeeper. And even now, with this strange man in his bedroom, making him feel suddenly so very vulnerable and defenceless, Marklew had to consider the principle of the matter. But the truth was, he didn't *want* the boy's skull. Fifty thousand pounds was by no means the most expensive purchase he had ever made at auction, but this was surely the most unjustifiable. He had heard tell of stories of even the shrewdest collectors who had made, at some points in their careers, hideous misjudgements—their honed instincts deserting them momentarily, buying fakes, damaged goods, art of no skill or value, even in one apocryphal anecdote a Dark Ages skeleton fashioned largely from plastic. Marklew did not think he had made as much a fool of himself as all that—not quite—no, not nearly. But he regretted the whole enterprise, and wanted to put it behind him. If his rival was prepared to buy the skull, then he felt he could move on with his dignity intact. He might even make a little profit.

Marklew said, ironically, "If we are to talk business, may I at least get dressed?" And the solicitor gestured slightly with his hand that Marklew may do as he liked. But the solicitor made no movement to leave, and Marklew stayed exactly where he was.

"My client wants you to understand that this will be a one-time offer. The agreement we come to will be reached here and now, or not at all. And no mention of this conversation shall ever be made again once our business is concluded." Marklew nodded at that, that was all the better.

"My client further wants to state that the skull has no intrinsic worth, to him or to anyone else. But it interests him nonetheless, and accordingly he is prepared to offer you a generous sum as a gesture of good faith. In return, you will give up all rights to the skull in perpetuity, and all prospects for the future acquisition of the skull will transfer to him."

"Yes, yes," said Marklew. "And what is this sum?"

"Ten pounds."

"Ten pounds?"

"As a gesture of good faith."

Marklew laughed. "I paid fifty thousand for it."

"Indeed."

"I don't think you've quite worked out how these negotiations are supposed to work."

"May I have your answer?" asked the solicitor.

Marklew stopped laughing.

The solicitor went on, "My client is not a sentimental man. But he would have the skull. The boy, you see, is one of ours."

Marklew did not pretend to understand that. He licked his lips. "If your client would be prepared to reimburse me the fifty thousand pounds I have already spent," he said, "and offer me some little extra for the sake of honour. Then. Then, I think, we would have something to talk about."

The solicitor stared at him. His face did not even flicker with a reaction. Then, he said, "You are rejecting my client's offer?"

"Wait, now. Look here. Even just a small token. Even just ten pounds."

"You are rejecting my client's offer."

"Or even. Damn it. You bid how much at auction? Three thousand, I think? Then offer me that three thousand. Forget the fifty, you just offer me the three."

"No."

And Marklew said, "Why not?" And he sounded like a little boy, and he was ashamed of himself for that.

"My client's offer is, as I say, to be accepted, or not at all. If you do not give my client the skull now, we will not be prepared to take it from you later. It will belong to you forever. You will never be able to be rid of it. You will never be able to sell it, never able even to give it away. This is your final chance. We need offer you nothing. Instead, we offer you ten pounds."

"As a gesture of good faith," said Marklew, feebly.

The man didn't even bother to agree.

The bed seemed cold to Marklew now. The sheets were rough. The bedside lamp was too bright, the glare seemed to sear into his head, it made him feel nauseous. "Not for ten pounds," said Marklew. "You must understand. I can't. I can't. I can't."

There was a moment's pause, and then the man got to his feet. If he were disappointed, he didn't reveal it. And Marklew wondered whether even now it was too late, whether he could change his mind, accept the insulting offer, or at least reopen negotiations—but any little animation the solicitor's face had shown had faded away, there was nothing there now but the cool and the stiff.

And then, an afterthought. The solicitor turned back to Marklew.

"A question, Mr Marklew? Why do you do it? Why do you surround yourself with the trappings of the dead?"

Richard Marklew said nothing.

"My client instructs me to say he takes no interest in the matter himself. I ask merely to satisfy my personal curiosity."

"Get out," said Marklew quietly. Then, shouting now, "Out! Out!" And stupidly, childishly, he threw his pillow at the solicitor. It bounced off him. The solicitor didn't seem to mind.

"Goodbye, Mr Marklew," said the solicitor. And he was gone.

Marklew had to get out of bed to retrieve his pillow. There was a draught in the room, he shivered in his pyjamas.

He flew home to London the next day. The day following, he took receipt of two guillotine blades and a coffin lacquered with bone. Of the skull, of course, there was as yet no sign.

The next year the convention was in Marrakech. It was a better convention. One of the senior members had died, everyone was delighted. At auction Marklew won a collection of shrunken heads, and a mummified body from the Chimu people of fourteenth century Peru. The mummy looked like it was made of faded newspaper, and when Marklew got close to it he thought it smelled sweet like toffee. He looked for the solicitor, but he was not in attendance.

The year after that, the convention was in Leningrad. It was a reasonable convention. At auction Marklew bought an authenticated tooth from the head of Tsar Nicholas. He asked if anyone had seen the solicitor, but no one had; no one admitted even to knowing whom he was talking about.

The year after that, the convention was in Tehran.

Later that year, his eldest son died. It was a shock, but only inasmuch that most of the time Marklew forgot he had any sons at all. They had gone away years ago to live with his wife in Italy. Some of the time Marklew forgot he had a wife either. She had a lover there, and they shared a house on the banks of Lake Como. Marklew's wife let him keep the house in Richmond, and granted him an annual pension.

He flew to Italy to attend his son's funeral. He couldn't remember when he had last seen his wife; she had always been petite, but now she had put on weight as if she wanted to look like a plump Italian mama. Husband and wife stood by the side of the grave, threw in clumps of earth that sounded too faint against the coffin. It turned out that the son had died fighting some war. Marklew hadn't known his son had been a soldier. He hadn't actually known there was a war on, wasn't that all over by now? "There's always a war going on somewhere," said his wife. She asked him how he was, and he said he was doing well. She reintroduced him to their younger son, who wore his hair foppishly long and looked to Marklew like a homosexual. He stayed the night with his wife and his wife's lover at their house in Bellagio. The décor was charming, but he thought the room was too cold.

When he returned to London, there was a parcel waiting for him. It looked like a hat box, although he knew he hadn't purchased a hat; he picked the box up, and with a cold thrill he knew what it must be. He took it into his study and opened it immediately.

Inside there was a rock. Presumably it had been put in there to weigh the box down. He lifted the rock, and he supposed that yes, it was about the same basic shape as a young boy's skull. Underneath the rock there was a sealed envelope. Inside, a simple, typed message:

'Not Dead Yet. But Coming Soon.'

The following year the convention was in Johannesburg. It was a disappointing convention. At auction Marklew bought some bones, some skeletal fragments, a jar of pickled skin. In the bar on the Sunday night he asked whether anyone had seen the solicitor. He did so, evidently, with increasing volume. It was eventually requested that he retire quietly to his room.

Some months later his wife died. It had either been murder or a suicide pact, it was hard to be sure: whatever the details, both she and her Italian lover were dead, shot in the head at point blank range, and maybe it didn't really matter which one had pulled the trigger. Marklew was not invited to the funeral. On the day his wife's body was laid to rest, he received another hat box at his house. Once again, it weighed like a skull. Once again, there was no skull inside, just a rock.

The rock was wet to the touch, and Marklew fancied it was covered with bubbles of solid spit. The bubbles wouldn't burst when he pressed down on them. The message inside the envelope, too, was the same. Maybe it was the type size, or maybe the font, but it seemed a sadder message this time: 'Not Dead Yet,' it apologised ruefully. And then, brighter, a cheery promise, 'But Coming Soon!'

Marklew by rights inherited his wife's estate, but there was some little legal difficulty about it: her Italian family were claiming a substantial share. Marklew knew that the matter would resolve itself in his favour eventually, but in the meantime was obliged to let several of his staff go.

He still liked to hold dinner parties before going to a convention. He didn't attract as many guests as he once had, and the ladies seemed much more reluctant to fuck him. Still, he would show them his favourite skull, he'd talk to them of ritual sacrifice, and he'd invite them all to put their fingers between the cracks. The night before he flew to Buenos Aires he gave a dinner party and no one wanted to touch his cracks at all. And he was telling them some anecdote or another that seemed to be heading towards no discernible ending, when his one remaining maid interrupted him to say there was a young man at the front door to see him.

"I am not expecting any more guests," said Marklew.

"He says he is your son."

Marklew asked that he be shown into the drawing room.

His son was pale and shivering, but Marklew was pleased to see he had at least availed himself of a haircut. Marklew asked what he wanted. The boy helped himself to a brandy without even asking; his hand was shaking as he poured it. "I'm sorry," he said. "I'm sorry. I don't know who else to turn to."

Marklew told him at least to sit down.

"Oh God," the boy said. "Do you ever feel that someone is watching you? I mean, all the time. It's there in the shadows, waiting for me. Oh, not just in the shadows, oh God. It's there when I wake up, I wake up so frightened I think I'll have a heart attack. Do you feel this? Does anyone else feel this? Is it just me?"

Marklew asked his son if he were taking any drugs. The son said he was, a bit. Marklew suggested he should stop.

And suddenly angry, getting to his feet: "What is all this bloody stuff? Why do you want this bloody stuff?" And he was at the shelves now, he'd picked up one of the skulls, he was grimacing at it, as if the very touch appalled him. "What do you want with all this *death*?" And he raised it high, he raised it so he could smash it down upon the floor.

"Put that down," said Marklew. "Put that down, very very gently."

His son froze, and he was like a little boy again, and Marklew suddenly had a memory of him, of them playing together, or having a picnic, how old would his son have been, six or seven? "I'm sorry," said the boy. "Really." And he put the skull back on the shelf. And he burst into tears.

"If it can take me whenever it likes," he sobbed, "what's it waiting for?"

Marklew wanted to get back to his guests. He told his son he was flying to Argentina the next morning, and he had no time to deal with this right now. The boy asked if he could stay in the house whilst his father was away. Marklew pretended to consider, but he knew he couldn't have his son there, he couldn't trust him around all his fragile things. Did he have any money? He could give him some money for a hotel. The boy said he didn't want money, he already had money. "Here, take some money," said Marklew, and his son did.

"Well," said Marklew.

"Well," said Marklew's son.

"You'll be all right," said Marklew.

"Can I see you once you're back home?" asked his son.

"Yes," said Marklew. "Maybe. In time. Once you've straightened yourself out."

"I'll do that then," said his son. "I'll straighten myself out."

The convention in Buenos Aires was dreadful. At auction Marklew didn't buy anything at all.

On his return he found his maid had left the hatbox in the study. The rock inside was wet again, and perhaps just a little sticky. The note was very enthusiastic. 'Not Dead Yet. But Coming Soon!!!!!!!'

There was also a message from the police, asking him to get in contact immediately. They had tried to reach him abroad, but the maid had given them a hotel name that was untraceable. Marklew's son had committed suicide, and had hanged himself with such force that he'd been virtually decapitated. The police expressed sympathy for his loss, and Marklew thanked them, but told them that he hadn't known his son well.

The following year Marklew didn't receive an invitation to the convention. It would usually come in the autumn; this year the leaves turned brown and fell from the trees, and then there was the cold; and then, snow.

Richard Marklew rented a four-roomed flat in Lambeth. A bedroom, a kitchen, a bathroom, and one room left to do with whatever he pleased! Some days he even quite liked the flat. His landlady was called Mrs Gascoyne. She never smiled much, or said anything very nice, but she had a heart of gold. Mrs Gascoyne didn't like him moving in with all his dead things, she said it was unnatural. But she agreed to turn a blind eye if she upped Marklew's rent, and refused ever to do any of the cleaning. Marklew agreed, and a happy bargain had been made.

Of course, there wasn't room for all of his collection. He had to get rid of the gossamer wire puppets from Mexico, and his coffin lacquered with bone. He might have got a good price for them at auction, but the convention had never invited him again. As it was, he was able to donate some pieces to the British Museum. A lot had to be binned.

Marklew filled all the wardrobes and cupboards with what artefacts he had left. There wasn't much room left for clothes, but Marklew didn't need many clothes. Two complete skeletons lay spread out in his bath, one balanced on top of the other, and sometimes it seemed to Marklew that they were making love, and sometimes that made him laugh. On good days he'd open up all the cupboards and pull open all the drawers, and he could see his collection all around him. This expression of who he was, somewhat diminished, and in borrowed circumstances.

If the weather were fine he might take the omnibus into the city. He'd walk by the Thames, by St Paul's, sit in Green Park. If the weather were bad, he'd stay at home.

At night he would lie in bed, and stare into the shadows, and fancy that they rippled.

Dear Mrs Gascoyne had no choice but to raise the rent again. He wrote to the six biggest collectors of *memento mori* in Britain, men he had shared drinks with at the conventions, men who were very nearly old friends. Two of them replied. Between them they bought his shrunken heads, his canopic jars and death masks, his skulls. They paid so much that he could now pay the rent for four whole months, and he treated himself to a steak dinner too. No one wanted the cracked skull, though; they said it was damaged.

Most of all Marklew liked getting the omnibus to Waterloo Bridge. It was his favourite bridge. He liked to stand at the midpoint, he'd paced the length of it to find out precisely where the midpoint was. And he would tilt his body over the rails, as far as it would go, and stare straight down into the Thames. He could stare into the Thames for hours. Sometimes he saw shadows moving in there. He wondered whether they were the same shadows from his bedroom.

One day he treated the cracked skull to an expedition to London. "You'll enjoy this," he told it on the bus—only a whisper, he didn't want people thinking he was mad! He took it to the midpoint of Waterloo Bridge, and dropped it over the side. He thought it would make a bigger splash. It somewhat disappointed him. The skull went straight down, it didn't even struggle for air. He watched for ages to see if it might float back to the surface, and then it began to rain, so he gave up, and went home.

The shadows in his bedroom reached out some nights and stroked him, and their touch was so very soft.

And one day he was on the omnibus, and it was very crowded, but nevertheless Marklew managed to get a seat anyway, people always gave up their seats when he came near—and for the life of him he couldn't remember whether he was going to Waterloo bridge or was coming back from it, and that was funny, but he was sure he'd work out which one when he got there!—and suddenly, by the doors, he saw him.

He had never expected he'd ever be able to recognise the man. There had never been anything remotely distinguished about his features, nothing that Marklew could ever recall to mind. But there was no question. He looked no older. But still cool, still stiff, his face a pose of professional blandness. Wearing a suit that was smart but not dear, not tailored but practical.

And just as soon as he'd seen him, the doors were opening, and the solicitor was getting off the bus. "Hey!" called Marklew. "Hey!" But the crowd was surging forward to fill up the little space that the solicitor's body had taken, and the bus was starting to move. "Hey! No, stop!" And he was pushing his way through the other passengers now, and they were pushing back, they were angry. And he was pulling at the door, but the door wouldn't open, and then the driver brought the bus to an abrupt stop, and the doors freed, and Marklew hurled himself forward and tumbled out on to the street.

The crowds were no easier here than they had been on the bus, it seemed the whole world was out in London that day. "Hey! Stop! Stop!" called Marklew, but he wasn't even sure whom he was calling at any more. And then—and then he saw him, the solicitor was maybe twenty feet further down the pavement, and he was moving fast, how could he move so fast in all this crush? "No, please!", and Marklew was running too. "Please!" Elbowing people away, waving his arms, breaking into little sprints on the spot when he got blocked and could advance no further. Marklew jumped off the pavement. Horns. Screams. The screech of tyres. He was running down the road. He was catching the solicitor up.

And he reached him at last, and he grabbed him by the shoulder, and he didn't know what to expect when he touched him, he half-expected his fingers would go straight through, or that he'd feel cold to the touch, or burn like fire—but no, no, he felt like an ordinary man. Swinging him around so they were face to face. And that face wasn't so bland now, it was frightened! He'd lost that cool, that stiff poise was gone for good. Now he had him. Although there was a beard, and there hadn't been a beard before—and this man's hair was grey, and he was old, and he was shorter than Marklew had remembered.

"Help me!" Marklew begged him. "You know me! Do you know me?"

"Please let me go!"

"You know me! You know who I am!"

"I don't know who you are, please!"

Marklew let go of the man, and he thought he didn't look much like a solicitor at all, not in that cheap brown coat, Marklew thought the man was probably in trade. "Please help me," said Marklew.

And the man hesitated. As if unsure whether to run, or whether to call the police. And then he said, "Go home. Go home, Mr Marklew. It's waiting for you."

The hatbox was sitting outside on the pavement, where anyone might have stolen it. Still, no one had.

Richard Marklew picked it up, and it felt no heavier and no lighter than the boxes he had been sent before. He tucked it under his arm as he struggled with the keys to his flat, and it suddenly felt like such a disrespectful thing to do to a dead little boy, and he hoped that the front of the skull was at least pointing away from his armpit. He went indoors. He set the box down in the middle of the floor. Gently, carefully. He sat on the floor beside it. He looked at it.

He decided he wouldn't open the box.

He opened the box.

He saw only the top of the skull whiter and shinier than he had ever thought a skull could be. He prodded it, daintily, with his finger. It was warm. It was cold.

He reached into the box so he could lift the skull out, and one hand grabbed it by the back of the head, the other fingered the eye sockets. The skull was free, but he wouldn't look at the skull, not for the moment, he looked instead to see if there were another envelope to read, some special message to announce the long-awaited arrival. Maybe even a receipt!—there wasn't. There wasn't, and all there was was the skull, and he was still holding it, it was in his hands, warm, cold, and he was looking at it at last, he was daring to look.

His heart beat so fast and he wondered if he were going to die. But he didn't, he just sat there on the floor, and the skull sat in his hands, and they were both touching each other, and yet neither had anything to say. To be honest, it was more than a little awkward.

The skull was perfect. It had not a single blemish. No browning discolouration around the temporal bones, as was common—the mandibles were in immaculate condition. The eyes were two round holes that seemed wide open in innocent surprise, the jaw was intact and allowed the mouth a reassuring smile.

And now Richard Marklew knew why he'd spent his lifetime building up a collection of the dead. He thought he'd known before, what the urge was, why he had to satisfy it, why he had *never* satisfied it, not till now. But he'd been wrong, and now he knew the truth, and the truth made him cry. He was crying with happiness. Was it happiness? Yes, probably.

He didn't want to let the skull go. He wasn't sure if he even could have. He got to his feet, and his old bones cracked with the effort, but he didn't care. He held the skull tight, and he swayed a bit because he felt so giddy now, and it seemed to him they were dancing. He went to lie down upon his bed. He was still wearing his clothes. He couldn't get undressed without putting the skull down, so that was all right, he wouldn't get undressed again. It was simple.

He thought maybe he dozed a little, and when he awoke the little boy in his hands was watching over him. He felt comforted, he dozed some more. It got dark. It didn't matter. Some little light streamed in from the window, a streetlamp maybe, or the moon.

The shadows moved around them both, but he didn't need to look at them any longer.

And there was the crack—just the one crack, running horizontally from side to side, just above the chin. It wasn't damage, it was a beautiful crack, wide and inviting, and it was studded with bright white teeth like smooth pebbles, not a single tooth was missing. He dared himself to touch the crack. Would he touch the crack? He would. He pulled the crack closer to his face, right against his very lips, and he pushed his tongue inside, past the pebble teeth and onwards, deeper, he pushed his tongue into the smiling crack as deep as it could go.

And the old woman says:

- *So much great treasure can be uncovered in an excavation. To appreciate the archaeologists at work, turn to* **Dig Deep** *(story 38, page 633).*
- *The greatest memento mori of all would have to be a horror story scratched upon the inside of a coffin lid. To read it, turn to* **And This is Where We Falter** *(story 49, page 811).*
- *Can we ever consider the dead to be our slaves, as this story suggests? Consider what happens to the* **Angels in Australia** *(story 59, page 995).*
- *If you dare to peer a little further into the shadows, turn to* **The Shadow Mother** *(story 71, page 1229).*
- *"There's always a war going on somewhere." True enough. It's a statement repeated in* **72 Virgins** *(story 72, page 1257). Try and find it.*

95

Carry Within Some Small Sliver of Me

BEVERLY MCROBERTS LOOKED like both her parents, and that was quite a feat, considering that they in no way resembled one another. She had her father's nose, large and bulbous and with nostrils that had a propensity to flare—she also had his deep blue eyes and his cold thin lips and his hair. And she had her mother's skin with all of its strange milky pallor; Beverly sometimes imagined that her mother was a big sack of milk and that if she were cut open all the milk would come pouring out, and if that were true of her mother she supposed it was also true of her, and she'd pat at her stomach and listen to all the milk sloshing about inside—she also had her mother's little hands and her crooked teeth and her ears. Whenever she got lonely at school, and missed the parents who loved her, Beverly would go into the toilets and gaze into the half-length mirror by the washbasins. And there she'd see her parents gazing right back—Beverly would gaze at different body parts dependent on which one of her parents that day she'd decided to love the most.

And she'd asked if she could have her ears pierced, just like her mother's were, and her parents had always said no, no, she was too young—and then she'd turned eleven, and they'd changed her minds, because eleven meant she was very nearly a teenager, and a teenager meant she was very nearly grown up! And Beverly's mother had one ring in her left ear and two rings in her right, and that looked unusual but had apparently been quite the fashion once. That's what Beverly wanted, just the same style, please. Mother pierced Beverly's ears herself. She told Beverly to keep still and be brave. Beverly couldn't sit still but she wasn't frightened, she was excited, it was a completely different sort of not sitting still—Mother used some rubbing alcohol and a needle and made three little holes in Beverly's lobes, and she gave Beverly three little stud earrings, just like the ones she wore, and Beverly was proud.

And when her parents weren't watching Beverly might take out her father's pipe from the cabinet in the drawing room. She'd never seen her father smoke a pipe—he once told her, laughing, that he'd only smoked it when he was young and pretentious—but he'd kept the pipe anyway, didn't it make a nice ornament, it was wooden and looked so grand. And Beverly would put the stem of the pipe into her mouth, and imagine her father's lips had been there once, years ago, before she had even been born, before she'd even been dreamed of. She didn't like to suck at it, the stale taste made her tongue curl. She liked to blow down it as if it were a whistle, if she blew hard enough a sound might come out too high for human beings to hear.

But the best days were when they all went out together. Perhaps to the park—and they'd all hold hands, and Beverly would be in the middle, Father to one side, Mother at the other, they'd march to the big pond, and her parents would let her throw bread for the ducks, they'd let go of her hands just so she could do that, her aim was getting better, sometimes she'd hit those ducks right on the head! And if not the park then the supermarket, but they couldn't walk hand in hand there, it blocked the aisle. And even the worst days were like the best days—not to the park, not to the supermarket, just staying at home, watching television, eating dinner, sitting about not doing much at all—but they'd still be *together*, that was the main thing, they'd still be a family.

Beverly had friends at school, but not too many, and none very close. They thought she was a bit odd.

The letter for Beverly arrived on a school day. And so her parents could have easily intercepted it. They could have opened it, or destroyed it unread, and they didn't because they loved their daughter and they didn't believe she'd ever betray them. And so the envelope sat on the table for hours, unassuming, flat, waiting for Beverly to come home and find it.

Beverly didn't receive many letters, not unless it was her birthday, and it wouldn't be her birthday for ages. It was exciting. She took the letter upstairs, and lay down upon her bed, and opened it, and she hoped that the message inside would be terribly long and full of great incident and detail.

It wasn't very long at all. "You should know this," it said. "Your father has died."

That was it. Beverly turned over the letter, and then turned it over again. She looked down at the bed as if some other words might have slipped off the page without her realising. The handwriting was small and mean, the message at the top of the sheet and the rest of it left blank, it seemed oddly cruel so much of the paper had been wasted.

The handwriting on the envelope was just as mean, and Beverly shivered to see her name and address written there so coldly. On the back was a series of numbers, and Beverly thought it might be a telephone number, but when she counted it was a few digits short.

And then she was crying—*bawling*, so that it hurt her throat—and she didn't even know why, only that she felt grief, though she had no idea whom or what the grief was for.

Mother came in and sat on the bed next to Beverly, and held her hand, although she didn't hold it too tightly, as if that were no longer allowed. Father stood at the doorway, tall and upright and so serious. Father told Beverly that she was adopted. He told her that it didn't matter she was adopted, he and Mother loved Beverly very much, and surely that was what was important? In the scheme of things? He told her that they hadn't been able to have children of their own, but they'd been given the chance to make one very special girl the happiest and most beloved darling there ever was, she was lucky really, didn't she feel lucky, even a bit? "We were going to tell you when you were older," he added, and he looked away, and Beverly knew he was lying.

"They shouldn't have written," said the woman Beverly had thought was her mother. "It was supposed to be confidential!"

"We love you very much," said the father figure by the door.

"Did you know my real parents?" said Beverly.

"No," said Mother, and let go of Beverly's hand.

"No, kiddo," said Father, and tried to smile.

"Do you know where I can find them?"

"It was supposed to be confidential," said Mother again, and she seemed close to tears herself. "We have to move away!"

"Would you like that, kiddo?" said Father. "Shall we move away? Somewhere they'll never ever find us, so we can be left in peace?"

Beverly wasn't a spiteful girl, and she knew what they said was true, that their love was all that mattered. During dinner she tried to behave the same way she always had, she was nice, she smiled from time to time, she even laughed when Father made one of his terrible jokes. But it seemed to her that she was watching herself from a distance, and her laughter sounded so false, as false as everything else in the world, and the smile made her face hurt. The parents offered her extra pudding because she was being such a good girl, and she thanked them both politely, she asked to be excused, she wanted to go to bed.

She got into her pyjamas, brushed her teeth. The toothpaste tasted off. She looked at herself in the mirror, she looked really hard. She realised she didn't resemble either of the grown-ups downstairs at all.

She went to sleep.

And maybe she dreamed it, but in the night she thought she looked up and saw her mother standing over, watching her. Not her mother, of course, she'd have to correct that, she'd have to find something else to call her, but what, what? "Hey," said Mother softly. "Hey. I don't want to disturb you."

"It's all right," said Beverly.

Mother sat down on the bed, and began to stroke Beverly's hair.

"I love you so much," said Mother.

Beverly promptly said the same thing back.

"We lied earlier," said Mother. And she continued to stroke the hair. And then, nothing else was said, not for a while, and Beverly thought that that was it, that she wouldn't have to hear what the lie was, maybe it was all a lie, every single scrap of it, and she closed her eyes tight and pretended she was still asleep.

Then Mother spoke on, so very softly, never raising her voice. "We *can* have children. We had a child once. A proper child of our own. I hated it, darling. I hated my own daughter, can you imagine? I could feel it, for months, growing inside my stomach. Eating the food I swallowed. Kicking me. Making me feel so sick, sick like you can't believe, sick that just wouldn't go away, and then giving me so much pain. I wanted to get rid of it. I didn't want it in me. I didn't want this monster." All the time, still, still stroking Beverly's hair.

"Mother," said Beverly. "I'm asleep."

"When it was born, I pushed and strained, I wanted it out of me. Parasite. And out it came, and how it screamed. What did it have to scream about? What did she. She wasn't the one who. She wasn't the one who had to. She had nothing, *nothing*, to scream about."

"I'm asleep now. Please. Please let me sleep."

"They said I would adjust, feel differently. Give it time. I gave it time, but I never did. I never did. We gave it away. We gave it up for adoption. But this is the truth," Mother said, and she loomed ever closer to Beverly, Beverly thought she would bite her ear she was so close, "I always wanted a daughter. Just not that one. Not her. I wanted to love someone who had never hurt me. Was that so wrong? Was it wrong to adopt you, my perfect little girl? To want all the good times, and not have the bad? I don't know. I don't see why. I don't know."

She kissed Beverly then, and got up off her bed, and left the bedroom, and closed the door behind her.

Beverly cried one last time, and she knew now what she was grieving, and it wasn't a father she had never met. And then she decided she was never going to cry again, not ever, not about anything. That was all over now. And so it was.

She waited until the house was still. And then she studied the row of digits on the envelope that was too short to be a phone number, and she went downstairs, and she dialled the number anyway.

It rang for several minutes, but Beverly was patient, it wasn't as if she had anything else to do. And by the time the woman on the other end picked up, Beverly knew exactly what she wanted to ask her.

Beverly was strangely relieved that the woman lived so very far away. Had she been close, Beverly could have slipped out of the house to meet her and been back before her parents knew it. She might have had some thin hope that everything could be put back to normal, and that hope would have made her anxious, it would have been something to fight for. But the woman told her she was in a town Beverly had never heard of, and the name didn't seem real, it had too many syllables and too few vowels, and when Beverly found it on a map she could see that it would take her all day to get there, all day and part of the night, there was no way her mother and father wouldn't realise she'd abandoned them. So, that was that.

She left home in the middle of the night. By the time she reached her destination it was the middle of the night again—the next night, probably, or maybe the one after. Beverly had had to catch so many trains, all of them so slow and winding, and she'd slept only fitfully on each of them, she couldn't tell how much time had passed.

The café was exactly where the woman said it would be, out of the railway station, turn right, then turn right again—but the town was so dark, all the houses were shut up and still, there wasn't even a single street lamp to throw any light. And Beverly thought the café wouldn't be open, it couldn't be open, not when the rest of the town was so dark and dead. But there it was—lights poured out abruptly from the windows and gave the pitch black outside it some little warmth. Beverly went up close, shivered in that warmth. There was chatter indoors. Something like laughter. Even music from an old jukebox.

A bell tinkled as Beverly pushed open the door, and she went into the café, and everybody looked up at her, just for a moment. The café was full, not a single table was free, and it seemed to Beverly that all manner of people were there—policemen, bikers, men in pinstripe suits. Women in ball gowns who looked as if they'd just escaped from a dance, their hair up in beehives, and their faces heavy with make-up. Entire families with children and grandchildren and great-grandchildren besides. For that one moment they looked at her, and some of them smiled, and most of them looked tired, and one of the ballgowned women burst into tears.

And even now Beverly thought this must be a mistake, that she'd be told by some grown-up that she couldn't come in—she thought that with all these people inside, the one she'd come so far to meet wouldn't be there. But then, from the other side of the café, sitting in a pink plastic booth by the window, a woman gave her a single wave in greeting.

Beverly went to her. The woman looked her up and down appraisingly. Then shrugged. "Well, sit down then," she said. Beverly did.

"You wrote to me?" said Beverly. "About my father? We spoke on the phone?"

"Yes," said the woman, "and yes, and yes. And they changed your name to Beverly? Well. Why not? Why not indeed? It's as good a name as any other."

"I was called something else?"

"It doesn't matter now. May I pour you a coffee?"

"Mother says I'm not old enough to drink coffee," said Beverly, and then blushed bright red.

"If you can have your ears pierced, you can drink coffee. And if you can drink coffee, we can talk like adults." The woman pulled back her hair, showed Beverly there were rings dangling from her lobes. "See? We're both old enough." She poured the coffee, it came out thick and slow like treacle, she pushed the mug across the table to Beverly. The coffee smelled strong and bitter.

Beverly stared at the woman closely. Her skin wasn't milky, but dull like sackcloth. Her nose wasn't bulbous, the nostrils were well-behaved and refused to flare. "Are you my mother?"

The woman looked scandalised, and then barked out a laugh. "Good God, no! I have children. I have three fine sons, and I got them the normal way. I don't need *you*. Look. I have photographs. Look. Look." From a neat little purse she took three photographs, spread them out on the table. "That's Harry, he works in insurance. And that's Gary. And that's Larry, he works in insurance. You can keep the photographs if you like," the woman added helpfully. "Really. I have plenty."

Beverly thanked her. "Do you have a photograph of my mother?"

"No."

"Do you have a photograph of my father?"

"Before or after he died?"

"Um. Before."

"No. I thought you should be told he died." And she screwed her face into something that looked somewhat sympathetic. "I always think the children should be told."

"How did my father die?"

"Good God! It's not as if you even know how he lived! Ask how he lived first!"

"I'm sorry. How did my father live?"

The woman gave this some thought. "Clumsily. I always thought he'd die horribly one day."

"And did he die…?"

"Horribly? Yes. Suffocation. Believe me. It's not as painless as it looks!"

Somewhere on another table a small boy began to cry, and his mother comforted him. On another table a policeman started crying, and no one cared. Beverly looked for the ballgowned woman, but she had gone, all the women in ballgowns had paid up and left. "Can I see my mother?" she asked.

"Your mother doesn't want to see you."

Beverly felt tears prick at her own eyes, and she blinked them away, she wasn't ever going to do that again. "Why not?"

"She doesn't want to see any of the children. Not afterwards. Don't," and she touched Beverly's arm in a sudden act of tenderness, "take it too personally. Or, rather," she added, letting go of the arm, and sitting back, and shrugging, "*do* take it personally, if you like. It probably is personal."

"Oh."

"Was there anything else?" And the woman was making for her purse, closing it with a tight snap. Beverly felt a last chance slipping away from her.

"Please," said Beverly. "Do you know her? Are you her friend? Please. Tell me what she's like."

The woman gave this some thought. "You could say I'm a friend of your mother's," she said, at last. "I suppose, in a way, I am. I care for her. I do the best I can. She's not easy to care for. Your mother is a very demanding person. But special. We all think she's special." The woman frowned, as if assessing the accuracy of her response, then gave a single nod, and pulled herself up from the booth. "I'm sorry for your loss," she said. "Losses are irritating things. I've taken care of the bill. Don't try to follow me."

The woman left.

Beverly sipped at her coffee. Just for show, so the woman would think she wouldn't follow. It was too hot, but the taste was surprisingly sweet, Beverly wanted nothing more suddenly than to stay and finish it. It took effort to set it back down on the table. And as soon as she heard the bell on the door sound, and she knew the woman had left, she made to her feet. Her legs felt weak, she had to grasp on to the booth to steady herself, and the pink plastic was soft and yielding, her fingers sank in deep and it would have been the easiest thing in the world to let them sink further, to sit back down on to the comforting warmth of the padded seat, to drown in it.

With all the nonchalance she could muster she walked through the café, walked to the door. This time none of the customers looked up at her, they had their own lives to worry about, and that was just as well, Beverly didn't want anything to do with them, all she wanted was her mother—and even as she thought of that, of that word, 'mother', it seemed like such a precious lie, all her life she had never understood how precious, and if it were a lie, well, so, what of that? And so excited, and so nervous, almost walking on air, she stepped out into the dark. She'd forgotten how very black the dark was, and this time even the lights of the café couldn't penetrate it, and there was a moment of panic, she couldn't see which direction the woman had taken. But then—there—just a few metres away—she was leaning against the wall, she was fiddling with something, her purse, her hair, her shoelace, it didn't matter—she had delayed, and that was a stroke of luck.

And now the two of them were walking on into the night—Beverly trying to tread quietly so she wouldn't be heard, trying to keep her distance—the woman striding into the pitch black with such confidence, as if she knew every junction, every corner, every loose paving stone (and perhaps she did)—her heels tapping out on the ground a beat for Beverly to follow. Every so often Beverly thought she'd lost her, that the woman had got too far ahead, but the woman would always stop and deal with that meddlesome shoelace again, and Beverly would catch up. They walked on like this for an hour, maybe longer. Until at last the woman stopped, and turned to one of the houses lining the pavement, and it was only then that Beverly realised there were houses there at all, it had been so dark and the houses so bland; the woman took some keys from her purse, and marched up to the front door. She unlocked the door. She turned around. She looked back out, she seemed to stare right at Beverly. Beverly froze, tried to make herself invisible, or at least see-through, or at least as black as the night—and maybe it worked, because the woman turned around again, and entered the house, and closed the door behind her.

So this was the house where her mother lived—and Beverly felt a strange recognition, a *belonging* somehow; it was an anonymous house, it was no different in shape or size to the others either side, but it was so very special. She wanted to know what the address was, what this special house was called, but there were no street signs, and there was no number on the front door. She looked around for any landmarks, anything that might help her identify the house again in the daylight—nothing—really, nothing. And she thought that she'd just have to stay there, then—she'd stand on the pavement outside her mother's house all night, just to be sure she wouldn't lose it, she would *never* lose it now, she wouldn't even take her eyes off it in case it slipped away—and then, suddenly, there was light. So startling and dazzling that for a moment Beverly was blinded, and she thought the house might have vanished in the flash, that when her eyes adjusted to the glare the house would be gone and her mother would have gone with it, gone forever. The woman had pulled open the curtains to the front room, and Beverly could see inside so nice and bright, and the woman was smiling, it was as if she *wanted* her to see.

And there was her mother.

Her mother was pregnant again. Beverly realised she had expected her mother to be pregnant, so this was no shock. All she knew of her mother was that she could pump out babies, it made some strange sense to find her like this. The shock was how pronounced was the pregnancy, that it made her mother so fat and swollen. And ugly too —because it wasn't the stomach that was swollen, Beverly thought she could have accepted that, no matter how gross and distended that stomach might have been. It was the head. It was the head. The head was swollen. Somehow balanced upon what was still a perfectly slender neck—and it was to this neck that Beverly kept lowering her eyes, the neck was the beginning of what was normal and the end of what was obscene—balanced upon that stick-thin neck was a head maybe four or five times the size it should have been. It looked like an enormous balloon, filled with air to the point of bursting—and yet, not like a balloon at all, because balloons are neat and round, and this head had grown into such a lumpen shape, bits of the skull rising sharply out of the skin like crude horns. The nose had been smoothed down to a point; one of the eyes had been stretched thin and wide across the face, the other seemed almost normal, though sunken rather, and a little dull, and a little teary, as if it knew it wasn't as impressive as the other. And the jaw looked crushed with the weight of it all.

When the first thrill of horror had passed, Beverly felt a surge of such pity. Her mother was in pain. Her mother was *trapped*—she was sitting upright on a hard wooden chair, and her ankles were tied to the chair legs. And a thick leather strap ran around her mother's forehead, fastening the back of the head against the wall—and she could see how tight the strap was, how the fat skin pooled and bulged white against it. The woman from the café—her captor?—was smiling still. Her mother couldn't smile back, she wouldn't have been able to frame that contorted mouth into any sort of reciprocal position—but she did raise a hand in greeting. Beverly wondered whether the strap was a restraint at all. She thought that maybe the strap was there to keep the head balanced. She thought that maybe, without that balance, the head would simply fall off.

And then there was, what? A ripple, yes, across her mother's face? Something passing close underneath the skin, something on the move. And the ripple passed over the flat eye, and it popped out big and wide and shining, it seemed to attempt an almost flirty wink.

The woman from the café was talking now. And then taking something out from a metal box on the table, it looked silver and so glamorous, like an old cigarette box. Chunks of meat—and they looked to Beverly red and raw, was it beef, was it something else? Talking again, and waving the beef at the mother playfully; Beverly could see her mother start to drool, a whole stream of it spilling out over the flab of the bottom lip, gushing now like a geyser. The woman went up to the mother, and with both hands grabbed hold of those fat lips. And then she began to prise them apart, to pull the mouth open—it was obviously quite a strain, and the woman put her all into the job, and the mother didn't have the strength to help her, she sat there looking down at the woman's efforts uselessly and apologetic—the woman set her own mouth hard with the effort, and her mouth was so puny and ridiculous in comparison—the woman heaved, she was up to the task, she had done this before, she was expert at opening Mother's mouth, Beverly could see that and could admire her for it—and was there some give?—was there some dark hole peeping out between those lips?—the mouth finally gave way, it swung open large and wide and wet. And quickly the woman produced a block of wood, she wedged it in to keep the mouth from slamming shut again. There weren't many teeth left, and they were small and fractured—they were pebbles bobbing to the surface on a sea of hard red gum.

Time to serve dinner. And the woman tossed the lump of raw steak into the gaping maw. The steak was lost from view—and then, just for an instant, Beverly could see it again—it was held aloft—it was held high and proud—it was gripped tight within the grasp of a tiny hand. A tiny hand sticking out from the mouth, and it looked so neat and so perfect, the little knuckles, the little fingernails.

And then—and then, the woman turned to the window. She looked straight out. She looked straight out at Beverly. She gave a smile. Maybe it was a smile of triumph. It wasn't a cruel smile.

And the mother at last looked towards the window too. She strained against the straps, her head slowly turned. She stared out at her daughter—at her own child, pretty and smart and wearing earrings like a grown-up. Beverly could see that in spite of everything, the mother did look like her. Somehow, there was a resemblance.

Mother raised a hand to her. In greeting? In need?

And the little baby that was growing inside her mother's mouth raised a hand in greeting too.

There seemed to be a sound in her head. It couldn't really be there—but maybe it was like a blast from a whistle too high-pitched for human beings to hear.

So warm in here, big sister. But soon I'll come out to play. And oh! What fun we shall have.

And that's when Beverly turned and ran.

She dozed on the trains, she didn't know for how long. But whenever she opened her eyes it was always dark outside.

And at first she had nightmares, but they soon wore off, soon her dreams were sweet and peaceful. She slept soundly, even though she now knew what she was.

At one point she decided to open her mouth wide, as wide as possible. All those years and she'd never thought to see how far it could go, now it would be such fun to find out. She let her jaw droop, she stretched and stretched, she had to grit her teeth hard and concentrate, these were muscles that were weak and lazy, but Beverly had no patience with weakness any more. She heard something splinter, and she tasted blood, but there was no pain, or not much, at any rate—and soon she could fit her hand inside her mouth, the whole hand even with the fingers splayed, and then her whole arm, she could push in the arm right up to the elbow, she could push it in as deep as she liked.

At first she wasn't sure she would even recognise her old house. But there it was, she found it on the street side just where she'd left it, looking up at it seemed like such sweet nostalgia. Had she really made that her home for the past eleven years? It was dark. All was still. She found a key in her pocket, and she put it into the lock, and it fitted, and it turned, and the door was open, and so she went inside.

She could see her parents had been worried. There were leaflets about missing children, 'what to do in the event of..'. and 'how to cope with…'—thick pamphlets that made merry with words like 'grief' and 'trauma'. They were scattered all around the sitting room, and that was the main clue something was wrong, her old mother and father had been so neat and tidy. She felt a stab of guilt, she hadn't wanted them to suffer. She wondered how long she'd been away.

But when she went into her parents' bedroom, when she stood over their sleeping bodies, they looked so calm and carefree, they looked innocent as babes.

She stood over them for quite a while. She enjoyed the peace. She didn't want to disturb it.

Eventually, with a soft sigh of resignation, she went to her father's side, and she picked up his pillow, and his head went ker-thunk! down upon his mattress, and that was funny, and he didn't even think to wake up. And she pressed the pillow down hard on to his face, right over his mouth and that bulbous nose, and that's when he stirred from sleep, too little too late, he struggled so limply and then stopped struggling at all. She lifted off the pillow, and he just lay there, still, and he didn't look any different in death—suffocation agreed with him, if indeed it *were* suffocation, as she pressed down she had heard a little snap and had wondered vaguely whether she had broken his neck.

Her mother slept on. She walked round to her mother's side, she lifted her pillow, the head did the ker-thunk thing again but it wasn't so heavy and wasn't so funny. She considered. Her mother wasn't old, she was healthy. Beverly sniffed, and there was a faint coppery tang to the air, and she knew her mother was still fertile. The heart thrummed, Beverly could hear it, and it sounded confident and strong, it sounded strong enough to support two. Beverly put down the pillow. She sat down by her mother's side. She stroked her hair, she stroked her milky skin. Her mother gave a little whimper at that, and cuddled into Beverly closer, and Beverly felt happy.

When dawn broke Beverly stood up and left the bedroom. She took her father's pipe from the cabinet. She took his other things too—the whisky that only he ever drank, the collection of commemorative coins, all the photographs, every single one. She put them into a sack, and left them outside by the dustbins. And then Beverly came back inside, and made herself a coffee, good, strong and black, and sat at the kitchen table, and waited for the woman upstairs to wake up.

And the old woman says:

- *To read a tale of adoption from the mother's point of view, turn to* **Talent Will Out** *(story 57, page 953).*
- *It's not hard to follow someone. I know. I do it often. No one expects anyone could want to follow them, they never turn round and see me. Watch another girl pursue someone through the streets of a totalitarian regime in* **The Touch of Baby Stalin's Skin** *(story 67, page 1165).*
- *When you stop to consider, the mouth is such a peculiar thing. The perfection of the face is offset by some bloody great hole—it looks unfinished, like slovenly work done by cheap builders. You half-expect to see a disused cement mixer left around it. For a tale in which the mouth is wrenched fatally open, turn to* **The Ineffectual Photoscopy of Cats** *(story 77, page 1351).*
- *How about something lighter? Another little girl finds use for her father's pipe in* **The Rainman** *(story 36, page 603). See what it can be.*
- *If this story wasn't dark enough for you, go darker still with* **Custard Cream** *(story 17, page 291).*

96
Ruin at Knossos

On the coroner's report it said that James Grizzell-Jones had suffered 'death by euphemism'. Those were the actual words, I saw them for myself. And it's certainly true that my poor husband had his whole life shied away from matters of delicacy. He was not a man to call a spade a spade, not unless it were a good solid British spade with no nonsense or flim-flammery about it; offer him a spade that in any way suggested the sloppier, seedier, steamier side of life and he'd have refused it politely, thank you very much.

He died on a bus tour, high in the Cretan mountains. We'd just done some museum or another, now we were on our way to Knossos. The bus tour didn't cater exclusively for the English, the commentary the guide gave us was in French, German, Spanish too, and one other language we couldn't identify, James thought it might have been Dutch. I suppose you get what you pay for. "We should have gone for the more expensive one," my husband muttered to me as we drove along. "Twice the price, but at least we wouldn't have to put up with all this jabbering." I was inclined to agree with him; we agreed about most things, really. And I think they may have been the last words he ever said to me. He tutted. I tutted back in sympathy.

He'd had a moussaka the night before that hadn't agreed with him. Or maybe it had been all the retsina, that nasty little waiter kept on filling our glasses though we'd told him not to. Or the vine leaves. Anyway, James had been up and down all night, out of the bed and into the bathroom. "Are you all right?" I asked him, and I could tell he was embarrassed, he told me to go back to sleep. But it was hard to sleep with all that commotion going on, when the bathroom door didn't close properly and kept letting the light in, with the electric fan that turned on every time he went in there, with that smell.

Now on the tour I could tell he wasn't feeling quite right. He kept on wincing, and grabbing at his stomach, and I'd hear the odd gurgle from within—and he'd clasp his hand to it to muffle the sound. It's all that oil they put in their Mediterranean dishes, it can't be good for you, though apparently all those Greeks seem to live a long time. Anyway, at one point he got up from his seat, and struggled down the aisle to the front of the bus. The tour guide was at that moment telling the French all about Minoan pottery; we'd already heard the English version, it was nothing to write home about. I could tell it genuinely pained my husband to interrupt her. He tried to whisper to her, but she was holding a microphone, and bits of their conversation were broadcast all around the bus. "Please sit down, Sir," she said; I'll give her her due, she'd clocked we were British, right from the start. "I need to use the whatsit," said James. "I beg your pardon, Sir?" "The thingummy. You know. I need it very badly. Very urgently." "I don't know what you mean, Sir, please sit down." And so he turned around and came back down the aisle, and his face was burning red, and he was doing his best to walk proud and tall but he was starting to stagger. And there was some little laughter, but I couldn't tell whether it was at my husband's expense, or at some foreign joke that the guide had made about Theseus and the Minotaur.

"Is there anything I can do?" I asked, and I got up so he could sit by the window. But he shook his head, angrily, as if angry at me, and he gritted his teeth, and he turned his head to look at the Greek countryside whipping fast past the window, and he died.

It's not the way I would have chosen for him to go. But then, what sort of death would I have chosen? It's not as if I was presented with a set of options, and frankly I'm rather glad the matter was taken out of my hands altogether. They say that the best way to go is peacefully in your sleep, and it's certainly the one most people seem to pick. But who can tell? Maybe, at the very point of death, you suffer the most terrible nightmares. You look all peaceful on the surface, but inside something is raging. Maybe that's what actually kills you. And all the nightmares you ever had as a child, the really big ones you never quite forgot, the ones that left you forever scared of the dark, or of spiders, or of great heights—all the nightmares come back for one last hurrah, and they torment you, and they fill up every inch of your sleeping body and crush your heart.

Really, these days I'm frightened to go to sleep at all. These days I keep the bedside lamp on, the television loud, the windows open wide and cold, anything. Just in case I never wake again.

The coroner's report said 'death by euphemism', and I thought, how could they have known? And was it even true? If my husband had been able to overcome his embarrassment—if he had more cogently expressed the immediacy with which he needed to relieve himself—would it, really, have made much difference? It wasn't as if he suffered for much longer, he returned to his seat and his kidneys ruptured and that was it.

But I do wonder whether had the tour guide given him some reason to *hope*—an assurance that his concerns would be addressed, or that looking for a rest stop would be made a matter of high priority—then it might have given James something to live for. I think the truth was, James just gave up. He was given two options. He could either die, or he could speak forcefully before a large group of strangers about his bowel problems. He went for the easy way out.

Sometimes I get cross with him for that. That after nearly fifty years of marriage I wasn't worth fighting that little bit harder for. I wasn't worth that small humiliation.

I mean, had it come to it, he could have dropped his trousers there and then and done his business in front of everyone. He could have pooped right there in the bus aisle, and yes, it might have embarrassed both of us, but it would have saved his life maybe. I'm sure that's what the Mediterraneans would have done.

'Death by euphemism' seems rather an odd thing to put on a coroner's report. Unless I read it incorrectly, and it really said, 'Death by (euphemism)', as in, 'Death by (insert euphemism here)'. It's just possible that the coroner had opened James up and looked at the fatal accumulation of moussaka and vine leaves, and recoiled, and was still trying to find a pleasant way to describe it. Which would be reassuring, because it would suggest that James' death wasn't caused by any hesitancy on his part. But only a *little* reassuring—because we're then left with this rather squeamish coroner who, like my husband did, shies away from the sloppier parts of life and wants to cover all that up with niceness and obfuscation. I'm all for tactful politeness, but it isn't what I look for in a coroner. I want someone out there who isn't afraid to confront death head on, warts and all, and who can express it clinically and without shame. Because if even the coroners are forced to hide behind euphemisms, what chance have the rest of us got? And how awkward, how embarrassing, how cross-your-legs-tight and screw-up-your-eyes appalling must death really be?

Or maybe. The coroner *was* suggesting that James was killed by a euphemism—but not his euphemism, my own. Because even though I knew my husband was dead, or dying, I didn't raise the alarm on the bus. There was his body lolling next to me and I chose to ignore it. Instead I read the guide book, I listened to the English bits of the tour commentary, I looked past James' dead head out of the window at the scenery. And when the passenger across the aisle asked, "Is your husband all right?", I smiled and said, "He's just a bit under the weather." 'Under the weather', of course, being a euphemism for 'dead as a doornail'. I didn't want to say anything. I didn't want to make a scene. I didn't want to interrupt the tour guide, because my husband had already interrupted her once, I didn't want her to think the elderly British couple sitting near the back were troublemakers. I didn't say a word, in fact, until the bus had come to a designated stop outside a market selling souvenirs. I spoke up, after everyone else had go off, and said, "I think there's a slight problem with my husband," and they took a look at him, the bus driver and the tour guide, and they called for an ambulance.

I didn't ever get to see Knossos.

They assured me they'd get James' body flown home in time for the funeral. I made a joke. I said, "I hope he is home in time, I know he'd hate to miss it!" No one laughed. Perhaps no one understood it? Adam and Marcia took charge of all that, everything to do with the funeral. They were very proper and solemn, and I thought how adult they'd suddenly become, and how unknowable. They kept on coming to visit me to see if I were all right, Marcia more than Adam, of course, because Adam's kids are younger. They talk to me about how James was a 'good man' and a 'good father', as if they'd only barely been introduced.

Of course, it had all been Adam's fault. James would never have eaten moussaka if we'd been on our usual holiday in Totnes. But Adam did insist, he said, "You should travel the world a bit, you're not getting any younger, you don't know how long you've got!" He would keep going on about it. One day James found in the local Oxfam a guide book, and it was only going for two pounds fifty, and it was all about the Greek Islands. And once he'd bought that, James had to have the holiday too, the book would have been useless otherwise and James did so hate waste.

The night before the funeral Marcia and her two girls stayed over with me. And I found her outside in the garden, in the dark, late. I asked her what was wrong. Her shoulders kept heaving. She said to me, "I can't make the tears come out, no matter how hard I try. What's wrong with me? Am I a bad person?" I said I didn't know.

During the funeral everyone was very polite. It was said that James Grizzell-Jones had gone to a better place, although I rather doubted that—he hadn't believed in God when we'd met, and he'd not told me of any new beliefs he might have acquired since, that was one of the things he would have found embarrassing to discuss—and besides! where could he have gone to that was better than Crete, the travel agent had told us it was one of the top tourist destinations. They told me that he was a good man, a good father, a good friend, a good husband. They told me that everyone would miss him.

It hadn't been euphemisms in the beginning, had it? Between Jimmy and me. Back at the start we could hardly keep our hands off each other, he was always pulling me into corners and kissing me, on the mouth, *in* the mouth!—and sometimes with my parents in the next room! We said we'd know each other for the rest of our lives. And he wasn't shy, and do you know, I wasn't shy either, and we'd make love, and we wouldn't worry about what to call it, we'd just rummage around with all of our bits until it felt good. He wasn't ashamed of his thingummy then; I wasn't ashamed of my whatsit. And I wondered, as the vicar droned on, as we stood up to sing a hymn Jimmy wouldn't have liked, I wondered—when did we let the euphemisms creep in? When did we find the reasons to stop talking? Because once in a while James would say, do you fancy a bit of business this evening? Without even looking at me, he was blushing bright red. We did business a few times, but I never liked the word for it, it sounded so cold and formal—and maybe that's exactly what it was, maybe the word changed it into something that was cold and formal, I don't know. And after a while he'd ask if I wanted any business, and I'd say no—I'd say that I had a headache, needed to wash my hair, that I was feeling tired, that I was feeling anything, anything but the truth. And eventually he stopped asking.

Sasha was being noisy. Sasha, that's Adam's youngest. Sasha was saying, "But where's Granddad? Is Granddad in the box?" And Adam and that wife of his were shushing her, they told her to be quiet. Yes, Granddad was in the box, ssh now. "You said he was with the angels! Are the angels in the box?" They didn't know where the angels were, the angels were waiting for Granddad when he got out of the box. "How can he get out? He's dead, isn't he? Isn't he dead? Isn't he dead?" My son and that wife blushing to hear the word mentioned, and telling her to shut up, and looking so embarrassed, and trying to find the right phrase that would cover 'dead' up and make 'dead' all right again—he's at rest, he's asleep, he's at peace now, ssh, he's in a better place, he's with the angels in the box, ssh ssh.

And I realised that it is the children who bring on the euphemisms. It's the children who make us feel awkward, and send us retreating behind soft words and smooth blather. We look at the children, and we know that we've made them, and we don't know how, they're so fragile, and so very strange, we did it with body parts we no longer will describe in front of them, we did it by methods we'd sooner now do with the lights off, or once a month, or not at all. And we'd do anything to protect them, anything to save them, we don't fear death for our own sakes, but for them we'll do everything we can to hide death away where it can't get them.

"I said, that's enough!" hissed Adam, and he smacked Sasha hard, and she burst into tears, and he had to take her outside.

Oh, I don't let on. People would think it were odd. That I knew he was already dead, and did nothing. Sometimes I even pretend to myself I didn't know, just to take away a little of that oddness.

I saw the actual moment he died. He grunted, turned from me towards the window, and sort of slumped. And in a moment he was gone. It didn't look so bad, it didn't look so frightening.

He'd closed his eyes, and I was grateful for that, I could carry on as if he were just sleeping, or shielding himself from the glare of that Mediterranean sun—I wouldn't have wanted to have closed them myself, that would have felt wrong, my skin crawls at the very thought of touching a dead man's eyes. But I didn't mind holding his hand. I took his hand.

And I pointed out bits of the Greek scenery to him. There wasn't much scenery, we were on a motorway, but I did my best. I chattered about Knossos, all the things we were going to see together. All the things we'd ever see. And I told him I loved him.

"I love you," I said; the very words, no substitutes, and this time he couldn't flinch, this time he couldn't back away, change the subject, leave the room or go and hide in the garden shed. "I love you," I said, and he was mine now, he couldn't help but listen; "I know we both thought I'd be the one leaving first, but I think it's better this way." It *was* better this way. His hand was still warm. His bare arm brushing against mine, it had started to tan. "I love you," I said again. I had run out of ways to say it. I let go of his hand, picked up that old guidebook he'd bought.

I'm not saying my husband's death was a good thing, that I'm glad it happened. But at last the suffering was over. His suffering, my suffering. Same difference.

It's not the way I would have chosen for him, death by euphemism. And yet, it makes me smile. It's a mistake, I think, to read too much into the way a person dies, that it in any way sums up the way they lived. James' death was silly. He was not a silly man. It was therefore an inappropriate death. But he'd had a sense of humour once, hadn't he? I'm sure of it, I remember it from back in those days of youth and wildness and sex. It's true, it hadn't peeped out of him in quite a long time. I am glad, at the very end, that he let it peep out once more in spite of himself.

I was glad it was quick. To save him the need for some long drawn out goodbye. To save him that last embarrassment.

When the doctors said I was dying, James refused to discuss it. Not with the doctors, and certainly not with me. He insisted we mustn't tell the children. We'd upset them. I said to him, "But they're going to find out sooner or later, aren't they?"

Now James is gone I could tell them. I could phone Marcia right now, and Adam too, I suppose. I haven't yet. I don't know why. I might do it tomorrow.

The doctors say I could go off at any time. I shouldn't be frightened. It could happen in my sleep. I don't want to die in my sleep.

It's a mistake, I think, to read too much into the way we die. But sleeping isn't right for me.

I wrote an ad for the personals column in the newspaper. I said that I was a widow with a dicky heart that could give up the ghost at any moment. And that I wanted to die in the arms of a young man. Oh, not in his arms, that's a euphemism. Not just a young man, either, a stud. I said I wanted to die with a stud's thingummy jammed high inside my whatsit. I wanted to die better than I'd lived.

I wrote it, rewrote it, replaced all the euphemisms I had put in. The newspaper published it, and put in lots of new euphemisms of their own, I hadn't even heard of some of them.

No one has called yet. But it's a big world, and there are lots of people out there. I have faith. I have faith someone will find me in time.

Because—will you excuse me? If I speak bluntly? Because death is a mean-spirited old cunt. And if she's coming for me, she can catch me with my knickers down.

And the old woman says:

- *One would never choose one's last words to be an embarrassed request to use the toilet. One would want something heroic and noble—or, at the very least, witty and memorable. But can it really matter? At the moment of death, who cares whether you shuffle off this mortal coil with a quip on your lips? Consider* **Famous Last Words** *(story 78, page 1363).*
- *What else could be with Grandad in the box? Turn to* **And This is Where We Falter** *(story 49, page 811) to find out.*
- *In* **The Pillow Menu** *(story 48, page 799), another elderly couple go on holiday. See whether they have a better time.*
- *If you too are in mourning, then I am so sorry. Consider* **Good Grief** *(story 39, page 647).*
- *Of course, grief is really just a form of love story, one of the sweetest and saddest there is. Turn to* **101 Heartbeats** *(story 101, page 1695).*

YOU'RE EITHER
VERY NEAR THE END,
OR SOMEWHERE IN THE MIDDLE,
OR RIGHT AT THE BEGINNING.

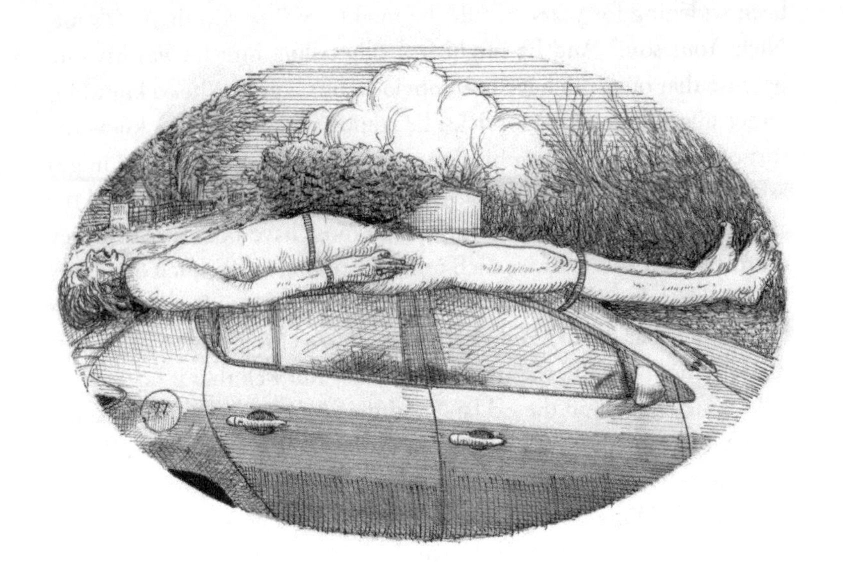

97
THE HOLLOWS

a

NICK BLAKE HADN'T liked his father, but in other respects he broadly supported the concept of fatherhood. If he sat in front of the telly, beer in hand, and watched a movie, and it was in some way about fathers and sons—and they all were really, weren't they? and so seldom about mothers, what was up with that?—if a movie were on, and there was some rift between a dad and his arsehole son, he'd always take the side of the dad over the arsehole—and when, in the final reel they'd be reconciled—and they always would, wouldn't they? and didn't that mean it could happen in real life?—then Nick would watch agog, with tears streaming down his face.

Sometimes, after seeing one of these movies, he'd felt the urge to phone his own father. Reach out to him, bridge the chasm that had been widening for years: "Dad," he might say, "are you there? It's me, Nick! Your son!" And he might feel silly telling him he was his son, because that ought to have been obvious, but how was he to know, his father might know lots of Nicks, he couldn't be expected to know the sort of people with whom his father would associate. His father might ask him how he was, and Nick would ask the same—and then feel the absurd urge to apologise, because there must have been a *reason* they didn't talk any more, or see each other any more, or like each other any more—he didn't want to be just another arsehole son! But he couldn't think what that reason could be. He could never remember. And so he might natter on to fill the silences, he knew full well that if he stopped talking silence was all there'd be—and then he'd have to find an excuse to get off the phone, quickly, *now*, now before the silence broke through—"Got to go, there's someone at the door, the cat needs feeding, it's Molly's bath time. Got to go, I am about to run out of words. You have drained all the words from me, and I am hollow."

So he'd had a system. He'd finish the movie, he'd finish his beer. He'd dry his eyes. Then he'd look at the clock, and give himself half an hour. Just to see if the urge to call his father would have faded by then. And if it hadn't, he'd give it half an hour more, and that usually did the trick.

b

Nick hadn't slept in days, and you might suppose he was thinking of his father. But the truth is, he didn't think of anything much. He just lay there in bed, on his back, still—and there were no thoughts inside him at all, there was *nothing* inside, the hollow was absolute.

And if a stray thought somehow did manage to creep in from somewhere—through the cracks in his skin, maybe, from somewhere outside, because surely not from within, Nick was a void where nothing could grow—if some lonely little thought crept in, Nick fancied he could hear it rattling around the emptiness, battening against the inner shell of his body, like a desperate housefly on a window pane. He'd listen to the thought knocking away trying to escape, until it did the decent thing, and gave up, and lay down, and died.

His wife, Charlotte, beside him, could sleep. Their daughter, Molly, in the next room, she could sleep. Everyone in the entire world could sleep except Nick.

At times it almost made him feel special.

c

As perplexing as the message was, no matter how grave its implications, it was good to hear someone criticise his father. At last—it was all getting too much to bear. There'd been a flurry of letters and condolence cards, and each one had told of how he had been a good man, or how he had been a kind man, and a special man. And the funeral, the coffin just lying there at the front, and everyone staring at it with such respect—a vicar spouting on about the impact his father had made upon the world, committing him to God's hands as if God could barely wait to get hold of him. Nick had done it too, he hadn't been able to stop himself; all these friends and colleagues and well-wishers he had never heard of coming up and saying how grateful they were his father had touched their lives—"Yes," Nick would say, "yes, indeed, we are all very lucky." And at night, in bed, the funeral done at last, Charlotte even, even Charlotte, saying to him so sleepily: "He was a good man, your dad." When he'd thought Charlotte had never liked him either. When Charlotte had always moaned if they'd had to visit him at Christmas.

But then, the day after the funeral, on the answering machine, the message. From the crematorium—"Your father won't burn," said some woman bluntly. "Come and collect him at the earliest opportunity."

d

"I'm sorry for your loss," said the woman, but she didn't sound sorry, and Nick rather liked that about her. She made a phone call. She tutted when she was forced to leave a message: "Jim, the Blake body needs picking up from the warehouse." She glared at Nick as if it were his fault Jim wasn't answering; Nick tried a smile, but this woman wasn't for thawing. "Sod it," she said, "I'll take you there myself. Let's just do it quickly, all right?"

They walked across the car park to the warehouse, and Nick struggled to find the right questions he should ask. "What seems to be the problem? Was there not enough heat, or was my father too damp, or…?" She seemed to ignore him, took out a heavy set of keys, pulled open the corrugated steel door and went inside. Nick followed.

There were lots of bodies, mostly propped up against the breeze-block walls. The woman checked her clipboard—"That's the one," she pointed. And Nick's first instinct was to say, no, that's the wrong man. Because the corpse was at least seven foot tall and altogether too thin—and it was odd but at that moment it was that mean thinness that seemed the more surprising. Then Nick realised that the body had been distended somehow, stretched out like a piece of chewing gum—and though the cheeks were sallow and the eyes were white, it was certainly the right face: an older, paler and decidedly deader version of Nick's own.

"It rather wasted our time, trying to cremate your father's body," said the woman. "Frankly, you should have warned us. Frankly, you should have read the small print." She rapped her knuckles against the naked corpse, and it let out a dull clang.

"He's metal?" said Nick.

"More than that," said the woman. "He's hollow too." And she felt for a catch just above Nick's father's exposed genitals, and gave a tug, and a hatch door fell open. His whole stomach swung aside, she slapped her hand against the inside walls to demonstrate it was nothing but an empty box. "Nothing," she said. "I mean, maybe there were some organs before the cremation. But if so, where's the ash?"

"I don't know," said Nick, and she nodded at that, as if she'd proved some point.

"We tried burning your father three times," she said. "Never even scorched him. That's time and fuel we could have spent on real flesh corpses, more deserving corpses."

"I didn't know," Nick heard himself say. "I'm so sorry."

The woman raised an eyebrow, she clearly didn't believe him. And Nick felt the rightness of that—what sort of son wouldn't realise his own father had no skin or bone? An arsehole son, that's what.

With practised efficiency the woman tipped Nick's father on to a trolley, and she wheeled him out to the car park. "Where's your vehicle, Sir?" she asked, and Nick indicated his little Mini Metro. "I've got some rope," she said. "We can tie him to the roof."

"Can't we just get him sitting in the back seat, or…?"

She laughed sourly. "It's a hunk of metal. It doesn't have hinges to it. If you think you can fold it up, be my guest." And Nick thought—he must have seen his father sit down at least once in his life, surely? Wasn't there a time his father had stooped to play with him when Nick had been a little boy, or sat him on his knee to read him a story? Maybe not. Probably not.

The body was heavy, but Jim was back from lunch, and his mate Jerry too, and between the four of them they heaved the corpse on to the roof of the car and secured it in position. The woman took most of the weight in the lifting, she was stronger than she looked. They laid the father on his stomach, the genitals were pressed fast against the back window but that couldn't be helped. Face downwards was good. Nick didn't want to see his father's face. The face stayed implacably calm, and showed not a hint of apology for all the trouble he was causing.

"I'm sorry," said Nick one last time, and the woman handed him a brown envelope.

It was an eight mile drive home, *and* through the town centre, *and* in rush hour—and Nick felt very embarrassed, and acknowledged the hooting of car horns with a wave and watery smile.

When he reached home he sat in the driveway for a good ten minutes and tried to cry, but he couldn't. He opened the brown envelope, and inside there was a bill, and he threw it away.

e

Nick brought indoors the body of his father. Charlotte was sympathetic but practical, just as she'd been when his father had died in the first place. "Let's find a place to put it," she said.

They tried standing Nick's father in the sitting room, face to the wall. "It looks as if he's sulking," said Nick, and Charlotte agreed, and so they turned him around so he was looking inwards, and that was even worse. They put him in the cupboard under the stairs, but he didn't quite fit, the elbows stopped them from getting the doors closed; he'd fit if they took out the vacuum cleaner, but as Charlotte said, "Then where are we going to put the vacuum cleaner?" They put him under the bed, but on one side his legs stuck out, on the other his head was revealed down to his white eyes.

"The pity is," said Charlotte, "that if we lived in a more temperate climate, like the south of France, somewhere the rain isn't such a bother, we could keep him in the garden." She mused on this for a while. "But we don't."

In the end the best plan was the entrance hall, flush against the wall. The downside was that as soon as you came home from work you'd see it, this stark reminder of death. But, as Charlotte pointed out, that also meant you quickly got it out of the way. From the moment you passed the corpse, the rest of the evening would just get better.

f

Charlotte admitted she had misgivings having her dead father-in-law displayed in the house, but she wanted Nick to understand she wasn't being selfish. She needed him to understand. No, but *do* you?" she asked again. Nick said he did.

Molly had just turned four years old, and the heftier of the child-rearing manuals told Charlotte it was high time that she should be exposed to the concept of death. An early appreciation of the limits imposed by mortality, the book insisted, forced the intelligent infant to narrow the parameters of its imagination and ambition. This, to be sure, was natural and healthy.

And so every Saturday Charlotte turned off the children's channel on the television, and sat Molly down in front of black and white movies made before the war.

"That man speaking," Charlotte would say, "the one with the monkey? He's dead now."

"When did he die?"

"Oh, long ago."

"What did he die of?"

"I don't know. And that man, getting out of the car. The fat one. He's dead too."

"Does the man with the monkey know that the man with the car is dead?"

"They're not dead in the story. Only in real life."

"Were they dead when they made the movie?"

"No. They died after."

"Did they know they were going to die?"

"Yes, I expect so. We all know we're going to die."

"Oh."

"The movie couldn't save them. Nothing could save them. Nothing can save any of us. The movie was made eighty years ago. Chances are, by now, everyone who worked on the movie is dead. All those people in the background with nothing to say, they're dead. The ones behind the camera, who built the sets and made the costumes, they're dead.

Dead, and gone, and they can never come back, and we'll never see them again."

"We're seeing them now," said Molly.

"And in another eighty years, probably much sooner, I'll be dead, and Daddy will be dead. You may be dead too, and if not, you'll be dying. This is important, Molly. Are you listening?"

"I want to hear the movie," Molly said.

Charlotte told Nick they would have to handle the fact Nick's father was now standing in the hallway very carefully.

"She might not even recognise him," said Nick. "Not all elongated and naked with his dick hanging out."

"Your daughter is smarter than you think," said Charlotte.

Charlotte told Molly to close her eyes, she wanted to show her something, and Molly got all excited, was it a present, was it a present? "Not exactly," said Charlotte, "this is something horrid." "It'll be all right, sweetheart," said Nick.

Molly opened her eyes. She stared in wonder. "It's Grandad!" she said.

"Yes," said Nick.

"No," said Charlotte. "This isn't Grandad. This is just an empty shell. This Grandad doesn't love you, he doesn't like you, he won't play with you or send you a card on your birthday."

That night in bed Charlotte perused the manual with a frown, then put it aside. "Maybe it's a good thing," she said. "Maybe this can work for us. But I need you to promise me. We mustn't sentimentalise your father. In Molly's hearing we must only refer to him as 'the dead man', or 'the corpse', or, at solemn moments, 'the late Mr Blake.'"

"Please turn off the light," said Nick.

She was soon asleep. Nick envied her for it.

g

When Charlotte got up to go to work, Nick kept his eyes closed so she'd think he was sleeping. Once he'd heard the front door close, he got up too. He went downstairs and made Molly a nice breakfast.

"What would you like to do today, sweetheart?" he asked her.

"Can I play with Grandad?"

They went into the hallway, and Molly stared up at the distended man.

"Lift me up," she said to her daddy, and Nick did as he was told. "Shake hands!" she said, and Nick supported her at the right height so she could put her little hand inside her grandfather's. It was so very tiny in comparison, Nick never usually bothered to look at his daughter's hands but he did so now and he thought they were just marvellous. Her fingers clawed tightly around her grandad's; Grandad, naturally enough, did not reciprocate. "How do you do?" said Molly. "And how do you do again?"

They played the hand shaking game for quite a while, and then Nick said he was tired, and put Molly back on the floor, and Molly didn't complain. After that she seemed to lose interest in Grandad, and was happy enough when Nick sat her in front of the television.

"I love you, Daddy," she said.

"That's nice," said Nick.

He checked the post. Most of it was for Charlotte. There was a brown envelope addressed to him, he opened it.

It was from the crematorium. It was another bill, 'for services rendered'. He was about to throw it away when he saw the sum of money they were after.

He tried phoning the crematorium. The line was constantly engaged.

He fumed.

He went into the television room. Molly looked up from a programme that was extolling the virtues of the letter 'g'.

"We have to go out, sweetheart," he said. "On a little adventure. Come on, I'll help you with your coat." Molly clapped her hands in glee. She liked adventures.

h

The woman behind the desk clearly recognised Nick, she watched him beadily as he approached her. He tried to be forceful, but it was a hard thing to pull off beneath her withering glare. He passed over the bill. "It says 'for services rendered'. But there were no services rendered."

"Are you saying we didn't burn your father's body, Sir?"

"You didn't successfully burn it, no."

"Are you saying Jim and Jerry didn't do the best they could? Do you want me to call them in here now? So they can defend themselves?"

"They didn't do a very good job."

"Do you want to say that to their faces, Sir? That what they do every day, no matter how grisly, no matter how repulsive, is something they're not even very good at? Jim, with his diplomas? Jerry, with his employee of the month badge? Sir, do you think you could do better?"

"I'm not paying the bill," said Nick. "It's twice what you charged me yesterday. And I'm going to stand here until the matter is resolved."

"That's up to you," the woman said, and began to read a magazine.

Molly yawned.

"I'm recently bereaved," said Nick. "You're exploiting me in an emotionally vulnerable state."

The woman ignored him. Molly tugged at her father's trouser leg, then sat down hard upon the floor.

"Everyone who comes here," said Nick, "we're *all* in emotionally vulnerable states. You should be ashamed of yourself."

The woman finished her magazine. She sighed, looked around. She looked at the phone, frowned to see that it was off its cradle. She put it back on its cradle. Immediately it began to ring, and the woman winced, and took it off the cradle once more. She sighed again, studied her fingers, the backs of her hands, her wrists, yawned. Looked, at last, straight at Nick.

"Since you're here anyway," said the woman. "Do you want to have sex or something?"

"What?"

"There's the break room out back," she said. "It's got a sofa."

"Why?"

The woman shrugged. "I don't know. The fleeting futility of life. The grim certainty of death. Because death is all around, each and every day, and it's cold, and it's relentless, and it's *boring*, I can't tell you just how boring it is. Because there are only so many chances we'll ever have to enjoy ourselves, and that's even fewer than you think, and not a single one of the corpses that get wheeled in here ever died of happiness. Because the sofa's soft and spongy. It's up to you."

"Yes," said Nick. "All right." Molly was dozing on the floor by his feet. He picked her up, and kissed her, and said, "Just sit in the waiting room, sweetheart. There are magazines for you to look through." The woman lifted the counter, and led Nick through a door marked, 'Staff Only'.

The sofa was indeed spongy. "I tell my clients, it sometimes helps to think of the chimneys outside belching the black ash of burned flesh high into the air," and Nick was surprised that she was right, that *did* help.

The woman didn't smile once throughout the entire process, but when it was done Nick kissed her on the cheek and she didn't seem to mind.

"I wasn't too long, was I, sweetheart?" he asked Molly, and Molly looked up at him and beamed and said she was quite all right, she'd been looking through a lovely brochure about coffins.

i

Nick stared up at the stolid face of his father, and tried to find some expression in it—anger, disappointment, forgiveness. "I'm sorry," he said. "All of these years, no matter what else you may have been, you were a faithful husband. You're a better man than me." And he realised he had no idea whether that was true.

j

Nick didn't know what woke Charlotte up, maybe it was parental intuition. Nick pretended to wake up too. They raced down the stairs, and they saw in the hallway that the floor was littered with thousands upon thousands of tiny white packing beads—and that Molly was amongst them, the little bits of polystyrene dribbling out of her mouth as she choked—that Grandad was looking down upon her and doing nothing to help.

Charlotte put her arms around Molly's waist and was trying to do the Heimlich manoeuvre, but wasn't she doing it wrong, shouldn't she be behind her, and there were too many polystyrene pieces, she'd never get them all out of Molly that way—and Molly was even now still stuffing more packing foam inside her mouth as if it were sweets—"Stop, stop!" Charlotte cried, but Molly wasn't listening—"Grab her arms!" said Nick, and Charlotte held Molly fast, and Nick had his fingers inside his daughter's mouth, he was plucking out every tiny bead he could find, digging down deep, making her gag, tugging out one last bit that wouldn't come free, it had to come free, he realised in time it was her tongue.

Then Molly was breathing, Molly was safe, and Charlotte was

carrying her up to her room, "It's all right," she kept saying, "it's all right."

Nick looked out across the floor at the sea of polystyrene beads and wondered where they could all have come from. From his father, obviously—but as giant as his stretched body was, there was still no way that they could all have fitted inside. Unless they had been compressed somehow, very *very* tightly. Yes, Nick thought vaguely, that would make sense.

He began to put all the polystyrene beads into rubbish sacks. He'd almost filled his fourth when Charlotte came down to join him.

"She's sleeping," she said.

Nick nodded. She helped him clear away the rest of the mess.

"That corpse is a death trap," she said.

Nick opened up his father's stomach cavity and looked inside. "He's empty now."

"Better safe than sorry," Charlotte said. So for the next hour or two they worked to make Nick's father's body childproof. They couldn't tell from which of his orifices the packing foam had leaked, so they sealed them all. They taped his mouth and nose, they put a bung up his backside and jammed a cork up his dick. And they wrapped wire around the stomach, and pulled it so tight that it cut a groove into the metal skin, and secured it with a double knot.

"We have to take better care of Molly," said Charlotte.

"Of course," Nick said, but she was already walking up the stairs to bed, and she didn't look back, as if this were all somehow his fault.

k

The next morning Nick asked Molly if she were all right and she smiled at him and laughed. "What would you like to do today?" he said.

She wanted to stay at home and play with Grandad, but Nick was mindful of the promise he had made to his wife, and now he'd had torrid sex with a stranger at a crematorium he decided he should try in all other ways to be a conscientious husband. "Let's go to the park," he said. "Is there a park nearby? I bet there's a park nearby. If so, let's go to it."

There was a park nearby. Nick bundled Molly up nice and warm, made her put on gloves and a scarf, and felt quite the responsible father. He made them both sandwiches—"We can have a little picnic," he said—and he made sure to cut the crusts off Molly's because she didn't like crusts.

The park was bleak and largely deserted. There were some swings, but the seats were caked with mud. There was a bench marked in memoriam for some poor dead sod. On the bench sat an old woman on her own and she was smoking and shouting and crying. There was a river. "Let's go to the river," said Nick, and Molly agreed.

And they stood at its bank, and ate a sandwich, and shivered in the cold. The river tried its very best to flow, but the water was thick and black and shit.

Molly asked, "Where does the river flow to?", and Nick said that it went out to the sea.

"Do you think all those little droplets know where they're going?"

"No. Yes. I don't know."

"If they knew where they were going, that'd make them feel better, wouldn't it?"

"Yes."

Molly bent down by the river and told it not to worry, there was something big and magical for it to look forward to.

"Can we feed the ducks?"

"Yes."

Because there were ducks in the water. They looked perfectly pissed off to be there, as if they too had thought a day at the park might be fun and relaxing.

Molly took off the cheese from her second sandwich, then broke up the bread into little pieces. The ducks quacked in excitement, and slurped their way through the mud water over to her. When she threw the first scrap there was a flurry of wings and beaks. Molly laughed. "There's no need to fight," she said. "There's enough for everyone!"

Nick removed the cheese from his sandwich too. He threw clumps of his bread into the water. The ducks ignored it. So he threw bread directly at them. The ducks swam away to avoid it.

"Hey," said Nick. "Hey!"

"They prefer my bread, Daddy," said Molly, with a smile.

"But it's *all* my bread," Nick told the ducks. "Her bread, it's *my* bread, it's all mine. Hey!" And he broke a larger piece off the crust, and threw it hard.

The crust hit a duck upon the head, and Molly laughed. But the crust must have been sharper than it looked, or the throw must have been very keen—either way, it didn't bounce off the duck's head—instead it *stuck* there—and then there was a bead of blood welling around the point of entry, and it was too red and it was too thick—the shard of crust had cracked the duck's skull.

The duck's eyes seemed to bulge. It panicked, fluttered its wings. And the blood was spouting now, there was a whole arc of it raining down on to the stagnant river like a fountain. And the duck seemed to scrabble about for hands so it could press them upon the wound and staunch the flow, and you could see the horrified realisation cross the duck's face, B*ut I don't have any hands*, it thought, *I'm just a fucking duck*, and at this it gave a strangled squawk of terror that was all too human, and keeled over onto its side dead.

"Oh dear," said Nick.

The little ducklings looked confused. They nudged their mother's body. Some chattered, as if it were all just a game.

"Can I go home and play with Grandad now?" said Molly. "I'm bored."

"Yes," said Nick. "Let's go home. And you can do what you like."

1

"Do you want me to lift you?" asked Nick, but Molly said that was quite unnecessary. She pressed hard with both hands under the ribcage, and then pulled herself up. The left knee was her first step, the second was in the testicles. "Careful, careful!" said Nick, he'd get it in the neck if Charlotte came home to find Molly had hurt herself—but Molly cheerfully called out that she knew exactly what she was doing. And so it seemed. She reached up to the shoulders and dug her nails into the metal skin, then climbed still further—now she'd reached the summit, she draped herself across the bald head, her hands tight around the throat so she wouldn't fall off, and laughing hard as if she were performing the cleverest trick in all the world.

"I love you, Grandad," she said. She looked at Nick. "And I like you too."

She started fiddling with the tape pulled over Grandad's mouth. Nick warned her that Mummy had gagged Grandad for a reason, be careful, you *will* be careful, won't you? And Molly winked, and it seemed such a peculiarly adult thing for her to do, and he shut up, he was out of his depth.

"Just a little hole," she said, "just wide enough," and Nick heard a faint rumble from deep within his father's body, as if a can of drink was being dispensed from a vending machine. Out of the hole in the gag appeared a single polystyrene bead. Molly pulled it free. She put it into her mouth and chewed it as delicately as you like.

"Do you want one?" she asked her father. Nick said no. Oh, come on, there are plenty!—she held out a fresh little white strip that had popped out to replace the first. Nick put it to his nose. He sniffed it. Molly nodded, egging him on.

It was foamy on the tongue. It melted. It tasted like chicken.

m

When Nick set out in the car the next morning, he actually thought he was going shopping. Charlotte was working from home that day, and so could look after Molly whilst he ran errands. He was worried that Molly might get up to games her mother wouldn't approve of—she'd become quite expert at scurrying up and down the whole length of her grandfather's dead body like a squirrel on a tree—but Molly whispered that she knew the value of discretion. That they both had things they wanted to keep secret.

It was only when he refused to take the right turn towards the supermarket that Nick realised where he was really going.

He had to wait before the woman came to the reception desk. At last she appeared, straightening her skirt, and the customer who accompanied her looked both mournful and sweaty. "Hello, yes?" she said to Nick.

"I received another bill."

"Yes?"

"It came this morning."

"And?"

"I just thought. After what we did. That maybe." She just stared at him. "It's gone up," he said.

"Interest," she said, flatly.

He said, "What we did was a mistake, and it isn't going to happen again."

She led him to the back room. She'd made it up really nicely, there were scented candles everywhere.

She told him to think of all the corpses lined up for cremation next door. How much would they give for just another moment of life?

How much more, if that moment could be spent fucking? And there they were, rotting, and here they were, fucking, and maybe not for long, but now, at least for now, they were the better off.

Afterwards he felt so calm and drowsy. It had been so long since he had slept, and he could now curl up next to this strange woman and drift away. Oh, it would be delicious—"No time for that! Up you get!" she said, and so he did. "And you'd better settle your account soon," she went on, "or we'll take you to court."

Nick said, "I don't even know your name."

She said, "It's better without names."

Nick said, "But you know my name."

She said, "But I don't care." And then she got back behind her desk, and read her magazine.

n

During the actual moment the sex was guilt-free. It wasn't that he didn't think of Charlotte, or of their marriage, or of the family they had created, or of the home they had built. If anything, all of that was an anchor, it was what brought him down to earth and stopped him floating away. He was grateful for them. They kept him safe.

One night he got up from bed and went to the bathroom. He stared at his reflection in the mirror, looking for any sign of remorse. "I don't like you," he said. The reflection didn't care. It stared right back, implacable, shameless, smug.

He hadn't intended to cut deep. But because there was blood just under the surface it didn't mean the hollows weren't lurking further down. He looked at himself in the mirror once more—"No, I really don't like you"—and that's when he drove the nail scissors into his arm, hard, *fast,* he wanted to see that guiltless face wince.

It didn't wince. Or not enough, anyway. And there was blood everywhere now. Just as well he was over the sink! That had been a good plan! Maybe he should stop digging. Maybe that would be a good plan too. He thought of his father, and of that perfectly smooth, perfectly empty cavity inside his body—and he said, what the hell, and carried on.

He couldn't find that hollow space, and it was annoying, because he knew it had to be somewhere. He wondered whether he should call an ambulance. "No," he said, and the mirror reflection agreed with him. It was the first thing they'd found in common all night. "You know, you're not so bad," he told himself, and himself gave a big, cheesy grin, and said that he was glad to see at last he was coming to his senses.

He wrapped up the arm with a towel. He went downstairs, softly softly, he didn't want to wake the house. In the hallway he said hello to his father, and held up his bloody arm ruefully. He wasn't sure his father understood.

His arm was hurting rather badly now, and he supposed that was to be expected. The pain gave him a marvellous sense of clarity. Right then he saw what was wrong with his life, and how it could be better. It was obvious! He decided to write a letter to his wife to tell her exactly how he was feeling. He thought it would be a confession, but it came out much angrier than that. Into that letter he poured everything that he had inside him, and he wasn't hollow at all, it turned out he was full to bursting. This is what he learned—that all this time he'd thought he loved her, he actually hadn't! Everything was her fault, who would have thought it? And wasn't this a good thing to realise, and if it had taken his father's death to show him the truth of that, wasn't it a good thing his father had died too? Everything had a meaning. It *was* a good thing. He was pleased. One day he was going to die too. Just like his father. And he hoped it would be as helpful to Molly as his father's death was now being to him, maybe she'd realise she didn't love some future husband, maybe it would give her the impetus to change her own life in time. So that when *she* died (perhaps yielding marital revelations to children of her own in the process, really there was no reason this procedure couldn't go on ad infinitum down the generations) she'd know enough to make sure that that husband was no longer a part of her world, just as Nick now knew when he died he wanted Charlotte to have long since stopped being any part of his. He wanted Charlotte gone. He wanted her out. He wanted to waste no more of his life breathing her air, seeing her face, hearing her voice, sharing precious seconds with someone he couldn't stand the sight of any longer.

He wrote until dawn, and his arm had stopped hurting, and the towel had dried. He looked over the finished letter. It was perfect. He would give it to his wife immediately. It was perfect. It was twenty-eight pages. It was perfect, but it did go on a bit. He would give it to his wife, after just a little edit. It was perfect, but he hadn't quite finished it yet.

The next night he waited for Charlotte to fall asleep, and then he stared at her for a while, filling his head with an antipathy that seemed to him both literate and succinct. He cut into his arm a bit, just to sharpen his grammar, and then went back to work on another draft of the letter, and this time he removed all the unnecessary words, and all the embarrassing bits, and all the wheedling self-justification, and all the parts that felt insincere, and replaced them with something brighter and wiser and better. And by the time the sun rose he had managed to cut down twenty-eight pages of bloated prose to a lean and taut forty-four.

o

So, this is how Nick fills his days:

He says good morning to his dead father. He makes Molly breakfast. He watches her eat. He lets her loose on her grandfather, he loves the way she scales the heights of him so effortlessly, it's like she's defying gravity, it's like she's a wild animal. He then does a spot of writing. The edited version of his forty-four page draft comes to seventy-one pages, the seventy-one page version gets honed down to one hundred and three. And each time the letter feels more urgent and meaningful and he's starting to feel very proud of it, and he fantasises that after he's given it to Charlotte and shattered her heart he may get it published somewhere. When he needs to take a break he'll go to the bathroom, and try to find out where his hollows might be. It's not in his thigh, but he may start on the chest soon, that could be promising. And when he wants to take a break from *that*, he can drive over to the crematorium for a spot of adultery. "I'm going out!" he calls to Molly, gripping his towel to him and keeping his voice level so she won't think he's in pain. "You just do as your grandad tells you!" He knows it's wrong he's spending so little time with his daughter, but he's never pretended he's any better a father than he is a husband. Besides, she's with Grandad, Grandad will look after her.

It may not be the perfect life—but it has some structure to it, and that alone is very calming, and for the first time in such a long while Nick wonders whether he might even be happy.

p

"Have you lost your parents?" Nick asked the woman in the crematorium one day.

They were lying together on the sofa, an old blanket wrapped around them. Nick didn't think it was a very clean blanket. It smelled of dogs. He'd been about to ask whether the crematorium owned a dog, but somehow the dead parent question had popped out instead.

She looked at him. "Because you think that would make my job easier?"

Nick said, "Maybe. A bit. Or harder. A bit. Maybe."

She didn't reply immediately, and so Nick played with her hair in a manner he hoped she'd interpret as a conciliatory gesture.

"No, they're not dead yet," said the woman. "But Dad's pretty ill with the cancer, he doesn't know when to give up. And Mum is fat and smoking, I can't see her going on forever."

"I'm sorry."

"I don't know whether I'll cremate them myself when the time comes."

"Because you'll be too close?"

"No. Who's going to pay me?"

She was quiet for a minute or two. She said, "Maybe I'll fall apart. I think I'd like that. For it to mean something and be special. But they're not special. And I'm not special. It's no great tragedy when your parents die. They all do, sooner or later. Everyone acts as if they're the first to ever go through it. It makes me laugh. Every single day thousands of people die, and most of them are parents. It's the least special thing in the world. Do you know what's special? Every day your parents *don't* die. Every day they're not dead. You should throw your arms around them and hold them tight, and feel them quivering in your grip, and treat it like a fucking miracle."

Nick said, "Is this a dog blanket? I'm not complaining. I like dogs."

She turned over, and rolled on top of him, and they fucked once more. And he held her tight and felt her quiver in his grip, and he supposed that meant she was alive, but he didn't know for sure, she could have been faking it.

q

The thing is, it hurts him to watch Molly play. His daughter and his father have found a bond that he has never enjoyed with either one of them. But he knows he ought to watch, and he makes himself do it. Because Molly won't be a little girl forever, soon she'll be at primary school, and then she'll be a teen, and then she'll be an adult and she won't want to know him any more—all these little versions of his daughter, and no sooner will he get used to one than she'll be replaced by another, all these Mollys dying one by one. Is it even worth the effort to form a bond with this Molly, shouldn't he just cut his losses and wait for the next—because she is definitely growing up, he can see the changes in her day by day, she'll be too big to scamper up the body of her grandfather and lie spread-eagled on his bald dead head and swing him backwards and forwards like a rocking horse; backwards and forwards, over and over, it makes him feel quite giddy to see it.

It was when the letter to Charlotte pushed past the seven hundred page mark that Nick finally admitted that maybe it was lacking the focus it required. One morning he went down to the breakfast table and found that she'd left him a letter of her own. It said, "Whatever strange crisis you're going through since your father died, I can no longer be a part of it. I am leaving you. Goodbye." And Nick thought, yes, clear and direct, *that's* the way to do it.

r

The next time Nick felt a craving for sex he found a new receptionist sitting behind the crematorium service desk. She was bored and dismissive, but in all other respects entirely dissimilar to the woman he had been shagging.

When he asked for the other receptionist, she just shrugged. She'd gone. No, didn't know where. No, she wouldn't be coming back. "Is there any way I can contact her?" Nick asked. "It's funny, but I think she may have been my best friend." And he felt a shudder of grief. "Could you at least tell me her name?"

The new receptionist said, "The old receptionist only shared her name with special people."

"Did she share her name with you?"

The new receptionist smiled. "Oh yes," she said. "It's lovely."

In the years to come Nick would think back on the old receptionist and pretend that she was dead. It was easier that way. She had fallen into an open grave and broken her neck, she had cremated herself by mistake in the oven. She had drunk a bottle of formaldehyde, and now her body was pristine and unchanging and beautiful forever, beautiful even though in life she had been somewhat plain.

"Can I have sex with you instead?" asked Nick, and the new receptionist said no, and advised him to pay his outstanding invoice before she sent the heavies around.

s

The heavies arrived nice and early the very next morning. They rang the bell, and waited patiently on the front step for Nick to open the door. They smiled and explained who they were; they offered Nick the option to pay his debt, and when he refused, asked permission to enter the house so they could beat the living shit out of him. They carried baseball bats and there were top hats perched upon their heads; they wore knuckledusters and respectful black suits.

The heavies stopped short when they saw Nick's father looming over them in the hallway.

"Is this the body that's causing the financial dispute?"

"It is," said Nick. "As you can see, it's hardly been cremated at all."

"You've got a point," said the heavies. "Don't let them push you around. You should stand up for your customer rights."

They started work on Nick's kneecaps, but the joke was on them.

"I don't even feel it!" screamed Nick with laughter. "I can't feel anything! Is this how you expect me to pay, you stupid bastards?"

The heavies said, "There's no need to be rude, Sir."

At length Molly came down the stairs. "What are you doing to my daddy?"

Nick told her to run along and play, the heavies wouldn't want a little girl watching them.

"But I want to play with Grandad," she said.

The heavies said, "We don't mind if the little girl wants to watch. But you're her father, what do you think?" Nick gave permission for Molly to watch his beating for a little while, so long as she wasn't a nuisance to the men. "Lovely little girl you've got, we've got little kids ourselves, don't they just break your heart?"

The men didn't break Nick's heart, but they did break two of his fingers, and possibly a rib.

"I think that's quite enough now," said Molly, at last. "I mean it."

The heavies looked at each other. "Can we just give him one last crack on the head if we're quick?"

Molly considered. "Just the one," she said, "but then you be on your way."

They cracked Nick over the head, and Nick thought that it split open like a piñata, and there was blood, and then there was no blood, and then there were polystyrene beads.

"That is enough," the heavies agreed. "We've quite literally knocked the stuffing out of him." And Nick wanted to thank them—he was hollowed out, at last he was hollowed out, he'd found the emptiness he'd been searching for. He wanted to offer them a tip, but wasn't quite sure of the etiquette.

The heavies said their goodbyes, and tipped their top hats in unison, and Nick giggled, they were so charming and funny. And he looked across to Molly to see if she were giggling too, and she wasn't.

"You saved me," said Nick. "You saved me, there's my brave little girl." But she wasn't such a little girl any longer, was she? Molly picked up one of the polystyrene beads that had fallen from Nick's skull. She put it up to her mouth, stuck out her tongue. She touched the bead gently with the very tip. She pulled a face.

"Don't you like it?" said Nick. "You prefer Grandad's?" He tried to give her a hug, he realised how much he wanted a hug, but Molly pushed him away, maybe it was all the blood he was covered in.

"You should go upstairs and have a lie down," said Molly. "You look as if you need a rest."

"But I'm not sleepy," said Nick.

"Oh, for Heaven's sake," said Molly. "Haven't you caused enough trouble? Why can't you just do as I tell you? I want to spend some time alone with your father."

"All right," said Nick. He picked up one of the beads, and popped it into his mouth. It didn't taste *that* bad. Maybe a little bitter. He turned away, and behind him he heard his daughter huff and puff as she heaved her bulk up her grandfather's torso.

t

He lay on the bed for hours, he didn't know for long—Molly hadn't told him when he was allowed to get up. Day turned to evening turned to night. And he tried to sleep just as she'd instructed, he closed his eyes and didn't move a muscle and pretended that's what sleep was.

When the crash came he refused at first even to open his eyes, it had nothing to do with him. He listened for a second crash. If there were a second crash, perhaps he should investigate. There was no second crash.

He lay there for another hour or two, and wondered what that first crash might have been.

"Molly?" he called out at last. "Molly, did you hear the crash?" And he got out of bed and went downstairs, he hoped she wouldn't mind.

There was another sound then, and it was something like a shriek, and Nick irritably wondered where the hell all these strange new noises were coming from, and then he supposed the shrieking was probably coming from him. And it was a single word that was being shrieked, over and over and over.

"Molly," he cried, "Molly, Molly,"—because his father's body had toppled over, the dead body had finally fallen face forward, Molly had been playing on her grandfather and rocked him too hard and brought him crashing down. And he'd brought down Molly too—Molly—look, there were her little legs poking out from beneath her dead grandad's midriff.

No, he told himself. No. Remember. You're hollow, you don't feel this. You're hollow now.

And so that was all right.

And maybe Molly was safe! Because maybe Molly was hollow too. Maybe she hadn't been damaged when the metal corpse had collapsed on her, maybe she had a metal shell just like her grandfather and her cold unfeeling Dad, he would lift the heavy weight off her and she'd be there giggling at the sport of it—maybe—oh, but no—no—because there was so much blood, there was blood everywhere, that put paid to that little theory.

Nick lifted up his father and looked down at the crushed body of his daughter beneath.

He wanted to do the right thing. He'd have given her mouth-to-mouth resuscitation but he couldn't be sure where her mouth was.

u

When he called the crematorium a pert answering machine told him that he was blacklisted and laughed.

V

The park looked different at night. Its bleakness was softened by the dark. It looked like a happy place, and Nick felt happy to be there.

The moon was out, and the river sparkled and the water seemed fresh, and the flow of the current was strong.

Nick carried his family to the river bank. His father was light in his arms. His daughter sat high upon his shoulders, her dead arms tied in a knot around his neck.

He lay them side by side on the grass so they could look up at the stars. And he lay down with them too.

To his father he said, "Thank you for giving me some extra time to be a son."

To his daughter, "Thank you, that even for the shortest time, I was a father."

The words sounded trite, they were lies, but he spoke them regardless and the speaking made them true.

And in the darkness his father was no longer a giant but a frail and gentle old man, and his daughter was still beautiful.

He lowered his father into the river. He bobbed lightly on the surface—"Wait a minute!" Nick laughed, as the current tried to pull him away too soon.

He opened up the door to his father's chest and swung it wide open. With tender care he placed his daughter inside.

Nick wished he'd kept all the polystyrene packing, Molly would rattle around that enormous cavity if he weren't careful. He padded the space with pages from his letter, he screwed up the paper and made soft little balls to keep his daughter safe. He didn't stop until every last scrap was used up.

He kissed her then, and in the dark he seemed to find a forehead, and his lips didn't come away sticky.

He kissed his father too, and he thought it would be embarrassing, and it wasn't.

He let the current take them then; it tugged the bodies away, and Molly was riding on her grandfather, and Nick was sure she would love that, and Grandad was keeping Molly safe, he would love that too.

w

And he watched at the bank as the little boat began its long journey to the sea—and Nick suddenly wanted them back, he wasn't ready to say goodbye yet, and there was room inside his father's chest cavity for him too, there was room for *everybody*—he could jump into the river and swim and catch up with it, he could climb aboard, they could set out on the voyage together.

But he didn't chase it. This had been a perfect moment, maybe the only perfect one he'd ever had, and he had such a habit of spoiling everything, isn't that all he ever did? Just let it be.

x

The hallway looked bare without his father standing there.

He sat on the floor and at last he cried. The sheer force of all the tears made his head ache, but it was a good ache—he felt light and muzzy and he wanted to sleep.

y

Charlotte was under the covers and snoring gently. The lights were on, she must have been trying to stay awake for him. He stared at her. Like Goldilocks in the little bear's bed—he had forgotten how beautiful she was, could he have forgotten so easily?

She stirred when he got in beside her.

"You came back to me," he whispered.

"I did."

"Thank you."

There was silence then, as Nick waited. She would ask him why his father wasn't in the hallway, why Molly wasn't tucked up safe in bed. And what that large thick bloodstain could possibly be at the foot of the stairs.

And the seconds went by, and still she didn't ask.

"I love you," he said, and he reached for her hand. She squeezed it.

The silence no longer felt awkward, it was peaceful, it was so full of peace.

Maybe she would never ask. Was that even possible? Maybe she would never ask the questions that would bring the whole world crashing down about their ears. Because sometimes you need to hold on to the tragedies of your past just to give them meaning. And sometimes—sometimes, it's just right to let them go. You have to let go of the past, if you want any chance of a future.

She kissed him on the lips, and it wasn't an invitation to make love, but an invitation for something better yet, maybe, maybe.

And she was asleep. He turned off the light. He cuddled close. Her body seemed so warm, and so *full*, there were no hollows to it. And the rhythm of her breath rising and falling, the regular ease of slumber, was a comfort to him. If he could just match her rhythm, he might follow her.

Tomorrow there would be the questions. Or tomorrow there would be no questions. Or tomorrow there would be new questions, ones he couldn't even imagine. But right now there was the darkness, the feel of his wife's body, and rest. And at last Nick stopped clinging to the side of the world, and closed his eyes, and let go.

z

zzzzz

And the old woman says:

- *It is quite a thing to forgive without recrimination. Contrast with the married couple in* **A View From the Clifftop** *(story 20, page 327).*
- *The hero of* **Good Grief** *(story 39, page 647) learns how to mourn in a radically different way. Check to see which method will be of more use to you, next time you have to do it.*
- *Why not try something lighter? Another man watches as the greatest relationship of his life is put to flames. Find out what it is in* **Some Unusual Facts About Laurel and Hardy You May Enjoy** *(story 60, page 1013).*
- *There must be a lot of free space afforded by the hollows. Find out how it can be put to the best use in* **Mummy's Little Miracle** *(story 86, page 1477).*
- *If this story wasn't dark enough for you, really and truly, you can go darker still with* **Baby Sick** *(story 66, 1137). On your own head be it.*

98
THE CURTAIN FALLS

I AM DYING, BUT THERE are compensations.

Firstly, I have already read my obituary, and I think it's rather fine. It pays tribute to my distinguished career in glowing terms, and concludes that I am 'arguably one of the finest actors ever to walk upon the post-war stage.' I like that use of 'arguably', it sounds so modest, and yet doesn't brook argument at all. I also like the use of words like 'neglected' and 'undervalued', and the phrase 'criminally undervalued'. I did not write my own obituary, but I did suggest a few areas that the journalist might like to pay particular attention. I have spoken to the editor of *The Stage and Television Today*, and he has given me no reason to believe the obituary will be trimmed.

Secondly, I have left in my will a grant to my old boarding school, the money to be put towards the creation of an award given out every prize day. It is to be presented to the boy judged that year to have made the most notable contribution towards the excellence of theatre, and there will be words to that effect inscribed on a silver cup, and my name will be upon the cup too. I am hoping it will encourage some resurgence of interest in drama at my alma mater; when I last visited, a few years ago now, their Christmas production of *Twelfth Night* was desultory at best. I think it's important to give back. I have had a long and successful career—even if not quite as successful as my talents promised, but hey ho—and if I can make some children benefit from that, and have good reason to thank my name, all to the good.

And thirdly, and finally, and most frivolously—I am looking forward to those final moments when your whole life flashes before your eyes. For all these years I have given pleasure to untold thousands of audiences, sitting in rapt and respectful silence as I dazzle them with my arts. The one person, alas, who has never had the opportunity to see me on stage is I myself. But now, at last, as my entire existence passes in front of me, I can afford to settle back and experience my greatest successes, one after the other, watching from a front row seat.

I am especially looking forward to my celebrated performance of King Lear, as given at Hornhaven Playhouse in the summer of 1979. We had a full house every night, and people travelled far and wide to see me, some travelled from as far away as Shaddock. It wasn't a perfect production by any means, and Anna Walker-Smith made a rather adenoidal Cordelia, but the critical notices regarding me were especially warm. *The Hornhaven Gazette* said I was 'definitive'. Bless.

It's my heart that's killing me. But I never take much notice of it. It's not giving me any pain.

It starts to happen. I can feel it. I am not afraid. I am prepared.

I prop myself up high on my pillows, and watch as the house lights go down and the curtains pull apart.

My childhood is unremarkable. As I play with my school chums at hide and seek, cowboys and Indians, cricket, you can see my talent is there, all that imagination, that innate sensitivity. But it is as yet without discipline. I resist the urge to shout out and tell my younger self to project, but I doubt he'll be able to hear me. It doesn't matter; this is what my three years of voice training at RADA will be for.

It's nice to see my parents again, though they are not quite as I remember them. My father, I thought, was taller than that—but I suppose all performers look shorter close up than you expect; oh, that season I worked with Larry Olivier at the National, and my shock on finding out he was a borderline dwarf! I hadn't realised my mother had such a lantern jaw.

First kisses, first sex. Some of the girls I vaguely recall. Most I don't.

It's not until I get my first job, as Merriman in *The Importance of Being Earnest*, with ASM and light understudy duties, that I recognise something is wrong. Merriman isn't a major character in *The Importance of Being Earnest*, he's just a butler who turns up once in a while to announce the arrival of gentry and dispense cucumber sandwiches; it takes until act three before I get enough of a glimpse of Merriman to assess him properly.

The actor playing Merriman isn't me. Or, rather—the actor playing *me* isn't me.

My heart may be weak, but my brain is as sharp as ever, thank you very much. I recognise him, vaguely. I know I've seen him before. I think maybe I've even worked with him. But it's been a long time, and it takes me past the curtain call and into that first night party where I felt up Angela Dunstall before I'm able to put a name to the face.

And then it hits me, hard—and there is a coldness on my heart, and I think that's it, I'm bowing out early, I'm going to die right here and now of shock, or disappointment, or simply rage. I breathe deeply, and slowly. I steady myself.

I get out of bed. I pace a bit. I'm not going to die, not like this. No death allowed until I get this matter sorted out.

To discover that I'm not seeing my life pass before my eyes accurately is galling enough; it's just a reconstruction, this is someone's *interpretation* of it. But to realise that I've been so woefully miscast, that the actor who is representing me in my dying moments is so grossly unsuited to the job—it feels like a calculated insult.

Because it is Nicholas Milton, the very same Nicholas Milton I worked with for an entire season of weekly rep back in 1978, the same Nicholas Milton who was my enemy. He looks a bit older, yes, a bit greyer, certainly—but it's him, it's him, it's him.

I think I'm going to be sick. I'm not sick. I need all the strength I can muster.

Nicholas Milton was a very bad actor.

I think I shall be remembered for a certain generosity I display towards fellow performers. I do not call someone a bad actor lightly. I accept that good actors can have bad performances in them; they can be miscast, they can find themselves out of their depth, they can lose their way in rehearsal because of insensitive direction or unflattering costume choices. Anna Walker-Smith may have given the world a Cordelia stymied by adenoids, but the following week her Lady Sneerwell in *The School for Scandal* was perfectly adequate. Even I myself—I accept that I may have got the wrong end of the stick with *Waiting for Godot*, though I do maintain that at least my particular portrayal of Estragon kept the audiences amused.

But Nicholas Milton was a very bad actor; more than that, he was the worst actor I ever worked with; more than that, he was the *only* bad actor I ever worked with, all the others excelled in comparison.

Alan St John cast him in the 1978 summer season, but I do not blame Alan. I always told Alan I'd leave all the casting up to him—if he wanted any help he could ask, but I had every faith in his abilities. Alan took me at my word and never asked. Every year, around May time, he'd give me a ring—he'd say, "Dear heart, are you free for another spell treading the boards under the thumb of yours truly?" He was joking, of course—I was never under his thumb; Alan may have nominally been my director, but in rehearsal he always looked to me for guidance. We'd do a season of eight plays in weekly rep, the whole commitment lasting two and a half calendar months; two weeks of preliminary rehearsals, followed by a block of performances, acting the latest show in the evening, breaking in the next one during the day.

I'd say to Alan, "I shan't commit yet, something better may turn up," and that was my little joke too really, I always kept myself free for a St John season, he and I went back such a long way. I'd ask him whether he wanted me to give my King Lear to the masses, and some years he'd say it was too soon after the last one, we didn't want the audience to take it for granted—and some years he'd say yes.

And each season Alan would cast new actors into the troupe, some straight out of drama school. He knew the value of fresh blood, that these baby-faced hopes might be stars of the future. He knew too that when I wasn't on stage giving it my all the audience would need something young and pretty to look at.

I thought nothing of Nicholas Milton at first. He was just another juve, a bit wet behind the ears, a bit gauche—bless their hearts, I *liked* meeting the juves, how I'd tease them the first days of rehearsal, I'd instruct them on all their supernumerary duties which involved making me tea and calling me Sir, until, laughing, Alan would tell them I was joking.

They'd come to the rehearsals with lots of things they'd learned in class, of course, but practical experience would soon drum that out of them. You can't learn how to act from a book, or from a 'workshop environment'—you stand up on stage before a crowd of strangers, with nothing more than a doublet and hose and spotlighting for protection, and you soon find out the hard way when they're enjoying themselves and when they're not. There is no sound more deathly, I tell you, than the sound of an audience that's bored. You stare into the darkness, you can't see anyone out there because the lights blind you a little, but you can *hear* them—you can hear how still they become, how numbed they are, how in each cough and rustle of sweet paper they long only for the interval and a chance to escape. It's the sort of silence that any good actor dreads. It's the sort of silence that gives you nightmares.

Nicholas Milton was all fancy theories. He told me, I think it was on the first day even, he told me that in order to act our parts successfully we had to discover some inner truth to the characters. I told him, quite amiably I thought, that the most important thing we had to do was to face out front, talk loudly, and not bump into the furniture. And if we could get the odd laugh now and again, that was a bonus. He smiled at me then, and I remember his smile well, it was wide and friendly. I think, looking back, that smile was the best bit of acting he ever did.

Those first few days of rehearsal went well. It was a season Alan wanted my Lear, and of course that suited me like an old glove—and it was nice for the other actors too, there was a ready-made production they could fit around. And in breaks, in the green room, if the cast had done well, I'd sit in my armchair and treat them with a few anecdotes about my life on the stage. They were funny stories, I could always make them laugh, and I'd tell them of times I'd worked with Ralphie Richardson, or Johnny Gielgud, back in the days when none of us were knights. And if they listened closely, the clever actor would realise there were useful lessons to be gleaned from these anecdotes too, handy little instructions that would give a juve something to feed off when *he* had to be on the stage.

I'll admit, I enjoyed telling stories in the green room more sometimes than I did the actual acting. Those young faces, so full of spirit and idealism, with years of performances ahead of them, of Restoration comedies and Feydeau farces and Lears of their very own—they'd look up at me, they'd hang on my every word. And I liked that old armchair too. It had been officially mine since the season of '74 or '75—it was the only comfortable chair there, really, all the others were the plastic sort you'd get in schools or village halls—and we'd been doing a rehearsal of *King Richard II*, and I'd been especially good in the first-half run-through, and as we traipsed into the green room to put on the kettle and have some char Martin Dempster (who was playing Bolingbroke) pulled out the armchair and waved his hands over it most amusingly, and said, "Your throne, my liege!" And we all laughed, and I played up to it, of course, and I sat down in it with all due pomp and ceremony, and from that point on it became *my* chair, at the very top of the room, and there I would tell my stories and make jokes with the cast and dispense advice.

I remember that first day of rehearsal, and it may have been before Nicholas Milton came out with that arse about inner truth, but it may have been after—and there I was, I was telling them all some anecdote about my time in the London West End and how I once met Sir Terence Rattigan. And then, even before I'd properly reached the end of it, Milton started speaking. And I thought for a moment he was building upon my anecdote, trying to explain it to his fellows, and that was bad enough—I don't need any *help*, thank you very much—but then I realised that no, worse, he was telling an anecdote of his own! This scrap of a kid who hadn't even *done* anything yet! I gave him enough rope to hang himself. I let him finish his story, trivial as it was. His fellow actors laughed politely. And then I continued with another story, a better one, one of my all-time classics. Milton didn't seem put out by this. He smiled that smile he had, and I recall a faint feeling of triumph—he'd realised he'd been bested, and I felt a little sorry for him, it was rather like using an elephant gun to kill a fly. And I finished my story, and brought it to the punchline, but before I'd even taken breath to start another there he was again, telling some new yarn of his own, something about his days doing a school play of all things! I got up and left. I didn't want to punish the whole cast. It wasn't their fault one of their number was speaking out of turn. But I had no choice.

I spoke to Alan at the end of the day. I told him what the problem was. He said he'd see what he could do. I have no idea what he did, but Nicholas Milton never interrupted an anecdote of mine again. Indeed, he usually wasn't in the room during the break at all.

He was a bad actor, as I say, and this wasn't merely because of his behaviour in the rehearsal room. He had a sort of earnestness about him on stage that doesn't reach an audience—any seasoned actor knows that it's what you can push out to the dress circle that counts, not all the *sotto voce* mumbling you do in the name of *verité*. The audience loved him, and the poor fool hadn't the wit to understand they loved him only because he looked nice, it was nothing to do with the impassioned sincerity of his emoting. In *King Lear* he was playing Oswald. It's a nice part, Oswald. Not many lines, but a bit of sneering, a joke or two, and a lovely death scene, it's a gift for the right juve. Whenever Oswald made an entrance the audience straightaway would start to laugh at him, and he wasn't supposed to be *that* funny; at the curtain call when he stepped on stage for his bow the clapping would get louder, and there'd even be cheers. There wasn't much applause left for the rest of us, the crowds got all clapped out. It was embarrassing. Milton's popularity was overwhelming the production.

He had to be taught a lesson, and only I could do it. One evening, in act one scene four, I cut a page or two of the script altogether. I cut out Oswald's first major entrance, and his subsequent exit. One moment I was chatting to the Earl of Kent, the next I was calling for my Fool. Donald McDermott was playing Kent, and he looked a bit horrified, but I squeezed his arm so he'd know it was all right, and Nicholas Milton was left stranded in the wings without any chance of coming on and stealing the limelight. He would turn up later in the play for his death scene, but now it would be without any context, he'd just be another oik getting stabbed in the carnage. I apologised to Milton later, and pretended it had been a mistake. But I said to him, "*Lear* can do without its Oswald, but it can't do without its Lear." And I tapped my nose for emphasis, yes. I think he got the message. I think it was a point well made.

That must have been the Thursday, or the Friday, I think. It would have been on the Monday before that we'd had the technical rehearsal, and during the break Alan asked if I could go to see wardrobe about a wig fitting. I suppose the rest of the cast thought I'd be gone for longer, but the Lear wig was a simple matter—we'd had one made a couple of seasons before, five minutes with the hair tongs and we were done. When I went into the green room, all the cast were laughing—not just the juves, *all* of them, even the Goneril I'd served with for five seasons, even the Duke of Gloucester. And there was Milton, and he was sitting in my chair, sitting in *my* throne—and he was telling a story to them all, some stuff about how he'd met Henry Irving which couldn't *possibly* be true since Irving had died a hundred years ago, and his voice was different, and I wondered why he sounded so old and so queasy, and then I realised he was impersonating me.

Some of them had the decency to stop laughing when they saw me there. (Some of them later apologised, although I told them there was no need for that—young Milton had been very funny, he'd certainly got the measure of me!) Milton stopped talking. He stopped, at least. But he didn't get out of my chair. He didn't get out of my chair and let me sit down.

Nicholas Milton was a very bad actor, and a charlatan, and a man of mendacity, and a shit.

I haven't seen Nicholas Milton in over thirty years. Not in the flesh—once in a while, back in the eighties, he'd turn up on television, and as soon as I recognised him, I'd change channel. Never anything very fancy—bit parts in sitcoms mostly, or turning up as some victim in *The Bill*. I had to change channel quite frequently for a while—and then, as the years went by, less and less.

I haven't *thought* of Nicholas Milton in several years either, I'm sure, not actively. I don't know. It's hard to tell. Once in a while your memory will just toss random stuff at you, something will just flit unexpectedly back into your mind, it has nothing to do with you. How am I meant to stop that happening? It's not my fault.

I don't know, after so very long, why Nicholas Milton has managed to pop back into my life, right at its very centre, to take all I have ever done and make a mockery of it. I have to find out. I'm not standing for it. It's too late at night to call anyone, I should go back to bed, but

I don't want to do that if it means I'll die accidentally in the process. I'll keep myself awake, and keep myself alive. I go down to the kitchen, drink lots of coffee, take some vitamin pills, one or other should do the trick.

I would call Alan St John, I know he would have helped me find him. But I remember reading that Alan himself died only a year or two ago. He didn't get a very big obituary in *The Stage and Television Today*, and on balance I think that's right—he was a nice man, but not a very good director, his only real skill was in steering actors around the set, he had no verve, no imagination, you could hardly say theatre is poorer for his loss.

For the first time, though, I miss him, and wish he was still around.

As soon as day breaks, I phone Equity, the actor's union. I tell them I'm trying to contact an actor called Nicholas Milton. They tell me he hasn't been a member of Equity since 1994. They tell me which agency he was with. I phone the agency. I tell them I'm looking for Nicholas Milton. They tell me they stopped representing him in 1994. I say I know that. I say I'd like to contact him anyway. They tell me they can't give out his home address to just anyone, and I tell them I'm a famous actor who used to work with him. I give them my name, but they don't recognise it until they look me up on the internet, idiots. They tell me the last address they have on file; it's in Hull.

I've never been to Hull. I wasn't looking for any new experiences in this lifetime, and if I had been, visiting Hull would not have been on the top of my list. I go to the train station. I buy a ticket for Hull. It's a five-hour journey. I hope I don't die on the way.

I didn't hate Nicholas Milton, I don't want to overstate the matter. Really, he was beneath my contempt. But I think I have demonstrated ample reason for my hatred had I bothered to harbour any, even before the incident with Maureen. It was Maureen that was the final straw.

Maureen and I had an arrangement. She didn't run the nicest theatre digs, nor, it must be said, the most convenient. Her bed and breakfast was a good twenty-minute walk from the theatre—fine if the summer weather was living up to the name, frustrating if, as common, it wasn't. But since 1972 Maureen had only charged me half-price.

And in return I got her front row tickets to all the shows, and had a port and lemon waiting for her at the interval, and I shared her bed.

And Sundays, I remember, were the nicest—no performance in the evening, and no rehearsals either, and we could just stay in bed till noon. She'd have to get up early to make the breakfasts for all her other lodgers, but she'd soon return, bringing me my own breakfast on a tray, and she'd have cooked me an extra sausage. And then we'd doze, or read the Sunday papers, or we'd have sex, or I'd tell her some of my theatrical anecdotes. She liked my anecdotes. But you had to be careful with Maureen, she didn't know much about theatre, she didn't care a rat's arse about Ralphie Richardson or Gielgud, the stories I told her had to be rather fruitier than the ones I'd tell the actors in the green room. She used to laugh with me. She was a pretty little thing.

That was the arrangement—ten weeks each year, and nothing more. Not even a card at Christmas. We'd have celebrated birthdays had they coincided with the summer season, but my birthday was in March, and hers was Heaven knows when, so it was never an issue. On the final night of the eighth play I'd say, "Well that's it for another year, ducks," because she liked being called 'ducks'; she'd ask me if I would be back the following year, and I said I'd see if something better turned up, but I expected I would. Then sometime around May, after Alan St John called me, I'd give her a ring—I'd say, "Do you have a room for the forthcoming season?", and she'd say, "Yes," and I'd say, "Our usual arrangement?", and she'd say, "The usual." She always sounded happy to hear from me.

She told me we had to keep it secret. This was just a bit of fun. I agreed. I didn't want the cast to think less of me. I'd told them tales of dalliance with Peggy Ashcroft and the young Judi Dench, I didn't want to disillusion them.

And the best nights of the show were always the one when Maureen was in. I'd get her a seat right on the front row, so that if I stood downstage centre for my big speeches I knew I was just in front of her. And then that night in bed she'd tell me how good I'd been.

Maureen was predisposed to dislike Nicholas Milton, of course. I tried not to gossip about rehearsals with her, I'm not really a bitchy sort of actor. But I'm sure that Nicholas Milton cropped up in conversation every once in a while. To the point, I remember, that when we went to bed after she'd seen *King Lear*, and told me how regal and tragic I had been, I was almost as keen to find out what she had made of Milton's Oswald. "Oh," she said, "I didn't like him too much," and that pleased me.

Milton's big break was as the titular inspector in the Priestley potboiler, *An Inspector Calls*. He played the part too young, and with too much charisma. Maureen saw it three times, once on the ticket I gave her, and on two subsequent visits she paid for herself. I assumed she was taken with my comic turn as Arthur Birling. Even then, I wanted to believe the best of her.

She stopped wanting to have sex with me during *A Murder is Announced*, and right in the middle of *Easy Virtue* told me she didn't want me even sharing her bed. She said she was having a relationship with Nicholas Milton. She wasn't sure how serious it was, but she wanted to find out. She said she didn't want to hurt me. I said, "You little idiot, you think he cares one fig for you? He only wants to spite me!" That made her cry, and I'd never seen her cry, we'd never had that sort of relationship. She said that I was talking nonsense, we'd kept our arrangement secret all this time, Milton wouldn't even have known about it. But of course Milton knew about it—I talked about Maureen in the green room—I dropped hints—couldn't she see, I was so proud of her?

She said I could take another room in the house, but I said no. I found a room in the inn just out of town, it was a half-hour walk, and uphill, but what of that?

There were only two shows left to the season. It was a wonder I got through them, but I'm a professional. We did *Gaslight*, and *Gaslight* was no trouble, I'd ridden the back of that old warhorse so many times I could have acted it in my sleep, there could have been earthquakes going on all about and I'd still have given a solid performance.

The final show was another matter. It was a new play, or a newish play at any rate, I'd never heard of it. It was billed as a comedy, but it was one of those modern comedies that doesn't have many jokes in, and everyone stands around looking miserable. You know the sort. Once in a while Alan would choose a play he thought could 'push the boundaries a bit', and I never knew why, audiences pay good money so we'll keep our hands off their boundaries altogether.

I didn't have a big part, but it was, of course, significant. And I don't know, maybe it was the noise at the inn I was staying in, maybe it was my own little irritation with the Maureen incident, but whenever I tried to learn the lines they just wouldn't stick.

During one rehearsal, Milton stopped me mid-speech, and said, "I say, I'm afraid you're paraphrasing."

I said that I never paraphrased.

He said that I *was* paraphrasing, and that it made it rather hard for him to find his cue.

I said that if I *were* paraphrasing, it was only because the play was no good, and I was making the lines better.

He said that that was fair enough, but could I just decide which paraphrase I was going to stick to. Unless I would rather he just take pot luck every night. Unless I'd rather he just jump into my improvisation whenever he thought best.

He said it all quite affably, as if he were giving me considered options, as if he had only my best interests at heart. He gave that friendly smile. I told him he could do whatever he damned well chose.

For weeks I had contrived never to be on my own with him. I would avoid the pub when he was there, I would change my entrances so I came on from opposite sides of the wings. But now Maureen had confessed everything, I couldn't care about that any longer. Indeed, after the performance that night, when I'd said good night to everyone, I doubled back to find him alone in the dressing room.

He looked up in the mirror at me when I came in. He was sponging off his eyeliner. "Hello, old man," he said, "what can I do you for?"

My first punch took him off his chair. I couldn't reach down to punch him again, so I just kicked him a couple of times.

He didn't cry out. And he didn't retaliate. I thought that maybe this was because I was beating him so hard, but I knew I wasn't, really; I'd never hit anyone for real before, and even now I was resorting to stage-fighting techniques, I was making my own sound effects. Then I thought that maybe he felt guilty, that he was getting only what he deserved.

And I looked him in the face, and I saw that actually he just pitied me.

I kicked him once more and left. I kicked him in the stomach—I remembered the stage directions of the new play had said the hero had a clear and handsome face, and I didn't want to do anything to compromise the show.

I thought he might tell the company what I'd done, but he didn't. He didn't say a word to anyone. Except, perhaps, to Maureen. I wouldn't put it past him.

The following May I had the annual phone call from Alan St John. "Me again, dear heart," he said. "Fancy getting back into harness for another eight weeks of fun and merriment beneath the aegis of yours truly?"

I said I would like that, on condition that Nicholas Milton wasn't part of the company.

Alan went quiet at that. Then he said to me, "But I've already offered him the season. He's doing Orsino."

I said that he had better unoffer him the season then. That it was Milton or me.

There was silence, and I went cold, and I thought—he's going to take *him*, he's going to take him after all. The bastard—and then Alan said, "All right." He was quiet and rather flat, and I'd never heard Alan sound like that before, so lifeless.

I asked him whether he wanted me to give my King Lear again that year, and remembered as I was doing so that of course he wouldn't, we'd had it just the season before—but Alan just sighed, and said in that same flat voice, "Sure, why not?"

That would become the proudest King Lear of my life, in fact, and even Anna Walker-Smith couldn't spoil it.

I stayed at the inn again, and found that once you got used to it, it had its own particular charms.

Maureen had taken her name off the digs list, and didn't come to any of the performances. I supposed that was just as well, though she missed a terrific season.

I don't die on the train to Hull, and that's a good thing, although looking out of the window as we pass through Grimsby I'm sorely tempted.

I get a taxi to take me to Nicholas Milton's last known address. It doesn't take long.

And only now I am wondering—what am I going to say to him? Am I going to have to hit him again? Do I suppose that this time he'll just lie there on the ground, and take it, and pity me—because he'll have to, if he hits me back it'll certainly kill me, even the exertion of my swinging a fist may finish me off. I don't feel angry any more. Confused, yes, and a little sad. And lost.

I ring the doorbell, and only then do I realise who's going to answer it. She opens the door, and there she is, small, and still pretty, in her own way. "Hello, Maureen," I say.

She is surprised to see me, of course she is, but not as surprised as I might have expected.

"I'm sorry to trouble you," I say. "Is your husband there?"

She hesitates. She says, "You'd better come in."

She shows me into her sitting room. It isn't as nice as the one she had in Hornhaven. Naturally enough, I don't tell her this. "Nice," I say.

"Nick is dead," she says, and there's no emotion to it.

"I'm sorry," I say. "What did he die of?" And she doesn't answer that, and why should she, it's none of my business. "But he was so young," I say, "wasn't he?" And to this at least she reacts, she twitches one of her shoulders into a half-shrug, and I look at her, and she's *old*—and I think, quite right really, is anyone I ever knew young any more?

"What do you want?" she asks me, and it's not unkind.

"I don't know."

"Do you want a cup of tea?"

"A cup of char!" I say. "Yes. Yes. Thank you. Yes."

I sit down at her kitchen table. She tells me that Nick has been dead a long time. She tells me he died eight long years ago.

I am going to ask when it was that he recorded my life story, and who approached him, and how much he got paid for it, but I'm distracted when Maureen puts my tea in front of me, and that's just as well.

"He gave up acting years ago," Maureen tells me. "He helped me run my B&B. We had two kids. We did all right."

"He was a good actor," I say. "This business can be very cruel."

"I don't think he was a good actor," she says. "He wasn't an actor like you." And I look for something cutting in that, and I don't find anything, but that doesn't mean it isn't there, and I thank her cautiously.

"What do you want?" she asks me again.

"I was thinking of Nick," I say. "I'm sorry. I came to say sorry." And it doesn't feel like a lie, it's what Nick would have called an inner truth. "I miss you, ducks," I say. And I reach out and take her hand, and she doesn't resist, and that's not quite the same thing as accepting it, I know, but it's better than I am hoping for.

She says, "Come to bed with me."

"I miss you," I say again.

"I miss *him*," she says. "So much. And you knew him. At least you knew him. Come to bed with me."

I don't want to tell her that I'm on the point of death, I really don't want to put her off. But she's very gentle with me, and sweet, and when my heart starts to speed it's as if with new life.

We lie there in her bed, holding each other. Maureen begins to doze.

I close my eyes too.

When I do, my life starts to flash before my eyes. Back from the beginning.

And now I'm on the lookout for it, and of *course* I recognise my father! That's Alfred Potter. He began his career in the days of music hall, and he was in my first professional season, already an old man, and a kind one—I remember him saying to me that he thought I would go far. And that lantern-jawed mother of mine, that's Mildred Hewitt, I worked with her on *Hobson's Choice*, she was delightful, and used to cheat at cribbage. Both long dead, I can't even guess how long. It's so nice to see them again.

I'm not scared of death. I know that whatever happens next there will still be a job for me.

I shake myself awake, I force my eyes open. It would be so easy to sleep, and sleep forever, but not here. Not beside Maureen. She deserves better than that.

I kiss her on the forehead. She doesn't stir.

I leave her a little note, put it on the dressing table. It says 'Thank You'.

I get the taxi to the station.

The evening train from Hull has been delayed by engineering works, and by the time it finally arrives and I clamber on board with all the angry commuters I am so tired. I had wanted to finish the story of my life in my own bed, but I don't think I'm going to get there. It doesn't matter. I hope I don't alarm anyone. I squeeze myself in opposite a couple who look hale and hearty and unworried by fears of death, and I put as peaceful an expression on my face as possible.

Nicholas Milton is dancing before my eyes before the train has even left the platform. His King Lear is quite good. Subtler than I'd have played it, and the boy could work harder on his projection—but he's good, he's got something, he's got talent.

I settle back, and I smile, and start to enjoy the show.

And the old woman says:

- *Do you dream of a world in which the text of King Lear forever vanishes into thin air? If so, turn to* **Canon Fodder** *(story 12, page 199).*
- *Within a year of its first performance, King Lear was censored by the court for its explicit criticism of social ills; by the eighteenth century a happy ending had been grafted on to it. Turn to* **The Censor's Report** *(story 99, page 1679).*
- *If you want to get regular work as an actor, you have to stay trim and keep the weight off. For dietary advice, turn to* **Taste Me** *(story 75, page 1301).*
- *For the struggling actor, sleeping with the landlady is a perfectly legitimate way of cutting down on your expenses. Turn to* **Bobbo** *(story 82, page 1407).*
- *Staged performance as a commemoration of death is all very well, but it doesn't last long. For something with more staying power, turn to* **It Flows from the Mouth** *(story 85, page 1459).*

99
The Censor's Report

THERE WAS ONCE A MAN who liked reading books. He would take a book to work with him every day. It was back-breaking work, building the Wall, and the task seemed never-ending, there was always more wall to be built. But he didn't let it tire him, he knew that at lunchtime he would be able to find a nice quiet spot and eat his sandwiches and read his latest novel. The state-sanctioned novels were just a little bit thick and stodgy, but still the man found things to enjoy, still they offered him glimpses of lives that were not his own. For one designated forty-five minute break period per day, he could lose himself in another world. One afternoon the foreman summoned the man to his office.

"You're a little shit," said the foreman. "You think you're smarter than me, don't you?"

The man said he was sorry he was a shit, and he certainly did not think that he was smarter than the foreman.

"You've been observed," said the foreman. "The state thinks you have potential that is wasted building walls. You are to report to Government Block C tomorrow morning for reassignment."

The man said he would go there bright and early, and thanked the foreman for the opportunity.

"You're a little shit," said the foreman.

When the man went home that evening and ate supper with his wife and son, he didn't tell them he had a new job because he didn't know what it was yet nor whether he had permission to discuss it. And that night he tried to read another chapter of his novel but was unable to concentrate on the words properly, and he didn't know whether that meant he was excited or he was scared.

The next morning he put on his Sunday best and he went to Government Block C. He was directed to his new office. The office was very small. It had inside one wooden table, and one wooden chair. On the table there was a pile of half a dozen books, all in plain covers. There was a typed note telling him what to do. It seemed peculiar that a note was going to explain his job rather than a foreman, but the man liked it, he had always preferred words to people.

The note said:

"*You are the state censor. Your responsibility is the approval or disapproval of all state literature. Put approved books in the tray marked Approved Books. Put disapproved books in the chute that leads to the furnace.*"

He sat on the wooden chair, by the wooden table, and picked up the first book, and began to read.

That day he read two short novels, and he enjoyed them very much. They were fresh and clever, and he had no hesitation in putting them both in the Approved Books tray. The next day, he read a much longer novel, so long he didn't finish it until the third day. It was a little overwritten, maybe, and the ending was forced—but it was good overall, and so the man approved that too. Next was a novella of satirical intent, but the satire was *very* subtle, and the man thought most people wouldn't even notice it. The next book was really not very good at all. The prose was flat. The ideas were thin. And the man was going to put this one in the chute, but then he reasoned to himself—maybe this book only *seemed* bad because he'd read better books before it. It only suffered by comparison, and had he read this weaker book to begin with, he might have enjoyed it much more. It seemed unfair to condemn a book because he had been reading stories in the wrong order. He gave the novel a lot of thought, and he imagined the poor writer who had slaved so hard on it, and how crushed he might be if his book were destroyed, how it might discourage him from going on to write something better. So he put it in the Approved Books tray with all of the others.

This was turning out to be the best week of his life, and he was buzzing with new ideas and with new energy, and that night he made love to his wife, and they really hadn't done that for quite a while.

He returned home from work the next day to find his house had been ransacked. The windows were broken, furniture was overturned. His son had been beaten, and his wife was missing. The man asked the son what had happened, but the son could not speak, his face was too broken. Instead he gave his father a typed note. The man struggled to make out the words through the bloodstains.

The note said:

"Read faster.

"Read more critically.

"And you will get your wife back."

The next day he read three books, and burned two of them. He put the manuscripts in the chute, and they were sucked down so eagerly, and he could feel the heat from the furnace as its door opened ten storeys below.

The day after, he read five books, and burned three.

The day after that, he read eight books, burned eight.

He soon realised he didn't have to read the entire book to damn it. He could do that from the first chapter. From the first page. The first sentence.

'The' was such a predictable and dull way to start a novel; anything else, ostentatious.

One day he found it hard to open the door to his office, it seemed jammed. There were books everywhere, on the floor, on the desk, piled high in collapsing heaps. The chute could only take one book at a time, he spent all day feeding it with manuscripts, one after the other. He howled like a wolf.

The next day—and the office was bare. Except for one single short story, typed, neatly lying square in the centre of his desk. For want of anything else to do, he picked it up, and read it.

The story was of a man who had lost his wife. He didn't mean to lose her. He missed her dreadfully. He was angry and hurt that she was gone. He retreated into books to try to find her. Presently he had read every single book that had ever been published in the world. And still—still, she wasn't there.

Because the man in the story didn't realise the obvious truth. You never find quite what you're looking for in books. The good ones, the bad ones, all of them, they give you what *they* want, your feelings don't come into it.

In the back of a library, an old woman in the dark said she would read him one hundred and one strange stories of her own, and if he picked the correct sequence to hear them, he would get his wife back.

The story didn't seem to have an ending. The censor hoped the man in the story would succeed. And then he burned the pages.

The next day there was another short story on his desk, neatly typed like before. And so there was the day afterwards, and onwards, every single day. Some were short and funny, some touched him, some repulsed him. There was the story of the man who built skyscrapers upside down, or the girl who posed as a cartoon dog. There was a cat that could recite Homer, a boy who carved his own tongue from a tree, a girl afraid of bathtubs. Giant spiders, balloon animals, men made of rainfall. And God, many times over. God was a monster, God was an ordinary man, God didn't exist. There was life after death. There was death and nothing else. And there was love, so much about love, and it was just as nebulous as God, and twice as unlikely.

And all the tales were about grief. The sad ones were about grief, very obviously, and all the horrific ones, that made some sense too—but so were all the happy ones, and the silly ones, and the ones he didn't really understand. This man who had lost his wife, the man listening to one hundred and one stories in the dark—it was as if that loss was seeping into all the stories he heard, as if he was tainting them at their very core. The censor felt sorry for the man. The censor hoped he would be all right. But he also hoped he might, you know, just *get over it*, and stop ruining all the fun for everybody else.

So the censor read the hundred and one tales. He didn't like them all. Some of them bemused him, some offended him. All of them made him weep. All of them felt personal specifically to him. And he couldn't quite tell why.

He burned them all, of course, but that wasn't his fault. It was the times that he lived in. Sometimes burning stories is what you have to do to get by. The day he came to work, and the desk was empty, and he knew that the stories were over now—it broke his heart.

The next day there was nothing to read. The day after, nothing. He checked in at eight o'clock, left for home at six, ate his sandwiches in his designated forty-five minute lunch break.

The next day he took in paper of his own, and a pencil. And he began to write.

He didn't have any great stories he wanted to tell. So he told the story of his life. It was an unfinished story. He didn't know how it ended yet.

At the end of the day, he sent it down the chute to the furnace, and that felt good.

The next morning there were still no stories to read, so he wrote his own again. It was a little longer this time, he had a whole new day to relate.

He burned it before he left for home.

The next day he wrote it again, still just those few words longer, and burned it.

And the day after that, he finished the story. And he looked at the Approved Books tray. Nothing had touched the Approved Books tray in quite a while, even the spiders were avoiding it. He thought, what the hell. He dropped the story of his life into the tray, and then put on his Sunday best coat, and closed the door to his office, and he went home.

The next morning he went to his office in Government Block C, as punctual as ever.

They were waiting for him, as he knew they would be. One was in his office chair, the other standing by the desk. He told them he was sorry—but he wasn't sorry, and besides, they didn't care.

They took him from his office, one held him by the arm, the other walked behind.

As they marched down the corridor, the door to the adjacent office opened. Out came a woman, flanked by two guards of her own. She looked so tired, so spent, but he recognised his wife immediately—he saw how thin she was—he saw her hands were bandaged. As they passed, she looked at him. He called out to her. She didn't call back.

He turned around, strained to see where she was being taken. The guard pushed him forward. Not before he saw her being led into what had been his office.

And he was led into hers.

The guards left him there, and closed the door.

The office was very small. It had inside one wooden table, one wooden chair. On the table there was a stack of white paper, and a typewriter. There was a typed note telling him what to do.

The note said:

"Write faster.

"Write less self-critically.

"And you may get your wife back."

He sat down, and typed until his fingers bled.

And the old woman says:

- *Have you yet read that story about—*
- *The boy who carved his tongue from a tree?* **Sounding Brass Tinkling Cymbal** *(story 13, page 211).*
- *The girl who is afraid of bathtubs?* **The Bathtub** *(story 61, page 1037).*
- *The man who built skyscrapers upside down?* **A Short History of Tall Buildings** *(story 33, page 539).*
- *Or the giant cockroach—***Detached** *(story 81, page 1397)—or the balloon animals—***The Popping Fields** *(story 14, page 227)—or the man built out of rainfall—***The Rainman** *(story 36, page 603)?*
- *Or are you tired? Have you had enough of such silliness? Have you reached the end of the road, the end of the line, the end of your patience? Have you heard all the stories you can possibly hear—and still, still life feels just the same, and still, still you carry your grief about you like a huge great bloody sack? If so, turn to* **Scheherazade's Last Story** *(story 100). It's nearly over.*

If this were the Arabian Nights, there'd be 1001 of these stories to get through. Be grateful.

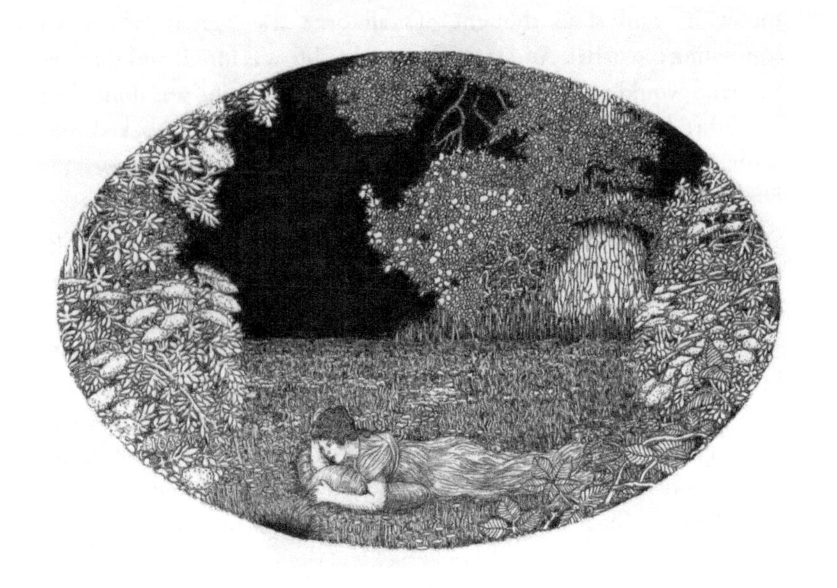

100
SCHEHERAZADE'S LAST STORY

ON THE ONE THOUSAND and first night after she completed her *1001 Nights*, Scheherazade wakes up from a dreamless sleep with the idea for a brand-new story.

She sits bolt upright, she may even cry out in surprise. She looks across to the body of her husband, the sultan, and he hasn't stirred. And she considers waking him too, because all of her stories are *his* stories, aren't they, and wasn't that what she promised him on their wedding day? His face seems so gentle in sleep, she almost feels she loves him. Let him have his rest.

All of her sleeps have been dreamless for the longest while. Ever since she told that final story to her husband, could that just be a coincidence? She remembers how she felt as she dragged herself to the finishing line of that one thousand and first tale, and her tongue was thick, and her head emptying, she knew there were no stories left to follow it—and she'd thought, it's all over, it's over at last. With something like relief. And if that meant her life was forfeit and that her husband would put her to the sword, then so be it. She was done. But he didn't kill her. As her last words dribbled out her cracked and aching lips, as she croaked 'The End' straight at his face, he clapped his hands and told her that he had fallen in love with her. Her extraordinary ordeal had melted his cruel heart, and he vowed not only to spare her life, but to spare those of any subsequent wives he might marry when one day she'd died of natural causes. Congratulations!—and Scheherazade knew she ought to have been pleased, but really, she just felt so very sleepy.

Always sleepy, but always dreamless—sometimes a lone spark of imagination will creep into her head, but finding only rock and sand and nothing there to water it, it soon withers and dies. And she sleeps on a bed of silken sheets and the softest of mattresses and pillows scented with rosewater and honeysuckle—she is the wife of a sultan, after all, and no slumber of dreadful, empty void is too good for her.

But now it is there in her head—impossibly, it is there—the one thousand and second story. And it isn't just some fleeting wisp of an idea that'll dissipate the moment she turns critical attention to it—it's got a beginning, a middle, and an end, and helpfully in that very same order: it makes sense, and has both theme and point, it is a story fair ripe with subtext. And it's an actual physical presence, it's *huge*, it makes her brain feel fat.

She gets out of bed very carefully. And she now doesn't want to wake her husband, mustn't wake him. As if the story's life depended on it.

She'd forgotten how uncomfortable having a fully-fledged story in your head can be. She's been wanting to get one in there for so long. Nothing necessarily complex, just a funny anecdote, maybe—because recently she's been going to dinner parties, her husband is always being invited to dinner parties, and she has to go along too, that's her job—and she wants to entertain, she wants to be an asset to him. To charm the hearts of the populace and to poleaxe foreign ambassadors, all with her raconteur wit. She was once so good. She once knew all the right words. She once saved her life from a psychopath by telling him one thousand and one stories in a row, one after each other, just like that! But she's been broken. The words are wrong, and the order of the words is wrong, and the reason for the order of the words is wrong—

she can no longer even tell a joke properly. The very simplest stories of all, and yet she'll botch the punchline, she'll stammer over the set-up, she'll forget the reason she was telling the joke in the first place. And all around the banqueting tables everyone looks embarrassed, and there might be coughing, there might be some intense plate staring, until someone, thankfully, mercifully, starts a new topic of conversation. She'll steal a glance to her husband the sultan and all she wants is that he's proud of her. But he won't meet her eye, and she knows that all of his subjects feel bad for him—why did he end up with such a clod as a consort, and one so inarticulate, and one so dull? He hasn't had sex with her in months, and with good reason. Where is the sparkling storyteller he once knew?

Every so often Scheherazade thinks she loathes her husband the sultan. She had all the stories of the world inside of her, and he has ripped them out. And she'll grasp onto that vague fury for all that she is worth, because sometimes a little flutter of hatred seems very similar to creative inspiration. But it isn't.

She tiptoes to the bedroom door, and she is carrying her chin in her hands so the new story won't get jolted about—like her head is a delicate crystal vase, like her head is a goldfish bowl filled to the very brim, like her head is a soap bubble that will burst into nothing at the slightest misstep, like her head is stuffed with similes again, look at all her lovely similes, she can't wait to set them all free! There are armed guards outside the bedroom; she doesn't know what excuse to give them for her departure; she says she is going to check on Baby. They shrug. They don't care what she does.

She doesn't want to see Baby, but now she supposes she'll have to. Baby is sleeping in its crib. She'd once tried to tell Baby her stories, isn't that what you did with babies? The nice ones, the ones with magic and adventure and easily adopted moral conclusions. But Baby hadn't liked her stories, he'd screamed himself hoarse and pissed himself, everyone's a critic. "You have a bright, bouncing, baby boy," the doctors told her. "What story could you hope to create that'll ever be better than that?" She has tried to think of Baby as a new story, she really has. That this tiny man is one tale more perfect and more complex than any of her *1001 Nights*. But she doesn't like Baby. Baby gurgles and cries and pukes and shits out yellow poo, if Baby is a story then it's not a very sophisticated one.

She suddenly knows that she will never see Baby again. That this new story in her head will change her life forever. "Goodbye, Baby," she says. She considers kissing it on the forehead, but decides not to: one thing she's always tried to do with her storytelling is to be sincere.

She supposes she'll never see her husband again either.

Scheherazade makes her way through the dark corridors of the palace, until she reaches the spiral staircase that will take her down to the ground.

She's often thought her husband the sultan might be having an affair. There's been a new bounce to his step, and she hasn't put it there, not with her stale plots and meandering prose—who's spinning stories for him now? She could find out for sure. It wouldn't be hard. Follow him through the bazaar and see where he goes, she could disguise herself as a peasant, or a beggar, or a magic genie. Until at last she might find him in the arms of some other woman. Catch them both in the act!—mid-narrative maybe, and he'd be lying flat on his back with that hungry grin he'd once used on her and he'd be feeling up her dramatic segues and structural quirks—and the woman might reveal how far through her own labyrinth of tales they'd got: is this the first Night, or the forty-first Night, or the four hundred and fourteenth? (Does she think she's got one thousand and one in her. Oh, let her try.) Yes, she could do that. But what if he isn't having an affair? What if this is just some half-baked story she likes to tell herself, a helpful little fiction that gives character motivation to why he's now so cold to her, why he doesn't touch her, why he can't stand even to be in the same room as her if he can help it? In her *1001 Nights* Scheherazade has learned that one of the rules of storytelling is not to destroy the fantasy by subjecting it to too rigorous an examination. Her husband the sultan is having an affair. Her husband is having an affair, and it doesn't matter. Sooner or later his new love will run out of stories to tell him; they always do.

Down, all the way, until she's at the bottom.

She needs paper. Where will she find paper? She goes to the library. There will be paper in the library. The library has the largest collection of books in the known world, they tower to the very ceiling. Her husband the sultan doesn't like books much, but he thinks they make the shelves look nice. She takes down a book to write her new story in. But the pages are already full with other people's stories. There's barely any room for hers. She starts to write in the margins, but it makes her words look like an apologetic afterthought. It's not right. This is not the way she told her stories. This is not her way at all.

She goes out into the garden, and the night air is cold, it bites at her.

Her husband the sultan once told her that her voice had a flavour to it. That when she told him her stories, he could taste lychees and cream. She shall use that voice now to tell her new story, and if she has no one she can tell it to, why, then she shall tell it to the earth. She gets down upon her hands and knees, and she claws at the soil with her fingernails. She shall dig a hole, and into the hole she shall whisper the tale, and then at least her tale shall be free. Wasn't there a story like this once? Was it one of hers? She can't remember. Because sometimes it seems that all the stories that have ever been told are hers, really—and other times she doesn't own a single one of them, she can dimly remember plotting them and giving them form but they're out of her head now and making their own way in the world without her and they never call and they never visit and they never care and it's as if they've forgotten she ever gave birth to them at all.

She wonders which sort of story the new tale is, will this be one of the ungrateful ones? The hole is deep enough now. She lowers her head right inside it, until her lips brush the soil. She feels such power within her. She had forgotten she ever had this much power.

Because people miss the point of the *1001 Nights*. They think that Scheherazade is the victim. Courtiers go quiet when they see her in the palace corridors, and lower their heads and mumble and look sympathetic. As if Scheherazade has been abused. She hasn't been abused. Yes, it's true, her husband had wanted to kill her, and each night it was only her stories that saved her. But it is precisely that—her stories *saved* her. He'd had his sword, she'd had the stories, and the stories had won. Theirs had never been a marriage of equals. For one thousand and one nights they'd gone to battle, his brutality against her imagination, and for one thousand and one nights she'd been the victor. And to his credit, her vanquished husband had never sulked or complained. He'd taken each and every defeat on the chin with the grace of a good sportsman. His conduct had been exemplary, and Scheherazade couldn't be sure that if *she'd* lost one night, and he'd got to slice her head off, she'd have been quite so sanguine. "You have seduced me with a voice that tastes of lychees and cream," he'd said.

She loved him. Of course she loved him. He listened to her. He had used to listen. Whatever stories she fed him, it was as if he saw through the fictive carapace and knew the very essence of her. And it was sad, desperately sad, that she'd run out of stories he wanted to hear—and that he'd never had any stories of his own to tell.

She tells the earth her story. And there is a flavour to her voice, it had once been lychees and cream, but age has curdled it, it now tastes of sour lemon. But that's what it is, and that is all right.

This will be her last story, she thinks.

The tales she'd given her husband had been full of flying carpets and monsters and spells. But she doesn't have to tell any more stories that will please a sultan—or please a baby—or please anybody else in the world. And she realises that this new story is the story of her life. All of her life, the awkward bits, the lumps, the bumps, the unvarnished truth. The border between fiction and autobiography is a nuance of literary conceit Scheherazade has never had to worry about before. And if she runs out of incident, then that's surely because her life has never been allowed much incident. And if she chooses to enliven the narrative with some flying carpets and monsters and spells after all, at least this time they're hers. They're hers, and she'll make their magic work for her alone.

Scheherazade tells her new story, and the world doesn't change. Her husband doesn't soften, her baby doesn't become worthwhile. Men are still cruel and women are still cruel and the world is still cruel. But something is created that has never existed before, and that won't do anybody any harm. And maybe that's the real achievement, and maybe that's good enough.

She's told better. She's told worse. Not every story has to change the world. That would be irritating.

It's over. It's done.

She doesn't bother to fill in the hole. Let the story escape if it wants to.

Her last story. And yet not the last. Last sounds so terminal. This can be her last but one. This is her penultimate story. She can feel a one thousand and third poking about inside her, the one thousand and second has dislodged it. She'll make that one her last instead.

And every story can be your penultimate story, so long as you keep changing your mind about when you'll come to a halt. Every story you write, and every story you read, and every story you live.

This is not a sad story, or a happy story. It's simply yet another story, in a book that's filled with stories.

Scheherazade wonders where she'll tell her next one. She picks a direction at random, and begins to walk.

And the old woman says:

- *Continue to story 101.*

101
101 HEARTBEATS

1

AND WHAT WAS LUCKY was this, was that they both fell out of love at the exact same time! The exact same moment. And they had friends who had got divorced, but they hadn't fallen out of love at the same time—and that meant one of the couple had always been left floundering, clutching desperately to the wreckage of a relationship they hadn't the wit to see was damaged beyond repair. It was embarrassing to watch. You know what?—it was tedious.

But not in this case. The very same second, they couldn't have planned it better. They looked at each other, and they both said in unison, "I don't love you any more"—and then they laughed a little, because it was weird to hear those same blank words echoed straight back. They shook hands, they said farewell, and they parted. And with a slight sense of sad regret, yes, but mostly in relief. And in amusement too—because they'd never been in sync before, not ever, not even during the good times; it was funny how, only in breaking up, they were at last perfectly compatible.

2

These stories are for all the women I've ever told I loved. Especially for the ones I was lying to.

3

They both fell out of love, but not at the same time. She fell out of love first.

He's noticed that she's stopped calling him 'pookie'. He'd never liked being called 'pookie'. She'd always called him 'pookie', he thought, just to annoy him—she'd ruin perfect days with it, suddenly using that silly name when they'd been having fun, she'd call him it at dinner parties when he was about to make an intelligent observation. He'd tell her off, and he'd sulk; she'd laugh, then kiss him on the back of the neck, "Does that feel better?" she'd say, "Better now, my little pookie bear?" and she'd smooth the humiliation away.

But one day she'd just stopped. He doesn't know precisely when. Only that she doesn't do it any more. The moment passed without announcement, there was no fanfare to his depookification.

In bed he lies there in the dark, wide awake as she sleeps still beside him. He racks his brains. Certainly, she hasn't called him 'pookie' for a couple of weeks. And before that there was the business trip, and before that there'd been those days she'd visited her mother—no, he didn't suppose he could have been her pookie for well over a month.

He wants to ask her why not. He wants to wake her right now, and ask. Isn't he her pookie, what is it that he's done, how can he put it right. He'll beg her, please, let me be your pookie once more. He stops because it seems like the single most pathetic thing a grown man could ask of a woman.

He'll just have to work on it. He'll just try to be as pookieish as he can, and hope it'll reawaken her love.

He never realised before that a broken heart was more than just a turn of phrase. Because he feels the shards of his heart rattle around inside his chest, it's as if he's swallowed glass.

30

So they fall out of love, and she thinks he falls first.

She considers it odd how little romantic gestures have become attacks, accusatory and passive aggressive. He'll kiss her on the cheek but no longer on the lips. He takes her hand whilst crossing the road, but will drop it as soon as they reach the kerb. He's polite, when he was never *polite*, he'll say he loves her but it smacks of that same cool politeness. She starts to realise how every small precious act they ever shared, an unforced smile, a brush of arms against the other as they watched TV, the lowering of voices to whispers in the dark—every single one of them he will carry on performing, and they are exactly that, they're a performance. He'll fart in bed, and then turn to her with a leer, as if to say, "But you never *used* to mind, and if you mind now, if you dare say you mind, it proves it's all over, it means we'll have to confront what you're so scared to face, it's *over*; it's over, and you'll never get this love back, each and every day it just gets ever more tarnished, it's over now, baby."

And it's true, she used to love his farts, once upon a time his farts were the whole world to her.

85

They broke up, but there was no animosity to it. They decided they would be best friends.

He suggested he should move out, but she said there was no hurry, she didn't want him put to any inconvenience simply because she didn't love him any more. He could stop in the spare room—although, on second thoughts, *she* could take the spare room if he preferred, whatever he found nicer! He decided the spare room would be fine.

They arranged a rota so they could use the kitchen at different times, the bathroom, the lounge. That way they wouldn't have to see each other. It wouldn't be awkward.

The first night he put a note under her door. "I know you're hurting," he said, "and I feel so sorry for you, and I promise you things will get better."

She put a note under his door. "You're the kindest sweetest man. I worry about you too."

He left her a note the next day propped up against the toaster. "I hope I didn't disturb you last night with my crying. I want you to get the best night's sleep you can, and be all fresh to tackle the day!"

She left him a note on the toilet seat. "I was crying too. Don't think I wasn't crying. But I muffled it by putting my head under the pillow."

He left her notes every day, telling her how he was doing, little anecdotes that had happened at work.

She left him notes, and she'd talk about how she *felt*—her happiness now the weather was improving, it might be nice and sunny at the weekend.

Every note was marked with 'x's. And they would secretly count them on each new note they received to see whether there were more 'x's or fewer 'x's than before.

"I think you're adorable. I never deserved you," he wrote.

"You're my entire world, and even now you're gone, you always will be," she replied.

"xxxxxxxxxxxxxxxxxxxxxxxxxxxxxxxxxxxx," they both concluded.

One day he wrote her not a note, but a letter, a long letter. He told her that this was silly. That he still loved her with all his heart, and he was pretty sure she still loved him. He knew they had their differences, but surely with all that love they shared they could find a way to put them aside—or, if not that, face up to them squarely and discuss them and make them right? Because now he was alone there was such an ache within him, he knew she was the only woman for him, there would never be another. He wrote the letter, put more 'x's at the bottom than ever before, left it for her to find, and went out to work.

When at last he came home he found an old suitcase waiting in the hallway. All of his stuff had been packed inside it higgledy-piggledy, a single white sleeve lolled uselessly out of the side. There was no letter, just a simple note, and it told him to get out.

10

Let's get one thing clear.

I think it's important not to get bitter when love fails. When someone breaks your heart. Love is an impossible, confusing, frustrating mess—why should the person who's hurt you have any better understanding of how it works than you do? Look back on all the times you've shared. Rearrange the order, put all the good memories together, one directly after another, like a glorious happy story. And forgive.

I believe that completely. And yet sometimes I wake up in the night so angry that you've left me. I still hardly believe our extraordinary future is something you just threw away.

44

Oh, I have so many plans for you.

34

They met, and they got on so well, the hours seemed to fly by. The hours, and then the years. They got married within the whirl of their twenties. Their thirties brought them children, a boy and a girl, they were learning to walk, then to speak, then they were applying for college—the children were there and then they were gone, the nest was empty again, and still on they raced, accelerating now into their fifties. "Faster, faster!" he cried, and she shrieked with laughter, and she matched him every step of the way, "let's see how fast we can go!", and it was so fast now, the world around them seemed to blur and they just didn't care, they gobbled up the years together but not a single one was wasted.

And then, one year, so suddenly, the race stopped. The brakes were thrown, and she'd been running so fast the jolt gave her whiplash.

She sits alone at home. Her children come to visit, and they say bland things to comfort her, they hold her hand and make her tea. She's never had time to look at them properly before, who are these people? And time seems so slow now, is this how long time is supposed to feel? How can she stand it? How can anyone?

They think it's grief she feels, but she hasn't even got to the grief yet, this is all still motion sickness. The world still and fixed, and it takes her a day just to walk into the kitchen, it takes her a year to fall asleep at night. And as she lies there in bed, and sleep is so very far away, she thinks back to her only love and how she misses him. And her heart is the only thing still speeding—come on, it urges her, come on. How fast can you go?

31

He asked her whether she loved him. "Oh yes!" she enthused. "Because you're like a clown. Because you're like this sad, pathetic clown." He wasn't sure what to make of that, but he looked at her, and her laughing sympathetic face, and she was so beautiful, and he decided he should just be grateful and take what he could get.

4

She'd fallen in love with him, and it gave new colour and meaning to her life, and the only problem was he made her sick.

It wasn't his looks; she supposed there may be more handsome men out there, ones whose features were more classically proportioned, but that meant nothing to her, his was a body that suited her tastes. Not his looks then, his smell? No—she did wonder at first whether this was the source of the difficulty, but she gave hearty experimental sniffs in his presence, and both his eau de cologne and the odour of his sweat were pleasant enough. And nor was it his manner. He was charming, and funny, and courteous. He was clever when he needed to be, and, when it was her turn to sound intelligent, not. She loved him, she loved the whole package.

On the third date she had sat opposite him at dinner, gazing at him and wondering what it would be like to kiss him, and wondering what it would be like to kiss him forever and never let go. And she thought, yes, he could really be the one—and at that moment it overcame her in a wave, she felt so sick she thought she was going to faint, the room spun and she nearly fell off her chair. She gagged. He stopped being witty. He looked so concerned. He took her by the hand, and drove her straight home.

And on the fourth date she was able to keep herself together. She felt so queasy as he put his arms around her, but she fought the nausea down, she was winning, she was winning. And they went back to his place, and they made love for the first time, and he was so gentle and loving, she'd never felt passion like it, and just as she climaxed she looked up at his face bobbing away just above her own, and she thought it was already so dear to her, and she threw up all over it.

He made her sick, in spite of all her best efforts. She hoped there might be something to be done. Sailors adjust to the tossing and turning of ships at sea; workers at rendering factories overcome their revulsion to the stench. She went to the doctor.

He gave her an examination. He told her she was suffering from motion sickness.

"But I sit perfectly still with him," she said. "And lie perfectly still when appropriate."

"But your insides," he said. "Ah, your insides!" And he laughed, though not without sympathy. "Your heart, it is jumping about like a wild beast in a cage. It is twisting this way and that, spinning around and around and around. I must admit, just looking at it on the X-ray, I feel pretty nauseous myself."

She asked what could be done. He said there was no cure. She must protect her heart, if she didn't stop it clowning around it could puncture itself on a rib, and then where would she be? Dead, that's where. Her body simply wasn't equipped for the extremities of love. If she wanted to live a full life, she must resign herself to tempered contentment rather than unabandoned joy.

This disappointed her, but she reined the disappointment in, she didn't let herself feel *too* upset—and the doctor was right, straight away her heart began to calm and her nausea began to fade. She telephoned her lover right there from the surgery. There was no use in prolonging it. Not now she knew there was no future for them both. Down the receiver she could hear him crying, he didn't understand, he loved her, didn't she realise that? She was quite surprised by the force of his declaration, but proud she'd already found a way not to care.

She met someone else, a man she couldn't love but didn't dislike. She felt vaguely repulsed when he touched her, but only vaguely, and only *repulsed*—she never felt nauseated. They had two children, and when they were born she felt a rush of such love for them and straightaway a sea of vomit rose in her throat—and then she swallowed it down, she took a big gulp of air and told herself not to be so silly. These children would never amount to their full potential, they'd never repay the nine months of pregnancy and the pain of labour, they would always be less than they should. And so it came to pass.

This is not a sad story. She lived long, and happy in her own controlled way. She reached one hundred and one, old enough to see great great grandchildren she could disdain.

As for her ex, he was fine. He had the ability to inspire other women to love him, and just as ardently, he was lucky that way.

96

Her future husband keeps following her about. He lurks around her favourite aisles in the supermarket, the bank she uses, the café she goes to in her lunch break from work. At night he stands outside her house in the dark and stares up at her window. At first she found it all a little disconcerting.

She knows he's her future husband, because he has evidence. He's kept it neat in a brown manila envelope. He has shown the marriage certificate, and a few of the love letters she'll send him in her own handwriting, and some photos of them on their wedding day. She's all dressed in white. She looks so happy.

Her future self is pretty. So why isn't he with her instead? Wouldn't that be better for everyone, rather than going back in time and stalking the plainer, duller past version? But he won't answer that.

And whenever she asks to see his time machine he refuses. He says that'd create a paradox that could wipe out all life on earth. He says the physics would be too much for her, she's such a silly goose, she wouldn't understand things like that! He knows who she'll become, she'll *never* understand things like that. And he presses his finger to her lips, and shakes his head, and gives her a slow and knowing wink, and all in a manner she has to suppose one day she'll think adorable.

48

Shortly after they'd begun dating, he used a time machine to nip into the future and judge the quality of his successor. He was impressed by the boyfriend who'd come after him—nice teeth, nice hair, easy on the eyes and no slouch in the brains department. It made him feel proud that his new girlfriend had the good taste one day to dump him for someone so much better. Many of his exes had had such poor judgement—frankly, he'd been passed over for idiots.

63

He tries to warn her. He knows he is a shallow man. He loves her *now*, yes—but he's loved before, many times, and it always ends the same way. One morning he will wake up beside her and realise the passion is over, it'll have dribbled away whilst he wasn't looking, and he'll do his best to fire it up once more but it'll be gone, it'll be gone. He'll break her heart. He is a shallow man. He'll break her heart. And she smiles at this, and kisses him on the lips, and it feels soft, and she tells him not to worry. There's no need to cry. Don't cry. And that night when they go to sleep he wraps her up in his arms and holds on to her so hard and so desperately.

33

He thought she might leave him when he grew old. But she said that every one of his wrinkles was a story, and she hadn't finished reading them yet.

86

If I read all the love stories in the world, and followed their instructions, I'm sure I could win you back. If I only could read them in the right order.

47

There's a quantifiable amount of love in her, she realises that now. On her wedding day she loves him almost fit to burst—he looks so handsome in his suit, and he's so nice, and he's so happy, and he's so happy because of *her*—he speaks at the reception and is clever and just a little bit racy and as she looks at him over the cake she thinks she can just about eat him up. She loves him so hard and so furiously that day that when she wakes up the next morning she discovers with horror that she's burned her way through a good forty percent of it already—nearly half of her love has been squandered, and they haven't made it through the honeymoon yet! So she tries to ration out the love she feels for him for the remainder of the holiday, she's cool and reserved about him every time he's not directly with her, when he's in the bathroom, for example—but it's no good, it's a honeymoon for God's sake, and Venice is *so* romantic. By the time they return home to begin ordinary married life she's used up sixty-eight percent of all the love she can ever feel for him, and her heart feels chilled and a little empty, the remains of her love seem to rattle around inside like dry peas in a tin can.

They're both young, they might have fifty years of marriage ahead of them. Maybe it'll be all right. Maybe, if she resents him throughout the year, but uses up half a percent every birthday as a gift. Or hates him during the daytime, really truly learns to *hate* him—but at night, when all is still and peaceful, she can love him a little in her dreams.

45

Scientists have announced the discovery of a new planet in the solar system—and it's my wife's head. It was on the news, everyone seems very excited by it. It's odd, because at first glance my wife's head doesn't seem to fulfil any of the standard criteria given to planet classification—it doesn't revolve exclusively around the sun, for starters, nor does it have sufficient mass to assume hydrostatic equilibrium. And compared to some of the more familiar planets my wife's head is really rather small. I'm not quite sure what to make of it all. My wife, of course, is as unflappable as ever, she's a rock. "That's nice," she says.

NASA are going to launch a probe to examine my wife's head. There are discussions about whether the head is gaseous or not, could there be any life on my wife's face, could it even one day be habitable? There'll be no answers for a while. My wife's head is so distant that even with the latest space technology it'll take at least ten years for the probe to reach her.

Some speculate that beneath the surface there may lie frozen oceans, capable of supporting simple organisms, and with that new knowledge at last would come the reassurance that in this vast cold universe we are not alone. I love my wife so much. I ask her what she thinks. She says she's not sure it'll make much difference; it's not as if we take care of the life we already have here at home. She doesn't seem very interested, and in her nonchalance her face hangs slack and there's no feeling in it. I lose hope. It seems absurd to think there could be any life in there at all.

But sometimes, just recently. Sometimes. When she doesn't know I'm looking. When she thinks I'm asleep. I'll catch her at the bedroom mirror staring at her reflection, and she puts her fingers to her cheeks and traces the outline of all the craters with something like awe. And I don't know whether she's just another cold dead rock world hanging in infinite space, or whether she's something extraordinary—but either way, my heart flutters.

87

I want to be her satellite, her moon.

83

They carried about the ghosts of their love. His was thinner, even svelte, and dated from before he'd grown the beard. Hers looked much the same at first glance—but on careful study you'd see that the ghost smiled more, and its eyes were brighter, and its shoulders less hunched.

They kept the ghosts in the spare room. In bed they could hear them through the wall, giggling and whispering to each other. They were pretty sure they were whispering about *them*. And every single night the ghosts would make love, and to be fair they weren't inconsiderate, even in the days of their passion neither of the couple had been given to demonstrative squealing. But even so, the walls of the house were thin, they could hear each and every ghostly grunt of pleasure.

And she might lose her temper, and she'd bang on the wall, and tell the ghosts to keep it down, shut up, shut up, shut up. And he'd say, ssh now, it's all right—and she'd say, it's *not* all right, nothing about this situation is remotely all right. And she'd cry, and he'd want to comfort her, and he wouldn't know how.

25

They carried about the ghosts of what their love would become. His was fat, and old, and why did his skin have that rash, and why did he scratch it so? Hers looked much the same at first glance—and that was somehow even worse, that meant there was nothing to distinguish the happy from the sad at all.

They kept their ghosts in the spare room. In bed they would strain to hear them—but they didn't talk much, these ghosts, they didn't have much to say. The silence between them was unbearable. It seemed to leak through the wall. If they weren't careful, the silence would reach them, and smother their love to death.

"Let's make love," she'd say every night, and her eyes would be wild, and he'd say, but I'm so tired, can't we just sleep instead, can't we sleep for a change? But she was insistent. Her eyes weren't wild with lust but with panic—we can't become *them*, she said, we mustn't become the ghosts next door, so passionless, so spent—make love to me right now, seize each moment of love that we can!

And they'd bounce around with all the energy they could muster, they were both so tired and getting tireder, they just wanted to stop, they'd bounce about until they heard the ghosts bang on the wall in complaint. But what if one day the ghosts didn't *need* to complain, what if the ghosts saw through their forced passion? They grinned at each other through gritted teeth as they slammed their bodies towards climax—"I love you," he'd say, "I love you," she'd say, and they'd think of the ghosts next door and wonder which one of them had stopped saying I love you first.

9

There's a haunted look in her eyes each time he tells her he loves her. At first he wonders whether she just looks randomly haunted, it doesn't necessarily have anything to do with his love. So he stares at her face when he talks about the weather, what's on the telly, the day he's had at work—and no, she never seems the least bit haunted by any of that, it's only when he uses the 'L' word. He supposes this ought to worry him. But it doesn't. He likes her looking haunted, it lends her face new mystery. And he keeps throwing declarations of love at her, out of the blue, to see how quickly the face will transform. He should cut down, he thinks. Her face might break. But it's so hard to stop—what a lovely surprise it is, after all these years of marriage, to turn his wife into a toy.

57

The second date was sweeter than the first date. The first had given them something to be nostalgic about. "Do you remember that time the waiter asked if we wanted wine?" "Ha! Do *you* remember how we said 'yes'?" They ordered exactly the same food as before, just for tradition's sake. They laughed at the same jokes together, together nodded soberly at the same forays into current affairs. And when they said good night, and promised there'd be a third date soon, they kissed—and that was new, they hadn't kissed before. The taste and texture of each other's lips seemed familiar and reassuring. And both kept their eyes open so they could recall and mythologise every detail for next time.

67

They'd had five dates, they'd gone to five different restaurants. They'd had Italian, Indian, Chinese, Thai. It was during the Mexican meal that he told her he was in love with her, and she was so pleased.

"I knew it right from the start," she said. "But I didn't dare say anything. Now I can admit it. All those magical times together, I kept souvenirs. Look." And she reached into her handbag, and pulled out a little plastic bag. Inside there were serviettes. He saw that there were bolognaise sauce stains on one of them; on another, a mark that might have been sag aloo.

With one hand she stroked at the serviettes fondly, with the other she reached out for his arm and took hold of it hard. "Whatever your lips touch," she said, "it's mine now, it belongs to me." He knew it was romantic, and he should be flattered. But he looked down at the little paper towel with which he had dabbed his lips clean from chimichanga, and he felt this insane urge to keep tight hold and never let it go.

60

She decided she would throw a party, and all her friends would be invited.

It had been seven years since she had dumped him—and she had made many mistakes in the last seven years, but that was one thing she had never regretted, not even once. And if things were getting on top of her or she felt she had put her foot in it again, that was one specific achievement she could look back at with pride—she had dumped him, and that had been so *good.* He'd been charming, certainly—that was the first thing everyone noticed about him, that easy unforced charm. And his clear blue eyes. And his hands—she had never even bothered to look at a man's hands before, what was the appeal of hands?—but his were perfect, large and rugged, and when he'd taken her own hand within his she had felt instantly *enveloped,* so safe, and warm. Oh, dumping him had been hard. It had required strength. It was something that even now, seven years later, she congratulated herself on every single day.

Since she had dumped him she had taken a good long look at herself. She looked in the mirror and could see herself age, see herself *change*—the skin shedding, the hair greying. Every single cell in her body was dying and being replaced in a constant circus of decay and renewal. Year by year she has watched as the body she had worn when she'd dated him has flaked off. In a very real sense, she was no longer the same woman who had loved him so unwisely.

There was now just a final patch of cells that had survived the last seven years. They'd been practically infants at the time of the break-up. One last single grouping of cuticle and dermis, and when that was gone she would be free—not a part of her body would ever have been touched by him, or been breathed on by him, or influenced by him in any way—the last invisible trace of his fingerprints would be erased—she would be virgin pure. She went to the doctor, and he looked at the patch, and said it'd be dead come Sunday. She was pleased.

So she decided to throw a party, and all her friends would be invited. Friends and family too, and even the people at work she didn't like very much, why not? Why not, let them all see her transformation. If this wasn't worth celebrating, what ever else would be? She'd have a barbecue. On Saturday afternoon the weather would be nice. They could all give her dying cells a send-off. She'd get in a big cake, and lots of wine, and some of those little picnic eggs she liked.

77

The day of her party. And Mother arrives early, like always, bringing cake, and sausage rolls, and sparkling wine, and Father. "I've already got food in, Mum," she says, but Mother bats aside her objections with a swipe of her hand; "The cake's homemade," she says, and, "dish it all out, Gerald," and Father wordlessly does as he is told.

Melanie comes soon after. She's known Melanie since school. "I can't stay long," says Melanie. "Jack's not well." Jack is one of her two boyfriends. Neither of her boyfriends are ever well, she collects men who are sick and then nurses them to health. "I like to feel useful," she explains.

Then there are the girls from the marketing department, all in short skirts and heels and wearing the little devil horns they wore at last week's hen party. There are the next door neighbours, Muriel, and Muriel's husband, and they accept glasses of wine, and paper plates for their hot dogs, and talk only to themselves in whispers. Jackie pitches up; Jackie is her favourite hairdresser, and Jackie's had her own hair done up for the occasion, she is quite a sight! She brings along her little assistant Marvin, and they're all over each other, and that's a surprise, she always assumed Marvin was gay.

Her own sister keeps to herself, and sits in the corner of the garden, and drinks a lot, and smokes a lot, and she isn't much used to either, it seems she can't decide from moment to moment whether to put wine glass or cigarette to her mouth next. It looks as if her sister has been crying. She tells her parents about it, and Father grimaces silently, and Mother says, "She doesn't know what she wants. You know your sister."

And there's the smell of dead wine bottles, and fags, and burned meat. There's a fight between the girls in marketing, shrill obscenities and pulled hair. Two of them have dated the same man, and now they can't agree which one hates him the most. She has to separate them, she takes one of them into the kitchen. "It's not fair," the girl says. "She was only with him for a week, I dated the fucker for nine months!" She begins to cry, and rocks her head backwards and forwards, and her demon horns seem to flash on and off in time to the motion.

At some point there's a speech. She didn't realise she'd be giving a speech, but the words seem to come so easily now she's pissed. She stands in the centre of the lawn, and tells everyone to shut up, no, shut up now, and they all stop talking and stop eating burgers and her mother's homemade cake. She thanks them all for coming. They are her friends. Her very dear friends. She loves them all. She explains why they're all here today.

"Well, let's see it then," someone shouts out.

She doesn't want to show them, she's not as drunk as all *that*—but they're soon crying, "Off! Off! Off!" and Melanie is joining in, and so is Jackie, and she looks across to her mother for support, and her mother seems to be leading the chant.

She strips down, and displays the little patch of dying skin cells. Everyone comes closer, and stares at it.

"Looks horrible," says one.

"It looks *contaminated*," says Jackie, and people mutter agreement, and Jackie seems pleased with herself.

"And this is the last bit of your body that bastard touched?" asks Melanie.

"Yes."

"I hate it," Melanie says. "Ugly, nasty thing."

She confirms it will be dead by Sunday afternoon. Sunday evening at the latest.

"I want to spit at it," says Mother. "Can I spit at it?"

She says she would really rather her mother didn't spit at it, no.

She puts her clothes back on, tucks away the last relic of her ex-boyfriend's love. And people stop talking about it, and drift back into their conversations, and their wine glasses, and into their stupors. She feels rather sorry for the patch of skin; after all, it wasn't as if it asked to be touched in the first place, and it'll soon be gone, shouldn't she find some forgiveness for it now? Mother is now smoking and drinking with her sister, Father is asleep. Jackie and Marvin are tonguing each other on the patio. The girls from marketing are now hugging and laughing.

She goes indoors, and starts to clear up.

21

She rubs at the little patch of dying skin with her finger. It feels numb. She hopes it isn't suffering, it doesn't deserve that. She hopes that when her time comes it will be like that, she hopes she'll be numb.

She picks up the telephone, dials the number impulsively.

She is surprised when he picks up.

"Hello?" she says. "I didn't expect you to be there. Are you still there? Is that you?"

He knows who she is right away. "Are you all right?"

"No."

"Do you want to see me?"

"No."

"Do you want me to come over? I can come over. Where are you?"

"I'm still here," she says. "Where I've always been. It's never changed. I've never changed."

He comes right over. He rings the doorbell. She opens the door.

He is so different. Older. All the skin on him, she knows this, by now all his skin she'd ever known will have been replaced, he has stranger's skin. His eyes shine. He smiles that smile. And those hands. He is exactly the same.

"I'm sorry I called," she says.

"Don't be."

"No, I'm sorry."

She shows him in. She tries to remember whether she's made any refurbishments to the house since he's last been there. "The carpet's new," she points out.

The kitchen is still full of paper plates and bottles from her party. And picnic eggs, no one had got through all the picnic eggs. "You been having fun?" he says. "Want some help cleaning up?"

"Please."

"You sit down," he says. "It's all right. I'll take care of this." And she watches as he runs the tap, puts the plates into soapy water one by one.

As he cleans, she tells him the reason for the party. He doesn't seem to react, his attention is on the crockery. And her explanation runs out before the washing up does, and she falls silent, and all she can hear is the slap of his gorgeous hands against the water.

He dries his hands, he turns to look at her. He says, very gently, "Let me see."

She nods, she pulls off her top. "There," she says, "that bit, right under the armpit?"

"May I touch?" And she says yes, so long as he's careful not to touch anything else, just that patch of skin that's already contaminated by him, nothing else.

"Poor little thing," he says. He strokes it with his finger. He kisses it.

She closes her eyes and enjoys it, it isn't numb at all.

"Come to bed," he says. And he holds out his hand to her. And she knows she mustn't touch him, because she'll be right back at the beginning, and the last seven years of watching her skin flake off will count for nothing. But he is charming, he's always been charming. And when she puts her hand in his it envelopes it altogether, it feels so warm and safe.

71

"We should have a child," she says. "A child will renew the spark of our love, will be a bridge to the yawning chasm between us." He can't disagree with the simple logic of that. But wishes she had found more loving words on their wedding night.

89

They had a child, and it was strange, the capacity of the love they had for each other was cleaved exactly in half. The baby took its own share, and that seemed right. So she still loved him for his smile, and his patience, and the way he held her in the night and kept her safe from the bad dreams—but she no longer loved the way he'd cut his toenails in the kitchen and let the clippings ping across the floor.

84

They thought they should stay together for the sake of the kids. The kids took a vote to see whether they wanted this responsibility. They decided seven-four against.

92

She wanted a man who was just like her father, and when she found one she seized him with such insistent passion he couldn't resist. "You'll have to grow a moustache," she said, "and smoke a pipe, and tell funny stories about the war." He did his best to comply. She was delighted. She sat on his knee, and hugged on to him tight, and played with the downy coat of his chest hair. "This is wonderful," she said. "I can't wait for us to have children, just so I can see what my daughter makes of you."

49

The nape of your neck. The first time I ever found a 'nape' attractive—it seemed like such a silly word before. But then I saw yours, and I thought, oh, I get it, now I understand.

18

They broke up over the pronunciation of words. He liked to say 'either', she preferred to say 'either'.

51

He wakes in the night, just to watch her breathing. He likes the way she breathes, the way she sucks the air in, then lets it out between her teeth with a hiss. He likes the way she breathes, when the rest of her body has shut down, when that is all it is. If it could just be about the breathing, he thinks, he could love her forever.

53

And so she wrote him a love letter, and she said he was so wonderful she didn't deserve him, and she wrote it with such sincerity that, sad to say, he believed her.

7

He wrote a message in her Valentine's card, and this year he was inspired, he filled all the blank spaces with words of love, and he had still more words to spare! It seemed silly to waste them, he went out to buy more cards, he decided to write next year's early. He had enough love to fill another five years Valentine's cards, and he was clever, by the last one he'd factored in the little physical differences that would come with age, he started referring to her wrinkles and greying hair. "I still love you," he wrote, "even though you're old now, even though your looks have faded, even though all your friends have become weird and annoying." It felt good to get the homework done early. He hid the Valentine's cards of years to come where she'd never find them, right at the bottom of his sock drawer, then turned on the telly, and cracked open a beer.

36

She told him she was going to be the perfect girlfriend. "But not for you," she added. "I'm working towards my final draft, and I still need to iron out some quirks and kinks. Think of yourself as a beta lover." He agreed he'd give her notes. She was already very good, he said. The sex and the cooking were great, and she had that docile smile down pat. All he had were a few minor tweaks to suggest—perhaps she could take the man's coat when he came home from work, perhaps she could take up less space in bed? She thanked him for his help, and they broke up—they shook hands, and she went on her way. She promised she'd give him a call when she was ready to launch; there'd be a party, she said, and she'd be sure to put his name in the acknowledgements.

52

Tears in the night. He thinks it better not to ask. And, sure enough, by the morning she's stopped.

88

It was after midnight, and there had been complaints about the noise, and the hotel security were forced to knock upon the door. "Could you keep it down, please?" "I'm sorry, we're on our honeymoon!" explained the husband; the hotel clerk smirked and winked, and said he'd leave them to it. The door closed. And the married couple went back to their first blazing row as man and wife.

20

And there was that night we caught the overnight bus back from the beach. The storm was raging, we sat at the back and we were so drenched we stuck together. And I made a joke, a silly joke, that we should watch out for lightning! "Don't," you said quietly. "Please, don't." And then there *was* lightning. It seemed to arc around the freeway, the rain was now so heavy we could barely see out of the windows, but every now and then, by the side of the road, it struck. I had never seen lightning so close. There was a field in flames. And I said sorry, because I felt I'd somehow conjured it into existence, and you squeezed my hand to let me know I was forgiven. You said you were frightened and hugged on to me. I was frightened too. I can tell you that at last. I thought we might burst into flames. I thought we might die. But as we huddled there together, I thought—if it *is* now, then let it be now. With you here beside me in the dark, as I shushed you calm.

6

Now that he can't speak or move, she tells him how much she loves him. She sits beside his bed, and she holds his hand, and she talks of their marriage, all their years together, how much he has meant to her, how much he always will. These are things he has never doubted, but even so, he has never had confirmation of them before. So much love she's felt, and he's surprised how every time she visits she finds some fresh way to express it. It frightens him rather.

5

No. No. No. Yes.

22

If he sleeps on his right hand side, he'll dream of her, and only her. On his back, or on his left, he's safe. Those dreams will be black and numb, and he won't wake up crying, and with so much regret for the things they never did, or the things they could have done better, or the things they did perfectly well but he should have grabbed on to tighter, clung them to him close, and never let go.

If he sleeps on his right hand side, and tucks his arm about the pillow just so, and says the same words before he turns off the light, and holds the image of her fast in his mind's eye—then he'll dream of her, and only her. It's terrible. How he wishes he could make it stop.

95

Halfway through dinner he said he no longer loved her, and she'd spent all afternoon on that casserole, she'd thought it was his favourite. Weeks ago now, and still she can't bear to wash up the plate he's left. The knife he'd gripped so tensely when he said he'd found someone new—the fork that had touched his lips, touched his spit, been deep inside his mouth.

She keeps the plate in the fridge. All the food still on it, just as he'd left it. The knife in the same position. She sometimes picks up the fork, and sniffs at it, and presses it against her tongue—but she makes sure after she puts it back just right.

Every day she takes out the plate and studies it. Only once a day, and in the evening, so she has something to look forward to. The meat now mottles with white spots. Vegetables turn from solid, to liquid, to gas. In the fridge she starts to keep the plate on its own separate shelf.

The white spots become pustules, and the pustules swell and thicken. They turn green. They look like eggs. She stops thinking about the man she's lost. She thinks only of what he's left behind. She wonders what will happen when the eggs hatch, what will come out, and she hopes that it's a creature that's fresh and strange. A brand new act of creation. She sits by the fridge on a hard chair, she watches over the plate now day and night, she wants to witness the moment everything cracks.

17

They get back their wedding photos, rolls and rolls of them, and she goes through them all with a red pen, and each one he's smiling in she obliterates with an X.

40

When he breaks up with her, she lost eight kilos in a week. She had never realised how heavy love can be, how it weighs you down.

97

Blessed with a supernatural gift of precognition, he knew precisely when, years hence, he and his wife would get divorced. And he calculated the exact midway point of their marriage, and took her out for a fancy meal to commemorate it. They had oysters, and *confit de canard au gratin*, and three bottles of the best champagne. It was during the third bottle that he told her what they were celebrating. He cried a lot, and laughed, and twice the waiters had to ask him to keep the noise down. "It's all downhill from here, baby!" he cackled. "Only two thousand and eighteen days to go!" As much as she loved him his wife felt a sudden stab of pure disgust that was entirely new, and she wondered whether she could hold out quite that long.

66

They'd been together for so long, and yet were as happy as they'd ever been. Indeed, he became more devoted to her with the passing of every New Year—he could actually feel it happen inside of him, like a grinding of gears: at midnight as the bells rang out in celebration his heart seemed to click inside his chest, and he'd be flooded with new passion for his wife sweeter than he'd ever known before.

And sometimes he'd see through the rush of that passion his wife's smile wobble—she bit her lip, she looked pensive, she looked guilty. But what of that? He chose to ignore it. He took her to bed, and he pleasured any little worries away.

One year, before the clock chimed, she said, "I can't bear the deceit any longer." And she confessed that she wasn't the woman he thought she was. Really she was a wicked witch. She'd plucked hairs from his head, and cut nails from his toes, she'd mixed them with his blood and his spit and his urine and cast a spell on him. She'd made him love her, she'd blinded him with love. In truth she was an ugly old crone. And the older she got the more his love grew stronger, and the uglier she grew the greater his desire.

"But I love you too," she said. "I didn't expect it to be this way, but it's true. And each year the older you get, I put up with it. And each year the uglier you grow, I accept it. But it's hard. It's hard when I'm the only one who has to forgive the compromises of age. It's hard to be doing all the work myself."

She set him free then from his enchantment. And the clocks struck midnight, the new year was rung in. And all over the town there were fireworks, they lit up his wife's face, the face he had never seen before. He recoiled. And she cried because he recoiled, she cried at the sure inevitability of it.

But still, he stared at that face. Of a woman he had shared his life with, and laughed with, whose company he had treasured as a best friend, whose conversation gave him such delight. The woman who had taken his silly little empty life and filled it with purpose. He stared at her face, at the wrinkles, and the boils, and the maggots that were growing out from those boils—he stared *through* the face, and there it was, there she was. There was the darling he still loved.

56

I know that the love between us is dying. It's so badly sick now, and honestly, I don't think there's a cure. It can't last much longer. But I promise you this. I won't let our love count for nothing. I won't let the years pass, and never see you. You'll still matter. You'll still count. Yes, of course. Yes, of course we can still be friends.

23

Suddenly everyone in the world loses their mirror image. Now you no longer see your own reflection, but instead the face of one of the principle cast members of *Friends*. Only the reflection—other people still see you as you really are. But when you brush your teeth, to all intents and purposes you're scrubbing away at the plaque of Matt LeBlanc or Jennifer Aniston.

It's astonishing how quickly everyone adjusts to the phenomenon. And who could feel worse off—because everyone loves the cast of *Friends*, there's not really a bad one, is there? Though there's a certain status attached to which Friend you see. Most men are David Schwimmer. Most women are David Schwimmer too. Matthew Perrys tend to be people who've been through higher education and have a comfortable disposable income, and congregate around other Matthew Perrys. Jennifer Anistons are rare.

Even the actors from *Friends* are affected. When Lisa Kudrow looks in the mirror, all she can see is Courtney Cox.

And for a while there may be a nagging sense that something has been lost—but, really, it's silly to suggest that your identity is threatened. Aren't you the same person as before? You still work in a bank, you still have sciatica, you still have two kids. You still blush too easily and can't be witty on cue. But you have a little more self-confidence, don't you? Even if it's only a common or garden David

Schwimmer winking at you over the bathroom sink each morning to encourage you on your way. It's good to spend time with your Friends.

Your true appearance, of course, is still fixed in photographs and recordings. You can look at the real you whenever you want to. But why would you want to? And at your wedding you wear a mask of the Friend you feel closest to, and so does your spouse—on a really big day like that, you want to be preserved for posterity the way you know yourself deep inside.

TThey met at work. She thinks he's sweet and funny and gentle. He thinks she's the prettiest girl he's ever seen. When he asks her out for a drink, she eagerly accepts. The drink goes so well it rapidly transforms into a meal, and then the meal into an easy four-hour chat over coffee about everything and anything that only ends when the waiter tells them he'd really like to shut up shop and go home. She asks him what his star sign is; he's an Aquarius. She asks him his Friends sign; he's a Matthew Perry. "Oh!" she says. "Well, I'm a Gemini and a Lisa Kudrow!" They share their first kiss on the pavement, and it's raining hard, and neither of them cares, and both of them think – maybe this time it'll be all right, maybe this time it'll be love, real love. And if it is real love, maybe the love will be strong enough that they'll one day tell the truth. A truth they've never told anyone, not their doctors, not their families, not their closest friends. That when they look of them in the mirror the only reflection either of them has ever seen staring back is Marcel the monkey. Those of us who are the Marcels, we make sure we are always seen smiling when we look in the mirror, we fight that daily disappointment down.

(50)

(There is no 'fifty', there is no middle to my love.)

68

Did anyone actually like that monkey on *Friends*? I was never a big fan, but I've seen a lot of the episodes, who hasn't? And I saw lots of the ones that featured the monkey. I remember that bit where the monkey keeps getting hold of Ross's hi-fi system and playing his own CDs, that was pretty clever. But clever isn't funny. We can admire clever, but we never love it. Funny is funny; clever puts us off.

There were two hundred and thirty-six episodes of *Friends*, but Marcel the monkey only featured in eight of them. The character was written out at the end of the first season, the producers claimed there was just one too many cast members. Apparently it had been a toss-up between Marcel and Lisa Kudrow.

I'm no expert on the monkey from *Friends*, okay? I make no claims for that. But there was this one time I met someone who was.

I was at a television convention in Toronto a few years back. I was representing some British sci-fi series you probably haven't heard of. I'm sure the Canadians would rather the BBC had sent an actor, but they'd got a writer instead—and they were very polite, being Canadians, but it was a pretty chilly politeness. I felt quite lonely, and so when I wasn't promoting my own show I would check out some of the others. They had *Lost* there, they had *The Sopranos*, and all the different incarnations of *Star Trek*, past, present and future. There was one panel that advertised the cast from *Friends*, and I had no idea the cast from *Friends* were at the same conference as me, and I was intrigued. I went to the *Friends* panel. When I got in, though, and took my seat among all the *Friends* fans, I saw that up on stage there was just this one woman I didn't recognise, sitting next to the monkey.

The audience would ask the monkey questions. The monkey considered each question carefully, and then would chitter at the woman, and she'd lean into her microphone and translate. Yes, Marcel had loved his brief stint on *Friends*! Yes, he was still in regular contact with all the other cast members, they hung out sometimes and always exchanged cards at Christmas. Yes, if Central Perk were a real coffee shop and he could order coffee there his favourite coffee would be a monkey macchiato.

The monkey never acknowledged the woman, and when the panel ended and he thanked the audience for coming, he didn't so much as look at her. I saw her in the bar that evening, and no one was talking to her, I thought she might very well be the only person there less famous than me. I asked if she'd like a drink. She said she would. She looked grateful.

It didn't take many drinks before she was telling me the truth. Marcel had had a miserable time on *Friends*. The rest of the cast had never made him welcome. Jennifer Aniston, Matt LeBlanc, Courtney Cox... as soon as the cameras stopped rolling, they wouldn't even speak to him. Lisa Kudrow and Matthew Perry actually bullied him; they never laid a finger on him, but it was *psychological* bullying, and that was worse somehow. They'd hide his bananas and call him 'apebreath'. Only David Schwimmer was nice to him—and that sucked, who'd want David Schwimmer being nice to you? When Marcel was sacked he was almost relieved. Almost—but sometimes he'd drink too much, and take too many pills, and then he'd get maudlin, he'd say he was a washed-up chimp and he'd missed his one chance for superstardom. Sometimes, she said, Marcel couldn't cope with the questions on stage, and he'd snap, and he'd come out with stuff that was borderline obscene. Sometimes she didn't merely translate, she had to make up the answers altogether.

She was a monkey wrangler, she told me. That was her official job description. She had been a monkey gaffer, but she'd worked her way up.

"My parents are ashamed," she said. "This is what you do with your life, my father says, you wrangle monkeys? And not even a successful monkey, a has-been monkey, a faded star. And what does that make me? I'm not a has-been, I'm a never-was, I'm a never-gonna-be."

"Yeah," I said. "But Hollywood, right? That's got to be nice!" The BBC had filmed most of my stuff in Cardiff.

She asked me back to hers. She said it casually enough, but when I said I might as well she looked so delighted her eyes began to water. Outside her bedroom door she gave me a kiss on the lips, and that was very nice, and she said, "I won't be long, wait here," and I said, "What about the monkey?" and she sort of snapped, "I'm dealing with it, aren't I?" She left me out in the corridor for about ten minutes. Once in a while people would emerge from the lift, and I would pat at my pockets as if trying to find my keys.

The bed looked big and soft, and she'd got undressed and there was a lot of flesh on display. But I couldn't help it, my attention kept being drawn to that little cot by the television. Inside it was Marcel the monkey, and he was stretched out on his back, and his paws were sticking up rigid, and once in a while the paws would start to pedal the air. "Forget about him," she said, "what he doesn't know won't hurt him." We began making out. But I don't know, whenever I closed my eyes I pictured the monkey's face, I thought it was the monkey who was nibbling at me, the monkey who was grunting—and perhaps the grunting was the monkey's, because even drugged to the eyeballs he was clearly having vivid dreams of some sort or another. "This is for me, this is just for me!" the wrangler kept saying over and over, as she ground away.

At length I just had to push her off. "I should leave," I said. I told her I felt sorry for Marcel. He'd been betrayed all his career, and now we were betraying him as well. She, his best friend and only confidante, and me, a guy who'd quite liked the episode where he played with Ross's hi-fi. "Bullshit," she said. "You don't feel sorry for him, you feel ashamed of me. You wouldn't leave if it were Matt LeBlanc I'd been wrangling." And I didn't say so, but I suppose she had a point.

A few years later I read in the newspaper that Marcel had killed himself. He was doing a stage adaptation of *The Lion King*, it was only a small part. They found him hanging in his dressing room during the interval, and it's hard for monkeys to hang themselves to death, hanging is pretty much their most comfortable position. Right to the end Marcel had been very clever—but not necessarily very funny.

Of the wrangler no mention was made, but that didn't mean anything. She might have found another job ages ago.

26

Dear God, but I miss you.

80

"Do you love me enough you'd die for me?" she asked, and he said, "I'd really rather not, no." And after long discussion he conceded he *would* die for her, but only under certain conditions—if there was no hope of rescue, and he would have died soon anyway, and it wouldn't be a painful death, and he would be anaesthetised beforehand by a trained doctor. It wasn't the romantic response she had hoped for—but he was lucky, she just happened to find wheedling pragmatism a massive turn-on.

39

"I'd give my life for you," he'd told her, and she had thought that sweet, but just one of those things lovers say. But one day it had happened. In a rather dramatic and tragic turn of events, he'd kept his promise. And now he was gone and she was still here, here and only here because of him, he'd proved his love in the noblest way imaginable. And it made her guilty to think it, but she really wished he hadn't bothered. What was the use when she was now left all alone?

72

He'd proposed to her at the top of the Eiffel Tower twenty-five years ago. She'd always been nervous of heights, but somehow the thought of going up to the very top wasn't a problem, not if he were there with her. He'd asked her afterwards whether it was really such a surprise he'd proposed, hadn't she been expecting it? And she hadn't been!—even when he'd got down on one knee she'd assumed he was tying his shoelace. When he took out the little jewellery box and opened it and showed her the ring, when he told her how much he loved her, for the longest moment her brain couldn't make sense of it at all. She'd said yes to him right away. Of course she had. And the first kiss she shared with a man she already thought of as her husband was to the amused applause of several dozen Frenchmen and tourists.

They had never been back since. And once in a while he'd suggested it, wouldn't it be nice if…? And she'd always said, oh yes, yes please, one day! So now they were actually *booking* it, a full weekend in Paris, they'd paid the money, they'd got the email confirmation, and it had all been so simple to do, it still seemed unreal.

There would have been changes, they knew that. And no francs, for example, they'd have to get euros. But he said, "Try as they might, they can't change what Paris *is*," and she agreed, "No," she said, "Paris will go on forever."

She thought they should stay at the same hotel. It had only been a two star hotel, that was all they could afford back then, and they looked it up on the internet, and now it had three stars! Things were looking up! When they got to Paris and checked in they couldn't see what the extra star was for, the room was pretty shabby. And he said it wasn't too late, they could find another hotel altogether if she liked. But she told him it didn't matter. And she pulled him down on to the bed beside her.

They were too tired to go out that first night, so they ate in the hotel restaurant. They both had steak and chips, and it was delicious. "They cook better than they clean," she said, and they agreed it was a very nice meal. They ordered a second glass of wine each, he raised a toast to her, and she blushed.

The bed was pretty hard, and the walls were thin so they could hear their neighbours talking in the adjoining room. It didn't bother her; "It's lovely to hear French the way it *should* be spoken," she said. "Isn't it a beautiful language?" And they were so tired, and when they woke the next morning they both said it had been the best night's sleep they'd had in ages.

19

They went to Notre Dame, and then they walked around Montmartre. He asked her if she'd like to be sketched by one of the artists there, but she didn't really. It'd be nice, but where would they hang it? Their walls at home were filled already, and he thought that was a good point. For lunch he had a croque monsieur, and, not to be outdone, she had a croque madame. They queued to get into the Louvre, and they both thought the Mona Lisa was smaller than they remembered, but that was it prettier too. "She knows something I don't," he said, and she said, "She knows *tons* more than me!" As they looked at the painting he held her hand and stroked at the back of it with his fingers.

They went back to the hotel to eat, because the steak had been so good. And that night they made love. He was worried the neighbours would hear through those thin walls. They made love very quickly, and it was nice, and they both agreed it was the best sex they'd had in ages.

The next morning he said they should go back to where it had all begun. To the Eiffel Tower, and pay their respects. She agreed, but could they walk along the Seine first, it was so sunny, and the river looked so calm. He bought them both an ice cream, even though they'd just had their breakfasts, even though they didn't much like ice creams—and he didn't eat his fast enough, it melted over his hand, and she laughed, and helped him to lick it off.

And then they went to where the Eiffel Tower had stood. There was a longer queue than for the Louvre, and he thought that was strange, and she thought it was nice—it showed that people were essentially good, that they wouldn't let things like this happen again. There was a plaque on the ground, marking the exact centre point of the tower.

They both got on to the plaque, and he looked up, as if trying to see where he had proposed to her all those years ago, and she looked up too. Then they moved on, other tourists were wanting to stand at ground zero. There were other plaques all about, and on them were the names of the people who had died. There were flowers, and there were banners, and some of them said, "Jamais Encore."

"I love you," he told her, and she said she loved him too, but it didn't seem entirely appropriate.

27

For the third night running they had steak and chips at the hotel. "Why change it, when we're on to a good thing?" he said. They ate, and didn't speak for a while, and then he said, "Paris has changed, of course it has. It would have done. But I think I'm surprised by how much of it is exactly the same. In spite of it all, it's the same." She wasn't sure if the steak had been cooked differently, it seemed tough and tasteless. "Over all," he said, "I'm glad we came."

She lay on the bed beside him, and she thought of how they had stood on the top of the Eiffel Tower, and she'd been scared, but he had kissed her scares away. And he'd got on one knee, and everyone had applauded, and some of them were French people, and a lot had been tourists. You got all sorts at the Eiffel Tower.

She cried.

"I'm sorry," he said. He held her. "I'm sorry."

And it wasn't that there were bad things in the world, because she'd always known that. And it wasn't that the place so precious to them had been destroyed. It had been a good marriage, and she loved him, even if she thought the love had a different taste to it these days. They'd never had children, and they'd never bought that cottage in the country and never would, and they'd never done half of the things they'd promised, and they'd been so young when they'd first come to Paris, and now, somehow, they were old.

"I'm sorry," and he was still saying it, and none of this was his fault.

"I don't want to go home," she said. "It's been such a lovely holiday." And he kissed her, and he held her close, he held her all night long.

55

I love you. It breaks my heart that only a few weeks ago those words would have thrilled you—and now just make you cross.

35

They had promised they would stick together through thick and thin. They agreed it was the most important of all their wedding vow—that was the bit of the service when they looked most deeply into each other's eyes, and she'd given his hand a squeeze, and he'd squeezed right back. Neither of them had liked it when the water had turned to blood, but they put a brave face on it—she said she'd just get used to the coppery taste in her coffee, he still helped with the washing-up even though the plates got so sticky. She was frightened of locusts, but he took care of them for her, every time they entered a room he'd swat them all dead and let her know when it was safe to come in. He'd never been much fond of frogs, he hated the touch of them, the sliminess repelled him—but with frogs she was a trouper, frogs held no fear for her, she'd snap on some rubber gloves and scoop them up with her hands, she'd keep him safe, she'd protect him. When their skins burst open with boils they didn't complain—yes, they were both ugly now, but they were both ugly together, and that's what mattered.

And when their only son was swept away in that plague of the first born—well, they were devastated, of course. He'd had his father's eyes, he'd had his mother's smile. But they held fast. They refused to give in to despair. They kept close, they kept faith with one another.

It seemed to them that every adversity could only make them stronger. No matter what life threw at them, they each had their own secret weapon—and it shared their bed, it held them in the night and kept them warm. Together they would face down anything. And together, each evening, they would go out into the garden, and stare up at the night sky, stare past the stars and up towards heaven. They would shout out to God a challenge. Do your worst, you old shit. Do your worst. We're still standing.

24

Their son died just before Christmas. He'd been eight years old. It was an awful thing. It had been a simple accident, and that was at least better than the agony of a long illness, but still—awful, unspeakably awful.

The parents were devastated. The Christmas tree was already up, and they hadn't the heart or the strength to take it back down. In the early hours of Christmas Day the husband found his wife frantically wrapping up all their dead son's presents and putting them under the tree. "Don't say anything," she told him, "just help me,"—and he did.

In the morning they found their son waiting by his mound of presents. He was grinning from ear to ear, and jumping up and down, he was so excited. He didn't seem to know he was dead, and his parents didn't know how to tell him. They let him open his presents, he tore off the wrapping paper and how he squealed to see his shiny new toys. There was a board game and a model aeroplane and a radio controlled car—"I want to play with them all!" And he did, he played with every single one, and they watched him have fun until it was past his bedtime.

They wondered whether he'd still be there the next morning, and he wasn't. Because it had been a little Christmas miracle. Because he was dead and gone, and that was the way of it.

They packed up all his new toys, and put them away in the attic.

And it wasn't as if their grieving was any easier. Or that either of them could talk about what happened, even to each other. But they both knew they'd had the gift of spending one more day with someone they loved more than they could express, and they'd seen him happy.

And they carried on, in spite of their grief, and they survived.

One day, a year later, the husband caught his wife bringing a little radio controlled boat in with the groceries. "What's this?" he asked, and she started, and looked guilty, and told him she wanted to get their son some new toys for Christmas, something that would lure him back.

They didn't think that it would work. But they wrapped up lots of new presents, and all the old presents they'd stashed in the attic, and put them under the tree. And it *did* work—on Christmas morning their son was back again, bouncing about with glee. He didn't appear to have aged. He didn't appear to know he'd done this all before, and he played with both new toys and old toys with the same joy.

Each year the parents got their eight year old boy back for Christmas. And though it made the three hundred and sixty-four days they spent without him all the more painful, maybe that special twenty-four hours of unadulterated love made up for it.

93

The parents grew old. Their eight year old son didn't seem to notice that Mummy and Daddy were no longer as fit as they'd once been, that they could no longer play with him without panting for breath.

The husband died just before Christmas. It was an awful thing. It had been a long illness, and that was at least better than the random stupidity of an accident, but still—it was awful beyond words.

And for the first time the wife felt properly alone, and she had to wrap all her son's toys by herself, and without her husband to hold down the ends of sellotape.

She wasn't sad. She refused to be sad. People were surprised, even thought her rather callous. But she knew everything would be all right. Because Christmas was coming, and she would have her family back.

On Christmas morning she got up from bed, and her bones cracked, and her back ached, and she didn't care. For one day at least her love would see her through. She raced down to the tree to see what was waiting beneath it.

There was her dead son, bouncing about as always, he couldn't wait to tear into his presents and play with his toys. But he was on his own.

"Where's Daddy?" she asked the boy. "Where is he? Didn't you bring Daddy with you? Where's Daddy?" Because she'd got her husband all the things he liked—the shaving kit, the socks, the slippers—she'd wrapped them up and put them under the tree.

She rounded on her son. "Couldn't you bring a present for me?" she said. "Isn't it my turn?"

Her son didn't answer, he was too busy with his board game and his model aeroplane and all the pointless gadgets that were radio controlled and shiny and brand new, and she understood that she'd never see her husband again, that all that love she'd planned to keep inside forever was useless now and needed to be let go.

70

Their love was foretold by Nostradamus, it was referenced in the Koran, there was a footnote about it at the very bottom of the Ten Commandments. Cut down the largest living tree and count the rings in the bark, and there you'd find enumerated every single day since they'd first met and fallen in love. Each time he had declared his love for her and she had declared it right back. And sometimes, when the night was clear, when there were no clouds, the stars in the sky would spell out their names in a giant celestial heart.

That said, they didn't have a whole lot of friends. There was something just a little bit smug about them, you know?

38

Since Father had gone her mother hadn't had many good days, and so he was surprised to hear her on the telephone, she sounded so excited, so happy. "I've such good news!" she said. "You must come and see!"

The house seemed bigger now Mother was living on her own, she didn't have anything to fill the empty spaces with. Mother told him, "Your father's back, he's come back to me!" And she pointed at the dog.

He endeavoured to explain that Father was now living in a flat in Bayswater, but Mother shushed him. "He isn't your father," she said. "Your father would never have left me and broken my heart. Your father would never have run off with some hipless bitch. That's just the shell of your father. His spirit stayed here with me." The spirit had hung around the house the last month or two, trying to find some way to communicate with his darling wife, to reassure her it still loved her. And eventually, perhaps as a last resort, it had entered the dog.

"I saw it go in," added Mother. "There was a sort of whoosh!"

The dog had been in the family for years. It still looked like a dog. It didn't now walk on two legs, like his father had, nor smoked a pipe. It lay on the rug by the chimney, eyes barely open, it was probably trying to sleep. "I prefer him in the dog," Mother said. "Now he can be with me whenever I want. I sit him on my lap whilst I watch my soaps, I keep him in the bedroom at night. He can't open the door. And he doesn't ask for sex. Go on. Go on, be polite. Go on, say hello to your father."

He bent down. He bent close. He put his face up to the dog's. "Hello, Dad," he said.

"I only feed him his favourite things," he heard his mother say. "Roast beef and Yorkshire pudding. Wine. Cake. The way to a man's heart is through his stomach." The dog was panting for breath, he could see now how much weight it had gained, it could barely move. But otherwise it seemed happy, it gave him a smug smile. And his father had had a smile that smug, who was to say he wasn't hiding in there, really?

"It's just so good to have him back," Mother said, and the dog seemed to nod in agreement, and it farted, and the fart smelled like chocolate.

74

If she had to lie to her husband, she thought at least the lies should be interesting. Just because she was cheating on him, it didn't mean her excuses couldn't entertain him. She created a new best friend called Stacey she could say she was out with when she was shagging her boss in that motel outside Ipswich. Stacey was great. She was so glamorous, and the things she got up to, and the jokes she told! That time she'd gone skinny dipping, or spent all night with a judge off *X-Factor*, or come into work without wearing knickers! "That Stacey!" he'd say. "She's a crazy girl!", and he'd laugh and shake his head. And she noticed that whenever Stacey was mentioned her husband would stop what he was doing to listen, and his pupils would get bigger, and his body stiffer, and the tip of his tongue would peek out from his lips like a snake's.

73

When his mistress broke up with him, saying she could waste no more of her life on an adulterous cheat, he was strangely glad, and felt suddenly single and free—and it wasn't until he got home he remembered he wasn't.

62

He insisted they gave their first child his own name, so that when one day they got divorced she'd have something to remember him by.

64

He was surprised just how quickly the love for his wife had turned to hate. And he wondered whether that was a property unique to her, or whether other passions in his life could be transmuted so easily. He spent the whole afternoon summoning to mind all the things he held dear, just so he could turn them sour, he concentrated so hard it made his head ache—Christmas, Pink Floyd, bread rolls straight from the oven, long summer days sunbathing by her side, winter evenings huddled together for warmth, football, chocolate, sex.

78

And so he was the one selected to take up the matter with God. He set off into the desert, and fasted in readiness, then climbed to the top of a high mountain. God manifested himself as a burning bush—"What seems to be the problem?" said God.

The man explained there was a design flaw with the heart. It was just too sensitive. It kept getting bruised, or pecked at, or pulled about in all directions. It'd flare up for the wrong person, often for lots of wrong persons all at once, often when you really truly cared for the right person but they were just starting to seem a tad boring. It'd pang, it'd flutter, it'd beat like a drum, and all at inappropriate moments. It'd ache. Oh, it could ache. It made no sense. No man, woman nor child could fathom the human heart.

"What do you expect me to do about it?" said God.

The man suggested that maybe the heart was in the wrong position in the body. That it'd be considerably less vulnerable or irksome if it were moved elsewhere. The human frame was a fine piece of craftsmanship, he added hastily, because he could see the bush was rustling in irritation. But having the heart balanced on top of the head? It just didn't work.

So God hearkened unto what the man had said. The heart was relocated just between the thighs. That seemed better for a while, but it didn't half chafe when you walked. God moved it again, this time to slap bang in the middle of the face—and no one liked that much because it was hard to peer round the tricuspid valve sticking out the side. God moved the heart a third time, to the crack of the arse, but it kept on getting covered with shit.

"You again," said God, as the man climbed once more up the mountain. "I never have this problem with the squirrels. What now?"

Man said, "How about we just do without the heart altogether?"

"Fine with me," said God. "Anything to shut you up." And the bush snapped its twigs like fingers, and lo, the heart was gone for good. Instead he set deep within Man's chest a clock, a silly little clock, and the clock didn't do anything useful, it just ticked away inside where all mankind could hear it, counting down the days of our existence until death.

29

God himself is there to welcome you both through the pearly gates. "These guys," he says to the angels, "these guys, just look at these guys!" There have been a hundred billion people who have lived on Earth, and none of them ever quite managed to get love right—until you two came along. There are balloons everywhere with your faces on, there is bunting. Angels shyly line up to take selfies and ask for your autographs. God tells you he's been watching everyone get it wrong for millennia—they never find their soulmates, kept apart by oceans or centuries or just catching the wrong bus—and instead they've all put up with someone who doesn't quite fit, doesn't quite work, they've muddled through on compromise. But you—you—you alone, you both found the person you were always destined for. "I never intended it to be *easy*," says God. "But I never intended the odds against it to be so astronomical either!" He tells you he has no idea whether your success is down to genius, or divine providence, or just dumb luck. You agree it's been a good marriage, and it had a simple formula: listening to each other's problems, finding hobbies you can share, never going to bed on an argument. Date night every other Friday, and cocoa in bed on a Sunday morning. "Really, it's not rocket science," one of you says; the other agrees, "We're each other's very best friends!" God's autograph book is the biggest autograph book of all—in it you write, "To God—Never stop believing," and you sign your names beneath with perfectly compatible flourishes.

13

Even after all these years, they only mouth their 'I love you's. The words carry so much power, they might break something if they said them out loud.

46

I count the ways I love you. It is not romantic. The time for romance is past now. This procedure is purely practical. I need to sleep at night. The doctors tell me I need to sleep. And I can't sleep for missing you. So I don't sleep.

Some people count sheep, I count the ways I love you. That I've always loved you. Ever since we met, all those years ago.

76

She died one stark day in February, and the rain was turning to sleet, the sort that makes his joints ache—and he cried—and so he had her buried in Barbados, thousands of miles from home, far away from the cold because she had never been a cold woman, her gravestone facing the sea—and each time it's her birthday he flies over to pay his respects to the only love he's ever had—"I miss you," he says—he stands upon the beach and feels the sun upon his face and the waves beat at his knees, and he feels happy, he feels happy that he knew her.

12

She begins taking lessons in French, just so she's got an entirely new language with which to ignore him.

82

She'd only slept with men famous enough their deaths would be reported in the newspapers. And now every morning after breakfast she turns first to the obituary column, pen in hand just in case she gets to cross another one off her list.

16

He thought her growing disdain was literally killing him, it felt like his insides were being torn apart. She'd glare at him over the dining table and how his guts would twist. But when he went to the doctor the diagnosis was far more prosaic—she'd been grinding up glass and putting it in his food, oh, what a relief.

32

Pretty soon, he thought, I'll be so old that the only people left to love me will do so out of nostalgia.

65

First time in bed, and she said to him, "You know, you have all the bearings of a Greek god."

"Really? Okay. Wow."

"But which god? Let me see. Let me look at you properly. Well then. There's a touch of the Hermes about you. He was the messenger god, he was very nimble, and you've certainly been nimble with me. Or Hades, god of the underworld. Because there's the very devil in you! But no. No, I think you're Apollo. Very handsome, but also very wise."

"I'll be your Apollo for you. I'd like to be your Apollo."

"And which Greek goddess do you think I can be?"

"Venus," he said. "Definitely Venus. Oh yes."

She turned away. "I said *Greek* gods, dipshit," she said. And they had sex again soon after, but somehow the spark seemed to have gone.

11

When she dumped him it hurt so much he thought she'd broken his heart—but the X-rays proved he was merely suffering from a bruised ego.

90

The first kiss isn't very good. Was he too excited? Too drunk? He was out of practice maybe, but he remembered what to do, surely, where to put his lips, his teeth, his tongue? She pulled back, said, "One last try." He nodded. He took a breath so deep his cheeks bulged. He knew this had to be the clincher.

94

If he'd known it was to be their last kiss, he just might have opened his mouth a little wider.

59

When she broke up with him she sent him a long essay detailing all his faults and failings—delineating the difference between the ones that were psychological and the ones that were anti-social, in clear bullet point form, with diagrams. He was offended at the time. But he had to admit, when he resumed dating a few months later, they gave him some useful pointers, and the colour coded areas about personal hygiene were especially helpful.

28

Only two weeks into the relationship, and he had already eclipsed her. He was smarter, kinder, dressed more nattily, and was better at telling jokes. He'd sometimes look over his shoulder, and see her shivering in the darkness of his shadow, and he'd ask, "Are you all right?" And she'd shout back she was fine, but her voice didn't travel very far, she wasn't sure he could hear her.

37

His first girlfriend had a cluster of small moles upon her back. And after they had made love—clumsy with inexperience, but so joyous, so exciting!—he'd lie next to her as she dozed, and he'd stroke the moles with his finger, and it seemed to him like a map, he'd trace the journey from A to B to C to D. He forgets about those moles now, he forgets about that first love of his. Except sometimes when he's with his wife, and he stares at her sleeping beside him, and he longs for a map to be printed somewhere on her skin, that he might know her better, that he might have a clue where they are going.

91

A couple in the holocaust exhibition break into a snog right in front of them, blocking their view of a scale model of Dachau. "We used to be like that," she tells him. She tries to hold his hand, but he's too busy reading about dead people.

14

Four years were up, it was time for another election. The country would go to the polling booths to decide who would be his next girlfriend. For months now there'd been hustings and televised debates, and people knocking at the door canvassing votes—frankly, he thought, it'd be a relief when it was all over, and did it make that much difference who was in power really? He hoped the voters would put in office a better girlfriend this time, he hadn't enjoyed the last one's policies on how much he smoked and who had control over the TV remote. But he wouldn't complain; he knew it wasn't perfect, but democracy was still the best system they had.

43

He knows that when he's with her she's the best she'll ever be. He's seen the photos taken before they met, and she was really nothing special. He's heard what her friends have said, how she's improved in leaps and bounds since they started dating. And he's followed her about, stealthily, and it's true, the further away from his influence she gets the more she seems to regress into a dull and dowdy bore. He's so happy he can do such wonders for her. That his love is so transformative. It makes his heart swell with pride. She's worth all the effort he puts into her, to make her shine, if he can derive this sort of satisfaction for a job well done.

81

He knows that when he's with her, he's the best he can ever be. That's enough.

41

You think back on all the people in history, and wonder, did any of them love with as much passion as you love now? Any caveman, anyone from the Middle Ages, anyone from the nineteenth century, your parents? Because this feels like a new thing. It's such a new thing.

79

It was his parents who bought them the holiday as a wedding present, and he knew they couldn't afford it, and he tried to talk them out of it. "But it'll be the perfect honeymoon for you," said his mother; Father said, "Ever since it was discovered your mother has been *dying* to go." So they should take the present back, they should go themselves—"No, no," said Mother; his father said, "No, it's too late for us. We're old now. Our time is over."

The flight alone was cripplingly expensive. Left to their own devices, the holiday could only have been possible if they were to stay in a cheap hotel once they got there—but there were no cheap hotels, everything built around the Encounter cost a fortune. And that was the awkward thing, neither of the two honeymooners much wanted to go. Their tastes were simple, and neither of them were religious. "Can't we sell it to someone else?" she whispered to him. "To someone who'd care?" Even though she knew they couldn't.

They flew in, they were met at the airport by a chauffeur, they were taken to their luxury hotel. They didn't see the Encounter that first day. No one ever went to the Encounter the first day. It was something that had to be anticipated, then savoured, it was not to be compromised by jetlag. They spent their time instead by the pool. The hotel was perfect, of course it was. The guests fell into distinct categories: those, like them, who were waiting for the Encounter. And the others who had already been—eyes shining, cheeks flushed, looking so beatific, so *transformed.*

Entry to the Encounter was strictly timed; their tickets allowed them access to the tower the next morning. Even so, the queue they joined still snaked out on to the streets. Access was granted in groups of two, and restricted to three minutes and not a second longer—three minutes didn't seem long when you had flown halfway across the world to see it, but it was the only fair way to ensure everyone could get a turn. They joined the queue at five o'clock, as advised, and it was still dark outside; by the time they reached the elevator that would speed them the one hundred storeys up to the top it was past eleven. "You're very lucky!" cooed the elevator attendant. "Eleven o'clock is the *perfect* time for emotional metamorphosis!" They guessed she said something similar to everybody, but it made them feel good.

They sped up into the sky, taken to the perfect vantage point to witness the spectacle; their stomachs lurched, they held hands tightly, they smiled. There was a sort of courage to those smiles. What if it didn't live up to the hype? What if it was all a crushing disappointment? You couldn't start a life of love with a disappointment. They didn't know what that would say about the world. They didn't know what it would say about them.

And out of the elevator, and over to the observation deck, and to the telescope. Fixed firmly into position, pointing upwards at just the right angle. The view never changed—clouds would break around the Encounter, as if they would never dare obscure it. He was going to let his new wife look first, but the elevator attendant laughed and said there was no need to be gallant, it was designed for two.

No one quite knew what had caused the split in the sky. Whether it were a natural phenomenon, an 'air quake' as the scientists would have it. Or whether it were a deliberate gift from God. But one thing was clear. A fissure had opened in the firmament, and through it one could see Heaven.

There were no cherubim or seraphim. No bright lights. Jesus wasn't dangling his feet over a fluffy cloud. But it was Heaven, and it was real, and it was indisputably true. He didn't take his eyes off it; he wanted to get his full three minutes' worth. He grasped blindly for her hand; she found it.

"I love you," he told her, and for the first time he knew that he believed it.

"I love you too," she said.

And the three minutes was enough, because they had each other.

The attendant had gone. Another had taken her place, a young man, and he silently ushered them to a different elevator. They got inside. They kissed on the lips. The attendant pushed a button, and they dropped back to Earth.

The attendant said, "We hope you enjoyed your visit to the Encounter. On leaving the elevator turn to the right, there will be postcards in the gift shop, there's a restroom." He looked down at his feet.

She said, "It must be a wonderful job, you get to see the Encounter every day!"

He didn't look up from his feet, and he didn't reply.

They spent the rest of the week in the hotel. They swam in the pool. They ordered room service. They made love.

They had those beatific smiles on their faces, and they flashed them at everybody.

75

They didn't mind flying home at the end of the holiday, they had seen what they had needed to, and the rest of their lives stretched out ahead of them.

They soon found out she was pregnant. They liked to think that the conception had been on the day they'd seen the Encounter, wouldn't that be lovely? The pregnancy was easy, the delivery smooth, their baby son was beautiful.

They often talked about the Encounter. To anyone who would listen, and when no one would listen, at least to each other. Some evenings that's all they would do, and they'd get out their postcards and look at them for fun. None of the postcards were of the Encounter itself, of course—no camera could capture its ineffable rightness. They were of the hotel reception, of the pool, of the airport.

In time they had a second child. And it wasn't quite as easy a pregnancy, and they supposed this new baby would be flawed because he wasn't conceived in the light of heavenly protection. But, actually, he was just as healthy a son as the first, and rather better natured to boot. They just didn't love him as much.

They talked about the Encounter less and less often. Both privately thought the other was describing it wrong. He would say he'd heard harps, she knew there'd been no harps. She said she'd glimpsed the heels of angels' feet, and it was all he could do not to laugh at her. They both wondered whether there was something wrong with the other—was the memory failing? Or were they just crass, had they always been so?

And she found as time went on she dreamed not of the Encounter itself, but of the boy in the elevator afterwards. Not his face, she couldn't remember what he'd looked like. Just his weary despair.

The children grew up, and they'd been good children, but they made indifferent adults. One married someone neither parent could like, the other took a job neither could understand.

He said, "If we save up, we could see the Encounter again. What do you say?" And she said, "Maybe."

He had an affair, and he didn't even bother to hide it from her, and she forgave him, but the truth was she didn't really mind.

He said, "We can start again, we can go and see the Encounter. Would you like that?" And she said, "No."

When she was diagnosed with cancer he took it worse than she did. He felt such grief, and she wasn't even dead yet! And the grief made his stomach lurch as if he'd been dropped through the air.

"You have to fight it," he said, "please, for me, for the children." And she said she would, but she just looked down at her feet.

It made no difference to either of them that they knew there was a heaven. And her body was cremated, and he poured the ashes off the top of the house, which wasn't really that high up at all, and for a while they seemed to rise, they were buoyed up by the wind, but soon they rained down hard to the ground.

54

Some nights he stares up into the dark sky and wonders whether she's up there.

He wonders if there are harps. He can't remember.

And he thinks that he should make a return visit to the Encounter. It would use up all his savings. His sons tell him not to—what good would it do him? He needs to get over Mum's death, not obsess about her. And it's so expensive. Is he taking his pills?—he should be taking his pills.

58

God summoned them to his side, and he was sore displeased. The married couple quaked before his fury. "You make me sick!" thundered God. "Love is the greatest gift I bestowed upon Man, it's a work of genius even I can't understand! And you kept it all to yourselves? Why didn't you shag around like everyone else?" They stammered their explanations: they were devoted to each other, their love had defined them, it had made them complete—God really wasn't interested. "It's time to make up for lost time," he said. "Put on the rubber suits. The angels will come in batches of fifty."

69

They've been married nearly forty years, and she loves her husband, she does. But from the very first day they met she knew there was something about him that bothered her, though she could never quite put her finger on it. And she's still searching for it: eyeing him over the breakfast table, or as they cuddle on the sofa watching TV. As he sleeps, his arms wrapped around her as if she were a security blanket. One day, she knows, she'll figure out what's wrong, it's on the tip of her tongue, sometimes she can almost taste it. And then she can divorce him.

15

They've been married nearly fifty years, and he doesn't know how he will live without her. But he'll have to, and soon. It'll take months, but she's dying right before his eyes, the only woman he has ever loved. The only woman he *can* ever love—and it's all so precious now, every single day counts, he knows that each moment is something he'll need to look back on and savour once all the moments run out. And he knows that at some point he's going to have to ask her how the washing machine works.

61

They've been married nearly sixty years, and privately both of them wonder when they'll start to get it right the way their parents did.

42

They're still married, and it's been so long since they fell out of love with each other that they've started to sentimentalise that too. "I was happy back then," she thinks, "those first years when I loathed him." He says to himself, "Nothing has ever been so good as when I first realised everything was bad." She fell out of love with him on a summer holiday on the Dorset coast, and it had rained every single day, and each time it rained he sulked as if it were somehow her fault, and in one glorious moment something inside her had just snapped. Now she remembers that rain as light and refreshing, wasn't rain so much cleaner back in the old days? He fell out of love with her in a local restaurant halfway through his chicken alfredo. He suddenly knew as a pure and obvious fact that his wife was never going to understand anything he said to her, she was never going to understand *him*, or any of his needs, or any of his failed ambitions, and how much those failures hurt. And hadn't she got fat, and hadn't she got dull? He liked that chicken alfredo. He thought back on how it had burst with flavour and melted on his tongue.

Each year he says to her, where shall we go on holiday this time? And she always wants the Dorset coast. Each wedding anniversary he takes her out to dinner, and he always orders the chicken alfredo.

And for a while at least that stale antipathy they feel for each other gets a bit of spark to it, they still despise each other but it's a beautiful thing—or, at least, a comforting thing—or, at least, it's theirs. It's theirs, and only theirs. They've earned it. And they'll go to bed and make something like love, and hold each other all night long.

8

And at last they knew each other completely. It had taken eighty years of marriage, but they'd got there. They'd sifted through every scrap of their innermost selves, they'd measured them all, they'd decoded them. Each tic, and quirk, and affectation—and she knew why he seized up each time his father was mentioned, he knew why she always wept at happy endings. There was total understanding. And, what was better yet, there was total forgiveness.

She offered him her hand to shake in farewell, just as he knew she would. And he instead lifted it to his lips, and kissed it, in a way she found romantic but entirely predictable. They smiled in unison. And then they left each other, forever, and went to find some new puzzle to play with.

98

I walk about the city and there are hundreds of people around and I feel there is an entire universe within me. I am too vast to be understood. It's a secret. I can't tell anyone. I don't want them to realise they're standing next to a universe, I don't want anyone to be intimidated. My brain is the most advanced computer in creation, and I'm only using ten per cent of it, and I still don't know where to find the on / off switch.

The only thing as advanced as my brain is the brain of every other person in the world, all seven billion of them.

I don't like to think about that.

I like to pretend that everyone is simpler than me. That child being noisy in the park, the teenager selling me a cheeseburger. The old woman who has just walked past and glared at me for reasons I cannot guess and shall never know. They are all bit parts in the story of my life, they are the background artists, I shall never know their names so as far as I'm concerned they don't *have* names. I will never speak to these people, or remember what they look like, or think of them again. They are without character. They are without dimension. They cannot hold universes the way I do.

My brain is constantly judging and appraising everything I catch only the merest glimpse of. It often judges negatively. It's easier that way. I cannot bear the thought that I'm just the bit part in thousands upon thousands of other lives, the strangers whose paths I cross and then dismiss within the blink of an eye. I cannot bear it, that they turn their universal intellects upon me, assess me, then discard.

Knowing this truth—that the same mass of contradictions make up each and every one of us—that everyone is like you, has the same potential as you, has the same capacity for love—how, then, can you not be awestruck by every single person you meet? How can you not be terrified of them, in all their enormity?

I cannot help but feel that the reason I dislike anyone is that I've seen the wrong pieces of them, the bits that without proper context don't seem to make sense. That if I only knew them well enough, I couldn't help but love them. The only barrier to loving every single person in the world is that I judge them with far too little information. It's like saying you don't read books because you hate encyclopaedias, abhor France because you don't like croissants. You refuse to trust any of the elements on the periodic table because you've never been especially fond of boron.

I cannot know more than a fraction of myself. What hope of my knowing anybody else?

What hope is there for love?

But still we try. Still—I'll try.

I will never know you, but if it makes you happy, I'll pretend. If it makes you happy *now*, in this moment, before your mind changes, because we know your mind will change, you are such a mass of contradictions!— I'll pretend.

I am a million billion different short stories assembled in random order. And so are you. And whichever order you read my stories in, no one else will ever be able to read them in quite the same way.

And no one will pretend to love the same you that I pretend to love. I promise.

This little sliver of my universe is for you, and you alone. I love you. Enjoy.

99

So what was lucky, what the lucky thing was, here's how they were lucky: they both fell out of love with each other at the exact same time! And the moment of that love dying was so undramatic, so bloody casual. It was like the fade of summer. It was like a silent fart. Neither of them even noticed. Their love had withered away into something so very small that when it finally disappeared it didn't leave on either heart even the slightest pockmark. They carried on in this loveless state until one of them died—him, maybe, or her, it doesn't matter which. And it was only at the funeral that the one left alive realised that he or she really didn't *care*—there was this coffin in front, and people dressed in black all around, and some of them were even crying, and everything was supposed to be so sad—but to the remaining spouse it wasn't clear what impact this death was supposed to make. No tears. No grief. And, in a way, that was rather a good thing. And, in a way, it was desperately awful.

He (or she) would sit at home, lost and lonely—and yet not so lonely, and that was the hardest part. She (or he) would feel the rhythm of the day pass over, and it was strange how little that rhythm had been interrupted. And the survivor might go to the photo album, and pick out the wedding pictures, and stare at them—him in his best suit, her in the white dress. And remember that time when in front of the whole world they had made their vows to love each other forever.

"I do," he had said; "I do," she had said back. Not in sync, not quite simultaneous. But so nearly, really so very nearly.

100

Now it's all over—and really over this time, with no chance of reprieve. And I look back on our years together, and I can't help but feel they're tainted somehow. As if the certainty of our end makes all those times of happiness seem foolish or wanting—or even worse, a *lie*. That time you told me you loved me in the rain, you know when—did you mean it? Was any of it ever real—if it isn't real now? If love is going to stop one day, what is the point of loving at all?

I suppose we interpret our lives best as if they're stories. We love stories. With an ordered narrative, and consequence, and *meanings* to that consequence. When we tell someone our history, we do it like a fairy tale, we impose upon it a structure with a series of events and decisions leading on to the next event and the next decision, and then again, and then again.

And I think of love in the same way. This happened, and that caused that to happen afterwards. And if the final consequence is that love died, and we broke up, and we never wanted to see each other again—then that was some inevitability planted into the narrative structure of our love. Any reader would be able to see it, that when we first exchanged kisses in chapter one, the flaw that would wreck us by chapter fifteen was already in place.

I tell you this. I didn't decide to love you. I just did. No decisions, no correspondingly planned consequence. My life, my love—it's a bunch of things that happened in a certain and not necessarily ideal order.

Stories teach us to define our lives, our loves, our achievements, by where we finish up in the final chapter. But a man's life cannot be summed up by the likelihood he'll die amongst strangers in a hospital bed—and the love we felt for each other cannot be summed up so coldly either, just because it too is now dead.

When I think of the fact I'll never again stroke your hair or touch your skin—it makes every remembered stroke or touch seem exquisitely sweet and cruelly ironic. I won't touch you again. I miss that. Not for the sex. But for the million and one nanoseconds just before, and the million and one nanoseconds straight after. That's when we loved the best.

Love isn't a single story with a structure. When I think of you, some of it makes me happy, some of it bitter and angry. It's one hundred and one stories, and they've been assembled in random order by an idiot.

I loved you, you know. I did. And it was immediate, and it was real. Even if now it's done it's starting to feel like a story, with all the artifice of that—with a beginning, a middle, and, of course, an end. Always an end.

Goodbye, my darling.

101

Once upon a time there was a man who lost his wife, and he tried to find her by reading all the stories in the world.

He missed his wife terribly. He didn't know what to do without her. And he thought that maybe he could bring his wife back from the darkness—he never claimed that his love was greater than anybody else's, but it *was* love, and if love isn't a more powerful force than life or death, really then, what is it for?

But if love cannot transcend life and death—then, still, maybe stories can. If you read just the right ones. If you read them in just the right order.

He read books. He read all the books in the world, fast, one after the other. He was entertained, enthralled, distracted, amused—but he could not find his wife on any of the pages. At the end of the day he still had to put the books down and return to the emptiness of his life. And he even listened to the stories which *hadn't* been written—he sat in the dark and listened to an old woman, and the old woman's words meant nothing to him, the whimsy of it all made him sick to his stomach.

There was once a man who loved his wife, and he sought to save her in the realms of fantasy. And maybe, in spite of all, he will succeed.

And the old woman says:

- *This is the final story in the book.*
- *There are no more. It is over.*
- *Did you take the correct path? Did you read all one hundred and one stories? If so, turn to* **Epilogue (a)**.
- *Did you take another path? Have you left these tales unfinished? If so, turn to* **Epilogue (b)**.
- *Either way, I hope you enjoyed your journey.*
- *Goodbye.*
- *You may find your own way out. Be careful not to trip over yourself in the dark.*

EPILOGUE (a)

THE MAN HAS NEVER expected he would get his wife back. It is an impossible dream. He has finished all one hundred and one stories, but some time around story twenty-two he put aside all thoughts of his wife; by story forty-eight he was enjoying them for their own sake; by story ninety-three he was ploughing on for the sake of bloody-minded completism.

The day at the library has been very long, and when he emerges from the pitch-dark room he can't adjust to the sudden brightness of the world. He feels disorientated; he feels changed. He goes back home, and walks into the library, and sees his wife sitting in her favourite armchair—and he can't even cry out, he can't even muster surprise, for the longest moment he just stares at her.

"I'm sorry," he says. "I'm sorry I burned your books."

She is smiling. "It doesn't matter."

She rises, and gives him a hug—and that contact is all he needs, he sobs with relief, his wife is really back.

He says he'll cook dinner, her very favourite meal, would she like that? She says that will be lovely. The last few months, whilst she was dead, she was just aching for a good prawn risotto.

Afterwards they go to bed, and they make love, and it is so very sweet.

The first few days are idyllic. He reacquaints himself with the touch of her skin, the sound of her voice, her smell. He thought he'd got them preserved in his head, he thought he had never let them fade—but they weren't like this, not like this.

But then the cracks appear.

There's a problem with his memory.

Sometimes they'll be talking, and all at once his mind will go blank. He'll get the sense that something is shifting in his head, is detaching itself and melting away. It frightens him. He tries to grasp hold of what he has lost, but how can he find it when he's already forgotten what it was supposed to be? The stories. The stories—he can no longer remember who was the mayor of Casterbridge, who was the man in the iron mask. And those tales he heard from the old woman in the dark—oh, he doesn't mind losing _2, and he didn't enjoy 6_ at all, but he knows he found 5_ amusing, and _8 meant more to him than he can tell. Fading fast, then gone—and he'll burst into tears at the tragedy of their loss.

To begin with his wife finds it frustrating, then she gets cross. At last she admits something is very wrong.

They go to the hospital. The doctor runs some tests. He asks him questions, so many questions—it's like that interview he went through to join the library all that time ago, picking into every aspect of his life. He's distressed. He begs for it to stop. He's given a brain scan. There are no lumps or bumps or lesions—but what's lurking under the surface, who can guess?

"Probably just age," says the doctor. "Try not to worry." He's given some pills.

But what he doesn't tell the doctor, and he cannot tell his wife—sometimes he lies next to her in bed, and he feels so warm and comfy that she is beside him, and he knows he should be grateful for that.

But he thinks—it was better before. It was better when I had the stories. And he thinks he might hate his wife. And he doesn't turn the light on. He doesn't want to turn the light on. He doesn't want to make it a fact.

He tries to go back to the library, but the building is no longer there.

He stands in the checkout queue at the supermarket. In his trolley there are packs of prawn risotto—it's his wife's favourite, but for him it's rather lost its appeal. Over the hubbub, suddenly, he hears a familiar voice from a customer at another till. It's a voice he knows he'll never forget, even though he's lost all the words that were spoken. "Hey!" the man shouts. "Hey!" He abandons his shopping, chases the old woman out on to the street, he grabs hold of her.

He has never so much as glimpsed the old woman before. The room was too dark. The old woman does not look as he expected. She is taller, and thinner, and stares at her assailant boldly.

The man tells him what is wrong.

The old woman says, "You keep your stories, or you keep your wife. It's as simple as that."

"Let me come back to the library."

The old woman considers. "I shall give you no more stories. But I will give you the choice."

She walks away into the crowd, and is gone.

And that night, the man goes to bed with his wife. And there in the darkness he thinks about all his stories, and he thinks he can almost touch them, because we all hear stories in the dark. And he makes his decision.

Make your final choice.

- *If you choose to keep the stories, turn to page 373.*
- *If you choose to keep the wife, turn to page 706.*

EPILOGUE (b)

THE MAN HAS NEVER expected he would get his wife back. It is an impossible dream. And besides, he hasn't finished all one hundred and one stories; the enormity of all those words has finally defeated him.

The day at the library has been very long, and when he emerges from the pitch-dark room he can't adjust to the sudden brightness of the world. He feels disorientated; he feels changed. He goes back home, and walks into the library, and sees his wife sitting in her favourite armchair—and he can't even cry out, he can't even muster surprise, for the longest moment he just stares at her.

"I'm sorry," he says. "I'm sorry I burned your books."

She is smiling. "What books?"

She rises, and gives him a hug—and that contact is all he needs, he sobs with relief, his wife is really back.

He says he'll cook dinner, her very favourite meal, would she like that? She says that will be lovely. She frowns. She asks him to remind her what her favourite meal is.

Afterwards they go to bed, and they make love, and it is so very sweet.

The first few days are idyllic. He reacquaints himself with the touch of her skin, the sound of her voice, her smell. He thought he'd got them preserved in his head, he thought he had never let them fade—but they weren't like this, not like this.

But then the cracks appear.

There's a problem with her memory.

Sometimes they'll be talking, and all at once her face will go blank. She is smiling, she always keeps smiling—but he realises she hasn't any idea what he is telling her about. He mentions Ray from work, it is clear she can't remember him. Their holiday in Sicily. Mutual friends. A shared antipathy for grapes. The date of his birthday. The date of *her* birthday. How they first met. How they first loved.

And she has completely forgotten she ever liked to read books, and once upon a time he'd have loved her to have put away all her silly books, and now this seems to him the saddest thing of all.

To begin with he finds it frustrating, then he gets cross. At last he admits something is very wrong.

They go to the hospital. The doctor runs some tests. He asks her questions, so many questions—it's like that interview he went through to join the library all that time ago, picking into every aspect of their lives, and sometimes she knows the answers, and more often she doesn't. She's distressed. She begs the doctor to stop. She's given a brain scan. There are no lumps or bumps or lesions—but what's lurking under the surface, who can tell?

"It may just be age," says the doctor. "Try not to worry." And he gives her some pills.

And what the man doesn't tell the doctor, what he cannot tell his wife—sometimes he lies next to her in bed, and he feels so warm and comfy that she is beside him, and he knows he should be grateful for that—but he reaches across to hold her, and he can't find her; he grabs hold and it's as if his arms are passing straight through a ghost, and he's sure if he turns the light on to look he'll discover she's barely there at all. And he doesn't turn the light on. He doesn't want to turn the light on. He doesn't want it to be a fact.

He tries to go back to the library, but the building is no longer there.

He stands in the checkout queue at the supermarket. In his trolley there are packs of prawn risotto—it's his wife's favourite, but he has to keep telling her so. Over the hubbub, suddenly, he hears a familiar voice from a customer at another till. It's a voice he knows he'll never forget. "Hey!" the man shouts. "Hey!" He abandons his shopping, chases the old woman out on to the street, he grabs hold of her.

He has never so much as glimpsed the old woman before. The room was too dark. The old woman does not look as he expected. She is shorter, and fatter, and more frightened.

The man tells him what is wrong.

The old woman looks so sad. She says, "You didn't hear all of the stories. So you didn't get back all of your wife."

"What can I do to put it right? There's no more library. The library has gone."

And the old woman says, "We shall bring back the library just for you. It shall be there tomorrow."

That night, the man goes to bed with the remnants of his wife for the last time. And in the morning he kisses her on the forehead, so gently for fear he'll break her—he says goodbye, and that he hopes he'll see her soon. And he sets out, to hear more stories in the dark.

Go back to the beginning.

ACKNOWLEDGEMENTS

ALL THE STORIES WITHIN this book were conceived as being part of the same project, but a number of them sneaked out into the world early, often in very different versions, and with different titles.

THE GRAND ADVENTURE. First published as 'A Grand Day Out', in *They Do the Same Things Different There,* Chizine Publications, 2014.

SHAGGY DOG STORY. First published as 'Joke in Four Panels;, in *The Best Science Fiction and Fantasy of the Year Volume Seven*, edited by Jonathan Strahan, Night Shade Books, 2013.

BEDTIME STORIES FOR YASMIN. First published in *Shadows & Tall Trees 4*, edited by Michael Kelly, Undertow Books, 2012, Subsequently collected in *The Best British Short Stories 2013,* edited by Nicholas Royle, Salt, and *The Year's Best Dark Fantasy and Horror 2013*, edited by Paula Guran, Prime.

THE DISAPPOINTING STORY IN THE BOOK. First published in Czech as 'Rozczarowujace Opowiadanie', translated by Pawel Dembowski, in *Fantastyka*, 2017.

ICE IN THE BEDROOM. First published in *Fearsome Magics*, edited by Jonathan Strahan, Solaris, 2014.

NINE LETTERS ABOUT SPIT. First published in *A Carnivale of Horror*, edited by Marie O'Regan and Paul Kane, PS Publishing, 2012.

THE WAR ARTIST. A section first published as 'Our Fallen Sons', in *They Do the Same Things Different There*, ChiZine Publications, 2014.

THE ALL-NEW ADVENTURES OF ROBIN HOOD. First published in *They Do the Same Things Different There*, ChiZine Publications, 2014.

SOUNDING BRASS TINKLING CYMBAL. First published in *They Do the Same Things Different There*, ChiZine Publications, 2014.

THE POPPING FIELDS. First published in *Nightmare Carnival*, edited by Ellen Datlow, Dark Horse, 2014.

THE SWIMMING POOL PARTY. First published in *Shadows & Tall Trees 7,* edited by Michael Kelly, Undertow, 2017. Reprinted in *The Year's Best Dark Fantasy and Horror 2018*, edited by Paula Guran, Prime.

THE SIXTEENTH STEP, First published in *The Burning Circus*, edited by Johnny Mains, BFS, 2013. Subsequently collected in *The Mammoth Book of Best New Horror 25*, edited by Stephen Jones, Robinson.

CUSTARD CREAM. First published in *Remember Why You Fear Me*, ChiZine Publications, 2012.

UNFINISHED. First broadcast on BBC Radio Four, directed by Jeremy Osborne, Sweet Talk Productions, 2018.

THE CONSTANTINOPLE ARCHIVES. First published in *The Cutting Room*, edited by Ellen Datlow, Tachyon, 2014.

THAT TINY FLUTTER OF THE HEART I USED TO CALL LOVE. First published in *Psycho Mania*, edited by Stephen Jones, Robinson, 2013. Subsequently reprinted in *The Best Horror of the Year Volume Six,* edited by Ellen Datlow, Night Shade Books, and in *Best British Horror 2014*, edited by Johnny Mains, Salt, and in *Nightmares: A New Decade of Modern Horror*, edited by Ellen Datlow, Taychon. Shortlisted for the Shirley Jackson Award.

JASON ZERRILLO IS AN ANNOYING PRICK. First published in *Remember Why You Fear Me*, ChiZine Publications, 2012.

BLOOD. First published in *Seize the Night*, edited by Christopher Golden, Gallery Books, 2015. Subsequently reprinted in *Year's Best Weird Fiction Volume Three*, edited by Simon Stranzas and Michael Kelly, Undertow.

THE MONOGAMY OF WILD BEASTS. First published in *Dangerous Games*, edited by Jonathan Oliver, Solaris, 2014,

TOM IS IN THE ATTIC. First published in *Phantoms*, edited by Marie O'Regan, Titan Books, 2018.

THUMBSUCKER. First published in *New Fears 2*, edited by Mark Morris, Titan Books, 2018. Subsequently reprinted in *The Best Horror of the Year Volume Eleven,* edited by Ellen Datlow, Night Shade Books. Shortlisted for a British Fantasy Award.

SUFFER LITTLE CHILDREN. First published in *Fearful Symmetries*, edited by Ellen Datlow, ChiZine Publications, 2014. Subsequently reprinted in *Best New Horror 26*, edited by Stephen Jones, PS Publishing.

BLUE CRAYON YELLOW CRAYON. First published in *Remember Why You Fear Me*, ChiZine Publications, 2012.

GOOD GRIEF. First published in *Haunts*, edited by Stephen Jones, Ulysses Press, 2011.

LUMP IN YOUR THROAT. First published in *The 2nd Spectral Book of Horror Stories,* edited by Mark Morris, Spectral, 2015.

CLOWN ENVY. First published in *Remember Why You Fear Me*, ChiZine Publications, 2012.

ALICE THROUGH THE PLASTIC SHEET. First published in *A Book of Horrors*, edited by Stephen Jones, Jo Fletcher Books, 2011. Shortlisted for a World Fantasy Award and a British Fantasy Award.

DIGITS. First published in Spanish as 'Digitos', translated by Maria Pilar San Roman in *Cuentos Para Algernon,* 2019.

THE DARK SPACE IN THE HOUSE IN THE HOUSE IN THE GARDEN AT THE CENTRE OF THE WORLD. First published in *House of Fear*, edited by Jonathan Oliver, Solaris, 2011. Subsequently reprinted in *The Best British Short Stories 2012*, edited by Nicholas Royle, Salt.

DUMB LUCY. First published in *Magic,* edited by Jonathan Oliver, Solaris, 2012.

AND THIS IS WHERE WE FALTER / AND THIS IS HOW WE FALL First published in *Terror Tales of the Ocean*, edited by Paul Finch, Gray Friar Press, 2015.

THE DESPERATE WOMAN WITH THE RAIN-SODDEN HAIR. An excerpt first published in the introduction to *Year's Best Weird Fiction Volume Five*, edited by Robert Shearman and Michael Kelly, 2018.

PECKISH. First published in *Fearie Tales*, edited by Stephen Jones, Jo Fletcher Books, 2013.

MOND. First published in *They Do the Same Things Different There*, ChiZine Publications, 2014.

I SAY (I SAY, I SAY). First published in *Tales From the Shadow Booth Vol. 3*, edited by Dan Coxon, Shadowbooth, 2019. Subsequently reprinted in *The Best Horror of the Year Volume Twelve*, edited by Ellen Datlow, Night Shade Books.

TALENT WILL OUT. First published as 'Accursed', in *Horrorology*, edited by Stephen Jones, Jo Fletcher Books, 2015.

THE BATHTUB. First published in *Remember Why You Fear Me*, ChiZine Publications, 2012.

THE GIRL FROM IPANEMA. First published in the ebook edition of *Remember Why You Fear Me*, ChiZine Publications, 2012.

THE COCKTAIL PARTY IN KENSINGTON GETS OUT OF HAND. First published in *This Dreaming Isle*, edited by Dan Coxon, 2018.

ERUPTION. First published in *Riptide: Carpe Diem,* edited by Virginia Baily and Sally Flint, Dirt Pie Press, 2016.

72 VIRGINS. First published in *They Do the Same Things Different There*, ChiZine Publications, 2014.

PAGE TURNER. First published in *They Do the Same Things Different There*, ChiZine Publications, 2014.

SLOW HANDCLAP FOR THE MORONIC HORDE. First published as 'The Play's the Thing', in *Zombie Apocalypse! Fightback*, edited by Stephen Jones, Running Press, 2012.

THE INEFFECTUAL PHOTOSCOPY OF CATS. First published as 'Simon Harries' in *Hauntings*, edited by Ian Whates, Newcon Press, 2012.

BOBBO. First published in *Uncertainties Volume III*, edited by Lynda E Rucker, Swan River Press, 2018.

PUMPKIN KIDS. First published in *The Mammoth Book of Halloween Stories*, edited by Stephen Jones, Skyhorse Publishing, 2018.

IT FLOWS FROM THE MOUTH. First published in *Shadows & Tall Trees 6*, edited by Michael Kelly, Undertow, 2014. Subsequently reprinted in *The Best Horror of the Year Volume Seven*, edited by Ellen Datlow, Night Shade Books.

MUMMY'S LITTLE MIRACLE. First published as 'One More Bloody Miracle After Another' in *Remember Why You Fear Me*, ChiZine Publications, 2012.

MEMORIES OF CRAVINGS LONG GONE. First published in *They Do the Same Things Different There*, ChiZine Publications, 2014.

MERELY A HORROR WRITER. First published in *Remember Why You Fear Me*, ChiZine Publications, 2012.

BRAND NEW SHINY SHINY. First published in *Flotsam Fantastique*, edited by Stephen Jones, Jo Fletcher Books, 2013.

CARRY WITHIN SOME SMALL SLIVER OF ME. First published in *The Spectral Book of Horror Stories*, edited by Mark Morris, Spectral, 2014.

101 HEARTBEATS. Extracts first published as 'Simultaneous' in *Solstice Shorts: Sixteen Stories About Time*, edited by Cherry Potts, Arachne, 2014, and as 'Squint And You'll See Me', in *Postcards From Impossible Worlds*, edited by Peter Chiykowski, ChiZine Publications, 2018.